The Wounded Land

by
Roger Thomas

To Rudy
who appreciates

Books in the *Watchful Sky* series:

Under the Watchful Sky

Rising Darkness

The Wounded Land

The Tattered Web

With special thanks to my gimlet-eyed editorial assistants,
Ellen and Annette

Published by JCK
Fort Gratiot MI

ISBN 978-1-7330809-1-0

This is not a story for children. This is a story about the struggle between good and evil in the midst of the decaying remains of what was once Western Civilization. It grapples with the types of evils that arise in such moral environments, which requires describing them. These descriptions are done plainly, with no choreographing, special camera angles, or other embellishments that are used by the entertainment industry to make evil appear glamorous and alluring. Those who have never encountered unretouched descriptions of evil may find them shocking, dismaying, and even revolting – as well they should, for that is what depravity looks like. This story deals plainly with kidnappings, rapes, beatings, murders, and other brutalities.

But why describe such things? Certainly not to revel in or celebrate them, nor to shock or affront deliberately, but rather that the reader might appreciate the good that rises to combat the evil. For there is good, though the weapons of combat are not the glowing sabers or technological super-suits or magic hammers so beloved by modern legend. Instead they are the only weapons that have ever been effective against evil: humility, longsuffering, determination, obedience, forgiveness, and most of all love. This story and the others in the series are also clear about the cost of the struggle, the fact that the Faithful of every age "fill up those things that are wanting in the sufferings of Christ." Redemption costs.

This story and others in the series also present plainly the Unseen Real. This is not in the interest of making them Fantastic Stories (as we moderns like our tales categorized), but because the Unseen is as real as the tangible reality present to the senses. The Seen and Unseen Real stand closer than we moderns like to admit, even in the face of St. Paul's warning that our enemies are not flesh and blood. Because of this, and because "where sin abounds, grace abounds all the more," I believe that we will see both evil and good, hitherto unseen, manifested more and more plainly in the times that are upon us. These stories reflect that belief, and those who read them should be prepared for that.

Roger Thomas, Easter 2019

Michigan's Thumb Region

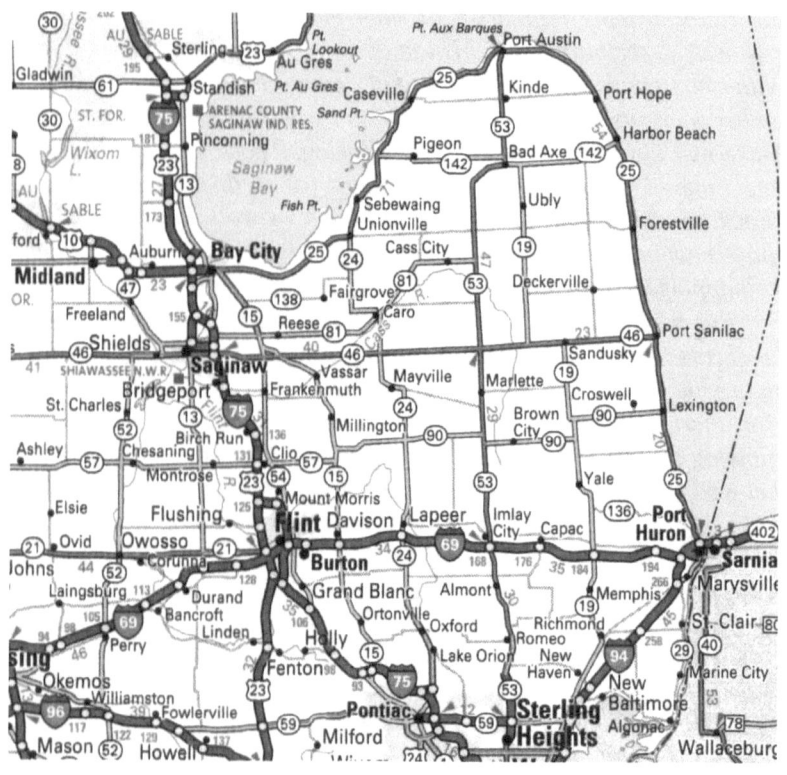

Sault Ste. Marie and Eastern Lake Superior

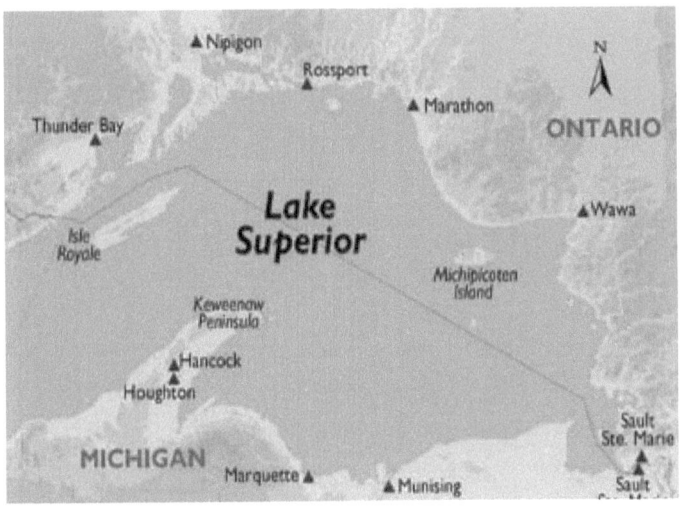

Journal

"Dr. Harris?"

Dr. Brian Harris looked up from his desk to see an unfamiliar man standing in his office doorway. The man was wearing a worn flannel shirt and faded jeans and held a dirty trapper hat in his hands. He seemed to be in his mid-30s, with stringy brown hair and a scant beard. He looked out of place in the academic surroundings, but not awed or intimidated. He was clearly no student.

"I'm Dr. Harris," Brian responded, rising to his feet.

The man broke into a broad grin and stepped into the office. "Good, good – security said you'd probably be here. I'm Peter Durant, and I live here in town. They said you'd be the most likely person to help me."

"In town" meant Sault Ste. Marie, Michigan, where Lake Superior State University was located. Dr. Harris taught history and political science at the university, and typically not even his students troubled him during office hours. He wondered what would bring a town resident to his door.

"I'll certainly try, Mr. Durant," Brian said, shaking the man's hand and gesturing him to a seat. "What's on your mind?"

"Oh, just call me Pete, Dr. Harris," Peter replied, draping his jacket over the adjacent chair, but not before removing something from the pocket.

"Then call me Brian," Dr. Harris replied. "We Yoopers don't stand on ceremony, even at college."

"All right, Brian," Pete grinned in response, then gingerly laid on the desk the item he'd taken out of his jacket pocket. It was black and brown, and carefully sealed in a plastic kitchen bag of the kind that closed with a zipper. Whatever the item was, it looked old, and was probably quite fragile. Brian raised his eyebrows.

"May I?" He gestured toward the item.

"Of course," Pete replied. "That's why I brought it. It's so old and tattered that I reckoned it would best be handled by an expert. Jeremy – that's my buddy – thought the same when I asked him. He's the one who thought of putting it in a Ziploc."

"That was good thinking on Jeremy's part," Brian confirmed, carefully taking the item from the bag and laying it on the corner of his desk. It was a book – a very old book of simple construction, being nothing but two pieces of dark, stiff leather bound on one edge with a thong of brittle leather and holding several rough-edged pages made of coarse, yellowed paper. Easing the cover off and laying it to one side, he saw that the first page was filled with small, close writing in badly faded ink. He could not make out the language, though it looked vaguely like French. Glancing quickly down the page, his eyes caught a phrase he recognized.

Anno Domini 1640.

Brian looked up at Pete with wide eyes. "Am I the first person you've shown this to?"

"Yes," Pete nodded, "except for Jeremy, because he –"

Brian held up a hand to silence him while he picked up the phone handset and punched an extension. "Lucy, could you come in here?" he asked, and within a minute a young woman appeared at the doorway.

"Pete, this is Lucy, a student of mine," Brian explained. "Lucy, Pete Durant from here in town. Lucy is my aide this year, and I wanted her in as a witness. Lucy, do you see this book?"

"Yes," Lucy affirmed, leaning over to peer at the faded writing.

"Mr. Durant has just brought it to me in this bag. As you can see, the binding thong is brittle and broken, enabling me to remove the cover. Can you see the writing on the first page?"

"Just barely," Lucy said.

"Do you notice this line?" Brian pointed at the page without touching it. Lucy looked closer and her eyes grew wide.

"Is this for real?"

"I'm about to ask Mr. Durant for the particulars, but it does appear genuine. Can you contact the library, or whomever you can, to obtain a suitable receptacle – preferably one opaque to ultraviolet – and some specimen gloves?"

Lucy bustled away while Brian turned his workstation on the book in the middle of his desk and adjusted the camera so it took in both men in their seats. Keying the recorder, he began.

"Dr. Brian Harris, Department of History, Lake Superior State University. I've just been visited by Mr. Peter Durant of Sault Ste. Marie, Michigan, who brought me this artifact. It is a book or journal of some type with a notification on the first page indicating it may date from 1640 Common Era. If you would be so kind, Mr. Durant, could you please explain how you came into possession of this book?"

"Not much to explain," Pete shrugged, glancing from the workstation to the book to Dr. Harris. "I live here in Sault Ste. Marie, as did my aunt Evelyn Cooper. She had no kids, and lived in a small house in an older section of town. The house had been in the family a long time, and our family has lived here in the Soo since – oh, long as anyone can remember. I've got family on both sides of the river."

Brian nodded – this was a testimony as to how old the family was. Sault Ste. Marie was one of the oldest still-occupied cities in North America east of the Mississippi, and for centuries had been a single settlement until the boundary between the United States and Canada had been drawn down the middle of the St. Mary's River in 1842. Subsequently there had been "two Soos", one in Ontario and one in Michigan. But historians and those from old families remembered the days when the Sault had been one city.

"Anyway, my aunt passed a while back, and it fell to me to go through her house. Not much there, mostly old worn out things, some going back to the middle of the last century – photos of her dad from World War II, and such like. She was eighty-four when she died, and had lived in that house all her life, by herself for the last seventeen years."

"Did your aunt give you this book?" Brian asked.

"No. She may not even have known she had it," Pete explained. "Jeremy was helping me go through the attic, where we found a great old chest in a corner – the kind with the locking tab like they used to make, right? It was locked and looked like it hadn't been opened in a century at least, so that made us more curious. Jeremy had a pry bar in his truck, so we broke the tab. Sure enough, the chest was filled with old stuff – pictures, a Bible, an old hat, a fan, that sort of thing."

"Family mementos, then?" Brian asked.

"Looks that way – things from all through history. There's a bonnet that I want my sister to look at, and some names in the Bible that I'm sure somebody will care about. But off to one side, wrapped in old, yellowed paper, was this book. Minute I picked it up, I could tell it was really old and rare. Jeremy thought so, too. We just opened the front cover, like you did – that's when the leather straps cracked. Once we saw how old it looked, I fetched a plastic bag and tucked it in."

"When was this?"

"Just this past weekend. I put it away safe and brought it to you as soon as I could."

"Thank you for your trust," Brian said. "May I ask – what are you expecting of us regarding this book?"

"Well, now, I don't rightly know," Pete replied, scratching his head. "It may be nothing but the diary of some long-ago relative with nothing much to say. But it looks old, and it looks French, which would put it way back, so I figured that some scholar might be interested. Jeremy and my sister agree. It's not like it's doing me much good, other than as a real old family heirloom."

"So, you'd like us to examine it, and you'd be willing to entrust it to us?" Brian asked.

"Oh, sure. You might be able to figure out what it says. I wouldn't mind knowing that, but I sure can't read it."

Dr. Harris took a deep breath and let it out slowly. This was almost too good to be true. Perhaps the book was nothing much, but perhaps... "I'll be frank with you, Pete: this book may be of considerable historical value. Even if it's just the diary of an ordinary person, it will be a welcome addition to the rare documents from that period. But if it is from the area of the Sault, and the date is accurate, then – well, that would be from the times of the earliest Europeans in the region. If there was a literate man in these parts at that time, it could be a historical record of substantial significance."

"Whoa," Pete said with wide eyes.

"I don't want to speculate, or get your hopes up," Dr. Harris continued. "And furthermore, I have to caution you that 'historical value' rarely translates into 'monetary value'. A find such as this is a treasure of a different sort. If this book is as significant as I suspect it may be, you'd be recognized and thanked, maybe with an article on a news site or an interview, but probably no more than that."

Pete looked crestfallen for a minute, then grinned and shrugged. "That's all right. I wasn't expecting nothing."

"If it's any consolation, nobody else will get rich off this, either," Dr. Harris assured him, then assumed a more formal tone. "Understanding that this book is and remains your property, are you entrusting this artifact to me and to the university, that we may examine and investigate it?"

"Yes, sir," Pete answered.

"Though we will treat it with utmost care, the age and condition may mean it will suffer some damage in the course of the examination. Are you willing to accept that risk?"

"Well, I figure you're going to handle it better than Jeremy and I did."

"We'll certainly try," Brian assured him. "Do we have your permission to make images of the artifact and its pages in the course of our examination?"

"I figured you would, so sure."

"And lastly, do you want a written and signed record of this agreement, or will this video record suffice?"

Pete glanced at the monitor and nodded. "You seem like an honest man, and I trust you. No need for anything written."

"I thank you, and the university thanks you," Brian replied. "And I'm guessing that scholars from all over will eventually be thanking you."

"Oh, you're more than welcome. If that'll be all, Dr. Harris –" Pete turned toward the door, clearly anxious to depart this unfamiliar environment.

"Wait, Pete – how can we get ahold of you?"

"Oh, yeah," Pete replied. While he gave his contact information to the video recorder, Brian stared at the book and pondered. Pete might be right. Just because this book ended up in Sault Ste. Marie didn't mean it had anything to do with the area's history. It might be the diary of some Parisian maid of that era, full of maundering and romantic fluff. But his gut told him it was more – possibly much more. He said goodbye to Pete and sat down to collect his wits while he awaited Lucy's return. He needed to notify someone official about this, so he dictated a voice message to his dean, his fellow history instructor Alexa, and the university president. Yes, the president should know about this. That finished, he began to consider the problem of how to best preserve this artifact while getting good images of all the pages. It should be handled by a properly trained and equipped ancient documents team, but LSSU didn't have any of those. Maybe Michigan State or the University of Michigan, but the last thing he wanted to suggest was shipping this precious treasure elsewhere. He wanted to exhaust all his university's resources before doing that.

But who? Ah – maybe the university's Criminal Justice Department? Their forensics people were accustomed to handling evidence, some of it fragile and delicate. They had preservation methods, too, as well as sophisticated imaging. Perhaps they could help. He reached for his workstation to punch up the forensics lab.

Three weeks later, Pete Durant returned to the university at Dr. Harris's invitation for an evening meeting in the department's conference room. Seated at the table with Dr. Harris was a strong-featured woman with light brown hair, warm brown eyes, and a ready smile. Beside her was a stocky gentleman with a receding hairline, a bushy salt-and-pepper moustache, and a friendly but businesslike manner.

"Peter Durant, permit me to introduce Dr. Olivia Picotte, assistant professor of French studies from the University of Western Ontario in London, and Dr. Andrew Newell, professor of First Nations studies at the same institution." Pete shook hands and took a seat.

"On behalf of the university and the scholarly community," Dr. Olivia beamed, "permit me to thank you most earnestly for your generous contribution of this artifact. It is an item of immense historical value and a substantial addition to our sources from that period."

"Really?" Pete blinked. "It's that important?"

"Put it this way," Dr. Newell said in a slightly more subdued tone. "This journal may not be a gold mine, but it's certainly high-quality silver. It's a verifiable first-person document dating from the earliest days of European presence in this area. It's in good condition considering its age, which means that most of the writing should be recoverable, especially with enhanced imaging. The scholarly community owes a considerable debt to your family for preserving it, and to you for bringing it forward."

"Well," Pete shrugged. "It seemed like the obvious thing to do. Jeremy thought so, too – he's my buddy."

"Then please extend our thanks to Jeremy as well," Dr. Newell granted. "The point is, where someone else might have pitched this into a drawer, or into the trash, you had the presence of mind to bring it to Dr. Harris. He, in turn, had the stroke of genius to bring in his forensics experts, who have been doing a superb job of handling the journal. They've been separating the pages and sealing them in argon-filled ultraviolet-opaque evidence sheaths." At this Dr. Harris held up a stiff, thin, clear plastic object about the size of a piece of copy paper. In the middle of it Pete could see one of the beige pages from the journal.

"Dr. Harris has been scanning the pages and sending us the images," Dr. Newell continued. "Since the language is French, the project was referred to Dr. Picotte's department. Dr. Picotte?"

The professor smiled and tapped a keyboard, bringing up an image of the journal on the monitors that stood back-to-back in the center of the conference table.

"First, Mr. Durant, your little silver mine is the personal journal of Fr. Thomas D'Aubigne, a Jesuit priest. Does the name sound familiar?" Pete shook his head. "I'd have been surprised if it did – we're having research done in the Jesuit records in France. He volunteered to come to the New World as a missionary 'For the Glory of Christ and the advancing of the Message of Salvation,' in his words. He left France in 1640 and arrived in the Sault area sometime in 1641. He began this journal to keep a record of his journeys.

"We've only begun the translation effort. Not only do we have to deal with the condition of the document, but the writing itself is difficult for a couple of reasons."

"How can writing be 'difficult'?" Dr. Harris asked.

"For one thing, the physical letters are small," Dr. Picotte explained. "When paper is at a premium, you write as small as you can. That's enough of a challenge, but the French is idiosyncratic. Latin was the scholarly language of the time, and when Fr. Thomas uses that, he's quite clear and structured. But the vernacular languages of the time were still finding their footing, so spelling and grammar is much less predictable.

"Thus, our first effort is to transcribe the document, working around the tiny writing, faded ink, and irregular language usage. I've got a team of grad students and senior undergrads working on that. Interspersed through the journal are sections written in Latin. We guess that those sections were intended to be his semi-official report back to his superiors, in case he didn't return but his journal did – a common enough occurrence with these forward missionaries. We don't know yet, but we're guessing that the fact that the journal was hidden here for centuries means that Fr. Thomas never made it back." Dr. Picotte tapped the keyboard, and the image of the journal was replaced by the image of one of the journal pages in its plastic sheath, and beside that a page written in neatly printed French.

"Right behind our transcribers come our translators. They're doing a couple of things – one is 'regularizing' the French into conventional form to make it more readable to the modern eye. The other is translating the pages into English to make them more universally readable. The Latin will be left untouched, grammatically, but will be also translated into French and English. When we're finished, each original page will have a direct transcription, a 'regularized' French version, and an English translation."

"Wow," Peter said. "All this from a trunk in my aunt's attic!"

Dr. Picotte gave him a brilliant smile. "Understand, Mr. Durant, that in the scholarly world a journal like this is the find of a lifetime. When Dr. Harris sent the news, our entire department was electrified. The competition to be assigned to the project was fierce. We're in touch with scholars in France, Quebec, and the Jesuit Order, all of whom are eager to see our results. We've just gotten organized, but we hope to be translating at a good pace very soon. This find is important for many people – which explains Dr. Newell's presence." At this she nodded to her partner.

"Yes," Dr. Newell rumbled, tapping the table. "My inclusion in the project is in hopes that Fr. Thomas's record will include accounts of First Nation life and activity from the period. We're optimistic about this, since most Jesuits were diligent about recording nearly everything. But since the translation effort is still in the early stages, all we yet know is that Fr. Thomas was a missionary to the area, and that he initially worked with Fr. Claude Pijart. Fr. Pijart we know of – he was very active with the Huron Nation around the Georgian Bay area for many years. Beyond that, the nature of Fr. Thomas's work, how he – or perhaps just his journal – ended up here at the Sault, is yet to be discovered.

"The timing of his record is especially important. In 1640, European contact had not yet significantly impacted First Nations' lives. Aside from the occasional trapper or missionary, the Nations had little contact with outside influences and were still living as they had for centuries. Even traded goods were only beginning to reach the tribes in this area.

"All of that changed radically in the decades that followed. The fur trade and the economic changes it wrought, Iroquois incursions, an increasing flow of Europeans into the area, and many other factors changed First Nation lives irrevocably. Since their transmission of knowledge was oral, much was lost when tribal elders died. Personal written accounts by early visitors such as Fr. Thomas provide a vital source not just for European scholars, but for the First Nations as well. It gives them a glimpse of how their ancestors lived before substantial European contact. We're hoping Fr. Thomas's journal will enhance a too-sparse fund of information about those times."

"Well," Dr. Harris said, looking around with a broad smile. "How exciting!"

"To scholars, certainly," Dr. Picotte added with a nod to Pete. "I hope you can appreciate how important your family artifact is, Mr. Durant."

"Oh, maybe not as much as you professors can, but I get the general idea," Pete answered. "I'm just a shop manager by trade, but my family roots go deep in the area, and history has always interested me. My study has been more around the Revolutionary War and the War of 1812, but this is interesting too."

"Good, good," Dr. Newell replied. "Then you'll appreciate some of the steps we've tried to take. If it's acceptable to you both, we'd like to bring in a First Nations scholar who lives very near, just north of the Canadian Sault. His name is Gerald Solomon, and he's a member of the Anishinaabek Nation, specifically the Salteaux Ojibwa. He's quite a scholar and a fascinating man. Though he's well educated – he has an MA from Oxford University – he prefers to live with his people on the Garden River Reserve, trying to preserve their life and lore. Fortunately, modern communications enable us to keep in close touch with him. On occasion, he's even guest lectured for my classes via videocast.

"With your permission, we'd like to make Gerald our First Nations contact for this project. As the pages are translated, we'll send the content to him for his evaluation and input, and also for distribution to the First Nations," Dr. Picotte explained. "If you'd like, we can ask him if he would schedule some sessions to sit down with you both to go over the translations and explain the findings."

"We'd like that very much – in fact, we'd be honored," Dr. Harris said, glancing at Pete, who nodded enthusiastically.

"It's the least we can do for you both, for providing this wonderful opportunity for us. We wish we could come up ourselves to take part, but the distance is an obstacle. Once we get a set of pages translated, we'll send them along with Gerald and you can set up a meeting," said Dr. Picotte.

Assignment

Jason Pelletier paced the conference room anxiously, his thoughts churning. As he passed near the floor-to-ceiling windows, he looked out over the bustling hive of activity that was suburban northern Virginia – the mirrored high-rises, the nonstop traffic, the ever-present helicopters loitering in the air. He could easily see the major landmarks from here: the Washington Monument, the Capitol dome, and the rounded top of the Jefferson Memorial at the edge of the Tidal Basin. He could even see some of the low, block-like office buildings that lay within the District. To neophytes, these were the coveted addresses, a couple of floors away from Cabinet officials, a brisk walk away from Capitol Hill to attend hearings or consult with staffers. Only the more experienced knew that those offices were show quarters, puff jobs fobbed off on those who had reached their level of incompetence preparing talking points or gossiping with other Administration officials in the District's many bars. The true centers of power, the addresses you really wanted, were out in the suburbs like Alexandria and Fairfax and Tysons Corners, which was where he was now. Here, amidst the anonymity offered by the hundreds of office buildings that dotted the region, was where the real decisions were made. An office in the District with your name on the door meant you had an office in the District with your name on the door, and everyone knew who you were and where to find you. You were the one to be summoned before the subcommittee, it was your name tag on the desk in front of you and maybe a clip of your testimony on the news sites. But the positions you explained and the policies you defended were drawn up out here, by people who didn't have their name on the office door, and might not even have an office. Maybe they had a cubicle, or maybe just a mail slot in the lobby, and an e-mail address and a phone number. Those who mattered knew how to find you. You were one of the decision-makers, the ones who crafted the direction of the agency and executed its policies.

Jason forced himself to sit down. There was no reason to pace like an anxious job applicant. He'd been here before. Never *here* to the eleventh floor, of course, but that didn't matter. He knew that some things were unsettled at the moment and decisions were being made. Maybe this summons had to do with that. Maybe he was here to receive some news. It would be good news, certainly, favorable news – why else be called here to the eleventh floor? He'd been effective, he'd helped the division achieve its goals. Of course, there had been the debacle in Salt Lake City, but they could hardly hold that against him. He'd been called in toward the end of that, and the DOJ had been lead agency anyway. Without thinking he stood up and began pacing again. The downside of not having an office with your name on the door was how easy it was for you to vanish, to be shunted aside to some backwater or even dismissed. Dismissed? Surely it wouldn't come to that. Think positive, think positive, he encouraged himself. He knew there was a position opening. Dare he hope this summons meant he was being notified of a promotion? No, no, don't get your hopes up that high, don't risk jinxing it.

Realizing that he was pacing, Jason angrily forced himself to sit back down and assume a relaxed posture. But his agitated mind did not relax. He wished he could grab a smoke, and was beginning to regret the cup of coffee he'd hastily swilled on the way here. He looked at the conference room door and pondered what he could expect. Who would come through it? If it was some nameless functionary, or even worse, a terse text message summoning him to the Director's office, that wouldn't be good. That would forebode a swift reassignment or dismissal. He'd find himself standing before the Director's desk with an aide hovering back by the door, ready to open it at the right moment. On the other hand, if the news was good, the Director himself might come through the door, followed by a flock of staffers coming along to bask in the cheer and good wishes. Which would it be? Jason glanced at the clock above the door. Come on! The call had said to be here at 10:00, and it was already 10:20! He clenched his hands and forced himself to remain seated. Think positive. Think positive.

The door opened abruptly. Jason jerked his head up, then swiftly schooled his features to appear unconcerned. He was glad he hadn't been caught pacing. Through the door walked a woman, alone, who closed the door behind her and turned to him. Jason wracked his memory – mid-length black hair, sharp features, no-nonsense expression – he should know who this was. That's right, she was Director Miller's aide, Cynthia, Cynthia somebody. He rose and tried to smile.

"Hello, Jason," the woman said, setting her tablet on the table and sitting down without introduction. "The Director sent me to inform you that he's selected Kevin for the position."

Jason nodded and gave the obligatory smile, though he was clenching his teeth while doing it. So it was Whitman who was getting the happy visit right now, the bastard. "How fortunate for him," Jason said emptily, because appearances had to be maintained. But what did this mean for Jason?

"Director Miller wants to be sure you know that he appreciates your contributions to the division, but many factors influenced his decision. I'm sure you'll understand," Cynthia threw him a bone.

"Certainly," Jason acknowledged.

"However, given that you are at loose ends after your last posting, Director Miller was wondering if you would consider a special assignment," Cynthia continued, tapping at her tablet and then looking up at him expectantly.

The subtext here was unmistakable. His last posting had ended in embarrassment, even if it hadn't been his fault, so the promotion had gone to his rival. However, he was being offered an opportunity for redemption. What choice did he have?

"Possibly," Jason said noncommittally. "What is the nature of this special assignment?"

Cynthia forced a quick smile then turned the tablet toward him with a suitably sympathetic expression. "I'm afraid it's another interdepartmental screwup. Not DOJ this time, though. Health and Human Services."

"HHS?" Jason asked in mystification as he skimmed the details. "How the hell did we get involved in an HHS project?"

"Because of how it ended," Cynthia reached over to scroll the page to the bottom. "Big domestic terror incident up in Michigan that brought a critical pilot program to a crashing halt. Over twenty killed, including a high level official from HHS who'd been the director of the project and its chief architect."

"*Twenty?*" Jason asked in astonishment. "You'd think a domestic terror hit like that would have made the news."

"That's the thing – the project was so black that it had to be hushed up. It was let out as an industrial accident with just a couple of local casualties. Few people know the real story."

Jason felt like he'd stepped into an alternate universe. What kind of HHS project could be considered "black"? "Any leads or clues?"

"None, but whoever the terrorists were, they knew exactly where and when to strike to maximize impact. The hit was completely unexpected and precisely timed to decapitate the project down to the shoulders. No survivors."

"Sounds sophisticated," Jason acknowledged. "Any idea who would have been behind it?"

"In the course of shaking out the pilot, some of the HHS operatives had uncovered evidence of a clandestine domestic terror network in the region working to frustrate the project's goals. Their investigation was just beginning to bear fruit, and they'd even apprehended a couple of the perps, when the network struck back ruthlessly. Even killed their own people."

"Wow," Jason said, as he continued to review the scant details on the summary sheet. His mind was racing – he had to find a way to leverage this. "Over two years now and no substantial progress?"

"The project was so secret that HHS wanted the need-to-know circle drawn as small as possible. That meant that once the cover story was released, other agencies formally stepped back, though they've been lending us quiet support."

"And we got stuck with it because of the domestic terror angle?"

"That, plus we lost a few people in the blast ourselves," Cynthia added.

"Ouch," Jason winced. "That makes it personal."

"It does, though they were low-level functionaries – just field agents."

"Hmm," Jason mused, sitting back and eyeing Cynthia critically. He had to set the right tone here: cautious, judicious, not too eager. "I see here some detail about our operations, but precious little about the HHS project. I'm reluctant to sign up without knowing more."

"Understandable," Cynthia acknowledged. "But that's a bit of a Mexican standoff with them. They need help, but are reluctant to divulge full details to someone who hasn't yet signed on. They are getting more pliable, though – this thing has been a bleeding sore in their side, and they're getting anxious for resolution. Frankly, so is Director Miller – he's tired of seeing this listed on his summaries with an 'Unresolved' status next to it."

"Well, we're the only other agency with skin in the game," Jason added, pretending to examine the tablet but thinking furiously about how to play this. His gut was telling him to go for the gold, that this situation called for bold strokes. "All right," he said suddenly, leaning forward and tapping the table as if he was negotiating from a position of strength. "Two questions: what does the Director want? Does he just want that status cleared? Or does he want the whole smash? Is he only looking for the domestic terror investigation to be resolved, or does he also want to help HHS get their project back on track? Catching the saboteurs is one thing, but repairing the broken machine and getting it working again is the ultimate goal, right?"

"Well, now," Cynthia replied, looking at him sideways. "The Director would certainly wish our responsibility in this situation brought to a satisfactory conclusion. As far as helping HHS get their project restarted – you know what a proponent of interdepartmental cooperation he is."

Jason knew how to interpret that. If Director Miller could deliver to HHS not only the resolution of the incident but also their stalled project restarted due to Department of Homeland Security action, it would score major points in the endless game of one-upmanship that was the D.C. world.

"All right, then. Next question: how much authority would I have? You know that was the biggest factor behind the Salt Lake City debacle – I was given responsibility for almost everything, but the DOJ wouldn't give up any authority." He forced himself to stop there, though he could have gone on for hours. It wouldn't do to sound like a whiner.

Cynthia nodded sympathetically. "I appreciate your point. Simply put, you'd be given plenary authority over the entire situation, both DHS and HHS. On our side, we've got plenty of resources, given that it's a border area. Agents, investigators, facilities, and other assets would all be yours to tap. There's also an aerial base in the region, with high- and low-level drone assets."

"Weapons capable?"

"Of course," Cynthia affirmed. "You'd have a free hand."

"So far as Homeland Security is concerned. What about Health and Human Services? How much authority there?"

"That's something that we'd have to negotiate with them," Cynthia qualified. "But I can assure you that if you are willing to go in with intent to advance this situation, you can count on complete support from Director Miller. He will make clear to his equivalent in HHS that they either give you the authority you need or we're walking away."

"So, I wouldn't be going around with a gaggle of policy twerps breathing down my neck?" Jason pressed.

"No. If you take on the problem, you get what you need to resolve it – within reason, of course, but we trust your judgment. But there is one proviso you should be aware of."

"What's that?"

"Given the authority you'd be granted, the Director doesn't want this run remotely from here in D.C. You'd need to be on site for the duration," Cynthia said.

Jason fell silent for a minute as he pondered this. It was a big consideration. A project of this magnitude would take several months to resolve, possibly as long as a year. Moving hundreds of miles away for that long a period risked becoming seriously disconnected from his environment. Out of sight not only meant out of mind, but also out of the circles of power that flowed and morphed constantly. On the other hand, if he returned in triumph, not just over the enemy but over another department, that could cut right through the circles and open doors that had always been closed to him. Besides, it wasn't all that far, not even out of the time zone. He could do one day drop-ins, flying down in the morning and back in the evening, just to show his face from time to time.

Jason was aware that Cynthia was eyeing him as he thought. She knew as well as he that this facet of the project was a major issue, and was watching his response. "I presume," Jason ventured cautiously, "that I'd be required to report progress in person from time to time?"

"It would be permitted," Cynthia replied. "But given the latitude you'd have, the Director's expectation would be that you'd be spending most of your time at the site attending to details. Most reporting and consultation would be either written or by teleconference."

That required some interpretation: we'll put up with your checking in from time to time, but don't want to see you hanging around when you should be off solving our problem. Jason kept his smile relaxed and forced himself not to squirm in his seat as he began to appreciate the tightness of the corner he'd been maneuvered into. All of this – the mysterious summons, the private interview with the Director's aide, the confidential project – was starting to smell like a setup. If he declined, he'd be told "we understand" and "we'll try to find a place for you", then be shunted off to some obscure corner to wither and die. But if he accepted, he'd be out of the loop for months, missing all the developments and nuances and opportunities to edge out his rivals. That son of a bitch Whitman had to have his hand in this.

Jason fought against the bitter animosity that threatened to overwhelm his judgment. He felt like he was always getting dropped into these impossible circumstances, requiring him to kite off to remote corners of the country while his rivals worked the ropes here in D.C. He took a deep breath and forced himself to calm down. This sounded like a minor situation. In all likelihood, the only reason it hadn't been resolved was because nobody had given it proper attention. It had been a C-list problem, easy to shunt aside. He'd faced circumstances like this before, and had always come out on top. All it took was a little self-confidence. He willed himself to calm down and face the situation rationally. He'd tackled worse than this; he'd tackle this as well.

Besides, it wasn't as if he had any choice.

"Well," he said as lightly as he could manage. "When do I start?"

Cynthia bared her teeth in response. "Wonderful. The Director will be pleased to hear that you're on the job. I'll start making arrangements immediately, beginning with the briefings you'll need. I'll be in touch." Tapping her tablet screen, she rose and departed, leaving Jason to ponder what he'd gotten himself into.

Just outside the door, Cynthia stopped long enough to open a window on the tablet and tap out a brief message.

"He bit."

Jason never liked visiting HHS facilities. The subtle air of low-grade grievance that the staff carried around with them seemed to permeate even their buildings. As he sat alone in the basement auditorium awaiting the arrival of the staff giving the briefing, he could hear the ventilation system groaning. Jesus, even their offices complained! The HHS logo projected on the wall-sized screen had a slight greenish cast to it, and one of the panels in the upper left of the screen was dead. Minor defects, but Jason wouldn't have tolerated them for a week in a DHS facility – he would have found someone to fix them. But this was HHS, so it was, "That's just how this screen is," and "We've had a call in to Maintenance for months."

A side door opened to admit a tall, heavyset man followed by a short, officious looking woman who was carrying a briefcase. They walked to the table on the dais at the front of the room, where the woman placed the briefcase on a table and they both thumbed the biometric pad to open it. Only then did the man turn to Jason.

"Agent Pelletier, thank you for coming," the man said as he shook Jason's hand. Jason decided that this was not the time to point out that he wasn't any sort of agent. To most HHS workers, anyone from DHS was an "agent", and only one missed dosage away from whipping out his service pistol and emptying it into some hapless therapist.

"I'm Jerry Casey, and this is Alice Nagan, both from the HHS Office of Strategic Planning," the man continued, as behind him Alice bustled about pulling binders and tablets from the briefcase and slipping a chip into the projection controller. "We've been assigned to brief you on the pilot project spearheaded by Dr. Tasker." He tapped his phone and an ominously worded message appeared on the screen, warning the viewer that the contents of the presentation were Top Secret, not to be discussed with unauthorized personnel, etc. Jason had seen plenty of these warnings in his time. The bustling Alice bustled over to lay a binder and tablet on the table before him.

"Put your thumb here, please," Alice muttered, and Jason dutifully thumbed the biometric pad. The tablet screen sprang to life, showing an array of icons for documents, presentations, and summary sheets.

Jerry tapped his phone again and the next image appeared on the screen. It showed a heavy, balding man with a pronounced red cast to his skin, holding a drink and talking to another man. "This was Dr. Kevin Tasker," Jerry explained. "Dr. Tasker was an analytical supervisor here at OSP. He had two doctorates, an MD and a PhD in Economics. He was a brilliant man with a keen mind and tremendous foresight." Jerry paused and took a breath before continuing. "He was also an irascible bastard with a short fuse, fierce temper, and little patience with anyone not as smart as he was – which was nearly everyone." Jerry glanced at Alice, who pursed her lips primly but said nothing. For his part, Jason appreciated the frank appraisal, and nodded for Jerry to continue.

"I know this, because I worked closely with him from the time he transferred in from Accounting. He was the most demanding boss I ever worked for, but he got results. No matter how many toes he stepped on or egos he bruised, his projects succeeded – except, of course, his final one."

Jason parsed this summary. Tasker's track record must have been impressive, if he'd advanced as far as he did despite a short temper and a blunt manner. Particularly in the HHS environment, weighted as it was with staff from the helping professions, being harsh and undiplomatic was a serious handicap – yet this man had succeeded nonetheless.

"Dr. Tasker's particular strength was creating computer models. His models were complex and wide-ranging, incorporating the most unexpected elements. They were also astonishingly accurate, which was part of the reason he was both loved and hated. Sometimes his models would predict outcomes that would sharply contradict conventional wisdom and settled policy. That ruffled many feathers, particularly when he was so consistently right.

"After working for many years in budget forecasting, he was transferred here to OSP to help guide emerging policy. He got to work on his most ambitious project – a broad evaluation of the future of publicly funded healthcare. The results of his modeling efforts were distressing. Let me illustrate." A new image filled the screen, one that looked familiar to Jason. It was a line graph with a light blue line that sloped gently upward from left to right as well as a dark blue line that sloped more sharply, intersecting the light blue line about two-thirds of the way across the graph.

"This graph indicates anticipated healthcare revenues and expenditures," Jerry explained. "The light blue line represents revenues, while the dark blue represents expenditures over the same period. As you can see, expenditures are currently below revenues, but are expected to catch up quickly and overtake them at a point in the near future. This point, where the two lines intersect on the graph, is the drop-dead point – where we run out of money to pay the bills."

"Where are we currently along this timeline?" Jason asked.

"By this projection, right about here," Jerry illuminated a vertical yellow line about a third of the way along the graph.

"We don't seem to be very far from the drop-dead point," Jason observed. Jerry chucked darkly in response.

"Oh, you have no idea. This is our graph for public consumption, the one approved by the Secretary for inclusion in our reports and submission to Congress. This is what you'll find on our online site. This," Jerry brought up the next image, "is the projection according to Dr. Tasker's model."

The new graph was much harsher, with a reddish-brown background, a bright yellow line angling slowly upward, and a glaring red line climbing swiftly to cross it about halfway along the horizontal axis. The red line didn't slope smoothly, but curved more sharply upward as it went, until it was almost vertical by the time it reached the right edge of the graph. A vertical white line stood nearly halfway along the graph, disturbingly near the point where the red and yellow lines crossed.

"On this graph, the yellow line represents revenue and the red line represents expenditures. As you can see, by this projection revenues grow only modestly while expenditures climb far more dramatically than on the official graph. This model projects a much more calamitous situation."

"And we seem to be much closer to the drop-dead point," Jason noted, pointing to the vertical line.

Again Jerry gave a grim laugh. "Oh, that was where the line was six years ago, when this graph was first presented to HHS leadership. Here is where things stood at the beginning of this fiscal year." He brought up the next image and a lighter set of lines were overlaid on the graph – a yellow one that closely paralleled the existing yellow one, and a red one that roughly followed the first line. Jason noticed that the new, lighter red line sloped upward more sharply. The vertical white line stood just past the point where the light red and light yellow lines intersected. "Once again,

Dr. Tasker's model predicted the unfolding of events with distressing accuracy. These new lines represent actual revenue and expenditures over the projection period."

"And the vertical line is where we are now?" Jason asked.

"That's where we were at the beginning of the fiscal year, about five months ago," Jerry replied.

"But…that's past the drop-dead point," Jason pointed out.

"That's right."

"Then how are bills getting paid?"

"You can do amazing tricks with accounting," Jerry admitted. "But there's no denying that this is the foremost issue pressuring HHS leadership, especially since the pilot project collapsed."

Jason tapped the table. "You mentioned this being presented six years ago. Was that part of this pilot project?"

"That was when Dr. Tasker first proposed the project. Since his model projected a much more severe situation much sooner than our staff analysts were predicting, he wanted to propose a solution at the time he presented the problem. He came up with the Chengdu Project."

"Chengdu?" Jason asked.

"He never explained that, even to me. It's a city in central China. From a hint or two he dropped, I think he knew of something that had happened or was happening there."

"So what was the thrust of this Chengdu Project?"

Alice looked stone-face while Jerry fidgeted a little. "Please keep in mind that this material is Top Secret, and cannot be discussed outside authorized facilities or with unauthorized personnel."

"Please keep in mind that I'm DHS, and have extensive experience handling Top Secret material," Jason replied coolly.

"Very well," Jerry nodded, and brought the next image up on the screen. It was an oddly shaped bar graph, with a vertical axis that had horizontal bars extending from it to the left and right. The outline of the bars formed a shape that roughly resembled the outline of an apple. "You're familiar with a population pyramid?"

"Somewhat," Jason admitted, fishing in his memory. "The horizontal bars represent age brackets, don't they?"

"That's right," Jerry replied, visibly relieved that he didn't have to explain the graph from scratch. "You've got the country's population divided into age brackets, represented by these bars from bottom to top, and by sex. So, this bottom bar on the left represents females between ages zero and four, and the equivalent one on the right represents males in the same age bracket. The next set of bars up represent females and males in the five to nine age range, and so on up the ladder to the one hundred to one hundred four bracket at the very top. Have you ever explored the economic implications of this view of population?"

"Can't say that I have," Jason replied.

"Well, to greatly simplify a more in-depth explanation," Jerry said, flicking through several slides that overlaid shapes and text onto the population pyramid, "The populations in the lowest and highest brackets are net resource drains. It's the populations in the middle, from ages fifteen to sixty nine, that generate the GDP. All the wages, taxes, and economic production comes out of these population brackets. These workers do it all, including supporting the nonproductive brackets."

"Ah," Jason observed. "People in that stage of life are strained enough just making a living, much less supporting noncontributors."

"Well, the lower brackets, the children, are normally an accepted burden," Jerry said, "but the pressing problem is the upper brackets – those who have passed out of their productive years and represent net drains on the economy. It gets even worse when you consider medical expenditures. This next graph shows how dramatically medical expenditures increase as the population moves up through the age brackets, particularly after passing age fifty…"

"Jerry, I get the idea. I'm somewhat familiar with the problem," Jason interrupted. "Skip to the part where you discuss what Dr. Tasker proposed – the Chengdu Project."

"Oh...ah, yes," Jerry stammered, thrown off his stride by the interruption. He started flicking through images at a rapid pace until he came to the ones he wanted. "Well, then, the project itself. The goal was simple: as efficiently and unobtrusively as possible cull out high cost recipients who were beyond their economically productive years. Since the potential for social fallout and consequent political backlash was high, the project focused on recipients that fit a particular demographic profile."

"What demographic profile?" Jason asked.

"Recipients who either had no immediately concerned parties, or who were separated or estranged from them. For example, a divorced male who never had children, or a single mother who has had no contact with her daughter for years, and so forth."

"You can determine that kind of thing from the data you have?"

"There are ways of interpreting various data elements that allow you to assign probabilities. You start with obvious things like census and tax filing data, but there are a myriad of other things you can evaluate. Dr. Tasker was a genius at figuring out which factors to include in the models. And, of course, once you got to the actual field work, your point agents could look right at the actual data and provide further feedback."

"Field work?" asked Jason.

"I'm getting ahead of myself," Jerry said apologetically. "Dr. Tasker convinced leadership that his models could identify population segments that could be culled in order to reduce costs. Leadership green-lighted a pilot project to allow him to test his theories. We did an extensive analysis of the economy, geography, and demographics of various regions of the country." An image clicked onto the screen showing an outline of the nation with small shaded patches scattered across it. "Dr. Tasker determined that the best location for an effective pilot program would be this section of eastern Michigan known as the Thumb." All other patches faded while the one covering a portion of east Michigan glowed brighter.

"Michigan?" Jason asked.

"There were a number of reasons this region was chosen, which you'll find in the documents on the tablet in front of you. The biggest two reasons were that it contained a high concentration of recipients who fit the demographic profile, and it was easy to isolate geographically. There are a limited number of acute care facilities servicing the area, and that reduced the number of field operators we had to manage." The image on the screen zoomed in on the eastern portion of the familiar mitten shape of Michigan. Some lines and dots appeared on it, indicating borders and cities and roads. Larger shaped areas around the edge of the region indicated more populated cities, and bright dots with text beside them appeared in the areas.

"This was our geographic framework for the pilot of the Chengdu Project. Our first challenge was getting a network of field workers in place. The initial phase focused on the acute care facilities, with a long-range goal of expanding into long-term care facilities as well."

"What would one of these field agents do?"

"The field workers, the point-of-the-spear agents, would administer the cocktail that would cull the recipient from the population," Jerry explained.

"The 'cocktail'?" Jason asked.

"I was getting to that," Jerry replied peevishly. "Since discretion was one of the goals, the pharmaceutical combination compiled for the recipient had to be personalized to produce an outcome consistent with their condition. For instance, if a recipient was being treated for a heart condition, you'd craft a cocktail heavy in digitalis, which would induce the cardiac failure everyone was expecting. You'd use a different mixture for a case suffering renal failure. For one thing, too many losses of the same type would skew the outcome profile and trigger undesired responsive protocols."

"Okay, so the kill mix was tailored to the patient's condition, to make the fatal event more believable," Jason translated.

"You…you could put it that way," Jerry confirmed, while Alice pursed her lips. "But that meant we had to have pharmaceutical workers to prepare the cocktail for the end workers, and a supervisor to coordinate timing and delivery. We also needed data analysts to evaluate individual recipients for suitability."

"Where did you get all these people?"

"Some we moved up from our offices here, but most of the workers we recruited from the facilities in the region. Obtaining and retaining workers was the supervisor's primary responsibility."

"Really?" Jason asked in astonishment. "How did they do that? Just ask, 'Hey, Nurse Kelly, how'd you like to off a few patients?'"

Alice looked more stone-faced than ever, and Jerry nearly winced. "Dr. Tasker could be very...idealistic at times. He was convinced that the right workers with reasonable intelligence could be convinced of the necessity of the effort, and the importance of their role in it. He was big on "buy-in". Foundational to the project were extensive education and persuasion efforts, in an attempt to get 'buy-in' from the workers. He wanted to create a dedicated corps that was as devoted to the goal as he was."

"How well did it work?"

"It started off well enough, especially given our limited budget. Dr. Tasker found some competent managers who got the field operations up and running, and they got a foothold in the acute care facilities. Initial outcomes were close to target, and things looked promising," Jerry explained.

"'Initial' outcomes?" Jason asked.

"Well...yes, as we found out later. The first unusual sign we saw was a slow drop-off in target attainment. This was unexpected, since the targets were based on Dr. Tasker's models. It was maddening for him. He'd spend weeks on end honing the models and feeding back actual field data, but the results kept falling short of projections. Leadership was beginning to question the efficacy of the pilot."

"What was the problem? Was field staff falling short of their goals?"

"There was some of that. Trained agents would be reliably productive, but turnover was unexpectedly high, siphoning off resources from management into recruiting and training. But the biggest factor was one we least expected: a shortage of suitable recipients. We had figured that would be a constant: from the given population, a certain number of candidate recipients would cycle through the system, of which a predictable percentage would be suitable, and that's where we'd focus our efforts.

"But about six months into the effort, the pool of candidate recipients began to drop, and it continued to drop steadily over the next year," Jerry said.

"What, old people just stopped coming to the hospital?" Jason asked.

"Nothing so noticeable," Jerry answered. "The admission flow wasn't substantially lower, but fewer and fewer admissions met the selection criteria. We even started to wonder if the project had been compromised, and details leaked out."

"Could that have happened?"

"We thought it unlikely, since there was no public hue and cry. We considered that some party might have worked backwards from the mortality statistics, but we thought that unlikely as well."

"Why did you think that?" Jason asked. "There are plenty of smart people out there."

"One aspect of the pilot was coordinating with public opinion management to ensure the statistics released had been suitably adjusted to mask the effects of the pilot. It was good practice for them, against the day that the project was rolled out more widely. There's almost no chance that anyone reading the published reports could have discerned that we were running a pilot in the region," Jerry explained.

"Did you ever find out what it was?"

Jerry sighed. "We did, but it wasn't until right…toward the end. Some of our field supervisors were beginning to suspect fishy things."

"What kind of 'fishy things'?"

"Just anecdotally, they thought the drop-off in suitable recipients to be so odd that it had to have some cause. There were also the unusual discharges. Some recipients who met the selection criteria and had been admitted to acute care were being inexplicably discharged before they could be treated. Ultimately, that proved to be what blew the conspiracy wide open. One of our workers had been dispatched to administer a cocktail to a selected recipient, only to find that the case had been discharged by the time she got there. That was the smoking gun – our manager was able to investigate on the spot and verify that the discharge had been irregular. We knew then that we were facing deliberate, coordinated opposition that was working to sabotage the pilot."

"Let me get this straight," Jason interrupted. "Not only did you see a drop-off in the number of suitable patients being admitted, but some of the ones that had been admitted were being discharged before you could… ah…treat them?"

"Exactly. And we know they weren't routine discharges, because almost all of them were tagged with exit codes that were hardly ever used," Jerry confirmed.

Jason pondered this for a minute. "That level of sophistication implies data system penetration, as well as personnel assets inside the hospitals."

"And more," Jerry added. "Their operation was extremely sophisticated, not least in their level of secrecy. They operated in a high-security environment right under our noses for two years, and we knew nothing until that one incident."

"What did this secret operation do with the people?" Jason asked.

"The people?"

"Yes, the 'recipients', as you call them. The folks slated for the cocktails."

"Oh…ah, them. The best we can figure, they hid them."

"Hid them? Where? And why?"

"We don't know, exactly," Jerry admitted. "From surveillance and other clues, we suspect they had a network of clandestine facilities across the region. They certainly had a supply network, and seemed to have communications and coordination capabilities. That's what Dr. Tasker went up there to root out. But they must have caught wind of it – no idea how, because his movement was top secret – because that's when they struck, taking out him and the entire leadership of the project."

"But you still have no idea who 'they' are, or why they would be spiriting away lonely old people to prevent them from being served a cocktail by one of your field agents," Jason pointed out.

"No. The closest we came was identifying one man. He had some connection to this mysterious group – he was at least running supplies for them, and could have been one of their inside contacts at the hospital. We'd taken him into custody, and had him and his friend, one of our workers, at the facility where Dr. Tasker was. We'd hoped to get intelligence from him about this group. Instead, he was blown up with everyone else."

Jason gave a low whistle. "How brutal – killing their own guy."

"They may have thought the trade-off worth it. They got a lot of good people in the process, effectively the brains of the entire operation."

"Well, I'm having a briefing on that the day after tomorrow," Jason said. "For now, what's the status of the pilot project?"

Jerry glanced at Alice, who did not respond, then shrugged. "It doesn't exist anymore. I mean, all the files are still there, but once Dr. Tasker was...that is, he didn't come back, his position was eliminated and his office dismantled. The pilot project was simply terminated."

"Oh? Then what's being done about the situation?" Jason pressed.

"The situation? What situation?" Jerry asked in confusion.

Jason sat back, stunned, and then scowled. "The fiscal situation, numbskull! The drop-dead threshold, and the fact that we're already past it! The situation that drove this whole damn effort!"

Alice winced, but Jerry seemed to shrivel. "That's...that's been a subject of vigorous discussion in leadership circles, vigorous discussion indeed. As of yet no consensus has been reached. To be frank, much hope had been placed in the pilot project, and everyone was quite taken aback by its abrupt...ending."

Jason bit back a sharp retort and considered this response. He guessed that this Dr. Tasker had been a rarity in his circles: someone who recognized an imminent catastrophe and was able to envision the bold steps necessary to head it off. Furthermore, he was able to recommend decisive action and push it through, not caring how many toes he stepped on in the process. Jason suspected he and Dr. Tasker would have understood one another, and may have been able to work together. Probably with a fair amount of shouting, but they would have made progress.

After Tasker's murder, though, the HHS bureaucrats had dithered and wavered while the precious days had ticked away. No doubt some – perhaps many – had been glad to see their abrasive colleague get his comeuppance, but they'd squandered the time he'd tried to take advantage of.

"So, nothing's been done to restart this pilot, and no other initiative has been envisioned to replace it?" Jason asked.

"None that I'm aware of," Jerry confirmed.

"And you were his chief analyst throughout the project?"

"Well, yes, but it's best to say that Dr. Tasker was his own chief analyst. I was his main aide, and was with him throughout. At its peak, the pilot had a staff of six analysts, who I supervised, but they've since been reassigned."

Jason considered it unlikely that HHS would have started anything new without at least consulting Tasker's right-hand man, so if Jerry hadn't heard of anything, that probably meant nothing was going on.

"Well," said Jason, tapping the tablet. "I'm going to want to do a lot more research on the project. You say all the documents are on the tablet here?"

"And in the binder," Alice confirmed. "Feel free to contact Jerry or myself, and we can coordinate times for you to come and review them."

Jason smiled and shook his head. "Sorry, I don't have time to jump through the hoops. I'm taking this with me. I'll need to study it carefully, and probably refer back to it over time."

Jerry's jaw dropped and Alice blinked in shock. "I'm...I'm afraid that won't be possible," Alice stammered. "This is highly classified and sensitive material. It cannot leave the facility, and can only be reviewed under direct supervision of authorized personnel such as myself. You'll have to come here, file an access request, and have someone bring you the material."

Jason reached into his folder and brought out what looked like a business card, but had only a two-dimensional bar code printed on it. He handed this card to Alice. "Call your supervisor, and while you've got him on the phone, scan that."

"But...this is –" Alice blustered, but Jason interrupted.

"Just do it. It'll save a lot of wasted time."

Nonplussed, Alice took the card and walked to a corner of the room where she began fiddling with her phone. Jerry stood fidgeting and looking embarrassed. Jason started paging through the binder while Alice carried on an animated conversation in the corner. After some time, she returned and gingerly placed her phone on the table in front of him. The screen showed only a standard biometric square.

"Could you put your right thumb on the screen, please," Alice asked timidly. Jason obliged, and got the confirming flicker. Alice took the phone away for more conversation, returning in a minute looking chastened and a little humiliated.

"You have been authorized to take these materials – oh, damn!"

"Damn what?" Jason asked.

"You're authorized to remove them and use them, but I forgot to ask about the briefcase."

"What about the briefcase?"

"These materials are required to either be locked in a safe or in this briefcase when not being actively used. I forgot to ask if that condition still applied."

Jason threw up his hands. "I concede the briefcase. Get me authorized to open it, and I'll ensure the materials stay it in when I'm not reviewing them."

Somewhat mollified, Alice made a few more phone calls. Shortly thereafter a technician arrived with a tablet which he plugged into the briefcase, then had Jason scan his thumbprint again, then did some fiddling with the tablet, but when it was all over Jason was standing by the conference room door, holding the secure briefcase that contained the precious materials, shaking hands with Alice and Jerry and thanking them for their efforts.

"I'm sure I'll be in further touch with you, Jerry," Jason assured him. "I'll have plenty of questions as I review this material."

"I'm just a phone call away," Jerry assured him, which earned him a burning glance from Alice. Jason was sure that in Alice's books, Jerry was guilty of giving aid and comfort to the enemy.

Jason's mind churned as he walked to his car. He had a lot of studying to do – good thing his next briefing wasn't until the day after tomorrow. This seemingly backwater assignment was turning out to have unexpected depths. One thing was becoming clear: the mass assassination might be a matter that needed resolution, but the burning issue was this HHS pilot project. If Jason could get that back on track, it would get noticed. He needed to get intimately familiar with the Chengdu Project – what Tasker had been trying to do, how he'd gone about it, and what obstacles he'd encountered. Yes, he had encountered organized opposition, but Jason was sure there were innate structural problems with the pilot as well. If he could come up with a cleaner solution that accomplished the same goals, he might be able to resurrect the project.

Jason's phone chimed. It was a message from Cynthia.

Ruffling feathers already?

It was impossible to tell whether that was in jest or censure. Jason tapped out a response.

Had to cut through HHS admin BS. Got what I needed. Ambitious project.

A minute later the response came back: *Do what's necessary, don't yank chain too hard or often. Best of luck.*

Jason considered this ambiguous directive. Oh, don't worry, Cynthia. I'll be judicious about my chain-yanking – and I'll time it for maximum impact.

Shadow of Death

The old woman looked at Luke with bright eyes as he touched the thermometer to her forehead. He tried to keep his face impassive as he read the number he'd both expected and feared, and put on his best encouraging smile as he slipped the cuff on her arm and read her blood pressure. She submitted to his ministrations with a gentle expression that was marred by her flushed skin and shallow breathing. Again, Luke tried to keep a poker face while reading the blood pressure numbers, and was nearly successful.

"I'm dying, aren't I?" the lady asked seriously.

Luke started automatically to shift to his cheerful bedside persona, but her penetrating eyes were on him, and he knew he was concealing nothing. With a sigh he stripped off the cuff.

"I'm afraid so, Mrs. Reese, barring a miracle," Luke admitted ruefully. "I've reached the limits of the treatment I can provide. If only I had –"

"Luke," Mrs. Reese interrupted gently, laying a hand on his arm, "it's all right. I'm ready for it. Without your help and everyone's care, I would have died long ago, alone and unknown. But because of you all, I'm ending my days surrounded by love and appreciation."

Luke was about to reply when a quiet sob interrupted him. Turning, he saw young Julie, just eleven, standing at the door with her hand to her mouth and her eyes glistening.

"Oh, darling, come here," Mrs. Reese said gently, holding out her arms. The girl ran across the room to be enfolded in the old woman's embrace.

"Mrs. Reese, Mrs. Reese, I don't want you to die!" Julie sobbed into the blanket while Mrs. Reese consoled her. Blinking back a few tears of his own, Luke left to give the two some privacy. Stepping into the kitchen, he found Anna sitting at the table. She poured him a cup of coffee and patted his shoulder as she set it before him.

"It's bad, isn't it?" Anna asked.

Luke nodded. "The only antibiotics I have aren't working. It may be a resistant strain – I couldn't tell without lab tests. And her diabetes doesn't make it any easier."

"How long would you give her?"

"A week, maybe ten days," Luke said glumly. "But no telling. Sepsis can move quickly. She may not make it through tonight. If only I could –"

"Luke," Anna said gently. "You've done all you could have. She's at peace, we're at peace. You should be, too."

"Yeah," Luke conceded, taking a melancholy pull at his coffee. "Well, as long as I'm here, why don't I take a listen to that cough of William's?" He grabbed his bag and headed for the boy's bedroom, where he did what he could to comfort the lad and treat his bronchitis. When he returned to the kitchen to pack up, Julie was sitting at the table with her mother, sipping tea and sniffing.

"Julie says she's sleeping again," Anna assured Luke.

"Look for more of that as things progress," Luke said. "In a way, it's the most desirable outcome."

"Mr. Doc Luke, what's wrong with Mrs. Reese? Why did she get sick so suddenly?" Julie asked.

"Well, sweetheart, it's probably from that deep cut she gave herself a couple of weeks ago while working in the kitchen," Luke explained. "Your mother did a great job of cleaning it, as good as I could have done, but something probably got left behind in the cut, something that started putting dangerous germs into her body."

"That's mean," Julie chipped in.

"In a sense," Luke said with a smile. "But germs are kind of like…like houseflies. They're not mean or kind, they just do what they do. But these germs got into Mrs. Reese's blood, causing a condition called sepsis. Generations ago this used to be called blood poisoning, and many people died of it. But about a hundred years ago they discovered some medicines that would help kill the dangerous germs, so deaths from sepsis became much less common."

"Then why don't you give Mrs. Reese some of the medicine to make her better?" Julie asked.

Luke grimaced and glanced at Anna. "I've given her the medicines I have available, and they may have helped contain the infection, but to get rid of it completely, I'd need different medicines, more powerful ones that would completely remove it."

"Why not get some of the better medicine?"

"I wish it was that easy," Luke said, tousling her hair. "But I promise I'll do everything I can."

"Okay, Mr. Doc Luke," Julie said, smiling slightly and looking at him with hopeful eyes.

With that Luke packed his gear into his travel bags, said his goodbyes, and went out to his snowmobile. Going through the routine vehicle checks he noticed how low he was on fuel. He had enough to make it to his next stop, but he'd have to fuel up there. Fortunately, it wasn't far, though it was another situation where he wouldn't be much help beyond palliative care. He wrapped his scarf tight and buckled his helmet before turning into the biting north wind and heading up the trail.

*   *   *

The same north wind was cutting across the ice that covered Georgian Bay and sweeping unhindered across the farmlands of the northern Windsor peninsula, bringing an Arctic greeting to the bare trees and snowbound farmsteads. The calendar said spring was just around the corner, but winter still wanted its say. Overhead the unbroken layer of gray clouds blocked even the least ray of sunshine from reaching the bleak landscape.

The young woman stood at the edge of the gully, looking down at where a trickle of water still managed to weave its way past the frozen banks and ice-clad rocks. She barely noticed the bitter wind, partly because of the thickness of her parka and knit cap, but also because her attention was riveted by the water. All her life it had been this way, though she did not know why: she had a grim, almost morbid fascination with water, particularly flowing water. At a very deep level water terrified her, yet she was also drawn to it. She could sit and watch it for hours while images whirled in her imagination. Sometimes they were neutral or pleasant images, but most often they were disquieting: deep, dark torrents surging with irresistible power, or great waves smashing against the base of a high cliff. At times she felt like the waters were calling to her, whispering her name in low voices that sounded like a current flowing through reed beds. In her darker moods she felt an urging to respond to that call, to surrender to the summons and follow the voices down into the shadowed depths.

These darker moods had been increasing of late, though she had spoken to nobody of them. Sometimes they came upon her when she lay awake at night in her spartan dorm room, listening to the peaceful breathing of her roommate. At those times she heard a call to come outside, clad only in her nightshirt, to seek the frozen ponds and gullies. Early in the term, when the students had taken a day trip up to Georgian Bay, she'd found herself standing on the edge of a cliff, entranced by the crystal waters below and fighting the urge to cast herself down. But often the fears had no image or goal, coming instead as vague, unattached moods of darkness, emptiness, and falling. At times her hopes for the future of her relationship with Todd Beck crumbled into certainty of failure and consequent rejection. Her mother's condition, her brothers' futures, her own life goals all overwhelmed her in an avalanche of doubt and uncertainty. Her more frequent friction with her roommate this year didn't help matters. She found herself increasingly seeking solitude, ostensibly to think, but in actuality to brood on these dismal themes, turning them over and over in her mind but never resolving anything.

"Hey, Grace," came a subdued voice from behind her. The young woman recognized the voice, and did not turn.

"Hey."

"I'm...I'm sorry," the voice said humbly.

Grace set her teeth briefly, then released her tension. "Yeah," she sighed. "I'm sorry, too."

The speaker stepped closer and spoke again. "We seem to be saying that a lot this year. But I really am sorry."

"I know," Grace said, then sighed again. "Though I'm not saying it as often as I should be."

The speaker took another step and Grace felt an arm slip around her shoulder. She tensed slightly, then forced herself to relax. There was a hint of vulnerability in that sisterly embrace, a hesitance that shouldn't exist between such close friends. Yielding her sense of grievance, Grace tipped her head slightly to lean against her friend's shoulder, and was rewarded by a gentle squeeze. She thought she heard her friend sniff slightly, which was to be expected from someone whose emotions lived so near the surface. Grace's feelings were buried deeper, which had confused and frustrated them both, especially this year. But at least her friend was learning – having gotten the reassurance of her touch, she stepped away to give Grace some room. Grace turned and smiled, then compromised by reaching out a gloved hand, which was taken eagerly.

Felicity Peterson embodied Grace's ideal of loveliness: tall and graceful with delicate features, bold brown eyes, and wavy brown hair. Her classic beauty was accentuated by the fur trim of the hood framing her face, which was illuminated by one of her brilliant smiles. She carried herself with poise and confidence, and was never at a loss for admirers. Every boy on St. Anselm's small campus always knew just where to find Felicity. Even with the smudge of ashes on her forehead she still looked like a leading actress on opening night.

"Susan told me I might find you out here," Felicity said. "Katie and Thomas are planning a simple tea – cheese and crackers and such – just before Vespers. I thought you might want to come."

"Thanks. I'll think about it," Grace replied with a little smile and a nod. Felicity recognized the tone and nodded in response, letting go of Grace's hand. Grace turned back toward the gully in silence, while Felicity stood behind her, wrestling internally. Being fellow students and roommates at the tiny school, and the only American ones at that, meant they were in each other's lives constantly. As a result, they tried not to pry or intrude, but to wait for the other to open up as she wished. But Grace's increasing withdrawals and isolation had not gone unnoticed by Felicity and several others. Of course, the two of them were having more disputes this semester, which Felicity mostly attributed to the tight living quarters and stressful pace of study this year, but there seemed to be deeper causes. After nearly a minute of tense silence, Felicity was about to risk asking when Grace spoke again.

"Such things can be a trial for me, a drain on my energy."

"Excuse me?" Felicity asked, a bit mystified.

"The tea," Grace explained. "I don't think I can, not today, Feliss. Being around people brings you out – your charm, your grace, your natural beauty. I'm not like you. Lord knows, I wish I were, but I'm not. Socializing can be a real struggle for me, and it costs me a lot. I'm not like you."

Felicity opened her mouth to object, then checked herself. It was true that Grace regularly underestimated herself – not just her petite elfin beauty, which had a charm all its own, but her disarming way of setting people at ease, of getting inside their defenses so that they always felt comfortable around her. But Felicity didn't want to risk hindering this unanticipated flow of candor, so she kept quiet, letting Grace continue.

"To be honest, it can be a little intimidating at times, being with you in social situations. It's not like you're doing anything but being yourself, but you're *so* radiant, *so* fetching, that it's hard not to feel overpowered. You probably aren't even aware of it, and I'm certainly not blaming you, but at least half the guys you meet end up with a crush on you. I've never met anyone like you."

A thousand protests swarmed into Felicity's mind, and a surge of indignation threatened to rise within her, but she quieted her heart and sighed. "Actually, I am aware of it, far more than I let on," Felicity admitted. "I hope I don't do it on purpose, but I never fail to notice, and to get a little thrill of satisfaction when I see another guy giving me that look. I like to rationalize that I don't lead guys on deliberately, but I can play the coquette as well as any – ever so chastely, of course – and keep a mental list of the guys I know who'll come running if I whistle."

Grace turned with wide eyes at this admission. "Felicity, I didn't at all mean –"

"Of course you didn't, dear heart," Felicity interrupted. "But I did, and I mean it. Vanity. It's been my biggest curse since puberty, when I learned I could turn a boy's head by batting my eyelashes. I struggle with it every day, because in the end it's nothing more than a big ego fest for me. So I'm pretty. Great. But as Dad used to say, the only pretty that matters is a pretty heart, one that loves everyone, even young men whom it would be much easier to use as props for my own conceit."

Grace was astonished at the bitter edge in Felicity's voice. "I think you're being a little hard on yourself," she cautioned. "I see you as being very loving and considerate to everyone, even the guys."

"Do you? Good," Felicity gave a chuckle. "That means I'm keeping the struggle inside, where it belongs. But it's been hard this year, a very difficult struggle. I hope that by being honest with myself, and with good friends like you, I can make some progress. After all, aren't we beginning the season for facing our faults and weaknesses?" She touched the smudge on her forehead.

"We are," Grace affirmed. "And I appreciate your honesty, though I don't think matters are as dire as you paint them. I will pray for you, though."

"And I for you," Felicity assured her.

"For now, I really have to get to that Virgil. Give my apologies to everyone at tea. I think I'll say Vespers on my own tonight."

Grace started trudging back toward the house, leaving Felicity to watch her go while struggling with self-doubt. Had she jumped in too quickly again, turning the conversation to herself like she usually did? Should she have let Grace do more talking, in hopes that she'd open up about the moodiness that was plaguing her? Felicity looked out across the snow-clad fields, plagued by uncertainty. Something was definitely wrong this year. Maybe it was just the pace of the studies. Maybe deciding to accelerate the curriculum to end the year by Easter hadn't been such a good idea. But no, it was more than just that. Grace had changed, and Felicity was sure she had as well. The strain was certainly showing in their relationship, and in other areas of life as well. Maybe the familiar discipline of Lent would help, as well as the prospect of returning home in just over a month.

Felicity turned her back to the bitter north wind and headed for the warmth of the house.

*   *   *

The old man eased the door open just enough for a bar of light from the hallway to fall against the far wall, bringing a bit more illumination into the dim room. He watched the still figure in the bed, listening carefully. After half a minute he began to back out again quietly, but the figure stirred and a soft voice spoke.

"I'm awake."

"Oh…ah, good," the man said, swinging the door wide enough to let him slip in with the large tray he was holding. "I wasn't sure. Did you rest well? Are you still tired? I brought you some lunch, if you're up to it."

"I am still tired, but if you held off lunch 'till I wasn't, I'd never get any," the figure replied, sitting up to reveal an older woman with disheveled hair and a wan complexion. But her smile was warm and welcoming, and the old man smiled in return as he set the tray on the table beside her bed. He patted her hand as he sat on the edge of the bed, trying to keep his expression encouraging, though concern haunted his eyes as he scanned the woman's face.

"I brought you a bowl of Ruth's chicken soup. Harmony made the noodles herself." The man held up the bowl as the woman spread a napkin in her lap and sampled the soup.

"Ooh, delicious, but a little hot yet," the woman said with a wince.

"We'll give it some time to cool, then. How about a biscuit? There's grape jam," the man said, spreading butter on a biscuit half. He was so encouraged by any sign of appetite that he would have fetched her anything she wished. She nibbled the biscuit half while they chatted about minor matters. Then she tried some tea, and had a few swallows of the soup, before announcing she'd had enough. She allowed him to leave the biscuits and tea on the bedside table.

"I think," she said as she brushed biscuit crumbs off the blanket, "that I may come out for dinner this evening. I might even do a little knitting."

"That's wonderful, sweetheart," the man replied. "Just don't tax yourself. Luke should be home tonight, and he can give you a look-over. Also, Teresa messaged that she got permission for a night away, so she'll be coming down for a brief visit."

"That's wonderful," the old woman said with a broad smile. "I haven't seen her since Christmas. Now, if you'd help me to the bathroom, I'll take care of the necessaries and then do a bit of reading."

Once she was settled back in bed, the old man gave her a kiss and took the tray back to the kitchen. There he found his granddaughter Cathy bustling about with dinner preparations.

"Hi, Grandpa!" she said cheerily as she took the tray from him. "I'll clean these up. How's Grandma?"

"Holding her own, holding her own," Grandpa replied absently. "Thank you, sweetie." He wandered away, concern etching his brow, while Cathy looked after him with worry in her eyes.

*   *   *

In another corner of the same house, five people with yellow legal pads in front of them sat around a table sipping coffee. Though Ruth Winters actually lived in the house, by convention Gil Peterson acted as informal chair. Also present were Gerald Fitzgerald, universally known as Fitz, Steve McLean from the northern area, and Shelly Peterson from Lapeer.

"Welcome, everyone," Gil began. "Thanks for coming. As you know, we're here to squarely address the question that we've been dancing around for nearly a year. In the simplest form, it is this:

has the time come for us to close down the ranches and return the guests to the regular system for their medical care?"

"I think that's the gist of it," Steve agreed. "Though there are nuances that complicate matters."

"Agreed, agreed," Gil replied. "But that's the core of the question: is it safe to go back in the water?"

The five looked at each other guardedly. The group in this room represented most of the handful of people who knew the complete story of what had happened at the remote factory north of Imlay City a couple of years earlier. They'd reviewed the video footage that Sam had captured with his concealed monitors – not just of the evening of the blast, but all the other footage as well. From these secretly recorded conversations they had learned that the clandestine effort in the area had been a pilot project, and that nearly the entire leadership team of the project was in the factory when it had been destroyed. Since nobody had survived that blast, it was a reasonable guess that the project had been decapitated, possibly completely, since the director from D.C. had been there. He'd been senior enough to have an aide, supervise a project that spanned a region, and summon a paramilitary force from an adjacent state. Since he and a good number of his subordinates had perished, it was a reasonable guess that the project had suffered a severe, possibly permanent, setback.

But was that enough to stake lives on?

"I think there are many facets to the question," Shelly said. She'd done the most careful research into the video footage, transcribing all the dialog for careful study. "The first is the external threat. Is any part of this project still in operation, or close to being reactivated? I think we've already answered that in part when we stopped taking new guests last autumn. We hadn't heard a whisper of any activity for a long time before that. Our decision speaks clearly that we don't perceive an apparent threat."

"That's true," Fitz observed. "But there's a difference between not removing people from the system and putting people back into the system after they've been away from it for a while."

"So, you're saying that it might be safe enough for people who are out there already, but that people reappearing might draw notice?" Steve asked.

"I'm just saying it's possible," Fitz replied. "It's also possible that we're jumping at shadows two years after the actual threat was blown to flinders over in Lapeer County."

"We could well be," Gil admitted. "But even if we knew the actual level of threat out there, we have other considerations, the foremost being our ability to maintain the operation. Ruth, could you speak to that?"

"Sure," Ruth said, looking at them with her usual sober expression. "Honestly, this is unsustainable. The drain on our resources is too great. We can't keep living like this. We started this operation in a big rush in response to a crisis. We've made things up as we went along. We've broken some laws and bent a whole bunch of others. I know that we're no longer doing the most dangerous stuff, like snatching people from hospitals, but we're still living in the shadows. We've had to modify our lives just to reduce the risk of detection. It isn't normal, and the strain is starting to show. Smuggling pharmaceuticals, caring for people who probably don't need to stay hidden any more, maintaining our own systems for communications and distribution – I tell you, we can't keep this up! The cost and risk are too great!"

"Now, Ruth, things aren't quite that dire," Shelly offered in a conciliatory tone. "I know we've had to make accommodations, but most of the families and guests are getting along just fine."

"That may be true over in Lapeer, where most of the ranches have one guest, or two at most, but it's a different story here at Rivendell, where we're caring for almost a dozen people, and at St. Anne's," Ruth retorted.

"Ruth, I know you have a special burden here, and we can make any changes we need –" Shelly began, but Gil cut in.

"Please, folks, we're not here to discuss how to fine-tune the system, but to address the question of whether it needs to continue at all. We all acknowledge that Ruth has many valid points. Because of what we're doing on behalf of the guests, we are living in the shadows, on the border of legality, and sometimes across it. The fact that we've become accustomed to it shouldn't blind us to the abnormality of the situation, the risk it introduces, and the strain it puts on all our lives." This got general nods from around the circle.

"But even with these points, there is more at issue," Gil continued. "I've been talking at length with Luke, and he's asked me to bring this to everyone's attention. He's seeing increasing instances of serious illness and death from conditions that he doesn't have the resources to deal with. Treatments exist for these conditions, but he can't get access to those treatments, or get his patients to where they could get them. There are many examples, but the foremost one he's encountering is limited access to antibiotics. We can get him first-line antibiotics, which are almost as common as aspirin, but there are so many resistant strains floating around that everyone administers these assuming they're going to fail half the time. For most providers that means reaching for second-line drugs, but Luke can't do that. This is just one example. He's also dealing with advanced cancer, cardiac, and pulmonary issues that guests are dying of even though they could be treated with modern methods."

"The guests knew of, and accepted, the risks of reduced access to medical service when they came into our care," Steve pointed out.

"Yes, but that was when there was an active danger of the alternative being a needle in the night," Gil answered. "Is that still a real concern?"

"Another factor here is simple demographics," Fitz observed. "None of the guests were spring chickens when they came to us, and many had known chronic health conditions even then. We've been caring for them for anywhere from two to five years – it stands to reason that we'd be dealing with terminal conditions and fatalities. St. Anne's is pretty much set up for end-of-life care, and there's a waiting period to get people in. None of this is unexpected."

"True, but people in those conditions still take a lot of care, expected or not," Ruth replied.

"Granted – and especially so for Luke," Gil said. "Just from talking to him, I know it's severely draining for him to lose patients that he knows would respond to treatments he can't get for them. From his perspective, the compelling question is whether there's still any reason to deny them access to those treatments."

Shelly, who had been sitting in mild agitation for a while, burst out. "Whatever we do, it shouldn't be a wholesale shutdown of the ranches. Yes, it takes resources to care for the guests, but many of them have found families for the first time in their lives. And it isn't just the guests – the host families benefit, too. I know we've got a few problem situations, but on the whole residents of the ranches have found love. They've become little caring communities, and we shouldn't just rip them apart because we're afraid, or because they've become too costly to deal with!"

"That's true," Gil acknowledged. "Be assured that whatever we decide, we won't be making any radical, abrupt changes if we can help it. I think incremental adjustment is the right path. We have several options. For example, the other Farthings are structured along much less intense models than ours. We could consider adopting some of their practices. But it seems to me the most urgent issues revolve around the question of medical care. We currently provide care completely outside of the mainstream channels – which was the very reason we set the ranches up in the first place. Is that extreme degree of separation still required? Or could we loosen that up a bit, on the assumption that the threat is past?" Gil looked around at the others, who gave nods or murmurs of agreement. There seemed to be a consensus about this aspect. "All right, then. I'll talk to Luke about candidates for easing back into the regular medical care channels, and we'll come up with a plan. Fitz, you and I will have to confer on strategies for protecting identities as we proceed. We'll take this slow and easy at first, and hopefully won't find any ugly surprises waiting for us."

Mysteries

The DHS briefing facility was more like what Jason was accustomed to. A well-lit midsized conference room, it had tables arranged in a square around a central area that was tiled instead of carpeted. There was a gap in the table arrangement right in front of the double doors, through which a couple of workers were wheeling a hand trolley laden with boxes and briefcases. A tall blond woman wearing a DHS badge strode over and gripped Jason's hand firmly.

"Jason Pelletier? I'm Susan Yost. A pleasure to meet you. Could I get a scan of your badge? Thanks." She toyed with her phone, bringing up an image on the screens at both ends of the room while the other workers began setting out cases and items on some of the tables.

"These are agents Nicole Trask and Frank Courser from the ATF Forensics Lab," Susan continued. "They've been working closely with us, and will be handling the more technical aspects of the briefing. Ready? Let's start."

Nicole placed a chip on the projection console, and the familiar logo of the Department of Homeland Security Domestic Terror Division glowed on the screens, followed by the standard verbiage about classified content. She quickly clicked to the next image, which was a photograph of a nondescript tan industrial building made of cinder block sitting on a dusty lot. There were some numbers in the upper left-hand corner of the image, and the words "Imlay City".

"The Imlay City blast was a demolition detonation that resulted in the complete destruction of the structure, twelve vehicles, and the loss of twenty-three human lives. The detonation was effected by about two dozen charges of various strengths placed strategically within the building and detonated simultaneously," Nicole explained. As she spoke the picture of the building was replaced by a line outline which rotated. Small red dots appeared at corners and on walls within the line drawing, which Jason guessed indicated the locations of the charges.

"So, it was a carefully planned incident," Jason added.

"Very much so," Nicole confirmed. "In fact, we asked a professional demolitions expert about it, and he confirmed that the charges were placed almost exactly where he would have placed them. The state police report confirms this, but also comments on the anomalous nature of the blast."

"Anomalous nature?"

"First, bringing down a building of this size with explosives is unnecessary. A bulldozer and crane would be cheaper, safer, and nearly as fast. Second, the quantity of explosive used far exceeded any reasonable requirement."

"So," Jason commented. "This was a demolition-style blast, but its purpose was terror?"

Nicole grimaced slightly and glanced at Susan. "That's another anomaly we've been contending with. Had this blast occurred in a populated area, or in a building full of, shall we say, ordinary public, I'd say yes, clearly a terror strike. But it happened in a remote location, and nobody has ever claimed responsibility. The motive is a mystery."

"But the building was full of strategic personnel, at least from the perspective of HHS," Jason said.

"That's more than they've told us," Nicole replied. "We know they're the interested agency, because they keep pushing for information, but they haven't told us anything about who the people were or why they were in the building.

"The totality of the destruction made forensics work challenging. Many of the bodies were so severely mangled by the explosion that we had only fragments to work with. The secondary fires from ruptured gas tanks did further damage."

"Question," Jason interrupted. "Why were so many cars parked inside the facility?"

"We can only speculate, since HHS has been so tight-lipped," Nicole replied. "Our guess is that part of the original appeal of the site was that it had plenty of room for parking inside. That way people meeting at the building could be out of sight while there."

"Really? In the middle of the country?" Jason asked.

"Cars are distinctive, more so than people in many ways," Nicole explained. "They have makes, models, colors, and identifying tags. These features stand out even more in sparsely populated areas. If you wanted to meet regularly, and not have locals driving by notice that you were doing it, hiding your car would be one of the first things you'd want to do."

"Ah," Jason nodded. This squared with what he knew of the project from the HHS documentation. He waved for Nicole to continue.

"With careful sifting, we parsed the wreckage into what we'll call the expected and the unexpected. The expected were the people, vehicles, equipment, and the like that we'd expect to find there. Again, discerning this was very one-way, since HHS didn't give us a list of personnel or vehicles to work from. We'd have to tell them, 'we've isolated some human remains, here's a sample for DNA testing', or 'we found a piece of wreckage with a vehicle ID number on it'. All they'd tell us was whether it checked out or not."

"Sounds like slow going," Jason said. "What about the unexpected finds?"

"There were only a few items, but they were mystifying." Nicole nodded to Frank, who placed a couple of blackened items on the table in front of Jason. "Two were video cameras of some sort. One was mounted on the wall in the office area and the other was in the ceiling of the shop floor. Our people speculate that there may have been more, possibly as many as three, but the others were destroyed by the blast. They would have transmitted to this device," Frank put another blackened item before Jason, "which was located in the office area as well."

"Video monitoring?" Jason asked. "Would this have been live monitoring?"

"That, we don't know," Nicole admitted. "Our techs guess that it was a simple store-and-forward monitoring setup, with motion-activated cameras transmitting video footage to the storage device, which was physically wired to a transmission station on the roof." Here Frank reached into the box on the cart and lifted out a couple of pieces of dirty, twisted metal, one of which looked like it had been a dish antenna. "It may have had real-time monitoring capabilities – we just can't tell."

"And this wasn't placed by HHS?"

"The only thing they'd tell us about it was that it was 'unfamiliar equipment'. I think they thought that saying more might tip their hand about what this site was used for, and who all those people were. Our guess is that it wasn't theirs – the items look too makeshift to be anything but a jury-rig. Not even HHS is that sloppy."

Jason considered this. Perhaps the deep dark project that HHS had worked so hard to keep secret might not have been as secret as they'd thought. Whoever had installed this video monitoring setup might have had connections to the mysterious group sabotaging the pilot project, and almost certainly had an influence on the devastating timing of the blast. It wouldn't have been difficult to know when to press the button if all you had to do was count heads.

"We wouldn't have any idea who would have placed this equipment, or where it would have been transmitting, do we?" Jason asked without much hope. Nicole shook her head.

"All we know is that the antenna indicates line-of-sight, which from that height would have been about twenty miles. Since we have no idea which direction the antenna was pointing, that narrows it down to about 1250 square miles. As far as the who, that leads us to the next unexpected find amidst the wreckage: a vehicle and a body."

"A body?" Jason asked in astonishment.

"And a vehicle," Nicole clicked the next image onto the screen, which showed numerous pieces of blackened and twisted pipes and wheels laid out to resemble a motorcycle-like thing. "This we pieced together from scraps littered around the shop area. It's some kind of scooter, apparently with close-set tandem wheels in the front, a drive wheel in the back, and a small displacement four-stroke engine. The frame was slightly smaller than a full-sized motorcycle."

"Sounds odd – what manufacturer builds something like that?"

"Nobody. That's what had our investigators pulling their hair out and running in circles for months before we finally concluded that this had to be a custom construct. The rear wheel is from one model of dirt bike, the two front wheels are from a different model by a different manufacturer, the engine is from a lawn mower, and the transmission is from yet another motorcycle. The frame is a complete custom weld job, and the controls are cobbled from several sources."

"Who builds his own motorcycle when you can buy used ones for a few hundred bucks?" Jason asked.

"Or why? We have no idea," Nicole conceded. "Our best guess is a serious hobbyist. However, it was built to a smaller scale – about three-quarters the size of a full-sized motorcycle – which may mean it was built for this person."

The next image Nicole brought up showed a digitally blurred shape that was clearly a human body. Jason was grateful for the blurring, for the body wasn't just blackened and twisted, it was in several parts which were laid out to approximate a human figure.

"This is the sole unidentified body on the site. We were able to recover enough of every other body – sometimes no more than a tooth – for HHS to verify that the person was known to have been there. This party was the only one they couldn't verify."

"And we have no idea who it is?" Jason asked.

"Of course we don't. Male, early 30s, no identifying documents, no labels in his clothing. Caught right in the midst of the blast, literally blown to pieces which were subsequently charred by the secondary fires. It was quite a feat to locate all the parts and reassemble them. Once that was done, our forensics team was able to identify two distinctive and puzzling things about him.

"One was that his bones, joints, and what musculature we could reconstruct indicate he was handicapped. Particularly his lower body was distorted in such a way as to make mobility difficult. Whoever he was, he probably got around with canes or a walker," Nicole explained.

"Could that be a clue to his identity?" Jason suggested.

"We followed that lead but came up empty," Nicole said. "We checked all the local service agencies and disability facilities, but couldn't find a match. Anyone who came close to the description was still around. We even checked the area medical service records for anyone with those sorts of conditions. No luck."

"So you're saying that this guy didn't officially exist?"

Nicole shrugged. "That's our best guess – either that, or he came from far, far away. We queried a broad base of conditions – anything remotely resembling this disability configuration – and tapped every medical database covering the region. We even checked Canadian data, which has to be taken into account given the geography. Every patient with anything like these conditions is accounted for."

"So he just appeared out of nowhere, showing up just in time for the blast that killed him?" Jason asked. "Suicide bomber?"

"No, for a couple of reasons. First, if he'd been the center of the blast, we wouldn't have even this much of him left to work with. And remember that this was a structural blast – the charges were carefully placed around the building and detonated at the same time. Suicide bombers wear vests or carry satchels."

"Hmm," Jason shook his head in mystification. "But you mentioned two puzzling things. What was the second?"

"He was shot."

"Shot?"

"That's right. Two clear penetrations: a thoracic impact that broke two ribs and pierced the left lung, and a pelvic impact that shattered the right hip socket. He also may have sustained a graze along his left outer thigh, but the burning was too severe to be sure. But even that wasn't the oddest thing."

"Okay, what was the oddest thing?" Jason asked, wondering how this bizarre situation could possibly get stranger.

"The impact trajectories indicate he was shot from below."

"Below?"

"Yes, below," Nicole confirmed. "The entry points and angle of travel are from beneath – much like they'd be if you were standing on the ground shooting up at a bear in a tree."

"So this guy was above whoever was shooting at him?"

"Either that, or lying on the ground with his feet toward his assailants, who would also have been lying on the ground."

"Was he shooting back at them?" Jason asked.

"No. He was unarmed. We've identified all the arms in the building, and have even isolated which guns fired the bullets that killed him. Compared with identifying the humans, that was relatively simple. One of the bullets was fired from a DHS pistol, and the other was known to HHS – we can't get more detail from them than that."

"A DHS pistol?"

"There were four of our people known to be on the site," Susan chimed in. "They were on loan for an emergency response to an urgent need. I'll fill you in later."

Jason nodded. "So, our mysterious cripple shows up, presumably riding a custom motorbike, somehow enters a closed secret facility that contains armed guards, and gets positioned so he can be shot from below just before a blast levels the building."

"That about summarizes it," Nicole confirmed.

"And we have no idea why they were shooting at him?" Jason pressed.

Nicole glanced at Susan, who shrugged. "HHS has been playing this so close to the chest that we don't know what communications were going on with the site."

Jason figured he could dig out that information later. "Do we have any idea if this person is related in any way to the parties that rigged the charges and, presumably, detonated them?"

"We've speculated that –" Nicole began, but Susan interrupted her.

"Excuse me, but that topic touches on some sensitive DHS internal matters. I'll be giving you a classified briefing before we're finished."

"Of course," Nicole smiled thinly at Susan. An uncomfortable silence fell until Jason could think of another question to ask.

"Does the forensic evidence give any indication of how this unknown party got into the facility, and when?"

"The best hint we have was gleaned from the aerial surveillance video that was taken at the time. I've got that on the next image, if I'm permitted to address the material?" Nicole looked at Susan with arched eyebrows. Susan's only response was a bland expression and a wave of her hand, so Nicole brought up the next image. It was an aerial view of the blocky, ugly building that Jason recognized as the HHS field headquarters north of Imlay City. From the grainy texture and high contrast, Jason guessed it was either low-light or infrared video.

"This was taken by the drone that was monitoring the site at the time of the blast," Nicole explained. "I've cued it up to nine minutes and thirty seconds before the explosion. The angle of the drone isn't good for what we're looking for, but watch." She clicked the video into motion, and Jason noticed the slightly jerky effect on the picture as the drone circled the building.

"At this point, all the HHS and DHS people are inside," Nicole went on. "Here's the driveway." A white line appeared on the screen briefly than vanished. "The main door, which is a large lift door like a garage door, faces the drive. You can't see it directly from the drone's current angle, but watch the drive, right here." A white arrow appeared on the screen, and Jason peered as the video rolled. Suddenly a fast, light blur flicked across the driveway.

"What was that?" Jason asked.

"We're not certain," Nicole admitted. "We suspect it may have been our visitor. We can't tell exactly where it came from, but it seemed to move toward the east face of the building where the main door was. Unfortunately, the drone was at this point passing to the west of the building, so the blur was on the fringe of the image. If it was him, we know that he got inside the building, but exactly how isn't clear. There's a contrast flicker on the driveway as he approached which may have been the main door opening and closing, but it's impossible to be sure."

"Can you replay that?" Jason asked, so Nicole re-cued the video and ran through the segment a couple of times, once at normal and once at slow speed. Jason squinted at the tantalizingly brief flicker, trying to glean more detail.

"Can we zoom in closer? Do we have footage with a better angle?" Jason pressed. The area of interest was in the lower right corner of the screen, barely within the field of view.

"You can zoom in, but the resolution is poor and grainy," Nicole replied. "As far as any other footage, it may be best for an authorized DHS representative to answer that." She nodded to Susan, who pasted on a frozen smile in response.

"The drone was under command of DHS Border Patrol Aerial Surveillance," Susan said. "It had been tasked with scanning the area surrounding the field HQ, concentrating particularly on roads and other potential approach vectors. The building itself was not considered in need of surveillance, and the woods were not believed to be a source of threat at the time."

"They were concerned about threats approaching the site?" Jason asked.

"It's standard procedure when conducting a major regional operation," Susan explained. "I'll brief you on that shortly." She smiled sweetly at Nicole, who grimaced in response.

"That's about it from the ATF side," Nicole concluded. "There are a lot of technical details in the files on the briefing chip. If you're interested, we can forward the video to the footage of the blast itself."

"Sure," Jason agreed, so Nicole cued the video forward. The drone's location had changed, placing it well to the north of the building. Most of the screen was showing roads and fields, with woods and other barren areas scattered throughout. The building was on the edge of the image. Everyone jumped when it suddenly vanished in a bright flare. The image whitened then blackened and whitened again as the sensors tried to adapt to the abrupt brilliance. Just as the image stabilized, it was disturbed again by the shock wave from the blast buffeting the drone. Once it had been brought back under control, the drone veered in and centered the blast site in the image. Jason nearly gasped. No building remained, only a vast circular field of rubble and twisted metal in which several distinct fires were beginning to burn. Even some of the nearby trees were flattened.

"Twenty-two lives lost – well, twenty-three, including our unknown party. Sixteen HHS staff, four DHS staff, and two locals, all annihilated. Massive overkill – about ten times the amount of explosive that would have been necessary to demolish a building of that size. Any questions?" Nicole asked.

"I have plenty of questions, but I think you've told us all that forensics can," Jason replied. "I have your contact information and the briefing data, so I'll get in touch if I need anything more."

Nicole nodded to Jason and Susan as Frank started packing up the items he'd laid out. Susan sat expressionless in the chilly silence as Nicole pulled the chip from the projector and followed Frank out the door. Only then did Susan rise, go to the door and key in the code to lock it, then go to the projector to insert a chip of her own. Again, the logo of the Department of Homeland Security Domestic Terror Division displayed on the screen, only this time with a scarlet "Top Secret" text emblazoned across it.

"That was informative," Jason said.

"Yeah, the lab rats are great at what they do," Susan admitted. "Very helpful support staff. But now we can get down to the meat of things." She brought up the next image, which Jason was coming to recognize as the standard map of eastern Michigan. A section of the map was shaded pink.

"This area of Michigan is called the 'Thumb', for obvious reasons: lower Michigan has the rough outline of a mitten, and this section would be the thumb of the mitten. It's bounded on the north by Lake Huron, on the east by Lake Huron and the St. Clair River, on the south by Interstate 69, and on the west by Interstate 75 and Saginaw Bay. It consists of all or part of five counties and is largely rural. It is due north of the most populous region in the state, the metropolitan Detroit/Ann Arbor area. Along the western edge of the Thumb lie Saginaw and Flint, once major manufacturing cities that have lost ground over recent decades.

Years ago, Bay City and Port Huron were significant shipping ports. Other than those, the cities and towns are all rural, agricultural settlements, with smatterings of light manufacturing and tourism.

"The area is of interest to DHS because it contains a major international border crossing: the Blue Water Bridge, running from Port Huron to Sarnia, Ontario. This directly connects the U.S. and Canadian freeway systems, so is a major transit point for commercial and personal traffic. The U.S./Canadian border runs down the center of Lake Huron and the St. Clair River, across Lake St. Clair, and down the Detroit River. There are a couple of cross-border ferries on the St. Clair River and three crossings in the Detroit area. As a result, the Border Patrol has a sizeable footprint in the region. Vehicles, marine vessels, aircraft, and physical plants are all located there, along with an aerial surveillance unit out of Selfridge Air Base."

"So, is that how we got involved in this?" Jason interrupted. "Because we have a big presence?"

"That's part of it," Susan acknowledged. "But there's also the domestic terror component. The region has a recognized anti-government disposition dating back at least forty years. Violent activists have been traced to the area, and the population tends to be reactionary and difficult to govern. We had no idea that HHS was running a covert operation in our own back yard; if we had, we could have warned them off."

"Really? Is it that dangerous?"

"Well, the last overt danger was back in '95, when some local radicals were connected to the Oklahoma City bombing. Since then things have been on a simmer, and frankly the recent unrest in the major urban areas has drawn most of the Federal attention, leaving little for investigating rural backwaters. Last summer a story broke about a corrupt private operation in the region that had links to human trafficking, with rumors of cross-border drug smuggling and possibly piracy, that had apparently been going on for years. But everything had been low-key until this HHS operation stumbled into it."

"How did that work, exactly?" Jason asked. "What was discovered, and how did we get dragged in?"

"It was our aerial recon group that was first contacted, asking for help with a warm pursuit. A party suspected of interfering with this HHS project had slipped through their surveillance net, and we were asked if we had any drone footage that might help track her."

"Did we?"

"Yes and no. We happened to have a bird in the air at the time, but our footage was too general, and didn't help – the suspect got away. But our surveillance guy offered to do more drone overflights to watch for more irregularities."

"Really? Why did he do that?" Jason wondered.

"The excuse he offered was that there was a loose domestic terror connection, along with the border security issue. I've spoken to him, and you'll probably get the chance – my take is that he was bored, and wanted to do more than just routine patrol flights up and down the rivers. More focused surveillance offered him a bit of a challenge," Susan explained.

"So that was our point of entry? Interdepartmental cooperation?" Jason asked.

"That, plus the HHS honcho running their op had some contacts in DHS leadership. Once HHS was tipped to the possibility that their operation had been compromised, one of their data analysts, Ron Porcher, began running some queries that turned up these irregular situations. Based on that, the project leadership determined that there was a support network facilitating this sabotage. Figuring this for a flavor of domestic terror, the honcho called his DHS contacts to ask for help. One thing our analysts did was start working with this Porcher to scope out the breadth and complexity of this subversive network. The results of their analysis, along with some aerial surveillance footage, convinced HHS that there was an immediate threat, and HHS asked us to pull the trigger."

"'Pull the trigger'? What does that mean, exactly?"

"We have a variety of protocols for addressing regional domestic terror threats," Susan explained. "In this case, a task force was dispatched from the Fort Wayne Fast Response Center to stand by for wide-ranging strikes at suspected sites. That's what I couldn't mention while ATF was here – the strike force was staged at a geographically central location, standing by for authorization to move."

"Did they get it?" Jason asked.

"No," Susan shook her head. "The key component was an intelligence asset who'd been taken into custody. There was compelling evidence that this asset was plugged into the subversive network. HHS called on us to help apprehend him, and he was taken to the field HQ for interrogation. The intention was that his information would give us what we needed to break the terror network. Instead, he was blown up with everyone else before he could tell us anything."

Jason recalled the drone footage of the building exploding, and all the questions that had been left unanswered. "This HHS analyst, Porcher – any possibility I could talk to him?"

"No – he was in the building, too," Susan explained. "We still have his queries and data sets, but it's hard to make sense of them. If we knew more about the purpose of this HHS project, we might be able to make more progress."

Jason recognized a fishing attempt when one was cast at him. Susan knew he'd been briefed by HHS, but she was doomed to disappointment.

"Yes, this was a secret project," Jason confirmed, telling her nothing she didn't already know. "I'm sure I'll be able to dig up some details in time. But I've been wondering something all along: this was a major domestic terror strike, one of the deadliest in years. Why hasn't there been a bigger push to resolve this? It's not like we're talking about that big an area – it's just a small corner of the state. Why haven't we saturated the area with resources and shut down this subversive network?"

Susan zoomed the slide out until it showed the entire state, with the Thumb region still shaded. "It only seems small by comparison to the rest of the state, but the Thumb area is roughly half the size of New Jersey. It's also sparsely populated – 92 people per square mile, whereas the state as a whole averages 175 people per square mile. For comparison, New Jersey has about 1250 people per square mile."

"What's the significance of that?" Jason asked.

"Firstly, fewer people means your agents are more conspicuous. In urban areas, you can achieve anonymity simply by avoiding uniforms and using unmarked cars. Out there, being a strange face will get you noticed. Secondly, a spread-out population means that certain options aren't available. In an urban area you can seal off a neighborhood and go house-to-house. You can't do that in the country – even if you tried, word would get around, and people have ways of slipping away."

"I see. Have you ever been up there, Susan?"

"Me? No. This investigation got dumped on me a year ago, possibly because I did some time up in the Detroit office some years back, supervising agents on the bridges. Hated it."

"Where else have you worked?"

"All over. San Diego, Atlanta, Seattle, Houston."

"Border Patrol mostly?"

"Some Border Patrol work," Susan confirmed. "Immigration, TSA supervision, a bit of FEMA, and finally here at Domestic Terror."

"Ah," Jason acknowledged, making a mental note that her service had mostly been in large urban areas. "So, what assets do we have working this investigation right now?"

"We have two agents in the area who've been assigned to make inquiries in addition to their regular duties. They'd been doing some investigating at the time of the blast, and we added the ongoing investigation to their tasks."

"*Two* agents, part time, are all we've assigned to investigate this incident?" Jason asked in disbelief.

"Look, I told you HHS is playing this close to the chest," Susan shot back defensively. "They haven't been pushing for resolution, and we have other fish to fry. By all indications, this was a one-off stroke. Sure, it took out a boatload of HHS weenies, but there's been nothing since: no threats, no action, not even anyone claiming responsibility. If HHS isn't demanding action, we sure won't."

"I understand," Jason assured her, though he was puzzled that the official reaction hadn't been stronger. Action against Federal operatives, especially lethal action, normally drew a swift and fierce response no matter what department was struck. Perhaps the shroud of secrecy wrapped around the project had something to do with it, but Jason had to wonder if this Dr. Tasker had been so obnoxious to his colleagues that a good number had been secretly glad to see him killed. "Well, thank you, Susan, you've been most helpful. I presume that all the relevant documents and contact information are on the tablet here?" He tapped the tablet that had been placed in front of him.

"Yes, and it's been keyed to your biometrics. I'll assume the usual precautions about leaving it lying around, dissemination, et cetera, have been read."

"Indeed. Will anyone be using this conference room in the near future, or can I camp here for a bit to study?" Jason asked.

"It's free for the afternoon, so you're good. Do you need the presentation chip? All the slides are on your tablet."

"No, take it. I'll lock up when I'm done and find my own way out. Thanks again for the help."

"No problem," Susan replied as she slipped the chip out and headed for the door. "Good luck!"

"Yeah, thanks," Jason muttered as she departed, leaving him alone in the silent room. He could dimly hear the bustle and traffic in the hallway and cubicles outside, but that only made him feel more isolated.

Well. Well, well, well. He was, it would seem, well and truly screwed. This had to be Whitman's handiwork, the bastard. Jason was stuck with a cold case in a backwater location that nobody really cared about resolving. Even if he charged up there and solved the mystery of the blast in two weeks, he'd never be recognized publicly, because HHS would want it kept quiet, and he'd get few points within DHS for resolving another agency's problem. Oh, sure, there were the four DHS staffers, but they were only field agents. Hell, even if he uncovered the entire terrorist network, what would that get him? Nailing subversives always counted for something, but if the last terrorist act these guys did was two and a half years ago, DHS definitely had more pressing problems. The most he could expect would be a tepid attaboy.

Damn Whitman, and everyone else who'd conspired to stick him with this no-win assignment. What he needed right now in his career was a major triumph, something to expunge the taint of Salt Lake City and prove that he could tackle a big project. He needed the equivalent of bringing the enemy's heads home on pikes to make the necessary impression, and the DHS side of this situation didn't give him enough to do that.

But the HHS side, now, that had potential. Not so much bringing the killers to justice – that would count for some points, but if Jason read this situation aright, some of Tasker's colleagues thought the terrorists had done them a favor by getting rid of Tasker and his underlings. But something like the Chengdu Project was still needed. The looming budget crisis that had engendered it had not gone away; in fact, it had become more urgent with each passing day. Tasker might have been an irascible bastard, but he'd given the bureaucrats the kick they'd needed to get something started. Of course, when Tasker had been blown to bits in rural Michigan, the bureaucrats had lapsed back into their dithering and waffling while the clock had ticked away.

Could a solo DHS operative succeed in rekindling a project encumbered by such colossal bureaucratic inertia? Tasker had proven he could light enough of a fire to get something moving – could Jason do the same? He knew little about the world of health care funding, and had no contacts within the HHS bureaucracy. But as he'd paged through Tasker's proposals and plans, and one thing had become obvious: the man may have been a mathematical genius but he was no engineer. He'd been correct that swift and decisive action was needed, but the plan he'd constructed had far too many layers, too many moving parts. Perhaps someone steeped in the protocols of health care and experienced in the intricacies of HHS bureaucracy was precisely what the situation *didn't* call for.

Maybe it needed someone who could design a simple, clean solution that would be easy to execute.

If there was one thing Jason could do, it was design things.

Jason spent the next few hours poring over the HHS and DHS documentation and jotting his thoughts on a pad. Finally he rubbed his eyes and shoulders and glanced at the time. If he didn't head home soon, he'd get caught in the worst of the afternoon traffic. He was just packing away his things when his phone chimed with a message.

It was Cassie.

Damn, he'd been wondering how he was going to break all this to Cassie. Mostly he'd been ignoring the issue, mentally pushing it aside, but now she was messaging him.

Busy tonight?

Jason considered simply ignoring the message, pretending that it never got through, but that would just mean tackling the problem later. He sighed and messaged back.

Sorta. Packing & stuff. Leaving soon on special assign. Be gone a while.

Actually, he wouldn't be leaving until later in the week, but this would be easier all around.

Leaving? Again? Can I call? Came the reply

Just what Jason didn't need right now was a long, cloying phone conversation with Cassie. He sent a quick reply.

In mtg. Call or msg later.

The response was swift. *Hoppy's tonight? 9:30?*

Jason flinched. He'd been promising Cassie drinks and dancing at Hoppy's for weeks now. He felt bad that he'd kept putting her off, but couldn't face the inevitable tears and clinging and pouting, even if it did mean ending up back at her place afterward. Why did he always end up in these high-drama relationships? He messaged back.

We'll see. Lots of packing & planning, but maybe cut loose.

Goody! Came the response. Jason felt another twinge of guilt for his vacillating, but he'd have to feel a lot more up than he did now to be able to face both Cassie and Hoppy's.

Strains

"Wait – why nine seats?" Phillip asked, glancing at the table crowded with plates and glasses.

"Martha and Evan are coming over," Elizabeth said hesitantly.

"And bringing Leo!" Tabitha bubbled, oblivious to the tension in the air. Phillip stared at the table with a stony expression while Elizabeth kept setting out the silverware and casting wary glances at him.

Phillip said nothing, but turned on his heel and stalked out the back door. Alarmed and frightened, Tabitha looked from the door to where Elizabeth stood with tears in her pain-fraught eyes, then back to the door again. "Phillip!" Tabitha called, dashing out into the yard just in time to see the taillights of the pickup turn onto the road, gravel spraying from the tires. "Phillip! Phillip!" her cries echoed in the evening air, but the truck just sped away.

*　　　　*　　　　*

The bar outside Marlette was drafty, noisy, and smelled of cheap beer – except the bathrooms, which stank of urine and vomit. Phillip was watching his cousins Cletus and Sixtus play pool, trying to choke down the tough, tepid hot dog that he'd gotten from the bar.

"Damn, I hate this crappy bar food," Phillip grumbled. "I don't know why I waste money on it." He was close enough to the bar that the bartender heard him, and gave him a glare that Phillip returned.

"Why are you eating it, then? Didn't you have some dinner before you came?" Cletus asked.

"No," Phillip replied. "They were having Martha and the kid over, and I just couldn't face it. My poor sister. When I think of what that animal did to her! Hell, she should be having sleepovers and going on horseback rides, not having to care for a kid!"

"I hear you, man," Cletus said. "And the perp got off with a 'new life'. I'd like to give him a new life!" He smacked the edge of the table with his cue, eliciting a sharp "Hey!" from the bartender.

"Better be good, man, or you'll get us kicked out," Sixtus warned as some of the guys at the bar glared at them darkly.

"Dammit, I'm tired of being good," Cletus growled. "I'm also tired of the same old grubby, stinking holes playing the same stinking music."

"Hey, at least you can go out in public without risking your family's safety," Phillip said, pitching the remains of the hot dog in the trash and draining his beer. "Which reminds me, I'm supposed to be home by nine, so I'd best be going."

"Especially since it's nine thirty," Cletus added.

"Don't let me keep you from your game, which you might want to wrap up," Phillip said as he headed for the door. "You've been monopolizing the table for two hours, and I think some of the others are noticing." He nodded toward the surly looking guys at the bar.

"T'hell with them," Cletus pronounced. "We'll play as long as we want to."

"All right, then. G'night," Phillip called as he headed out into the chill night. He took his time driving home, so it was pushing ten o'clock by the time he pulled into the driveway. The house was dark, as he'd hoped it would be. He eased through the back door into the kitchen and walked quietly toward the stairs.

"We missed you," came a quiet voice out of the darkened living room. Phillip stopped and sighed. It was Mom. He'd known a conversation like this was inevitable; he'd just hoped it would be tomorrow. He felt a twinge of guilt and a slight flare of anger.

"Martha and Evan missed you, too," Linda continued. "This is the third time they've come and you've made a point of being elsewhere. They asked you to be Leo's godfather for a reason –"

"All right, Ma, all right," Phillip blurted out in exasperation. "I'm sorry, but I just couldn't face…couldn't face it."

"Couldn't face what?"

"Ma, I'd rather not go into this right now."

"When, then?" Linda asked gently. "Phillip, the problem isn't going away. Leo is here. You're obviously distressed, but you never make clear exactly why. We're all confused and hurt, especially Martha, who loves you and wants you in her life, and in her son's life."

"Of course I'm distressed! Why wouldn't I be?" Phillip answered. "Look at our situation!"

"What about our situation?" Linda asked.

"Bah! What about our situation?" Phillip stormed, pacing the floor. "How can you even ask that, Ma? We worked hard, tried to do everything right, even put ourselves at risk to protect people, and how are we repaid? My siblings are kidnapped, my sister is raped and impregnated, we're driven into exile and hiding by our own government, where we live in constant fear of exposure. I liked our old home and our old life! Now it's all lost, partly because of that scum who raped my sister!"

"So, it's God you're mad at?"

"No," Phillip snapped, then paused. "I don't know. I just hate it all, the whole situation."

"You know Leo is innocent, as is Martha. And Evan is being generous and noble, and is a fine husband and father."

"I know all that, Ma," Phillip interrupted peevishly. "And I've nothing against them, really. It's just that that animal...and she just...I would have torn his head off!" He bolted up the steps, leaving his mother in the dark quietly rocking her youngest child while praying for her eldest.

* * *

"Dammit!" Luke swore as he stepped off his ATV and plunged his leg into frigid mud over his ankle. Getting a good look at where his front wheels were buried axle-deep, he swore again. This was worse than he thought, and he desperately hoped he'd be able to extricate his four-wheeler from this slough without having to call for help. He was already late, cold, and hungry, and having to summon someone to rescue him on this remote trail would be one more burden on some already overtaxed friend or family member. He slogged around the back of the vehicle and unstrapped the short-handled spade, then began scooping as quickly as he could in hopes of getting the wheels down to solid earth. It was frustrating and backbreaking work, made worse by the bitter north wind that cut through his parka. This spring was late, cold, and sloppy, rendering the trails completely impassable by snowmobile but only barely navigable by any other means. Many stretches were flooded, forcing him to take more roundabout routes on his ATV, and what trails he could use were soggy and treacherous, prone to unexpected soft spots like this one that had entrapped him. Gritting his teeth, he slashed and stabbed at the cold mud with the spade, but made little progress. He'd never had to deal with this many problems in all the years he'd been doing this – it was like the land itself was fighting him.

While his body toiled against earth and water, Luke's mind churned around several matters that were vexing him. He was under strain from many sources, one of the biggest being the situation toward which he was currently heading, but compounding everything was the bleak futility that overshadowed it all. For some reason, during this harsh winter and dismal spring, Luke had been feeling more keenly the strictures and limitations of his life. When he'd first submerged into this hidden world, he'd felt relief at being rescued, a sense of acceptance and belonging, satisfaction at truly making a difference, and a bit of a thrill at the subterfuge of it all. But now, over two years later, many of those feelings had worn thin or vanished entirely. The danger now seemed distant, and the security protocols by which he had to live constraining. The family to whom he was closest had been uprooted and moved so far away that he was rarely able to see them. The increasing losses he was experiencing among his patients, and his limited ability to do anything about it, was depressing him. The sheer volume of work was burdening him, and the initial appreciation for his help was being replaced with casual familiarity and being taken for granted.

But looming over all of Luke's dismay was uncertainty and dissatisfaction about his future. At first, he'd simply been grateful to have been rescued and hidden, and the fact that he'd been officially declared dead had been a convenient coincidence. But he was becoming increasingly aware of just how sharply his unusual status constrained his prospects. Surfacing anywhere as Derek Stevens would probably result in arrest, imprisonment, and no small amount of danger for the people he loved. Crafting a completely new identity was extremely difficult in the modern world, which had so many safeguards to prevent just that. But did that mean he was effectively imprisoned in this hidden existence, to live out his life never being able to do the simplest things like drive and open a bank account? Would he always be dependent on others to manage critical aspects of his life and keep him hidden from danger? As things stood now, he wasn't even able to contact his mother. Were she to die, he wouldn't be able to publicly attend her funeral.

Trammeled, Luke thought as he gouged at the mud with his little spade. That's what he felt: trammeled and constrained. He'd been over the Thumb from Reese to Lexington and from Almont to Port Austin. The trails were well-worn and wearying, and the little towns were starting to look all the same. Was this his entire future? Was this all he had to look forward to? His prospects seemed as low and gray as the ceiling of clouds over his head.

Finally, Luke got enough of the mud shoveled aside that his wheels could get traction, and he carefully worked the ATV clear of the slough. Repacking his gear, he continued up the trail, a distressing mixture of chilled, sweaty, filthy, and late. He had one more stop before he turned toward home, and he hoped he'd encounter no further mud holes.

It was nearly ten at night when Luke finally pulled into his quarters at the little campus of houses known informally as Rivendell. He desperately wanted to shower and collapse into bed, but he first wanted to look in on Grandma. Stripping off his muddy outerwear and changing his boots and trousers, he headed for the Big House with his bag. Quietly entering the little suite that served as quarters for the elder Petersons, he found Grandpa Mike dozing in his recliner in the sitting room. Luke tried to ease past him, but he slept lightly, and stirred as Luke passed.

"Sorry, Grandpa," Luke apologized.

"No, no, I wanted to catch you," Grandpa said. "She's been resting, but still isn't eating much. Teresa's in with her now."

"Teresa's here?" Luke asked.

"She came down with Sister Margaret to pick up Mrs. Baden. They're staying the night and will return to St. Anne's in the morning," Grandpa explained, heaving himself out of his chair. "We can poke our heads in."

In the bedroom they found Teresa sitting beside Grandma's bed, holding her hand and conversing quietly. Teresa gave Luke a warm smile and affectionate hug, which Luke returned gratefully. Teresa was one of his dearest friends, very much like a sister, but due to the rhythms of their lives he rarely got to see her these days. She stepped back from her chair so he could open his bag and extract his gear.

"Good evening, Luke dear," Grandma said with a smile.

"Good evening, Grandma," Luke replied. "How are we doing tonight?"

Grandma chuckled. "'We' are varied. You, I'm sure, are doing well. I have been struggling to stay awake, and have an abysmal appetite."

"Actually, I'm not doing as well as you might think. I got stuck in a mud hole on the way home and had to dig myself out," Luke replied as he listened to her breathing, took her pulse, and did the other things that made it look like he was accomplishing something. Everyone in the room played along, but nobody was fooled: Grandma was dying of respiratory failure. It was another condition that Luke was certain that more advanced treatments could alleviate, and oddly, Grandma could have gotten them. She was neither one of the guests nor "hidden" off the grid, so she could have sought public medical care. But when Luke had first explained their options to Grandma and Grandpa, the two had considered them prayerfully and had decided to stay at home, under Luke's limited care, until the end. Grandma had explained that she'd rather die sooner in her home, surrounded by those she loved, then move to a sterile medical environment just to live a few months longer amidst tubes and wires. That had seemed reasonable at the time, but now that death was drawing closer, Luke wondered if they were having second thoughts.

"So," Grandma asked with a smile as Luke finished his examining. "How am I doing, Doc?"

"About the same as last time," Luke said as he started packing away his gear. It was true enough – there was no perceptible decline since he'd last checked her.

"Well, considering that I'm dying, that can't be good, can it?" Grandma joked. Luke smiled and patted her hand. "Oh, I'm sorry," Grandma continued when she saw Luke struggling to keep his face impassive. "I'm trying to lighten the mood and it isn't working."

"It's okay," Luke said, kissing her hand. "Love you, Grandma."

"Love you, too. And thank you for all your care."

"My privilege," Luke replied, then stepped out of the room, followed by Grandpa.

"So – how is she?" Grandpa asked him as they walked toward the kitchen.

"Like I told her – about the same. She's holding steady, but in her condition, things could turn any day," Luke replied. As much as he wanted to comfort Grandpa, he had to be honest. "I'm sorry, Grandpa. If I had access to more sophisticated treatments –"

"No, no, you've done a fine job," Grandpa patted his arm. "Thank you for all you've done, and continue to do."

"Yeah," Luke replied with a shrug. He couldn't imagine what that had been, other than to make Grandma more comfortable in her decline. With no tool more sophisticated than a stethoscope, he was powerless to determine the cause of her pulmonary condition, much less properly treat it. Feeling more helpless than ever, he made his way to the kitchen where Ruth and Travis were sitting at the table. He would have greeted them, except that Travis was on the phone, listening with unusual intensity, while Ruth looked on with an expression of alarm mixed with – anger?

"What's up?" Luke asked, but Ruth waved him to silence while Travis nodded and muttered into the phone. Grandpa sat down beside Ruth and patted her shoulder.

"All right, then," Travis said at last. "I'll be right up." He hung up and grimaced at Ruth. "I'm going to need to hit the reserves to cover bail for both of them."

"Wait – bail?" Luke asked. "What's going on?"

"Travis has to drive up to Sandusky to get Cletus and Sixtus out of jail," Ruth said in clipped tones. "They were picked up for taking part in a fight behind a bar in Marlette."

Luke was stunned. Cletus and Sixtus? Fighting publicly? Grandpa patted Ruth's shoulder again, and though his expression was grave, Luke couldn't help but wonder if there wasn't the hint of a twinkle in his eye.

"It'll be okay, Ruth," Grandpa assured her. "I'm sure Sheriff Corrigan's men will handle them gently."

"I'm not worried about how gently the police will handle them, Dad," Ruth replied testily. "I'm worried about –"

"I'm off," Travis interrupted as he bustled back into the room, tucking an envelope into his jacket pocket. "Don't wait up for me – I have no idea how long I'll be."

Grandpa waved goodbye, but Ruth didn't seem to notice, being intent on resuming her tirade. Not wishing to become embroiled in this family discussion, Luke grabbed his bag and quietly slipped out the back door to make his way to his apartment. The rooms were dark and chill, and smelled a bit musty – it had been days since he'd been here and weeks since he'd had a chance to clean it properly. He turned on his desk light and collapsed into his chair, overwhelmed with confusion and discouragement. What else could go wrong? Grandma's failing health was bad enough, but that was expectable at her age. But Cletus and Sixtus arrested? Granted, they had feisty personalities, but at least one could be counted on to be level-headed at any given time, thus keeping the other out of trouble. But this was both of them, in serious enough trouble to get them arrested! Luke stared glumly at his desk, feeling lost and confused. The secure, comforting world into which he had been adopted seemed to be unraveling at the center. It had been bad enough when the Schaeffers had been attacked and uprooted last year, but everything seemed to have gone downhill since then. These days he hardly ever saw the Schaeffers, and when he did, their once-harmonious home was haunted by some kind of discord that he couldn't trace to any specific source. Of course, Martha was off with her new husband raising her baby, but Phillip wasn't around much, either, and Kent was moody and withdrawn. What was happening? How could something so stable and beautiful decay?

Luke sighed and pushed aside his prayer book so he could unpack his bag. It had been weeks since he'd opened the prayer book, but he'd been too busy and scattered. There was still time for evening prayers, but he was tired, and even the thought of trying to find the proper pages taxed him. Wearily he took out his gear, setting some items aside to be cleaned and others to be restocked. Damn, it was cold in here! He went over and turned on the space heater even though he knew it would burn expensive heating oil. For what he gave to these people, a warm bedroom wasn't too much to ask, was it?

Back in Grandma's room, Teresa sat beside the old woman's bed, listening to her shallow breathing and holding her chilly hand. Teresa prayed for strength to hold back the thoughts and fears crowding around her in the dark. Old terrors whispered from dark corners, terrors she'd thought had been left behind. She'd been abandoned by two mothers already. Now the mother who'd adopted her and helped bring her out of the darkness seemed about to leave her as well. Teresa bowed her head, trying to fight the fear. What about her was so unlovable that mothers kept leaving her? Her rational mind argued that Grandma couldn't help her illness, but her heart wasn't listening.

Grandma stirred in her restless sleep, and Teresa slipped her hand away, lest her movement disturb the old woman. Teresa tried to pray, but found it nearly impossible. She buried her face in her hands and sobbed quietly.

Arrival

As the plane banked on its approach, Jason got a glance at the water that bordered the area. The sprawling expanse of metro Detroit was bounded on the south by the Detroit River, which was a bluish-gray channel that cut west beneath the city before turning south to flow down to Lake Erie. The water over which they were descending also looked bluish-gray, but had white blotches scattered here and there. The map told him this was Lake St. Clair, and he supposed the blotches must be ice floes, still lingering in the frigid waters. The landscape was bleak, mostly bare trees and open land in various shades of brown. How he hated these icebound northern states with their interminable winters!

The plane shuddered slightly as it leveled off and the pilot lowered the flaps for landing. Never before had Jason been able to take the departmental shuttle which winged around the continent transporting important DHS officials. But he now had not only had the rank, but the excuse that he needed to meet with another DHS official at the shuttle's first stop, so he'd been able to reserve a spot on the elegant twenty-seat jet, bypassing the hassle of baggage checks and seat assignments, and even the security line. At least there were some benefits to this god-awful assignment.

The plane was descending quickly over the water, approaching Selfridge Air Base from the east. Jason would be greeted by a Major Collins of the Border Patrol's Aerial Surveillance division, and he hoped the guy wouldn't be a jerk. Jason didn't like dealing with the uniformed types, who tended to be stuffy and officious, but he wasn't getting many choices on this assignment. The wheels shrieked and the plane bumped as it touched down on the runway.

After a brief taxi the plane stopped and dropped the boarding ladder. It was clear who Jason's greeting party was: a man in the light blue of the Department's uniformed division stood beside a black SUV, his gold ornamentation contrasting with the rumpled black utility uniform of the underling beside him. The man stepped forward briskly and extended his hand.

"Mr. Pelletier? Major Chad Collins, Border Surveillance. Welcome to Selfridge. Hines here will fetch your gear. If you'll come with me." They got into the SUV while Hines piled Jason's luggage into the back and then got in to drive.

"As you requested, I've reserved a conference room for our briefing," the major continued as Hines drove across the base. "Don't worry about security – the room is hardened and secured, with all the hookups and devices you might need. Here at Selfridge, we're accustomed to all levels of security clearances."

Jason smiled and nodded. Whatever else this guy had going on, he had the stuffy and officious down perfectly.

"My team was in on this effort from the beginning, when they first discovered they had a problem," Major Collins explained once they were settled in the conference room. "We first got a call asking for surveillance footage along the riverfront up in Port Huron. A party of interest had escaped their containment, and they asked us to help track her down."

"Excuse me – who's 'they'?" Jason interrupted.

"The HHS people. My office got an urgent call from one of their analysts, and we responded," Collins explained. "Anyway, we weren't able to help that time, because all we had was general footage that we examined after the fact. They didn't notify us beforehand, so we couldn't get assets into position, and we weren't given targets. That first call, they just gave us a vague description of what they were looking for, and we couldn't find anyone fitting the description."

"But they asked for ongoing assistance?" Jason asked.

"Yes."

"Did they ever explain why?"

"No, but I assumed that was because of mission confidentiality, and I was right. We offered them more assistance than we've ever offered anyone – in fact, I was the one who picked up their project director, Dr…Dr…"

"Tasker," Jason supplied.

"That's right, Tasker. He and his aide flew in here to Selfridge."

"On the shuttle?"

"No, special flight straight from Andrews."

"Did you drive him up to the site?"

"No, some of his people picked him up at the gate. I was needed here to direct the surveillance support of the evolution. It was a regional effort – we had eight birds loitering, waiting for the go-sign. We even had to task a low-level asset for close-in surveillance and tracking of some suspects. Got 'em, too – they couldn't have done it without us," Collins boasted.

"Great, but we're getting ahead of ourselves," Jason said. "Let's back up to your initial support. After that first contact, what kind of help did they request?"

"General surveillance," Collins answered. "Looking back, it should have been a clue to them, how easily their first suspect slipped through their fingers. This terror network they were facing was well trained, deeply embedded, and stealthy as hell. They asked me to do wide-ranging overflights, looking for something – anything – suspicious. I obliged as best I could, without compromising our own mission."

"Did they ever explain why they were asking? Reveal anything about the project they were working on?"

"No, but I didn't press them too hard. I know about OpSec! I helped as I could, which was difficult at times, because some of them could be quite testy. One woman in particular was almost abrasive. I tried to understand – it's hard when you discover that your confidential project has been compromised and undermined. They were under a lot of pressure.

"My main contact was one of their data guys, Ron. He and I met and conferenced a lot. He was decent enough, and smart as a whip. He's the one who figured out how widespread the infiltration was. He ran the queries which estimated how many people had been diverted from their program. He figured out that the hospital systems were being manipulated, and he made the big breakthrough that blew the whole thing open."

"What breakthrough was that?" Jason asked.

"They found a firm connection, a specific person to track. That was their big frustration – they knew people were doing stuff that was adversely impacting their operation, but they couldn't tell exactly who. Even the HHS auditor brought into the hospital wasn't finding anything concrete. But then, somehow, they got a track on a guy. Something about spending and travel patterns. Turned out to be something they could run with."

"This specific person – was it this Derek Stevens?"

"I think that was him. It all got kind of fast-paced there toward the end. I remember driving out to the HQ for a conference on the day of…that is, on the last day. Ron had isolated some specific anomalies and asked me to share the aerial footage for corroboration. We found a few things, not as much as we would have liked, but enough to justify bringing the guy in for questioning," the major explained. "In fact, it was largely our footage that convinced them they had a genuine lead on the terror network, enough to justify a large-scale response. I helped make that call."

"You and who else?"

"Just me, Ron, and this Melissa person. She could be a bit of a bitch at times, but she knew her stuff."

"Anyone else that you know of?" Jason asked.

"Not on my end," Collins replied. "I don't know who Ron was talking to, but I got the impression it was mostly to D.C. A little bit to some data analysts at the Fort Wayne FRC, but locally it was just me and maybe some Border Patrol field agents."

"So, no idea how the terror network would have known when to strike?"

"None," Collins shook his head. "But the terrorists were sophisticated and experienced. In fact, the HHS people actually lost track of the target for a while – this Stevens guy. He slipped through their fingers, and it was only by sheer luck that they recovered him. We helped with that, too."

"Really? That wasn't in any of the documentation," Jason said.

"Well, it wouldn't have been. Not only was it embarrassing for them, but nobody lived long enough to write it all down," Collins explained. "Once the call was made to bring Stevens in for questioning, there was some sort of delay that provided enough time for someone to slip him word. By the time they showed up to apprehend him, he'd escaped. They called me in to see if overflight footage could help, but it was just enough to show him getting away. He showed some nice tradecraft there, too – somebody had taught him how to use cover to elude overhead surveillance. Also, the geotrackers on both his phone and his car had been tampered with, so Ron couldn't trace him that way."

Jason raised his eyebrows. He was going to have to adjust his estimation of this terror network – they clearly knew a few tricks. "So, if he got away so smoothly, how did they get him back?"

"That was Melissa's guess, and it turned out to be a good one. She figured he'd return to rescue his nurse buddy, who was still at the hospital. This nurse had been questioned, and they'd intended to detain her, but let her go on the chance that he'd come back for her. Needless to say, they had all sorts of assets tracking her closely the entire time, including a helidrone controlled from this office. I've got the takedown on video, if you'd like to see it."

"I'd like a copy of that. Was there any indication that this nurse buddy of his was involved in the terror network as well?"

"Hard to tell, but I'd guess not," Collins replied. "They talked about her like she was one of theirs, but I don't know if that just meant a hospital employee, or active in this secretive HHS project. They certainly suspected him, and he was her friend, so I'm sure they intended to question her as well."

"Hmm," mused Jason. "I wonder if that's it. One thing I've wondered all along was why the terrorists blew up the building with their own people inside it. Is it possible they didn't know he'd been captured?"

"Could be," Collins replied. "But the way the techs were talking when they were tracking her, especially once she picked him up in her car, they were guessing he had assistance. From his actions and field skills he looked like he was executing a coordinated plan, and may have been in active communication with some agency."

"So they probably knew that both Stevens and his friend were in custody," Jason confirmed. He didn't mention the video monitoring equipment that had been found in the wreckage.

"And they blew it up anyway," Collins added. "Cold hearted bastards."

"It's what fanatics do," Jason replied. "You actually witnessed the blast in real time?"

"Well, one of my techs did. But we replayed it immediately. Want to see the footage?"

"I've got it here," Jason tapped the tablet. "Just a couple more questions. This regional evolution with the troops from the Fort Wayne Fast Response Center: how was this office involved in that? How closely were you tied into the effort?"

"Very closely," Collins assured him. "We were tasked to be the overhead eyes of the action. We had birds in the air across the whole region, and control teams for each one tied into the TacNet awaiting targeting information. Once we got that, my people would vector in the aerial assets while the ground troops moved into position. The goal was to strike as many terrorist sites as possible at roughly the same time, to minimize the risk of them alerting other cells. Of course, we were prepared for that as well. We had a two-layer deployment strategy, with the low-level assets providing close-in support, while the high-level birds scanned for anomalies in the –"

"I'm sure we can go into the details later," Jason interrupted. "Last question: was there any activity you were asked to perform subsequent to the incident? Fly any further surveillance, or provide additional intelligence?"

"Nope," Collins shook his head. "Not a damn thing. Once the dust settled from the blast, it became all forensics work. The FRC teams were pulled back, I grounded my drones, and no further instructions came. It was like everything just…died."

"Well," Jason replied. "Everything did. The entire project leadership was taken out by the blast."

"Sure, but I would have expected some kind of follow-up. There is one thing, though: several weeks later, due to the severity of the domestic terror threat, I was granted permission to fly my drones further from the border, and to arm them if necessary."

"So I understand," Jason replied. "Have you ever flown them armed since then?"

"Only a of couple times, for training and drills," Collins almost pouted. "The weight of the ordnance reduces the aloft time, and my techs whine about all the extra protocols they have to observe when working with live weapons. Also, I have to be careful with armed drones near the Canadian border due to diplomatic considerations. But, by hell, we've got the standing authorization to do it, if we ever get the chance."

"Well, then," Jason grinned as he started to pack up his briefcase. "You may get the chance soon. I've been commissioned to resolve this situation, and I intend to resolve it decisively."

"Damn straight!" Collins whooped.

*   *   *

Jason sat in the drab, sparse conference room of the chain motel in Imlay City and stared at the black television screen on the wall. When he'd asked the desk clerk if he could use the room for his meeting, she'd just shrugged and told him nobody was using it at the moment. From the looks of things, nobody used it much after the cheap continental breakfast ended in the morning. The TV was not only off but unplugged, and the carafes on the coffee service stood bone dry, their bottoms stained with coffee residue. Apparently, there weren't many conferences in Imlay City, at least in the motels.

Jason hadn't yet decided what to do about his living situation while he was assigned here. The simplest thing to do would be to stay near places where the DHS had facilities, like Selfridge or Port Huron. But he didn't want to barge into an established domain and start requisitioning resources. That was a sure way to foster resentment, as well as raise difficult questions about who he was and what he was doing there. His instincts told him that the fewer people who knew he was here, the freer his hands would be. So for now he'd checked into a hotel near were the blast had been. Eventually he might rent an apartment or efficiency in whatever place made the most sense.

Unfortunately, complete stealth was not possible. Jason needed to talk to the two agents who'd been working the case for the past couple of years, if "working" was the applicable term. They were currently driving over from Port Huron, bringing his rental car with them. He wanted to get what information he could about their investigations, and ask them about the best way to get familiar with the area. He had no clue where to begin looking for the threads that would lead to this terror network, but he suspected that it wouldn't be in the urban areas. That meant getting familiar with the countryside, which looked vast and empty on the map.

A couple of men stepped into the conference room. One was taller and heavyset to the point of approaching pudgy, with thinning brown hair and glasses. The other was shorter and thinner, with black hair and an incipient five-o'clock shadow. His eyes and features were sharp, and he had a slightly unkempt air.

"Mr. Pelletier?" the tall one asked.

"I am," Jason responded. "I presume you're agents –"

"Sanderson, sir," the tall one gripped his hand. "And Agent Harris. Welcome to the Blue Water District."

"'Blue Water'? I thought this was called the Thumb Region," Jason said as they all sat down.

"It is, sir, but the eastern counties that border the water are locally referred to as the Blue Water Area. If you get over there, you'll see why – the lake and river are amazingly blue. Since the international border is our main concern, the department adopted the name."

"I see," Jason explained. "I appreciate your driving my car over on a Saturday. I've been assigned the task of getting the investigation of this blast back on track, and I understand that you two have been the lead agents so far?"

From the slight stiffening of the agents' shoulders and a narrowing of their eyes, Jason saw that he could have chosen his words more tactfully.

"Well, sir," Sanderson bristled. "Not to make excuses, but we got this whole thing dumped on us without any direction or additional resources – on top of our existing duties. We were never even told why our department pulled the duty. It's more rightfully the domain of the FBI or ATF, not the Border Patrol."

"Well, they haven't been totally absent," Jason explained. "The ATF did a thorough forensic workup of the site, and I have their report right here on my tablet."

The agents looked at each other with a mixture of astonishment and rage. "Those bastards!" Harris blurted out. "They never –"

"Calm down, Stan," Sanderson patted his arm. "Mr. Pelletier is new here." Harris bottled up while Sanderson turned to Jason. "You see, sir, this is just the sort of thing we've been dealing with. We're supposedly the lead agents on the case, and we were never told there was an ATF investigation going on. We didn't know you were coming until the day before yesterday, we don't know what your mandate is, and we don't know if we're supposed to start reporting to you. We're held responsible, but we're told nothing."

"I appreciate the difficulty of your position," Jason assured them. "And I'm not here to blame you. I hope to provide the resources you've been denied to this point. I'll keep you as informed as I can given security constraints. I've got your written reports here," he tapped the tablet, "but I'd like a summary from both of you on your feeling for the incident, the follow-up, and the current state of affairs."

The two agents looked at each other with a mixture of relief and skepticism, and proceeded to unload on Jason their tale of two years of frustrating interviews, worthless leads, and wasted effort. Sanderson did most of the talking, with Harris chipping in from time to time. As the story unfolded, Jason began to suspect that these two agents weren't the sharpest knives in the drawer, and that their pursuit of the investigation hadn't been as wholehearted as they were trying to get him to believe, but the gist of what they told him was true: they'd been given the assignment with scant resources and no direction. Jason suspected that this was more so that their manager could maintain that "an investigation is ongoing" rather than in hopes that they'd resolve anything.

That was about to change.

"All right," Jason said after fifteen minutes of explanation. "I get the picture. I can see that you were handed a difficult mission and got no support. I'm here to give you support. Starting right now, it's a clean slate. Everything you've done, and haven't done, is in the past. I can't promise you immediate results or a frustration-free project, because I can't promise myself that, but I can promise you that we're going for results, not make-work and wheel-spinning."

Sanderson and Harris looked at each other again, their expressions difficult to read. There may have been some relief, but there was certainly a good measure of skepticism.

"That's good to hear, sir," Sanderson ventured cautiously. "How will that affect our organizational placement? Will we be reporting to you?"

"My assignment is temporary," Jason explained. "But my authority is plenary in this matter. You will be reporting to me in regard to any work on this. Don't worry, you won't be caught in any crossfires. I'll work with your supervisors to ensure your responsibilities are clear. If there are any questions or problems, bring them directly to me and I'll resolve them."

"Oh, that reminds me," Sanderson pulled out his phone and looked something up. "Our supervisor, Madison, looked up special positions like yours and it turns out you rate a car and a driver."

Jason raised his eyebrows. "But I have a rental car –"

"I know, sir, and you'll need that, too, but Madison suggests you consider it. A driver would free you to work while traveling, and he knows the area well, and could take some responsibilities for coordinating and scheduling."

Jason pondered this. A driver? One of the most coveted perks in the Capital area, one he wouldn't have dreamed of earning for years yet, but out here in the sticks he qualified for one? Granted, he usually preferred to do his own driving, but the prospect of having a secretary as well was alluring.

"Could he handle coordinating effectively? I don't want to get some lout who I have to instruct in every detail."

"Oh, he'd do fine, sir," Sanderson replied. "We know who she's got in mind, and he's a competent guy. His name is Ethan Patterson. Madison just got him dumped on her by another supervisor, and she's wondering what to do with him. Just between us, sir, he's on probation, so she doesn't know how long she has him."

"Probation? Am I allowed to know why?"

"We don't officially know ourselves, though we have our suspicions. Nothing dangerous or disabling, or she wouldn't dream of assigning him to you," Sanderson assured him.

"Ah. Well, have her send him around tomorrow at ten, and I'll interview him. The car has to be nondescript – no federal plates, and he shouldn't be in uniform."

"Sounds good, sir," Sanderson said. "Will there be anything else, sir?"

"Only this, gentlemen: I intend to take this investigation seriously. This was a major attack on national soil with heavy casualties, many of them important government officials, and it's been swept under the rug. The investigation hasn't been given priority or resources, as you're well aware. There are a lot of dots scattered around: long simmering anti-government resentment, rumors of cross-border drug smuggling, clandestine supply chains, sophisticated communications capabilities, and secret networks dedicated to lawbreaking. Nobody has been connecting these dots, but I intend to, and I intend to use what I learn to impact them heavily. At the least I intend to bring those who masterminded the blast to justice, and hope to go much further.

"You both can be part of this, if you wish. You'll have the resources you've been denied to this point, and we'll be pursuing things aggressively. I'm not returning to D.C. without accomplishing major things, and there will be recognition and promotions for those who help me. Are you on board?"

"I...uh...we are, sure," Sanderson stammered. "We're on board, aren't we, Stan?"

"All the way, sir," Harris assured him.

"Good," Jason said, standing and offering his hand. "I'm still working out a plan of attack, so go back to your usual work. As I formulate things, I'll be in touch with you and your supervisor to coordinate your hours. I'll look forward to seeing Patterson tomorrow morning."

"Okay, then, sir," Sanderson assured him. "We'll look forward to hearing from you."

The two agents went out to Sanderson's car for the drive back to Port Huron. Harris sat sullenly and stared straight ahead as Sanderson pulled out of the parking lot.

"Well, hoo-rah, Captain effin' America," Harris growled. Sanderson grimaced – they both recognized a pep talk when they heard one.

"I hear ya," Sanderson replied. "But maybe he means it, Stan. We haven't yet had anyone from D.C. assigned here."

"I'll believe it when I see it," Harris retorted. "Until then, he's just another beltway blowhard. Say, are we off shift yet?"

"Not really," Sanderson pointed at the dash clock. "We could consider ourselves so by the time we got back, though. I sure don't plan to head back to the office."

"Okay, then, if you could drop me at the rental place, that'd be great – it's where I left my car. Can we stop at Bill's Market on the way? It'll save me a trip later."

Sanderson glanced at his partner. The silence was thick in the car, because they both knew what he'd pick up at Bill's, and what he'd do with it once he got home.

"You...ah...sure about that, Stan?" Sanderson ventured cautiously.

"Yes, dammit, I'm sure," Harris barked. "I don't need a damn wife – or mother!"

"Okay, Stan, okay," Sanderson replied quietly. "No need to jump down my throat. I'm just trying to help. I'm covering for you as best I can, but people are starting to talk."

"Yeah, yeah," Harris grumbled. For a moment the mask of his anger dropped, and he looked pained and exhausted. "I know you're trying to help, and I appreciate it. I'm on top of it, I really am." Silence fell in the car for a minute before he spoke again. "How are you doing? I mean...you and Kayla?"

Sanderson stared at the road and licked his lips. "We're...okay, I guess. Some progress, in the sense that our lawyers hope to work out a hearing date sometime in the next few weeks. They say it'll be quick, because it's so cut-and-dried."

"Well, at least you won't have to go through custody hearings. Those are a particular type of hell," Harris said bitterly.

"Yeah, that's one thing," Sanderson agreed. "Stepdads don't have to worry about custody hearings. Jasmine and Brent will just...go with Kayla." He drew in a big breath and let it out slowly, keeping his eyes firmly on the road.

"I'm sorry, man," Harris said quietly.

"Yeah," Sanderson said in a thick voice. "Yeah, so am I."

The afternoon was fading toward evening, but Jason figured there was enough daylight to squeeze in one more task. Taking the main road north out of town, he drove until he came to a dirt side road where his car's navigational system told him to turn east. He traveled almost two bumpy miles to where the road curved north again. At the curve was a locked gate made of rusty iron pipes that closed across a dirt driveway.

Jason had to park in front of the gate because he didn't have the key to the lock. He made a mental note to find out who did – perhaps that could be a task for his new driver/secretary. He squeezed his way around one of the gate posts, getting his shoes dirty and his pants legs wet from the tall grass.

What had been the parking lot was littered with debris and was beginning to be retaken by weeds. Beyond the lot lay grassy meadow and scrub, with a thick belt of woods pushing very near to the east edge of the parking lot. What remained of the building had been enclosed in a tall chain-link fence, which also had a gate that was chained and locked. The gate had not been used in some time, as the area within the fencing was overgrown with tall weeds right to the edge.

Jason walked slowly around the overgrown lot, listening to the chill breeze whisper in the bare branches of the trees and rustle through the weeds. There was something fine and fresh about the desolate loneliness of the site. Jason looked out across the twilight-shrouded fields, spotting a few distant lights but no movement. He realized he was listening for something he wouldn't hear: the constant low-grade hum of urban life – the traffic and people and aircraft, punctuated by the occasional distant siren or honking of car horns. For most of his life, whenever he'd been outside, that auditory tapestry had been a constant backdrop. Here, the silence was so great that it almost pressed on his ears. He could hear nothing but the soft breeze and the muted crunch of the pebbles beneath his feet. It was peaceful, in a wild and remote way.

But, Jason reminded himself, appearances could deceive. He walked to the fence and gazed through it at what had once been the building. Barely visible amidst the innocent looking weeds were blackened bits of cinder block and twisted, rusting pieces of angle iron, mute testimony to the blast that had devastated this placid spot. Twenty-three people had met a sudden and brutal end here, victims of blind rage and senseless malice. He closed his eyes and tried to recall the aerial footage of the explosion, imagining what it must have been like at the site, what the fireball had looked like or how the shock wave must have felt. He struggled to understand the hatred that would do such a thing.

Jason stepped back from the fence and looked about. The darkness was deepening quickly and the peace he'd felt had vanished. The derelict clearing now felt haunted, overshadowed by death. He glanced at the woods, which now seemed shrouded in menacing shadow. The innocent-looking surroundings hid dangerous secrets. He wanted to flee back to the warm, familiar bustle of his urban home, far from this ominous desolation.

But unfortunately, he was here not to run from those secrets, but to face them, to delve in and expose them. He retreated to his car and his hotel room.

Missionary

When Pete and Dr. Harris pulled up to the tribal center on the Garden River Reserve, they were met by a dark-haired man who greeted them without smiling, but whose eyes were alert and whose handshake was welcoming. He introduced himself as Gerald Solomon and invited them into the center. The interior looked like any generic township hall or community center, right down to the coffee service off to one side right under the bulletin board.

"I'm afraid we'll have to grab a corner here," Gerald said, gesturing to a round table on which lay a few loose leaf binders. "I tried to get one of the smaller meeting rooms, but there are only three. There's a finance meeting in one, and the ladies are taking up the other two for their knotting and weaving."

"This'll be fine," Dr. Harris assured him, sitting down and opening a binder. "So, are these the first results of the translation effort?"

"Yes. Before we begin, I want to reiterate the thanks which Drs. Picotte and Newell stated. This work is a substantial find. A quick skim through the journal indicates that it provides details of this early missionary effort in the Sault area. We hope that it will prove a critical source of knowledge about the First Nations life at that time. On behalf of my tribe and people, I thank you both for so generously making it available."

"Oh, no problem," Pete waved dismissively. "I was glad we found it. My family's Old Sault – though not as Old Sault as yours – and we're happy to do anything we can to help the area."

"Nonetheless, we owe you a debt," Gerald continued. "Now, to the translation." They opened the binders to see a brief introduction page, then the pages of the journal laid out in a facing-page format. On the left-hand page was a scaled-down image of the journal page itself, and beneath that a French text of what the page said. On the right-hand page was the English translation, with footnotes at the bottom. Gerald began flipping through the pages as he spoke.

"The initial pages of the journal give a bit of background. Though this was a private journal, Fr. Thomas clearly kept it with the constant consideration that it might someday be public. This was typical of missionaries entering hostile environments – they knew that perhaps the only thing that might tell of their deeds would be a journal like this. As such, he recorded things that would enable a chronicler to place his writings in proper context.

"Fr. Thomas was from Nantes, in western France. He was the sixth of seven children, and the third of four sons. His father was the scion of a minor branch of the nobility who had the foresight to enter into trade. Thomas grew up in the family's manor. Most of his brothers seemed to follow the family pattern for the time: the eldest inheriting the father's position and lands, the second son entering the army, and Thomas entering the priesthood. Reading between the lines a little, one gets the idea that Thomas's Mama didn't mind him entering the priesthood, but would have preferred him to become a diocesan priest and settle in a parish in France rather than joining the missionary Jesuit order. But Thomas was convinced that he'd heard the call of God on his life. He waxes poetic about it here on this page, contrasting his choice with that of his next elder brother: 'He has chosen the army of the king, and I the Army of the King of Kings.' It's speculation, but it's possible he was pushing back against some pressure he'd been feeling."

Gerald paused, flipping past a few pages in the binder before continuing. "He writes a little about his training and formation, but doesn't go into detail. He probably presumed his readers would be familiar with that process. He was ordained in 1637, and served for a while with the Jesuits in Paris. He must have done well, because in late 1639 he received news that he had been selected for missionary work in New France. He goes on at length about that. He embarked for Quebec in April of 1640, at which point the journal becomes current."

"'Becomes current'?" asked Pete.

"Forgive me, I should have been more clear," Gerald replied. "The journal actually begins, in the sense that he puts pen to paper, in April 1640, shortly after Easter. He was in the port of Le Havre, waiting to take ship. He purchased the paper there and began writing, but the first thing he did was fill in his history. Everything we've covered to this point has been backstory; his first current entry was on April 28th. See here on the ninth page – *I have engaged passage on a merchant ship named for King St. Louis, and am bound for Quebec. The mate says he had sailed with Champlain and knew him well. I admit the possibility, but do not believe everything these sailors say.* They set sail two days later.

"The relentless march of cultural imperialism," quipped Dr. Harris as he turned a page. Gerald paused, gazing at him for a long moment before responding.

"You speak as you have been taught, and indeed that view is pervasive among western intellectuals. But we of the First Nations, especially of the upper Anishinaabek tribes, take a different view of the black-robed Jesuits. Yes, their coming was the first footfalls of tumultuous change, for First Nation and European alike. But they were clear about their purposes and, in the main, true to their principles. They had personal integrity and deep respect for us as a people and as a culture. By the standards of their day, they were incredibly adaptive, coming to live in our midst and learn our ways so they could better understand us. They came to spread their faith, and were always clear about that. But given their worldview, that was the highest compliment they could have paid us, and the greatest sacrifice they could have made on our behalf. They were men of their time and culture, of course, as are we, but the Blackrobes were not the worst influence we encountered. To see true cultural imperialism, look to the fur trading companies that spread their influence through the region in the decades that followed. Neither English nor French agents cared how many First Nations fathers were torn from their homes and families, to the devastation of our way of life – they just wanted more men out hunting the beaver and the marten. Remember, Fr. Thomas could have stayed home in a quiet parish in France. Instead, he chose to come to an unsettled land to live a primitive life with strangers, and ultimately to die here, out of concern for our souls. Whether you agree with his principles or not, you cannot deny his heroic choices."

Dr. Harris mumbled something while looking down at the pages of his binder.

"There are several places where Fr. Thomas recounts the difficulties of his travels, his arrival in Quebec, and his superiors arranging transport to the interior," Gerald continued. "He was assigned to assist Fr. Claude Pijart, of whom we know, who was desperately in need of help with his work among the tribes around Georgian Bay. Fr. Thomas records little of his passage up the rivers and through the woods in the hands of First Nation and *métis* voyageurs."

"*Métis*? This early?" Dr. Harris asked.

"Well, yes, since first contact between French and First Nations in the area had been nearly thirty years earlier, *métis* offspring were sure to follow – but this would have been the first generation. As I said, his entries were sparse during the passage, possibly because the rigors of travel left him little time or energy. He writes of his arrival in the area, and his welcome by Fr. Pijart. And here," Gerald turned a page with a triumphant flourish. "We come to the first scholarly jewel this document has given us."

"Which is?" Pete asked.

"We'd known that Fr. Pijart was active in the area during this time. We even know that he sent a couple of Jesuits on a missionary journey to the Sault – Fr. Charles Raymbault and Fr. Isaac Jogues, who was later martyred by the Hurons. What we hadn't known, until this journal told us, was that a third Jesuit accompanied them, with the intention of staying and establishing a permanent mission at the Sault. That third Jesuit was Fr. Thomas D'Aubigne."

"Whoa," Pete looked up with wide eyes. "So – this is an account of the first attempt to establish a mission?"

"Yes," Gerald grinned. "Twenty-five years before Marquette. Of course, that's how we know Fr. Thomas failed, because there was no mission here by the time Marquette arrived, but it's an important piece of history to know that the attempt had been made.

"That's as far as the translation effort has gotten. The last page they've translated records how excited Fr. Thomas was to be chosen for the mission, and his preparations to accompany Frs. Raymbault and Jogues. Hopefully the next set of pages will tell of his arrival and early efforts. Those binders are yours to keep, so you can read the translations at your leisure. Bring them the next time we meet – I'll just print out the newly translated pages and punch them for you."

"Will we meet here?" Pete asked.

"I've been thinking about that. Given the state of things between our countries, it might be easier for me to come there, if you can arrange a meeting place."

"Really?" Pete asked in surprise. "I'd think it would be harder for you as a Canadian to get over."

"It would be – if I were just Canadian," Gerald explained. "But the First Nations status usually eliminates any problems."

"Ah. Then we'll wait to hear from you when the next set of page translations comes through?" Dr. Harris asked.

"Yes. I'm guessing it'll be about two weeks."

Introductions

Figuring out ways to address complex problems had always been Jason's strong suit. Time and again he'd been thrown into knotty, almost intractable messes, and had always been able to work out solutions that would at least move matters toward better order, if not outright solve the problem. He had something of a reputation as a wizard in that regard.

But this situation was beyond anything he'd yet had to face.

Jason stared at the notes he'd scrawled where they lay spread across the conference room tables. He'd essentially co-opted the hotel's space, after the breakfast hours were finished, which nobody seemed to mind – they'd even cleaned out the coffee service so he could put on a fresh pot. In time he'd have to make permanent arrangements for a workspace, but he had more pressing concerns just now.

He'd been over and over the scant evidence they had. The forensic report on the blast, which raised as many questions as it answered. The aerial footage from the drone. The figures on the patients who had been spirited out of the hospitals while the Chengdu Project had been running, and the estimates of how many potential patients had vanished before they could be admitted. The name of a suspect, Derek Stevens, along with some of his purchase records and a few minutes of overhead footage of him doing various things, always ending with him driving out of range. Some cryptic queries from Porcher, the data guy who'd blown things wide open only hours before being blown to pieces himself.

Jason had never had so little to work with. Just about everyone who'd been involved in the project was dead – not just dead, but killed within a few days of the problem being uncovered, before they'd had time to document anything or even have many discussions. There was almost nothing to go on.

Jason was both trained and experienced in domestic counter-terrorism. He understood cyber-detection, how to analyze incidents to discern operational patterns, how to scrutinize communications patterns, and a host of other things that were part and parcel of domestic terror work. But most of these methods presumed an urban environment, and all of them presumed a network of parties of interest who were active and communicating, with immediate and long-range goals they were coordinating to achieve.

None of that could be assumed here.

Not only did Jason not have a handle on how the parties coordinated their activities, he didn't know what a coordinated activity would look like. The one time they'd nearly caught one of the parties in the act, inside a hospital no less, she'd slipped through their fingers with almost stunning ease (and there was precious little documentation about that incident, either). The only other party they'd been able to connect even remotely to the operation had been blown up as well.

So he didn't know who he was looking for, how the mysterious parties coordinated, any details about how they did what they did, or even if they were still doing it. After all, the HHS pilot project had come to a crashing halt just over two years ago. Had this hidden group continued their secretive operations beyond then? Possibly not, since they were certainly the ones who'd engineered the blast and thus would know that the threat was past. That would mean that not only was Jason's data thin and his clues nearly nonexistent, but the trail could be stone cold – the parties he was hunting might have been inactive for perhaps two years.

Jason began to feel the desperate, walls-closing-in panic that he almost always felt at this stage of a new initiative. They were asking far too much for how little they'd given him. They'd dumped this impossible project into his lap and exiled him to this backwater. He'd never figure this out. His career would die here, and he'd slink back to D.C. in ignominy, to be banished for his failure.

Jason stood up and took a deep breath. He walked around the table, pressing the heels of his hands to his eyes and forcing himself to center. He always felt like this initially. He always felt like this. He had felt like this in Knoxville, yet he'd figured that out. He'd felt like this in Seattle, and had worked that out. He'd felt like this about the Mont Belvieu case at the outset, yet he'd conquered that as well. He'd even felt this way at times in Salt Lake City, and though that had ended up poorly, he was confident about the part which had been his responsibility. It always started out feeling this way. He'd figure it out. He'd been in spots like this before. He'd find a way – he always did. He just needed to calm down and focus, to break this problem into manageable chunks.

The conference room door opened and a short man with curly black hair and the wisp of a moustache stepped in. He looked at the screen of his phone and then at Jason.

"Jason Pelletier?"

"Who's asking?" Jason replied.

"Ah," the man responded. "Ethan Patterson, DHS Border Patrol. I was told I could find Jason Pelletier in here."

"You have," Jason replied. He glanced at the clock, which showed just past noon. No wonder he was feeling off – he'd had a bagel and coffee for breakfast, and was long overdue for lunch. "You're late – I was told you'd be here about ten."

"Well," Ethan shrugged as he got himself a cup of coffee. "There was some confusion over in Port Huron, and then we had to find a car, and – yuck! Who brewed this battery acid?" He dumped the coffee down the drain.

"I did – hours ago," Jason said frostily. "If you want fresher coffee, show up earlier."

"Well, I'm here now," Ethan sat in one of the chairs and grinned at Jason. "At your service. What can I do first?"

"First, you can drive me someplace to get a decent lunch."

"I suppose this is as elegant as lunch spots get in Imlay City?" Jason asked as he looked around the diner at what appeared to be the usual midday crew. The waitress who'd taken their orders had addressed them both as "Honey", and people at the other tables were talking to each other with easy familiarity.

"Actually, the steak house up by the expressway isn't too bad, if you'd like to go there," Ethan answered.

"You'll have to prove your value before I get you any steak for lunch," Jason warned.

"Tough boss," Ethan grinned. "Actually, there are one or two nice places in Lapeer, and a few decent spots around Flint. The restaurants over near Frankenmuth are all right, especially if you like chicken, but that's a bit of a drive from here. There are some fine microbreweries in the Saginaw-Bay City area. Of course, there's Port Huron, with some pleasant waterfront outfits that have a great view. But if you're looking for sophisticated elegance, you'll have to go down to metro Detroit."

"You seem to know the area fairly well. Are you from around here?"

"No, I'm originally from near Pittsburg. But I've been assigned here for nearly a decade, and I like to get to know the areas I'm working in."

"So you know the Thumb region?" Jason asked.

"Well enough," Ethan said with a shrug. "I've been all around and through it over the years. I know how to get from Vassar to Pigeon to Harbor Beach to Capac – that, plus I can read a map."

"Great," Jason replied. "You want to tell me why you're on probation?"

Ethan grinned again. "You don't miss a beat, do you?"

"I am an investigator," Jason pointed out.

"I'm afraid my supervisor and union rep have asked me not to discuss the topic with anyone. However, if you were to file a formal request, I'm sure –"

"No need," Jason interrupted. "I just want to be sure it's nothing that will hinder you in the performance of your duties."

"I ain't a drunk, if that's what you're asking, and I don't do dope. I'm a competent, responsible, and safe driver."

"That's a good start," Jason replied. "But I was told you could do more than drive. I need someone who can contact people for me, set up schedules, follow up on tasks – in short, someone to cover details that I won't have time for. I need a cross between a chauffeur, a secretary, and an investigative assistant. Are you up for that?"

"Hey, boss," Ethan answered as he picked up his massive cheeseburger. "Making arrangements is my specialty."

"Great," Jason said. "Because I need you to make arrangements for us to visit this guy tomorrow afternoon." He slid his phone across the table so Ethan could see the name and contact information.

"Major, eh?" Ethan asked around a mouth full of burger. "What is he, Air Force?"

"Border Patrol Aerial Surveillance. I spoke briefly with him when I arrived yesterday, but I need to interview him in more depth. I also need to examine some video footage he has."

"So you'll need, what? Two or three hours?"

"That should cover it," Jason said.

"So, if I can ask," Ethan ventured. "What's all this about? Will I be able to sit in on these interviews, or will I have to stay in the car because of security considerations? It's all the same to me either way, I'd just like to know."

Jason eyed the man keenly. This was an important question, especially if Ethan would be doing more than just driving. On one hand he didn't have a need to know, and there was highly classified information involved. On the other hand, Jason had been sent out here with scant resources. A secretary and coordinator would be a major asset, but working with him would be clumsy if Jason would always have to be dancing around what he was cleared to know. Besides, Jason suspected that Ethan's breezy, irreverent mannerisms hid a keen mind and perceptive insights. He couldn't afford to ignore that kind of help when facing this nearly impossible task. His long-ingrained caution tempered his ambition, but this wasn't D.C., and he'd supposedly been given all the authority he'd need. Time to use it.

"What's your security clearance?" Jason asked.

"Classified, which is usual for my job level," Ethan explained. "The probation didn't change that."

"All right. What I'm dealing with is an interdepartmental investigation to resolve a set of longstanding, interlocking problems. The security classification of some of the material goes up to Top Secret, and some of it you wouldn't want to know. But the immediate challenge pertains to an event that is somewhat public knowledge already. Do you remember the Imlay City blast?"

"Can't say that I do," Ethan replied.

"Happened a couple of years ago, just north of here. It was let out as an industrial accident that killed a couple of local medical workers."

"Oh, yeah, I remember now," Ethan said. "Little add-on story at the end of the newscasts, faded quickly. But I assume that if it was 'let out as' something, that there was more to it?"

Jason glanced around. There were no diners at nearby tables, and their waitress was chatting with some customers who were ringing out. He lowered his voice a little.

"There was. In addition to the medical workers, sixteen high-level government workers were killed, along with security staff and…an anomaly."

"Ooh, an anomaly," Ethan quipped. "Very dangerous."

"And it was no accident, but a carefully planned and timed explosive demolition. Domestic terror involvement is strongly suspected."

"Ah, those domestic terrorists, committing the unforgivable sin of killing bureaucrats. Kidding, kidding!" Ethan backtracked his quip under Jason's humorless gaze.

"The domestic terror side is hardly incidental," Jason continued. "The assassination probably happened because some of the officials had stumbled across the activity of a domestic terror network, and were preparing to take forceful steps to destroy it. That's the part I can't tell you much about. The terrorists learned of their plans and struck first."

"Well, that certainly sounds hazardous," Ethan said lightly. "Where do you come in?"

"The loss of so many high-level personnel left the investigation in…disarray. I've been asked to pick up the threads and try to bring it to a conclusion. There are other issues floating around as well, but it may be risky trying to get them restarted if the terrorists are still active."

"I see. How does this involve the major down at Selfridge?"

"His team got aerial footage of the blast when it happened. Plus, he was tangentially involved in the investigation that first uncovered the terror network. He briefed me yesterday, but I want to interview him more closely, and review all the footage he has."

"'Tangentially'? Can't you talk to anyone who was more directly involved?"

"No," Jason replied. "They were all killed in the blast."

That, at last, seemed to sober Ethan up just a little.

So the next day they were back at Selfridge spending the afternoon going over and over the footage of the blast, dissecting every detail and grilling Major Collins for everything he could remember about the investigation that led up to the fateful night. Unfortunately, many of the details had faded from his memory, for he had been counting on the HHS staffers to write up everything and they'd never gotten the chance. But replaying all the footage helped bring some of it back, and a few more details emerged.

Ethan was in on the sessions, but sat at the back of the room taking notes. He interjected rarely, but when he did it was with a penetrating question or cogent observation. In contrast, Major Collins was an endless source of threadbare speculation and harebrained theory that Jason found tremendously distracting. Collins seemed to think that by virtue of the fact that he had known and assisted some of the HHS personnel, and had witnessed the blast, that made him an inside expert on the matter. Jason was impressed by Ethan's restraint when, on the drive home, he described the major's contributions as "less than helpful."

The following morning Jason and Ethan met in the hotel conference room to try to sort out where they were. Jason applied a helpful filter he sometimes used to cut through masses of partial details and speculation.

"What do we actually know?" he asked as he paced the room. "Major Collins's guesses notwithstanding, what facts do we know for certain?"

"We know that the building was demolished by carefully placed and precisely detonated charges," Ethan pointed out. "We can safely assume that the charges were placed there before the day of the blast, since the building was occupied for most of that day."

"You're right," Jason affirmed. "We know that a party suspected of involvement in the terror network had been apprehended, along with an associate, and taken to the site by Border Patrol agents. The vehicles carrying them were the last two to enter the building."

"We know that the agency who had them apprehended expected to obtain vital information from the suspect, because they had lots of domestic terror units staged up in Sandusky awaiting instructions," Ethan added. "I actually remember that. It was explained afterward as a readiness drill. Do we know if everyone who was expected at the site was present when the blast occurred? Had all the vehicles arrived?"

"I *believe* so," Jason replied, checking his notes. "I think the vehicles carrying the suspect were the last ones, and they'd been long expected. I think we can safely say that we know that, because Collins had told his team to have the drone monitor the access roads and to consider any approaching vehicle suspicious."

"If that's so, then we also know that nobody entered or departed the building from the time the suspect arrived until the blast occurred," Ethan pronounced.

Jason looked at Ethan sideways. The man might be flippant at times, but he was intelligent and thoughtful, and the only personnel resource Jason had. He wouldn't be able to help if he didn't have sufficient information, even if that information was classified. Jason made his call, and leaned over to speak more quietly.

"Actually, we're not sure of that. Remember that anomaly in the drone footage yesterday, the one I had Collins run and re-run several times and zoom in as best he could?"

"The anomaly about which he had about a hundred theories? Yeah, I remember that, and I remember wondering why you kept giving him repeated opportunities to bloviate."

"What I'm about to tell you is classified at least secret, if not top secret. It was from a report commissioned by DHS, not the other agency, so it's 'in house', in a sense. But not only can you not speak of this, you can't let slip that you know it. Understand?"

"Got it, boss."

"That anomaly? The forensics investigation on the blast site turned up an unknown body, along with an unknown vehicle. The vehicle was something like a homemade motor scooter. All the known parties were identified by the other department, if only by clothing scraps, but that one party remains a mystery. Nobody knows who he was, what he was doing there, or how he got there. The scooter is the only clue."

"Oh, *really?*" Ethan asked with high interest. "Well, now, that changes things. Suicide bomber, perhaps?"

"The forensic techs don't think so, and I agree. For one thing, the charges were planted about the structure, not on him. His body was caught by the blast, but wasn't the source of it. For another, he'd been shot by weapons belonging to security staff within the building – one of them a Border Patrol sidearm and the other from the other agency."

"Ah. So whatever this guy was, he was perceived as hostile by security within the building," Ethan observed.

"One more thing: the forensics investigation also turned up what seemed to be part of a video monitoring system that hadn't been placed by the other agency. It's a reasonable guess that this secret site was being monitored by parties unknown."

"Now *that's* interesting," Ethan replied. "And fills in a lot of gaps. If these unknown parties were watching the site, they would have had a good guess at what it was being used for, and could have slipped in when the structure was unoccupied to mine it. They also could have known when the critical personnel were inside the building."

"They would also have known that the informant who'd been apprehended was inside the building – maybe. But we're getting ahead of ourselves here, off into speculation. Let's refocus on what we know," Jason suggested.

"Okay, we know that an unknown party was inside the building at the time of the blast, and he was perceived by the occupants as being hostile."

"I think we can assume he wasn't in the building when people started arriving," Jason expanded. "The place was simple, just a few rooms and no corners to hide in. Anyone inside would have been spotted as the building filled. That must mean he had to have arrived later."

"Which would mean very tight timing, but squares with the timing of that anomaly that the drone footage barely caught. But...but..." Ethan paused, thinking furiously.

"But what?" Jason prodded.

"That's more important than you might think," Ethan replied. "We know this unknown person was there, and he had to have been the last guy to the party."

"Are we sure of that?"

"Yes. You said that one of the guns that shot him was a Border Patrol firearm. The only Border Patrol guys there came in the last vehicles, the ones that brought the suspect."

"Good point. Why is that important?"

"It's important because it means we know how he didn't arrive: he didn't come by road. The drone was watching the road by that time, and didn't see a sign of him."

Jason stared at Ethan. Why had that obvious point not occurred to him? "Which makes the anomaly in the drone footage much more important, because it's probably connected to the mystery party's arrival."

"It means more than that. It gives us a likely time of his arrival, but all these factors considered together mean there is a very restricted set of options for his approach. We know it wasn't by road – so how did he get there?" Ethan asked.

The men looked at each other. "We need to take another look at that blast site," Jason said.

Jason still found the blast site unsettling, but not as much in full daylight and with a companion. They parked outside the gate again, and Ethan promised to track down the keys the next day. They inspected the ruined building through the fence, but Ethan quickly wandered over toward the woods. Jason hung back, not just because of the damp grass and mud but because of the vague sense of menace he felt under the shadow of the bare trees. Ethan seemed unperturbed, striding through the knee-high grass and scanning the grounds.

"Well, well, looky here," he called from the edge of the woods.

"What?" Jason answered, tentatively venturing into the field.

"You can see better from over here," Ethan pointed. Jason set his jaw and approached the woods, occasionally stumbling over debris and irregularities in the ground. He finally reached Ethan, who was standing beside a cluster of bushes and looking into the trees.

"We're going to have to get some proper boots and trousers if we're going to be doing much of this," Ethan said, glancing at Jason's mud-stained pants legs.

"Do you think we will be?" Jason asked.

Ethan half-smirked. "You didn't play in the woods much when you were a kid, did you?"

"Not really."

"No matter," Ethan said with a shrug. "We can pick up what we need at Tractor Supply. Anyway, if you come around this thicket of shrubs and look down this way, you can see it more clearly."

Jason followed Ethan deeper into the high weeds and looked where he was pointing. All he could see was bare gray tree trunks, scrubby bushes, and brown plants waving in the chill breeze.

"What am I looking for?" Jason asked.

"The path. It's quite overgrown, and that small tree has fallen across it, but it's clearly a path. Follow the high weeds – see how it curves? The area where there are no trees growing?"

"I think I see it," Jason squinted.

"Believe me, it's there. In woods like these, treeless stretches like that don't just happen. This is a deliberately cleared and maintained trail – at least, it was. This weed growth indicates the trail hasn't been used in some time. Probably just over two years." Ethan looked soberly at Jason.

"So you think our mysterious visitor may have come this way?"

"He couldn't have come by any other route. You said there was a vehicle, a scooter or small motorcycle, right? That kind of vehicle can't go through thick woods, or even meadows like those over there. But it could use a groomed trail, which I suspect this is, under all the weeds."

"But who would have a trail here, and why?" Jason asked.

"As for why, trails like this are common in wooded rural areas. They're used for ATVs, dirt bikes, horses, hiking, perhaps snowmobiles in the winter. The woods near where I grew up were honeycombed with them. They were usually cut and maintained by the trail users, with the permission of the property owners."

"Where do you think this one goes?" Jason asked.

"Trails like this don't necessarily 'go' anywhere," Ethan pointed out. "They just run through woods or scrub to facilitate general use by whomever. But people can use them to go places without taking public roads. So the real question becomes, if we were to follow this trail to its various outlets, what might we find there? More trails? If so, where would those take us?"

"So, what's next?" Jason asked.

"Let me take some pictures of this, and we can go back and consider things," Ethan said, pulling out his phone to snap some shots of the woods and trail from various angles. Then they packed up and headed back to the hotel.

The next day Ethan didn't show up at all because he was chasing down "resources". Some of these were the keys to the locks at the blast site, which apparently required driving to two different locations in metro Detroit to acquire. Ethan was vague about the others, but assured Jason they were necessary.

Jason took advantage of the off day to set aside concern about the terrorist incident and try to focus on what he hoped to make the other facet of his task here: the aborted HHS pilot project, and how to get that back on track.

What did he know for sure about that? One thing was that the Thumb region was suitable for the Chengdu Project because of a number of factors – or had been four years ago. The basic conditions were unlikely to have changed much, so the place to start would be the original data, the medical and demographic summaries that identified the target population for which the pilot had been tailored. He called Jerry Casey at HHS, who seemed surprised to hear from him.

"The original data sets? Why, yes, they're still in place. The data is rather stale, not having been updated in two years, but the framework remains," Jerry explained.

"How hard would it be to get the data current and keep it updated?" Jason asked.

"Simplicity itself," Jerry assured him. "The data is drawn from a wide range of sources, but the load scripts are still in place. There may have been some minor alterations to the base data, but that should be easy to locate and –"

"I'll leave the details to you, Jerry," Jason interrupted. "I'm presuming the data for the project was refreshed regularly?"

"Daily. It also had several levels of detail – what do you need?"

"I'm sure the summary data accessible through VQI should be fine – I can contact you if I need more detail. One thing: will I be able to time tunnel with the VQI level summary? I'd like to be able to examine current data side-by-side with data from when the pilot was running."

"I can provide that ability," Jerry assured him.

"Great. Let me know when you have that set up."

"Certainly, sir."

Jason was no data analyst, but one of the smartest things he'd done in his career was take a night class in Visual Query Interface, the standard for viewing information using icons, colors, and graphs. He wasn't an expert at it, and certainly couldn't delve into the text code like Jerry could, but he knew enough to get around without having to conference in a data tech to hold his hand. He had a set of VQI tools on his tablet, but he would need more powerful computers if he was going to hammer this data like he needed to. He messaged Ethan that he needed to requisition one – no, two – large-screen workstations. He also mentally advanced the priority of finding more permanent quarters and a workspace – he couldn't camp out in the hotel's conference room forever.

Forced to wait on others to complete their tasks, Jason spent the rest of the afternoon reviewing documents and thinking out options. He only took a break to wander down to the farm supply store in the strip mall near the expressway to purchase some jeans and work boots. It was a rather different venue from his usual stores in Alexandria and Crystal City.

The next morning Ethan showed up in an unexpected vehicle: a big four-by-four pickup towing a flatbed trailer on which sat a hefty ATV. There were logo decals on the truck doors that said *GeoTech* and a couple of hard hats on the dash.

"What's all this?" Jason asked as he walked around the rig.

"Specifically, the ATV is for the trail exploring I'm hoping to do today. But the pickup is our long-term vehicle, unless you'd rather not. It's plenty comfortable," Ethan said.

"No, it's fine, but where did you get it all? Is it rented?"

"No, I requisitioned it. It's Border Patrol stock – the pickup, trailer, and four-wheeler are all inventory," Ethan explained. "The Border Patrol never knows where it's going to have to go, so it has many types of vehicles. Granted, there are more ATVs on the southern border, but we have a few."

"Okay, but what's with the decal and hard hats?"

"Camouflage. Sometimes you want a prominent presence, so you arrive in cars with stripes and Federal plates and lights on the top. Other times you want to be discreet, at which point you want vehicles that blend in. The Thumb is a rural area, and the towns are small and intimate. The locals notice strange cars stopping in town, and take note of who gets out of them. Without an explanation near at hand, they start asking questions. But if you offer them a something satisfactory, they settle for appearances."

"Clever," said Jason. "What does GeoTech supposedly do?"

"Doesn't matter. Could be anything from surveying to field tiling to mineral work. Point is, people are accustomed to seeing that sort of thing. Wherever we go, we'll become part of the background."

"Especially in the hard hats, eh?" Jason grinned.

"For sure. I'll even get a couple of road vests to go with them. A tablet completes the look, though for best effect you need a clipboard and transit."

Ethan had also scared up a couple of workstations, which were older but still functional. They tucked these into Jason's room and drove up to the blast site. There Ethan backed the ATV off the truck and donned one of the hard hats.

"Well?" he asked, beckoning to the rider's seat on the big four-wheeler. "You coming?"

Jason looked at the bare trees standing against the gunmetal gray clouds. The vague sense of uneasiness returned. "No, I don't think so," he replied. "I've got some data work to tackle. What will you be doing, anyway?"

"Following this trail to see where it leads. I can't hope to be so lucky as to hit on the exact path our mysterious visitor used, but trails lead to more trails, and if I can find a link into a broader network, that'll be something."

With that Ethan tucked a small saw and what looked like a machete into the ATV's carrying case and roared off. Jason drove the pickup, with the empty trailer bouncing and rattling behind him, back to the hotel to await Ethan's call.

Jason had to set up the workstations in the conference room because it was the only place with enough table space. Jerry had sent him the links and logon credentials to the HHS databases and had even given Jason access to the icons and definitions that Tasker's crew had used. It didn't take long for Jason to connect one workstation to the historical data, reflecting the state of affairs when the pilot program had opened, and the other workstation to the current data. This enabled him to view past and current situations side-by-side.

"Oh, big computers!" declared the housekeeper who came in to refresh the coffee.

"Yeah," Jason acknowledged. This lady, whose nametag read "Allie", frequently serviced the room and had a tendency to chatter as she worked.

"Y'know, I remember when those things were really small screens on top of really big boxes, and you had to dial in to get to the internet."

"That's great, Allie," Jason muttered as he set up the icons and keys.

"Set a new pot brewin' for ya, Mr. Pelletier," Allie announced as she put a new bag in the trash can.

"Thanks, Allie."

Allie puttered out murmuring to herself while Jason completed his setup. A quick initial review of the current data confirmed what Jason had suspected: the conditions which had so alarmed and motivated Dr. Tasker still applied – in fact, they looked worse than ever.

The demographics of the Thumb region were heavily weighted toward what Tasker's team had dubbed OPELs – Old, Poor, Expensive, and Lonely. These were distributed fairly evenly across the area, with greater concentrations in the east and the north, primarily clustered around smaller towns and villages. Jason brought up the icons indicating where the OPELs got most of their acute health care, and sure enough, a thin chain of glowing white dots traced along the western and southern edge of the Thumb. There was a smattering of sparkles across the interior, indicating smaller hospitals, and a few dots further south near metro Detroit, but the preponderance of care facilities lay in the cities found along the two expressways that bordered this corner of the state. No wonder this area had seemed so suitable to Tasker – the geography lent itself perfectly to his project.

Jason spent the rest of the morning comparing the original model which Tasker had constructed with the actual data recorded across the region during the life of the project. There was such an abundance of information that Jason almost got lost as he drilled down and rotated and summarized and qualified, but eventually he could clearly see what had driven Tasker and his staff so mad: about six months after the Chengdu Project had kicked off, admissions of OPELs to acute care facilities had started to drop off for no apparent reason. Every other economic and clinical factor remained constant, but an increasing number of people from that demographic group stopped going to the hospital – slowly at first, but at a steadily increasing rate.

This had to be the anomaly that Ron guy had spotted, Jason thought. Fewer OPELs had been culled from the population because fewer had come in to be culled. The model had projected a steady demand for acute care services by the OPEL population; in actuality demand had dropped once the pilot had begun. There was no apparent cause for this, but since there had been no public outcry, it was assumed that it could not have been because the project's secrecy had been compromised.

Jason wasn't so sure.

Though he hadn't worked with Tasker, Jason had worked with a few savants before, and had noticed they tended to have a blind spot: they assumed that people who weren't as smart as they were had to be simply stupid. But Jason had found that people could be plenty smart when it mattered, particularly on issues that touched on their own survival. Though the theories behind the Chengdu Project were too arcane for common folk to understand, and the implementation was a closely guarded secret, it didn't surprise Jason that when people had started not coming home from the hospital their friends and neighbors had noticed. Jason had seen the effect time and again: theorists assumed that the impact of their action on an environment wouldn't change the environment, that people would just keep doing what they had been doing. But it rarely worked that way.

Jason tapped a few icons and brought up the map of the region that highlighted the acute care facilities. He leaned back and tried to think as Tasker had. The allure of those hospitals was obvious: they were strung along the edge of the Thumb, a glittering net in which to catch his OPEL fish. Acute care admissions were a firm, steady number, the kind of metric theorists loved. They were just the thing to use as the foundation of the Chengdu effort.

Until they weren't anymore.

For all his sophisticated abstracting, Tasker had lost sight of one everyday human reality: being admitted to the hospital was a big deal, even for old people. It was something people noticed, talked about, planned for, and – most importantly – could avoid if they wished, with the occasional exception of emergency admissions. Lots of doctor visits and courses of treatment were geared specifically to keep people out of hospitals, and in the end, people could simply refuse to go.

How to deal with that, Jason asked himself as he gazed at the map littered with glowing icons and tiny numbers. The basic elements hadn't changed – the demographic, economics and other factors were, if anything, more suitable now than they had been four years ago. But restarting the Chengdu Project as it had been originally designed was out of the question. What *would* work? What could he come up with that would avoid the errors of the pilot project while achieving the same goal?

That was a challenge worth tackling.

Storm Clouds

The bar in Avoca was nearly empty, like the rest of Avoca, so it was easy for Jake Kyle to spot his friend sitting alone at a table toward the corner. They'd taken to getting together like this, toward midafternoon on Saturdays, after the day's chores were finished but before the bar's evening clients crowded in. Neither of the men knew exactly why they did it, but it was a comfort to them both, especially since last summer. They enjoyed each other's company, and besides, it paid to be on good terms with a man who could end up being your brother-in-law.

Though that was seeming less of a sure thing these days.

"Hey, Todd," Jake hailed as he approached the table. There was a half-finished plate of nachos on the table and two empty mugs, and the waitress was bringing a third mug along with Jake's order.

"Hey, Jake," Todd replied, picking up the mug and draining about half of it. "Pull up a chair. Plenty of nachos if you like."

"Thanks," Jake said, grabbing some chips and sipping his beer. Even considering the dim lighting, Todd was looking strained and unfocused, and Jake wondered if that was only Todd's third beer. It was a concern he'd had more than once of late.

"So," Jake continued after a lengthy silence. "Hear anything from Grace?"

"Naw," Todd replied, shaking his head. "I was wondering if you had."

"Not hardly," Jake said. "Even allowing for the roundabout channels, she's writing a lot less this year. I think she mentioned that the school was doing an accelerated study schedule – something about trying to be wrapped up by Easter."

"Yeah, I seem to remember that," Todd acknowledged, nibbling another chip while working steadily at his beer. Jake grimaced – there was a definite slur to Todd's voice. The men chatted for a while about how the week had gone, with Jake doing most of the talking. When Jake ordered another beer, Todd was about to as well, and Jake felt he had to say something.

"Todd, man, are you sure you want another? You still have to drive home, remember?"

Todd looked at him keenly, as if ready to make a sharp response, then slumped. "Yeah, you're right, I guess. Better knock it off." He fell silent for a minute before asking, "You hear what happened to Cletus and Sixtus?"

"No, what?"

"They got picked up in Marlette last night for getting in a fight outside a bar. Their dad had to go up and bail 'em out."

"I bet it was Cletus," Jake said. "That guy's a hothead."

"Didn't used to be," Todd replied darkly. Jake said nothing, because they both knew what the other was thinking. Things were different now. "Well, you're right, I gotta go. Catch you later. Let me know if Grace gets in touch." Todd drained his mug and wandered out, leaving his friend looking after him with concern. Todd was definitely feeling the strain, of Grace's absence at least. But then, so was Jake. He started at the nachos with a gusto he hadn't wanted to display before Todd. Work had been slow recently, and the consequent shorter hours meant less income, and one of the places he skimped was lunches. He didn't like to eat too much at home, because things were tight there as well, what with Mom's deteriorating eye condition and all the other kids.

Jake was just cleaning the plate and thinking of ordering another beer when he noticed a girl sitting by herself in a booth. She was looking at her phone, and on the table before her was a small beer that she'd barely touched and a half-empty bowl of bar popcorn. Jake thought she'd been watching him, only to turn away when he'd looked around the room. She was decent enough looking, with blonde hair bobbed in the current style, bright eyes, and high cheekbones. She was thin, almost too thin, and kept her jacket on and zipped. Jake guessed her thinness was due to more than fashion – there was a lot of that going around these days.

The girl looked up and caught Jake's eyes. He was tempted to look away, but instead held her gaze, and she gave him a smile. He smiled back, and gave her a little nod, which she returned. Jake was suddenly conscious of how long it had been since he'd had a conversation with a girl. He'd been so occupied with work concerns and family concerns and all manner of concerns that he'd almost forgotten how to be social. He thought about the content of his wallet and figured he could manage a light dinner for two, if he drank moderately. He picked up his beer and wandered over to the booth.

"Hi. I'm Jake."

"Hi, Jake. I'm Avery."

"Hi, Avery. I was wondering if you'd like to split a plate of those nachos. I just finished my friend's half-plate, and they're mighty good."

Avery's eyes sparkled eagerly. "That…that'd be really nice, Jake."

Ah, he'd guessed correctly. "How about another beer to wash things down?"

"That'd be nice, too," Avery replied with a smile as he sat down across from her.

*　　　*　　　*

Jake awoke to the sounds of people bustling about downstairs. He glanced at the clock and groaned – he hadn't meant to sleep this late. But then, he hadn't meant to do a lot of things he'd done in the past twenty-four hours. He rolled out of bed and headed for the bathroom.

"Well, good morning! Or nearly good afternoon, I should say," Dad said as Jake made his way down the steps and into the kitchen.

"Morning, Dad, Mom," Jake muttered, heading for the coffee.

"Late night with Todd, eh?" Dad continued jovially. "Where'd you catch Mass? Yale?"

"Ah – yeah," Jake replied, feeling a twinge of conscience. Mom gave one of those odd head-twists that she did these days, as if she caught more in his tone than she let on. As her sight faded, her hearing seemed to grow more sensitive. He wondered if she'd heard him creeping back home at 3:00 a.m.

"Someone called for you last night," Dad said. "Named Gustav Davis. Didn't leave a message, just said to tell you he'd called and to call him back. We tried contacting you, but your phone was off."

Jake's conscience gave him another twinge. He'd turned off his phone when he and Avery had gone back to her place. But he was alarmed to hear who the caller had been. Gustav Davis was Chip Keller. It was a code name, his actual first name and middle name, which they'd used while training last summer. The fact that Chip was trying to contact him at all raised suspicions; that he would use that name to do it lent an air of urgency to the situation.

"Thanks," Jake muttered into his coffee as he headed back to his bedroom. Out of the corner of his eye he noticed Mom still watching him with her nearly sightless eyes, not saying a word but wearing a pensive expression.

Up in his room, Jake turned on his phone and saw the two messages – the first from Chip's personal phone, which Jake had logged as Gustav Davis, and the second from home, undoubtedly to let him know that Chip had called. Tentatively he keyed Chip's number.

"Hello?"

"Hey, Chip, it's Jake."

"Jake, thank God you called. You were the only one I hadn't heard back from. Listen, can you make it up to Bad Axe for a 2:00 p.m. meeting? There's something I need to tell everyone."

"Um, okay," Jake fumbled as he glanced at the clock and did some quick calculating. If he showered quickly and got moving, he could just make it.

"Great. We're meeting at The Sugar Bowl, in the meeting room just inside the doorway. You won't have to even go inside. Shouldn't take more than fifteen minutes."

An hour and a half of driving for a fifteen-minute meeting? "Chip, can you tell me what this is about?" Jake asked.

"I'm sorry, but I'd rather tell everybody once, and in person. See you there," Chip replied in a somber tone, and rang off. This did nothing to reassure Jake, who had no doubts as to who "everybody" was. He hastened through his shower and headed north under a cloud of guilt darkened by trepidation.

The Sugar Bowl was bustling with Sunday afternoon diners, but the mood in the meeting room was sober. Chip was standing at the front of the room, while Cletus and Sixtus Winters, Todd Beck, and Phillip Schaeffer sat around a table. Todd looked sallow and puffy, and Sixtus had a bandage on his jaw. Phillip was just staring at the tabletop. Jake had seen most of these guys individually at some time or other over the past months, but this was the first time they'd all been assembled since last summer.

"Ah, good," Chip said as Jake entered. "You're the last one we've been waiting for. Could you close the door?"

"Wait," Phillip interjected as Jake swung the door closed. "'Last one'? What about Dan?"

Chip sighed heavily. "It's about Dan that I've called you together. Last night at about nine o'clock Dan...took his own life."

There were gasps around the room, and Jake was smitten by even more guilt. Last night at nine, he and Avery had been –

"While in the service, he'd had several overseas deployments," Chip continued. "Some of those he discussed with me, others he didn't. Anyone who knew him knew that he struggled with many demons, particularly since...that is, over the past several months."

Tears seeped out of Jake's eyes as he remembered the briskly professional yet friendly veteran who had worked so hard to train them all. Suicide? Dan? How could that be? Jake didn't have to ask that out loud – he knew full well how it could be. Everyone in the room knew where and when Dan had turned the corner that had ended where it did, because they'd all turned that corner together. Jake glanced over at Phillip, who'd been Dan's partner on that mission. Phillip wasn't saying anything, but still stared at the tabletop, his fists clenched before him. Everyone else either had their heads bowed or were staring around in shock.

"Did…did you…was there any indication…?" Todd asked haltingly.

"None that I saw," Chip shook his head. "But Dan was a very private person, and there aren't many veteran support organizations in this region. His family said he'd been no different recently, doing his tasks, managing his responsibilities, until last night when he went to his room and –"

Jake knew that every man in the room was thinking the same thing: was there anything he could have done? Any contact, any service, anything of any nature to help their comrade, to tell him that he wasn't alone, that they loved him? But whatever opportunities there might have been had passed unnoticed in the bustle of daily activities, and now it was too late. A harsh, blank silence filled the room as each man wrestled with his own internal torment.

"Services are being arranged by the family," Chip finally said. "I'll keep you all informed. That's all I had."

The men stood and headed for the door in silence, but Chip spoke just loudly enough for Cletus and Sixtus to hear. "Except for you two – hold on a minute." Standing like scolded schoolboys, the twins hung back while the others filed out.

"Al told me what happened," Chip continued once everyone else had left. "Was there anything going on other than what showed up in the police report?"

"Nope," Sixtus answered sullenly. "Just a garden variety bar fight."

"What were you guys doing at The Rooster, anyway? That dive is for losers."

"Drinking beer and playing pool," Sixtus replied with a touch of defiance.

There was a moment's silence before Chip continued, nearly pleading. "This isn't at all like you two. Is there anything going on that you want to discuss, or let me know about?"

Cletus just glared at him, and Sixtus responded shortly. "No. Is that all you want, Sheriff?"

"Yes, that's all," Chip responded, a little stung. They'd had a good rapport when they were training together, but now he was begin treated like a hostile. His voice took on a more official tone. "You two watch yourselves. I'll put in a word for you with Al, and with Prosecutor Duncan, but no more of this, y'hear?"

"Don't bother, Sheriff," Sixtus called back as they headed for the door. "We can look out for ourselves."

Yeah, the hell you can, kid, Chip thought as the door swung shut. He felt responsible for those two, for them all, especially now that Dan was gone.

If only he had any idea what to do.

*   *   *

Jake wandered out to the parking lot to find Todd standing beside his car, staring toward the north. The sky was overcast with dark gray clouds and the wind was blowing chill from the northeast. It had been the best part of a year since Jake had been up here near Bad Axe, and the last time it had been summer. He'd forgotten how close to the lake it was, and how cold the spring winds could be as they whistled across the water, which still contained ice floes this time of year.

"Hey, Todd," Jake said as he walked up behind his friend.

"Oh...ah, hey, Jake," Todd stammered as if he'd been interrupted in some deliberations.

"Hard news about Dan, eh?"

"Yeah," Todd agreed. "Hard news." Silence fell for a minute before Todd spoke again. "I was thinking of dropping into Kerrigan's before heading home. Want to join me?"

"Kerrigan's?"

"Yeah – a little bar just west of town along Van Dyke."

"Nah, I've got to get going," Jake excused himself. He couldn't help but notice that Todd suddenly seemed to know where every cheap bar in the Thumb was. Again, he wondered if he should say something. But it wasn't Jake's business, and they all had concerns enough, especially with the weight of Dan's death lying on them like a pall.

Just then Cletus and Sixtus came storming out of the restaurant after their private conversation with Chip – not difficult to guess the topic – and stalked to their pickup. With much slamming of doors and squealing of tires they departed the parking lot without even greeting Todd and Jake.

"All right, then," Todd said in a subdued voice. "See you around, then?"

"Yeah, see you around," Jake replied. Todd pulled out of the lot and turned west, leaving Jake feeling crushed and desolate. He supposed he ought to pray for Dan's soul, but prayer wasn't coming easy at the moment. He didn't want to go home to the inevitable questions, but he didn't know where he could go.

Or again, maybe he did. Jake checked his phone, and sure enough, he'd recorded Avery's number. Maybe she'd be home, and wouldn't mind if he dropped by, especially if he brought a bag of groceries. He was sure she'd appreciate that. Appreciate it a lot.

*   *   *

The knock at the door startled Luke awake. He'd been going over some patient records and had nodded off where he'd been sitting. "Come in," he called, rubbing his face and stretching.

Gilbert Peterson stepped in holding a folder. "Hey, Luke."

"Hi, Gil," Luke answered. "Have a seat. What can I do for you?"

"Well, it's about something that's been pretty quiet to this point," Gil replied, sitting down and setting the folder on Luke's desk. "We'd prefer to keep it that way for the time being, but we're at the stage where we need to bring you into the discussion. So we need to ask for your discretion, but we know we can always count on that."

"Uh...thanks," Luke said, wondering what this was all about.

"Some of us have been talking about the ranches and the guests, and the cost and effort and risk of keeping everything running..." Gil began, and proceeded to relate the gist of the discussion about releasing some of the guests back into the public medical care system. Luke recognized some of the points he'd been making about some of the guests needing access to better medical technology. All the reasons Gil discussed made sense: the costs of maintaining the network of ranches, the need for better medical care for the guests, the probability that the risk had passed – all these justified reexamining the need to have everyone hidden away.

"So," Luke asked when Gil had finished. "What do you need from me?"

"We're hoping for your input on likely candidates for trial cases," Gil explained, opening the folder. "Ruth and Shelly have been considering the ranches themselves, and Fitz has been examining the legal framework – the trusts and executorships – and we've come up with a preliminary list of guests for you to go over."

That figured, Luke thought as he took the folder and skimmed down the list. These guests were at the ranches for medical reasons, but consult the medical guy last. "What criteria are you looking for?"

"Well, nobody who's at death's door – those we should see through to the end," Gil replied. "Maybe guests who need urgent medical care that you can't provide, and who might benefit from more sophisticated treatments."

"That would be almost everyone who isn't in active decline," Luke cautioned. "Should I consider issues like how content they are in their current situation?"

"That's a factor, but Ruth and Shelly are doing most of that evaluation. If you could look over that list and get back to us with guests who best fit the medical criteria, that would be great. If that's most of them, so be it."

"Sure, Gil," Luke acceded with a yawn. "Can you give me a couple of days? I'm trying to get caught up with some other things, and I'd like to check the patient records before deciding anything."

"No rush, Luke," Gil replied. "Take your time."

After Gil left, the still-sluggish Luke gazed blearily at the list of names for a while before setting the folder aside and rubbing his face in an attempt to focus. This all made sense, and had even been somewhat expected, but the more Luke thought about it, the larger loomed an aspect which nobody seemed to have considered.

What about him?

The ranches had been created, and continued to operate, because of the threat to a certain portion of the population. If the threat was truly gone – which these trial cases were intended to test – then there was no reason to continue to incur the cost and risk of running the network of ranches. Everyone could get back to a normal life – except him. Loneliness and desolation closed in on Luke as he gazed at the folder of names. Was he being asked to cooperate in rendering himself obsolete? Or had that consequence of closing the ranches not occurred to anyone? That seemed most likely. He longed to talk to somebody, to seek reassurance, but the best person for that was Kent Schaeffer, and Kent now lived over an hour away, and had plenty of problems of his own. Grandpa? Maybe Grandpa was free. Luke checked the time – it was still early evening. He could take his gear over with the excuse of checking on Grandma, and see if Grandpa was available to talk. He grabbed his bag and headed over to the Big House.

The house was quiet. Dinner was over, and almost everyone was probably back settling the guests for the evening. Luke made his way to Grandma and Grandpa's suite, only to find Cathy coming out with a tray of dishes.

"Is Grandma awake?" Luke asked. "I thought I'd check on her."

"She's sleeping. She seems to be doing okay – or at least no worse," Cathy said.

"Best not to disturb her, then," Luke replied. "Is…Grandpa back there?"

"He's resting, too. The whole ordeal has been very trying, and he rests when he can so he can be awake when she is."

"Ah, yes," Luke replied as bleak loneliness again surged within him. "Good thinking there. I…I'll check back later."

"Is there something you need help with?" Cathy asked. "I could get Mom or Dad if you need."

"No...no," Luke said, turning for the door. "I'll catch him later."

Cathy watched as Luke walked away. Presently Harmony Peterson came in, having completed her evening rounds of the guests.

"Is something up?" Harmony asked when she saw Cathy's pensive expression.

"I'm not sure," Cathy answered. "I wonder...I think something might be going on with Doc Luke. He was hoping to see Grandpa."

"That shouldn't be hard – Grandpa lives right here."

"He's resting at the moment, but I think I'll mention it to him when he wakes."

Back in his apartment, Luke was struggling not to feel isolated, unappreciated, and forlorn. He considered calling Teresa – it was still hard not to think of her as Janice, but he knew she preferred her new name – but decided she was probably busy with her responsibilities. He looked around the darkened apartment, dreading the idea of trying to sleep there that night.

He knew what he'd do. Luke checked the time and glanced at his schedule. It wasn't too late. He was due to start a circuit early the next morning, with the first stop up in Melvin to check on Al Becker. Gary and Olivia had a guest room that Luke sometimes used. If the guest room wasn't occupied, maybe he could get a jump on tomorrow's schedule by running up there tonight. The evening was mild and dry, and he could be there inside of an hour. He called Gary and verified that it would work, then bustled about packing his gear for a multi-day circuit. The ATV was a little low on fuel, but it would get him as far as Melvin. Within fifteen minutes he was heading north along the trails. He might as well make himself useful while he still could.

About an hour after Luke left, a quiet knock came at his door. When there was no answer, the knock was repeated, then Grandpa stuck his head in. "Luke?" he called. "Luke?" But no answer came from the darkened quarters. Grandpa stepped in and turned on a light. There were papers scattered about the desk, and the prayer book Grandma had given Luke for his Confirmation lay off to one side. But of Luke there was no hint, though the apartment bore signs of a hasty departure. Grandpa sighed and turned away, clicking off the light and closing the door behind him.

Ensnared

The next day was Friday, and Ethan showed up in the morning with the pickup and ATV to do more "trail exploring". Jason suspected he was doing at least as much joy riding on the government's dime as legitimate research, but he let it go. Ethan returned just after lunch to report that there were indeed numerous trails cutting through the woods and along the fields in the area. He'd followed several for many miles in all directions, and it seemed like there was no shortage of them.

"Do you think these terrorists could be using these trails to get around?" Jason asked.

"I wouldn't go that far, given how little we know," Ethan cautioned. "All we're reasonably sure of is that one guy used them one time. However, the guy did use them to act within a very tight time frame – the decision makers hadn't been on that site for very long before he showed up to wreak his havoc. When you combine that with the video monitoring, it's a safe bet that he knew when to show up and acted quickly. All we can presume from that is that *this* guy knew these trails well enough to use them to respond urgently. However, if we assume that he was part of this broader network, then it's also reasonable to assume that the broader network knows of and uses them as well. They did look unusually clear and well-tended for simple recreational traffic."

"Okay, if this network is spread across this region, then they could be using these trails to move between sites," Jason said. "But with roads extending to every corner of the state, I can't figure out why they'd use more cumbersome, less efficient off-road travel over simply getting in their cars and driving."

"Well, I'm sure driving remains the most common means of transport," Ethan replied, "but something did occur to me as I was dodging low branches on those trails. It isn't as obvious now, when the leaves are off the trees, but in a few weeks, it'll be more clear: coverage."

"Coverage?" Jason asked.

"Sure. Most citizens don't think about overhead surveillance, even though it's almost constant, particularly in this area. You and I are only attuned to it because we're DHS. But if you were running a hidden network to do illegal things, you'd have to be very conscious of that surveillance or your network wouldn't last long. Every car on a road can be tracked from overhead, down to the license tag, if the surveillance is diligent enough. But these trails run through woods and other unexpected places, which provide cover from eyes in the sky."

"Hadn't considered that," Jason replied. "Could these trails be used to travel completely out of sight of overhead surveillance?"

"Not completely. The Thumb isn't totally covered – there are patches of woods scattered among the fields. Anyone using the trails would have to come out from under cover now and again, but it's still a more hidden route than a road would be. Some of the trails I found ran through tall grass and weeds alongside fields. There's no overhead cover there, but it would still be very hard for a drone to spot someone on them – it would have to be in just the right place viewing from just the right angle."

"So it's a reasonable guess that this hidden network could be making use of covered trails for some of their transportation," Jason pointed out. He was remembering the portions of his briefings that discussed the one man who had been known to be part of this network, and how he seemed to have been trained in "tradecraft", particularly behavior aimed at avoiding overhead observation. "I'm guessing that they were taking precautions before things – ah – blew up."

"Nobody said they were stupid," Ethan agreed.

They made plans for the following week, then Ethan began making noises about returning the pickup and ATV to the depot, and headed back to Port Huron. Jason was left with an afternoon to kill and a weekend stretching before him. He wrote up his status report to send to D.C. and had a desultory message conversation with Cassie. He'd been toying with the idea of catching a weekend flight back to D.C., but he doubted he'd be able to expense it, and besides, one of Cassie's school buddies was in town, and they'd planned to spend the weekend doing the art fair in Fairfax. He'd be a fifth wheel there, so it looked like he was stuck here, knowing nobody and having nowhere to go. For dinner he tried the steak place. The food and ambience were okay, and probably superb for its target clientele, but it was much less sophisticated than he was accustomed to even if the prices were low.

Jason slept as late as he could on Saturday. When he woke completely enough that it was clear he couldn't fall back to sleep, he rose and went to the diner for breakfast. His server was friendly enough, and pretty in her way, but it was a busy shift, and she didn't have time to linger and chat.

Back in his hotel room, Jason paced. He had work he could be doing, but there was no place in the room, and he was tired of the four walls of the conference room. Besides, nobody would be working down in D.C. on a fine Saturday morning. There were no good shows on, and all his gaming gear was back in his apartment. He considered messaging some acquaintances in D.C., but quickly rejected that idea. The last thing he wanted to provide was gossip fodder for the Saturday evening get-togethers, how poor pitiful Jason had messaged first thing Saturday morning from his exile in Michigan.

In frustration Jason pulled up a map of the Thumb region. He wasn't all that far from the metro Detroit area, and the map showed a few venues that looked promising – or at least the best that the area could offer. He sighed in discouragement. It had taken him a long time (and plenty of effort and funds) to learn the ropes in D.C., which spots to visit and whom to meet there. He didn't want to go through that all over again up here, not least because he had no idea how long he'd be around. Besides, he was itching for something to do right now, not later in the evening.

Zooming the map out, Jason's eyes strayed northward, to the area that was his region of concern for this assignment. Susan had been right: it was larger than it appeared at first, especially for one guy. He was surprised at how few cities there were, and how small their names were on the map. He wondered if there was a city above ten thousand people anywhere in the interior. Yet all the data indicated there was a terror network hidden among those small towns, a network capable of operating with lethal effectiveness. Beyond question there was a geographic aspect to this assignment, an aspect he couldn't completely delegate. Sooner or later he'd have to get out and familiarize himself with these obscure places. It wasn't his first choice of what to do with a Saturday, but it was better than being stuck in his room waiting for Allie to show up and change the sheets. He grabbed his keys and headed for his car.

He decided to avoid the expressways, since he'd undoubtedly have plenty of occasions to visit the cities along them. His goal today was exploring the interior of the Thumb, so he headed out along the two-lane road that led west out of town. He had driven for several miles before it struck him how empty the road was. Accustomed as he was to D.C. area traffic, it was outside his experience to be able to count on two hands – and often on one – how many other vehicles were in sight. He enjoyed the unhindered driving, but the empty road made him feel strangely exposed.

On top of this, the scenery was uninspiring, if not depressing. The sky was overcast and the wind blew chill from the north. Jason drove past muddy brown fields interspersed with stands of bare trees with gray trunks nodding and swaying in the wind. There were meadows filled with rustling brown grass and dotted with thickets of dense brush. The road was rough and patched, and he'd pass drab houses or dingy little business sites, a good number of them empty. Occasionally there were nicely tended homes, usually on large, well-groomed lawns with the occasional pond, but most of the houses were old and worn –ill-kempt bungalows with dirt driveways and litter in the side yard, or aging farmhouses half grown over with their gutters falling off.

An increase in the number of small businesses, shabby bars, and big-box stores told Jason that he was approaching the next town, which the car's navigation console told him was Lapeer. He passed along what had undoubtedly once been a major commercial strip, but was now mainly empty storefronts and weed-edged parking lots. At the intersection with the main north-south road in the center of town Jason turned north, toward the center of the Thumb region. This road was also thick with old and seedy buildings, but the terrain turned more hilly and wooded. As he drove through pine forests, he found himself slightly unnerved by their shadowy depths. There were fewer homes among the pines, and longer stretches of untamed meadows and dark, ominous woods.

Jason shook himself. This was getting out of hand. It was just countryside. There was no reason to let it depress him. He flicked on the car's sound system only to find that his car was one of the more limited models, with broadcast and satellite bands but no streaming capability. His tablet could stream, but he didn't want to stop and go through the hassle of setting up the link between the tablet and radio. He turned off the radio and tried to listen to streaming straight from his tablet, but the sound quality was dismal, and the music he normally enjoyed while commuting struck a discordant note while he rolled along through the vacant country. The talk channels were even more depressing, filled as they were with Capitol-area buzz and chatter about D.C. area events that weekend, which only served to remind Jason of his exile. He turned that off, too, preferring to drive in silence.

Jason finally approached another small town which had a confusing road layout, so he got a bit lost. At one of the town's three stoplights he took a wrong turn and ended up driving through a small residential area. This was dismal, for there were only old homes, some of them abandoned and all in varying states of disrepair. Overgrown trees pushed up broken sidewalks and weedy lawns were streaked with mud. There were many older cars parked in the streets and on front yards. Few people were outside on the chilly morning, but Jason saw a couple of older guys in grease-stained work jackets and dirty ball caps standing by a pickup that had its hood up. They stopped talking and stared at Jason as he drove by, continuing to stare until he turned at the next intersection. Ethan had been right: in these small towns, strangers would be noticed and watched with an unfriendly gaze.

Jason eventually made it back onto one of the main roads out of town, but found that it was taking him west toward Saginaw. Wanting to stay in the interior of the Thumb, he turned north again and soon found himself passing through flatter land, with more tilled fields and fewer woods, though dark stands of trees were never out of sight. A chill drizzle started, gray sheets of rain falling on sodden fields that already contained swaths of standing water. It seemed like the land couldn't make up its mind whether to be woods or swamp, earth or water. Everything seemed to run together. From time to time he passed through little towns – empty main streets lined with vacant storefronts in dingy brick buildings, with perhaps a handful of cars parked near a party store or bar. But he drove through these near-ghost towns almost without noticing, barely registering their existence before he was passing the cemetery or school at the edge of town and heading back out into the dreary landscape.

Though Jason found the bleak emptiness of the fields unsettling, he was unnerved enough by the patches of woods to start wondering why. He was accustomed to trees – Virginia was thick with them. But then, maybe that was it – around D.C., trees were decorations planted around buildings and along parkways to shade sidewalks and provide pleasant views from office windows. Out here, the dark stands of bare trunks and scrub were like entities in their own right, shadowy and a bit menacing. He found himself unconsciously taking routes that would keep him clear of them, but they were never completely out of sight, always lurking on the horizon no matter which direction he looked.

Eventually the rain ceased, but the overcast grew thicker, giving the afternoon a dark and heavy air. Jason drove north, not attending to the navigation console where he was supposed to be tracking his progress. Finally, after coming through a stretch of wood-lined road to find himself panting and gripping the wheel, he shook himself. What the hell was wrong with him? For pity's sake, it was just woods and farmland, both of which he'd seen before. He had to be feeling the pressure of this assignment, he reasoned, or was missing his friends and usual haunts. This shamed him – he was tougher than this. He had to get out of this mood and get back to business.

Recognizing that his goal of familiarizing himself with the region was a lost cause, at least for today, Jason took the next right turn and headed inland. He had been skirting the western coast of the Thumb, along Saginaw Bay, and wanted to head east to find M-53, also known among the locals as Van Dyke, the main north-south road that cut through the Thumb region from bottom to top. That would take him back to Imlay City. He didn't know exactly where he was, but didn't bother to bring up the map on the nav console. He was heading east, and would hit the road eventually. He drove along for some time, thinking about the assignment and watching the small amount of traffic, when suddenly the road he was using came to an intersection, beyond which it became dirt. Blast. Jason hated driving on dirt roads, but the only paved roads departing this intersection were the one he'd come in on and the one to his left, heading north – he thought. He took that, resolving to turn right again as soon as he could. But the road curved, and then came to a Y-intersection. Taking what seemed to be the eastbound road, he came to a few more odd intersections, and ended up having to drive for a bit on a dirt road anyway, resulting in him totally losing track of which direction he was headed or where he was. Frustrated with himself, he pulled over and punched up the map on the navigation console. He shouldn't need to be doing this – he'd always had a good head for direction, and the mostly arrow-straight directional roads through this farmland were nowhere near as convoluted as the roads in Virginia which he navigated with ease.

It took Jason several frustrating minutes to determine that something seemed to have gone wrong with the console. It displayed a map of the area, but the little blue dot that was supposed to indicate his position was missing. He zoomed in and back out, but nothing displayed. He brought up the mapping tool on his tablet, but it didn't even register where he was – it just displayed the last map he'd used, which was for Tysons. He pulled out his phone and opened the tool for reporting position, but it gave him a red band with the text "signal error".

Jason felt a slight shiver of panic. He'd never had to navigate without knowing where he was. He forced the panic down – whatever was wrong with the devices or the signal, he just had to make it to M-53 and turn south. He was sure he'd not yet crossed that road, so it still lay to the east. No matter how confused he or his electronics had gotten, all he had to do was head east – which he was pretty sure was that way. Turning the car, he proceeded along the dirt road, determined to keep his heading no matter what.

As Jason drove, he noticed something unusual ahead. The fields through which he was driving looked unkempt and overgrown with weeds, but farther up the road to the left was a stand of woods. That was not unusual for the area, but what was unusual was the tall chain-link fence topped with barbed wire that surrounded it. Slowing down as he approached, he saw that the fence had been erected right at the edge of the road, enclosing even the shoulder and the drainage ditch that surrounded the wood. This was very strange.

Jason's curiosity overcame his aversion to woods and cold. Pulling to the side of the road, he got out and walked over to the fence. It looked new, and was at least ten feet high. There was no gate in evidence, and about every fifty feet along the fence was posted a generic sign stating that this was private property and no hunting or trespassing was allowed.

It was odd enough that the chain-link fence was right at the edge of the road; what was even odder was that inside the fence, on the far side of the reed-clogged ditch, stood another fence – in fact, what looked like two fences, or one fence and a try at a second. At the edge of the woods ran a standard wire fence, with the posts about ten feet apart and fencing wire with about four-inch squares. This fence had trees and bushes growing right to the inside, and looked older and more distressed – at points the wire was bent, and some of the posts were crooked. But along the post fence in places stood vertical metal panels immediately outside the wire. Jason recognized these as standard interlocking panels designed to be driven into the ground and linked at the edges to make a solid, opaque fence. This was more expensive than chain link, but with enough of the panels you could quickly erect a wall for any purpose.

It appeared that enclosure was what had been attempted here. For stretches along the inner fence these panels stood firmly driven into the ground and tightly interlocked, making a solid, sturdy fence about eight feet high. But then there would be a gap, perhaps with some panels driven in at an angle or lying on the ground, and then a little farther along there would stand some more well-set panels. It looked to Jason like someone had tried to erect a wall of the panels, but had failed for some reason, only putting up sections of it before giving up. But why erect a solid fence right up against a standing wire fence? And why hadn't the solid fence been finished? Had the chain-link fence been the next step? What was inside here that needed fencing in so badly?

Looking through a gap in the panel fencing, all Jason could see beyond the wire fence was dense shrubbery, with large trees all through it, towering above the bushes and at places dropping great branches down outside the wire fence. The floor of the overgrown woods was in deep shadow, and as Jason clung to the chain-link fence and peered in dread fascination, it seemed like the shadow had actually congealed, and was roiling and churning like a thick, dark fog just inside the wire fence. That which had been troubling Jason all day – the murky, shadowed eaves of distant woods – here seemed to have taken form and acquired substance. Like a rodent transfixed by a viper's gaze, Jason peered at the wisps and tendrils of darkness as they coiled and twined, ever morphing and shifting before his eyes. One part of him shrank back from this embodiment of the darkness which had so frightened him, but another part was held in grim fascination. The shadows seemed to beckon, promising mysteries revealed and desires satisfied if he would but plunge into them. He even glanced up to see if the chain-link fence could be surmounted. Not seeing a way, his eyes were drawn back to the hypnotic shadows shifting among the branches. He was caught in a fierce tension, part of him desiring to flee this dread place and part of him yearning to gaze just a little longer.

Then some of the lower branches rustled, and a low rumble came from the underbrush. Jason realized that there was something in there, something waiting for him, something possibly watching him as he stood at the fence. Panic suddenly surged within him, choking his reason. Backing away from the fence even as he kept his eyes locked on the shadowed foliage, Jason saw some branches move again, more violently, and thought he caught a glimpse of a low, dark form moving in the murk.

That was too much for Jason. Terror overwhelmed him, and he hastily stumbled back to his car. Slamming it into gear, he tore away in wheel-spinning haste, scattering pebbles and dirt behind him. He turned blindly and sped down the road at a speed he would never before have dared on dirt and loose gravel. He swerved close to a weedy ditch, overcorrected, and veered into the oncoming lane. Thankfully there were no other vehicles in sight, for Jason was driving like a madman in his panic, caring for nothing but putting as many miles between himself and that darkness as he could.

Jason came to a crossroads and turned right, then turned again at the next corner he came to. These were all dirt roads, but Jason didn't care, so long as they took him away from that hellish fenced wood. Still uncertain of where he was, Jason peered ahead in hopes of spotting M-53 or any other paved road. None of the intersections had road signs, and had no idea which direction he was headed. Seeing nothing around but the ubiquitous fields edged by patches of woods, he turned yet again.

Driving straight for a while, Jason finally spotted something ahead. It looked like a building or wall along the road, but he couldn't be sure at this distance. Peering carefully, he slowed down as he approached so as to better ascertain what it was. Finally, he got a good look.

It was the chain-link fence.

Taking a deep breath, Jason kept driving past the fence. This section ran along a different side of the woods, and as he passed a corner he could see a longer stretch of fencing run along the edge of an overgrown field, just beside what looked like a drainage ditch that edged the wood, and a shorter length of fence that ran right along the road edge. Idling along the shorter section, he saw that it contained a gate that was securely locked with an embedded lock and an industrial padlock as well. Beyond the gate in the chain-link fence he could see another gate, this one in the wire fence, which had no visible lock. The metal panel fencing was complete along this stretch, running from both corners right up to the gate in the wire fence. Jason gazed in frightened fascination as he idled by, but could see nothing of the woods but the branches waving overhead.

How came it that he was back here? He'd been driving away, and felt certain that he hadn't done so much turning that he'd come completely around. Why was he back here at this ominous wood? And what was that noise? Jason glanced down to see that he'd forgotten to turn off the radio, and since it was dialed to a station that didn't reach this far, brief bursts of static were pulsing through. Annoyed, he punched the radio off and set his jaw. However he'd gotten turned around, it wasn't happening again. He pondered reversing course, turning right around and going back the way he'd come, but decided that straight ahead would do just as well. He sped off, his eyes on the horizon, determined to put the place behind him.

Before he'd driven half a mile, the road began to curve. Perhaps vagaries like this were why he'd gotten disoriented. Not far after the curve came an intersection, with one branch leading right, the direction he'd been heading. Should he take that? He decided to, but shortly the road ended at another, forcing him to turn left or right. In futility he brought up the map on the nav console, but the telltale blue dot that would indicate his position was nowhere to be found. His tablet was still useless. Turning right, he soon came to a branching, which led to another intersection, and soon after that to another T intersection where he was forced to turn again. If only he could see the sun! But the overcast was as thick and dark as ever, and the fields and trees all looked alike. He came to another stop which he didn't recognize, turned left this time, and...

The radio started spitting static as his turn brought him in sight – again – of the tall chain-link fence that enclosed the brooding, shadowed wood. He was looking along another, shorter length of fencing, possibly the opposite end from the gated stretch. This section had no gate, just unbroken chain-link fence, and inside that the wire fencing. None of the metal panels were visible here, just posts and wire. Some of the posts looked a little askew and the wire fencing looked strained, as if something had pushed at it from the inside. He got an unhindered view of the dark bushes, leafless in the chill spring, bowing and bobbing in the coiling darkness while the gray trunks swayed above them.

What was this place? What was this place? What was this horrible, horrible place that he couldn't seem to escape? Black panic surged within Jason, and he turned his car around right in the road, clipping the chain-link fence as he did, speeding back the way he'd come. He had no idea how fast he was going, but he didn't care. The frantic rattle of gravel hitting his undercarriage didn't matter, all that mattered was getting away from that terrible wood. He didn't even consider any turns, keeping straight on the road as far as it went. He ignored the spurts of static from the radio. He ignored everything but the road.

Then, finally, he saw an intersection ahead, a paved road with traffic flicking by on it. He slowed as he approached the intersection and noticed a few old, abandoned buildings around it. The radio was still sputtering, and he punched it off. He had no idea where he was, or which way he should turn. He glanced at the nav console again, and was amazed to see the familiar blue dot back in the center of the screen. Zooming out, he saw that the road he was on was labeled Nathan Road, and the paved road before him was M-53, the main road he'd been searching for. But how was it that he was approaching it from the east? That meant that he'd crossed M-53 at some point in his driving, but he couldn't for the life of him remember doing that. No matter. Turning left would take him south, which was the direction he wanted. He glanced in his rear view, half fearing that he'd see a chain-link fence, but all he saw was an unbroken vista of brown fields and dark patches of woods under a sullen, slate-gray sky. He turned left and sped toward Imlay City.

Jason awoke the next morning with a dry mouth and a splitting headache. God, he hated hangovers! He stumbled to the bathroom, trying to remember how he'd gotten here. Slowly it came back – the blind flight down M-53, the party store where he'd picked up some bags of chips, a jug of orange juice, and a bottle of cheap vodka, stumbling into his room and turning on all the lights, then drinking himself into a stupor. Why had he done that? Why? How long had it been since he'd fallen into that trap?

The more Jason thought about it, the more furious he became. What the hell was wrong with him? He thought back on the events of the prior afternoon, which after a night of sleep didn't seem so terrifying. Dammit! He scrubbed his teeth furiously, as if clearing the foul taste from his mouth could expunge his shame. What had he been so afraid of? So his electronics had malfunctioned and he'd gotten lost on some strange back roads. Why panic about that? Why should that cause him to crumple?

God, he hated this part of himself. He'd thought he'd left it behind, grown out of it, but it kept cropping up at the worst times. Like times he'd have to get up out of bed to shut the half-closed closet door because the shadows inside creeped him out. Or the times he found himself talking with buddies at the bar, staying far longer than he intended, just so he could leave with them and not have to face the darkened parking lot alone. And now he'd done it again, letting shadows under trees and equipment malfunctions panic him into a drinking bout. Weak, weak, weak!

Jason came out of the bathroom and looked over the debris littering his room, mute testimony to his frailty. Dammit, he was stronger than this! His tablet lay on the table. He brought up the navigation app, which dutifully showed the glowing blue dot right there in Imlay City.

"Damn you!" Jason growled as he hurled the tablet across the room to smash into the wall. "Why do you always fail when I need you?"

There was a timid knock at the door. "Mr. Pelletier? Mr. Pelletier?"

Jason recognized the voice. "Yes, Allie?"

"Are you all right? I heard a crash."

"Yes, I'm fine, Allie," Jason said with labored patience. "I just…tripped, and knocked something on the floor."

"Do you need me to clean it up? I've got the broom right here."

"No, no, Allie," Jason assured her. "I've got it. I'm fine. Give me half an hour and you can take care of the room."

"If you're sure, Mr. Pelletier," Allie sounded skeptical.

"I'm sure. Thank you, Allie," Jason walked over to where his tablet lay on the floor. The screen wasn't just cracked, it was shattered, and the device wouldn't respond to anything. Great. It was an older tablet, and had been getting flaky, and he'd been thinking about getting another one soon, but now he had to – and in his rage, he'd forgotten that he was out here in the sticks, where there weren't six suitable shops within ten minutes. *Maybe* there was a store or two over in Port Huron, or in the Flint area. There were probably stores down in the metro Detroit area. Maybe he could spend the day finding –

No! Jason pulled himself up sharply. He recognized what he was doing. He was already trying to brush yesterday aside, sweep it under the rug, pretend it had never happened and move on. But it had happened! He'd let himself be humiliated and routed by nothing more than shadows and getting lost in the countryside. His cheeks burned with shame and fury at the memory of his panic, his reckless flight, and his spineless lapse into the bottle. He was stronger than this!

Jason knew what he needed to do. He needed to drive right back up there and find that fenced wood, just to prove that it had all been nonsense. A timid corner of his mind recoiled from the idea, but his determined will frowned it down. He *would* do it, and if part of him found it distressing, that was the price he'd have to pay for being weak.

Jason stormed through the shower and went to his car without thinking twice. His queasy stomach begged for something to settle it, but Jason ignored that. He deserved the discomfort – maybe he'd remember it next time he was tempted to cave in. He roared up M-53, grumbling to himself and cursing the whole assignment. How he hated this place, with its petty people occupied with their petty affairs! He hated the dingy houses and the little two-stoplight towns and everything about this backwater hell-hole. God, he couldn't wait to be done with this job and get back to civilization!

When Jason got to Bad Axe (what an asinine name for a town!), the timid portion of him began to reassert itself, for it was just north of here that he'd found himself turning onto M-53. But Jason growled at himself and set his jaw. Of course, it helped that the day was clear and sunny rather than overcast and dark, but Jason ignored that. He *would* retrace his steps and find those woods, if only to prove to himself that there was no justification for his irrational panic.

Jason drove north out of Bad Axe until he spotted the intersection from the day before. The same cluster of run-down, abandoned buildings, the same dirt crossroad. Nathan Road, the sign said. This was where he'd come out, fleeing in panic like a frightened schoolboy. He silenced the shrill voice yammering in his head and turned east.

Straight ahead was what Jason remembered. His flight from his last encounter with the fenced woods had been a straight shot, no turns. He drove steadily, not too quickly, watching the road. It couldn't be more than a couple miles, straight ahead. It had to be coming up shortly – but what was this? He found himself approaching a T-intersection. Left, or right? He didn't remember this at all. Well, he knew he had to go east, so he'd just head south and take the next left turn.

As he turned, he began hearing those static bursts. Glancing down, he saw that the radio had come on again. Stupid thing – he knew he couldn't have turned it on, so it must be something in the circuitry. Maybe there was some kind of malfunction in the dash, which might explain why the nav console hadn't been working either. That made sense, Jason reasoned, taking comfort from a sensible explanation in the midst of all the confusion. He punched the radio off. Soon he came to an intersection and turned left, satisfied that he was back on track and soon would be at his goal. But before he'd driven a mile, the road dead-ended. What? He turned around to go back to the intersection and turn back north. Problem was, he couldn't find the intersection. He was driving steadily north, but passed no crossroads where he could turn either left or right. He seemed stuck on this straight dirt road extending straight ahead as far as he could see. What was going on? He was certain that he'd driven further retracing his route than he had driven to the point where he'd turned around.

Finally, Jason came to an east-west road, which was paved, and turned east again. Just when he was becoming convinced that he'd driven too far, he began to see signs for places like Port Hope and Harbor Beach. He knew that couldn't be right – however he'd gotten here, he'd come too far. Pulling over in frustration, he tried reading the map on his phone, but the screen was too small to be useful. He tried the car's nav console again, but the screen wasn't responding to his taps, and the radio started spitting out static bursts again. All the nav console could give him was a map, and from that he guessed he was north and west of where he'd intended to go. He turned around to try again.

Jason spent the next hour driving back and forth across the area, fruitlessly searching for the fenced-in woods. His mystification and frustration grew with every passing mile, and a frightened corner of his mind piped up from time to time, though he quelled it fiercely. Eventually he gave up, and though he rationalized that he'd accomplished his purpose by driving up and at least trying to face his demons, the frightened corner breathed a sigh of relief that he hadn't found them. By now hunger was his overwhelming concern, so he turned south to Bad Axe where he grabbed a meal, then returned to his hotel to begin the online search for a replacement tablet. Maybe he also needed to look into replacing the rental with a car that had a functional dash.

He'd be in the area for a while, Jason reasoned as he drove. He'd be all over the territory. He'd find the elusive woods again.

Stains

It was Thursday before Luke returned from his long circuit. He'd just put down his gear and was looking forward to a shower when a swift knock came at his door. He was reaching for the knob when the door opened and Cathy stuck her head in.

"Thank God! Doc Luke, you finally made it. Come quickly – it's Grandma!"

"Grandma!" Luke exclaimed, fear gripping his heart. "Has something happened?"

"Nothing dramatic, but she's been steadily declining. Her oxygen levels haven't broken eighty-five all day."

"Oh, God," Luke said, grabbing his bag and heading for the house with Cathy following. "Have you been supplementing?"

"All day," Cathy assured him.

"Why didn't you call me?"

"Grandpa said you were coming home anyway, and there weren't any dramatic incidents, just a steady decline."

They were at the house now, and Luke slipped into the suite where Grandpa sat beside the bed holding the hand of the sleeping – or unconscious – Grandma. She was wearing her cannula and the quiet hiss of the concentrator could be heard from the corner. There was only the soft light from the lamp on her bedside table, but even by that Luke could see that her skin had taken on the pale, parchment-like quality that he'd seen too much of recently.

"Has she responded at all?" Luke asked, alarmed by how significantly she'd declined in just the few days he'd been gone.

"She stirred a little about lunchtime, when we managed to get some crackers and chicken broth into her," Grandpa explained. "She's been murmuring responses to questions, and occasionally squeezing my fingers."

Luke clipped the oximeter to her finger and felt her pulse, which was weak but steady. Her breathing was shallow, and when he put the stethoscope chest piece against her skin, she roused a little.

"Oh, hello, Luke dear," she murmured, patting his hand.

"Hi, Grandma," Luke smiled back. "How are you feeling?"

"Sleepy," Grandma responded. "Everyone has been so good at keeping things quiet so I can rest, and I keep telling them they can go away, but they never do." She gave Grandpa a slight grin, and he patted her hand.

"They want to be by your side," Luke assured her as he prepped a hypodermic. "Listen, I'm going to give you a little shot here, some medicine that should help you breathe better."

"Oh, all right," Grandma allowed. "But only if it's not depriving somebody who needs it more than I."

"I've got plenty, and you've got as much right to it as anyone," Luke said. The first part of this wasn't quite true, but the last part was. She patiently endured his ministrations and patted his hand again when he'd finished.

"Thank you so much for all your help, Luke dear."

"It's my pleasure, Grandma," Luke replied. "Cathy is going to stay with you a minute." He nodded to Grandpa, who rose while Cathy sat down.

"Oh, pish, nobody needs to stay with me," Grandma waved dismissively. "But if somebody's here, I'm glad it's you, Cathy."

Luke and Grandpa slipped from the room and went into the kitchen. "I gave her a compound that can help with oxygen bonding in the lungs," Luke explained. "Sometimes it works, sometimes it doesn't, but I figured it was worth a try. Her stats are only slightly down, but she looks much worse. I'm worried –"

"Luke," Grandpa interrupted, laying a hand on his shoulder. "It's all right. We both know the end is near. We're at peace with it. It's in the Lord's hands now."

"Yeah," Luke said with resignation. Just then Gil walked in, and Luke seized the opportunity. "There's something I have to talk to Gil about – could you excuse me?"

"Sure, Luke," Grandpa replied, and headed back to the suite. Gil came over.

"So, how's Mom?" he asked.

"Frankly? Declining. I won't be planning any overnight trips in the immediate future, and I recommend you don't, either," Luke replied, fishing in his bag. He pulled out a paper and handed it to Gil. "I went over that list you gave me. Here are about a dozen guests that I'd consider in a suitable state for releasing back to public medical care."

"Oh – thanks," Gil said. "We weren't expecting you to get back to us so quickly. You could have taken your time."

"I wouldn't want your plans to be delayed on my account," Luke said. "Now, if you'll excuse me, I just got home and haven't showered yet."

"Sure, Luke. Thanks," Gil replied, watching with an uneasy feeling as Luke headed for his apartment.

Back in his quarters, Luke started unpacking his bag and returning things to their places. As much as he wanted a long shower, he knew he wouldn't be able to relax unless there was some order to his space, so he dug out his dirty clothes and set out his medical gear so he'd know what to restock. As always, it took him longer than he expected, until every minute was a frustration. By the time he emptied his last bag and tucked it away, he was more than ready for his shower and bed.

Just then a quiet knock came at the door. Luke glanced at the clock and rolled his eyes – it was far past time for him to be asleep, much less answering knocks. He was tempted to not answer, but there was too much chance it might be something to do with Grandma, so he called, "Come in!"

To Luke's surprise it wasn't Cathy or Ruth who stepped through the door, but Jake Kyle.

"Hey, Jake, I didn't know you were here," Luke said. "Did you just arrive, or was your pickup out front and I missed it?"

"I...ah, just got here," Jake explained. "I didn't drive – I came on trails by ATV."

"Really?" This mystified Luke. Granted, it wasn't all that far from the Kyle's home to Rivendell, but normally people only took the trails when they had to, especially in the cooler seasons. "What can I do for you, Jake?"

"I was wondering if you...well, if you had a minute to talk about a situation," Jake said haltingly.

Luke struggled against the urge to roll his eyes again. This was hardly a good time for chit-chat. But he disciplined himself and said, "Okay, as long as it doesn't take too long. I just got in from a long day of riding, and haven't even showered yet."

"Oh – well, if this isn't a good time for you, I could come back later," Jake said, turning toward the door. Luke almost let him go, but there was something in Jake's tone that caught Luke's attention.

"No, as long as you're here, let's tackle it," Luke encouraged him. He was now curious and a little apprehensive about what might have turned the normally upbeat and ebullient Jake into this timid, hesitant late-night visitor.

"Well, it's kind of hard to talk about, because of what people will think," Jake muttered.

"Jake, I shouldn't have to remind you about doctor-patient confidentiality. It's like the seal of the confessional. What's up?"

"I...I think I might have an infection."

"An infection?" Luke asked, beginning to suspect where this conversation was headed. "What are the symptoms?"

"Well, it...it burns when I piss," Jake admitted sheepishly. "And when I woke up this morning, my shorts were stuck – to me." He pulled a white wad of cloth from his pocket. Luke pulled on some exam gloves and took the underwear. There in the crotch was the light yellow staining. Luke sighed as his heart dropped. Jake?

"You were right to bring this to me, Jake," Luke said. "I'm going to have to physically examine you, and ask you several embarrassing questions, but they're necessary if we're going to fight this infection."

"I understand," Jake replied. "What do you think I've got?"

"I don't want to jump to conclusions, because to be certain I'm going to need to send a sample to a lab, but based on your symptoms I'd guess you've picked up gonorrhea," Luke explained sympathetically.

"Oh, no," Jake sank into a chair and buried his face in his hands. "Is…is it treatable?"

"It is, provided you haven't picked up a resistant strain," Luke replied. "Again, let's not jump to conclusions. I'm afraid I'm going to need you to take off your pants."

The forty minutes that followed were difficult for both men, as Luke stepped Jake through the standard examination that accompanied a suspected STD diagnosis. Luke had to look up some things, for this was a situation he'd never encountered in all his years. He gave Jake an antibiotic shot, which seemed to encourage him a bit, though Luke was not so optimistic. Well, there were fallback options, though they'd require Jake to go into town to visit one of the clinics that treated STDs at low cost and with few questions. The entire ordeal was humiliating for Jake and depressing for Luke, though the hardest blow came at the end of the exam, when Luke was trying to ascertain the exposure window.

"So, your first exposure would have been – last Saturday?"

"Yeah, we went back to her place and then I snuck home in the middle of the night. It's easy to remember because the call came the next morning about the meeting in Bad Axe."

"Meeting in Bad Axe?" Luke asked. Jake looked at him in surprise.

"You mean, you didn't hear?"

"Hear what?"

"Dan Knight, the Marine veteran who trained us for that operation last summer. He committed suicide. Sheriff Keller wanted to tell us personally, so we met in Bad Axe last Sunday afternoon."

"Wait – suicide?"

"Yeah, didn't you know? I thought you'd heard," Jake replied.

"I've been a little out of touch for the past few days," Luke explained. He hadn't known Dan Knight very well, only meeting him on that night last summer when the factory had been liberated. Luke had examined Dan after he'd suffered that inexplicable episode in the woods, and he'd seemed like a decent, level-headed guy. It wasn't until afterward that Luke had learned more of Dan's history, that he was a Special Forces veteran with several overseas deployments under his belt.

"I suppose only a few of us ever met Dan, but it was a shock," Jake said. "I never would have expected it of him."

"I understand that those clandestine missions can put a lot of stress on people that sometimes doesn't surface until long afterward," Luke replied. "Okay, I'm going to get these samples in for testing, and I'll want you back the day after tomorrow for another shot. I'll be sticking around here, but if you'd prefer, we can meet somewhere else." They arranged a few details then Jake slipped out into the night, enabling Luke to finally get his shower and topple into bed.

Despite his bone-deep weariness, Luke had trouble falling asleep. He was feeling bludgeoned – how much more emotional stress could he take? Grandma dying, Cletus and Sixtus getting arrested, Jake (of all people!) sleeping around, and even a suicide! And looming over it all was the question of his own future, and what he'd do if the ranches were all closed and the guests returned to the public medical care system. What options did he have? Sometime in the morning's small hours he slipped into a light and unsettled slumber.

The next several days were trying for all, especially Luke, as Grandma's condition steadily worsened. Grandpa hardly left her side, and Luke restricted his visits to ranches no farther than a couple of hours away. The word had gotten out, and a steady trickle of visitors made their way to the house to pay their respects to the dying matriarch. Luke bridled a bit at this, contending that the visits were sapping what little remaining strength Grandma had, but Gil took him aside to explain that Grandma would rather spend her few remaining hours seeing people she loved than live a few hours longer in solitude.

On Sunday afternoon, while Luke was tidying up his apartment, a welcome visitor showed up at his door – his friend Teresa. She wore her usual simple white blouse and skirt that looked vaguely like an old-style nurse's uniform and served her as an approximation of the white habit worn by her colleagues at St. Anne's House. Her firm hug and brilliant smile warmed his heart as little had over the past weeks.

"What brings you here?" Luke asked as he cleared off a chair for her. "I'd think you'd be up to your eyebrows in work at St. Anne's."

"Sister Joseph detached me," Teresa explained. "I think she figured the patient here was in as much need of end-of-life care as any at St. Anne's."

"Unfortunately true," Luke affirmed. "Have you seen her?"

"Just now, briefly. She was dozing, but I think she heard my voice because she smiled briefly."

"She's stopped eating completely, and only manages a few sips of juice now and again," Luke lamented. "I suggested an IV, but Grandpa wouldn't hear of it. She's probably in early renal failure even now, as well as –"

"Dear brother," Teresa interrupted his building agitation by laying a hand on his arm. "Everyone has been expecting this, and they're accepting it with peace and grace. You and I were trained in the medical profession, where death is fought for every inch along every front. Over the past few years, we've both had to get used to letting things take their course – me more than you, I think – and this is one more such case."

"I know, but this is a little more personal," Luke replied. "Which reminds me – how are you doing through all this? Grandma was much closer to you than even Grandpa was to me."

"No denying, it's been hard," Teresa admitted. For a moment her face fell into the old expression that Luke remembered from when he'd first known her: tired, stressed, and lost. "It's brought up many old fears that I thought had been left behind." She gave a short, hollow laugh. "Sister Joseph has been a great help. She's very wise, and can discern what's going on inside me when even I can't. She's been comforting me, but also challenging me to be strong. She thinks – and I agree – that we will soon face a period of trial and testing; in fact, that it's already begun."

"Well, that's wonderful," Luke said bitterly. "As if we need more of that."

"Why do you say that?"

Encouraged by Teresa's sympathy, Luke poured out his concerns – about Grandma's decline, the twins getting arrested, the plan to start closing down the ranches and the uncertainty that introduced into his future – everything but details about Jake's situation. Teresa listened to it all without interrupting, wearing the serene expression that was typical for her these days. When he'd finished, she knelt and wrapped her arms around him.

"These issues are clearly a great burden to you," Teresa said. "I won't diminish them by uttering cheery platitudes. But try to remember: our center is not the jobs we're currently performing, or the network we serve, or even the families who have adopted us. Our center is Christ, and while all those other things might change, He never will. The more we're anchored to Him, the less disturbed we'll be when things around us change."

"I know – but that's a lot harder than it sounds," Luke replied.

"True," Teresa replied, kissing him on the cheek and sitting down again without releasing his hand. "We look to others for help and stability, like you've looked to Kent and Grandpa, or I've looked to Grandma or Sister Joseph. To the degree that they strengthen and encourage us, that's great, but the day comes when we have to deal with their weaknesses. That's when we have to remember Who the real center is.

"That being said, let me assure you of one thing, dear brother – you will not be forgotten. You are too dearly loved, and you have served selflessly and faithfully. Whatever changes are coming, you will not be cast aside or left behind. You will be cared for just as everyone else will be."

"Thanks," Luke replied, squeezing her hand. Her reassurances were comforting, though they didn't quite offset the fears that clung to him. "Where will you be staying while you're here?"

"Over at the Big House. The room I used before I went to St. Anne's happens to be open, so I'll be in there."

"Good! I'll get to see you more often, then."

"For a while – and we both know it'll be a short while," Teresa stood to go, then turned back. "Have you heard? Felicity and Grace will be returning soon, possibly by the end of the week."

"Really? Their term is over already?"

"It's such a small school, and their course of study is only two years. When they started this year the students elected to accelerate their pace in order to wrap up by Easter. With word of Grandma's failing condition, Grace says she and Felicity got permission to take their finals early."

"Oh, you've heard from Grace?"

"Only sporadically," Teresa admitted. "You know how touchy communications are. But lately she's been contacting me more often. I think she's worried about Todd."

"Todd? What's going on with Todd?" Luke asked.

"If you haven't heard, it's not my place to speak," Teresa said. "Suffice it to say that Cletus and Sixtus aren't the only ones struggling these days."

"And Jake as well," Luke blurted out before he could stop himself. Teresa cocked her head.

"Jake? What's going on with Jake?"

"Not my place to speak," Luke replied. "But he's got struggles of his own."

A pensive look came over Teresa's face, and she turned toward the north wall of the apartment, which was covered with bookshelves. A faraway look came into her eyes, and her lips moved noiselessly, as if she was whispering to herself. She did this for so long that Luke began to get nervous.

"Teresa?" he finally asked.

"Have you heard from Phillip?" Teresa replied in a conversational tone, not turning her gaze from the north.

"Phillip? No, my runs haven't taken me up that way. Why?"

"You may want to – but no," Teresa began, then interrupted herself and turned. "I suspect we'll have reason to assemble soon enough, those of us who have passed under the Shadow. There is yet time, but it grows short."

"What on earth are you talking about, Teresa?"

Teresa patted Luke's arm and kissed him again. "Things will become clear soon, dear brother. All too soon, I fear. Stand fast and do not give in to fear."

"Okay," Luke replied hesitantly, a little spooked by Teresa's odd moods. Reading his tone, she gave a light, merry laugh and hugged him close.

"Be encouraged, Luke. All our lives will turn soon, if we manage to hold firm through the darkness. I must go. Bless you!"

With that she was out the door, leaving Luke to ponder how much she'd changed. Then he turned his attention back to tomorrow's visit list, and what he'd have to check on the guests he'd be visiting tonight over at the Big House.

It turned out to be the next day when Felicity and Grace returned. As usual, they were circumspect about the precise means by which they crossed the international border, but everyone was glad to see they'd made it. They were permitted to slip into Grandma's room, where Grandpa and Teresa were keeping vigil. Teresa stepped back to make room for them at the bedside. Felicity sat beside her grandmother and took her hand while Grace stood farther back. To everyone's surprise, Grandma stirred and opened her eyes to look at the girls.

"My beautiful granddaughters," she whispered with a smile. This was a courtesy as far as Grace was concerned, for they were no blood relation, but every young woman whom Grandma loved became her granddaughter. "I'm glad you made it back."

"So are we, Grandma," Felicity smiled through her tears and patted Grandma's hand. In response Grandma opened her eyes a bit wider, and her face lit up with a bright smile.

"Why, look at you all, come to visit me in your wedding dresses! How gorgeous you are, all three of you! Such beauty in my room all at once – I'm honored!"

The girls all looked at each other, and at Grandma, in mystification. They were all dressed in ordinary clothes, and in Grace and Felicity's case, somewhat wrinkled travel garb.

"So kind of you to let me see," Grandma continued, but then her brow furrowed a little. "But, if I may say, they're a little smudged in places. What is that, soot? How did that get there?" She waved a hand vaguely, as if trying to brush something away.

Felicity and Grace were even more puzzled by this, but to their surprise Teresa spoke up.

"It's from the Shadow, Grandma. It left stains when we walked through it."

"Oh, that," Grandma said dismissively. "You'll be able to clean them up in time, won't you, Teresa dear?"

"Of course, Grandma," Teresa replied calmly.

"Good, good," Grandma said, lying back on her pillow with a contented smile. "Be sure to call me for the ceremonies."

"Certainly," Teresa said. Since Grandma was clearly going back to sleep, the girls all slipped out of the room and stood in the hall. Felicity and Grace still felt a little bewildered, and would occasionally glance down at their clothes in spite of themselves.

"Was that just Grandma being punchy, or did something just happen in there?" Grace finally asked.

"Who can tell?" Teresa replied.

"She looks so frail," Felicity said, tearing up again. "She's very close, isn't she?"

"She is," Teresa acknowledged. "I'm glad you made it back in time. But you're graduates now! How exciting!" She gave her friends a hug.

"Providing we passed Finals, but I think we're all right," Grace said. "Though the graduation festivities may have to be put off for a little while."

"The graduation festivities may have to be put off for quite a while," Teresa added quietly.

In the middle of the night, when all was silent in the Big House, Grandma stirred and tried to sit up. Grandpa, who was dozing in the chair beside the bed, woke and patted her shoulder, urging her to lie back down.

"Shh, shh, it's all right," he said soothingly as she eased back down onto the pillow.

"What, you're still here?" she asked quietly.

"Where else would I be?"

"I don't know. Working. Sleeping."

"I've got no place better to be than right here with you," Grandpa assured her, stroking her hand.

"You're sweet. But you'll have to find someplace to go, 'cause I won't be here much longer."

"I know," Grandpa choked, bowing his head. "How...how do you feel? Are you in pain?"

"Mostly I feel sleepy, but I get tired of sleeping," she said, then chuckled. "That's funny – 'tired of sleeping'. Who'd have thought I'd ever say something like that? A bit thirsty, maybe. Is there any water?"

"There's water and juice," Grandpa offered.

"Water's fine – I just need to wet my whistle," Grandma sat up a little to sip from the offered straw, then lay back down with a contented sigh. "That was good. Don't you go worrying about me, now."

"I'm not," Grandpa assured her through his tears. "It's me I'm worried about. What will I do without you?"

"Well," Grandma replied, patting his hand. "Whatever it is, you won't have to do it for long."

"How do you know that?"

"Just a hunch," Grandma sighed, nestling back into her pillow. Soon she slept again, her shallow breathing the only sound in the quiet darkness.

She never woke again.

It was about ten the next morning when Luke was summoned to bring his instruments to verify Grandma's death. Grandpa stood silently by the bedside as Luke went through his checks, then without a word brought the bedspread up to cover her pale face. Luke never ceased being surprised at how small and frail people looked in death. Even the large and burly seemed shrunken and diminished when their breath left them. Luke stepped out of the room while Gil stood ready to escort his father away and Teresa attended to the body.

The arrangements had long been made. Father Gabriel had visited the day before. The funeral home was called and within half an hour the men had come to take Grandma's body away. The ever-prepared Ruth even had a tray of sandwiches out and coffee set up for the numerous people who would be passing through. Luke lingered around the house, not knowing what to do but not wanting to leave Grandpa and Teresa alone.

People arrived from all the houses at Rivendell, and Luke imagined it wouldn't be long before more people came from farther away as news of Grandma's death spread. Grandpa settled in the living room, looking stunned and wiping his eyes but insisting on seeing anyone who showed up.

Of course, some of the first to arrive were the Petersons from next door: Gil and Janine, their sons Christopher and Andrew, and Harmony and Felicity. As always, Luke's heart leapt a bit when Felicity came in – he hadn't seen her since before she left for St. Anselm's at the end of last summer, and she looked as stunning as ever. Understandably, she went straight to Grandpa, and Luke tried to walk away to give her some time with him, but found himself wandering back into the living room from time to time just to catch glimpses of her.

In time other visitors arrived, and Felicity stepped aside to make room for them. She looked around the room full of friends and relatives she hadn't seen in the best part of a year, and to Luke's astonishment walked right over to him. Her smile was warm and welcoming, but there was a slightly different quality to it. Rather than being perky and effervescent, it was shy and touched with gravity. Without a word she wrapped her arms around his neck and leaned her head on his chest, as she'd done twice before in the history of their friendship.

Somewhat surprised and wholly delighted, Luke wrapped his arms around Felicity and held her close. They stood in silence for a minute, sharing their grief and loss. Even in his sorrow he was conscious of the weight of her body pressing against him, the gentle movement of her breathing, the light floral scent that always seemed to accompany her. Relishing his good fortune, he stood still for as long as Felicity was willing to lean on him, which was quite some time. Finally she stepped back a little, though she kept her arms about his neck, and looked up at him.

"Derek, have I ever told you what a comforting man you are?" she asked. "In times of my greatest trials, there you are for me to lean on and draw strength from."

"I...I'm glad," Luke whispered, but no response seemed necessary. She was gazing into his eyes and her arms around his neck weren't easing an inch. He felt flushed and could hear the blood pulsing in his ears. He tried to listen to her words that spoke only of comfort, nothing more. He tried to remember that Felicity was a naturally affectionate person who touched often, and that embraces meant to her what a handshake would mean to others. He tried to ignore the fact that their lips were only inches apart. This was not the place, he scolded himself. He should be ashamed for even allowing such thoughts to slip in under these circumstances of grief. He was sure that Felicity was unaware of the effect her proximity had on him, and that the responsibility for taming his unruly passions was entirely his. But the intensity of the encounter was building to the point where Luke felt he must step back or flee entirely. "I...ah...I'm sorry for your loss," he fumbled.

"Thank you," Felicity replied. "It sounds so cliché to say she lived a full life, but in her case it's true. Her love blessed hundreds of people directly, and countless more indirectly."

"It was an honor to know her," Luke began, but just then Teresa walked into the room. Catching sight of her, Felicity smiled at him ruefully.

"There are so many people, and today..." she trailed off.

"I understand," Luke said.

"We'll talk more later, maybe this evening," Felicity added. "Promise me?"

"I promise," Luke replied.

But it was a promise easier made than kept, as the work needed to prepare for Grandma's funeral absorbed much of everyone's time. Felicity was nearly run off her feet preparing food, arranging lodging for people coming from a distance, and setting up and taking down items for varied uses. There were coffees and brunches and a wake on Thursday night. Through it all Felicity was a trouper, as were her siblings and cousins, but they barely had time to breathe and no time for leisurely conversation. The one talk they did have was brief and far from relaxing. It was right after the wake, as Luke was passing by the kitchen. Felicity grabbed his arm and pulled him into the pantry.

"What's up?" Luke asked, seeing her strained expression.

"I just spoke with Grace. She's really distraught, as is the whole family. Something's going on with Jake that nobody can figure out. He vanishes for long periods, then when he's around, he's withdrawn and uncommunicative. Nobody knows where he's going."

"Well, that's odd," Luke said noncommittally. He wasn't sure about all Jake's absences, but two of them had been to visit Luke for more shots. He was due for one more visit and checkup the next day. "Aren't he and Grace rather close?"

"Yes, and that's part of her pain," Felicity replied. "She thought he'd be excited when she came back, but it's like he hasn't noticed her. Oh, he says hello, but he's distant and distracted. Her parents are noticing, but they don't know what to do. And on top of that, there's Todd's behavior."

"What about Todd?"

"Well," Felicity said a little shyly. "They've never been secretive about their attraction, and Grace was hoping, based on some hints Todd had dropped, that when she returned this year, he'd start courting her in earnest."

"And that hasn't happened?"

"No, and to Grace that seems the strangest thing! He used to nearly haunt the Kyle home when she was there; now he's only dropped by twice. She's wondering what she might have done wrong."

"I don't know what's going on, but I doubt it's her. Let me do some checking," Luke offered.

"Thanks! Oh, there's Aunt Ruth – we'll talk more later, okay?" Felicity bustled off, leaving Luke to worry. He remembered Teresa's comment a few days earlier, and the implication that she knew more than she was saying about Todd's situation. Maybe it was time for him to look into it further.

Luke got his opportunity then next day when Jake paid his final visit for his last dose of antibiotic. To Luke's relief, the infection seemed to be responding.

"Good news, pal," Luke said. "You dodged a bullet on this one – the antibiotic seems to be working."

"Oh? You had a question about that?"

"I didn't want to tell you, but this is the strongest stuff I can get my hands on, and it's only effective about forty percent of the time."

Jake's eyes grew wide. "I did dodge a bullet, then."

"Chalk it up to your guardian angel," Luke said, then gave Jake a hard stare. "I presume that we've been avoiding further infection opportunities?"

"Yeah," Jake replied glumly, slumping down in his seat. "But it's hard. The situation is…difficult."

"Hey, I'm a guy, too. I understand," Luke assured him.

"It's more than just that. I mean, yeah, I've been feeling lonely lately, and horny, but Av – this girl really needs help, and she's grateful when I provide it. You can guess how she expresses her gratitude."

"Needs help?" Luke was puzzled. "What kind of help?"

"Let me put it this way: if I go over to her place for a big evening, guess what I bring?"

"Umm…a couple of six-packs and some schnapps?"

"Nope," Jake replied. "Groceries. Bread, peanut butter, lettuce, milk, maybe a frozen pizza or so. This girl is so poor that she can barely keep gas in her car and propane in her trailer's tank. The night I met her all I did was buy her a plate of nachos, and she was so grateful that she invited me back to her place, and – things proceeded from there."

"So, you show up with groceries, and she thanks you."

"Pretty much," Jake admitted. "I mean, she's a nice girl, but we don't have a lot in common. Not much of a conversationalist – her idea of an evening's entertainment is watching shows."

"Essentially she's prostituting herself for food," Luke observed.

Jake winced. "You…you could look at it that way."

Luke remained silent for a while before speaking again. "You know, you could just take her food and go for a walk. Or drive up to Yale, or down to Port Huron. You don't have to stay at her place."

"I know," Jake said glumly. "It was her idea, and I just…succumbed. I get the impression this isn't the first time she's paid for food this way, which makes me feel even worse. But –" Jake buried his face in his hands. "I've always been weak in this area. Lust has always been my vulnerability. But this winter it's been especially bad. I don't know what's come over me. I've prayed, gone to church, tried to fill my hours, but it just keeps getting worse. I'll look at a woman and all sorts of vile images flood my imagination. I'm just – defeated."

"Hey, buddy," Luke said, patting his shoulder. "I sympathize. I'm weak in that area myself."

"But it's never been this bad," Jake protested. "I don't know what's happened to me."

"I think you need to talk to Fr. Gabriel, or someone who can help you. I think you need to stop seeing this woman, even to drop off food – you can find other ways to get food to her, if you want to help. People are starting to worry about you. Grace in particular has been puzzled and hurt."

"Grace! I've felt too guilty to face her, and I miss her so badly."

"Well, then," Luke said. "Have that talk with Fr. Gabriel. And get back with your family."

"I'll try," Jake replied in a resigned voice. "Thanks."

"Sure thing. Say, before you go, a question, if you can answer: what's going on with Todd?"

"Oh, that's tough," Jake shook his head. "Todd has been hitting the bottle kind of hard. Something's stressing him, and that's how he deals with it."

"Stressing him? Any idea what it is?"

"Nope. And he gets touchy and withdrawn if you press him about it, or about his drinking."

"Obviously, Grace is concerned about him as well, so you may want to reassure her – but be circumspect about what you share."

"Yeah," Jake agreed.

After Jake left, Luke sat staring at the wall, his heart heavy. What a mess. Todd struggling as well, just when Jake was having such problems. Luke knew how much difference a close friend could make in times of vulnerability, but just when Jake needed him, Todd goes missing. And they'd been such good friends, especially since –

Wait a minute.

Todd and Jake had been together that night. In fact, they'd been a team. Todd had needed rescue.

It had been Grace who'd gone for him.

Who else had been there?

Cletus and Sixtus.

Teresa and Felicity. Oh, God, Felicity.

And Dan Knight.

And Phillip. Teresa had asked about Phillip. Luke hadn't heard anything, but maybe he needed to look into it.

Maybe he needed to look into it soon.

Oversight

Ethan showed up the next morning even as Jason was setting up one of the workstations in a corner of the hotel conference room.

"Mornin', boss," he said as he sat down with a cup of coffee. "How was your weekend?"

"It had its moments," Jason muttered. The tension and fear were quieter after a couple night's sleep, but his frustration and anger with himself were on a slow simmer. "Here," he shoved a slip of paper across the table at Ethan.

"What's this?"

"Your assignment for the day. I need you to make those calls."

"Oh, man," Ethan groaned, looking down the list. "I thought I'd do a little more field exploration today – I even brought the ATV."

"The exploration you've done has turned up all we need for now," Jason explained. "The time may come when you can do more four-wheeling on the clock, but for now I need those arrangements made."

"It'll take me a while to work through this list."

"I'll be right here."

Ethan retuned nearly two hours later. Jason had spent the time running and re-running models against the HHS data, and a plan was beginning to form in his mind.

"Okay, boss, this is the best I could do," Ethan explained. "Of the sheriffs, two could squeeze you in tomorrow or any time afterward. The other two aren't available until Wednesday at the earliest, and the fifth is out on vacation until the middle of next week. What's your preference?"

"Let's shoot for Wednesday," Jason decided. "See what you can arrange there. I'd like to make a sweep of it and knock off four in one day if possible. We'll pick up the fifth one as we can."

"Gotcha," Ethan noted something on the slip. "This second thing might take some time. 'Geographically central' is a nice idea, but the closest you'll get to that in the Thumb is a little town named Kingston – not much there. Sandusky would have more options, but they're about twenty miles east."

"That would be fine – check out what there is," Jason instructed.

"Okay," Ethan replied. "As far as Selfridge is concerned, Major Collins has some time this afternoon, if you're free."

"I am. Line it up," Jason said. "And call those two investigators, Sanderson and…and…"

"Harris."

"Right, Harris. See if they can meet us there."

It was 2:00 p.m. before everyone was able to converge on the Border Patrol facilities on the Selfridge base. Collins had them in a conference room that had screens on several of the walls. On one screen was projected a geographic map of the region, while on another was cued the video of the blast from the drone footage. Jason began by explaining what he and Ethan had figured out about the hitherto undiscovered trail through the woods. He had to tread carefully because the forensics report was still DHS Top Secret, but by alluding to unspecified anomalies at the blast site he was able to give them enough to understand why he and Ethan had reinspected the site and discovered the overgrown trail.

"So, you think that someone used this hidden trail to access the field HQ the night of the blast?" Collins asked.

"It's very possible, given a number of factors," Jason confirmed. "But more interesting is the fact that there seems to be a network of these trails that might be utilized for clandestine travel. Ethan, explain what your survey has turned up."

Ethan told of his explorations on the ATV, and the trails and paths he had found. He explained how he suspected that the trail network reached farther than his limited search had discovered.

"If you don't mind my saying so," Agent Sanderson interjected. "A network of trails by themselves proves nothing. They could just be used by farm kids on dirt bikes and four-wheelers. You admit that you didn't see anyone else on them."

"You're right," Jason replied. "But from classified details about the site and other evidence, we strongly suspect that there is an underground network operating in the area dedicated to spiriting away and hiding people. The existence of a hidden complex of trails that could be used for evading surveillance raises more suspicions. Weren't you two once assigned to investigate a missing person?"

"Yes – the lady who went missing from the hospital under unusual circumstances," Sanderson confirmed. "The details are in the file you have."

"Yes, I've read it," Jason said. "Have you, in all your investigations, seen or heard anything that would suggest people are using concealed methods of getting around?"

"Can't say that we have," Sanderson said. "But then, that hasn't been what we've been looking for."

"How about any other instances of people mysteriously vanishing? Just going missing without explanation?"

Sanderson and Harris glanced at one another before Sanderson replied, "I can't recall anything off the top of my head, at least not in connection with the blast investigation. Of course, we'd have to go back through our notes, but we gathered a lot of stuff that was irrelevant to the blast."

"Don't assume that. Don't assume anything," Jason said. "From here on, assume everything might be connected to the blast."

Sanderson looked skeptical. "So you're suggesting these vanished people might have something to do with the blast?"

"Yes!" Jason nearly barked. "The vanished people could be a connection to this clandestine, possibly terrorist network responsible for a deadly explosion and the terminal sabotage of a critical government program, about which I can't provide details."

Harris, who'd been fidgeting for a while, abruptly spoke up. "Terrorists? With due respect, we've been all over this area speaking to all kinds of people. These are rural folk living simple lives. Their idea of rough stuff is a brawl behind the bar after a few beers over pool."

"Is that what you know, Agent Harris?" Jason snapped. "If that's so, then why was a human trafficking network uncovered in this rural region less than a year ago? A sophisticated network with ties into the foster care system, slave labor, and the sex trade? A crime family that was operating undetected for years, and may be tied to the blast? Is that your idea of 'rural folk living simple lives'?"

Harris muttered sullenly and shrank back into his seat while Jason continued emphatically. "I want a full-court press on this. We're assuming everything's interwoven, but since we don't know which thread is going to unravel something, we pull on them all. Chad, what kind of aerial assets can we get scanning the region? And what kind of imaging analysis resources do we have on tap?"

"Well, now, we just got briefed on a new image analysis system that NSA is opening access to," Collins answered eagerly. "They claim it can infer activity patterns from even the most random data. As far as aerial assets, we have a few options –"

"Excuse me, Major," Jason interrupted. Glancing at the other agents, he asked, "Guys, could you give us a minute? Just step outside for a while – security matter."

"There's a break room just down the hall on the left," Collins called as they filed out, then he looked at Jason with a mystified expression. "Okay, what's so secret?"

"I've been thinking of requesting a RA asset for continuous overflights."

Collins raised his eyebrows. The RA surveillance drones were one of those projects that everybody seemed to know about but nobody officially acknowledged. As a surveillance specialist, Collins had heard more of the scuttlebutt than most: how the drones were partly solar powered and could stay aloft for weeks or months, how their camera array could simultaneously scan hundreds of square miles continuously while enabling their operators to zoom in on something the size of a skateboard at the same time, how their onboard storage could hold petabytes of information. None of it official, of course, but none of it surprising, given the capability of commonplace assets like he had in his hangars.

"You...have access to RA control?" Collins asked, trying to sound nonchalant.

"I do," Jason nodded. "When I was sent here, I was told how badly the Department wanted this situation resolved, and was given plenary authority. I'm going to push things, if only to see whether they were serious or just blowing smoke."

"Do you think they'll free up a RA drone for this?"

"If they're serious, they will. Of course, their status is all hush-hush, but my understanding is that they're mostly tasked to overfly urban areas because of all the unrest. But this project is important, too – few people know how important – so I think I can persuade them to retask one of the RAs to monitor the Thumb for a period. *If* they agree, would you be able to make good use of the imagery?"

"Hell, yes, I can make good use of it," Collins said with enthusiasm. "If I can get the kind of output the RA is reputed to deliver, and run it through this new IA system that NSA is advertising, we should be able to find anything that's out there. One thing, though."

"What's that?" Jason asked.

"Early spring around here tends toward steady overcast. We usually have to keep our birds below 8,000, sometimes below 5,000, just to see the ground. Those RAs are reputed to linger up there near 20,000. It may not work to vector in an asset that will only be useful every fifth day."

"I'll talk with them about that," Jason assured him. "I'm sure they have ways of dealing with overcast. But keep your other assets handy. My hope is that analysis of the high-level imagery will expose any traffic patterns that might exist. Once we have a line on those, we'll need lower level assets for more targeted monitoring."

"Hot damn!" Collins grinned. "Nice to have someone with balls calling the shots!"

They called the agents back in and everyone left with assignments. Collins was to contact the NSA while Jason investigated the surveillance asset. Sanderson and Harris were sent back to their office to scan their notes for any trace of missing people or clandestine traffic. They got into their car with the resigned disgust felt by government workers who'd just gotten their routines upended.

"This new guy sure is a firebreather, isn't he?" Harris grumbled.

"Yeah," Sanderson agreed. The car was silent for a moment before he spoke again. "Are you thinking what I'm thinking?"

"I dunno," Harris replied in exasperation. "What are you thinking?"

"That aside from that first case who went missing from the hospital, we've only seen one case of mysterious disappearance in all our years investigating. Remember that?"

"I...think so," Harris said.

"It was that family that vanished, the one whose kids had gotten swept into that corrupt foster care network. We never could find a connection between that and anything else, but it was really strange. Never found the family, either."

"Yeah," mused Harris. "And you know what else is strange?"

"What's that?"

"Both of those cases were connected to the same person."

"That's right, they were," Sanderson acknowledged. "Good old Counselor Fitzgerald."

"Do you...think we should mention this to Pelletier?" Harris asked.

"We may have to," Sanderson shrugged. "It's right there in the records. But we don't have to tell him today."

When Jason returned to his hotel room and logged onto his workstation, he found several messages waiting. One was from expense accounting, a curt denial of his request for long-term rental housing. It was a form message, with a list of about a dozen standard denial reasons, three of which were checked: "Expense unjustified by project scope", "Insufficient documentation provided", and "Departmental budget restrictions". There was nothing in the comments but "Request denied".

Jason almost slammed his fist on the desk, but caught himself. He was certain that Whitman was behind this – it was the sort of petty power game crap that he loved to play. Time to nip this in the bud. If they thought a request for an apartment rental was exorbitant, wait until they saw his broader plans. Now was the time to force their hand, to see how serious they were. Rather than clicking on "Appeal Denial" link at the bottom of the message, Jason forwarded the entire thing with a terse comment: "You said I had plenary authority."

There. That would either fly, or crash and burn. He knew he was further alienating colleagues by end-running standard protocols like that, but he'd been told that he had the authority to match his responsibility. Time to see how true that was. It was becoming clearer by the day that this project was for the highest stakes. If he didn't succeed his career was over.

And speaking of high stakes, it was time to compose that message requesting the RA deployment.

Two days later Ethan and Jason were driving northwest out of Caro, having just concluded their second interview of the day. Ethan had timed the appointments with the local sheriffs in such a way that the driving could be done in a great loop through the Thumb. They'd begun with the Lapeer County sheriff just by Lapeer, then visited Amanda Morris of Tuscola County in her office in Caro. Now they were on their way northwest to Bad Axe to visit Huron County's sheriff, and they'd end up in Sandusky with Sanilac County's sheriff Al Corrigan. The only base they weren't covering today was St. Clair County, and that appointment was set for a week from the following Monday.

Visiting the sheriffs was not strictly required, but it was considered a courtesy when conducting a law enforcement investigation in their own back yards. The discussions were made more difficult for Jason by the fact that what was being investigated was still largely classified. Jeff Murray of Lapeer County had been most understanding, since the blast had been in his county and his people had been among the first to respond. Sheriff Murray had simply nodded and kept his mouth shut while Jason had spoken of the blast as an industrial accident, because they both knew it was a smokescreen but couldn't admit that officially during a formal visit. The sheriff had raised his eyebrows slightly when Jason had alluded to the possibility of ongoing clandestine domestic terror operations, but he hadn't objected. They'd departed on cordial terms, with the sheriff promising all cooperation with the investigation.

Sheriff Morris of Tuscola had been a bit more reserved, and had kept her chief deputy with her throughout the interview. She'd gotten a bit defensive when Jason had mentioned searching for evidence of domestic terror activity, protesting that if there were any such activity in her county, she would have caught wind of it. Jason offered the usual platitudes, but it was hard to pretend to be a neutral agent in the area with the Halverson Protocols hanging over everybody's head. The Halverson Protocols were a policy implementation of some clauses in the Domestic Terror Act, basically holding that Federal law enforcement could demand any asset, including personnel, from local law enforcement at any time in the course of a domestic terror investigation. To Jason's knowledge, nobody had ever invoked the Halverson Protocols, and Sheriff Morris had seemed to be discreetly probing for reassurance that Jason wouldn't. To her increasing discomfort, Jason had offered no such reassurance. As far as Jason was concerned, if it made the locals jittery having him poking about, so much the better – it would make them more likely to cooperate if the need arose. Their departure from Caro had been cordial but strained.

Now they were driving through fields which Jason uneasily recognized from his drive the prior Saturday. The overcast wasn't so heavy and it wasn't raining, so the landscape wasn't as depressing as it had been, but the fields still looked waterlogged and the stands of bare trees slightly threatening. Trying to sound as casual as possible, Jason commented on the irregularity of the terrain – how some was level and tilled, such as the portion they were currently passing through, while other sections were hilly and wooded, and everything seemed to be perpetually wet.

To Jason's surprise, Ethan replied with an extensive description of the Thumb's geography and topology, and how it had gotten that way. He explained how the whole section of the continent had been worked over by glaciers during the last ice age, which had fouled up the drainage and created irregular high and low land not just in the Thumb, but across Ontario, Michigan, Wisconsin, and Minnesota. This caused the odd patches of woods cutting through the farmland. The western Thumb, close to Saginaw Bay, was flatter because it had once been lake bottom, just a few thousand years earlier when the bay had been a much larger inlet. He explained how the whole area had been completely forested when European settlers came, and how logging was the big industry for years as the huge pines were cut and floated down the rivers to market.

Through this lengthy and erudite mini-lecture, Jason looked at his driver with increasing amazement. "You seem to know a lot of things about a lot of things," he said when Ethan had finished.

Ethan shrugged. "I like to learn about the places I'm stationed."

"How old are you, Ethan?"

"Forty-two."

"If you don't mind my asking, why are you still a field agent? With brains like that, you could be a manager, or an investigator."

Ethan looked at him with an odd grin. "I got issues."

Jason tried to hide his nervousness as they rolled into Bad Axe. He was glad Ethan was driving even as he detested himself for his weakness. Leaving Ethan in the truck, he went into the sheriff's building and was soon being escorted into the office of a sturdy middle-aged man with a neatly trimmed mustache and a crisp manner. The man looked at him guardedly with brown eyes that looked alert but weary.

"Sheriff Keller, thank you for taking time to meet with me," Jason said, shaking his hand and giving him a card. "I'm Jason Pelletier from the Department of Homeland Security."

"A pleasure, Mr. Pelletier. Would you like some coffee?"

"No, thank you."

"Well then," Chip asked as both men were seated. "How may the Huron County Sheriff's Department assist the Department of Homeland Security?"

"I've been assigned to conduct a regional investigation of suspected domestic terrorist activity, so I'll be working in the area for a while. Today's visit is largely a courtesy call – I'm not requesting any resources at this time."

"I see," Chip replied cautiously. "Thank you for your consideration. Are there any specific indications of domestic terror on which you're following up? Anything you're free to share with me, of course."

"A scattering of clues is all we have so far," Jason said vaguely. "I've learned a few things since arriving, and we're bringing more resources into service."

"Would this have anything to do with the Imlay City blast?"

Jason blinked and then mentally shook himself. Of course these sheriffs talked to one another. "As you're aware, the official finding released about that was that it was an industrial accident, though I can confide that the investigation is ongoing."

"I can imagine that it is," Chip said with a knowing gleam in his eye. "That was a rather…ah… spectacular explosion."

"May I ask why you inquired about that particular incident?" Jason said.

Chip shrugged. "Simple industrial accidents are rarely taken over by the Feds to the exclusion of local authorities. That, plus the fact that the whole thing was locked down so tight, made me wonder if there was more to it than had been let out. Just casual interest on my part – it's more Jeff Murray's concern, if it's anyone's."

"I see," Jason replied. "I do have one question, though, Sheriff: has your department ever discovered movement of people or goods by trails through woods or along the edges of fields?"

Chip cocked his head a little. "You mean, off-road traffic? Dirt bikes, four-wheelers, UTVs, that sort of thing? There are always plenty of those. Not only do the kids love the bikes, but the farmers use the four-wheelers and UTVs as work vehicles. They're technically not licensed to travel on or beside roadways, but in rural areas like Huron we kind of wink at that, so long as it doesn't get too blatant."

"Well, I'm looking more for parties using these trails for getting around in ways that would make it difficult to spot or track."

"You think domestic terrorists are using ATV trails in Huron County for their activities?" Chip asked with a hint of incredulity.

Jason bristled a little at the man's tone. "Sheriff, we have credible indication of sophisticated domestic terror activity in this region. An important Federal pilot project was detected, stymied, and then decapitated by violent action. There are indications of clandestine networks facilitating illegal activity, including smuggling, illicit provision of services, and fraud. Yes, even in Huron County, where I recall there was recently exposed a regional syndicate that was running a human trafficking and sweatshop operation headquartered right here, was it not?"

"Yes, it was," Chip confirmed stiffly. "But that was good old-fashioned crime, not domestic terror."

"Indeed, but if that was happening right under your nose, what else might be going on that you're unaware of?"

Chip Keller tried not to let on that Jason had unknowingly struck a very sensitive nerve, and struggled lamely to answer. "Well, I wasn't sheriff when that took place."

"You weren't sheriff at the time," Jason pointed out. "Though the sitting sheriff 'died unexpectedly' just as the syndicate was exposed, and you were asked to step back into your old job. That appears a little...convenient."

"Are you accusing me of something, Agent Pelletier?" Chip asked coldly.

"Not at all, Sheriff. I was only pointing out the curious conjunction of events."

Chip's shoulders sagged and he sighed heavily. "Convenient isn't the word – tragic is. Truth is, Andy killed himself. He had connections with the family who'd been running the syndicate – his brother married one of the boss's daughters. When the whole thing was exposed, he left a resignation letter on his desk, went home, and blew his chest open. One of my deputies found him."

Jason nodded. He'd guessed something like this from the tersely worded death report, but it was good to have it confirmed. "And the finding of death by accidental discharge?"

"I signed off on that to buffer the blow on his family. The medical examiner, county administrator, and I all know the truth – and the deputies, of course. There was so much coming down right then that Andy's demise was minor news by comparison. I have a file back there with the full details."

"He was in office for less than a year, wasn't he?"

"Yes. In fact, I have my suspicions about how he got elected."

"What are those?" Jason asked.

Chip eyed him warily for a moment before speaking. "This is sheer speculation, understand, because I haven't a shred of proof of any of this, but some of us guess that Andy was put up to running, and his campaign financed, by the family running the syndicate for the purpose of getting me out of office. I was starting to pick up clues about the syndicate's operations and was alerting my deputies. Only after I did that did Andy announce his candidacy."

"I see," was all Jason said, but what he thought was that it was one possible explanation. Another might be that the longstanding sheriff had been moved aside just long enough for a dupe to be moved in to take the fall, after which he could safely be returned to office. Sheriff Keller had held that seat for years while the criminal activity had raged all around him. Maybe he hadn't known about it. Maybe.

"On another topic, Sheriff, I'll also be following up on reports of pockets of...shall we say undocumented parties who have been receiving services through unauthorized channels, and who perhaps have participated in other illegal activities. Have you or your staff heard of any such activity?"

Chip looked puzzled. "Are you talking about settlements of illegal immigrants?"

"No, ICE would be handling those," Jason replied. "I'm talking more about secluded and clandestine parties who have withdrawn from usual channels of supply and communication."

"Which laws are these secluded and clandestine parties suspected of breaking?"

Jason bristled a little. This was hardly cooperative. "There could be any number of them – tax evasion, receipt of unauthorized services, identity fraud, and the like."

"If you'll provide me with names, addresses, and indictments, I'll be happy to send my deputies after any lawbreakers in Huron County," Chip assured him. "But if these undocumented parties are living in peaceful seclusion, they're not likely to come to our notice unless they start breaking laws more visibly."

Jason nearly ground his teeth in frustration. "What I mean is, you and your deputies are all over this county continuously. If there were secluded parties being supplied and serviced by unorthodox channels, wouldn't you have heard something about them?"

"Not necessarily," Chip replied. "We've got our hands full dealing with criminals. It isn't unusual for peaceful, law-abiding citizens to live their entire lives without coming to our attention. If these parties are as secluded as you say, then avoiding the sheriff's attention is as simple as obeying the speed limit."

"What kind of criminals could keep your hands so full?" Jason asked sharply

"Mr. Pelletier, just because we're small town doesn't mean we're small time when it comes to crime. We've had three opioid overdoses this month, two of them fatal, and my deputies are trying to track down a major meth facility which we suspect is operating in the western part of the county. We've got the usual run of domestic violence, robberies, and assaults. And, as you've reminded me, there was a major family-run criminal syndicate that was broken open last summer – we're still cleaning that up."

"I see," Jason replied. "Well, I'd appreciate it if you'd notify your staff of my interest, and send along anything you might hear."

"I'll do that, Mr. Pelletier."

They parted with the usual courtesies and Jason headed back to the truck for the drive down to Sanilac County.

"So, how did that go?" Ethan asked.

"I'd say…marginal," Jason replied.

"Really? I thought these were supposed to be courtesy visits, introductions. Was he hostile? Uncooperative?"

"Not hostile," Jason said. "And cooperative up to a point. I don't know. I can't quite put my finger on it. Maybe it was just local skepticism of Federal involvement, but I can't shake the impression that something's going on up here. Don't worry about it for now, we can't let ourselves get distracted, but I suspect we'll be back up in Huron County."

"Okay," Ethan replied. "How about we grab some lunch then head down to Sandusky. We can talk to the Sanilac sheriff, then I've got some spots I've lined up for you to take a look at."

Back in his office, Chip sat behind his desk and pondered the interview he'd just been through. A DHS investigator, all the way from D.C., asking if he'd heard about hidden people and the network that supported them. Of course Chip had heard things, but he'd heard them as private citizen Keller, not in his capacity as county sheriff, and thus didn't feel compelled to relay what he'd heard to a Federal agency. Maybe he needed to drop a quiet line to Lawrence Stover about this.

Chip had been completely accurate in stating that his staff had more urgent demands than tracking rumors about law-abiding citizens. What he'd been less frank about was what a growing number of those demands were.

Every town always had a few peculiar people, hanging around the library or the park or the diners. The people with serious problems were handled by community mental health, but the innocuous ones were tolerated, even welcomed. But in Huron County the number of these odd characters had been steadily growing of late. The locals and the deputies had many names for them. The Zanies. The Crazies. The Nut Jobs. Whatever they were called, there was an increasing number of people who ranged from the merely strange to the clearly insane. The disturbing part was that they weren't local. Nobody knew where they had come from, though it was clear that many had come a long distance. Nobody knew why they'd come, but his deputies were having to answer more and more calls regarding disturbed people.

Starting last autumn.

A few of these people were quiet, sitting in corners and gazing about with wide, searching eyes. Some wandered about muttering to themselves, oblivious to those around them. Some were aggressive, startling people with sudden declamations, or trying to engage them in animated conversation. They turned up in the oddest places: in shaded corners of parks, strolling on docks in harbors, at campsites, or even in yards. Chip's deputies had picked some up wandering aimlessly down empty country roads. Some were eerie, some were pathetic, some were frightening. But they all seemed to be searching, searching for something they couldn't describe, at a location they couldn't specify, for reasons they could not articulate.

That was disturbing enough in itself. What made it worse for Chip was that he was fairly sure he knew all those things, even if the Crazies didn't.

Chip was overdue and he knew it. It had been almost two weeks, and he'd intended to make it a weekly discipline. He forced himself up and grabbed his jacket and hat. One thing he prided himself on was never asking his people to do something he wouldn't do himself. Since he couldn't ask his people to do this, that meant the task fell to him.

"See you, Chief!" Audra called from the dispatch desk as he walked out.

"Back in an hour, Audra!" Chip called back. "I hope," he muttered under his breath. He navigated to M-53 and turned north, trying to clear his mind, trying not to imagine what might be waiting for him.

"Here we are," Chip muttered when he reached the intersection. Some old battered buildings, empty for decades and falling down. He ought to get after someone about those. But not today. Today he pulled into the empty lot on the corner, took out his phone, and thumbed it off. He clicked off his tablet while he was at it, as well as the laptop mounted beside the driver's seat. Then he brought up the car's trip odometer and zeroed it. Taking a deep breath, he turned east onto Nathan Road.

Chip drove slowly, watching the odometer tick up. That was the secret. Don't look at the road, don't look at the fields, don't even try to look at the driveways and mailboxes. Just keep your hands steady on the wheel and watch the odometer, only glancing far enough over the hood to ensure you didn't veer into a ditch. He knew the mileage exactly, and as long as he kept going straight for that exact distance, he'd reach his goal. But if he looked up and around before finishing the distance, all bets were off.

Unlike the Zanies, Chip knew exactly what he was looking for. He even knew exactly where it was. The problem was getting there.

Nobody lived within sight of the woods – Ray Hubbart had made certain of that. Ray hadn't wanted to risk anyone accidentally spotting something they shouldn't, so he'd acquired all residences within line of sight by methods fair and foul. Thus, when everything had come collapsing down last summer, nobody was living in the immediate vicinity. Had there been, Chip was sure that he would have heard of the phenomenon earlier. It was his deputies who first reported the bizarre occurrences. If they happened to be driving through that area, they'd inexplicably find themselves elsewhere, along some road or at some intersection that wasn't near where they'd been going. It was never far – no more than a couple of miles displacement – but it was disconcerting as hell. There was no rhyme or reason for it, and some of his deputies had been starting to wonder if they were losing their minds or other faculties until they'd started talking among themselves and realized they were all experiencing this. Chip considered it a sign of trust that they'd all come to him and presented these baffling events. Pooling their experiences, they identified a region about four miles square north of Bad Axe and a little east of M-53. It was within that area that the mental or sensory confusion seemed to occur.

It was Chip who'd noticed, though he hadn't mentioned, that roughly at the center of that region lay the woods. It was Chip who'd noticed that a common thread among all the reports was that his deputies had all been driving along a route that would have taken them past the woods.

Until, inexplicably, they weren't.

Chip had verified this personally. It had been simple enough – he knew right where the woods were, and just how to get there. He'd gone north, turned east on Nathan Road, driven about the proper distance – and suddenly found himself heading into Rapson from the north. That had been spooky, but he'd turned around and headed back, only to find himself crossing the New River east of Kinde. Disturbed but determined, he'd spent the next hour trying and retrying to drive to where he knew the woods lay, but never even coming within sight of it. It seemed for all the world like someone or something didn't want the woods to be found, and had means of deflecting anyone who came looking. How exactly that was done he'd never determined.

That would have been even more surprising had Chip not known a little about the night the woods had been invaded, and the slaves set free, and all the alarming and inexplicable phenomena which had accompanied those events. It was still mysterious and creepy, but given those origins, Chip could understand why the woods might want to remain hidden.

Except when they didn't. Which was even worse.

It had been Tom Stover who'd found the first one. He'd been driving in another direction, not even thinking about the weird zone, when he'd turned onto a road and found himself driving down the eastern edge of the woods. There, along the fence, he'd spotted the body. It was right up against the wire, and when Tom had approached it, the body had toppled over, revealing that the man's right arm had been stuck through the fence and had been chewed off nearly up to the shoulder.

Tom had guessed that the man had died by bleeding out through that wound. He'd clearly been dead for a while – a few days at least, possibly a week. Nobody recognized him, and the general opinion was that he was one of the Zanies. But that left the distressing question of what had happened. There was no sign of binding or forcing, and no indication that anyone else had been there. By all appearances, the man had sat down beside the fence and thrust his arm through.

That had been horrifying enough. It had been even more so for Chip, who alone among his staff had a glimmer of what might be lurking in the brush behind the fence. But then had come the next incident, which had been Angela, who'd been heading elsewhere and had abruptly found herself driving along Nathan Road right past the gate in the fence that enclosed the woods. She'd spotted a backpack on the ground by the gate, and from its distinctive design recognized it as having belonged to one of the Zanies she'd spoken with in Pigeon just a few days earlier. Here it was lying in a ditch just outside the woods, and from a scrap of clothing caught on a bush just inside the fence, Angela guessed that the guy had climbed over the fence and disappeared into the murk beyond. Then, about a week after that, a couple had come rushing into town bringing a guy they'd found wandering along M-53 with a bloody rag clutched against the stump of his left wrist. He'd been a Zany, too, and all they could get out of him was a phrase muttered over and over, "They accepted it."

After these incidents, Chip and his staff had started paying more attention to the Zanies, and began to notice a frightening thing: they vanished after a while. They'd show up, wander around for a bit, then not be seen any more. Everyone had been supposing they'd just gone back where they came from. With dismay, Chip began to suspect what was actually happening: that whatever drew them from their far-flung origins to Huron County was ultimately drawing them from the corners of Huron County to vanish into the shadowed woods.

That was when Chip had called in every political favor he was owed and pushed for a fence to be built around that half-section. It had taken some effort given the county's financial state, but he'd finally gotten the okay. The original plan had been a tall iron panel fence smack up against the wire all the way around the property, one with sides that had no handholds, and was too tall to scale. A firm from Bay City had picked up the bid and had started work promptly. It was then that Chip had learned that convoys of three or more vehicles were less susceptible to the confusing effect that seemed to emanate from the woods. It was also one of their supervisors, Mick Ryerson, who had taught Chip the odometer trick to get to the site reliably.

The effort on the panel fence had started well, but things had soon begun going wrong. Equipment had malfunctioned, and there was the ever-present frustration of finding the place. But more serious were the personnel problems: tempers had frayed and workers had balked about coming to the site. Though nobody had told them anything, the contractor's men soon came to loathe working right beside the dismal woods. They had complained about sleeping poorly and nervousness and other problems. The project had started to fall behind, and when Mick had tried to schedule night shifts to catch up, the workers had flat-out refused to work after dark no matter how much site lighting was burning.

In the end Mick had come into the county offices and apologetically backed out of the job. The firm paid the non-completion penalty and walked away, leaving a half-erected panel fence and an unsolved problem. In the end Chip had settled for having a local firm throw up a tall chain-link security fence right at the edge of the road. It wasn't ideal, because it could still be scaled, but it was something, and Chip had resolved to check it every week.

At this Chip had mostly succeeded. As autumn had turned to winter, the wandering Zanies had tapered off, probably because it was too cold to get around easily. Chip had used the odometer trick to find his way, and at least drove around the woods, sometimes walking, looking for irregularities or evidence of attempted breaches. He'd found none, but that wasn't conclusive. It wasn't all that difficult to scale a chain-link fence, even one with barbed wire at the top.

The odometer ticked off the last tenth of a mile, and Chip pulled to the side of the road. Only after he'd stepped out did he look around. Sure enough, it had worked again. There was the chain-link fence, with the south-facing gate. Chip walked over and inspected both of the industrial-strength locks that held the gate shut. They were secure, showing no sign of being forced or abused. Chip walked east along the fence to the corner, then turned north. Today, he decided, he was going to walk as much as he could, inspecting every foot. He strolled briskly, relishing the exercise, eyeing the fence and barbed wire. Everything seemed to be in order. He deliberately didn't look at the woods beyond. The sun bathed the land in pale spring light, only occasionally occluded by the cumulus clouds scudding by, driven by the light west wind. The shade under the bare trees seemed typical for the season, and Chip knew the branches would soon be budding. In so many ways, it looked just like another patch of woods.

Chip reached the northeast corner of the fencing and scanned along the north-facing stretch. It looked smooth and undisturbed, but above one of the panels some of the barbed wire looked like it had been bent. Chip walked over and examined it carefully. Only one of the strands of wire seemed to have been pulled or stretched just a little. There was nothing in the ditch beyond the chain-link, nor any indications that the wire fencing edging the woods had been breached or damaged. Chip walked along the rest of the north stretch of fence to the northwest corner, looking for more irregularities and finding none.

With a sigh Chip looked down the west-facing stretch of fencing. The drainage ditch ran right up to the edge of the woods, and the chain-link fence had been erected along the western bank of the ditch. The untended field to the west was thick with weeds and scrub. It would be a prime place for somebody to hide if they intended to try scaling the fence. He would have to make arrangements to have that mowed, if he could find somebody willing to take the job.

With a heavy heart Chip headed back toward his car. His phone was back there, and he was sure he'd been gone nearly an hour, and he didn't want Audra worrying. He pondered the problem as he strode down the east-facing stretch of fence. A tall chain-link may look strong and intimidating, but to anyone with a pair of bolt cutters it may as well be made of twine. The weather was starting to turn, and given the troubles they'd had last autumn, he dreaded what the warm months of spring would bring. Chip had to figure out what to do about this, something beyond throwing up taller, stronger fences. He couldn't shake the impression that whatever haunted the woods wasn't the sort of thing that could be contained by fences, that even now something more powerful was binding it, at least for the time being. But that barrier was only so strong, and whatever lurked in those shadows seemed to be growing in potency by the day.

Chip dreaded to think what might happen if those bindings were ever broken.

Mission Field

It turned out to be closer to three weeks before the men could find a time to gather to discuss the next set of pages sent up by the translation team. Dr. Harris reserved a small conference room at the university and ordered in pizza, which Gerald appreciated, since in his opinion there were no good sources for pizza on the Canadian side. As they were settling down with their slices, Gerald handed around the additional pages for Dr. Harris and Pete to slip into their binders.

"So," Gerald began, flipping to the newest page. "This next set of pages is fairly mundane, though valuable to students of the period. Now that he's been dispatched on a mission of his own, Fr. Thomas seems determined to try keeping more regular records of his progress. For a while he makes an entry every day, even if there isn't much to say. See here on page 22 – *Rowed from before dawn until sundown today. Very sore, cold from spray. Offering it up for salvation of souls.* He records some interactions with Jesuit colleagues, which will excite some historians, since there is precious little recorded about St. Isaac Jogues when he was in the field.

"They arrive at the Sault, and Fr. Thomas isn't very impressed, because it wasn't very impressive. Though it was beginning to be a major trading center, it hadn't yet been built up in any way. I think that Fr. Thomas was expecting at least a couple of buildings. To find forest that ran down to the water's edge, with a few wigwams scattered among the clearings, must have been disappointing. I'm guessing it reminded him starkly of just how raw his mission territory was. He spends a couple of pages thanking God for this chance to minister to the heathens – maybe that was also to remind himself why he was there.

"When they arrived at the Sault, they were taken in by a *métis* named Jean LaPenseé, who was known to Fr. Pijart. He made room for the three Jesuits in his home, though Fr. Thomas was a bit nervous about that, since it meant living in close proximity to a woman: Jean's Ojibwa wife Nikikouet."

"Was that because she was a woman, or because she was First Nation?" Dr. Harris asked.

"Neither," Gerald explained. "It was because of the irregularity of the marriage. Jean and Nikikouet were married *à la façon du pays* - 'in the custom of the country'. In the modern idiom, Nikikouet was Jean's common-law wife, which made their children, to European understanding, bastards. Fr. Thomas seems surprised at how casually his fellow priests take this arrangement – but then, they'd had much more field experience.

"The household proved to be critical to the missionaries. Only Jean spoke both French and Ojibwe, though Nikikouet had learned some French. Fr. Raymbault spoke Algonquin, which would be like a different dialect, and Fr. Thomas tried to learn from him. But once Fr. Raymbault and Fr. Jogues departed, it was just Fr. Thomas, Jean, and his wife – and Jean often departed, leaving Fr. Thomas with Nikikouet. She was probably less disturbed by this than he was, but when he requested the tribe find or make a wigwam for him, they accommodated his request. He had hopes of eventually making his wigwam into a chapel."

"How often was Jean gone?" Pete asked.

"Often enough, sometimes for weeks at a time. This left Fr. Thomas with only Nikikouet to talk to. From what I know of Anishinaabek culture of that time, it probably didn't enhance Fr. Thomas's prestige to be seen primarily in the company of a woman. He couldn't trap or hunt or paddle a canoe, and though he might be able to fish or harvest, that was woman's work."

"Could Jean have taken him along when he left?" Pete asked.

"That would have removed Fr. Thomas from the village too often, and he was there to convert the village," Gerald replied. "Besides, by his understanding, he was a worker of the mind and the soul. To labor with his hands would have been a distraction.

"But that's guesswork on our part. What we know from the journal is that he tried to be diligent in his devotional practices, such as praying his Breviary and saying Mass. He tried to expand his Ojibwe vocabulary, and to help Nikikouet improve her French. He eventually learned enough to try to speak to the other villagers, if he could get them to converse. Their brusqueness and disinterest mystified him. I'm guessing that they couldn't figure out what kind of man he was, and thus could find no good reason to speak with him.

"He got a few of them interested in some of his European gear, such as his folding knife and his pen. It seems he managed to convey to some of them the purpose of his writing – to represent the words that they spoke in marks on the page. He is amazed how blasé they are about this capability. Of course, their indifference makes sense to us – the Anishinaabek culture learned and remembered via oral communication, so they could not yet grasp the massive impact that written transmission of knowledge would have."

"Does he record anything about their way of life? Their manners and customs?" Dr. Harris asked.

"Not in the way we moderns wish he had," Gerald said. "There are a couple of reasons for that. First, he's writing a journal to record his personal experiences, and so he can report his progress to his superiors. He's only going to record matters germane to those two goals. But also, at that point in history the idea of studying a social order was alien. They didn't think like that. Fr. Thomas knew that he was French and that these people were Ojibwa, but he had come to live in their midst and become like them in order to preach the Gospel to them. The idea of standing apart from them to examine them and their ways, in the manner that you might study livestock, would never occur to him. That mindset had yet to rise in Europe. Thus the anthropologists will have to be content with his occasional descriptions of how the fish traps were set in the river, and such minor things."

"Does that make the journal less valuable?" Pete asked.

"Not really, at least to people who study such things," Gerald replied. "Fr. Thomas was trying to establish a static mission, so he viewed everything through the lens of what was important to that. How many Masses were said, how many conversations held, how many children baptized, et cetera. Itinerant missionaries would record different things, more of interest to moderns – tribes contacted, geography and terrain, and so forth. As you know, Marquette was a great exploring missionary who kept careful records. But even this was not to satisfy the curiosity of students, but so that other missionaries could follow him and establish the kinds of outposts that Fr. Thomas was building at the Sault." Gerald turned a few more pages, glancing over them.

"Seems like mundane reading through here," Dr. Harris noted as he skimmed the pages. "He has a lot to say about the insects."

"Wouldn't you?" Gerald grinned. "Ah, here he records another conversation with Jean and Nikikouet after dinner one evening. Poor Fr. Thomas – Jean is his most likely conversion prospect, and the guy isn't the least bit interested. Nikikouet is following the conversation, though – partly to improve her French, I'm sure, but also because she's interested. And – aha!" Gerald turned a page and pointed. "We see some fruit of his efforts, though not quite what he'd hoped. Jean left on a journey, and about two days later Nikikouet approached Fr. Thomas asking about his god and how to follow him. Apparently, a god who took equal interest in men and women was outside her experience."

"Well, that's something, right?" Pete asked.

"It is, but by now Fr. Thomas has learned enough of the tribal culture to appreciate the delicacy of the situation. The Christian God is a god of men and women alike, but this is alien thinking to the Ojibwa, and probably all the Anishinaabe. If the first Ojibwe follower of this god is a woman, he risks creating the perception that Jesus is a hearth deity, a god of lesser things. This would repel the men. But he cannot deny the Gospel to anyone, and after so much frustration he cannot be choosy about his converts." Gerald muttered as he turned the page. "Seems her primary interest centers around eating the flesh and drinking the blood of the god. That sounds to her like powerful magic, and she wants that for herself and for her children."

"Wait – 'eating the flesh of the god'?" Pete asked. "What does that mean?"

Gerald looked up at the men, mystified in turn. "You know – the Eucharist. Part of the Mass." Seeing their continued befuddlement, he leaned back in his chair. "Don't either of you know anything about Christian teaching? Eucharistic theology?"

"I...well, went to a class once," Dr. Harris offered weakly.

"Some of my family was Catholic," Pete said. "I think my Mom was baptized, but we never practiced."

Gerald leaned back farther with a look of amazement. "Let me savor the irony of this for a moment. Here am I, an aboriginal, explaining this to a couple of Europeans? All right: in Christian theology – at least Catholic and Orthodox, I don't know about all the Protestants – the bread and wine offered at the Mass become the Body and Blood of Jesus Christ. Then they eat and drink that, thereby acquiring divine life."

"Really?" Dr. Harris asked skeptically. "I knew about the bread and wine, but they believe it actually becomes the flesh and blood of God, so they can eat it?"

"Yes. I remember getting into a discussion with a theology student and having this carefully explained," Gerald said. "Come to think of it, he was a Jesuit."

"But, how can – it's just bread and wine. Do they believe it gets...transformed somehow?" Dr. Harris asked.

"No. Trans*formed* is precisely what it isn't. It retains the same form, the same outward appearances. What changes is the substance, the essential nature of the thing. It's so distinctive that they had to coin a word to describe it: tran*substantiated*."

"So...it gets changed at the molecular level, or something?" Dr. Harris asked.

Gerald smiled and shook his head. "The world view in which you have been trained hinders you from grasping the nuances here. Even molecules are an expression of form, of externals. In this case, the externals don't change, but the essence does. Let me give an example by opposite: in our legends, Nanabozho sometimes take the form of *Mizabooz*, the Great Hare. When he does, we say he is a hare to the tips of his ears – or as you would say, to his DNA – yet in essence he remains Nanabozho. This would be a change in form – externals – while the substance remains the same. In the Eucharist, the inverse happens: the externals remains the same, but the essence changes into the body and blood of the god."

"I…it's just…" Dr. Harris stumbled.

"Look, I'm not asking you to understand it, or to believe it. I'm just saying that's what Catholics believe, and that's what Fr. Thomas would have explained to Jean and Nikikouet. I can see why that would appeal to her. Even to touch a god would be a tremendous thing; to eat the god's very flesh and drink his blood – that would impart unspeakable power," Gerald said.

Dr. Harris scoffed. "I can't believe…bread and wine? Surely she'd be able to see –"

"You think like a modern rationalist materialist, Doctor," Gerald interrupted curtly. "To you, the appearance of a thing exhausts its meaning. Nikikouet was under no such constraint. She, along with most other people throughout history, saw reality as multilayered, with visible and invisible realities interpenetrating. That a rite could be performed over some things, and they would retain their outward appearance while their inner essence completely changed – well, she would not find that unbelievable. To her, the only questions were how to obtain this power, and what would it do for her and her family? That was why she came to Fr. Thomas to get answers."

"Even so, it sounds so…crude, even gruesome," Dr. Harris said with distaste.

"Your sentiments reflect a particular aesthetic viewpoint," Gerald replied. "Nikikouet and her people would have had a different outlook. To them, even dining at the table of the gods and eating their food would have been an unspeakable privilege. That theme enters into some of our tribal legends, as well as the myths of many other people, such as the Greeks and Egyptians. But to eat the god himself, with all the power and essential unity that would bring, would have seemed too good to be true.

"Fortunately, the matter at hand isn't what any of us in this room believe, but what Fr. Thomas believed, and what Nikikouet was seeking when she approached him. By his account, she wanted further explanation of the Eucharist, which he provided. She asked if this was only for Frenchmen, and he explained that no, it was for all people, and that the French had gotten it from others. She asked if it was for men only, or for men, women, and children. She was glad to hear that even children could partake, if they were old enough to understand, and had been baptized and properly instructed. Fr. Thomas speculates that concern for her children was a major motivation."

"So this Eucharist was the biggest draw for her?" Pete asked.

"Fr. Thomas seems to think so. It looks like he told her to discuss it with Jean. Her husband could not forbid her to receive baptism, but she could not become Christian without his knowledge. Perhaps he was hoping that Jean would accompany her – and possibly give him a chance to bless their marriage.

"That's as far as this translation set goes. Olivia says she's got more volunteers working on the project, and hopes to have the next set of pages to me by the end of next week. Should we plan on that?" Gerald concluded. All agreed, and the meeting broke up.

Hunger

The expense denial which Jason had forwarded to Cynthia with his terse comment was returned with an even more terse response: "Cleared". Jason figured that would have Whitman shredding coffee cups in frustration. The authorization for the RA drone came through as well, so he connected the RA controllers with the aerial surveillance staff at Selfridge so they could coordinate schedules and downloads.

After inspecting some rental units in Sandusky, Jason had Ethan sign a lease on a house that was just a couple of blocks from the courthouse in the center of town. This meant Jason was finally able to shift out of the tiny hotel room. It hadn't been that bad – the bed had been comfortable, and the room had been scrupulously clean, but it was far too small. As he was heading for the desk with his bags, he passed by Allie in the hall.

"Mr. Pelletier?" she called after him.

"Yes, Allie?"

"I heard you were leaving us," she said, fishing in her pocket for something. "I just wanted to say thank you, that it was a pleasure having you with us, and I hope you come back and stay with us again someday." With that she presented him with a little greeting card. It was one of the sentimental types that usually set Jason's teeth on edge, with a rainbow and a smiling butterfly on the front, but inside was scrawled, "From Allie Vonn and the whole staff, thank you and God bless."

Jason smiled in spite of himself. "Thanks, Allie. It's been good. If I'm staying in the area again, I sure will stay here. But I won't be far, just up in Sandusky. I may drop in for a visit once in a while."

"That'd be great, Mr. Pelletier." Allie's smile was so genuine that Jason almost resolved to do just that.

The house in Sandusky was small, but had the main feature for which Jason had been looking: a large living room with an entirely blank wall. Unfortunately, there was also a large bay window in one of the walls, but it faced north, so there wouldn't be any direct sunlight pouring in.

"Ethan, this is great," Jason said as he walked around the living room. "We can set up all the equipment on this end and project onto that wall. You're doing something about this bay window, right?"

"Heavy blinds are on order," Ethan assured him. "The equipment you ordered is due day after tomorrow. The communications tech will be here tomorrow to rig the connections. Living space is back here – kitchen, dining room, bathroom, bedroom. Sorry it's all so small, but it's the closest I could get to your specs."

"Don't worry, you've done well," Jason replied. "The front room is the main thing. I'll be able to plan my whole agenda from there. How did you ever find such a suitable house for rent?"

"Actually, it wasn't – it was for sale. But it was vacant, so I convinced the realtor to talk the owners into renting it while it remained unsold."

"Great, but what if they want to do some showings, or to sell the place, while we're still here?"

"The real estate market is very slow right now, so I don't expect that," Ethan explained. "Besides, I slipped the realtor a few hundred to hold off showing the place as long as we're renting. At worst, we can pull rank and invoke domestic terror privilege."

"You think of everything. Where'd you get the few hundred?"

"Buried in the expense submission."

While awaiting the communications lines and equipment, Jason set up the workstations in the living room and got crunching on what he'd come to call his "side project" – the knotty HHS situation. That kept him occupied until all the equipment arrived, shortly followed by the local workman to hang the darkening blinds in the living room. Now Jason had a suitably equipped base for analysis and planning. Collins had already reported that he had some preliminary results from the RA image analysis, so Jason scheduled him to come up early the next week. He also had Ethan contact Sanderson and Harris to bring whatever they had.

The following Monday, Collins was standing in the living room of the Sandusky control center, as Jason had come to think of it, beside a large projection of a standard map of the region, over which was superimposed a network of thin blue lines connecting occasional blue blotches with fuzzy edges.

"We don't yet have a large volume of sample imagery, so this is very preliminary," Collins warned. "It should get firmer as we get more image hours. The NSA analysis software scans the raw images for the sorts of things we've told it to look for, then calculates probability clouds that reflect how likely it was that the monitored activity happened at any given place."

"So that's why the blobs are fuzzy?" Jason asked. "They reflect probability clouds?"

"Exactly. The software was told to look for parties traveling along non-standard routes. Based on the images, it determined that somebody's travels ended somewhere in here," Collins tapped a blob. "The denser and brighter the blob, the more probable the monitored event happened here. Denser toward the middle, more feathery toward the edge, but likely somewhere in there."

"And the lines? They indicate travel routes?"

"Right. The lines are also probability clouds; they're just very thin so they look like lines. Some are very definite, though, like this line here – nice and clean along this stretch, which runs along the edge of a right-of-way for these high-voltage transmission towers. When it ducks through these woods, it gets blurrier, because the images can't track the precise path the traveler used. On the other side it gets firmer again as it passes through this field."

"And this is imagery of parties actually using these trails, right?" Jason asked. "Not just analysis of what look like trails?"

"Oh, yes – that's one reason the analytical output is so thin. Somebody is using these trails and our high-level asset is spotting them. But a few days of imaging doesn't give us much to work with. As more time goes by, there will be more activity spotted, and these probability clouds will grow firmer."

"Could these be recreational users?" Jason asked.

"There are some," Collins explained, "but recreational users exhibit different movement patterns. Their routes tend to start at trailheads or residences, run around semi-randomly, and then return to the point of origin – a predictable out-and-back pattern. These other ones, though, indicate a source-destination pattern, so that's where we're focusing."

"Also, boss, it's early in the season for much recreational four-wheeling and dirt biking," Ethan chipped in. "The die-hards will be out there, but it's still too cold and wet for most riders. Give it a few weeks."

"That just makes these mysterious transients even more conspicuous," Jason pointed out. "Since recreational riders are uncommon this time of year, that makes it more likely that those who are out will be some of our suspect travelers. But here's what I can't figure," he walked to the projection and pointed to one of the blue probability lines. "This stretch has no cover, so it's useless for hiding. Why go to all this trouble when the whole area is laced with a network of roads? Even though most of them are dirt, they're still better than a trail through the woods."

"You're talking about undocumented people, right?" Ethan said. "Undocumented means no license, no passport, no financial cards, nothing. Not only can they not drive, they can't risk being caught in a car. You're right, it's got to be a big hassle not to use the roads. But there are people doing just that, so they must figure that the lower risk justifies the extra trouble."

"But is it lower risk? I'd think that dirt bikes and ATVs would be more conspicuous than cars," Jason pointed out.

"Maybe where you're from, but not here," Collins replied. "In this area they're part of the landscape. Besides, the region is so sparsely populated that riders could travel these trails for hours and not be spotted by anyone. The variations in terrain also help. The way the trails duck through woods every so often makes it that much harder to track those who use them."

"Will that be a problem?" Jason asked. "Especially as the trees leaf out, will these travelers be harder to track?"

"For a car or other low-level asset, yes," Collins confirmed. "Concealing cover would make it very hard to trace them. But for ultra-high level assets like we have now, we'll be able to track them wherever they break cover, which they have to do relatively often. There are very few large high-cover areas in the region. Mostly it's a patchwork of woods, meadows, and fields."

"So they can run, but they can't completely hide," Jason added.

"Right. And the more hours of imagery we have, the finer these projections become. What you're seeing today is only the beginning."

"Great. Thank you, Major Collins. It seems that the aerial axis of this investigation is looking productive already, with promise of more to come. How about our ground assault? Agents Sanderson and Harris? Did your review turn up anything?"

"Not much at all," Sanderson shook his head. "We searched back through our files for any hint of vanishing or hidden people, and came up empty. We talked to a lot of people about a lot of crazy stuff, but never heard anything about missing people. There was only one case that came even close."

"What was that?"

Sanderson glanced at Harris then slowly handed Jason a file folder. "It was an odd case that turned up simply because it hit a couple of the criteria we'd set. A couple had several kids taken from them by CPS, then the kids vanish, then the couple vanishes. Details are in there."

Jason flipped through the documents in the folder. "This is in the electronic files you sent me, right?"

"Yes, but that's got the printouts, with all our notes and jottings," Sanderson explained. "We never did figure it out, or find the family, but since it didn't have any connections to our main line of investigation, we just dropped it."

"But...wait," Jason said, scanning the paperwork. "These kids were at a couple of Wondercare homes. And they were never recovered?"

"Nope, nor were the parents," Sanderson confirmed.

"Well...well," Jason muttered as he flipped the papers and thought furiously.

"Is that important?" Harris asked.

"Maybe not," Jason said. "But it is the closest thing to a connection between mysteriously vanishing people and the human trafficking network. I wonder if that network is quite as dead as we thought. I want you to recheck this thread and see if you can turn up anything new."

Sanderson and Harris looked at each other for a long moment. Harris seemed about to speak, but Sanderson shook his head slightly. "We'll take care of it," Sanderson said.

"Good," Jason replied. As he was closing the folder to hand it back, a note dropped out onto the table. He picked it up to slip it back in the folder, but as he did so he saw that it was an address. The only part of the writing he could make out clearly was "Nathan Road". A chill shot through him, but he closed the folder and handed it back to Sanderson.

The meeting concluded and everyone headed back to their offices. Jason halted Ethan on his way out the door.

"Special job for you," Jason explained as he pulled out a sheet of paper. "You proved such a sharp real estate operator that I'm turning you loose on some serious acquisitions."

"Oh?"

"Yes. The precise specs are on this sheet, but I want you to go hunting for plots of land."

"Plots of land?"

"Yes. Vacant, not on main roads but not too far off them, about five acres, cleared and packed hard enough to be used for temporary buildings and parking. The plots should have electricity available, but be a few miles from towns or villages. Got that?"

Ethan still looked startled. "Plots of land?"

"Yes. I've shaded the general areas on the map where I want you to look. The details are on the sheet, including the purchase authorization codes."

Ethan stared at the paper and then at Jason. "Seriously. Five acre plots in what, four locations around the Thumb?"

"Seriously," Jason assured him.

"You going to tell me why?"

"Not yet. All in good time," Jason replied.

"Okay," Ethan shrugged as he tucked the paper away. "Anything else?"

"Yes. Book me a flight to D.C. on Thursday morning."

"All right. Out of where?"

"What's the closest airport?"

"Flint."

"Flint, then. In D.C. by 10 a.m."

"Returning…Sunday night? Monday morning?"

"Friday evening," Jason said. "If I'm successful, I'll have plenty of work for the weekend."

The D.C. visit was mostly to confer with HHS people, if Jason could set up the appointments in time, but he wanted to drop in and report to Cynthia. This meant he needed something to report, and his actual progress on the blast investigation so far was insignificant. The surveillance held promise, and he just might have a tenuous connection between the hidden people and the human trafficking network, but he wanted more. It was all still threads: waving, disconnected threads too insubstantial to support anything and not yet weaving into a discernable pattern. He knew proof was too much to ask for at this point, but he needed more than just vague speculation. That meant he needed to make one more appointment before he flew out, though he doubted the party would be happy to see him.

*   *   *

"Mr. Pelletier, how good to see you," Chip Keller stood and extended his hand. "How may I help you?"

"First, I'm hoping you can answer a few questions about the Wondercare operation," Jason watched the sheriff's face for any tension or caution, but all he saw was heavy sadness.

"That was a bad business from start to finish. All the investigative and court records are open, but I'll answer anything I can."

"Thank you. I'm aware of the basics, but one thing has intrigued me: when the children were found, they spoke not only of human trafficking through the foster care network, but also of a factory or facility where they'd been forced to work. But looking at the records, the prosecution focused exclusively on the foster care network. Why was there never any serious investigation into the alleged facility? Does anyone know where it might be?"

"Well," Chip sighed. "That would be a better question for the prosecutors than for me, but I can tell you what I've heard. The foster care abuse caused so much greater public outcry that there was more immediate payback for the prosecutors to pursue that. Also, the forced labor facility was only ever a rumor, so the prosecutors initially focused on the avenue that had the clearest evidence. Keep in mind that the whole matter broke less than a year ago, and the investigation is still ongoing and could last for years. It may be that they simply haven't gotten around to that yet."

"I see," Jason replied. "That's reasonable for the prosecutors, but how about you? Have you seen or heard anything about a forced labor facility?"

There was just the slightest flicker in the sheriff's eyes, the least moment of hesitation, before he responded in very careful phrases.

"I've never seen any such facility in Huron County. The only official word I have is what testimony was gathered from the children who escaped the foster care network."

"You spoke last time of picking up clues to the syndicate's existence, to the point of alerting your deputies. What were those clues?"

"That had to do with what seemed to be unusual trucks on the county roads. We were never able to connect that to anything illegal. Of course, I lost my job shortly after that," Chip explained.

"I see. So everything you've heard about a forced labor facility has been rumor and speculation?"

"That's right," Chip affirmed. "In all my tenure as sheriff, I've heard nothing official."

"All right," Jason said, and pulled a sheet of paper from his folder. "On the topic of vanishing or hidden people, I have here some details on a family who got caught in the Wondercare confusion. Their children were taken by CPS under suspicion of maltreatment. When the Wondercare scandal broke, theirs were among the children missing. But when the agents went to look for the parents, they had vanished without a trace. They're missing to this day. The details and timeline are on that sheet."

"Perhaps in the confusion they were able to reclaim their children from the Wondercare homes and high-tailed it lest they be taken again," Chip suggested, looking over the paper.

"I considered that, but you'll notice from the time line that the parents were found to be missing several days before the Wondercare affair broke. The agents speculate that they'd probably been gone for at least a week prior to that. Doesn't that seem strange to you? Parents going missing while their children are in probate custody?"

"It does," Chip admitted. "But that address is in St. Clair County. Even the Wondercare offices were in Port Huron. Why are you asking me about this? It's Tim Neal you want."

"I'll be asking him, too, because this is the closest thing I have to a firm clue to a reputed network of hidden parties that could be engaged in, or benefit from, illicit activities. Have you heard any word of this or any other family that might be living in hiding for any reason?"

Chip smiled. "Mr. Pelletier, if they're hiding from the authorities, then we'd be the last people to know, wouldn't we? Especially if they went missing down in St. Clair County."

"Well, another connection, admittedly tenuous, is that though the Wondercare offices were in Port Huron, the entire operation was controlled from here in Huron County. Which brings up another question I had: I notice in the fallout of the Wondercare exposure, many family members were identified as "Missing, Presumed Dead", including the reputed head of the family, Ray Hubbart. Who made the judgment that he was 'presumed dead'?"

"That was me," Chip admitted.

"If I may ask, upon what evidence did you base that conclusion?"

"The last evidence of his presence strongly indicated that he'd taken his own life."

"But no body was ever found?"

"No," Chip replied. "That's why he's recorded as 'missing'."

"But *presumed* dead, which is a disincentive for further investigation of his whereabouts. Might a man of such resources and sophistication have faked his own death, or left a false trail, so he could slip away, as some Wondercare executives attempted?" Jason asked.

"Mr. Pelletier, the state attorney general sat in that very chair and asked that very question. I'll give you the same answer I gave him: of course, we can't be one hundred percent certain, but based on the reports of those who saw him last, and the disposition of his personal effects, and certain physical evidence, our best guess is that he is missing because he is dead. We and several agencies across the state – and the FBI, for that matter – are on alert for any sign of Ray Hubbart turning up anywhere."

"Very well," Jason replied. He'd let that rest for now. "I only have one more question, which is more of a request. I understand that one of the Wondercare executives is still in your custody? Andrea Stevens?"

"Yes, she is. Her mother was moved to a state prison a couple of months ago, but she's still here."

"May I meet with her to ask her a couple of questions?"

Chip tapped the desktop thoughtfully before continuing. "Officially or unofficially?"

"I beg your pardon?"

"An official visit would be to gather testimony, and we'd have to summon her lawyer and notify the court and the prosecutor and all. But any inmate can receive visitors for personal reasons. Those conversations are unofficial, and information gathered in them cannot be used as evidence. They also depend on the inmate's preference – they don't have to receive a visitor."

"Oh. Unofficial, then – I'm not gathering evidence, just seeking to understand some things."

"All right," Chip replied. "But understand, Mr. Pelletier, the only reason Andrea Stevens is still with us, and not further along in the criminal justice process, is that there are some questions about her mental stability. She's currently undergoing a series of psychiatric evaluations to determine her competence to stand trial. She may not be able to tell you anything of interest, and what she does say may not be reliable."

"I understand, Sheriff."

Chip summoned a deputy who escorted Jason down to the visiting room, which fortunately was empty. Jason sat in a booth, and within ten minutes a woman was brought in and seated on the other side of the thick Plexiglas. Her blond hair was stringy and her face was slightly puffy. She glanced at him, but didn't hold his gaze, instead eyeing the walls of the booth and her own hands.

"Andrea Stevens?" Jason asked.

"Yeah," the woman admitted.

"I'm Jason Pelletier, and I'm from the government. I'd like to ask you a few questions."

"About the homes? Do you want to know about the homes?" the woman asked nervously, giving him a sharp glance before looking away.

"No," Jason assured her. "Not about the homes at all."

"About the factory, then? Do you want to know about the factory?"

Jason's attention leapt, but he forced himself to answer calmly.

"Well, maybe about the factory. What do you know about the factory?"

Andrea looked at him with mournful eyes. "Nothing."

"Nothing?" Jason asked smoothly, trying to hide his disappointment.

"No," Andrea shook her head sadly. "That was Nick. That was always Nick. That's all we knew. Pa kept it all separate. We weren't allowed to talk. That was Nick, and Caleb, and Eli, and Charity. Maybe others, I don't know. We weren't allowed to talk."

"Do you have any idea where the factory was located?" Jason asked tentatively.

"No, dammit! I just told you we weren't allowed to talk!" Angela exploded with unexpected ferocity, slamming her fist on the desk and glaring at him, then subsiding into quiet brooding just as quickly. "Not that it matters now. It's gone now, all gone."

"Gone? Where did it go?" Jason asked.

"Gobbled up. All gobbled up now," Andrea replied cryptically. "The water gobbled some, Ethan and Owen and…no, not four, only three, I guess. That's weird, I thought it was four, but I guess it was only three. I wonder why…" She trailed off into muttering.

"'Gobbled up'?" Jason prodded gently.

"The earth gobbled the rest," Andrea assured him solemnly. "All the rest. Nick and Caleb and Kevin and Eli and Pa and all. All gone, all gobbled."

"Pa, you said?" Jason asked, trying to make sense of this rambling. "Do you know what happened to Pa?"

"Gobbled, I said, gobbled all up," Andrea insisted. Then she leaned forward and fixed Jason with a piercing gaze. "Do you know what I think?" she asked in a conspiratorial whisper.

"What?" Jason asked, a little unnerved.

"I think Charlie did it." The whisper was barely audible, and the eyes flicked around nervously.

"Charlie? Who's Charlie?"

"You know – Charlie," Andrea replied scornfully. "How could you not know Charlie? I think he was the one who did it." She was whispering again, leaning very close to the glass.

"Did what?" Jason pressed, utterly lost by this.

"The earth. The gobbling earth. The hungry, gobbling earth," Andrea muttered vaguely. "Hungry earth, earthy hunger." She looked up sharply. "You can still hear it, you know."

"Hear it?" Jason asked.

"Yes, you can hear it if you're quiet and listen. I do, late at night when everything's quiet. It's not far, you know, not far at all."

"What's not far? The factory?"

"The hunger. The roaring, howling, crunching hunger. It has tasted, and it wants more. And more and more. Can't you hear it? Listen!"

The room fell silent as Andrea cocked her head slightly, her eyes scanning the upper corners of the room. The abrupt stillness pressed in on Jason's ears, and he found himself listening for something despite himself. After about thirty seconds of pregnant silence, he found himself feeling increasingly foolish and uncomfortable, though Andrea was still listening expectantly.

"Ms. Stevens, if we could –" Jason finally began.

"Hush!" Andrea silenced him with an urgent wave of her hands, continuing her expectant scan of the ceiling. After another half a minute, Jason concluded that he was wasting his time and began to gather his things.

"Ms. Stevens, thank you –" he began, but was interrupted by her abruptly standing and looking at him disdainfully, as if she had just noticed him.

"Who are you?" Andrea asked with scorn, then turned and walked away.

Startled and embarrassed, Jason picked up his gear and accompanied his escort to the door.

*   *   *

Chip Keller's phone buzzed, and he picked it up unthinkingly.

"Yes?"

"He's gone, Chief."

"Thanks, Bea." Chip hung up and tapped the desk some more. He wasn't certain what this Fed was really after, but it was clear that he suspected something. Damn. They should have put more forethought into how they documented that mess last summer. They should have considered the follow-through more carefully.

But everyone had been anxious to get it tied up, to put it behind them, especially after Andy's suicide. Chip had rushed the paperwork, leaving plenty of room for smart operators to come in behind and spot the discrepancies. And Jason Pelletier was beyond question a smart operator. But what the hell was he after?

Chip stood up and grabbed his jacket. Even if he didn't understand why, the fact that the Feds were asking these kinds of questions would matter to certain parties he knew. Parties it would be best not to contact by phone.

Chip had some visits to make.

*   *   *

In his car outside, Jason thought matters over as he tried to settle himself from that unnerving interview. Something was going on here. The carefully worded responses the sheriff had fed him were crafted as much to conceal as to reveal, or Jason's instincts failed him. But what was being hidden? Jason had plenty of suspicions but not a scrap of hard evidence. Just how interconnected were all these mysteries? How far did the rot spread? And what, if anything, did the ravings of Andrea Stevens mean? Under other circumstances Jason would have dismissed them entirely, but for the fact that he'd personally experienced some very unnerving experiences on this investigation – experiences that had happened not too far from here, for that matter.

Jason started the car and headed back to Sandusky. He had some preparations to make before his flight to D.C.

*   *   *

Gerald Fitzgerald looked up from his workstation as his admin walked into his office holding a letter and an envelope and looking puzzled.

"Whatcha got, Kelley?"

"Odd one, Mr. Fitz," Kelley handed him both the paper and the envelope, which had been hand-addressed with no return address, and bore a standard first-class stamp. He braced himself – lawyers got all kinds of screwball things in the mail, including threats. He looked at the paper.

On a plain piece of copier stock were scrawled three numbers, the phrase "Bay 3" and a little sticker with the universal circle with a red slash through the icon of a phone. The first number was 43 followed by several digits to the right of the decimal, and the other was an 82 followed by several digits as well. Fitz looked at these for a moment, then brought up the mapping application on his workstation and keyed in the two numbers. Ah – that made sense of the "Bay 3" comment. He gazed in mystification at the third number for a moment, then nodded and pulled up his calendar. Sure enough, a Julian date with a 24-hour time.

"Thanks, Kelley," Fitz said, handing back the papers. "Shred these, please."

As Kelley went back to handling the day's mail, Fitz pondered the cryptic message. Somebody wanted to talk to him, in person, under very private circumstances. But there was no indication of who or why. Risky? Perhaps, but whoever had sent that note had known how to take precautions. That probably meant someone who might not be on their side, but at least wasn't hostile, and who urgently wanted to talk under secure conditions.

Looked like Fitz had an early start tomorrow morning.

*   *   *

Well before dawn the next day, Fitz pulled his car into the parking lot of one of the local big-box stores that was open 24 hours. Leaving everything but a shopping bag, he went into the store and ducked into the restroom. There he changed his jacket for the one in the bag and donned the hat that went with it. Walking across the store, he went out a different exit, got into a different car, and drove away. He didn't have far to drive – the spot designated by the latitude and longitude was a self-serve car wash less than a mile from his office. As expected, it was empty at 4:30 on a frosty March morning. The fronts of the bays faced the street while the backs faced the woods behind the car wash. Fitz pulled into Bay 3 and turned off the car. Shortly thereafter the washing wand, which hung on the wall, clicked on and began filling the rear of the bay with thick white mist. Only when the bay had been sufficiently occluded did the passenger door open and someone sit down beside Fitz.

"Well, well," Fitz said as he raised an eyebrow. "Agent Sanderson. Not our usual meeting venue."

"Were you expecting me, Counselor?" Sanderson asked.

"I was expecting someone cautious and clever, and you meet both qualifications," Fitz replied. "I'm presuming you didn't ask me to this unusual place at this unusual hour simply to get coffee?"

"No. I wanted to let you know that D.C. has sent up a new investigator. His name is Jason Pelletier, and he's been assigned to solve the Imlay City blast. He's got all kinds of authority, apparently unlimited funding, and is operating independent of any agency hierarchy in the area."

"That's intriguing, Agent Sanderson, but how does it affect me?"

"Mr. Pelletier has his sights set higher than just solving the blast. He seems convinced that it was the work of a domestic terror organization, one that's running a clandestine network in the area dedicated to hiding people. He suspects this network of illegal operations, and seems to be trying to connect it to that human trafficking operation that was exposed last year. He's using some very sophisticated assets to track off-road movement of people along the trails that run through fields and woods throughout the area. He is even asking about that family you were working with last year, the one who had their kids taken by CPS."

"The Schaeffers?"

"That's them," Sanderson confirmed. "He thought it suspicious that they'd vanish so completely. That's only one thing. He's doing a lot more, only some of which we know about. He's intelligent, determined, and has a big toolbox. He won't settle for going home empty-handed."

"I see," Fitz said pensively.

"I'm not saying this has anything to do with you, because I know as that a lawyer you have to stay within the law," Sanderson continued. Fitz smiled but did not interrupt. "But if, say, you knew somebody who knew somebody who might be involved in hiding people for any reason, you might want to pass the word that scrutiny is going to be getting tighter."

"I...see," Fitz said again after a moment's pause. "Thank you for thinking of me, Agent Sanderson. I'll put some thought into what you've told me. Is there anything else I should know?"

"Not that I'm aware of just now. If anything comes up, I'll try to contact you, but meeting is already trickier than it was. Everything is being watched, all the time, a lot more closely than it's ever been." Sanderson pointed up, toward the roof of the car, and nodded knowingly.

"Thank you for the warning," Fitz replied. "Is there anything I can do in return, now or later?"

"No, no," Sanderson began, then paused. When he resumed, it was in a more tentative voice. "Do you...handle family law?"

"Not really. I'm more estates and trusts," Fitz replied gently. "But I know some good local family lawyers. Would you like their names?"

"Yeah, thanks," Sanderson said thickly. "I got this guy, but I just pulled his name off a site, and he doesn't seem to be the best, so I'm looking for another."

"I understand," Fitz pulled a notebook from his pocket and scrawled some names on it. "The top name is the best in the area, and a personal friend. Tell him I sent you."

"Thanks, Counselor."

"And, Agent Sanderson...I'm sorry."

"Sorry?"

"Any situation that requires a family lawyer is painful. You and your loved ones have my sympathy, and I pray that things work out."

"Thanks, Counselor," Sanderson said, pocketing the paper. "I think the sprayer time is about to run out here. If you could give me a few minutes head start before you go –"

"Certainly, Agent. Thank you again."

Sanderson slipped out into the chill mist. Shortly thereafter a car pulled out of an adjacent bay. Fitz waited until the spray ceased, then another minute after that, then drove out to return to the big-box store parking lot by a heavily covered route.

Tension

Grandma's funeral was on Saturday morning, and the church was packed. Luke was seated with the Peterson family, but Teresa sat with the small contingent of sisters from St. Anne's. As Grandma's adopted daughter, she could have been seated with the family, but Luke and Teresa still instinctively stayed apart in public settings. Though it was unlikely that anyone would recognize them from grainy photos of damaged ID cards shown briefly on a local newscast years before, there was no reason to tempt fate. Teresa was wearing a black dress and a black lace veil that she pulled forward enough to half-hide her face.

Luke sat next to Grandpa in the front row, with Gil and Janine and the Petersons occupying the rest of the pew. Felicity looked subdued and somber in her simple black dress. Harmony sat beside her, looking much more mature than her sixteen years. Christopher and Andrew sat at the end of the row. In the next pew back sat Ruth and Travis Winters, with Cletus and Sixtus looking mutinous and Cathy looking quietly distressed. Glancing over his shoulder, Luke caught sight of the Schaeffers lined up in a pew about halfway back in the church. Kent was looking slightly dazed, which was his default expression these days, while Linda sat beside him holding his hand. Next to them, nearest the aisle, sat Martha and Evan holding Leo. The other Schaeffer children stretched down the pew, and were busy managing wiggly little Miriam. Elizabeth noticed Luke watching them, and smiled and waved at him. He waved back, but kept looking for Phillip, who didn't seem to be in the same pew. Finally, Luke spotted him in the next pew forward, looking straight ahead with a stony expression. Luke didn't know why Phillip wasn't sitting back with his family, but it was depressing to see.

Now the music was beginning and the priest was processing up the aisle. Luke stood and sang with the rest, but his mind was roiling with concern over the stresses that were pressuring people he loved. He tried to focus on the Mass, but his attention kept skittering off. He paid attention when Felicity and Harmony sang a beautiful duet while Ruth, Shelly, and Teresa brought up the Offertory gifts. Grandpa sat stoically, with bright eyes and a settled expression, looking not so much pained as peaceful and accepting. All through the Mass his expression didn't change, which was another concern for Luke. Had the impact of the loss hit Grandpa hard enough to disable him? This was a disconcerting thought for Luke, for whom the gentle patriarch had always been a rock of stability. Luke suddenly felt insecure, which made concentrating on Mass even harder.

Finally, it was time for the final blessing over the coffin, and Luke remembered he had a role to play. As one of Grandma's sons, albeit an adopted one, he was one of the pall bearers. He went with the family down the aisle, following the coffin, and once outside helped Gil, Andrew, and Bart to transfer it to the hearse. Then there was some sorting into cars and the procession left the church. Luke barely remembered the short ride to the cemetery out in the country and the gathering at the graveside. It was a companion plot, and Luke was a bit unsettled to see that the headstone was already completely filled in for both Grandma and Grandpa, with only Grandpa's date of death left blank.

The sky overhead was a low sheet of slate gray, but the south wind whispering through the pines carried the promise of incipient springtime. Mourners clustered in groups as Fr. Gabriel began the brief graveside service. Luke tried to concentrate on the prayers, but his mind was still scattered and racing. He spotted Phillip again, this time huddled in a little knot with Cletus and Sixtus apart from their respective families. Janine Peterson wasn't standing with Gil, but rather with her sister Linda Schaeffer and her family. Grandpa stood by the graveside, still wearing that sad but serene expression as he gazed on the coffin. He was flanked on his left by Ruth, who looked distraught and spent, and on his right by Shelly and Teresa. Luke noticed that Teresa was wearing the same calm expression that Grandpa was, which struck him as odd. He'd been concerned that Grandma's death would prove very difficult for Teresa, maybe even traumatize her, but it appeared that she was taking the loss more sedately even than Luke was.

Finally, Fr. Gabriel was concluding the Rite of Committal, and Luke bowed his head with the others as the final prayer was said over the mourners. Then the funeral was officially concluded, though many people stayed to chat, moving about in a desultory manner. A few started drifting back toward the cars, but most seemed to want to linger, as if reluctant to take final leave of the woman who had meant so much to them all. Many people were walking over to Grandpa, including Lawrence and Annette Stover, though Annette was in a wheelchair. Luke knew there would be time to catch up with everyone at the funeral luncheon back at the Big House, but right now he wanted to talk to the ones he might not be able to find there. He went over to where Cletus, Sixtus, and Phillip stood huddled.

"Hey, guys, what's up?" he asked. "Haven't seen you in a while, Phillip."

"Yeah," Phillip acknowledged. "Good to see you, too, Luke."

"My condolences on the loss of your grandmother, guys," Luke turned to Cletus and Sixtus. "I know she meant a lot to you all."

"Yeah," Sixtus said bitterly. "First of many changes."

"Oh?" Luke asked.

Sixtus glanced at the two others, then half-turned so his back was to most of the crowd of mourners. "We've been talking, and we think we're going to move out."

"Move out?" A chill spread through Luke's insides.

"We know a guy who has an empty house down near metro Detroit who'll rent it to us cheap if we fix it up," Sixtus explained. "We were just talking to Phillip here, and he may join us."

"Oh," Luke replied, not knowing what else to say. His heart was sinking at the prospect of the tight, loving families to whom he was so close being broken up. Of course, young men couldn't be expected to stay with their families forever, but this change didn't seem like a peaceful, amicable moving forward with their lives. "Is there some…ah…reason for this?"

Phillip said nothing, but scowled in the direction of his family. Cletus just looked at the ground, but Sixtus replied with a hint of defiance in his voice. "I dunno – maybe a chance to get a decent job, drive a car that isn't a decade old hand-me-down, maybe live in a house of our own and buy some things for ourselves."

"And you want to leave home for that?" Luke asked. "Guys, I've lived out there, and I have a highly skilled degree. It's not like what you think. Good jobs aren't easy to come by, and life is expensive."

Sixtus said nothing in response, but glared at Luke resentfully. Cletus, however, answered pointedly. "I'd move out just to have a chance to breathe easy, to not always be under somebody's eye, to have a chance to live my own life and make my own choices."

Luke opened his mouth to reply, then shut it again. He didn't know where to begin to respond to this. His own experience as a single man – the bleak apartments, the poor diet, the unrewarding work, the aimless life – differed sharply from what his friends seemed to think awaited them. He'd been grateful to trade all his "independence" for the love and belonging he'd found among the families; they seemed ready to walk away from their families for that dismal life.

"Have you talked to your folks about this yet?" Luke finally asked.

"It's not like we need their permission, y'know," Sixtus said sharply.

"Whoa, guys," Luke said, spreading his hands. "I'm on your side. I was just asking."

"We haven't talked to them yet, but we'd appreciate it if you didn't mention it. Let us handle this," Cletus replied.

"Your call. I'm still your friend, remember?"

"Yeah, Luke," Sixtus affirmed, giving a ghost of a smile. The expressions of the other two softened enough that they looked more like the friends he was familiar with, though their eyes were still shadowed. Luke held out his hand and got a shake and a rough hug from each of them.

"Whatever you do, stay in touch, all right?" Luke asked.

"Sure thing, Luke," Phillip assured him.

"And do me a favor, would you? Don't burn any bridges. I understand where you're coming from, but don't say or do anything you can't take back, okay?"

The guys all nodded reluctantly as they looked away or at the ground. Luke headed for the car, his emotions in turmoil.

The luncheon back at the Big House was a crowded frenzy, to the point that Luke guessed that someone had badly underestimated how many people would attend. There was no possibility of seating everyone at the same time, so food and drinks were set out for people to grab as they tried to navigate the milling confusion. Grandpa remained in the living room so mourners could find him, but everyone else moved slowly about, chatting with friends and relatives and trying to find a place to sit.

The Rivendell residents were especially busy, trying to keep trays filled, pitchers and carafes topped off, and garbage baskets empty. The Hagerstroms were there, as well as the entire Peterson family, bustling about, greeting and directing and refilling cups. Luke saw Ruth briefly, and thought he caught a glimpse of Cletus and Sixtus, but thereafter didn't see either them or their mother. Lawrence and Annette Stover were there, as were the Schaeffers and the Becks, though Luke didn't spot Todd. He noticed most of the Kyles, including Jake and Grace. He'd just decided to go talk to Grace when he saw something that distressed him yet more.

Felicity had been hustling about like a mad woman, tending to innumerable practical details while somehow maintaining her indefatigable cheerfulness toward all the guests. She always had a smile and handclasp or hug for everyone – right until she walked around a corner and came face to face with Grace. Luke happened to be looking right at the two friends, and the contrast was shocking. Grace got no broad smile or welcoming hug from Felicity, who stopped short and seemed to stiffen. Clasping her hands in front of her, she gave Grace a cordial nod, which Grace returned with a neutral expression. They exchanged a few words which Luke didn't hear, then Felicity gave a cheerful but perfunctory greeting to Mr. and Mrs. Kyle before bustling off.

Distressed, Luke sought a quiet space to think. Something was clearly amiss between Felicity and Grace, who'd been best of friends before heading off to school together. A heavy trepidation settled on him – was everything going awry? Were all these close friendships and loving family bonds crumbling before his eyes?

"I'm roasting," a voice from behind him broke into his dark reverie. "Want to step outside with me for a bit to cool off?" Luke turned to see Felicity, looking sweaty and wiping her hands on a kitchen towel.

"Uh...sure," Luke stammered, surprised to have been asked. They slipped out the glass doors onto the rear deck, where the afternoon air was refreshingly cool after the stuffy indoors. The grass was still damp with the spring thaw, but the gravel path that wound back to the gazebo was dry enough for them to walk unhindered. Felicity strolled along, chatting about the guests in her usual bubbly manner, oblivious to the shadow which lay on Luke's heart.

"It's so delightful to be out here," Felicity said as they stepped into the gazebo. "And look how light it is! Those winter nights over in Canada seemed interminable. I just love it when the day gets longer, don't you?"

"Yes, but I like it even more when they get warmer," Luke replied. "We won't be able to stay out here long dressed like this."

"For now, it's refreshing," Felicity answered. Silence fell for a minute while Luke summoned the courage to ask what was on his mind.

"So, ah, how was your school year? Other than dark."

"It was fine. A bit intense, but we made it through. I'll miss St. Anslem's."

"And how was...that is, how did things go with Grace? This was your second year rooming together, wasn't it?"

Felicity seemed to stiffen a bit, and gave Luke a sideways glance. Then she turned away, looking out over the plowed fields, and replied in a slightly cooler tone.

"Things were fine, fine. We were both feeling the pressure of the studies, and being cooped up indoors during those long nights wore on everybody's nerves, but we made it through."

To Luke there seemed something hollow about the explanation. "But, you're still friends, aren't you?"

"Friends? Of course, we're still friends," Felicity replied, but she stepped away as she said it, her back to him, wringing her hands. "We had our moments, as friends do. Actually, we bickered, which…which we hadn't done last year. We bickered a fair amount, truth be told. Some…hurtful things were said, by both of us."

"But you made it up, didn't you? Forgave one another?"

"Why, sure we did," Felicity said lightly with a dismissive wave. "Of course, we did. But –" she trailed off.

"But what?" Luke nudged after a moment's silence.

"But some things are kind of hard to forget, you know," Felicity said emphatically. "I forgive her, of course, but it's not easy –" Her body tensed and her tone grew harsh. "You wouldn't believe some of the things she said! That little snip! Who does she think she is? I am not a prima donna! I am not condescending!" She wheeled to look at Luke with fiery eyes and a fierce expression. "Who does she think she is? I've heard things about her family that would make you cringe! Yet she has the nerve to lecture me –"

Felicity cut herself off abruptly when she noticed Luke's shocked expression. He stood frozen, stunned by this side of Felicity which he'd never imagined was there. He had no idea what to say, or how to respond. Then her expression softened and she stepped closer to him, slipping her arms up to his shoulders and gazing into his eyes. Instinctively he put his arms around her waist.

"Do you love me, Derek?" she asked in a near whisper.

This seemed like the moment Luke had been yearning for since he had first laid eyes on Felicity. Alone together, with her asking the question he'd only dreamed she'd ever ask. But despite that, all his instincts were screaming – something was wrong here, something was very wrong. He'd had his arms around Felicity before, but it had never felt like this. There was a stiffness, a tension in her carriage that was completely alien. Her normally vivacious eyes seemed shrouded and her expression was enigmatic, as if she was inviting him yet hiding something from him at the same time.

Luke was frightened. This was not normal speech, this was not normal behavior, this was not normal posture – nothing about this bespoke the Felicity he thought he knew. Trying to keep his voice steady, he took a half step back – not far enough to step out of her arms, but enough for a little distance.

"Why, sure I love you, Felicity," Luke stammered, wondering what he could say to finesse this situation, which was not unfolding at all like his fantasies had envisioned. It turned out that he needn't have worried. Abruptly Felicity's expression changed again. The wary guardedness seemed to drain from it, and he again saw his simple, honest Felicity – though she suddenly looked as stunned as he felt. Her eyes widened and she pulled away, her hand flying to her mouth in shock.

"Oh Derek," she whispered. "Oh Derek, I'm so sorry!" Before he could respond she'd dashed past him and up the path to the house. Luke stared after her, dumbfounded and dismayed, wondering what had just happened, and feeling like his entire world was coming apart at the seams. The combination of emotional stress and chill air became too much for him, and he trudged wearily to his apartment.

Meanwhile, a tense gathering was taking place in the control room of the basement of the Big House. Fitz had called the meeting, and had insisted that all the decision makers attend regardless of how hard their other duties pressed them. The funeral presented a prime opportunity since everyone was already present. Ruth had been the last to arrive, looking distressed and bringing Travis, who rarely came to these meetings. But now he stood beside her, holding her hand while she sniffed and wiped her unusually red eyes.

"Folks, I'm sorry to summon you on such short notice, and under these difficult circumstances," Fitz plunged in. "But I've received critical intelligence that I need to get into your hands as quickly as possible.

"The day before yesterday a source informed me that the Federal government has reinvigorated their investigation into the blast. A new coordinator has been assigned to the region with broad authority and a mandate to solve the case. Apparently, they're taking a closer look at any connections between the blast and a clandestine network devoted to hiding people. Unfortunately, there seems to be some confusion between our network and the human trafficking network that was exposed last summer. Whether that's genuine misunderstanding or intentional propaganda, I couldn't say."

Everyone was quiet for a while, looking sober as they digested this information.

"Was there some incident or event that triggered this renewed interest?" Steve McLean asked.

"My source didn't know. It may be that the blast has gone unresolved for too long, and somebody wants to bring the investigation to a conclusion. Or maybe something happened that my source didn't know about. The important thing is that the Federal government's interest has been renewed, or awakened, or whatever, and they've devoted new assets to the investigation. It's very possible that they won't quit until they achieve some sort of resolution," Fitz explained.

"Do we know what kind of assets are in play? What sort of steps are being taken?" Gil asked. Everyone still remembered the armored vehicles and heavily armed personnel carriers that had rolled into the area a couple of years before.

"The only asset my source knew of for certain was this one Federal official, but apparently he's been given broad authority and access to many material and personnel resources," Fitz answered. "One immediate application of this authority appears to have been much broader and more comprehensive aerial surveillance – far beyond the casual high-level overflights we've been assuming."

"So, we're probably being watched right now," Ruth said glumly.

"Almost certainly," Fitz admitted. "We've always acknowledged the possibility, but if my source is correct, we can assume intense, if not constant, aerial coverage – and that's only the first part of the program."

The room fell uncomfortably silent for a while before Ruth spoke again, rather sharply.

"Well, I guess this settles it for us, doesn't it?"

"What do you mean, Ruth?" Gil asked quietly.

"What do I mean?" Ruth rounded on her brother. "I'd think it obvious! We need to shut this down, all of it, as quickly as possible! It may already be too late, but we have to try what we can!"

There were some murmurs in response to this, but Shelly was the only one who spoke up. "Don't you think that's a little abrupt, Ruth? There are a lot of factors to consider!"

"Factors to consider?" Ruth's voice rose. "We've lived for years under the threat of discovery, and now we find that the government has redoubled their efforts to expose us. We've sacrificed our resources and our time and our families to this quixotic cause, and now we're at risk of being arrested! Those are the only factors worth considering right now!"

"I wouldn't call saving lives a quixotic effort –" Shelly began to reply, but Travis had pulled the agitated Ruth aside and was speaking to her in low tones.

"Ruth has a point, though I'd argue it is cause for urgent concern, not panic," Gil said gently. "Fitz, did your source indicate that this new regional official was planning any specific action? Were there any plans or timetables?"

"He didn't say, which makes me think there aren't any yet," Fitz replied. "He just wanted to alert me to the renewed interest and the additional surveillance assets."

"Did your source indicate where this official had come from?" asked Steve, who had once worked for the Federal government and had some insights into the bureaucratic mentality.

"He was sent up from D.C.," Fitz said.

"Hmm – that makes it either much better or much worse," Steve mused. "Being sent from D.C. to a backwater like this would be a serious demotion. This fellow might just bide his time, going through the motions until he can get transferred back out, either to D.C. or somewhere else. Or he might be a go-getter, determined to earn his way out by resolving this situation, by succeeding where nobody else has, thus proving himself. We don't know which type this guy is, but I must admit, if he's been given authority this broad, he may be of the go-getter stripe."

"My source would probably agree with you," Fitz added.

"So, what kind of pressure does this put us under?" Gil asked.

"Well, no matter how determined he is, he's still got the Federal bureaucracy to deal with," Steve answered. "That alone should give us some breathing room. He could spend a few months just getting his feet under him, establishing working relationships with local supervisors, and so on."

"But didn't Fitz's source say the stepped-up surveillance is already happening?" Ruth asked.

"He did," Fitz confirmed. "He also said that this official was operating independently of local hierarchies, and that he was treating this as a domestic terror situation."

"'Domestic terror' is the catchphrase these days," Steve explained. "It can indicate a higher level of urgency, or it can just be a cover to angle for more resources. We can't tell which it is in this case without knowing more about the official."

"Right," Gil reaffirmed. "Given that we're working in the dark here, it sounds like this is a case for urgency. How are things progressing regarding our trial releases?"

"Good enough," Shelly replied. "We've got a list of guests who are willing to give it a try. I've got interviews set up with them and their families this upcoming week. If everyone's agreeable, we can select a couple to proceed with as test cases. Once that's decided, the next steps are in your hands, Fitz."

"That's right," Fitz said. "Unfortunately, we have to deal with court filings and things, which means matters can only move so quickly, but the documents are boilerplate. Based on the guests we select to release, I'll be filing over the next couple of weeks. Then there are the practical issues like arranging housing, bank accounts, and so forth. I'm guessing that it'll be a week or two after Easter when the initial guests are released."

Ruth whimpered a little and wrung her hands. Travis patted her shoulder and muttered something soothing. Everyone else understood – they knew it was a difficult time for the Winters family.

"Easter is only two weeks from tomorrow," Gil reassured her. "We'll have plenty to do until then, what with all this and the Holy Week schedule. Let's put our trust in the Lord, and our hope in bureaucratic inertia, and pray that our actions are in time. Fitz, I know we've mapped out a rather drawn-out schedule for releasing the guests, allowing plenty of time for observation. Any possibility we can accelerate that a little?"

"Sure. Working up the initial paperwork is always the time consumer. Once completed, it can be used as a template, allowing for slight individual variations, so we'll be able to process guests in less time."

"Then why don't we plan on stepping up the pace of the releases once the pilot cases prove out?" Gil asked. "That, plus being double sure everyone's taking proper precautions – staying under cover, mixing up vehicles, you know the drill."

"Haven't we always recognized that the precautions wouldn't be effective against a focused surveillance effort?" Ruth asked. "Because that sure sounds like what we're dealing with here."

Gil resisted his urge to sigh, and tried to adopt his most encouraging tone. "Yes, Ruth, we've always recognized the limitations of our avoidance measures, but they're all we can do at this point. We'll just have to do what we can, pray, and trust."

For some reason that seemed to upset Ruth even more.

Manipulation

Jason settled into his seat for the flight back to Flint. His couple of days in D.C. had been productive, and he'd been able to slip in and out of town without Cassie learning that he'd been there, always providing that she hadn't run a locator trace on him. He could remove her permission to run traces, but that would cause other problems, so for now he just had to hope.

It was unusual for him to have spent most of his time at HHS, but that was what the situation called for. Jerry had found two contacts who were just what Jason had been hoping for. Rex Hollis and Lin Wei had been able to answer all Jason's questions regarding his two biggest worries: protocols and personnel. Lin had been the personnel expert, and she paid careful attention to Jason's requirements, asking good questions. Her eyes had widened a bit at the aggressiveness of Jason's proposed timetable, but she had pledged to do her best to find the people to staff it. Apparently HHS had a pool of personnel ready to do temporary duty on short notice wherever they were needed.

Rex was the medical protocol wizard, and had assured Jason that the administrative hooks were already in place to implement the protocol changes he'd envisioned. Rex took all the queries for the Chengdu Project, right down to Ron Porcher's hasty last-minute work, and promised to come up with a protocol implementation that should work with Jason's proposed timetable. He asked a lot of questions as well, including some that raised issues that Jason hadn't anticipated.

That had been Thursday. Friday morning he'd sat down with Cynthia and briefed her on what he'd accomplished, what he hadn't, and what he was planning. He'd avoided the temptation to prepare a frothy presentation that would make much of his scant progress, and he saw that she appreciated his frankness. She'd been noncommittal about everything, though his progress with the HHS project had intrigued her, perhaps mitigating some of her concern over how slow his headway had been in other areas. She'd encouraged him to persevere and to keep her updated. On his way out, Jason had spotted Whitman filing into a meeting with the other managers. Whitman had seen him, too, and had given a curt nod, which Jason had returned. Then Jason had put the incident out of his mind. He'd either be crowing or crying when all this was over, and in the meantime he couldn't waste time worrying about Whitman. The only thing he could do was succeed, and for that he needed to focus.

The rest of Friday had been spent talking to the FEMA people, going over specifications and capabilities. They'd been very cooperative, agreeing that his proposal would be a great exercise which would give their staffs valuable experience. When he boarded the flight back to Michigan it was with a sense of real accomplishment – an unusual feeling for having spent two days working with Federal bureaucracies.

Back in Sandusky, he found an e-mail from Ethan stating that he'd scouted out several plots of property around the Thumb region that seemed to fit Jason's specifications. On the basis of the purchasing codes, Ethan had had the realtors draw up sales agreements for the plots. Jason's weekend was spent driving to the four corners of the Thumb, inspecting soggy acreage and pacing off distances and trying to guess at traffic flow. By Sunday evening he'd settled on the four that seemed best. He went to bed satisfied that despite his frustration with one arm of his plans, the other arm looked poised to make stunning progress.

Monday morning Ethan showed up in the truck with the GeoTech logo, obviously ready to drive places. Jason let him know which of the plots had been the best and told him to execute the sales. To Jason's annoyance, this turned out to be something that couldn't be done online or by message, but required him to be physically present to sign papers. Thus he had to burn all of Monday driving to realtor's offices to go through the tedious business of signing and initialing stacks of papers. The realtors seemed puzzled by his exasperation, which didn't help Jason's mood.

"They can't figure it out," Ethan chuckled at their third stop as they waited for the realtor to get all the paperwork ready. "From their point of view, this *is* being executed quickly."

"I don't care what they think," Jason grumbled. "They're wasting my time."

"C'mon, now," Ethan cajoled. "They knew this was a Federal government purchase. They thought they had weeks or months to prepare."

"Then they can think again. They should have had this paperwork all set up and ready."

"Well, they've no cause to complain. These are the easiest sales any of them have had in years, and some of these plots have been on the market forever. Now they'll get their commissions and the plots will be put to use. Which brings up a question," Ethan's voice took on a wheedling tone. "Put to use for what?"

Jason glanced sideways. "Patience. All things in time. However, in reward for your diligent service, I'll let you pull the trigger when the time comes. Good enough?"

"It'll have to be."

Their final closing happened to be in Imlay City. After they'd wrapped up the paperwork, Jason had Ethan pull into the parking lot of the hotel where he'd stayed so he could duck inside for about ten minutes. When he came back to the truck, Ethan couldn't resist asking, "Making more lodging arrangements?"

"Just checking in with a friend," Jason replied with a slight smile.

"Full of mysteries today, aren't you?"

"Always. However, your promised reward is due. What's the time?"

"Four thirty," Ethan pointed at the clock on the dash.

"That's good enough," Jason said, pulling out his phone and keying a number. "Here, you can do it. When someone answers, simply say 'Execute'."

"'Execute'?" Ethan confirmed as he took the phone. Jason nodded, so Ethan listened until someone picked up.

"Hello?" A voice answered.

"Execute."

"To confirm, you authorize execution?"

"Execute," Ethan repeated.

"Very well, executing," the voice acknowledged, then hung up.

"You wanna tell me who I just talked to, and what I executed?" Ethan asked as he handed the phone back to the grinning Jason.

"That was a FEMA manager at the Fast Response Center in Fort Wayne. He's been awaiting my call, but D.C. asked that I not make the timing too easy. Right near the end of the workday on Monday is inconvenient enough."

"What are you talking about?"

"You just authorized the placement of four emergency response medical clinics at the sites we purchased. It's a FEMA installation. They've got these ready-to-roll, supposedly turnkey medical installations which can be deployed to disaster sites in short order. In theory, they can be set up and operational three days from initial notification. Your call just triggered a flurry of activity down in Fort Wayne. The FEMA staff is now scrambling to execute an emergency deployment."

"You mean, they had no warning at all?"

"The FEMA managers in D.C. have known about it since last Friday, but they wanted to keep it quiet, to make the exercise more realistic. They want to run this evolution as if it were an actual emergency, not just as another drill."

"But...shouldn't we be making some arrangements? Utilities, infrastructure, whatever?" Ethan asked.

"No," Jason chuckled. "These units are supposed to be completely self sufficient. The only accommodation they're making is wiring them to the electrical grid rather than using onsite generation. But other than that, they're standalone – water is trucked in, waste trucked out, they've got dorms and food service for staff, everything necessary is brought in and set up."

"Okay, but even so, we could contact some local operations –" Ethan began.

"Nope," Jason interrupted. "FEMA has protocols for all those things, and they want to test them. Everything's in their hands now. We just stand back and watch."

"So, by Friday there should be four complete, operational medical clinics on those plots we just purchased?"

"That's the theory. In practice, I think everyone will be happy if they're erected by this time next week. But that's part of the reason for running the evolution – to iron out the kinks and give the staff actual deployment experience."

"I see. And once they're erected, what will these medical clinics be used for?"

"That will have to remain a mystery for the time being," Jason replied. "Meanwhile, I think we've earned a nice steak for our day's work. We deserve a bit of relaxation."

"More than those FEMA schmucks are going to get."

Jason tried to resist the temptation to hover around the FEMA sites to monitor the progress, but he was only partly successful. On Wednesday afternoon, and on Thursday, and again on Friday afternoon, he and Ethan drove around and observed from afar. Initial progress seemed to be good, with little bulldozers clearing and leveling the plots and sections of buildings trucked in on lowboy trailers to be lifted off by cranes. But then things seemed to stall, and there were a lot of people walking around holding tablets and talking to each other. Then there were periods where nobody was visible on the sites at all, which Ethan found hilarious. Friday afternoon was a little better, with some of the building sections having been moved around and some large objects in wooden crates having shown up, but nothing looked any more assembled than it had. Jason disciplined himself to do only one drive-around over the weekend. The sites seemed busier, with people in hard hats swarming all over them, even well past dusk with the help of some large site lights, but things still looked fragmented.

On Monday morning a FEMA official called from D.C. to inform Jason with touchy formality that the deployment had encountered delays, but that it was back on track and should be ready within days. Jason tried to respond in a way that balanced understanding and firmness, pointing out that staff schedules were predicated on the centers being ready on time. In truth he had factored the anticipated delays into the schedule, but based on the slow progress the FEMA teams seemed to be making, he was starting to get anxious even about that. The FEMA official noted his concerns and promised to keep him updated.

Jason's spirits were lifted that afternoon by a lengthy video call with Rex Hollis of HHS. Initially Lin conferenced in to update everyone on the personnel dispositions, which were proceeding with no more than the usual hitches. Jason took the opportunity to warn her about the FEMA deployment delays. Once Lin rang off, Rex gleefully informed Jason that the requisite protocol adjustments were configured and ready to be deployed with the execution of a script. Chengdu Two was poised to proceed once the facilities and personnel were in place.

"Really? That quickly?" Jason was surprised.

"It doesn't take much," Rex explained. "It's the Regional Medical Administration offices that make the difference. Every provider is linked into them, so if there's some protocol we want the providers to follow, we just load it into their profiles at the RMA, and it's active immediately."

"You mean you can even stipulate individual health care providers?" Jason asked, amazed.

"Oh, Jason," Rex chuckled paternally. "Not only can we stipulate providers, we can take it down to individual patients and diagnoses. We can arrange things so that if Joe Lunchbucket goes to Dr. Strangelove for his blood pressure, we can tell the doctor exactly what to prescribe."

"Wow," Jason said. "I had no idea things could be targeted that precisely. That sort of removes the element of doctor's choice, doesn't it?"

"Well, the doctor can do anything he'd like, but we'll only pay for what we tell him to prescribe," Rex said. "Besides, we rarely get that proactive. We normally define protocols by diagnostic profiles, or for treatments that meet certain criteria. However, it's nice that we *can* craft very tightly focused protocols if we need to.

"That's what we're doing with Chengdu Two: setting up protocols for patients who fit a particular profile. Fortunately, all we have to do is identify them, and most of the heavy lifting for that was done by Dr. Tasker. We've only had to define protocols that match his criteria and load them into the RMAs."

"Okay, so how will it work?" Jason asked. "If Joe Lunchbucket fits the profile, how do we get him to one of these…what did we decide to call them?"

"RCCs – Rapid Care Centers," Rex replied. "It would happen when Joe goes in for medical care in any facility using one of the Thumb area Regional Medical Administration offices – which is all of them. The provider treating him would see a sunny yellow tab show up on the edge of Joe's record, and get a message that Joe had been selected to receive care at an RCC. The provider must refer him immediately and will not receive payment for any care provided."

"Ah – incentive for the provider to show him the door," Jason observed.

"Exactly. Wherever Joe shows up, and his patient profile fits the protocol, then the only place he'll be able to receive care is at an RCC."

"Won't there be an outcry? Interfering in doctor/patient relationships and all that?"

Rex smiled indulgently. "We manage the outcries. Joe might grumble to his circle of friends, but nothing further than that. If things start to get out of hand, we have ways of spotting and stopping them. Which reminds, me, I want to conference George in to discuss the POM side of things."

"I'm sorry – POM?" Jason asked.

"Sorry, I've been spending so much time with George that I'm picking up the jargon. Public Opinion Management. But before I bring him in, do you have any questions about Chengdu Two?"

"Not now," Jason replied. "You seem to be on top of things."

"Oh, I just remembered something," Rex checked himself. "We wrapped in one more consideration, based primarily on Ron Porcher's work. He'd done some pretty sophisticated query construction to identify people who'd disappeared, either directly from the acute care facilities or preemptively, before they could be admitted to the hospital. Part of the protocol we'll be implementing will identify any of these people if they ever show up at any provider working through our RMAs. Those records will be flagged with a green tab, and they'll be sent to an RCC, and you personally will be notified."

"Me?" Jason asked.

"Yes, unless you'd prefer it to be some other party."

"No, that's fine. If any of these 'lost patients' turn up, I'd like to speak to them," Jason assured him.

"Then we'll leave it as it is. Now, let's see if we can get George – ah, here he is. George Spader, this is Jason Pelletier." Jason's screen split to display a young man who was mostly bald, with a pointed nose and watery eyes. "George is the POM specialist who's been assigned to this initiative, and he's been a fountain of ideas. George, could you brief Jason on the POM offensive we're planning for Chengdu Two?"

"Hi, Jason," George looked up to give Jason a quick nod before returning his attention to something on the desk in front of him. "Rex has filled me in on some of the delays you've been encountering with erecting the RCCs. Vexing as that may be for you, it's a blessing in disguise for us here, because it gives us more breathing room to craft and implement our campaign. We want to soften the ground out there before Chengdu Two goes live."

"'Soften the ground'?" Jason asked.

"Sure. We want to shape public opinion so that the RCCs are not simply tolerated, but applauded. In preparation, we're working with a couple of popular outlets in that area to run a couple of S and O pieces on public health care –"

"Excuse me," Jason interrupted. "'S and O'?"

Rex laughed and George flushed a bit. "We're hammering him with jargon today," Rex said.

"Sorry," George apologized. "'S and O' means 'Scandal and Outrage'. These are spots designed to inflame public opinion over some topic. We had been thinking of doing just three spots, but I'm considering ramping it up to four, which should really seal the deal."

Jason just blinked at this, but Rex roared with laughter. "Slow down, George! You're losing him! Explain it slowly."

George smiled thinly and began again. "We have an axiom in Public Opinion Management: the first spot is a scandal, the second is an outrage, and the third calls for action. We're planning two initial spots through different media outlets. The theme will be the failure of health care provision, particularly in rural areas. The reporters will show long lines at doctor's offices, and spotlight a couple of patients who've suffered due to slow or sporadic care."

"Where will these media outlets find the patients?" Jason asked.

"We'll provide them, of course," George explained. "We'll provide almost all of it: the doctor's offices, the patients, the narrative, the theme we're seeking to stress, even the crowd in the doctor's waiting room, if that's needed. Outlet managers like those kinds of details to be arranged – that way, all they have to do is provide the camera crew and reporter, and maybe a little closing commentary, and the spot is wrapped."

"I see," Jason nodded. "Please continue."

"Anyway, we figured the first two spots would go out through more populist outlets that feed a certain class of news sites. That'll generate the scandal and outrage. Then we were considering a third outlet, but now we're thinking we'll engage a fourth as well. These last two would be more thoughtful, considered commentary, with statistics and such."

"What would the statistics say?" Jason asked.

"Whatever we want them to say," George said with a shrug. "The actual numbers would be irrelevant. The point is they'd support the narrative we're presenting. These would be the kind of editorial commentary where the senior reporter or outlet manager would soberly intone about the grave problem of inadequate medical care for our underserved rural population, et cetera. We'll have lots of factoids to back everything up – we're still working on the copy. One of these commentaries would probably do the trick; two is going to have the public eating out of our hand. I've even got a line with a couple of state representatives who'll release statements decrying the terrible state of affairs and calling for change."

"Really? You have state representatives who'll do that?" Jason asked. "How do you know what they'll say?"

George looked at Jason as if he'd just asked if water was wet. "It's the staffers who matter, and they're the ones we're working with. We supply the boilerplate text, they make a few tweaks, then shove it under the rep's noses for signatures, and behold! You've got clamor for action from the highest levels of state government.

"And then, amazingly, HHS will announce a pilot project, designed just for underserved areas – the Rapid Care Clinics. Scope will be limited at first, with only members of the most disadvantaged population segments designated for treatment at the new centers until they get ramped up to full capacity."

"Oh," Jason said hesitantly. "Do you think?...I was hoping not to draw too much attention to these centers, given their purpose."

"Couple things about that," interjected Rex. "First, we won't be publicizing their locations, and we'll be making clear that they'll only be serving selected patients. That way we won't have people pulling in off the street expecting service. Secondly, we'll be seeding the selection pool with non-target patients. A percentage of patients sent to the RCCs will be 'blanks', so to speak – ordinary patients who'll receive ordinary care and be sent home. This will serve as camouflage, and their testimony can bolster the narrative."

"Right," George added. "Plus, the RCCs themselves are a minor factor in the grand scheme of the POM effect we're creating. The main impression we're planning to leave is that public outcry makes a difference and that diligent activist journalism can still change the world for the better. When we're finished, the news outlets will walk away patting themselves on the back, you'll have your clinics and protocols in place, and the public will not only accept them, they'll be convinced that they are mechanisms for providing better health care."

"I see," Jason said. "You certainly seem to have this well in hand, but it looks to me like a lot of components to align – are you sure you can pull it off in the timeframe we're projecting?"

"Pah," George made a dismissive gesture. "A project of this scope is like falling off a log. I've done dozens that were much more complex than this. The only issue that's even close to touchy is the timing. We're already working with the outlets, and are hoping to get the spots scripted and rendered next week. Ideally we'd like the clinics online and training staff by the time we start airing the spots. That's the best timing for generating the outrage, rolling out the protocols to the RMAs, and announcing the government's response to the public concern. We can delay a little, but not too long."

"All right, I guess this is your project," Jason conceded. "It's just a bit of a shock, after all the secrecy shrouding the initial Chengdu effort."

"It's called hiding in plain sight," George assured him. "Hey, gotta go. Keep me posted on when those RCCs get active!" He clicked off, leaving only Rex on the screen.

"I'm sure FEMA will call tomorrow, assuring me that the sites will be up by Friday," Jason told Rex. "If not, I know who to call to put the heat on them. Those installations *will* be operational a week from today, so you can make your personnel plans accordingly."

"I will," Rex said.

"This does seem like a lot to pull together in a short time," Jason added. "Now that we're into it, I'm wondering if we can pull it off, at least on this aggressive schedule."

"We can," Rex assured him. "Between you and me, my management would have dithered until hell froze over. It took an outsider like yourself with a new perspective and some bold ideas to give us the kick we needed. This plan may need tuning over time, but it's something, which is a damn sight better than nothing."

It was actually Tuesday morning before the FEMA official called back to assure Jason that the clinic sites would be operational by Friday, so Jason relayed that word back to HHS for their planning. He added the caveat that it might be prudent to have the bulk of the personnel arrive later in the week, but there was no harm in scheduling supply deliveries for first thing Monday. If there were still installation crews at the sites – which he suspected there would be – it wouldn't hurt them to feel a little heat.

With the Chengdu Two project proceeding, Jason turned his attention back to the blast and the terrorist network he was supposed to be investigating. He had Ethan schedule another meeting with Major Collins regarding the RA overflight data, and had Sanderson and Harris come along as well. Collins brought along one of his staffers, a Sergeant Danvers, as well as an NSA data specialist to explain the results of the image analysis. When the results were projected onto the wall, they looked very similar to the prior projection, only with clearer lines and more focused blurs. There was nothing new to report, no breakthroughs.

"What we're lacking here is the same thing we were lacking a couple of years ago: specificity," Collins complained. "Since they didn't know exactly who they were tracking until the very end, they just had us watch everybody doing everything. All that footage ended up being marginally helpful, because once they got specifics we could go back through all the footage and cull images of particular targets. But the images were scattered and random, nowhere near as useful as if we'd been able to focus our assets on particular parties. For instance, once they gave us a specific vehicle at a specific place and time, we were able to tail 'em until we nailed 'em."

"So, what kind of particulars do you need to get better outcomes?" Jason asked.

"An address. A vehicle. A person. Hell, even a spot on the globe," Collins tapped one of the blue lines indicating an off road trail. "You can see that we can analyze the movement of all traffic, be it on roads or through the woods. That's helpful for discerning overall patterns – what everyone is doing in the aggregate. But if you give me an address, I can identify which vehicles stop there, and where they've come from and where they go next. I can identify people, and then spot where else they turn up. With a few specifics we can identify more specifics, and that enables us to identify yet more, and eventually we can whittle this generic outline of everyone's activity down to exactly the parties you're interested in."

"I see your point," Jason said. "The problem is, we're scant on specifics. All we have is rumors, deductions from population patterns, and a mysterious blast. The only party we were reasonably certain about was blown up in the explosion."

Then the NSA tech stood up and gave a detailed explanation of the algorithms that were being applied to the overflight images, and how dynamic network analysis could discern patterns of probability, and so on. Major Collins looked bored and impatient – Jason suspected that his enthusiasm for this project was fading. Jason couldn't blame him. All this high-flying technology could only do so much without specifics.

When the meeting wrapped up, Ethan drove the guests back to Selfridge, leaving Jason alone in the little house with little to do. He checked and cleared his message box, which made him feel morose. His colleagues and coworkers were busy about their projects down in D.C., while he was assigned to this backwater, stuck in a bare house in an insignificant town, trying to pull off a miracle. The lack of progress on the blast investigation was discouraging, and though the Chengdu Two project seemed to hold promise, there were still many things that could go wrong.

In short, returning to D.C. in triumph was anything but certain, and at the moment felt like a receding goal.

Fed up with message traffic that only made him feel his exile more keenly, Jason pulled on his jacket and went for a walk. The mid-April air was warm, promising a springtime just around the corner, but the branches overhead were still stark and bare and the ground underfoot was still drab and muddy. Dirt-stained piles of plowed snow edged parking lots, seeping trickles of meltwater toward the nearest drain. He got a coffee at the shop on Elk Street and then strolled back to the courthouse lawn, where he sat on a bench by the gazebo and sipped his coffee. For some reason it aggravated him even more than usual to see all the pickups and rusty older cars bustling past. Their drivers seemed to be either pudgy women with curly hair or shaggy men wearing dirty ball caps. Jason thought of the sleek, clean cars he was accustomed to seeing around D.C., carrying young professionals about their business.

As Jason was gnawing on this, an older couple came trundling along the sidewalk past where he was sitting. It was an old, obese woman riding a motorized scooter with an oxygen tube fitted to her nose followed by a stooped, gray-haired old man wearing the ubiquitous dirty ball cap and a vacant expression. From the handlebars of the scooter hung some yellow shopping bags bearing the logo of the local bargain store. Jason watched their torpid progress with revulsion. They were typical examples of worthless consumers, people certainly living at public expense, draining resources and contributing nothing in return. Useless eaters, and ugly into the bargain. Disgusted, he didn't even finish his coffee, hurling what remained on the grass and heading back toward his house. Tonight, he was going to drive down to metro Detroit and get a decent meal at a decent restaurant.

Vision

Felicity opened the door quietly and slipped into the chapel. The darkness enveloped her, and she paused to allow her eyes to adjust. The chapel was a small interior room with no windows, and none of the room lights were on, so the only illumination came from the pinprick of flame of the Presence Lamp by the Tabernacle in the corner and two candles burning on the altar. The candles flanked a crucifix that stood in the center of the altar, drawing all eyes to the roughly carved cross and corpus.

The chapel held the usual rows of chairs, but just in front of the altar about half a dozen kneelers had been set up facing the crucifix. This made sense, for the chapel got frequent use during Holy Week, but at the moment only one of the kneelers was occupied. Felicity quietly made her way down the center aisle and knelt beside the other woman, who took Felicity's hand and squeezed it briefly. The two spent some time in silent prayer before the first crossed herself, stood, and moved to one of the chairs in the front row. Felicity followed her.

"Thank you for coming," the woman said, giving Felicity a quick hug.

"Always happy to, Teresa," Felicity replied. "Though I was surprised to get your message. It's been a while since I've been up here to St. Anne's."

"It's been a wonderful place for me," Teresa said quietly, looking about the dark, warm space. Then she took Felicity's hands and gazed at her calmly. "But tell me – how have you been?"

Felicity sighed. "It's been tough. We've all been preparing for Grandma's passing, but it's always a blow when it actually happens. And there's been lots of tension around the homes – Aunt Ruth is still distressed about Cletus and Sixtus moving out so abruptly, and that stresses Mom and Dad in turn. I'm worried myself, to be honest – nobody knows exactly where they are, and they haven't been in touch. So that situation puts Aunt Ruth off-center, and the guests still need care, so the rest of us have to take up the slack. I've never been so busy, and Harmony's been a champ. Cathy's been a trouper, too, despite being torn up about her brothers, and Aunt Jillian and Angie have been chipping in as they can. Grandpa has been a rock, helping and encouraging everyone – and here you'd think we'd be the ones consoling him."

Teresa waiting patiently as Felicity rattled on, letting her spin down on her own. When she finally fell silent, Teresa smiled gently and said, "I'm sorry to hear your family is under such stress, and will certainly continue to pray for them. But how are *you* doing, personally and spiritually? It hasn't been that long since you returned from school – how was your year?"

Felicity blinked and then stammered a bit. "St. Anselm's? It was fine, fine. Latin conjugation still throws me, but I think I managed to pass the exam..." Seeing Teresa's steady, patient gaze fixing her, Felicity trailed off, dropping her head. She sighed and began again, this time in a heavy voice. "Honestly, it was very difficult. The studies were manageable, but Grace and I...weren't getting along."

"Weren't getting along? In what sense?"

"It...it wasn't at all like last year. When we were first thrown together she and I hadn't known each other very well, so there was the excitement of the new friendship, and the consolation of each other's company when we were homesick, and the bonding that comes with enduring struggles together. By the time we came home last summer, I was sure I'd made a lifelong friend.

"But then last summer when everything happened, and we returned to St. Anselm's so shortly after that, things seemed...different. We started to get on one another's nerves in ways we hadn't before. That's easy to do in the sparse quarters at St. Anselm's, but it was more than just cramped space. We found ourselves making cutting little remarks, or getting irritated by one another's mannerisms. Tempers got shorter, especially once winter set in and we were more cooped up indoors. I suppose it was mostly my fault –" Felicity stopped abruptly and gave a hollow laugh. "You know, I say that all the time, and have since I was little. I think my parents taught me. I say it, but I wonder how much I believe it. I recite it as a formula, then proceed to disregard the other person, or to justify myself. I say the words, but beneath the surface I think the other is wronging me more."

"We all do that," Teresa assured her.

"Perhaps, but this year has stripped me of some delusions. In the past, it's been easy to make light of hurtful words and actions. I'd recite one of Mom's maxims – you know, like 'consider the source', or 'I'm sure he has his struggles' – and then dismiss the person. I'd ignore what was said, letting it roll off me. Turns out it's easy to be generous when you can discount what others say because you're convinced inside that you're a superior person. It's harder when the words stick – and sting.

"And for some reason this school year, Grace's words did a lot of sticking and stinging. I couldn't just brush them off like I'd always done – they seemed to cling to me like invisible burrs, and they festered. Grace can be…honestly, Grace can be a vindictive little bitch when she decides to be. But then, so can I – and I was. Except that I was an aloof, arrogant bitch, and I'd be sure to pay her back with interest. I think I understood her better than she understood me. I knew just what to say, and when and how to say it, to inflict maximum damage. It was like…like she was flailing about with a meat cleaver, looking to hack and maim, while I stood back with a boning knife, awaiting the opportunity to move in and stick the blade in to the hilt. We both knew that I was more effective, and I took grim satisfaction in surgically attacking her and then standing back to watch her frustration."

"You've clearly been doing some self-examination over this," Teresa said. "I presume you tried to reconcile?"

"We tried. We'd go through the motions – asking forgiveness and granting it, the obligatory hug, confession. And it wasn't superficial. I meant it as best I could, and I'm sure she did, too. But letting go, truly forgetting, proved much more difficult. We'd often reconcile in the evenings, just before bed, when we'd be forced back into each other's company. I'd say I forgave her, but then I'd lie there in the dark, going over the offense again and again, chewing on whatever she'd said and imagining how I should have responded. A couple of times I thought we'd really broken through and cleared the air, but then the next morning we'd be right back where we had been."

"A very human tendency," Teresa assured her.

"Yeah, I'm learning that," Felicity replied with a grim laugh. "But it makes me wonder how much I've ever truly forgiven. Have I just dismissed offenses, walked away from them? Or have I really recognized them and forgiven them? Do I even know how to forgive? I'm learning that it's easier to forgive when you're feeling on top of the world, in charge of your life, and magnanimous. But when you're hurt, and weakened, and feeling ground down – that's the real test of forgiving."

"Indeed," Teresa said, with a quick glance at the crucifix on the altar. "It sounds like you've been having experience with that."

"Ha – to say the least," Felicity acknowledged. "Grace and I returned feeling drained and wounded, and like our relationship was a source of stress rather than strength. Then to come home and be hammered by everything here! Not just Grandma's death, though that took its toll, but all the other pressures in my family. I was expecting some of it, and intended to charge in and set everything right, only to find myself – collapsing."

"Collapsing?"

"Buckling might be a better term. I thought I could be a strong pillar, but found myself weaker than I've ever known myself to be."

"How so?"

"Since returning home I've been petty and impatient and shockingly…manipulative. I thought I'd be generous and gracious and helpful, but when it became clear that my ego wasn't getting stroked the way I wanted, I'd get petulant or snappish. Just when people needed me most, I'd be least cooperative. In my immaturity I may even have…damaged…a relationship with a dear friend. I just don't know what to do!" Felicity buried her face in her hands and sobbed.

Teresa reached over and stroked Felicity's shoulder, saying nothing but handing her a box of tissues from one of the nearby chairs. Eventually Felicity calmed down a little.

"What do you want, Felicity?" Teresa asked. "It is Holy Week, when we should be bold in our prayers and expectations. What would you ask of Jesus?"

"For it to be all right again?" Felicity answered with a wan smile through her tears. "I guess that's a little vague. If I had to be specific, I'd like my relationship with Grace restored. She and I had become like sisters, and the loss of that has been the tragic backdrop to all the other things that have been wrong recently."

"It may encourage you to know that she feels the same way," Teresa said.

"Really? I thought she'd want nothing to do with me."

"She was afraid you thought the same."

"How do you know?" Felicity asked.

"Because she told me so just this morning. Fr. Gabriel was here to hear confessions, so I invited her to join us. Afterwards, she and I had a talk much like this one," Teresa explained. "She, too, was very remorseful and repentant, and wanting nothing more than to have your sisterhood restored."

"Really? She was here?" Felicity asked with nervous excitement.

"Actually," Teresa said with a broad grin as she held up her phone. "She still is. She's been in the kitchen helping with lunch, but I've messaged her, and she should be here shortly."

Even as Teresa spoke, the chapel door opened, and Grace looked hesitantly into the room. "Grace!" Felicity cried, bolting to her. The two friends locked in a close embrace, sinking to their knees as they sobbed and clung to one another. For a time, all was tears and kisses and brokenhearted apologies and openhearted forgiveness. Teresa had to duck out for another box of tissues, but eventually everyone had calmed down enough to talk again. Grace and Felicity sat side by side holding hands tightly, while Teresa sat across from them, her face shadowed in the candlelight.

"Sisters, I called you both here during this week when we especially remember Christ's reconciliation of God and man, in hopes of achieving a reconciliation between you. Thank you for being humble and open to forgiving. I wish I could say that it will make things easy, but I fear that it's only a necessary prerequisite for our dealing with the difficulties that face us."

"Difficulties?" Felicity asked.

"Yes. I fear that all those we love, and especially we three, are about to be sorely tried. There is hope of some peace on the far side of the trials, but not before terrible sacrifice and loss," Teresa explained.

"What a cheerful thought," Grace said. "Do you have a reason to think that?"

"I've had many clues, some of them spoken by you two this very day. A common thread between your stories was that you've both felt unusually burdened, unable to move beyond offenses and struggling to be charitable. Let me ask you, Grace – what is your deepest, oldest fear? Has there been anything that has haunted you much of your life, some dark dread that's familiar to you?"

Grace pondered this for a minute before replying. "Maybe a fear of drowning in darkness? It's hard to explain, but I have these dreams of being suspended above some abyss or pit that's swirling with darkness. Whatever is beneath me is not just in shadow, but seems to be filled with a tangible darkness that swirls or surges like liquid. My position is always precarious – near a cliff edge, or clinging to a rocky slope, or on a narrow bridge, or something. I'm terrified of slipping and falling into the darkness, of drowning in it, yet I'm also fascinated by it, drawn to it."

"Wow, that's vivid," Felicity said with a shudder. "Sounds scary."

"Have you been having more of these dreams recently, especially though the school year?" Teresa asked.

Again Grace thought for a minute. "Come to think of it, I have. I'd just attributed it to the stress of schoolwork, or the strain in our relationship, but thinking back, I've had more of the dreams in the past year than I'd had for years before, and they've been more intense."

Teresa nodded, as if hearing confirmation of something she'd suspected. "And you, Felicity? Are there any deep-seated fears that you have?"

"Now that you mention it, there is one, though it doesn't sound as horrifying as Grace's. When I was young, one of my recurring nightmares would be that I was invisible."

"Invisible?" Teresa asked.

"Yes, but more than just invisible. I'd be in my home, but none of my family members could see me no matter what I did to get their attention. They'd look right through me, or walk past me, neither seeing nor hearing me. Not only that, but none of my books or toys would be there, and there'd be no place at the table for me, and my room would be decorated differently. It's like seeing my family like they'd be if I'd never existed. I'd always wake up from those dreams sobbing, and when I was very young I'd run into my Mom and Dad's room to make sure they were still there, and that they could see me."

"Have you had any of these dreams recently? Within the past year?"

"I don't remember my dreams very well, but I do recall several times during the school year waking up distressed and panicked. I wasn't sure why, but it was the same sort of feeling I used to have when I awoke from those nightmares."

Teresa nodded again, as if receiving expected news.

"Do you think this all means something?" Grace asked.

"I don't know for sure," Teresa responded. "I have my suspicions, based on some things you both have said, and on your dreams, and on other indications. But it's just speculation at this point, and I don't want to say more, lest I mislead you."

"Wonderful," Felicity said. "Dark mysteries are some of our favorite things."

"Unfortunately, very mysterious – and possibly very dark," Teresa said. "As soon as I learn more, I'll let you know. For now, let's spend some time in prayer."

This they did, concluding about twenty minutes later. Teresa escorted them to the front door of St. Anne's, giving them parting admonitions as they went.

"Stay close to each other, and to the Lord. Immerse yourself in the Triduum, and go to Mass and confession frequently in the weeks to come. Be prepared for trial, and do not let offenses fester. Pray for one another, and for me."

"When will we know more about…whatever's going on?" Felicity asked.

"What I learn, I will share with you as it seems prudent, but I won't trouble you with vain speculations," Teresa replied. "Go with God, sisters."

The two friends departed while Teresa returned to the chapel for more prayer. In spite of the emotional lift provided by seeing her two friends reconciled, her heart was still heavy with concern. Listening carefully to the accounts of their recent struggles, Teresa had heard disconcerting things, such as the steady sapping of spiritual and emotional strength, and the resurgence of old and deep personal fears. She wondered what she'd hear if she had a chance to interview some of the others.

Teresa knelt and tried to clear her mind. She was feeling light-headed – nothing but water had passed her lips since after dinner the day before, and nothing would until sundown Friday. It was difficult, but it was Another's strength that was needed just now, not hers. She, too, had been feeling her share of spiritual burdens and old fears. The bleak emptiness, the self-accusations which had never retreated far now seemed to hover constantly over her shoulder, ready to move in at the least provocation to engulf her heart and tug her toward despair. She knew she could not fight these fears in her own strength, so she lifted her eyes to the crucifix and prayed.

At first, Teresa had been alarmed when her darkest terrors had come creeping back to plague her the prior autumn, but she'd gotten good counsel which had helped her recognize these for the external assaults they were. But that had raised the question: from whence had these come? And why now? As she'd fasted and prayed, her heart had been led down dark paths to a distressing realization.

Of all her acquaintances, Teresa was the only one who had ever deliberately taken a human life. Though she had been forgiven and remade into a new being, she still recognized the dark spiritual imprint of that thirst for blood, that ravenous, never-sated maw. She had felt it when she'd depressed the plungers that had sent the poison dripping into the veins of her victims, and she detected it again now – distant and attenuated, but unquestionably present. This was the wellspring of the weakening, of the attacks on her and her friends – and, she suspected, attacks on several others.

Teresa even strongly suspected the source. She'd guessed, even at the time, that they had not vanquished the force that had been summoned last summer to veil the evil that Ray Hubbart and his family had been practicing. They had battled it, and had snatched some of its victims from its jaws, and had even contained it, but it was still there, brooding and lurking and hungry as ever. She bowed her head and tried to pray, to lift her heart toward light and peace, rather than letting herself be drawn down into the darkness. Her focus needed to be upward: not upon the horror, but upon the power that could destroy it. She would be involved, somehow, she was certain. She was willing to be involved, especially if it meant freedom for those she loved. But she guessed that the cost would be great, probably more than she was able to bear.

Teresa lifted her head to gaze upon the illuminated crucifix, her lips moving in silent prayer. She needed to remember – it was not her strength that mattered, but her willingness.

But willing took a strength of its own.

*   *   *

"So, Frieda, is everything clear to you?" Shelly asked the older woman who sat across from her in the small living room. Luke sat in another chair, while Andy and Frances Jameson sat on either side of Frieda on the couch.

"It seems so," Frieda replied, waving at the folder on the coffee table in front of her. "Mr. Fitzgerald explained all the money things when he dropped by yesterday, and said that everything's all arranged."

"That's right," Shelly assured her. "Your accounts have all been set up, and the payments to the home, and all the necessaries. Fitz signed the contract with the home on your behalf, so you're set to move in this weekend. We'll have a team of helpers here for the move, not that you have all that much."

"I wish I could contact your specialist for you, Frieda, but you know how that goes," Luke apologized. "Promise me you'll call him first thing after you've moved in."

"I promise," Frieda assured him.

"You don't have to do this, you know, Frieda," Frances said.

"Oh, posh, I've troubled you all long enough with my old bones," Frieda waved.

"Frieda," Frances scolded gently. "I keep trying to tell you that you've been no trouble. It's been a delight to have you."

Frieda waved some more and blushed in embarrassment, but clearly appreciated the reassurance. Shelly and Luke stood up to leave in order to give the family some time together.

"Can you give me a lift as far as Brown City?" Luke asked Shelly as they headed for the door.

"Farther, if you need," Shelly assured him.

"No, you've got enough on your plate. Ben Stover will be in that neck of the woods, and he can give me a lift from there."

"How far are you going?" Shelly asked.

"Just south of Ruth – there's a guest with serious renal issues. He'll be the other test release."

"I sure hope we know what we're doing," Shelly sighed as they got into her car. "We've discussed this to death, but it sure goes against the grain. I suppose it's all the years of working in secrecy, but the thought of sending a couple of our guests out there in full view, to plug back into the regular medical system – well, it makes me nervous."

"Yeah," was Luke's only reply. He preferred not to discuss the deep foreboding that had settled in his gut as the plans had progressed. He couldn't figure out whether it was concern for his patients, or distress over what his beloved families were enduring, or anxiety about his own future, or something else.

*   *   *

Teresa lay still in the darkness, exhausted from her shift yet unable to sleep. It was times like this that the fears crowded close, seeking entry into her heart and imagination: the aching emptiness, the feelings of inadequacy and insufficiency, the crushing certainty that she'd never measure up. She tried to fight these by reciting Scripture verses or quotes from the saints, but in the quiet darkness the mouthed words availed little against the pressure of emotions that had tormented her for most of her life.

Recently Teresa had been experiencing a more disturbing manifestation of these forces. Even as she would close her eyes at night and try to quiet her mind, images would flit in, vivid memories of that which she'd thought she'd left behind, dark yet enticing. These images would start unfolding before she even realized they were upon her, and she'd find herself watching in petrified fascination as they played out in her imagination. She'd be looking down at the smooth white skin of her thigh held taut by her left hand while her right hand approached with the knife. There was the momentary hesitation as the cold steel lay against her skin, then the light gasp as the blade bit in, the initial shock of physical pain distracting her from her emotional anguish. But it wasn't enough, it was never enough, so with trembling hand she'd draw the edge slowly through the flesh, watching the layers peel back and the blood well up, wincing at the very pain she relished, fighting the urge to go further this time, further and deeper –

Enough! Teresa shook her head and hurled back her covers, letting the shock of the chill air break the flow of the images.

Brusquely she yanked on her robe. Though her eyes ached and her limbs were heavy with weariness, there was only one place to go when she couldn't escape the haunting memories.

The chapel was dark, with only the glow of the Presence Lamp illuminating one corner. Teresa didn't want to sit in one of the few chairs, so she knelt on one of the kneelers and stared at the Lamp, trying to quiet her unsettled heart. She felt battered and depleted in mind, body, and emotions, and had no eloquent prayers or profound meditations to offer. In helplessness she bowed her head onto her hands and tried to follow Fr. Gabriel's advice – to offer up her weariness, her weakness, the horrible deeds of her past, the dark memories that plagued her now, her emptiness, her pain. She offered all that as best she could, even as she nodded where she knelt.

Then, somehow, Teresa was flying, soaring at a very great height, so high that her wide wings were leaving little trails of ice crystals in the clear air and the earth spread out below her like a mottled brown and gray blanket. She recognized the terrain – it was her home, the Thumb region, with the plowed fields laid out like little tiles, edged and broken by swaths of woods. She had to be flying north, for the shore of Saginaw Bay could be seen ahead on her left, and far to the right Lake Huron glistened in the morning sunlight.

Teresa would have been frightened of falling – she'd never been keen on heights – except that she felt utterly confident in her vehicle. She was somehow aware of how bitterly cold the air was at that altitude, but she wasn't feeling it due to the metal walls that kept the cold at bay. What she could feel was the low thrum of the engine providing the thrust that kept her airborne. It was a strange sensation, in one sense like being in an aircraft, but in another sense like *being* the aircraft, soaring high in the morning sky. Once the initial alarm had passed, she began to enjoy the feeling of being aloft and free.

Or, rather, somewhat free. In the same way that she "knew" of her metal skin and broad wings, she also "knew" that she was on a set course, flying according to a preordained pattern that she could not alter. Try as she might, she could not turn or bank, and could not fly higher or lower. Some authority had dictated her course, and she could not deviate from it.

Teresa also realized what there was to do as she flew along: look. Specifically, to look down. She had no power to look up, or even very far ahead of her. She could see directly beneath her, as well as a little to her left and right. To the left her vision took in the cities strung along the expressway – Flint, Saginaw, and Bay City – and about to the middle of Saginaw Bay. To her right, at the far edge of her vision, she could see the shore of Lake Huron, but not so far as Canada. Ahead she could see only land, which told her she was not yet close enough to the waters that formed the north edge of the Thumb. Her field of vision was fixed.

But within that field, Teresa was amazed at how much, and how well, she could see. The landscape was rich with detail, even if the colors were only drab earth tones. She could almost distinguish the plow furrows in the fields, and the needles of the pines that swayed in the breeze. Also, she found that if she concentrated on a spot, her vision would zoom in to provide more detail. There was a small city ahead that she suspected was Cass City; as she focused on that it enlarged until she could see in detail the building fronts and the cars waiting at the stoplights. She scanned the streets for a while, spotting houses and trees and even people walking the sidewalks. Then she willed to widen her vision, zooming out until she could again see the entire width of the Thumb.

This unusual experience was intriguing enough, but then Teresa's vision began to shift again. She was still looking down on the landscape, and seemed still to be flying northward, but as she watched, it seemed a lattice of thin gray lines was being woven over the region. It looked like these lines were being traced by a small object or entity that was shuttling around the area – first west, then north, then southeast, then west again, then back north. Wherever this object went, it left behind a thin trace of gray which remained like a glowing thread. She seemed to be seeing this phenomenon on an accelerated timeframe, because whatever the object was, it seemed to be very busy, scuttling all over and leaving light gray traces behind it. The result was a steadily growing web that draped like fine lace over the landscape. At first Teresa thought it was pretty, which it was, but as she examined it more closely, she saw that the gray traces were not soft and flexible, but hard and cold and sharp-edged. With dismay she realized that what looked like delicate lacework was in fact a deadly net. Alarmed, she sought to examine more closely the busy object that was laying down the traces. This was difficult, for the object was moving so quickly that it was hard to get a good look at it. Teresa began to get anxious, for it seemed imperative for her to learn what it was that was generating this dangerous lattice. Then she remembered what she'd been told about anxiety, and worked to calm herself. This whole scenario was already bizarre enough. What she would see, she would see; what she would know, she would know; but all of it was in the hands of Another.

While this was unfolding, Teresa's "flight" continued, the landscape scrolling by beneath her as she followed her northward course. The web of gray traces was being spun everywhere she looked. At the north edge of her vision the coastline was growing longer as she approached the Huron shore. But even as the blue expanded at the forward edge of her sight, another alarming thing came into view. Ahead on the right she saw what seemed to be a gouge in the landscape, an angry red spot that seemed to glow and throb. Teresa had no desire to examine this spot more closely – in fact she would have swerved away if she could have. But she was locked into her course, so she had to watch as the red stain came more fully into her field of vision. Fortunately, her flight path would not take her directly over it, at least on her current leg, for this oblique view was as close as she wanted to get. Despite her revulsion, she couldn't help her eyes straying to the sight time and again. The red blotch looked like an open sore, and even from this height she could feel the caged anger that lurked and prowled within it.

As if that was not dismaying enough, Teresa noticed that some of the gray traces had been run very close to the red spot, almost near enough to touch it. Even as she watched, the bustling thing that was laying down the traces flicked past again, drawing another trace almost on top of the red spot. It was as if the thing didn't see, or wasn't affected by, the stain. But the traces were affected – Teresa could see that the ones that lay closest to the gash were being stained red. With alarm, she saw the red staining begin to creep slowly along the traces, branching off when it came to a junction, spreading steadily outward from the red gash.

It was very hard for Teresa to remain calm while watching this. She had her suspicions about what the red spot was, and sensed how intensely it was straining against that which contained it. Seeing the stain spreading along whatever those traces represented drove her near to panic. Could nobody see? Could nobody understand? She struggled against the metal frame in futility. She watched the bustling little object as it flitted to and fro, laying traces as it went, and yearned for a voice to call out to it, to warn it. But she was helpless to do anything but continue to fly straight, and watch what she was certain was a disaster in the making.

As Teresa was approaching tears in her frustration, her view began to dim. She wondered if she was flying into some sort of mist or cloud, because her vision was becoming shrouded by a rapidly intensifying whiteness. Before she knew it, she could see nothing but uniform whiteness everywhere. Against this backdrop a different vision unfolded. She was no longer flying, but she could see the face of a man. He was not an old man, perhaps no more than ten years older than Teresa, but his expression was so determined as to seem fierce. Teresa had never seen him before, and had no idea what he was doing, but whatever it was, he was doing it with dogged intensity. It was as though she was spectating as he went about his duties with a focused vehemence that was almost painful to watch. She could only see his face, and occasionally his hands, but that was enough to convey his frantic urgency. He never seemed to rest, but turned his attention from one task to another without pause. Teresa got the impression of someone hounded and driven, someone anxious to make up for some shortfall or attain some impossible goal. Only once or twice did she catch him when he wasn't concentrating and his expression relaxed. In those brief moments, the man looked so bereft, so forlorn and forsaken, that she longed to take his hand and reassure him that he was loved. He was clearly a driven man, a wounded man, a desperately unhappy man.

Then that vision faded as well, leaving Teresa in featureless whiteness, confused and distressed. What had she seen, and what did it mean? Who was that man? Were the visions connected? What, if anything, was she supposed to do? She tried to be calm, but it was all so vague and confusing that she couldn't help but be a little unsettled.

As Teresa tried to calm down, what she was seeing changed again, though it took her a while to notice it. She no longer felt like she was flying, but rather standing on something, though still surrounded by what seemed to be a pearly mist. She began walking slowly forward, and before long a small white pedestal, about waist height, emerged. There was something atop it that she couldn't make out at first, but as she drew closer, she recognized it as a bouquet and veil. But what a bouquet! It was mostly brilliant white blossoms, though interspersed with flowers whose petals were streaked with richest gold. The ribbon was pure white as well. Teresa had never seen such a delicate and beautiful arrangement. The veil that lay beside the bouquet was just as exquisite, with the cap covered in fine white lace and the veil of sheer silk embroidered with delicate tracery.

Teresa stood transfixed by the beauty. For whom were these items? The purest, loveliest bride on earth could not do them justice. She yearned to reach out and touch them – not to pick them up, but perhaps to trace the lace of the veil with her finger, or to feel the silkiness of the ribbon. But fear restrained her, fear that her touch would somehow defile them, or that her clumsiness would cause her to jostle the bouquet, knocking it to the ground and ruining its exquisite perfection.

But even as she gazed upon this rapturous vision of loveliness, something began intruding on her consciousness. Someone was calling her name, and she was being shaken, and the vision evaporated, replaced by the hard, chilly chapel floor and Sister Catherine shaking her shoulder gently while Sister Kateri looked on anxiously.

"Teresa, are you all right?" Sister Catherine was asking. Teresa didn't know how to answer that – she felt disoriented. Apparently, she'd toppled sideways onto the floor and had lain there for some time, if the chill in her side and the numbness in her arm were any indication. The serenity that she'd felt during the final portion of the vision was dissipating quickly in her confusion and distress.

"Should I call Sister Gianna?" Sister Kateri asked anxiously. Sister Gianna was the sole other nurse at St. Anne's.

"No, no, I'm fine," Teresa protested, pushing herself to her feet. "I'm fine, physically. I've just had – I've been dreaming, I think. I came here to pray and nodded off." But as she spoke the vivid intensity of the early part of her vision returned, and with it the sense of urgency. "Is Sister Joseph Marie awake?"

"I think so – we're just getting ready for Lauds, and she should be along shortly," Sister Kateri said as the two helped Teresa to a seat.

"I need to talk to her. I need to talk to her right now," Teresa said.

"Can't it wait until after prayers?"

"No, it can't," Teresa pushed herself to her feet and headed for the door.

*   *   *

Sister Joseph Marie sat alone in her office, pondering and praying. A thousand details clamored for her attention, but she put them all off for a time while she considered what she'd learned that morning, and how it fitted with her own instincts and forebodings.

Teresa was one of Sister Joseph Marie's most interesting charges. None of the other sisters at St. Anne's knew the full details of her complex and tragic history, or what she had been rescued from. The mental and spiritual trauma that had accompanied those drastic life changes had devastated her personality, which Sister Joseph could tell was still being reconstructed. In some senses, that simplified things, for Teresa was a responsible and diligent worker, discharging her duties crisply and making good suggestions about administration and patient care. But she was prone to bouts of insecurity and self-doubt, which she could be very adept at hiding beneath a veneer of brisk efficiency. Sister Joseph was learning that she could not just keep shoving more duties at Teresa, regardless of how little resistance that path offered, but had to ensure that Teresa took sufficient time for spiritual direction and the cultivation of her devotional life.

Teresa's unique personal history made her a bit of an enigma to the other sisters. They loved her and appreciated her diligence, but the devotional elements that were second nature to most of them were alien to Teresa. They couldn't understand why she didn't eagerly join in the chaplets, novenas, and other practices in which the sisters regularly engaged. Teresa did participate in community prayers when her duties permitted, but otherwise her devotional time was spent alone, in her room or the chapel, with only her Bible, if that. Her spiritual life was very internal, and she was not given to the enthusiasms and urges that some of the younger sisters were.

Which made this vision she'd had all the more unusual – and sobering.

Sister Joseph Marie looked down at the notes she'd taken as Teresa had recounted the dream or vision or whatever it was she'd had. Though she had clearly been upset at the telling, she was precise and dispassionate as she recounted what she'd seen. Both of them acknowledged that the whole thing could have been no more than a lengthy and curious dream, but the more Sister Joseph considered it, the more convinced she was that what Teresa had seen was not only true, but intended as a message, though expressed in symbol and metaphor. Furthermore, the harsh and ominous elements of the vision indicated that the message was a dire one, possibly a warning. This would square with some cautions that Sister Joseph had been receiving in her own devotional times – words about strength in trial, and perseverance, and the price of obedience. If this mysterious dream of Teresa's harmonized with those words, then it was possible that their little community was being forewarned. But of what? And what action were they supposed to take, if any? Sister Joseph knew that there were some changes being considered among the ranches, and some things had come to light that were driving other changes. She wasn't certain how this mystical vision would square with what was known or assumed by the decision makers.

Sister Joseph closed her notebook and tucked it into a drawer. Duties summoned, and she'd spent enough time pondering this. Perhaps she'd discuss it with Fr. Gabriel when he dropped in later this afternoon. In the meantime, all she could do was pray.

*   *   *

Late that morning, in a donut shop at the north end of Port Huron, Gil Peterson slipped unobtrusively into a booth across from where Fitz sat nursing a dark roast coffee and nibbling a muffin.

"Hey," Fitz greeted him.

"Hey," Gil replied.

"Are all the moves made?"

"Yes, with no more than the usual complications. Our trial cases are moved out and back in circulation."

"Of course, the real test will be when they go for medical care," Fitz pointed out. "Has that been scheduled?"

"For one, a week from today," Gil affirmed. "The other is still trying to get an appointment, but it shouldn't be long."

Fitz toyed nervously with the plastic lid he'd removed from his coffee cup. "We're watching them, right?"

"Like hawks. If anything goes amiss, we'll alert everyone," Gil assured him. "Your end is all taken care of, right?"

"Best I can do. I contacted a couple of attorneys who specialize in this sort of work and implemented the procedures they recommended. As long as the guests keep quiet about where they've been, nobody will be able to trace anything back to us."

"You briefed the guests thoroughly, right?"

"Yes," Fitz said with great patience. "They're more motivated than we are – they love their families and don't want to put them in any danger."

"I know, I know," Gil fidgeted, sipping his coffee. Both men sat in nervous silence for a minute, absorbed in their thoughts.

"So, how are things back home?" Fitz finally asked.

"Tough," Gil admitted. "Ma's passing was hardly a surprise, but when it finally happens, it precipitates changes no matter how much you prepare. You know how it is."

"I do," Fitz nodded. "How's your Dad taking it?"

"That's the odd thing – he seems to be riding it out better than any of us. You catch him occasionally in a solitary moment looking bereft and lonely, but mostly he's upbeat and engaged and trying to cheer others up, which is fortunate."

"Fortunate?"

"The one hit hardest has been Ruth, not so much because of Ma, but because of the twins abruptly moving out. That's been tough on all of us, but it's rendered her almost useless. It's been depressing to be around her, and none of us can cheer her up. Dad's the only one who can take much of her company. I mean, I love my sister, but…" Gil trailed off. Fitz nodded in sympathy. Even at the best of times Ruth's dour and pessimistic temperament was difficult to work with, and the trying circumstances had to make it worse.

"How about you, Gil?" Fitz asked. "How are you holding up?"

Gil sighed and took a sip of coffee. "All right, I think. I guess part of me is still feeling Ma's loss, but her decline lasted so long that I'd already done most of my grieving. Part of me is relieved her suffering is over, and I trust that she's in good hands." He took another sip.

"But…" prompted Fitz, sensing there was more on his friend's mind.

"Home life is a little difficult as well," Gil admitted. "Principally it's been Felicity."

"Felicity?" Fitz asked in surprise.

"I know – strange, isn't it? She's always been our golden child, never much trouble, ever helpful. Never a plaster saint, especially in her early teens, but never a problem child either – none of our kids have been."

"So, what's going on?"

"She's been moody and withdrawn, and we can't figure out why. Maybe something happened at school, but she won't talk about it. For that matter, she'll hardly talk about anything, which is part of the problem. Normally she's chatty and outgoing. By now we'd expected to have heard all about school and the friends she'd made and the things she'd learned. Instead, she's kept to herself, staying in her room or going on long solitary walks."

"Maybe this is how she's grieving her grandmother?" Fitz offered.

"I thought that possible, but Jan doesn't think that's it. Sure, she's sad, but we've lost friends and relatives before, and Felicity's response has always been different. Her faith and temperament give her a natural optimism that makes her more likely to be the one reaching out and comforting others in time of loss. Not so this time, which has mystified her siblings, particularly Harmony."

"Hmm," Fitz mused. "Is it possible she met some Canadian lad at school who caught her fancy, and is missing him now? Or maybe they had a tough breakup?"

"I wondered the same, but again, Jan doesn't think so. Felicity has had her share of crushes and flings, most of which I've been oblivious to, but Jan says she responds differently to them. While it's going on, Felicity is reserved but will confide in those close to her, particularly Jan. Once it ends, she throws herself into relationships with friends and family to diffuse the pain. None of that is going on now. She's just…pulled back, seemingly from everyone. It's like she's under some kind of cloud, and we can't figure out what or why."

"Hmm. I wish I could offer you some advice, but I've nothing to suggest. I'll keep you all in prayer, of course."

"Thanks. Speaking of clouds, have you heard anything more from your inside contact about the ramped-up surveillance?"

"No," Fitz admitted. "That has me concerned. He clearly thinks the situation dangerous, which means I do, because I trust his judgment. The fact that he hasn't contacted me since that day means either the danger has abated, or that there have been no new developments, or that things are too delicate to attempt contact. The way he was talking makes me doubt the first two possibilities, which leaves the third."

"That's encouraging," Gil said dryly. "Could you contact him? Get a little more detail on the nature of this danger?"

"I daren't," Fitz replied. "Given the steps that he took to ensure our meeting was secret, I'm assuming he's concerned about constant and thorough observation. Anything that might connect me with him would be a danger to us both. I'm leaving all initiative in his hands."

"And it's into this environment we're releasing our first guests in years," Gil added, shaking his head. "Are we sure we know we're doing the right thing?"

"We've talked it to death, Gil," Fitz spread his hands. "We've taken every precaution and have all the contingency plans in place. We were going to have to do something eventually – you know better than I that what we've been doing is unsustainable in the long run. It has always been stopgap."

"Yeah, I know," Gil admitted. "I just wish there weren't so many unknowns."

"Speaking of unknowns, have you heard anything about some new facilities being thrown up in the area?" Fitz asked.

"Facilities? What kind of facilities?"

"That's the thing – nobody knows. A friend of mine mentioned seeing some buildings being erected on a lot at the corner of a field just west of Forester, and I didn't think anything of it. But when I heard of another similar facility south of Brown City, I began to wonder, so I took a drive."

"What did you see?"

"Not much – just a few generic, nondescript buildings being put up on empty lots far from anywhere. No signs, no labels, no indication of ownership or purpose," Fitz explained.

"Well, I haven't heard anything, but then I don't know everything that goes on in the region," Gil admitted. "Maybe something to do with utilities?"

"If so, it's the fastest utility work on record," Fitz said. "Those lots were cornfields just weeks ago. Plus, no excavations and no utility trucks. Don't see many people around at all – just No Trespassing signs."

"Hmm. I haven't heard a thing, but I'll ask around. Probably nothing of concern to us."

Pressure

The next morning Jason woke late, his head throbbing and his mouth gummy. He'd made it down to some suburb a couple of hours away – Troy, he seemed to remember, not that it mattered. He'd scoped out a few spots that seemed to be trying just a bit too hard to be hip and chic like those found in real cities. He'd hooked up with some girl – Sting? Thorn? That was it – Thorn, if that was her real name. They'd danced and drunk and ended up back at her place for a tryst, where she'd brought out some excellent weed. He couldn't even remember driving home.

Well, Jason thought as he showered, at least he didn't have to commute anywhere. That was one of the few positives in this depressing assignment – he hardly ever had to face traffic congestion. His message box contained a link from George Spader, the POM guy over at HHS, to the two spots that were going to run. The first would be on Saturday and the next would be on Monday. The POM people planned to gauge public reaction to the spots – however they did that – before airing the two follow-up spots that contained the commentary. Once they did that, which would probably be within a week, it gave Jason a hard deadline. The RCCs had to be ready to announce within two weeks. That gave him a moment of panic until he read the next message, which was from the FEMA supervisor in charge of the deployments, explaining about the unanticipated complications, et cetera, but assuring him that the sites would be "all but" ready by the end of the day.

Jason was pondering the implications of that when a reminder chimed to inform him that he'd deferred his tax preparation for as long as possible, and that if he wanted his returns to get filed on time, this was the last day he had to get his information to the preparer. That put additional pressure on the day, so Jason hammered out a hasty progress report to Cynthia, trying to put the most optimistic spin possible on the progress of the RCCs, then spent the rest of the day scrambling to assemble components to send to his tax preparation firm. That night he lay awake, his mind churning over whether he had remembered to include everything in his taxes, and whether the RCCs would really be ready, and what Whitman was up to, and whether he'd ever get his career back on track – if indeed he still had a career after this debacle.

Jason had intended to get started first thing in the morning to drive around and inspect all the RCC sites. His insomnia the night before caused him to wake later than he'd intended, so "first thing" ended up being about 10:30 a.m., but he wasn't worried – it was a Saturday, so the normally light traffic was even lighter. He had the addresses plugged into the car's nav system, so he just let that direct him to the sites in turn, going roughly clockwise from his house.

The first RCC was located to the east, on a dirt road not far inland from the coastal town of Forester. Jason had to admit that the site looked reasonably complete, with a packed gravel parking lot and freshly sown grass around the edges. There were four buildings on the site – a main building about twenty feet wide by eighty feet long, a smaller building about the size of a house trailer that looked like administrative offices, a blockish single-story building near the back of the property, and what looked like a combination storage facility and garage. No heavy equipment remained on the site, though there were a couple of panel vans. The buildings were all sided in shiny metal that gleamed in the sunlight, but when Jason looked closely at the corners and joins, the dents and poor fit bespoke "hasty" and "low budget". No matter, Jason reflected. They would serve their purpose.

The next site was just south of Brown City, ironically not far from the blast site. It looked nearly identical to the Forester site, except with only one panel van. Since this site wasn't far from Imlay City, Jason decided to take a quick detour to visit some stores there for household necessities. While walking the aisles, he saw a display of gaudy purses marked down – and still, apparently, not selling. He was about to walk past them when a thought seized him, and he put the reddest, gaudiest purse from the rack into his cart.

Jason's next stop was the motel in Imlay City where he'd stayed. Taking the purse in, he asked the desk attendant if Allie was working. She was, and a quick call soon brought her lumbering to the lobby where Jason waited.

"Why, Mr. Pelletier!" Allie exclaimed. "How good to see you!"

"Hi, Allie," Jason said, holding out the red purse. "I saw something at the store and thought of you, so I picked it up."

Allie stopped dead and gasped, holding her hands to her mouth, her eyes going wide with surprise. "Oh…oh…" she stammered. "Mr. Pelletier, you shouldn't have! My old one…just fine…but, it's beautiful!" She took the purse as gingerly as if it were a relic, turning it over in her hands with sighs of amazement.

"I know your old one is still usable, Allie, but I thought you could use another. This one is bigger, I think," Jason explained. In fact, he'd seen Allie's purse, tucked into her cleaning cart. It looked like it had even more frills and baubles than this new one, but had seen much better days, and was scuffed and stitched and stuffed to bursting. Now, watching Allie tear up as she examined the new purse with wonder, he knew he'd made the right choice.

"Oh, Mr. Pelletier," Allie nearly sobbed. "How can I ever thank you? It's…it's beautiful. What a wonderful Easter present! How can I ever thank you?"

"Maybe by calling me Jason, like I've asked you to?" Jason suggested with a grin.

"Oh," Allie gasped again, then leaned forward and hugged Jason impulsively. Jason returned the hug, slightly embarrassed, because it seemed like she was sobbing onto his shoulder. He patted her back clumsily, a little self-conscious but also wondering what kind of life she must live, that a tawdry purse off a sale rack could generate this kind of response. Finally she stepped back, sniffing and daubing her eyes, clearly embarrassed herself.

"Thank you, Mr. Pelletier. Thank you so much," Allie choked out. "I don't…thank you."

"Don't mention it, Allie," Jason assured her. "Look, I've got to go, but I'll drop back in soon, okay?"

265

"Sure, sure, I understand, Mr. Pelletier," Allie replied. "Happy Easter!"

Jason ducked out, still a bit embarrassed by Allie's excessive response but feeling better about himself than he had in a long time. He was starting to feel hungry, so he ignored the nav system's instructions and turned north toward Marlette, where there was a cozy, clean diner that served breakfast all day.

The third RCC site was near Fairgrove, a few miles west of Caro, and the sun was westering as Jason approached it. This site, too, had a panel van in the parking lot, but it also had a black sedan with government plates. Jason got out and began walking around the site, checking over the buildings. He hadn't been at this long when a door in the main building opened and some men came out. A couple of them wore coveralls and dusty caps, but one was in khakis and a polo shirt. Spotting Jason, the man in khakis came bustling over wearing a self-important scowl.

"See here, this is a classified government facility," the man blustered. "You'll have to leave immediately!"

"I know it is," Jason replied, handing the man his ID wallet. "I'm Jason Pelletier, Department of Homeland Security Domestic Terror Division. I'm the one who ordered these facilities, and I was given to understand that they'd be ready a week ago."

The man inspected Jason's credentials and handed them back, suddenly obsequious. "Of course, of course, Mr. Pelletier. Surely you understand the need for site security – I had to be certain –"

"What I understand is that FEMA was supposed to have these sites erected and operational three days after project initiation," Jason snapped. "This is the ninth day since that promised delivery date, making these installations three hundred percent over time budget."

The man bristled at Jason's censure, and came back sharply. "See here, I don't care who you are, we've been working twelve hour days to get these sites up and functioning, and I don't appreciate–"

"What you don't appreciate," Jason interrupted brutally, "is that these facilities are essential to a tightly timed interagency initiative that is due to kick off this weekend. Perhaps you'd care to explain to my boss, Director Miller, why FEMA was the cause of the initiative being delayed? Or would you rather have FEMA's director explain it?"

"Look, look, we're almost done," the man said with a frightened look. "It wasn't my fault; they just handed the situation to me. I was put in charge of finishing, but that's supposed to be things like paint and trim. They left me with unwired sockets and misfit doors that won't close. It's been hell getting workers back to do what they should have done in the first place."

"Never mind that," Jason replied. "What's your name?"

"Landon Hill, sir," the man replied sullenly.

"Well, Landon, why don't you show me over the site? Maybe I can get some help for you."

So Landon showed Jason around the main building, which was the clinic itself. It looked like most medical clinics Jason had seen, with a waiting area, reception desk, exam rooms, and a small lab. Everything felt very cramped, but Jason kept in mind that these were supposed to be temporary facilities. The place smelled of paint and had wires hanging out of the walls where sockets should be, ill-fitting hardware, and poorly seated desktops. Landon made sure Jason saw all these irregularities, and that he understood that they weren't Landon's fault. The office building was in slightly better shape, and the garage was just a garage. But as Landon took him back toward the blocky building at the rear of the lot, Jason got to ask the question that had been nagging him.

"What is this building?"

"This?" Landon replied as he punched in the combination to unlock the door. "Lodging for the workers. Remember, these are supposed to be emergency facilities deployed to a disaster site. There would be no telling what kind of lodging would be available, so these are part of the package." The building had a hallway running along the front with several doors along it, and what looked like a common bathroom at the end of the hall. Landon opened the nearest door to show a room that could have been a college dorm room, with a desk, a simple metal frame chair with arms, a bed, and a sink with a mirror.

"Looks small," Jason said.

"In a pinch, we can stack another bed in here and quarter two people," Landon explained. "But that would be quite crowded. Will we need to do that?"

"I'm not sure," Jason admitted. He was a bit confused, because he seemed to remember in one of his conversations with Lin that HHS was contracting with hotels in towns near the RCCs to lodge the workers. What were they planning to do with these dorms? He supposed they had plans – he wasn't in on every detail of the Chengdu Two rollout, and didn't need to be.

Jason left the Fairgrove site with a frostily cordial goodbye to Landon, making a note to line up some local labor to finish the clinics. The HHS staff were due to start arriving next week, and those spaces needed to be safe to work in.

The car's nav panel was directing him north now, through country that bordered Saginaw Bay. The fields had dried out a bit, and looked less like vast mud flats and more like farmland. After weeks of sullen gray overcast, the sky was clear and the final glow of sunset illuminated the western sky. The roads were nearly empty, and the world seemed unusually still. Jason cracked his car window and let the evening air wash over him. The breeze wasn't quite warm, but neither was it as bitingly cold as the weather here had been. It was cool and refreshing, untainted by any scent. Jason drove in peace, hearing only the rush of the wind, turning where his nav system told him to, until he arrived at the fourth site.

This site had no vehicles, but Jason had expected none this late in the evening. He got out of the car and, once his headlights died, was astonished at how dark it was. There was a pole by the main building that had a security lamp mounted on it, but the lamp was off – probably some complication with connecting up the electricity. This meant the site was blanketed by darkness like Jason had never experienced. The last touch of the sunset's glow rimmed the western horizon, and away across the fields there were dots of light indicating distant homesteads, but the sky overhead was pitch black and carpeted with more stars than Jason had known existed. He leaned back until he almost tipped over, then backed up against his car so he could lean back farther, then gave up on leaning and stretched out on the hood, mesmerized by what looked like a glowing, furry carpet splashed across the heavens. He had never seen, never imagined, that there could be so many stars. To add to the beauty, a huge, brilliant moon was just rising in the east, bright enough to cast shadows.

Jason didn't know how long he lay there, transfixed by the majesty. He felt like he was alone on the face of the planet, but he was not frightened. No clamor reached his ears. At one point his hand moved toward his pocket for a cigarette, but he stayed it. He didn't need a smoke. He didn't need music, or companionship, or anything but to gaze upon the vast, quiet glow of the sky overhead. He felt tiny against the starry expanse, minute and forgotten, but that did not distress him. For now, he was content to be forgotten, so content that he even forgot himself.

But his fascination couldn't last forever, not with the north wind chilling his fingers and stiffening his legs. He eventually levered himself up on his elbows and then stood, stretching and bending to loosen the stiffness. Looking around the night-shrouded land, he reflected on how unusual this was for him. He had friends who were into the outdoors, who camped and hiked and skied and such. That life had never appealed to him, but on a night like this, he could see how someone could come to love it. Of course, that presumed a campfire to warm chilled hands, but he had no campfire, so back into the car it was. Jason was just reaching for the start button when he paused. What was that sound?

The radio. Making little bursts of static.

Jason felt a chill that had nothing to do with the north wind. He knew he hadn't left the radio on. He punched it off, then tapped the address on his tablet to bring up the map. Zooming out a little, his fears were confirmed.

The fourth site, where he was currently, was located just a little north of that crazy area, the one he didn't like to think about since that terrifying afternoon. For that matter, the site might lie within the area, since he didn't know exactly where it was, or how far it spread. He might already be trapped!

Gripping the wheel, Jason forced himself to calm down. Wherever the borders of the strange area lay, the RCC site didn't lie within them. He'd visited the site several times and had always been able to make it there and back without incident. Yes, his mind told him, he'd always come from the east or west, as he had today. And, his gut reminded him, he'd always come in daylight, never at night.

Jason pulled out of the lot and onto the road. He didn't want to activate the navigation system's voice directions lest they steer him into the area. He'd gotten here by driving straight for a while, right? He couldn't recall – when he'd pulled out of the lot, had he turned back in the same direction he'd come from, or was he now going the opposite way? He didn't dare turn around, lest he start getting confused amidst all the turning. The dirt road stretched before him, heading straight toward a long gray shape low on the horizon – a patch of woods, waving and bending slightly in the north wind.

Suddenly the clear night didn't seem so peaceful and innocent. Jason didn't know if the road was taking him into the shadow of those trees, and he wasn't keen to find out. He began to look for somewhere to turn, but would turning be wise? He thought of activating the nav screen, but rejected the idea – he couldn't face the possibility of not seeing the blue location dot. He jumped as the radio flicked on, hissing static. He punched it off again and gripped the wheel tighter. The land spread out in all directions, empty and threatening, naked fields edged by ominous dark patches. He passed a crossroads, but did not turn, lest he get lost in the network of empty roads and unmarked intersections. The menacing woods grew closer, gray at the edge and fading into stark blackness in the center, the treetops casting ghostly shadows as they swayed in the wind.

Shadows?

Jason looked out his window to see the bright moon hanging there, a little higher in the sky than she had been earlier. The moon! Of course! That was the light that had bathed the landscape – good old moonlight! He almost laughed with relief. What had looked spectral and eerie now appeared normal and friendly. It was the moon lighting his way.

Lighting his way?

Wait – the moon hung in the sky. It wasn't subject to whatever odd whims haunted these ground-level elements such as roads and woods. Jason had only to follow the moon! Coming to an intersection, he turned left so the moon was roughly in front of him. It looked smaller than it had earlier, but it shone more clearly, almost enough to hurt his eyes. The road he'd turned onto ran straight through the vast fields, and even took him along the edge of some woods, but Jason paid them no heed. He kept his eyes on the moon, and steered to keep the car between the ditches. There were no other cars on this road, but it eventually ended at another road, forcing Jason to turn. He turned left, and then right again at the first opportunity, to keep the brilliant moon hovering before him. Not long after that turn he reached a main paved road with a sign giving the mileage to Harbor Beach and Port Austin. Lake Huron stretched before him, the brilliant moon reflected on its placid surface. He had reached the lakeshore road that would take him down to Port Sanilac, where he could turn west and get back to Sandusky. The moon had led him out of the labyrinth of earth and trees and back to the water. He was safe.

The next morning the rising sun woke Jason, shining through a gap in his poorly closed curtains and full onto his face. He sat up, unaccustomed to being awakened so early on a Sunday morning. He reflexively reached to close the curtains and roll back over when he realized he wasn't sleepy – he felt perfectly rested. He couldn't recall the full details of how he'd made it home, only that he had been tremendously grateful to find his own door and tumble into his own bed. The alarming feelings of the prior evening had faded, but what stood out in his memory was the vast, spangled sky, and being led unerringly by the brilliant moon to the glistening water. The terrors of the shadowed landscape faded into insignificance.

Jason rose, stretched, and threw open the curtains to let the sunlight flood the room. He felt more rested, alert, and full of life than he had in a long time. He pulled on shorts and a t-shirt and headed for the kitchen. Today, he was cooking himself a proper breakfast.

Shadow

When the three men met again, there was a bit more material to work with. Either Dr. Picotte had secured more translators, or they were getting more proficient, but the newly translated pages covered several months of journal entries. To Pete much of it seemed mundane and repetitive, but the two scholars examined the pages with interest.

"Now we're getting to something," Dr. Harris commented. "This is something the historians will be able to sink their teeth into."

Gerald gave Dr. Harris a slightly disdainful look, but Pete asked what he meant. Both Gerald and Dr. Harris began to answer at the same time, then stopped, and Dr. Harris deferred to Gerald.

"If I understand Dr. Harris's inference correctly," Gerald began. "He means that Fr. Thomas's record is moving beyond personal incidents and accounts of religious activity. He's becoming settled enough in his surroundings that he's making note of changes. He's noticing more European-made trade items, such as hatchets and kettles. Of course, being new to the Ojibwa environment, Fr. Thomas doesn't have a good idea of what 'normal' looks like, so he can't comment on how much change he's seeing. But more experienced historians with a broader perspective will be able to fit Fr. Thomas's account into the bigger picture."

"So, then, he's right there at the very start of the encounter between this tribe and the Europeans?" Peter asked.

"Yes," Dr. Harris confirmed. "Even by Marquette's time, a generation later, European influence had already irrevocably altered the lifestyles of the First Nations. This record gives us a glimpse, however poor, into a world yet unpolluted by European influence. It's a priceless window into a pristine, unsullied existence."

Gerald erupted in barely contained rage at this pompous monologue. "Romantic nonsense!" he cried, slamming the table with a great fist. "Rousseauvian claptrap! What do you, who cannot even conceive of a life without electricity, know of such things?"

Pete blinked, and Dr. Harris gaped at this unexpected outburst. Gerald's rage cooled as quickly as it flared, but he was quite emphatic as he continued.

"As a personal discipline, I once lived the way of my ancestors for a full year. Despite my preparations, it nearly killed me. There was nothing 'pristine' about the life which Fr. Thomas found among the Salteaux Ojibwa. 'Hardscrabble' would be a better term. For them, every day was a minute-to-minute struggle for survival. They had to wring even the most basic life necessities directly from the land and water with their own hands. Often, failure – or even just a run of bad luck – meant death. They – anyone – would grab at any improvement, even the slightest advantage, that gave them additional leverage in that unforgiving struggle."

"I…I'm sorry," Dr. Harris stammered. "I didn't mean –"

"Again, Doctor, you speak as you have been taught," Gerald interrupted with a wave of his hand. "The life of the First Nations has been romanticized and mythologized, sometimes by our own people, to the point that the essential reality has been lost. A few of us – just a few, mind you – try to grasp their lives as they actually were, and communicate that to others. It's like swimming upstream against ice floes.

"To take one example: fishing. Everyone knows about fish traps, the subject of countless museum displays and middle school dioramas. You can see them demonstrated at pauwaus across North America. But as a method for catching fish, they were chancy – difficult to set up, easily damaged, and dependent upon the fish to swim into them. Better than nothing, but not nearly as effective as the simple technology of the fishing net. With a net, I don't have to hope the fish is going to cooperate, and I don't have to wade through icy water to help them into my trap. I can stand in my canoe and hunt them where they swim. When my children are ashore on the brink of starvation, I'm grabbing every advantage I can. What I'm *not* going to care about are the opinions of a European *philosophe* holding forth in *salons* across Paris about people he'd never met."

"But...surely there was some impact," Dr. Harris offered, trying to salvage his position.

"There was, Doctor, undeniably," Gerald acknowledged. "But don't blame it on the technology, and don't romanticize First Nation lives of the time, any more than you should romanticize the lives of the ancient Franks or Celts or Goths or whomever your ancestors were. The struggle for survival is universal, and every advantage is embraced as quickly as it can be. The error is to take a mental snapshot of a particular place and time, then hold that up as an ideal, as 'how things should be'. Whatever situation you choose, you can bet existence at that point wasn't idyllic. It sure wasn't for the Salteaux Ojibwa, and people living then would have eagerly adopted anything that made life easier, be it cooking kettles or fishing nets or iron hatchets. Your ancestors did, and it didn't make them any less Franks or Celts for doing so.

"What really wrought the change was everything coming down at once. Sure, technology was the bait on the hook, but at least bait has nutritional value. The new customs, the alien principles – hell, the sheer displacement of population – all conspired to bring an avalanche of change. You Europeans brought things you didn't even know you were bringing, such as horses, disease, and political alliances. I've had discussions with other First Nations scholars about whether we could have coped with the influx of Europeans in a measured manner, kept you at an arm's length until we could work out a cultural interface based on parity. Maybe we could have, but it would have depended on our having sufficient population. Unfortunately, once the diseases took hold and devastated our numbers, there was nothing anyone could do."

Gerald paused and rubbed his face with his hands. Pete and Dr. Harris glanced at each other, wondering if they were expected to speak. Gerald relieved them of that concern by continuing.

"But that whole discussion goes beyond the scope of our study of the journal. Fr. Thomas didn't bring enough technology with him to have a measurable influence on the Salteaux Ojibwa, though he is helpful as an observer. Notice here on page fifty two, and again on page sixty four, he speaks of canoes of travelers arriving at the Sault, members of tribes with which the Salteaux would have been familiar. The travelers were moving light, with few provisions but carrying valuable trade goods. See here that Nikikouet comments to him that there are families in the canoes, which is unusual. Knowing what I do about the times, I suspect that what Fr. Thomas was seeing was what we would call refugees – people displaced by the Iroquois incursions to the east. They were most likely Ojibwa from other places, or Odawa, or perhaps Hurons from above Georgian Bay. Fr. Thomas notes that they didn't seem interested in hearing the Gospel, though they knew of Blackrobes and some knew Fr. Pijart." Gerald flipped a few pages, skimming as he went. "Ah, here we have something. A discussion with Jean and Nikikouet after dinner one evening. Nikikouet mentions that the village women are agitated because some of the men are being distracted."

"Distracted?" Pete asked.

"Yes. The summer is fading into autumn, which normally would mean shifting from fishing along the river to hunting larger game in the woods to the north. The elk and deer needed to be killed and salted for the winter months. But the travelers coming through are showing the village men hatchets and kettles and buckles and other goods that can be traded for beaver and marten pelts. Trapping and skinning beaver would seem a lot less difficult and dangerous than trapping and killing elk. When the women ask about winter provisions, the travelers say they can trade pelts for corn and rice raised by the Huron. This sounds good to the men, but the women aren't so sure."

"So here we have a clear, dated record of the tribe modifying their behavior in response to economic influence?" Dr. Harris asked.

"Yes," Gerald confirmed. "To Fr. Thomas, it seems Jean isn't too happy about this development."

"Why is that?" Pete asked.

"Fr. Thomas doesn't know exactly what Jean does. He disappears into the woods for periods, but is evasive about where he goes and what he does. But he's able to provide for his family, and even has luxuries like tobacco. That makes me suspect he was a *coureur de bois* – literally a 'runner in the woods'. They were trappers who were, as far as the French officials were concerned, poachers. Since supposedly all the furs in New France belonged to the king, only those with royal permission could legally take them. In time these would be the chartered corporations and the *voyageurs* who worked for them. But at this point there were just these freelancers trapping where they could, trading on the sly, and avoiding paying taxes.

"I'm guessing that up to this point Jean had had it relatively easy, working the area without competition. But if the men of the tribe catch on that there are trade goods to be had in exchange for a few beaver pelts, there goes Jean's cushy livelihood." Gerald grinned at the prospect.

"Competition – the great leveler," Pete grinned as well.

"Yes. It seems that Jean is encouraging Nikikouet to have the village women remind the men of their hunting responsibilities. Oooh, canny Nikikouet! She agrees, but chooses that moment to ask Jean about her and the children receiving instruction and baptism. Apparently Jean grumbled and puffed his pipe a bit, then grudgingly assented."

"So – the first success as a missionary!" Dr. Harris observed.

"Indeed," Gerald said as he flipped a few pages. "The next several entries pertain to Fr. Thomas's catechetical efforts with Nikikouet and the children. Apparently it's forcing him to substantially advance his Ojibwe – Nikikouet can speak a little French but the kids aren't interested. Occasionally other women drop in to see what the fuss is, but aren't interested in learning about the new god. Fr. Thomas finds this discouraging, partly because they seem to think that baptism will make them French women and he can't convince them otherwise." He turned a couple more pages. "More of the same – ah, here we have the date of the baptism, which happens on the Feast of the Holy Rosary, October

277

7th. They went down to the river, and about half the village came along to watch. It seems they weren't very impressed by the baptism, possibly because it was much less rigorous than the initiation rites of some of the Anishinaabe. They were much more interested in the Mass that followed, when the bread and wine became the body and blood of the god. Nikikouet and her eldest daughter took Communion. Fr. Thomas proudly records, in Latin, the names of the converts. The Jesuits will find that interesting, because they were certainly the first Anishinaabek Christians at the Sault."

"Hell, I find it interesting," Pete said.

"More instruction, more attempts to engage potential converts," Gerald muttered, turning pages. "A couple more mentions of canoes coming from the east, so something's going on over that way. And...what's this?" Gerald paused and read silently for a while.

"What's what?" Dr. Harris asked, flipping through his binder to find the spot that had captured Gerald's attention.

Gerald waved his hand impatiently as he pondered the material, then sat back in his chair wearing a puzzled expression. "Look here, the entry beginning on October 16th. It's a few days after the prior entry, and it's a break from what has come before, both in content and style. The entry is in French, but in a less colloquial style than his usual entries."

"I see it," Dr. Harris said.

With heavy heart and trembling hand I now recount the events of the past several days. I can make little sense of them, and admit to great trepidation about what we are facing. But I trust to our Merciful Lord, and His Gracious Mother, for their protection from all danger temporal and spiritual.

"That sounds ominous," Pete observed.

"Yes. And the slightly more formal style indicates that he's more consciously recording in anticipation of someone else reading this," Gerald mused. "I wonder why he didn't write in Latin. Perhaps he considered that the person who might read it, and need to understand it, might only know French."

"So...he was considering that he wouldn't be able to tell them himself?" Pete guessed.

"Certainly a possibility," Gerald replied. "Let's see what more he has to say."

I began the day as usual, with my toilet and my devotions, committing my work to St. Hedwig on this, her day. At midmorning three canoes arrived from the east, bearing goods for trade. The men were both Odawa and Huron, coming from the Nipissing region. None bore any news of Fr. Pijart or his companions, which I am always seeking. The travelers were made welcome and spent much of the day around the fire with the men of the village, smoking and trading news.

As Non was approaching there was a disturbance at the north of the village. Two natives emerged from the forest. They were greeted warily by the men and welcomed to the fire with the others. They were strange, and their garb looked different.

"What's 'Non'?" Pete asked.

Midafternoon prayer – it would probably have been about 2 or 3 p.m." Gerald explained. "It's interesting that they come from the woods."

"People didn't travel through the woods?" Dr. Harris asked.

"They could – there were trails, and they hunted there," Gerald answered. "But the forest was very dense, so the preferred method of travel was by water. You know what the woods are like even now, and all we know is second or third growth. You can imagine how difficult the original growth forest would have been to traverse. Let's see what more Fr. Thomas has to say."

The village residents seemed disturbed by the two natives, which is unusual for them, who see many travelers through the Sault. Nikikouet told me the natives were Cree, from the far north. I asked if that was why they distressed the villagers, and she said no, that the Cree came through from time to time. She did not wish to speak of the two natives, and would answer no more questions. I asked if I could speak to them and she told me that I would not want to, that it would not be good. She explained no more.

I was attending to my prayers when a disturbance broke out around the fire where the men were gathered. I ran to see that the peaceable circle had been broken, and all were on their feet, some with weapons in hand. The two Cree were clearly the source of the disturbance, for they stood apart, as if defiantly, facing all the others. The village man who had been serving to translate was still asking them questions, but in a manner sharp and angry. I wondered what the Cree had done to so infuriate such normally peaceful folk. When I turned to ask Nikikouet, I saw in her face what was written in so many others. It was not anger, but fear.

Abruptly the visitors who had arrived by canoe that morning quit the assembly to return to their vessels. They had intended to stay for some days to trade, but now departed with all haste, packing their goods and departing without the customary ceremonies. The men of the village closed about the two Cree. I feared that violence would be done, but the village men restrained themselves, only escorting the Cree away from the fire in the center of the village. They took them to the outskirts of the village, where they continued to question them.

I implored Nikikouet to inquire for me what the Cree had done or said that would so distress this fearless people. I also offered to speak to the men of the village, and act as a peacemaker in whatever manner I could. She said she would speak to the men.

Sometime later she returned with an older lore master named Mygizi. It seemed he had better knowledge of the matter, though his speech was soft and difficult to hear. Without Nikikouet's assistance, I should not have heard anything he said. Also, he was reluctant to speak of the topic, no matter how much Nikikouet coaxed him.

In time I learned from Mygizi that the Cree had spoken of coming from their land and passing through an area of forest filled with darkness. I asked if they had traveled at night, but he insisted that the darkness was not night (nakshig) or cloud (nigwaankot), but was some other thing (minjimii makadweaa). Nikikouet had not the French words, but the closest she could come was 'clinging blackness'. Mygizi seemed to know a name for this darkness that he would not use. He used other words to hint at it, such as dark emptiness and endless hunger. He also spoke of trees with dark bark (makadweane-gekozi) and of the woods being hungry, and of dark fog (awan bishagiishkaa) from wounded land (aki inaapinash). In the end he fell silent, shaking his head and refusing to speak more. What he did say clearly struck terror into Nikikouet, who began to speak of gathering her children into her wigwam.

The three men looked up from the binders. The Americans looked simply mystified, but fear edged Gerald's eyes, as if the terror his forebearers had felt was reaching across the centuries to chill his heart.

"I wonder why he didn't want to name this – whatever it was," Peter said.

"Because to name a thing is to draw it closer," Gerald answered hollowly.

"What?" Dr. Harris asked. Gerald gazed into empty air for a moment longer, then shook his head as if breaking free of something.

"You modern Europeans and your categories," Gerald began. "You think of names as simply labels to stick on things, arbitrary designations devoid of intrinsic meaning. That is not naming. Your ancestors knew better. Hell, your own tradition knows better. Does not Adam in your tradition, as Nanabozho in ours, name the creatures? To name a thing is to come into union with it, to establish a connection with it."

"I've never heard that before," Dr. Harris said with a frown.

"Of course you haven't," Gerald continued. "You're mechanistic postmoderns. I blame Albertus Magnus, and William of Occam, and Descartes."

"Now you've lost me," Pete admitted.

"Albert the Great, University of Paris, Teacher of Thomas Aquinas, considered an early father of modern science because of his taxonomies of plants and animals. Followed by Bacon, of course, and so many others. It was Albertus who first started assigning names as merely labels. But true names, real names, bind up a thing, so to know the name was to know the thing – not simply to know *about* it, but to *know* it, to be acquainted with it. Thus, to use the name was to draw the thing, to summon it. That was why Mygizi was reluctant to use the name. He did not wish to risk summoning it."

"Summon what? What are they talking about? Even Fr. Thomas is confused," Dr. Harris pointed out. "What dire thing is this Mygizi worried about summoning?"

"There are things," Gerald replied. "And there are…non-things, absences of things. Note the terms he uses: dark emptiness, the woods being hungry, the hollow darkness. There are tales, ancient tales, of the bottomless dark, of the insatiable hunger…" He trailed off into muttering, his gaze again growing distant.

"You mean, like…a wendigo?" Pete asked hesitantly.

Gerald looked at him and smiled slightly. "Again, you Europeans and your categories. You hear a term or idea, and you want to have a thing on which to stick the term – a demon, or a monster. Even your own tradition knows of the nameless hunger, the ravenous void, but you embody that in physical beings like vampires and zombies. When you came to this land and heard the First Nations reference such things, you created another monster to embody it."

"But...I thought that was a North Woods legend," Pete replied. "That you became a wendigo by committing cannibalism."

"I speculate now, for much of our lore has been lost," Gerald said. "But I wonder if a misunderstanding took place when our cultures came into contact. Perhaps it was language, or concepts, or translators seeking to fit things into familiar categories, but perhaps the idea got inverted."

"Inverted?"

"What if it wasn't performing cannibalism that brought upon you the Nameless Hunger, but being exposed to the Nameless Hunger that turned you cannibal?"

Pete looked at Dr. Harris in befuddlement, and Dr. Harris returned the look with skepticism. Gerald ignored this and continued.

"Again, I speculate. Let us return to Fr. Thomas's account to see what happens next."

While Nikikouet was leading Mygizi away and going to search for her own children, the whole village was disturbed by a great commotion. From the area where the men had taken the Cree there came many cries and shouts, and the sound of distress. I rushed there and saw many of the men trying to pull one of the Cree off a man he had knocked down. The Cree was clawing and biting at his victim, while others struggled manfully to remove him. I wondered if the Cree had suddenly gone mad, for I have heard that madness will lend an abundance of strength to its victims. The other Cree had been knocked to the ground, and many men were sitting on him, holding clubs and knives over him.

Eventually the men pulled the mad Cree off their fellow and proceeded to put him to death. Though I cried out for them to stop, they heeded me not, assailing the Cree with club and knife. It was terrible to watch, and I said prayers for the man's soul, unbaptized though he was. But when they turned to do the same to the other Cree, who had already been subdued, I could stand no more. I charged in to stop them, imploring them in the name of God not to kill an unarmed man who was in their power. They grew wroth with me, for they think me no great man, and said many things in hot anger that I could not understand. When some of them seemed ready to kill me as well, Nikikouet ran up and began to translate for me. The village men agreed not to kill me, but insisted that the Cree was very dangerous and must be put to death before he did the village great harm. He could not be returned to the forest and could not be left alone, and no man was willing to sit with him. They said the hunger was on him and his companion, for they had passed through the darkness, and no medicine would cure them.

At this the men looked up at each other before continuing.

I said to them that my God was stronger than any curse or darkness, and had even raised men from death. I said I would stay with the Cree and guard him, that he would do no harm, only that they should not kill him, for it would be no more than murder.

When Nikikouet had explained my offer to them, they desisted their murderous intent for the time and said they would consider matters. They bound the Cree tightly and set two men by him. Then they attended to the dead Cree in the most curious manner. They stuffed his mouth and nostrils with dirt, and then bound his head tightly about with leather. Then they tied the body from head to foot with cords. Bringing a canoe from the landing, they placed the body into the canoe and carried it to the river bank. There they tied it to another canoe, which was rowed out to a deep spot, where the body was tipped out and sank into the churning water. Having before never seen this form of burial, I asked after it. It was explained to me that this was necessary because water was the only thing that could contain the hunger. I asked if this hunger could flow from a dead body, and they admitted they did not know, but were taking no chances.

Then attention was turned to the remaining Cree, who appeared frightened and by no means dangerous. Since these people have no gaols, there was some discussion of how to deal with the man. Normally, undesirables are driven from the village, but they did not wish the Cree to haunt the woods around. Tying him to the edge of the village would require a guard, which job nobody wished. To leave him bound and unguarded would risk him escaping, or dying of cold. To my dismay, the suggestion of killing him outright was again raised. At this I offered to stay with the prisoner, either at the edge of the village or in my wigwam. After some discussion this offer was accepted, even by the men least friendly to me.

Nikikouet gave me some fish porridge for our supper, and a cloth and dish of water to clean up the Cree, who was still bloodied and bruised from his treatment. I prevailed upon some of the men to loosen the tightest of his bonds, which were cutting his skin and causing him intense pain.

Evening was now approaching, so I bathed the Cree's wounds and shared my porridge with him. Then two men came and carried the Cree to my wigwam, where they laid him, still bound, on the bed pile. I went in with my prayer book and lamp and holy water, and made the best bed I could against the opposite wall of the wigwam. Then the men closed the wigwam door and bound it tightly, leaving only the feeble flame of the lamp. By this flickering light I read my evening office, and said my devotions. The Cree glared at me throughout with sharp, fearful eyes. It was no use attempting to speak to him. Before retiring I sprinkled my bed and half of the wigwam with Holy Water, imploring the protection of the Blessed Trinity and Our Lady. I did not think it proper to sprinkle the Cree without his permission, so I said a prayer for him. Then I lay down, commended my safety to St. Joseph and my guardian angel, and closed my eyes.

I was awakened by a cold wind, and distant cries of distress and alarm. The bed beside me was empty and the wigwam door stood open, torn and broken. Beyond it I could see the gray light of a predawn sky. I could only surmise that the Cree had worked his way free of his bonds and broken out of the wigwam, though with what intent I could not say. I ran outside.

There had been some struggle, for here and there around the village people lay on the ground with others tending to them. The great fire had been kindled. Most tellingly, I saw a party heading toward the river carrying a canoe overhead, in the same manner I had seen them carry one the day before. I ran toward the party, crying for them to stop. When they turned to see me, they stopped abruptly and nearly dropped the canoe, so great was their startlement. As I went toward them, I heard a cry to my left, and turned to see Nikikouet running toward me, calling my name. She rushed up to me, while the men put down the canoe and approached me more warily.

Nikikouet explained that the Cree had broken out of the wigwam and attacked many people around the village before being subdued. They had assumed that I had been the madman's first victim, and lay dead in the wigwam. At this one of the men came close enough to ask a question which Nikikouet translated: how had I escaped the walking hunger? I answered that the Cree had left the wigwam without disturbing my sleep, but that I had invoked the protection of God before I slept. At this the men drew back, warier than before. I went to the canoe to see the body of the Cree bound as his companion had been. Having said a prayer over the unknown man, I stepped aside and let the men take the canoe down to the river. I allowed Nikikouet to lead me to her wigwam to rest from this ordeal.

It is now midday of that same day when the second Cree was buried in the river. I have taken time to record the incident while the details remain fresh in my mind. I still do not know why the Cree were so erratic, or why the Salteaux remain so distressed. It is true that one of their men was badly hurt when the second Cree broke out, but their fear is greater than that can explain. Nikikouet is grateful that I am safe but is now concerned for Jean, who is away in the woods and is not expected back for some days yet.

The translation ended there. The three men looked at each other, Pete with puzzlement, Dr. Harris with some skepticism, and Gerald with weariness.

"Do you think there was some sort of…mental illness?" Pete asked.

Dr. Harris made to respond, but Gerald raised his hand in appeal. "Please – it's getting late, and this is a lot to digest. Let's go home, read it all over a few times, and meet again when some more pages come in. Perhaps they'll shed more light on the situation Fr. Thomas found himself facing."

The men agreed to this and concluded the meeting.

Rollout

When Ethan showed up the following morning, Jason assigned him the task of lining up local tradesmen to finish up the trim work on the RCC sites. Then the messages from D.C. started coming in. One was from Lin Wei, copying him on the staffing schedules for the clinics. Another was from Rex Hollis, updating everyone on the rollout timetable for the new protocols. George Spader circulated a message about the S and O spot that had aired, and the second one that was due to air, and a cryptic analysis of online chatter following the initial spot. Most of the graphs and indices were opaque to Jason, but from George's commentary, he gathered that the analysis indicated the responses to the spot were mostly positive.

The week flashed by in a whirl of deadlines and frantic attempts to coordinate all the components of the HHS initiative. The least flexible of these was the rollout of the health care protocols to the RMAs and providers. Apparently, that required such delicate timing of "operational and informational infrastructure" that the schedule was basically set in stone – it had to come off at the arranged time. But once that was done, the RCC staff had to be in place to handle the patients, which meant that the facilities had be ready. Ethan did his usual heroic job in scaring up contractors to square away the sites, so they were ready to power-on and stock by Wednesday evening. The HHS staff started arriving the next day, and Jason received a fresh flood of requests to attend to this or that minor detail.

The flurry continued into the weekend, but by then the primary activities were out of Jason's hands, and he was relegated to stomping out administrative fires and running errands. George's group ran the first of the follow-up spots on Thursday and the second on Saturday evening, and in the judgment of the POM analysts, response was "quite satisfactory", according to meta-analysis of online communications. The HHS press conference on Monday morning should be a minor PR coup, showing how attentive and responsive the federal agencies were. George announced that for public consumption, the name given to the effort would be Underserved Population Active Initiative Response. When Jason dared to ask what an "Active Initiative Response" was, his question was dismissed. George pointed out that the important thing was having an easy-to-remember acronym, well suited as a conversation tag for online discussion. "UPAIR" filled that requirement, and they'd even had a logo designed which market research indicated was the perfect balance between active and friendly. The logo would be unveiled at the press conference. The POM aspect of the project was well in hand.

Jason was online and communicating, though mainly as a spectator, on Sunday when the new medical protocols were rolled out. The RCCs were staffed and ready to accept patients, and the public announcement would be made Monday morning. Jason had done his job – now things were in the hands of HHS staff. Jason took himself to dinner at the local microbrewery in celebration, and wondered what the morning would bring.

*   *   *

Lottie Pierce had been sitting in the doctor's waiting room for in inordinate amount of time. Blast it! This was why she made these early morning appointments, so she wouldn't get caught in the inevitable appointment creep that plagued later time slots. If this took much longer, Sue would be finished with her shopping and would have to wait when she got back. Lottie hated doing that to her friend, especially when she'd been kind enough to drive her down here from Sebewaing.

"Ms. Pierce?" One of the office staff was standing over her, gazing at one of those tablets with a concerned expression.

"Yes?" Lottie replied. Great. Now what?

"I'm afraid we won't be able to serve you today," the staffer said apologetically.

"What?" Lottie blustered. "But…I had an appointment! I made it last time I was here!"

"I'm sorry, Ms. Pierce, but you're subject to a new protocol, and you'll have to receive your care elsewhere. We're forbidden to provide you care." The staffer showed her the tablet screen, which was densely covered in text and lines and little colored blotches.

"Well, isn't that dandy?" Lottie harrumphed. "Just dandy! Dr. Keenan has been my pulmonologist for decades – what am I supposed to do?"

"Well, the good news is that you've been selected to receive care at one of the new Rapid Care Centers they're opening."

"Isn't that dandy?" Lottie repeated. She guessed what that meant – some office in a strip mall over by Saginaw or Bay City, and an appointment later in the week at the earliest. Oh, it was hard enough for Sue to drive her here! Well, bad news didn't get any better with age. "So, where do I have to go, and when will they be able to see me?"

"That's the good part. The RCC isn't far – just south of Fairgrove – and they can see you this morning. In fact, they're expecting you." The staffer tapped the tablet screen, and Lottie's phone chimed in her purse. Lottie pulled out the phone to see a new message with numbers and scan codes all over it. "Just hand them your phone at the reception desk and they'll know who you are."

"Well," Lottie said, slightly mollified. "I guess that's not so bad."

"Maybe that's why they're called Rapid Care Centers," the staffer said with a sunny smile.

"But I'll have to call Sue, and see if – oh, here she is now," Lottie said as Sue bundled through the door.

Less than an hour later, Lottie was sitting in a small exam room, awaiting the doctor. She had to admit, she'd been pleasantly surprised. She and Sue – blessed, helpful, good-natured Sue – had driven from Dr. Keenan's office to this clinic in the middle of nowhere laughing and joking about just how "rapid" this care would actually be. How much time would Lottie have to spend completing forms, filling in the same information she'd filled in for every other doctor? And how long before she'd actually see any kind of medical professional? (She wasn't such a fool at to expect she'd see an actual doctor.) Would this detour turn out to be another administrative stop, with the real appointment scheduled for later? But when they'd arrived at the RCC, the receptionist had just scanned Lottie's phone screen, said they'd been expecting her, and promptly escorted her to the exam room. Maybe this wouldn't turn out so badly after all.

Lottie had been waiting less than ten minutes when a red-haired young man bustled in wearing a lab jacket and a stethoscope and carrying the ubiquitous tablet. He seemed friendly enough, but was all business, shaking her hand and addressing her as "Lottie". He didn't make any move to examine her, nor did he ask any questions, but sat down in the exam chair and studied the tablet screen.

"So," the doctor said briskly. "We've been in touch with Dr. Keenan's office, and have all of your records and test results right here. Dr. Keenan has been your doctor for..." He swiped up and down the tablet screen.

"Twenty-three years," Lottie interjected. "No, twenty-four, because –"

"Quite some time," the doctor continued. "He's done a great job of stabilizing your condition, but there are some newer treatments available that he may or may not be aware of. I see from your last couple of visits..." He frowned at the screen a little. "You have been taking your medication regularly, haven't you?"

"Yes. I have one of those little plastic trays –" Lottie began to explain, but the doctor interrupted her again.

"Well, some of the recent incidents you've gone to Dr. Keenan for are consonant with irregular regimen adherence. How about we help you with that?" He tapped some spots on the tablet as he stood up. "We're going to give you an automated dispensing device for your medications. It's a smart device, and will be connected to your phone. It will chime when it's time to take your medicines, and if you don't take them, it will chime louder. If you still don't take them, it will use your phone to contact the center here, so we can get in touch with you."

"So I'll use this for my existing prescriptions, as well as any new ones you give me?" Lottie asked.

"That's right – all your medications," the doctor replied. "We'll preload it for two weeks and you can take it with you. At the end of that period, you'll be coming back for another appointment."

"Oh, so I don't have to get it filled somewhere? Or load it myself?" Lottie asked.

"Not this time," the doctor said with a smile, shaking her hand. "Check at the desk to get your dispensing device and have your phone configured for it. They'll also set up your next appointment." He walked out as busily as he'd walked in, leaving Lottie bewildered and a little flustered.

The doctor had never even told her his name.

Lottie and Sue were back on the road half an hour later, with Lottie cradling a white enamel thing about the size of a small teapot. She'd been assured that it was a smart device, though it didn't look very smart. When she got home, she placed it prominently on the kitchen counter. As three o'clock approached, she stood by it, phone in hand, and waited for the hour to turn. When it did, the device chimed, her phone chimed, and there was a little clatter as some pills were released into the covered tray at the base. She opened the cover and examined the pills – yes, her familiar midafternoon dosages, along with a new pill she didn't recognize. The process repeated at six o'clock for her dinner dosages, and at nine o'clock her bedtime doses were ready. Just to test the system, she didn't open the dispenser's cover promptly at nine o'clock, and sure enough, the chime on her phone began ringing louder and louder until it was almost painful, and a message popped up with a countdown timer indicating how long it would be before the phone dialed the RCC. The mute and volume controls on her phone were overridden – the only way to silence the alarm was to lift the cover and remove the pills.

Well, thought Lottie as she swallowed her pills, that's certainly effective. Maybe this new arrangement would work out after all.

*　　　　*　　　　*

By Wednesday evening preliminary reports from the RCCs were being tallied, and the initial results seemed promising. Each site had averaged over a hundred cases a day for the first few days, of which about ten percent were OPELs. They wanted to keep the ratio under fifteen percent for the first few weeks, just for appearances, after which they'd slowly start increasing the numbers. The dosing mechanisms were set to begin kicking in any day, and the cleanup crews were standing by.

The HHS folks were ecstatic, and effusive in their praise of Jason. Within a couple of months, he'd managed to restart a vital project with nowhere near the effort and cost of the failed pilot. Director Miller had been getting messages all day commending Jason and thanking DHS for their superb interdepartmental cooperation. On the HHS side, things were looking wonderful.

But, Jason thought as he wandered across the courthouse lawn sipping his coffee, he still wasn't in the clear. Cynthia had forwarded to him one of the glowing notes that a director over in HHS had sent to Director Miller, but her added comments had reminded him indirectly but unmistakably that almost no progress had been made on his main mission. He had to admit, the blast investigation had almost completely stalled while he'd pursued the easier to manage and more immediately rewarding activity of getting the RCCs up and running. But he'd been sent here to investigate the blast, and no amount of success in other arenas or with other agencies would compensate for failing at that. He'd be shunted off to some dead-end position, or asked to leave the department, and that bastard Whitman would get what he'd always wanted: Jason's ruin.

Glumly Jason sat down on what he'd come to think of as "his" bench beside the gazebo. All the satisfaction from getting the sites completed and the excitement of being caught up in the whirl of the HHS deployment had been washed away by the gray tide of bleak desolation that was so familiar to him. He had to deliver on the main mission or he was nothing. The problem was, he had no idea how. What had seemed like a promising beginning, Ethan's discovery of the trail networks, had so far produced no significant results. The RA overflights and sophisticated image analysis had established that *something* was going on, but lacking particulars, they couldn't tie that back to the blast or to anything else. He sighed and sipped his coffee. Maybe all the business with the high-level surveillance and NSA computers had been nothing more than chasing unicorns down moonbeams. As Collins had pointed out, they needed specifics, and everything specific they had on the case had been blown to dust in the blast. Maybe there was no way to resolve this case.

"Excuse me," a soft voice said. At first Jason didn't hear it clearly, but then it repeated, "Excuse me."

Jason looked up to see a woman standing near the bench. She had short, curly red hair and lively brown eyes that were shining in the evening sun falling on her face. She wore a simple white blouse and skirt. He wouldn't have called her pretty, but her smile lit up her expression, and she was looking on with a gentle kindness that he'd never seen any woman direct at him.

"I...I'm sorry?" Jason stammered, totally taken aback.

"You matter to *me*," the woman assured him with a warm smile.

"I do?" the mystified Jason answered.

"Yes." The woman paused, then continued. "There's a way out of where you are, but it isn't by any of the paths you're trying. Keep looking." Having said this, the woman turned and began walking away.

"What do you mean?" Jason called after her. "Wait – who are you?"

Just on the edge of earshot, the woman turned and favored him with another smile. "You'll find that out soon enough." Then she turned again and walked briskly to a van parked along Elk Street, beside which stood two other women. The others seemed to be waiting for her, and were dressed in unusual long white dresses, with some sort of draping white veil on their heads. Before the stunned Jason could even rise from the bench, the women climbed into the van and drove off.

Encounter

Teresa sat in a corner of the cramped kitchen, nursing a mug of tea and watching Sister Margaret bustle about preparing lunch. Teresa was nodding with exhaustion, but was forcing herself to stay awake. She'd promised to help with the midmorning rounds, and though that promise had been made before Sister Elizabeth was stricken by the respiratory ailment that had forced Teresa to take her night shift, Teresa wanted to fulfill the obligation. But she wouldn't be needed for another fifteen minutes, so she was taking a breather in a quiet corner, relishing a brief spell without responsibilities. It was soothing to watch Sister Margaret as she executed her tasks with competence and cheerfulness. It was comforting to feel the warmth of the mug in her hands. It was mesmerizing to gaze at the shiny wire racks on the other side of the table, crammed with pots and utensils and tools, to behold without trying to analyze the random pattern formed by the chrome and aluminum, by the shelves and handles and lids and pans...

And then Teresa wasn't looking at pots any more, but down through some kind of coarse metal meshwork. Mystified, she looked about at what seemed a tangle of pipes and grating. She quickly recognized that she was standing on a network of catwalks of the sort that she'd seen above stages to be used by stagehands to place lights or manipulate components of sets. The walkways underfoot were made of metal grating and the railings of metal piping. This was familiar territory to her.

But over what was she standing? Not over a stage. She peered down into what seemed to be a narrow hallway with dark walls and floor but no ceiling, so anyone standing on the catwalk could look down into it. Everything was quite shadowed, though enough of the dim light around the catwalks filtered down into the hallway to provide some illumination. Wondering where the hallway went, Teresa proceeded along the catwalk for a short way until she came to where the hallway she was following ran into another hallway which ran perpendicular to the first. Curiously, at this junction a ladder ran down from the catwalk into the hallway. If she'd wished, she could have climbed down, but having no desire to do that, she turned onto another stretch of the catwalk to see where this new hall led.

There wasn't much to see. The hall she was following went along for a distance before intersecting another hall, which ran off in both directions into dimness. Continuing on, she came to a spot where the hall terminated into another. There was another one of the ladders leading down, and the new hallway stretched off into the dimness in both directions, with walkway suspended above it.

The whole setup reminded her of something, and she struggled against her fatigue to summon to mind what it was. Of course! A maze! It was like she was walking above a giant maze, looking down into the runways from her vantage point on the network of catwalks. At her level, there were pipes and steps and grating-floored catwalks as far as the eye could see, suspended above the maze of hallways.

As she wondered where she was, and what this could mean, Teresa heard sounds coming from below. They were random sounds, muffled bumps and swishes accompanied by what sounded like hurried footsteps. Teresa couldn't see anything in the stretches of hallway beneath her, and the direction of the sounds was difficult to discern among the echoing hallways and bare metal grating. Whatever the source, it seemed to be coming nearer, and soon Teresa could clearly hear the sounds approaching her from her right. As she peered into the darkness, there came into view a man who seemed to be making his way through the hallways. Teresa was so excited to see another person in this mysterious place that she called out.

"Hello! Where are we? What is this place?"

The man gave no indication that he'd heard anything, but kept on his way. The hall he was following passed right beneath Teresa's feet, and as he drew closer, it seemed clear that he was struggling. His clothes were bedraggled, his hair was mussed, and his movements seemed forced. It looked like he was trying to run, but the best he could manage was a stumbling trot. He seemed to be impaired, by drunkenness or exhaustion or something else, because he kept careening off the walls or glancing off corners. Teresa wondered if he was well, and called again, waving to try to attract his attention.

"Hello! I'm up here! Are you all right? Can I help you?"

The man didn't respond at all, but kept on at his stumbling pace, drawing closer to where Teresa stood on the catwalk above him. At one point he tripped and fell, and as he pushed himself up, she got a good look at his face.

It was the same man she'd seen in her last vision, the intense-looking man who'd been so busy.

Teresa gasped. What could this mean? Who was this man, and why was she being given images of him? He pushed himself wearily to his feet and resumed his staggering progress. As he drew closer Teresa could see his strained features and exhausted posture, but there was a grimness to his expression that bespoke how hard he was driving himself. He passed right beneath where she was standing, and she called to him again but to no effect. Either he couldn't hear her, or was too focused on his mission. She watched as he came to the end of the hall and looked left and right in desperation, as if trying to discern which way to turn. He lurched to the left, and Teresa could hear him stumbling and panting on his way.

Since the man seemed to be the only thing of interest in this curious tableau, Teresa followed him. It was ridiculously easy – she just went along the catwalk until she came to another one that took her right over where the man now stood at the intersection of two hallways, looking about anxiously and clearly fretting over which way to turn. Ironically, he was standing two feet from a ladder by which he could have climbed out of the maze and onto the catwalks.

"Hello!" Teresa called loudly, kicking one of the pipes to make noise. "Up here! You can climb up here, and see where you want to go, and walk there unhindered! Hello!" She seemed to be no more than twenty feet from the man, almost directly overhead, and briefly it appeared that her hollering and pounding was having an effect. The man paused in his agitation and seemed to be listening, as if he'd heard something. She called to him again, but the moment passed – he shook his head and took off down the right hand passage, away from her, intent on his task.

As the mysterious man disappeared into the dimness, his footsteps echoing down the dark halls, Teresa's heart fell. She felt that she had failed him, that if she'd just said the right thing, or had had the courage to climb down one of the ladders into the maze, she could have reached him and shown him a better way than his anxious scurrying. She wondered if she should pursue him – from her unhindered vantage point she should be able to keep up with him easily.

Even as she considered this, she felt like she was being lifted up, or that the maze and catwalks were dropping away beneath her. She wondered if she was going for another high-altitude flight on wide metal wings, but no such view materialized. She was suspended in pitch darkness, rising higher and higher and turning as she rose.

Finally, something came into her vision. It was dim and red and far off. It looked like a distant forest fire, or the mouth of a volcano. She wanted to turn her back so she couldn't see it, but found she could not. To her dismay, she seemed to have stopped rising and turning, and was now moving through the darkness toward the red glow.

"No, no," Teresa cried, tears streaming down her cheeks as she flailed and kicked in protest. The glow, whatever it was, filled her with dread and loathing. She was close enough now that she was almost above it, and seemed to be descending. The closer she got the less it looked like a fire. It was still glowing angry red, but it looked more like a vast open sore, swollen and throbbing, more revolting than any she had seen in her medical career. It was laced with deep red veins and churned as if alive. She could feel a raw heat emanating from the core of the glow, and she nearly gagged on the fetid stench that rose from it. Though disgusted, she gazed in horrified fascination at the spectacle. Whatever it was, it was pulsing about the edges as if straining to burst free of its constraints. Had this been an infection or wound on a patient, she would have been very concerned about systemic infection, and would be treating it urgently to prevent blood poisoning. As it was, she had no idea what to do, and could only look on helplessly.

Just when Teresa thought she could bear no more, the vision dissolved, and she again found herself in the open white space, standing before the pedestal with the bouquet and veil. She felt wonderfully warm and comfortable. Even though she was surrounded by bright mist, her eyes were not strained. Her fear and distress evaporated, replaced by awe and contentment. Wherever this place was, it was safe.

Teresa's vision was again drawn to the objects on the pedestal. They looked even more lovely than she'd remembered. A delicate aroma lingered near the bouquet, cleansing away the stench that had accompanied the prior vision. She stepped closer to the objects, but felt torn – she was attracted to their beauty, but at the same time felt they were too pristine to be sullied by her common hands. She stood about two feet from the pedestal and gazed enraptured. Despite her hesitance, a deep yearning welled within her to reach out and barely touch them, perhaps lightly stroking a petal or gently caressing some of the embroidery on the veil cap. Surely that would do no harm? The yearning warred against her inner conviction that she was too coarse, too common to aspire to such beauty. But with her gaze fixed on that vision of perfection, it was hard to think about herself at all. Unwittingly her hand began to reach toward the veil, ever so cautiously.

Then came the call, and Teresa jerked her hand back, fearing she had been caught in some transgression. The call was fleeting, as clear as the tone from a crystal bell on a fine winter morning, barely heard before it was gone, vanishing without echo into the whiteness. The call was no more than a few words, maybe only one, but was so compelling that Teresa turned to listen in case it came again. There was no censure in the call, but rather a summons that awakened within her a keen desire to answer, to follow that beckoning. She knew the call had been directed toward, or had included, her. She looked and listened intently, hoping to discover the source of the call, or at least the direction from which it had come, but she heard nothing. The misty whiteness remained unbroken, and the still silence pressed in on her ears.

Teresa's heart sank. Perhaps the call only came once, not to be repeated. Perhaps she'd missed the only utterance and it was now lost forever. Sadness overwhelmed her, and she began to sob at the thought that she would never hear that summons clearly enough to respond to it.

Then came another call, closer and clearer – someone was calling her name. But it wasn't like the summons. It kept repeating, and by comparison was coarse and harsh. She wanted it to stop, to be silent, lest it drown out the summons, but it persisted, and now she was being shaken, and suddenly she was lifting her head from the table to see an alarmed Sister Margaret shaking her with Sister Kateri looking over her shoulder.

"Teresa, are you all right?" Sister Margaret asked.

"I…ah…" Teresa responded, disoriented. "I'm fine. Sorry, I must have dozed off."

"'Dozed off'?" Sister Kateri broke in. "Teresa, you were moaning and throwing your arms around. You knocked your mug onto the floor. I've seen you dozing, but I've never seen you so agitated. Do you need to talk to Sister Joseph Marie?"

"No, no, I'm fine," Teresa protested weakly. "I…I'm sorry about the mess. I'll clean it up –"

"Let us worry about that," Sister Margaret assured her. "You ought to get some rest. You've been pushing yourself too hard."

"I'm fine, really," Teresa assured them. For some reason she didn't want to discuss this dream with anyone, at least until she'd considered it some more. "I've got to go help with rounds."

"But, Teresa –" Sister Kateri began, but Teresa had pushed out of the kitchen.

*   *   *

Gil Peterson's phone gave the peculiar chirp which indicated that the incoming call was encrypted. Curious, he looked and saw that it was Helen Markham, which intrigued him even more. He keyed on the encryption and answered.

"Helen?"

"Hi, Gil," came the response after the slight lag that encryption always introduced. Helen's voice sounded tinny, another effect of the encryption, but it was recognizably her.

"What's up?" Gil asked. It was midday, which meant that Helen was at work at the hospital in Port Huron, from where she almost never called.

"Strange thing I thought you should know about soonest," Helen replied. "Word is filtering out that HHS rolled out some new patient protocols over the weekend. They do that periodically, but these ones have a provision our people haven't seen before."

"What's that?"

"Certain patients are flagged as unserviceable."

"Unserviceable?" Gil asked. That was a term he'd never heard before.

"Yes, as in we cannot provide them service. We have to refer them elsewhere."

"That's odd. Have you ever seen anything like that before?"

"Never," Helen replied. "We've seen limitations on services, and more commonly limitations on reimbursements, but never an outright ban on service. Strictly speaking it's a ban on payment – we wouldn't be reimbursed for any services provided – but it amounts to the same thing."

"Who are these people? Is there any discernable pattern?"

"That's the odd thing – the flagging seems to be totally random. There seems to be no tie to diagnosis or treatment or provider or demographic that we can see. There's no prior indication on their record, either – the clinical staff doesn't know who they are until they start processing the patient and the yellow flag pops up."

"Yellow flag?"

"Yes. That's the indicator the protocol triggers," Helen said. "A yellow flag in the corner of the screen. Tapping that opens a form that explains the situation, and where to send the patient."

"Where is that?" Gil asked.

"I'm not sure. I'm only hearing rumors from the clinical side. I've asked a few people to poke around and find out what they can."

"You mentioned it's an HHS protocol – is this change everywhere, or just there at Port City, or what?"

"No idea," Helen replied.

"Can you discreetly look into it? You have contacts at providers all over the state – find out what you can, would you?"

"Sure, Gil. It'll take some time, but I'll gather what I can," Helen assured him.

Helen rang off, leaving Gil to tap his phone on the desk and ponder. The odd circumstances seemed to be piling up. The warning from Fitz's mysterious contact that the Feds were renewing interest in the blast. An active investigator with a broad mandate and, seemingly, even broader ambitions. Now this – new medical protocols that identified certain patients for special treatment. Granted, they didn't know much about these protocols yet. They might be completely harmless. But Gil trusted Helen's judgment, and knew she wouldn't have called him had she not harbored some suspicions. For that matter, given the area's history, anything that flagged certain patients for special treatment made Gil suspicious as well. Furthermore, all this was coming down just when they'd decided to start releasing guests from the ranches because they had judged that the threat had passed.

Had it?

Gil shook his head. He was doing his usual thing, spinning catastrophes out of scant evidence. The blast had lain dormant for over two years now, and there was no hard evidence connecting Sam's rogue action to the network of ranches. The likelihood of there being any connection between this investigator and these new HHS protocols was miniscule.

Still, Gil thought, they hadn't successfully run the operation for this long by being complacent. Maybe he'd better review those emergency procedures, just to be sure. Then he sighed and rubbed his face wearily. Not today. He just didn't have energy. He was still recovering from losing Ma, and there were so many tensions around Rivendell these days, he was just worn out. Things were under control, and they'd drawn up those procedures with plenty of forethought. No reason to review them again just for the sake of doing it. He tried to return his attention to his work.

*　　　　*　　　　*

The sisters had intended to make the supply run in the afternoon, but the day had gotten away from them, so it wasn't until after supper that Sisters Margaret and Elizabeth, along with Teresa, were able to head to Sandusky with the van to pick up the load of goods. Making the supply run was a coveted duty, a brief opportunity to get clear of the walls of St. Anne's.

Before they left, Sister Joseph Marie slipped Teresa a gift card and told her to take the sisters for a rare treat: some drinks from the coffee place in downtown Sandusky. So on their way back through town after picking up the supplies, they parked the van by the courthouse lawn and dashed across the street to the shop. Sister Margaret indulged her sweet tooth with a rich mocha, while adventurous Sister Elizabeth chose the most elaborate creation the barista could concoct. Teresa, remembering she had midnight shift and wanting to grab a couple hours of sleep beforehand, stuck to a simple decaf. The sisters strolled around the courtyard grounds, sipping their drinks and chatting, relishing the balmy evening that held the promise of a springtime about to arrive fully and finally drive away the last of a long, bitter winter.

It wasn't until they were making their way back toward the van that Teresa spotted him. He was sitting on the bench by the gazebo on the courthouse lawn, sipping a coffee and watching the traffic. He was all by himself and looked utterly forlorn, like he didn't matter to anyone.

It was the man from her visions, the busy man, the man trapped in the dark maze.

Any shock or fright Teresa might have felt was swiftly buried in an overwhelming sense of certainty, even acquiescence. Of course he was there, and of course she was here to see him. It was unfolding as it should. His path was laid out, as was hers, and all that remained was to walk out the steps. And yet, at the same time, she was free. She could choose to turn, walk to the van, and drive off. Yet she knew that she wouldn't. She would walk over to him and say – something. She started toward the man, leaving the puzzled sisters standing by the van.

As Teresa drew closer, she could see more clearly how distressed and lonely the man looked. Her heart nearly broke to see his bleak and harried expression. She wanted nothing more than to comfort and reassure him, to be a friend to this fellow human who looked like he hadn't a friend in the world. Though innately shy herself, particularly around men, her compassion overcame her hesitation. She was now very close, but he still had not noticed her approach, so absorbed was he in his struggles.

"Excuse me?" Teresa said quietly. When the man didn't respond, she tried again. "Excuse me?"

The man, who had his face in his hands at the moment, looked up in mystification. It was clearly the same man from her visions – she felt as though she knew him.

"I...I'm sorry?" he stammered, clumsily. Teresa now had to figure out what to say to him. She could hardly tell him the conditions under which she'd seen him, so she said the first thing that came to her mind.

"You matter to *me.*"

Stunned and puzzled, the man could only stammer out a barely coherent response. "I do?"

His bewildered expression looked exactly like the one he'd worn when Teresa had seen him trapped and frustrated in the maze. That mysterious vision came back to her vividly, with its shadowy halls and steel catwalks.

And ladders leading up out of the maze.

"Yes," Teresa reassured him. "There's a way out of where you are, but it isn't by the paths you think. Keep looking."

The man gazed at her, dumbfounded, but within Teresa something seemed to click. She'd just delivered the message she'd been sent to deliver. It made more sense now – the mysterious visions, this seemingly routine supply run, this apparently random encounter on the courthouse lawn. It was unfolding as planned, and that man was central to the plan.

As was she.

Teresa turned and started to walk away. She could feel the man's eyes on her as she went, but still he'd said nothing. She didn't worry – perhaps there was nothing for him to say. But as she approached the van, he found his tongue.

"What do you mean?" he called, then with more urgency. "Who are you?"

Teresa turned. Who was she? That was the question, was it not? As she looked at him, she was given the sure knowledge that this man had the resources to find her, to uncover her identity – not just her hidden identity at St. Anne's, but her true name, literally dead and buried for over two years. He would discover her, and it would be all right.

"You'll find that out soon enough," Teresa said with a smile. As much as she longed to stay and comfort this lost soul, that was not her task. She'd delivered her message. Turning to the van, she swung in with a quiet prayer entrusting him to the Mercy.

"Who was that?" Sister Elizabeth asked.

"I don't know yet," Teresa replied. "I suspect – hope – that I will someday, but we both have long journeys before us first."

The two sisters looked at each other in mystification, then at Teresa.

"Teresa, we love you, but you're strange," Sister Margaret said. "Very strange."

"My dear sisters, you have no idea," Teresa replied.

Discovery

Lottie was pottering about setting up the morning coffee when the phone finally chimed. She fetched her pills, grumbling a little about the one drawback of this system – you couldn't advance the dispensing by even ten minutes. She'd awakened a little early this morning, and would have showered by now, except that she couldn't get to her medications until the dispenser released them, and she didn't want her phone to start squawking while she was in the shower. Gulping the handful of pills, she turned on the coffeemaker and headed for the bathroom.

*   *   *

"Lottie?" Sue called tentatively from the doorway. She'd seen the kitchen lights on from across the yard, and thought she'd drop over for a morning chat over one of Lottie's excellent cups of coffee. But there had been no answer to Sue's persistent knocking, so she finally stuck her head in to see what the issue was. The kitchen was vacant, though the light was on and a full pot of coffee sat untouched on the brewer. "Lottie?" Sue called again, stepping into the kitchen and looking around. No Lottie in sight, though she could hear a dim rushing sound. Peeking around the corner, Sue saw that the bathroom door was closed and the rushing sound was coming from behind it. Ah, that was it – Lottie was in the shower. Sue went back to the kitchen to pour herself a mug of coffee and wait.

Sue was nearly finished with her mug before it occurred to her that Lottie was taking an inordinate amount of time in the shower. Neither had Sue heard any of the expectable sounds of someone moving about in a bathroom, even if they were showering. The vague unease she'd felt ever since Lottie hadn't answered her knock intensified, warring with her reluctance to startle or embarrass her friend. Timidly she walked to the bathroom door and knocked. "Lottie?" she called gently, then more clearly when there came no reply. "Lottie?" There was still no sound but the steady rush of the shower. "Lottie?" Sue repeated, knocking more loudly as panic surged within her. "Lottie!" she hollered, hammering on the door. When there was still no answer, Sue threw restraint to the wind and opened the door.

There on the floor, sprawled halfway in, halfway out of the shower, lay Lottie. She'd clearly fallen, and in her fall had caught the shower curtain, dragging it and the curtain rod down with her. Cold water was spraying all over the bathroom as Lottie's lifeless eyes stared vacantly at the door.

"Oh!" Sue cried quietly. "Jesus, sweet Jesus." She backed away, her heart hammering. She'd seen death before, but never like this, never finding a friend, alone –

Suddenly there was a commotion at the kitchen door. Still in shock, Sue stepped around the corner to see two young men coming through the back door. They looked official, being clad in some kind of utility uniform with patches on the shoulders. One was carrying a bag while the other was struggling with a stretcher-like thing.

"Ms. Pierce?" one asked, looking at Sue, who just shook her head and pointed toward the bathroom door. The man came around the corner and looked in.

"Oh, no," he said grimly. "Bobby, bring the stretcher!" Then he turned to Sue. "We're from the RCC. We got an alert that something might be wrong, and we came as quickly as we could. Apparently we weren't fast enough."

"I'm Sue, Lottie's neighbor. I dropped in to chat, and only just found her."

"We'll do what we can," the man said, then his tone became grim. "Though that may not be very much."

*   *   *

Jason awoke that morning determined to get his focus back where it belonged. He contacted Ethan and told him not to come up to Sandusky, but to stand by in case he was needed. He archived the flood of messages about the Chengdu Two project – he'd catch up with those later. He even walled off his nagging questions about the mysterious red-haired woman with her cryptic statements. All of that could wait until he'd wrestled to the ground the issue of the blast.

Doggedly Jason returned to the most basic documents on the case. He set aside the reports on the RA overflights, and anything he'd written up since arriving. He wanted to start from scratch, reexamining every shred of information from every possible angle, to see if he could spot something that might have escaped his notice.

It was a long, tiring, frustrating day for Jason. He delved into personnel records, into the documents on the original Chengdu Project, into purchasing archives, into everything he could think of. He played and replayed every inch of video footage he had – the record of the blast itself, the images of the suspect loading supplies into his car, even the full drone video of the stalking and takedown of the suspects on the day of the blast itself. He kept coming back to the question, "What do we know?", which in turn brought him back to the harsh reality that almost everything they knew, or might have learned, had ended with the blast. That was the terminus, the full stop that left so many questions hanging with no hope of ever being answered.

It was midafternoon, well past the lunch break that Jason should have taken but hadn't, and his eyes were getting blurry with fatigue. He was following what was probably the most futile of threads, the Lapeer County sheriff's report on the blast, projecting onto the wall the images that had accompanied it. There were various photographs of the wreckage: the twisted and scorched car bodies, the shattered cinder blocks, the extent of the debris field. Some of the last images were of the ID cards that had been found in the shrubs, the cards of the medical workers. Jason examined the first image carefully, for it was of the county employee ID and the driver's license of the deputy medical examiner, Derek Stevens, the party who'd been identified as a possible link to the terrorist network. This Stevens had been the most promising avenue of investigation, so Jason was searching for even a sliver of unexamined evidence that might illuminate some new aspect of the case. He finally concluded that if there was such a sliver, it wasn't to be found on those ID cards – everything matched what was in the files. He took a minute to scrutinize the photographs on the cards, which were the usual official shots showing a pale, thin-faced, unsmiling young man with dark hair. Just an ordinary guy you'd pass on the street without noticing. He didn't look like the type to have connections to a clandestine terror network.

With resignation Jason flicked to the next slide, which showed images of the ID cards of the woman who'd been killed. Jason knew this story, too – her name was Janice Boyd. She'd been a nurse at the hospital who'd been recruited as a Chengdu operative, and had even gotten a few culls under her belt. She'd been at least a friend, and possibly a lover, of Stevens, and was under instructions from her supervisor to try to recruit him into the organization. That apparently hadn't gone well, and there had been some concern that the reverse was occurring, that she was being drawn toward the terrorist network by his influence. This speculation was generally discounted, though. She seemed to be a minor player, peripheral to the main action. She'd proved vital for one thing, though: she'd been the bait used to trap Stevens after he'd skillfully eluded arrest. That was how she'd ended up at the blast site, to be killed with all the rest.

Again Jason compared the details on the ID cards to the file records. Everything was accurate, so he prepared to click to the next slide, but stopped long enough to examine the ID card photographs.

Jason's hand froze on the controller, and a chill seized his heart.

It was she.

It was the girl who'd approached him on the courthouse lawn, the stranger with the kind eyes and beautiful smile and cryptic message that had been troubling Jason ever since. There she was, looking back at him from the driver's license photo, which was the usual official shot showing an unsmiling, unhappy-looking woman. But whoever had taken her hospital ID photo had caught her smiling, and that made all the difference. Her entire countenance came alive, the tired lines vanishing and the harsh edges softening and the dull eyes coming to sparkling life. It was a face full of hope and ready for joy.

It was the face that had smiled at him just yesterday afternoon.

Jason was sitting upright, staring at the wall, his hand gripping the controller and his breath coming in short gasps. This couldn't be. That woman was dead. Dammit, they *knew* that woman was dead! It was one of the sureties about this case, a matter beyond question, one of the few things they absolutely, indisputably knew.

Yet this absolutely, indisputably dead woman had spoken to him in broad daylight not twenty-four hours earlier.

What else about this case that they absolutely, indisputably knew was wrong?

What had she said to him? Jason turned her words over in his mind, kicking himself for not writing them down at the time. But he'd been so startled and bemused by her addressing him that he'd just thought them the random statements of someone who was at least confused, if not insane. What had she said? Something about him, Jason, mattering to her. Why would she say that? Then something about there being a path out of where he was, but it wasn't where he expected it to be, or something like that. And she'd said something else, too. When he'd asked her who she was, she'd said –

That he'd find out soon enough.

He stared at the images on the wall. She'd been right.

Who was this woman?

Jason's astonished bewilderment was slowly penetrated by a regular tone. His phone. It was right at his elbow, and it was ringing. He didn't recognize the number.

"Hello?"

"Mr. Pelletier?" came a man's voice.

"Yes?"

"This is Dylan Matthews over at the Fairgrove RCC. My supervisor asked me to call to let you know that we have a green flag in house."

"A green flag?" Jason was mystified.

"A patient, sir. One of the special ones. I'm not sure of the details, but our protocol says that if we're ever sent a green-flagged patient, we're supposed to call a special team, and notify you."

It was coming back to Jason now. Green-flags were people who fit the profile of those who'd vanished, presumably into the hidden network. People who might know valuable information about the clandestine operation they were seeking.

People who might know specifics.

"Who is this person? And where is he?" Jason asked.

"Her name is Pelton, sir. Frieda Pelton, and she's here at the RCC right now. We've got her in isolation, and the team from Flint is nearly here."

Teams? That's right, that had been in the documentation they'd sent him. Special teams, briefed on the ultra-secret details of the first Chengdu attempt and how it had ended, and experienced in patient interrogation. They'd know what to ask, and how to ask it.

"How long has this patient been there?" Jason asked.

"Almost an hour, sir. Like I said, we've kept her –"

"Why did you wait so long to call me?" Jason snapped.

"I'm sorry, sir," the man said. "This is our first green flag, and we're still sorting out the protocol."

Jason did some rapid calculating. The Fairgrove RCC was at least forty minutes away. He wanted to be there, but he didn't want to risk the patient getting away before they had a chance to extract the information.

"Look, follow your protocols. I'll be there as soon as I can, but next time, call me sooner!"

"Yes, sir," the man replied timidly.

Jason grabbed his tablet and headed for his car. This might be the break they'd been hoping for.

* * *

Frieda stared at the door of the little room, feeling increasingly apprehensive. This experiment hadn't turned out at all like she'd expected, and she still wasn't sure how it would resolve.

They'd all considered this move carefully. She'd discussed it with Doc Luke, and Mr. Fitz, and Shelly Peterson, and of course her host family whom she'd come to love so dearly. Doc Luke had explained how her heart condition was getting worse, and there were effective treatments for it, but he couldn't provide them. Shelly had explained how the leadership had discussed the situation, and how conditions had changed since Frieda had gone into hiding, and how they judged that it was again safe to start using the regular medical care system. It was scary to consider, but then so were the symptoms she'd been experiencing.

So, they'd moved Frieda out last weekend. Her modest trust fund could afford a room in a care home outside Caro, and the Jamesons had promised to come visit often. First thing she'd done on Monday morning was to call her old cardiologist, Dr. Oswald, and the earliest they'd been able to fit her in was today. So she'd shown up for the 11:00 appointment, only to find that there was some sort of hiccup. She'd expected some delays, given that she'd been out of the medical system for nearly four years, but it still been a very long wait before the receptionist had come out to tell her that they couldn't give her medical care, and that she'd been selected to get special care at a facility that had just opened.

This irregularity had made the already edgy Frieda even more nervous, but when she'd suggested that she just come back another day, the receptionist had explained that some drivers were already on the way to take her to the new facility. Shortly thereafter two smart looking young men with a brisk, professional demeanor had come in and escorted her to a waiting van. Frieda had still been hesitant, but one of the young men had explained about this new pilot program for providing swift care to underserved populations, and how they wanted to cut through the red tape and give patients like her the treatment they deserved in a timely manner. The young men were so earnest and upbeat that it had somewhat eased Frieda's concerns.

They'd headed west, toward Saginaw, which she'd figured would be the location of this new facility. To her surprise, they'd stopped after driving no more than ten miles, turning into the parking lot of some kind of small complex on the edge of a field. There was a main building that looked like a medical clinic, but the van didn't stop there, instead driving to another building in the back. Here the men had escorted her down a narrow hallway and into a small room with a narrow bed, a desk and chair, and a little stool. They'd told her somebody would be right with her, and then left.

Alone in the little room, Frieda had begun to get nervous again. Where was she? Why hadn't she been able to see Dr. Oswald? After sitting and waiting for some minutes, she got up and tried the door.

It was locked.

Frieda had begun to feel truly alarmed. Her breath began to come in shorter gasps, and she'd started feeling dizzy. She knew what that meant, and sat down again. Pills, she needed her pills. Looking around, she saw that she didn't have her purse. Those men had hustled her into the room so quickly that she'd left her purse in the van. She was just about to stand up and start knocking to call for help when the door opened and a young woman had come in holding a tray with some things on it. Frieda had explained that she needed her pills, and the woman had made a call. Then she'd explained that she needed to take blood samples, and to do that she'd need to strap down Frieda's arm "for safety". This mystified Frieda, who'd had many samples taken over the years, but she was given no choice – the woman had secured her elbow and wrist to a chair arm, and started probing for a vein. Just as she was sliding the needle in, another med tech had arrived, this one with an IV bag and tube. She'd gotten promptly to work, hanging the bag on a hook on the bed, then strapping Frieda's other arm to the chair. As the first tech had departed with the samples, the second one had slipped in the IV needle and started the drip. She'd then left, assuring Frieda that someone would be along "shortly". Frieda had called after her, but the only response she'd gotten had been the door clicking shut.

So here Frieda sat, alone in a barren room, strapped to a chair that was feeling harder every minute, with no way to leave or even summon anyone. She twisted her arms to see if she could loosen them, but the straps were thick and tightly wrapped. Her nose was starting to itch, and she had to visit the restroom. If this was new and improved medical care, she wasn't very impressed. In fact, she was getting increasingly nervous with every passing minute, and she could feel her heart rate inching up. She'd been expecting to be talking with Dr. Oswald by now, not stuck in a strange place with people who didn't even give their names.

Just then the door opened again, and a young man breezed in. He paid no attention to Frieda, but uncapped a needle and injected it into the port in the IV line. Frieda decided she'd had enough.

"See here, young man, I want to be let out of here, or at least out of these straps. And what are you doing there?"

"Patience, ma'am," the man said absently, capping the needle. "This is part of your treatment. The straps are for your safety. The doctor will be in very soon to explain everything." With that he slipped out the door.

"He better be!" Frieda called after him, rattling the chair in frustration. "Because I've had about enough of this!" Her heart was racing now, and she could feel her face flushing with anger. She knew that wasn't a good sign. "Calm down, girl, calm down," Frieda tried to reassure herself. "No need to get worked up. It'll all come out in the wash." She tried to breathe slowly and calm her thoughts, and to her surprise, it seemed to be working. She could feel herself relaxing, the tension easing from her shoulders. The strange situation and inexplicable treatment wasn't bothering her as much. In fact, it wasn't bothering her at all – nothing was. None of this seemed to matter. She tried to force herself to be anxious about being strapped to a chair in a locked room, and found she couldn't. All her cares and anxieties were floating away on a tide of unconcern. Part of her knew there was cause for worry, she just couldn't get worked up about it.

Frieda didn't know how long she sat there in a thickening fog of detached indifference, but eventually a grave-faced woman in a lab coat with a stethoscope around her neck came through the door.

"Frieda?" the woman said in a serious tone. "I'm the doctor who's been assigned to your case, and I have to tell you, I'm concerned. Gravely concerned."

"You are?" Frieda asked in amazement.

"I am," the doctor confirmed. "Someone in your condition – your test results are bad. If I'm going to help you, I need to know what kind of care you've been receiving, and who's been providing it."

"You do?"

"Yes," the doctor assured her, sitting down across from her and tapping her tablet. "Let's begin with where you've been living."

*　　　　*　　　　*

Jason pulled into the RCC parking lot and wondered where he should go. The lot was about half full, and he saw people in the clinic, but he doubted that was the place. He parked by the administrative office and went in to find a heavyset man with short blond hair sitting at a workstation. He eventually deigned to look up at Jason.

"Yes?"

"I'm Jason Pelletier, DHS DTD," Jason said, flashing his ID. "I was told you had a party of interest who'd been sent here?"

"Ah, yes, Mr. Pelletier," the man's tone changed. "Yes, one of the team is in with the party right now. Things are apparently going smoothly."

"Oh. Can I...see her? Participate? I have a few questions."

"Mr. Pelletier, are you trained in these kind of investigations? Have you ever taken part in an agent-facilitated interview?"

"Agent-facilitated?" Jason asked. "I don't understand. I've worked with agents –"

The man smiled indulgently. "Not that kind of agent, Mr. Pelletier. Assistive agents, to make the party more cooperative with questioning. There have been great strides in recent years, but the parties being assisted by the agent have to be handled very carefully by skilled interviewers. If you or I were to just barge into the interview, it could unsettle the rapport the interviewer has established with the party."

"You mean…truth serum?"

"Not precisely. New formulations have been discovered, using combinations of sedatives and psychotropic agents, that render such crude terms –"

"Look, I'm in a bit of a hurry," Jason interrupted. "I need some answers –"

Just then the door opened and a woman came in. She was wearing a lab coat and was tucking a stethoscope into her pocket, but something in her demeanor told Jason that she was no doctor.

"Hey, Justin," the woman said, laying a tablet on the counter. "Here it is, all recorded, including the most valuable thing: an address."

"Thanks, Alexis. In fact, the man you want is standing right here. Mr. Pelletier, this is Alexis, one of our best interviewers."

"Pleased to meet you," Alexis said briskly. "If you've got a tablet or phone, I can dump the recording of the interview. I made a special note of the address. You'll also want this – one of the drivers gave it to me." She put a battered purse on the counter.

"Okay," Jason said, handing her his tablet. "Is there…should I be talking to her? I have a few questions –"

"Like what?" Alexis asked.

"Pardon me?"

"What kind of questions? Names of people she's lived with? Places she went? People who made arrangements for her? Why she's been living like that?" Alexis rattled off briskly.

"I suppose, that sort of thing," Jason replied.

"Please, I do this for a living, Mr…"

"Jason."

"Jason. I've been briefed on the situation and the mission. I asked all those questions and more, and her responses are in the recording. There isn't much – the people running this operation know their stuff, and keep their participants isolated and in the dark. But what little she knows," she tapped the tablet, "has been recorded. You may be able to get more out of this," she waved at the purse, "but I doubt it."

Seeing that he was being stonewalled but recognizing that Alexis was probably correct that he wouldn't be able to learn more than a trained interrogator, Jason decided to fold. "Okay, I'll take these. Thanks."

"I can have the interview transcribed, if you'd like," Alexis offered.

"No, we have programs for that," Jason replied. "What's going to happen to her?"

"'Her'?" Alexis said, mystified.

"The patient," Jason prodded.

"Oh. Well, she's an OPEL, right?" Alexis shrugged as she turned toward the door.

*　　　　　*　　　　　*

Frieda was still feeling relaxed, but somewhat confused by all the doctor's questions. She also felt just a little unsettled, the barest whisper of unease, about how much she'd talked. Should she have said so much? Shelly and Mr. Fitz had warned her about talking too casually, but somehow she'd found herself babbling to that doctor. Why had the doctor been so curious, anyway? She was also beginning to feel her physical discomfort more keenly again. Why was she still strapped to this chair?

The door opened again, and again an anonymous medical tech entered holding a hypodermic. She barely glanced at Frieda, instead busying herself with the IV.

"Please," Frieda asked. "Can you loosen these straps? They're starting to hurt, and I really need to visit a restroom."

"Be patient, ma'am," the woman said. "This is the final treatment before we get you out of here." She slipped the needle into the injection port and depressed the plunger.

"The final treatment?" Frieda asked hopefully.

"Guarantee it," the woman responded as she capped the empty syringe. "I'll be back in a few minutes."

"Okay," Frieda said as the woman left.

*   *   *

Jason sat in the parking lot of a gas station and thought. He'd gotten out of the RCC as quickly as he could, but thirst and the need for a rest stop hadn't let him get far. Having attended to those needs, he sat in his car, feeling strangely alone and desolate, unable to muster the will to drive farther. He picked up the purse he'd been given. This should get into the hands of some investigators. Sanderson and Harris? Maybe. If they weren't able to do anything with it, they'd know who could. He opened the purse and began poking through the sparse contents. A hairbrush. Some lip balm. A pill bottle. A wallet with a few coins and a little cash. He felt uneasy pawing through the personal items of a total stranger, almost as if he were defiling someone's bedroom, but then realized that the owner would never be needing these items again. That made him feel even more uneasy. He was about to put the purse aside when he noticed a couple of devices toward the bottom. Both looked something like phones, and sure enough, one of them was, though it was so old that Jason was surprised it still worked. But the other device wasn't a phone at all, but a little photo viewer of the type that some people kept on their desks which would cycle through a set of images. This viewer had about two dozen pictures, mostly of children and sometimes children with a couple, whom he presumed were the parents. A couple of the pictures showed the children gathered around an older black woman with a wrinkled face and a broad smile. Maybe that was the party who – Jason flicked to the next picture, which showed the old woman on a dock, with one of the children, a little boy. She

321

was wearing a floppy hat and sunglasses, and she and the boy were both holding fishing rods and clearly enjoying each other's company.

Jason clicked the viewer off. The investigators should get this device. The images might contain useful information, and could be fed into facial-recognition software to try to identify the other parties. Yes, these images, along with the entire contents of the purse, should get to the investigators, Jason thought – then he slipped the viewer and phone into his pocket. Picking up the tablet, he tapped the file that contained the recording of the interrogation. He heard the patient, disciplined voice of the interrogator, and another voice, an older woman's voice, answering the questions in innocent simplicity and complete trust. She spoke of "her family" and "her kids" and "home", and Jason thought of the images, faces to go with the terms. Coldly and skillfully the interrogator's questions continued, unrelenting, carefully phrased to elicit maximum information.

Abruptly Jason killed the recording. Somebody would have to listen to that, but it needn't be him. He gathered up the debris from the drink and snack he'd purchased and walked it over to the garbage can. He hesitated for a moment, then pulled the viewer from his pocket and pitched it into the can as well, followed by the old phone.

As Jason drove back toward Sandusky he tried to put the incident at the RCC behind him and consider what he'd discovered immediately before the interruption. It didn't seem possible, yet he'd seen it with his own eyes. He thought about all the resources at his disposal, and all the video footage that he'd gone over, and by the time he got home he knew exactly what he needed to review. It was the footage from the helidrone of the tracking and takedown of Derek Stevens, the time he'd eluded arrest but had returned to rescue his friend the nurse.

As Jason ran the video again, he caught some footage of her going from the hospital to her car, but that mostly showed her back. Then there were lengthy segments of her driving, up to the point where Stevens had jumped into the car. After that the drone had followed more closely, not wanting to lose the car, but it stayed behind and above the car, preventing a good shot of the woman's face. Only after they'd parked in an alley and gotten out of the car did the camera get a good angle. It was less than a minute of footage, and was grainy and jerky, but it was her. When he zoomed and enhanced, it was clear that the woman who'd been arrested with Derek Stevens was the same one who'd spoken to him at the bench yesterday.

Janice Boyd. Known to have been killed in the blast.

Jason's head hurt at the implications of this. Part of his mind tried to gnaw at the problem, to fit it into their current understanding. What if the terrorists had managed to...what if they'd staged... Jason shook his head to clear his thoughts. Worthless, all these speculations. If their most fundamental assumptions were wrong, then everything should be scrapped. He should start from nothing, making no assumptions, and rebuild it all from the ground up. The prospect weighed on him, not least because he had no idea where to begin.

Sighing, Jason clicked off the projector. It was well past dinnertime, and he didn't feel up to cooking. Looked like another night of burger or Chinese or pizza – the options in Sandusky were limited. Before turning in that night, he dropped a message to Ethan to line up a meeting spot the next day somewhere in the Port Huron area, and to get Sanderson and Harris there, as well as Collins and one of his people. He fell asleep pondering the words of the mystery woman, the one who should be dead but was alive. Why had she said those words, and what did they mean? His dreams were haunted by images of old women in floppy hats fishing on piers with little boys.

*   *   *

Late the next morning Jason met with Ethan, Sanderson, Harris, and the Selfridge crew at a DHS facility in Marysville. Collins was last to arrive, with Sergeant Danvers in tow, looking frustrated and bored and unhappy to be there.

"I gotta warn you," Collins announced before Jason could even begin. "We don't have anything new for you. Plenty of general analysis, but nothing new."

"Well, I have something for you," Jason replied, pushing his tablet across the table to Collins. "An address."

"An address?"

"Yes. Confirmed to be one of the sequester sites used to house people who had disappeared," Jason explained.

"Really?" Collins asked, showing the address to a smiling Sergeant Danvers. "You know this for certain?"

"As well as we know anything," Jason cautioned, sharply aware of how edged that statement was. "It was…ah…obtained from someone who'd lived there for a while."

"Well," gloated Collins. "Well, now, this changes everything."

"Everything? One address?"

"Maybe not everything, but it's a solid foothold. With one known point, we can identify the traffic to that site, and then note where else that traffic goes, and analyze patterns and calculate probabilities. From those we can project other patterns and probabilities. Obviously, the more known points we have, the more accurate the calculations are going to be, but one is a damn sight better than nothing."

"Great," Jason acknowledged. "You do what you can with that, and we'll get more to you as they come in. Now, Agents Sanderson and Harris, I've got something for you, too." He shoved the purse over to them. "Find out everything you can about the owner of that purse."

"Okay," Sanderson said. "Will we be able to interview the owner?"

"No, that won't be possible. Just work with those contents."

"Missing person?"

"No, just…indisposed," Jason floundered. "Now, presuming we can put a crack in this wall of ignorance we've been battering ourselves against, what are our next steps? How do we go about widening the crack, and what do we do once we're through the wall?"

The discussion that followed centered on using the intelligence that the overflight image analysis would hopefully provide to gather more intelligence, this time by more direct action. Jason found that he didn't have a good mental picture of how he expected to proceed once they had a set of addresses. Agent Sanderson presumed they'd just walk up to doors and request interviews, but Ethan reminded him that they were dealing with unknown factors. These terrorists had proven themselves willing and able to perform mass murder, so they might want to come in a little more prepared this time. They all agreed that the domestic strike force that Dr. Tasker had been prepared to deploy last time had been overkill, but that some weight of force was probably justified. Major Collins reminded everyone that his drones could provide armed aerial cover as well as overhead intelligence. Jason shied away from using the term "raid" to describe what they were planning, so Ethan coined the clumsy phrase "investigation in force", or IIF for short.

The planning could go no further than that without better intelligence, so the meeting disbanded. Collins and Danvers returned to Selfridge to feed the new data into their algorithms, while Sanderson and Harris gathered what they'd been given and headed out. As they were leaving, Jason dashed out to the hall to intercept them.

"Yes?" Sanderson asked in answer to Jason's hail.

"I was wondering – how much do we know about the woman who was killed in the blast?" Jason asked.

"'The woman'?" Sanderson replied in mystification. "Weren't several women killed in the blast?"

"I mean the woman who was brought in with the intelligence asset, the nurse – Janice Boyd. The only woman who was publicly acknowledged as a victim."

"Well, we know she was killed," Sanderson said. "And that she'd been a participant in whatever HHS had been running. Other than that, we don't know much. I think she was seen as a secondary, important only because she was a channel to this Stevens."

"Okay," Jason said. "Do me a favor, could you? Dig up whatever you can about her. I know it won't be much, but anything will help. In the interest of…completeness."

Sanderson and Harris exchanged puzzled glances. "Sure thing, sir," Sanderson replied. "Whatever we find, we'll send along."

"Thanks," Jason said, and ducked back into the conference room, where only Ethan remained.

"So, you want me to start calling folk to line up teams to do these…ah…IIFs?" Ethan asked.

"Sure. Would Fort Wayne be the best resource?"

"That's what I'm thinking," Ethan acknowledged.

"Though I'm also starting to wonder," Jason continued. "If we deploy these teams all over the Thumb, is there going to be a PR fallout? Are people going to start asking questions about what's happening to their neighbors?"

"We are the federal government," Ethan reminded him. "In the end, it doesn't matter what people ask."

"Well, sure, but there's no reason to ruffle feathers we don't have to," Jason pointed out.

"You're thinking some sort of PR campaign?" Ethan asked.

"I'm thinking more Opinion Management."

"Best of luck there," Ethan replied. "Our POM guys aren't much, and they spend most of their time trying to get people not to hate the TSA."

"I've got resources," Jason said. "Make those calls, would you? I don't know when Selfridge will be getting back to us with results, but I want to be ready when they do."

That afternoon Jason got a message from the RCC over by Forester. Another Green Tag party had come in, from whom the interviewer had gotten another address. Jason forwarded the address to Collins, but he didn't drive to the RCC, even though it was only fifteen minutes away.

Exposure

"So, are you looking to herd or scatter?" George Spader asked Jason.

"Am I looking to what?" Jason asked.

"If you're doing public opinion management, you're either trying to get people to do things – herding – or get them not to do things – scattering. I was just asking what your primary goal was."

"I don't know – I thought it was educating people," Jason said. George shook his head.

"If you're simply educating, you're not doing POM. From what you've told me, you're going to need a POM overlay on this or you'll be facing backlash."

"You're the expert - why don't you tell me?" Jason suggested.

George pursed his lips and examined his notes for a minute. "It looks to me like you've got a basic scattering operation. That's good, because scattering is easier than herding."

Jason was getting lost in the jargon, but he struggled to understand. "It what way is it scattering?"

"You're dealing with hidden agents doing shady things: illegal provision of care, smuggling restricted substances, probably some kind of tax complications, possibly even darker stuff. Your concern is reaction and resistance. If you could count on the neighbors just sitting on their hands when your teams move in, you wouldn't be concerned. But you are worried that they'll react in some undesirable way, anything from confronting your teams to calling other officials or the press. Correct?"

"That's about right," Jason acknowledged.

"So we want them to scatter from their neighbors. We don't want them banding together, so we throw some FUD around – fear, uncertainty, and doubt. We warn the public that hidden in their midst are suspect parties engaging in suspect activities. We stress how they're skirting laws that everyone else has to abide by. We associate them with unpopular political figures or government agencies. We warn that anyone near them might be swept up with them. There is a whole repertoire of messages which, if properly deployed, can drive wedges in even the closest friendships and family bonds. Believe me, after two weeks of watching our spots, Joe Lunchbucket will be suspecting grandma. I'll have one of our teams tailor a set to your circumstances."

"Oh, all right," Jason said. "That sounds great, but also complex. We need this in short order."

"Would the end of next week do for a run-through? I can have the basic messages for you to review by mid-week, and get some teams working up some spots. We'll put the messages and spots together and, if you like them, we can start airing shortly thereafter."

"Wow – that fast? Don't you have to line up actors and film them, and all that?" Jason asked.

"Bah," George waved. "We stopped doing it that way over a decade ago. It's all digital 3-D animation now, with preset templates to use. I've had my techs work up spots during meetings, and be able to show them before the meeting adjourned."

"That's amazingly fast, especially for a government operation," Jason said.

"You guys are easy – small scope and advance notice. We often have to handle much more complex POM after a situation has broken open. That's a scramble," George replied. "I'll be back in touch."

Shortly thereafter Ethan called with an update on the IIF teams. Apparently, there were complications with arranging some of them, and other administrative headaches. One of the questions that needed answering was what the apparent threat level was.

"Apparent threat level?" Jason asked.

"Yeah, there are five of them. Level One is potential threat, Level Two is imminent threat, Level Three is –"

"Look, Ethan," Jason interrupted. "I don't have time for the full download. What threat level would enable the teams to do their job most effectively?" Jason was starting to feel saturated with all the minutiae he was expected to know.

"That would probably be Level Three – immediate threat. Levels Four and Five are essentially going in with guns blazing, and we don't need that. Level Three is probably the best balance between restraint and effectiveness. We can change the threat level as circumstances warrant."

"Fine. Set the default apparent threat level to Three, subject to review and adjustment," Jason said. "Have you been in touch with the Selfridge people? I've heard nothing from them."

"Briefly. Apparently now that they have some addresses, they're taking the overflight images all the way back to the start and feeding it into the analytical engine. That's a tall order, even for the NSA computers. They hope to have something later next week, was my impression."

"Okay, that'll work well. I have a status report to throw together. Have a good weekend," Jason rang off and got to work pulling together his weekly update. He reported on the RCCs being active, and hoped that was the last he'd have to do on those. That project was firmly in the hands of HHS now, and he hoped to leave it there. He alluded to the breakthroughs they'd had in the terrorist network investigation, but didn't say too much, lest something fall through. There'd be enough to report if these leads led to real results.

Once he'd sent off his status report, Jason went for a stroll in the spring afternoon. It was nearly May, and the trees and bushes were greening up nicely. He wandered over to the coffee place, where the owner recognized him coming and had his order ready before he even placed it. Jason took the coffee back to the bench by the gazebo and sat thinking disturbing thoughts.

The foremost thought disturbing Jason was why two Green-tagged parties had shown up when they did. Had these people truly been in seclusion, or had they just been caught by some faulty selection criteria? If they had been in seclusion, why reappear just as the RCCs came online? And if they hadn't been in seclusion, if they'd just not gone to the doctor for a while, then did the addresses have any significance? No, that first party, Frieda, had had a heart condition, and had been receiving care from somebody

– "Doc Luke", whoever that was. The Green Tags weren't false trails, but that still didn't explain why they'd showed up when they had, or why no more had appeared since the first two.

The other disturbing issue, the one that kept Jason glancing around the courthouse lawn, was the red-haired woman. It wasn't even who she was – Jason knew that. She was Janice Boyd, supposed victim of the Imlay City blast. But she was clearly not dead. What were the implications of that?

*   *   *

The following Monday morning Sergeant Abigail Danvers arrived at her desk with a purpose. She'd been working closely with Major Collins on running the overhead imagery through the NSA computers to try to discover the points of interest. As expected, the two addresses had been the big breakthrough. When doing network traffic analysis, each known point of interest enabled the system to discern more points of interest. But all the analyses could provide was probabilities. Starting with only two points that had a high degree of confidence – the two addresses had been assigned 95% – the immediate points of interest generated from them could get no higher than a 70% degree of confidence, and secondary points had even lower degrees. To the diligent Sergeant Danvers, confidence levels that low were not considered good results.

What they needed was at least one more good address, one with a 90%+ level of confidence. Three or more points with high levels of confidence would enable the algorithms to determine secondary and tertiary points with much higher confidence percentages. But their source had only given them two addresses, and there didn't seem any purpose in asking for more.

But Sergeant Danvers had an idea, one that she'd been gnawing on all weekend. There was a third address, one that she'd heard bandied about this project, one which those two agents had been assigned to investigate, the one where the family had disappeared after having a run-in with Child Protective Services.

Abigail had gotten a glance at that address, and it had jogged her memory. She remembered that address, and the courtesy flights they'd done about a year ago to gather video footage of children playing near it. Abigail could add two and two. A request to film children followed by a CPS prosecution meant that her group had been gathering evidence.

But – kids playing? What kind of evidence was that? Something had happened, because the family had subsequently gone missing. Abigail could make no sense of that, but one thing was undeniable – that address kept cropping up. That was what had been nagging her all weekend, and she'd come in this morning with an idea.

Research first. She sat down at her workstation and cued up the RA footage of that section. There were hours of footage, and even on 20x speed it still took a long time to go through. After finishing, she scrolled back and ran certain footage again. Her instincts were telling her that there was something there, but her brain and straining eyes were struggling to identify what. Back and forth she ran the footage, peering and thinking but seeing nothing. Returning to her workstation after a short break, it struck her. Of course! It wasn't what was there, but what wasn't there. She reran some footage to confirm her suspicions, then dumped a representative sampling onto her tablet and picked up the phone.

"Major Collins?"

"Yes, Abigail?"

"Do you have a minute? I've something I want to run past you."

"Sure, drop on in."

Shortly thereafter she was in his office, slipping her tablet onto his cradle to project the footage on the wall.

"Sir, I've been doing some research in hopes of getting another address to feed to the algorithms. I did some video review around an address that seems to keep cropping up, and I'd like to show you what I've found."

"Fire away," Collins said.

"I'm about to show you footage of the site covering about six hours of a typical day. It'll be stepped up about fifty times, so individual movements will seem quite fast and jerky, but watch for the overall pattern," Abigail explained, then started the playback. Several minutes went by, showing the lighting changing as the hours wore by, with vehicles zipping in and out of driveways and the occasional person moving across the screen at comically high speed. Other than that, the images showed nothing but road and treetops.

"I'm not seeing anything," Collins interrupted after several minutes. "What should I be looking for?"

"That, sir, is precisely my point," Abigail replied. "This house toward the top of the screen is the address that keeps turning up, the one we monitored briefly a year or so ago. It, and the two properties to the south, receive a typical amount of vehicular traffic in the course of a day. What you don't see is a typical amount of human traffic. You only get an occasional glimpse of a person moving from a car to a house, or checking the mail, or some minor thing. If you didn't catch vehicles moving in or out, you'd almost think these houses uninhabited."

"Okay, so where are the people?"

"My guess? Hiding, and doing a damn good job of it. Notice the amount of tree cover around the properties, and the features like attached garages and covered walkways. Even when a vehicle pulls in, you rarely see people, because it pulls into a garage or parks under a tree. If you were to view six hours of footage of any randomly selected properties, you'd certainly see more people walking around in the open than we're seeing here."

"You think they're doing that on purpose?" Collins asked.

"I think it's...suspicious," Abigail replied. "Certainly if people were trying to avoid being spotted by overhead surveillance, their behavior would look much like that. And remember when we had that helidrone tracking that car on the night of the blast? When that guy got in the car, and the analyst commented on how good his tradecraft was? If there's any connection between that incident and the people at these properties, you'd expect these people to observe good discipline in remaining out of sight – which is exactly what they seem to be doing."

"Y'know," Collins said with increasing interest. "The first time our unit got called in to help on this effort, it was to track a party who'd slipped away from the hospital. We weren't able to help because there was too much cover over where she probably was. I'd always thought that simply bad luck."

"If she was trained by the people who live at these properties," Abigail tapped the screen, "then quite possibly more than luck was involved."

"All right, I agree – it's suspicious," Collins conceded, leaning back in his chair. "What does our suspicion buy us?"

"Not much, so far. I'd like permission to task some low-level assets to monitor these three properties more actively for a few days. I'd like to get a closer look at what goes on underneath that cover."

"That's all? Authorized," Collins replied.

*   *   *

By midweek, Jason was deeply embroiled in a task he hadn't anticipated: helping to find living quarters for DHS DTD agents being moved into the region in anticipation of the action against the terror network. This time there wouldn't be any high-speed convoy of heavy equipment rumbling up from Fort Wayne, but there still were a surprising number of agents, and they all had to be housed. Ethan handled most of it, but it was a big enough job that Jason had to pitch in as well. Many of the teams were lodged in hotels near Port Huron, Flint, or Saginaw, but for strategic reasons they needed to be spread around, so rooms also had to be found in Bad Axe, Imlay City, and Sandusky.

Jason hadn't heard anything further from any of the RCCs, so he presumed they were running smoothly. He kept hoping for a call that would provide another address, but apparently no more Green Tags had turned up. He figured he'd eventually get some figures and percentages from Jerry on how well the RCCs were doing, but for now he had enough on his plate.

Jason was down in Imlay City, at the motel where he'd spent his first couple of weeks in the area, getting things arranged for the two dozen or so agents who'd be staying there. Though they arrived in civilian clothes, Jason was surprised to see so many short haircuts and wraparound sunglasses and weightlifter physiques. These guys carried themselves more like paramilitary than law enforcement personnel. Even their vehicles looked ominous – unmarked, but heavy black vans with thick padlocks on the doors and an excess of antennas sprouting from the roofs. Jason wondered what kind of tactical doctrine these guys were going to be following when they conducted their "investigations".

As long as Jason was in the building, he took a minute before departing to check and see how Allie was doing. The desk clerk had stepped away, so he wandered down the hall and stuck his head into the laundry room. A maid was folding towels, and looked at him with wary eyes.

"Hi," Jason said. "I was just wondering if Allie was working today."

The woman blinked a few times. "Allie's not…around anymore."

"Not around?" Jason asked.

"She took a long lunch about a week ago to see her doctor – because of her diabetes, you know," the maid replied, sniffing a bit and wiping her eyes. "She called saying she'd be out a little longer, because they were sending her to this new clinic south of Brown City. She came back from there all excited, because they'd given her a new dispenser that would remind her when to take her medicines. Yesterday morning, just after morning break, she slumped over. They took her to urgent care, but it was…too late." The woman pointed to a service cart in the corner of the room. From its handle hung a gaudy red purse, looking forlorn and abandoned.

Jason stared at the cart in shock. Allie. His friend Allie.

"I…thank you," Jason mumbled.

"I know," the maid said, tears running down her cheeks as she touched Jason's arm to offer a bit of comfort. "She was such a dear friend, and we all loved her."

"I...I'm sorry," was all Jason could manage, patting her hand. Then he turned and wandered down the hall, stunned. He went out the side door into the parking lot, where many of the agents who'd just been checked in were strutting about, swinging their arms and talking in loud, macho voices. He stared at them, seeing but not seeing, while a cold, dead spot settled in the center of his chest.

What had he unleashed on these people?

There's a way out of where you are, but it isn't by the paths you think.

Her voice replayed in his head so clearly that he started and glanced around. There was nobody near, but he'd heard as plainly as if she'd spoken in his ear. He'd almost put the appearance of the mysterious woman out of his head, but it all came rushing back now, bringing with it all the questions and quandaries.

Janice Boyd was alive. What else wasn't as he "knew" it to be?

*   *   *   *

Thursday morning Sergeant Danvers set up in the conference room to brief Major Collins on her findings. He could only spare twenty minutes, so she had to give him the condensed version. He breezed in sipping his coffee and waved to her to begin as he took a seat.

"Results of the low-level overflights of the properties in question," Abigail began. "Four sorties, three daylight and one nighttime. Details like duration, drone type, and surveillance methodology are in the presentation file on your tablet.

"My conclusion: there's something going on at these properties. Given that we know there's suspect activity in the area, I don't think it much of a stretch to connect the two.

"First, you've got three houses that look like they're one property. No barriers or fences between them; in fact, there are what appear to be paths. There are two major outbuildings, rather large, one a stable for livestock and one a long general-purpose building. There are some fields out back which look to be planted with hay. The houses sit on properties at the corner of an eighty-acre plot, and it's all registered to somebody Peterson." Abigail showed various views as she spoke, pointing out the features as she described them.

"The low-level overflights didn't spot any obviously suspicious activity on the properties – just the expectable cars pulling in and out, and people walking back and forth, and the like. But there seems to be a significant amount of foot traffic between the houses, so these people must be pretty close neighbors. Also, they either have the most conveniently placed trees and awnings in existence, or they're consciously trying to hide from overhead surveillance. Anyone who's outside is always – *always* – under some kind of cover. It's possible to go from the west door of the barn to any of the houses without exposing yourself to open sky. I saw people do this routinely. *Maybe* it's just lucky placement, but I'd be surprised. People consistently moving around by those patterns would be unspottable from anything over three thousand feet."

"I presume you only spotted it because you were watching from a lower angle?" Collins asked.

"Yes, sir. Stealth drones at five hundred feet, watching from a quarter mile out. Full flight details are in the file."

"And in your judgment, you think the combination of physical environment and behavior indicate deliberate intent, not just accidental circumstance?"

"Yes, sir – I'd state that with over ninety percent certainty."

"All right, Sergeant – please continue."

"Some other odd things, sir," Danvers clicked up an image showing a close-up of a roof that was overshadowed by near standing trees. "This is the center house, a large ranch. Due to all the trees in close proximity, it's difficult to see just how large. A typical ranch house is between thirteen hundred and seventeen hundred square feet. This one is over five thousand square feet.

You can see a large addition on the back, with a big deck adjoining, and a wing running out from this side. The window placement on the wing makes it look like it holds a set of bedrooms. The back yard is also large, and is laid out like a park, with a gazebo, benches, lawn chairs, and a pond. There's nothing unusual about nice back yards, but this one looks to be set up for a lot of people to occupy – plus, it's almost completely covered by trees.

"I had our friends Sanderson and Harris do a little research on the address. Turns out a few years back the owners got the site certified as an adult foster care facility. But the odd thing is, there's never been an AFC registered to operate at that address, even though the site certification was renewed last year."

"Wait," Collins interrupted. "I'm not sure I understand that."

"If you wanted to run an adult foster care home, you'd need a couple of things," Abigail explained. "One would be a facility that met all the physical requirements for an AFC – barrier-free access, door and hall width, conformance to fire codes, and so forth. Another requirement would be the business operation to use the facility, with things like appropriate licensing and properly credentialed staff. You could have one without the other – for instance, an AFC business might have a catastrophe at their site, and be temporarily without a physical facility even though they were still an active operation. Or you could have a certified site without a business occupying it. That's what we seem to have at this address."

"Why would someone go to the expense and trouble of building a house and getting it certified but never run a business there?" Collins asked.

"That's the question, isn't it?" Abigail observed. "But that's not the only oddity. Another is that this corner of the section sits under one of our probability clusters for a terminus of the off-road network."

"Oh, *really*?" Collins asked.

"Yes, sir," Abigail zoomed out and clicked up an overlay that showed a fuzzy line curving through some woods to end in a blurry-edged blob that covered an entire corner of the property. "This wooded patch covers the west portion of the property and goes into the next section. You can see how it runs right up against the outbuildings here. Not practical if you're a prudent livestock farmer, but ideal if you want people to be able to leave the property unobserved by overhead surveillance."

"Did you spot any off-road traffic?"

"Only twice did I get a glimpse of what might have been an ATV coming out of the woods, but it was hard to be sure. The angle was poor, and there was only a short distance between the woods and the barn."

"All right," Collins nodded. "Anything else?"

"One more thing," Abigail brought up some footage showing a low pass over a utilitarian looking brick building with deep eaves. "This outbuilding sits on the northwest corner of the property. Notice that the power lines for all three properties run into this shed, and then from here run out to the specific buildings. These lines on the north corner are incoming power, and the lines fanning out to the south here are outgoing power."

"Odd. What might be in the building?"

"A Navy electrician I spoke to speculated that it might be an on-site generation facility, a guess which is bolstered by these fuel tanks right up against the building on the east side. Furthermore, he said the capacity of these lines was far greater than buildings of these sizes would be expected to draw. Apparently, these lines could carry enough amperage to power an entire subdivision."

"Wow...amazing," Collins said vaguely.

"Well, unusual," Abigail said, looking at him curiously. "Not expected, but not outrageous, either."

"No, I was referring to your getting the Navy to cooperate with us," Collins explained.

"Oh, that," Abigail waved blithely. "I can charm with the best of them when the need arises."

"Obviously. So, where does this all leave us?"

"With a suspicious site. *Something* unusual is going on at those properties. Whether it has anything to do with this hidden terrorist network, I couldn't say, but I think it likely."

"Likely? Or just possible?"

"Likely," Abigail answered firmly. "We're looking for places that have been stashing people off-grid, right? This looks like a site designed to do just that. Furthermore, it seems to be connected to this off-road transport network. It's possible – and this is a stretch – that it's a command center. But even if it isn't, I think it's something."

"What degree of confidence?"

"Eighty percent."

"So what's next?" Collins asked.

"With your approval, I'd like to send these addresses to NSA to plug into their model with that eighty percent level of confidence. Then we can see what adding these sites does to the network analysis."

Collins winced. "How much longer will that set back the delivery? It's already taken longer than I'd thought, and Pelletier has to be getting nervous."

"That's not how these models work," Abigail assured him. "They're set up for iterative refinement. Initial analyses give you starting points, then from those you discover more points, which you feed back into the system, which refines your overall results and enables you to verify more points, and so on. They won't have to take the analysis back to the drawing board – in fact, more points should speed things up, if the point is of actual value. A mistaken point would set the analysis back."

"Oh," Collins said. "Well then, approved. Send whatever you wish over to NSA, and see if you can get a time estimate on results delivery, would you?"

"Sure, sir."

"And Sergeant – good work. Not least for getting the Navy to cooperate."

"Thank you, sir," Abigail said with a grin.

*   *   *

The next morning Jason was videoconferencing with some of his "messaging specialists" about the spots they'd worked up. Jason was amazed at how polished the spots looked, given how little time the POM people had been given. Some were almost like pep talks, with smiling faces in cheerful settings talking earnestly about the measures being taken to improve health care in the region, and the gallant efforts being made against challenging obstacles. The underlying message of those spots was to be patient and encouraged, and to trust. The specialists called these the "carrots". Another set of spots were the "sticks", with grave-faced narrators reminding citizens that receiving medical care outside of authorized channels was illegal and dangerous, and those who did so risked wide-ranging consequences. There was a whisper of a suggestion that those who did so were being elitist, considering themselves too good for the system that provided everyone else with care. Even though they were negative spots, Jason was impressed by how masterfully they were constructed. The tone was beautifully understated, like that of a benevolent uncle who was disappointed and just the smallest bit hurt that he would be so distrusted.

"Those are great, guys," Jason assured them.

"We started off with the medical care angle, because that's the biggest leverage point, and it's also in our wheelhouse," one of the specialists, whose name was Ken, explained. "We've got more spots perking that more directly address the issue of subversion and domestic terror, but we thought we'd begin with this set."

"Well, if the ones you have coming are anywhere near as good as these, they'll be killer effective," Jason assured them. "But when were you thinking of running these spots?"

"Actually, we slipped some of them out starting yesterday," Ken said. "We kind of anticipated your approval. Our buyer found some great time slots on a wide range of channels and sites, but we needed to jump on it. If you sign off, we can dump the full content into the channels and execute the buy."

"Amazing," Jason shook his head. "I can't believe how quickly you guys get things done."

"It's the environment we have to deal with," Ken shrugged. "The world of broadcast sites moves at lightning speed. We've had to time campaigns down to the minute. By comparison, you guys are almost lackadaisical."

"Well, you've got my approval," Jason said. "Um…how is this all getting paid for?"

"Out of HHS budget," Ken assured him. "They're considered part of the Chengdu Two initiative. Frankly, our bosses are so pleased with what you've accomplished that you could ask for anything and they'd cover it. But if you can tell me without violating security, do you have any idea when your people might be making their moves? When that happens may affect the timing of the later spots."

"That depends on our overhead surveillance team, who are currently waiting on NSA," Jason explained. "But if the rumors I'm hearing are accurate, we might be looking at the middle to end of next week."

"Okay, then. If there's nothing else, we'll get moving on these," Ken replied.

Jason clicked off and started composing his status report, which was easier to write this week because of all the events which had happened or were impending. He was grateful for this, not just because it looked like he was making progress but also because he wouldn't have to summon the mental energy to write up nothing as if it were something. His spirits were weighed down, as if they had a large, wet tarpaulin lying upon them. The prospect of spending another weekend in this town weighed him down further, but he didn't know what else to do. Driving down to metro Detroit to find company and excitement was too risky. Jason knew his moods, and the craving for a binge was lurking too near the surface. He couldn't risk indulging that with so much on the line. An ill-timed binge had seriously complicated the Salt Lake City mess, depriving him of judgment and prudence just when he'd needed them most. A weekend dash back to D.C. was inadvisable for the same reason. He resigned himself to the fact that he was stuck in Sandusky again. Perhaps he could video Cassie, who was getting chatty again, after getting over her sulks about him leaving.

Jason wrapped up his work for the day and wandered over to the corner brewery for dinner. He was getting to be recognized there, and the server had a recommendation from their new menu selections. Jason ate his dinner while watching a baseball game on the television over the bar. At one of the commercial breaks he was surprised to see one of the POM spots he'd approved earlier that day. It was one of the upbeat ones, with a handsome, healthy-looking couple bringing their cute, well-scrubbed youngster to a smiling doctor for some form of medical care. The voice-overs and captions assured viewers that they had a right to prompt, effective health care, and that steps were being taken to improve access to care for area residents. The spot closed with the happy couple walking away down a clean path through a trimmed lawn, with their spritely child cavorting in front of them. Everything looked so realistic that even Jason found it hard to believe that those were computer generated figures.

The game came back on, but Jason couldn't help but overhear snippets of conversation from a nearby table. "My sister took her son in to the pediatrician...had to take him...over near Carsonville...really upset...quick care." Jason presumed that had been one of the decoy cases, not the targeted population, the OPELs.

Like Allie.

That thought dropped Jason's spirits again. He lost his appetite and any interest in the game. Paying his check, he picked up a few cans of the house brew on the way out, which he took home and drank while watching a horror movie.

Saturday he frittered away by tidying up little tasks, and catching up on his inbox, and video chatting with Cassie. He was restless and unsettled, and his mind kept returning to Allie hugging him and sobbing over her gaudy red purse. He attributed his agitation to his ill choice of movie the evening before, so that evening he cued up a different choice of movie, which ended up causing a different kind of restlessness, but at least he wouldn't have dark dreams.

Or so Jason thought. When he finally dropped off to sleep, he quickly found himself in a distressingly familiar landscape, driving down endless dirt roads through empty fields, trying to escape, but ever finding himself turning a corner to come upon that dark, looming fenced wood. It didn't matter where he turned or how fast he drove, he'd find himself back there before long. The night was dark and the dash lights glowed eerily and the radio spat static that could not be silenced. Dark woods swayed on the horizon in every direction, the headlights illuminated nothing but mile after barren mile of dusty road, and he never knew when the bright metal gleam of the security fence would come back into view – he just knew with dread certainty that it would.

Jason finally grew sufficiently distressed that he thrashed himself awake. He lay panting in his dark room, not even attempting to go back to sleep. Eventually he threw on his jacket and stepped out on the front porch for a smoke to calm his nerves. The night sky was thickly overcast, and seemed especially dark toward the north. The air was still and heavy, and everything seemed wrapped in a brooding silence. As he smoked, Jason thought about how much he hated this place, where even the roads and woods could give you nightmares. Finishing his cigarette, he went back inside and sat down in his recliner to distract himself with his tablet. After a while he felt drowsiness overtaking him again, so he leaned back and dozed off.

Jason dreamt again, only this time the dream wasn't fractured and scattered like his nightmare had been, but as solid and coherent as waking awareness. He found himself near a long one-story building made of cinder blocks. He stood beside a stone about the size of a headstone in a cemetery. There was a bed of flowers around the base and some writing on the face of the stone, but in the manner of dreams the writing was too blurry to be legible.

The building and monument were at the edge of an open lawn. On the far side of the lawn stood some trees, which formed the edge of a lightly wooded area. Jason strolled over beneath the trees and found himself in a tidily trimmed yard, which was almost large enough to be a small park, with a gazebo and benches and a pond on one side.

As he was enjoying the blissful tranquility, Jason noticed that he was not alone. A woman was walking along the far side of the pond. She wore a plain black dress which looked to Jason like mourning garb. She was walking slowly, as if lost in thought, and her head was bowed. She was doing something with her hands, and as Jason drew near the edge of the pond, he saw she was holding some sort of string with beads on it. He had no idea what that was, but there seemed to be something familiar about her, though he couldn't see her face. Then he noticed that her close-cropped hair was red.

"Oh!" Jason cried in surprise. "It's – it's you!"

The woman lifted her head. It was indeed her, Janice Boyd, the woman who should be dead. Gazing at him with eyes fraught with grief, yet still kind and understanding, she spoke.

"There's still time to stop this, Jason."

Jason snapped awake so abruptly that he half sat up. The gray predawn light filled the room. His heart pounded as he tried to recover his equilibrium. The earlier nightmare had been terrifying in its way, but this dream frightened him at a completely different level. Who was this supposedly dead woman who delivered her cryptic messages in person and in dreams? What did her words mean? What did she want of him? He went into the kitchen for a mug of coffee and took it outside on the steps for a smoke to calm his nerves. This was spooky, damn spooky. The coffee was sour in his empty stomach, so he decided to shower – there was no way he'd be able to get back to sleep now, even if he'd wanted to.

Jason was so preoccupied that he went mechanically through the motions of showering and dressing. It was still early when he finished, so he decided to try the only thing he could think of: driving down to the blast site. The sky was clearing and the rising sun bathed the greening fields and woods with fresh morning light. Jason knew the way to the site without thinking, though he had to squeeze around the main gate again because Ethan had the key. This time he didn't even notice the mud on his shoes, nor the dew on his trousers wetting them nearly to the knees as he tramped madly through the weeds. He clung to the fence surrounding the destroyed building and gazed at the wreckage. He went over to the cluster of bushes at the edge of the woods and stared down the overgrown path which Ethan had found. He stomped around the perimeter of the site shaking the bushes and peering into thickets. He didn't know what he was looking for, or even why he was here, other than this was one of the two places he knew she had been. Here, and on the Sandusky courthouse lawn. And, of course, in his dream.

"I'm here!" Jason called to the heavens in desperation as he stood at the center of the site. "I'm here! Where are you? What do you want of me? What are you trying to say?"

No sound returned from the calm morning air, but Jason felt a growing sense of standing at a vortex, as if the remote and overgrown site of destruction lay at the center of an intertwined series of events that reached years, even centuries, into the past, whirling and interweaving as they converged on this point in space and time, then hurling forth from here with renewed and pointed passion to ensnare yet more threads in their violent career. Jason sensed that the line of his life was but one of these captured threads, and though his role was minor, it was pivotal, and the trajectory of many lives would be deeply affected by how he resolved the choices before him. The weight of this awareness pressed down on him; his knees buckled, and he fell forward onto the gravel.

"Where are you?" he whispered. "I need your help." Consciousness left him.

Jason awoke some time later. The sun was high in the sky and he was terribly thirsty. His face was dirty and his palms were scraped where they'd struck the gravel. Dusting himself off, he made his way back to his car and drove toward M-53. He needed a drink and a wash. He was just north of Imlay City, maybe he could – no, he checked himself. There was no going back there. The memory of Allie was still too fresh. There were shops all along the road north of here. He'd stop at one of those. Not Imlay City.

Somehow the dazed and weakened Jason made it back home. He spent the day haunting the courthouse lawn, lingering about the gazebo, watching the passing traffic for large white vans, eyeing all pedestrians for close-cut red hair. He felt impotent. Events were sweeping toward a conclusion, and he was being swept along with them.

Tension

It was late afternoon when Luke rode his ATV up to the back of the house. The Mills' home just outside North Branch was one of his favorite stops, and Betty was one of his more agreeable patients. Julie always made something delicious for dinner when she knew he was coming. Here came Terry and Julie's son, the irrepressible Casey, bouncing down the back steps.

"Hi, Doc Luke!" Casey called as Luke stashed his helmet and gloves and began pulling out his gear. "Did you have a good ride up?" Just into his teens, Casey thought that there could be no cooler job than one that required riding around the Thumb on an ATV, and Luke had given up trying to disabuse him of the notion.

"It was great, Casey. Drier and warmer than it's been lately, though still soggy in spots. I could wish for some more leaves on the trees, though."

"Oh, sure, Doc," Casey said with a conspiratorial nod. He was acquainted with the principle of keeping well under cover.

"Here, can you tote this in for me?" Luke handed him the heaviest case of gear. "How are your folks? And Mrs. Betty?"

Everyone was fine, as it turned out, though octogenarian Betty Fowler's various conditions were getting more serious. It wouldn't be long before he'd have to have the talk with her and Terry and Julie about possibly moving her to St. Anne's – she'd soon be beyond the level of care the Mills family could provide. This would be difficult for them all, for they were very close.

As Luke came out to the living room, he found Terry there with his usual welcoming smile, though it seemed tinged with concern.

"Hey, Terry," Luke shook his hand. "Dinner smells great."

"Chicken pot pie – Julie was expecting you," Terry replied. "Say, I've got something for you to look at." They sat down on the couch and Terry clicked a controller that brought up a video on the television. "This showed up on one of the sites Casey was watching last night. It, and others like it, have started playing on several channels recently."

Luke watched as the spot rolled. It was a typical government PSA, with the predictable platitudes and vague verbiage. When it finished, Luke asked Terry to run it a couple more times.

"Do you know anything about this UPAIR initiative?" Terry asked.

"First I've heard of it," Luke replied. "How long have these spots been running?"

"No idea – but then, we're not on the sites very much. I did some searching, though, and there have been a couple of news reports recently about the government getting concerned about underserved rural areas."

"Hmm," mused Luke. His deep mistrust of the government, deepened further by the events of a couple of years ago, made him very suspicious of any agency activity, particularly where it touched health care. He'd noticed that the spot had referred to serving "select populations". He wondered who the populations were, and how they were selected.

"Do you think this will affect us at all?" Terry asked.

"You? No – you're safely under the radar, which is right where you want to be," Luke assured him. "It may affect some others, though." Luke's mind was churning. Why the sudden concern about health care for area residents? The last time the federal government had focused attention on the Thumb, the results had been ominous. Should he look into this? Maybe alert someone?

Just then Luke's phone rang with the buzzing that indicated an encrypted call. He excused himself to step into the dining room and take it. He saw that it was Fitz.

"Hey, Fitz."

"Luke, you're up near North Branch right now, right?" Fitz asked.

"Yes – just got here."

"How quickly could you get to Mayville?"

"Mayville? About forty-five minutes by the routes I'd have to use."

"Can you get there faster? You're our closest man, and there are things I don't want to discuss on even an encrypted phone call."

"If Terry can drive me and the ATV, we could do it in about thirty," Luke said. "What's going on?"

"Frieda Pelton has vanished. Nobody's heard from her since she went to her cardiologist last Thursday. Also, Willard Crowley hasn't been heard from since last Friday. I need you to get up to Mayville to talk to the Jamesons about Frieda – they've got all the information. You've got their address, right?"

"Yes," Luke replied, his heart sinking. Frieda and Willard were their two test cases. They were old and sick and might have been admitted somewhere and couldn't communicate, but they'd both been carefully briefed, and knew that people would be expecting to hear from them. Suddenly the upbeat PSA spots about a new Federal initiative in the area seemed less innocent.

"Terry," Luke asked as he rang off. "How hard would it be to rig up a trailer and drive me and my ATV up to just north of Mayville?"

"Piece of cake," Terry said. "Leaving us so soon?"

"Afraid so," Luke said. "We've got an urgent situation that I need to look into. C'mon, Casey, you can run the four-wheeler up onto the trailer if you're careful."

*　　　*　　　*

"I spoke to her Thursday morning," Frances Jameson said soberly. "She had an appointment to see her cardiologist in Caro. She was supposed to call me with the outcome when she got home."

"She never called?" Luke asked.

"No," Frances shook her head. "The day kind of got away from me, and I didn't even think about the fact that she hadn't called until it was too late at night and I didn't want to risk waking her. I called her first thing Friday morning and got her voice mail. Then I waited to hear back, and when I didn't, I called Dr.

Oswald's office to see if she had come in. But by that time they were closed for the weekend, and I didn't want to leave a message."

"So did you go up to her care home? Caro isn't that far," Luke asked.

"I know, and I wanted to, but it was too late Friday, and then Saturday we were all occupied with the start of spring soccer season, and Sunday we'd arranged to visit Andy's folks because we hadn't been able to on Easter, and everything just got away from me," Frances wrung her hands in distress.

"Did you keep calling her?"

"I did, and I left a message every time, but I finally figured I'd talk to Dr. Oswald's office before I hit the panic button."

Luke kept his lips closed and smiled thinly. Gil had assured him they'd be watching these cases diligently for any irregularities. This hardly sounded like diligent watching, but what could be done?

"So, what did Dr. Oswald's office say?"

"They were very unhelpful," Frances said. "They kept saying they could provide no information on patient conditions, treatments, or referrals. I kept trying to tell them that I wasn't asking for any of that – I just wanted to know if Frieda had come in on Thursday. But they just kept saying that: no information on patient conditions, treatments, or referrals. It was maddening! And this was Jeannie Schultz, whose son plays soccer in my boy's league! We've chatted on the soccer fields! Yet all she'd say to me was 'no information on conditions, treatments, or referrals.' I could have screamed."

"And that was this morning?" Luke asked.

"Yes. After that Andy and I decided we had to run up to Caro to visit her foster care facility. She wasn't there, and the manager said she hadn't been all weekend. She remembered that the facility shuttle had taken her to Dr. Oswald's office, but that she'd never called for a pickup. I should have called there first – Dr. Oswald's office didn't tell me a thing."

"I don't know," Luke mused, pondering what the office had told Frances so repetitively. "Then you called Gil?"

"I called Shelly, actually – I hadn't wanted to alarm her unduly, but this seemed important."

"Indeed. Did you get a look around Frieda's room at the care facility?"

"Yes, the manager let us glance in. Everything looked as it should. Her purse was gone, but nothing else. It looked like she'd just stepped out for the day."

"Okay, let me call Gil to see what our next steps should be," Luke said.

"Oh, my goodness, I'm so worried," Frances said with agitation. "We should never have done this. You don't think anything happened to Frieda, do you?"

In fact, that was precisely what Luke was worried about, but he wanted to talk to Gil first. He knew that the leaders had responses in place for all kinds of possible reactions to the guests reappearing, from refusal of treatment to arrest. He didn't know if they'd anticipated the possibility of the guests vanishing without a trace. He called Gil and briefed him on what he'd been told, which didn't differ much from what Frances had told Gil over the phone.

"And the doctor's office wouldn't offer any information at all, even the most harmless?" Gil asked.

"I'm not sure about that," Luke replied. "The receptionist Frances spoke to was a personal acquaintance, and apparently she kept repeating that she couldn't provide information about conditions, treatments, or referrals. Everybody knows that providers can't give out information about conditions or treatments, but the fact that the receptionist kept adding that point about referrals makes me wonder."

"About what?" Gil asked.

"Maybe the receptionist was trying to communicate in an oblique manner that a referral was exactly what had happened. That would have answered Frances's question – that Frieda had shown up – and even conveyed in general terms what had happened to her."

"That's possible," Gil admitted. "It would have had to be a quick-thinking receptionist."

"Many are. But that still leaves the question of what kind of referral it would be. Normally referrals are made after seeing the provider, and take days or weeks unless it's critical. Frieda should have had time to go home, or at least call someone."

"Oh, my goodness," Gil breathed. "I just put something together. Last week Helen called to notify me that their clinicians were seeing a new HHS protocol on their systems, one that flagged certain patients for immediate referral to other providers."

"Wait…what?" Luke asked. "The computer system was telling the provider they had to refer the patient to another provider?"

"Apparently so. Certain patients were flagged as unserviceable, and the hospital couldn't provide them any care – or at least wouldn't get paid for providing care."

"Any idea where these patients were being sent?"

"Helen didn't know, but she was going to look into it," Gil explained. "In fact, she should have gotten back with me by now."

"And this was an HHS protocol that was being triggered?"

"That's what she said, and I presume she'd know."

"Odd – these protocols are usually universal," Luke mused. "Why would they be targeting…wait a minute. Gil, have you heard anything about a UPAIR initiative?"

"A what?"

"I just learned about it myself, when I dropped in on Julie and Terry Mills. Terry showed me a public service spot he'd seen that discussed providing better medical care to underserved populations. It was a vague propaganda spot without many specifics, but it did mention this UPAIR initiative."

"UPAIR?"

"Yes, UPAIR. Maybe you could do a search on it. I've no idea who placed the spot, but given the topic, it wouldn't surprise me if it was HHS," Luke said.

"I'll check into it."

"How about Willard? What's going on there?"

"Almost identical situation, though Ben and Rose were more on-the-ball about keeping us informed. Willard went in for his appointment with his nephrologist on Friday, and when they hadn't heard back by the end of the day, they went to his home to look in on him. Apparently, it looked like he'd left only intending to be gone briefly. They called Fitz immediately, and waited through the weekend, but no word."

"That's...alarming," Luke said.

"Especially in light of what happened to Frieda."

"What do we do?"

"Let us discuss it with the others, and we'll get back to you," Gil said. "We have several plans ready, so the question is which one to execute."

"I'd suggest considering the most urgent ones – this is getting scary," Luke replied.

"No kidding," Gil said as he rang off.

Luke walked back to the living room where Frances still sat looking upset.

"We're doing what we can," Luke assured her. "Gil and Shelly and all are discussing options now."

"Oh, good," Frances said with relief. "Can you stay? We've had dinner, but I could make you a sandwich. Frieda's old room is available."

"A sandwich would be fine," Luke said, trying not to think of a steaming plate of homemade pot pie. The idea of staying in Frieda's old room gave him an eerie feeling, but he tried not to be superstitious. "I'll get my gear."

*   *   *

Back at Rivendell later that evening, Gil and Fitz looked at each other grimly. They had Shelly and Steve McLean conferenced in on workstations.

"So," Fitz summarized. "Both our trial cases emerge from being underground for several years only to vanish without a trace upon their first encounter with the public medical care system. I'd call that an ominous outcome."

Gil nodded, but Shelly spoke up. "Maybe they've just run into a few problems, and we should wait a couple more days before hitting the panic button."

Steve tried to avoid rolling his eyes, and Fitz smiled thinly. Shelly was a valuable worker and could be counted on to bring a positive perspective to any deliberations, but there were times she could be unrealistic.

"Shelly," Gil said tersely. "Both guests thoroughly understood the importance and risk of what they were undertaking. Both had equipment and instructions to contact us if – especially if – anything unusual happened. The fact that we've heard nothing from them since they went to their doctors' appointments indicates that something happened that was outside anything we'd anticipated. That is ominous, and we'd better pay attention."

"Agreed," Fitz added. "In light of the warnings we've received about renewed federal government interest in the area, and word of some mysterious HHS protocols –"

"Oh," Gil interrupted. "And Luke mentioned seeing a spot for some new medical care related initiative being rolled out – UPAIR or something, I've got the details here – we can research it later."

"Okay, so that, too," Fitz allowed. "I don't know about you all, but I'm starting to feel a bit spooked. There seem to be a lot of factors converging."

"Well, that's the question, isn't it?" Gil asked. "Are they converging anywhere but in our imaginations? The guests vanishing is worrisome, but can we assume any connection between all these things? We don't know precisely what we're up against, which makes it hard to know which way to jump."

Steve sighed in exasperation. "Maybe not, but we can surely see that some jumping is called for. We're looking at circumstances that may be worse than our worst case scenarios. We need to respond!"

"Nobody's questioning that, Steve, but sometimes precipitous action can cause more problems than it solves," Shelly pleaded.

"All our emergency plans are very disruptive to the lives of the families involved, and some of our guests are in very fragile condition!"

"I'm aware of that, Shelly, but we can't dither and vacillate just because we don't know exactly the right plan to execute," Steve rejoined sharply. "Some action, no matter how disruptive, is better than sitting on our hands – unless you'd prefer to wait until they're kicking in our doors? I guarantee they won't care about the fragile conditions of our guests!"

Shelly's expression flared and she opened her mouth to respond, but then closed it again and bowed her head. After a moment's silence she continued in a choked voice. "Look, you guys decide what you want to do and let me know what it is. I'll accept your decision." She tapped a button and her window closed.

Gil was tight-lipped, but Fitz ventured a response. "Maybe a little harsh there, Steve?"

"Maybe," Steve sighed contritely. "Sorry. I'll call her to apologize. It's just that we're under a little strain up here, especially with Annette's condition. And, just maybe, the memory of those troop carriers amassing in Sandusky is a little fresher in our memories than it is down there."

"Yeah," Gil replied, still feeling stung on his sister's behalf. "I don't think the circumstances call for a full-on SCRAM, which would indeed cause plenty of other problems, but we need to move urgently. Perhaps plan Charlie Three? The nighttime option?"

"Nighttime I like, but I think the situation calls for more urgency than a Charlie level plan, don't you?" Steve asked. "Perhaps Bravo Four?"

Fitz and Gil clicked through their files to examine the plan details. "I see what you're saying, but Shelly did have a point about the life disruption, and the fragility of our guests," Fitz said. "What if we start to execute Charlie Three or Five, but be ready to switch to one of the Bravo plans if conditions change?"

"I'll buy that," Steve acquiesced. "Charlie Three looks good. Activating when? Immediately?"

"How about midnight tonight?" Gil said. "That'll give us time to get the word out and handle any implementation hiccups before we activate."

"All right, then," Fitz concluded. "Charlie Three at midnight."

"I'll call Shelly to let her know," Steve said.

*   *   *

Fr. Gabriel sat in his car by the side of the dirt road, watching the sun drop toward the horizon. From where he sat, it seemed to be descending right into the woods, its glow being dampened and blocked by the shadowed branches. No lingering golden illumination for that accursed patch, no gentle touch of a balmy spring evening to caress those stark branches to life. It seemed that light and warmth and all other goodness ceased at those darkling borders.

Fr. Gabriel knew all about the events of the prior summer. By interviewing some of the workers who had been rescued he'd gotten a good idea of what conditions had been like in the slave-staffed factory. He'd interviewed many of the direct actors of that dreadful night, including Chip Keller, the Winters twins, Phillip Schaeffer, and the three young women who had been used to execute the rescue. He'd even been briefed by Lawrence Stover about what had been learned about the renegade called Black Charlie and his occult proclivities. Fr. Gabriel was not a credulous man, and did not uncritically believe every breathless story of the movements of good or evil. But what he'd learned in the aftermath of last summer's events had convinced him that something extraordinary had taken place amidst those trees that night, that a battle had been fought between darkness and light, with dramatic rescues and tragic losses.

If only that had been the end of it.

Autumn had barely begun when Fr. Gabriel had started to hear of uncanny things, particularly toward the northern edges of his territory. He heard stories of people getting lost on familiar roads, and of devices malfunctioning unpredictably, and of nameless dread whispering in the windbreaks and rustling among the rushes that lined the ditches. He heard of farmers leaving prime fields fallow, and drivers going miles out of their way, in order to avoid certain areas. He'd almost concluded that the locals were suffering a touch of rumor-fueled hysteria that was feeding on itself when he took a shortcut just north of Bad Axe and found himself trapped in the same frightening and inexplicable phenomenon of which he'd heard hints. Fr. Gabriel was a faithful priest who had no difficulty acknowledging the unseen real, but like most men he tended to look skeptically on anything that seemed merely spooky. But the half hour he'd spent trying to drive away from those woods, only to find himself approaching them again, had shaken his glib rationality to the core. Once he'd finally extricated himself from that infernal trap, he'd pulled into a parking lot and knelt down on the pavement to repent of the superior attitude he'd adopted toward those who had reported such things.

But even more distressing than that frightening encounter was the steadily increasing stream of relational strains across the area, particularly in Huron and northern Sanilac and Tuscola counties. Fr. Gabriel and his fellow priests and ministers stayed in close touch with law enforcement and community mental health agencies. They were the frontline workers, always first to feel the effects of increasing economic or social stresses on their communities. Through the autumn and winter they had all been reporting disturbing increases in dangerous and destructive behaviors across the board – domestic violence, substance abuse, workplace friction, neglect, family distress, and other problems. Fr. Gabriel encountered plenty of it in the confessional and in counseling as well – patterns of sin and conflict that had been minor were starting to become major; patterns that had been major risked becoming dire. As one penitent had put it to him, "I feel like I'm fighting a headwind, Father. I mean, I've always been doing that, but never as sustained and hard as this – and it's only getting worse." From what Fr. Gabriel could tell, almost everyone he encountered was fighting a similar battle.

And then there were the Wanderers. Sheriff Keller had been the first to alert him, and then Fr. Gabriel had begun to see them himself – lingering around Bad Axe, camping up near Port Crescent when the weather allowed, loitering in the parks, and wandering along the country roads. He'd spoken to some of them, and had even given one a ride from Pigeon once. Fr. Gabriel knew lost souls when he met them, and these souls were as lost as they came. They'd mumble and maunder and ramble on about nonsense, never quite looking you in the eye. Some would simply walk away when they saw him coming. He thought they were just one more symptom of the troubles that had struck the area until Chip Keller had shared his hypothesis about why the Wanderers were here and where they were ending up. That had broken Fr. Gabriel's heart, but he hadn't a clue what to do about it.

One thing Fr. Gabriel had begun doing was what he was doing tonight. Despite his natural aversion, he forced himself to remember Whose son he was, and that he had been given spiritual responsibility and authority in the area. He got a hint from Chip about how to foil the confusion that wrapped itself around the wood, except instead of focusing on his odometer, Fr. Gabriel focused on the small crucifix affixed to his dash. It achieved the same effect – enabling him to get within range of the wood. He'd usually park within sight of it to pray and ponder, and to ask for guidance. A couple of times he'd gotten out of his car and walked along the fence, and once he'd stood by the gate, his hand on the lock, praying and seeing if he could sense anything. He'd had to admit that he couldn't, at least emotionally – the place appeared like any other densely wooded half-section, albeit with exceptionally dense and murky undergrowth. What made it more eerie was the air of dereliction all around the woods – the unmowed roadsides and unplanted fields and reed-choked drainage ditches. That, far more than his emotions, told Fr. Gabriel that something was desperately, dreadfully wrong. Nobody lived here, nobody came here, any sane man who wandered near fled as quickly as he could. The human spirit knew danger when it was nigh, and danger brooded in those woods.

Tonight, as Fr. Gabriel watched the sun set and prayed and considered the situation, he began to wonder if he should risk reaching out for some help. Matters were certainly beyond his abilities – maybe it was time to consider an exorcist? He could talk to his bishop. They didn't have any trained exorcists in the diocese, but they did down in Detroit. But this didn't seem like a typical exorcism situation. And how could he phrase the request? "I think I have some haunted woods in my parish that are poisoning the spiritual atmosphere?" That would go over big at the chancery. Maybe he could write to Rome, to see if anyone there had ever seen a case like this. Maybe one of the missionary orders – they were always seeing all sorts of strange things. Perhaps they had specialists, people with experience –

Fr. Gabriel was interrupted in his dark and intense musings by the curious sensation that he was not alone in the car. Alarmed, he glanced about and saw nobody, but the sense of a presence persisted. But rather than the ominous or threatening presence he would have expected, this one seemed light and carefree, indeed almost bubbling with levity. Despite the uncanny circumstances, Fr. Gabriel found he couldn't be frightened – it was all he could do to keep from chuckling.

"Is...is somebody here?" he finally asked with a smile. He got no audible answer, but was drenched with a feeling of mirth and well-being. He was almost overwhelmed, but he resisted. Lightheartedness seemed inappropriate in the shadow of that looming threat. He focused on the dark branches standing starkly against the twilight sky, trying to force himself to be sober, but failed utterly. He dissolved into laughter – not just light chuckles, but bellowing bouts of hilarity that had him clinging to the steering wheel and gasping for breath. There was no apparent reason for this outburst, but he couldn't seem to stop. Yet in the midst of it, a reserved corner of his mind was nearly scandalized.

"How...how can You be so glib?" Fr. Gabriel finally managed to gasp out between guffaws. "This is...this is a serious problem, and people are really hurting!"

The response was not audible, but came as clear in Fr. Gabriel's mind as if it had been spoken.

This serious problem that has you so concerned I will vanquish in one hour by means of the least and weakest of My servants.

This response, along with the shock of receiving so clear an answer, did sober Fr. Gabriel a little, though his heart was still light. "Really, Lord? How…is there –"

You need do nothing but wait and pray. I am aware of all the suffering, including yours. My hand is already in motion. You have but to wait, and watch for My deliverance.

"All…all right, Lord," Fr. Gabriel held up his hands in surrender. Then, as quickly as it had come, the sense of presence was gone, though the effervescence remained. Fr. Gabriel chuckled a few more times just for fun, feeling lighter of heart than he had in months.

"All righty, then," he smiled to himself. Figuring his time was finished for the evening, he started his car and pulled up alongside the fence surrounding the wood. Pointing a warning finger at the gloomy darkness, he intoned solemnly, "Your days are numbered!" Then he dissolved into laughter at himself and drove away.

*　　　　*　　　　*

After several days, the evacuation of the ranches was proceeding at an expectable pace. A handful of them had been completely vacated, but far more were delaying and dragging their feet. The coordinators across the Thumb responsible for the evacuations were running into a variety of snags. Sometimes there were complications with the family or the guest, sometimes the problem was at the destination – the site in one of the other Farthings which was supposed to receive the family. Sometimes the coordinator himself wasn't as organized as he thought he'd be. But the biggest impediment they were encountering was simple inertia. It was hard to pry people out of their homes under even the most drastic circumstances. Asking them to leave when there was no obvious threat, on nothing more than the judgment of their leaders, was proving to be the biggest hurdle the coordinators were facing. Most ranches were putting some effort into cooperating, but a small number were flat-out questioning the need to move.

"I'm really glad we didn't start with one of the Bravo plans," Gil sighed as he came into the planning room and laid his tablet on the table where Fitz and Shelly were seated at their workstations, headsets on, phones ready to hand.

"No kidding," Fitz said. "That would have been a major screw-up. What's the latest, Shelly?"

"Just got off the phone with Unionville, and heard from Minden City earlier," Shelly replied, slipping off her headset. They're both set to go tonight, which puts our percentage close to forty. Still far behind schedule, but we're getting some traction."

"Sheesh," Fitz shook his head. "You can see why big operations that draw up these kinds of plans also hold drills to shake them out. If things were really dire, we'd be in big trouble. By spec, this plan calls for us to be eighty percent evacuated by one week from trigger. We'll be lucky to make sixty, and those will be the easiest sites. The remaining forty will be much tougher."

"Especially since we've got a major site – two, actually – in noncompliance," Shelly said, tapping her workstation screen.

"Who this time?" groaned Gil, dreading the prospect of facing down another recalcitrant homeowner or guest.

"You all," Shelly replied, slapping the desk. "Right here at Rivendell. Given how many guests you have, and your household population, you should have started evacuating the first day. It's right here in the plan." She pointed at the screen while the men crowded around to look over her shoulder.

"You're right, Shel," Fitz admitted, shaking his head. "The most populous sites should be going first, and we haven't done a thing yet."

"The good news is that our destination sites will be less trouble. We always keep them ready," Gil said.

"Well, the bad news is that even with that, moving as many guests as you have here, as well as all the households, is going to be complex," Shelly reminded him.

"Not to mention livestock," Fitz added.

"Not to mention livestock," Gil echoed. "Let me go talk to Ruth. She can make calls regarding the animals, and we can move them out tonight. That'll be the easy part. The guests will be harder."

"How many guests do you have here?" Shelly asked.

"I think we're down to about sixteen. We've been anticipating this, and Ruth wanted fewer demands on her resources while Grandma was declining," Gil replied.

"You mentioned two sites," Fitz said. "What was the second?"

"St. Anne's," Shelly said with a grimace. Everyone gave a light groan.

"A lot of those guests can barely be moved," Gil said.

"Some simply cannot," Shelly confirmed. "And I guarantee you, Sister Joseph Marie and her sisters will not leave any of them."

The three looked at each other grimly. "Well, we won't accomplish anything if we don't start something," Gil said at last. "I'll go talk to Ruth and Jillian about Rivendell here. Shelly, could you call St. Anne's to apprise them? We can start working out what we can."

That evening Felicity, Harmony, Christopher, and John Hagerstrom did something they hadn't done in years: saddled up horses to drive their small herd of cattle across the fields to a neighboring farm which had sufficient stable space for them. Truck transport was being arranged to distribute them from there to other sites. Fortunately, the fields were dry, and the few cattle were easy to keep under control, so everything was wrapped up before midnight. ATVs would have been more efficient than horses, but the horses were going as well, and were left with the cows. Gil picked up the riders and their tack in his pickup and returned them to the stables, where they somberly hung up the saddles and bridles.

*　　　*　　　*

The following evening Luke was wrapping up another of his longer-than-expected days. Pulling up behind a house just west of Kingston, he packed away his helmet and gloves and grabbed his overnight bag. Fortunately, he anticipated no need to provide any medical care here, at least on this visit. Ryan and Jessica Feldman were young and healthy, and their kids were strong as horses. They weren't currently housing any guests, but had made clear that Luke was welcome to stop for the night any time he needed. He took advantage of this whenever he could, because the Feldmans treated him like a family member, not just as a functionary they were accommodating for a night.

Luke knocked at the back door then let himself it. They were expecting him, and were accustomed to the variability of his schedule. The kitchen was dark, but he could hear voices in the family room. "Hello?" he called as he set his bag on the floor. Nobody answered, but he could hear someone coming. It was Ryan.

"Oh, howdy, Luke," Ryan said hesitantly. There was something odd about his expression – he was smiling, but there was a wariness and reserve about him that felt different from his usual warm welcome. He stayed at the kitchen door and didn't walk over to help Luke with his bag.

"Sorry I'm late," Luke offered. "I called Jessica and gave her an estimated time, but my stop in Clifford took me longer than expected. She did talk to you, right?"

"Oh, yes, we've talked. We've been expecting you, and were just discussing whether to call you or not," Ryan said with a note of sheepishness, not moving from where he stood.

"Call me? About what?"

"About your coming here today, and…well, about some talking we've been doing," Ryan forced out, clearly uncomfortable.

"Talking? Ryan, what's going on?" Luke asked.

"It's got to do with a spot that showed up on a site today –" Ryan began to explain.

"Is this the one about this UPAIR initiative? Because I've seen those, and –" Luke said, but Ryan interrupted.

"No, we've seen those, too. This is different. It's a mandatory spot, too. If it comes on, it has to play, and you can't close it or skip away."

"What's the spot about?"

"Probably best if we show you – we've flagged it," Ryan waved him into the family room. Seeing him coming, Jessica smiled quickly but hustled the children from the room. This struck Luke as very odd – he got along famously with the Feldman children. Ryan brought the spot up on the screen. "We first saw it this morning, and it played again later in the afternoon."

The spot lasted about ninety seconds, and it had a much more menacing tone than the UPAIR announcement Luke had seen at the Mills' house. The visuals were dark, the voiceover was ominous, and the content was threatening. It was clearly meant to intimidate, and from Ryan's expression it seemed to have done a good job. Jessica came back into the room just as the spot was closing.

"Well," Luke said as the spot faded. "That was fairly dire."

"It is," Ryan affirmed, taking Jessica's hand. "Which is why we feel we have to - nothing personal, and we hope you understand - we have to ask you to leave, and not come back again."

Leave? Not return? Was this the family to whom he was so close? "I…I mean, sure, if you wish," Luke stammered. "But I guess I don't honestly understand. That was just a government service spot – they run them all the time."

"'Just a government service spot'?" Jessica asked sharply. "Did you hear what it said about children? How they'd be taken from families who receive unauthorized medical services?"

"Jessica, I think you're overreacting. This is probably just a generic spot being placed all over to remind people –" Luke began, but Ryan cut him off.

"It's not generic. We've contacted friends and family in the area, and across the state and country. It's running aggressively, but it's only running here, in the Thumb area. Not even in metro Detroit – just here."

"All right, then, maybe it's some kind of regional campaign that'll roll along to the next region shortly," Luke argued. "How could the government possibly know about you, or anyone, getting unsanctioned treatment?"

"We don't know how they could know," Ryan replied. "They're not supposed to know about any of this – you, the guests, the care network – yet for some reason they're targeting this area with spots warning against illicit care. The coordinators must know or guess something about this, or they wouldn't be evacuating the ranches. What else might the government know? We just can't take the chance, not with the kids at stake. We're reevaluating everything – our involvement in the network, our housing guests, our contacts with others."

"All right," Luke conceded, realizing that he wasn't getting anywhere. "This means – I presume you'd like me to leave now?"

"We're afraid...yes, Luke. We're sorry, but the risk is too great. Nothing against you personally, but –" Ryan replied.

"I understand," Luke said, raising his hands, though in truth he didn't quite understand, and felt not a little stung. "Can I take the time to make a phone call, to see where I could go next?"

Ryan and Jessica glanced at each other. "We...we'd prefer you to get going, and make the call closer to town," Jessica said apologetically, but with a hint of defiance.

"We don't know what kind of signal tracking capability they might have," Ryan added weakly.

"All right," Luke said, trying to bite back the tart responses that were swirling in his head. He was tired, and hungry, and had been looking forward to a warm evening with the Feldmans.

Instead, he was being sent back out into the chill night, by every indication never to be asked back.

"We're sorry, Luke," Jessica almost pleaded. "We just–"

"It's all right, I understand," Luke interrupted. "Goodbye, and say goodnight to the kids for me." He grabbed his overnight bag and let himself out. In deference to Ryan and Jessica's wishes, he drove about half a mile away before digging out his phone and tablet to try to scare up a place to spend the night. He hoped he wouldn't have to call to ask Gil to come up with a trailer and give him a lift home – the folk at Rivendell had enough on their plate without a petty interruption like that.

Luke's heart sank as he scanned the map for options. To be thrown out so abruptly, on the basis of nothing more than a spot broadcast on a site! Well, no, it was really the fear rising from the spot, and Luke had to admit that whoever had written that spot had known how to create fear. Ryan and Jessica had acted like every one of their emotional buttons had been hit hard. Small wonder they'd thrown him out.

Luke's eyes blurred as he stared at his tablet screen. He felt a surge of disorientation. Who had placed those spots, and why? They weren't saying anything that anyone didn't already know – why run them now? Were they really targeting the Thumb? If so, did that mean someone suspected something? Luke felt an overwhelming sensation of matters spinning out of control, of patterns and relationships he'd relied upon crumbling and coming apart, of things long hidden exposed to unexpected and hostile attention, of people he loved changing and separating from each another. He pressed his palms against his eyes and tried to get hold of himself. He needed to talk to someone, but who? He couldn't disturb Grandpa, not during this time of grief. The Schaeffers had enough struggles, and he didn't want to trouble Gil, not least because that might lead to bumping into Felicity. Luke hadn't seen anything of her since that strange incident at the gazebo, and he wasn't sure how he'd respond if he did.

Luke felt completely unmoored, adrift alone in a sea of uncertainty. The decision to shut down the ranches and slip the guests back into the public health care system had been made on the assumption that the danger was past. Was it? What had happened to Frieda and Willard? Now the plans had changed again. Not only had the plans to release the guests been halted, the ranches were being evacuated, and the families and guests moved to safety in other Farthings.

But where did all these changes leave him?

Feeling battered and overwhelmed by the swirling maelstrom of issues, Luke bowed his head and forced himself to breathe. He'd work himself into a panic attack if he went on like this. A place for the night. That was his immediate goal. Find a place for the night, hopefully without having to trouble the people at Rivendell. He looked over the map again. There – the Drummonds lived just southeast of Cass City. Maybe they had room for him. It wouldn't be far. He keyed their number and hoped they'd be home.

Desolation

Teresa was wearying of this pattern. She'd worked herself to exhaustion all day in hopes of dropping off to sleep quickly, which she had – only to awaken in the small hours of the morning. She lay still for quite a while, trying to fall back to sleep, but to no avail. When the dark imaginings and old fears came thronging around, she threw back her covers and pulled on her bathrobe. Might as well pray in the chapel as lie there fighting it out.

No sooner had Teresa knelt and buried her face in her hands than she was into a vision. There was no drowsiness or dreamlike sense. It was as if she'd closed her eyes only to open them again to find she was again aloft, soaring high above the countryside - only there was little countryside to see. The regular patchwork of tilled fields mottled by the dark areas of woods and scrub had been overlaid by the lattice of lines that she'd seen being woven in her earlier vision. Only now the lines weren't gray and crisp and clean-edged. Now they were an angry, sullen red, and seemed to glow slightly, throbbing and pulsing like a living thing. Alarmed, she employed the telescopic vision that was a feature of these visions to examine the lines more closely. Their sharp edges which had seemed so threatening before now looked rough and harsh. Wherever two of the lines intersected, where there had once been clean, strong joins, there were now rust-tinged seams that seemed to be seeping something.

Disturbed, Teresa pondered what this vision might mean. She wasn't sure what the gray lattice represented, but she was certain that whatever the reddish coloration was, it wasn't good. It appeared to be some sort of corrosion or corruption – her medical background caused her to keep thinking "infection" – that hadn't been intended by whoever had woven the lattice. One thing seemed clear: whatever the lattice represented had been weakened. When she'd watched it being built, one of its virtues had seemed that it was well-designed and solidly constructed. Whatever its purpose, it would serve well. Now Teresa doubted that was true.

Whenever this lattice was turned on or activated or used – and somehow Teresa knew that hadn't yet happened – it would not bear the load of whatever it had been constructed for. Its integrity had been compromised. Whatever the corrosion represented would cause it to buckle and break, with terrible consequences.

Teresa was dismayed, and felt she should warn someone about the situation. But who? And how? Was she the only one who could see the problem? And what did these symbols mean, anyway?

Before Teresa could spend too much time pondering this, her perspective changed. She felt a brief falling sensation which was over almost before she was aware of it. She found she was in the back yard of the Big House at Rivendell. She even knew when – it was the afternoon of the day of Grandma's funeral. The funeral luncheon was still going on, and she could see people milling about in the house. She was wearing the same black dress she'd worn that day, and her rosary was in her hand. But in this vision she was all the way at the back of the yard, and she knew she'd not come this far on that day. She didn't know what she was doing here, so she just walked slowly along the edge of the pond. The sky was overcast as it had been, but she wasn't feeling the biting chill from the wind that she remembered. The trees and bushes were still stark and bare, which for some reason saddened her. In fact, she felt sadder now, in this vision, than she'd felt on the day of Grandma's funeral. Her sadness had many roots: mourning Grandma's death, weariness with winter and yearning for spring, vexation with the fears and imaginings that still tormented her, puzzlement about the meaning of these mysterious visions. But she also came to realize that the greatest component was dread, dread of some impending calamity, and sadness over what it would cost those she loved.

As Teresa walked along, fingering her rosary beads and trying to pray instead of fret, she heard a cry from the other side of the pond. She'd thought she was alone, but looking up, she was not surprised to see the man she'd seen before, both in her visions and on a bench on a corner in Sandusky. The moment she laid eyes on him, she knew two things: that his name was Jason, and that he was the one with the authority to activate whatever the lattice represented.

"It's...it's you!" the man cried in astonishment, pointing at her.

"There's still time to stop this, Jason," Teresa said.

No sooner were the words past her lips than the entire scene vanished like smoke, and she found herself back in the pearl white environment, standing before the pedestal that held the exquisite bouquet and delicate lace veil. She sighed in bliss – wherever this place was, she loved it, and treasured every brief second she got to spend here. She feasted her eyes on the balanced beauty of the items and savored the delicate aroma that lingered about the flowers. She felt at home here in a way that she'd never felt at home anywhere in her life. She drew closer to the beautiful objects, yearning for them. Then, perhaps from the confidence that came with familiarity, or perhaps because her longing finally overcame her fear, she reached out to pick up the bouquet. She did not wish to take it anywhere, or even to touch a petal, but to hold it just a little nearer to her heart.

Barely daring to breathe, Teresa lifted the bouquet. The movement released more of its fragrance, enveloping her in ecstasy. She gently turned the flowers so she could look at the arrangement directly, and was again smitten by the splendor. She felt like she'd never seen floral beauty – had never seen beauty at all – until now.

"Teresa!" came a call. It startled but did not frighten her. Janice might have felt ashamed, as if she'd been caught doing something forbidden, but Teresa recognized that there was no censure in that call. Exactly what there was, she could not say for certain. It was warm and welcoming, and seemed slightly familiar. Still holding the bouquet, she turned to see if she could discern from where the call had come.

She hadn't even finished turning when it struck her. Like a falcon stooping from the eye of the sun, something transfixed her heart, flooding her with rapturous yearning that burned and pierced and lifted and ravished her. She had never known such longing;

she had never known such fulfillment in the midst of longing. It was utterly alien, utterly mysterious, yet at the same time familiar and welcome. In the midst of its fleeting passage she knew in a way she'd never known anything in her life:

The yearning was for her.

Then it was gone, passing more swiftly than it had come, tarrying not the tenth part of a second, known only in its departure, leaving behind a fathomless canyon of emptiness, an aching loss that caused her to crumple, gasping and sobbing.

Teresa awoke on the floor of the chapel, alone in the darkness, having fallen sideways off the kneeler. She was aware that she was cold, and that she'd struck her elbow painfully, but neither of these discomforts registered in the slightest. The only thing she knew, the only thing that mattered, was the loss of that ecstatic longing. No pleasure, no satisfaction she had ever known or dreamed existed could compare to being pierced by that desire – and now it was gone, leaving behind nothing but a bleak chasm yawning before her. How could she take pleasure in any earthly good ever again, having known that heavenly yearning?

"No," she sobbed. "No, no, please don't leave me. Don't do that to me and then go away. Don't leave me here all alone." But there was no reply. The only things piercing the darkness were Teresa's muffled sobs and the dim, flickering light of the Presence Lamp.

*   *   *

"Dad?" came Gil's voice hesitantly from the doorway.

"I'm in here," Michael Peterson answered from the sitting room. Gil entered quietly, nodding to his father who sat peacefully in the recliner which was his usual reading spot. A book lay open on his lap and the little table beside him held an empty tea mug.

The rocking chair on the other side of the table was conspicuously empty.

"I...ah...don't mean to disturb you, Dad, but it's getting late, and I was wondering if you –"

"Ah," Grandpa held up a hand. "Say no more. You're wondering if I'm ready to pack up and go."

"Well...yes, that's essentially it," Gil admitted. "I didn't want to run you out, but everyone's almost gone, and –"

"It's all right," Grandpa said, laying the book on the table and standing up. "I've got my scant things packed and have just been waiting for your word."

"Oh," Gil said in surprise. "You...you have? I'm sorry. Here I was waiting myself, to give you time enough to...well..."

"To say goodbye?" Grandpa filled in. He clapped Gil on the shoulder. "Son, I appreciate your consideration, but don't worry overmuch. Yes, your mother and I spent some wonderful years in this house. But there isn't a single earthly good we get to keep. One of the secrets of peace is learning to relinquish them with grace and gratitude. By the time you get to my age, that's about all you're doing."

"Yeah," Gil acknowledged. "I've been getting some experience in that recently." He gazed at the empty rocker for a while, then shook his head and glanced at his tablet. "Anyway, I've got some options to suggest for places you could go –"

Grandpa raised his hand to gently interrupt. "Again, I appreciate your good intentions and hard work, but I've already made my plans. I'm going to go visit Otto and Joan Fletcher for a bit before taking the long journey."

"Otto and Joan? But they're over by Allenton. We were hoping to have you out of state by tonight."

"I figured that, but I didn't want to bolt without spending time with such old friends. They're expecting me for a few days, perhaps a week. After that you can hide me away in whatever safe haven you've arranged down in Southfarthing."

"Actually, we were hoping Indiana – just a little farther," Gil explained.

"Westfarthing, then. I know you're already behind on a tightly timed plan, Gil, but grant an old man some time with his old friends."

"Okay, Dad. I'm sure I can trust you to keep a low profile."

"If you'll recall," Grandpa said with a bit of an edge, "I was the one who taught you about OpSec."

"Right," Gil acknowledged sheepishly. "I've got someone arranged to give you a lift –"

"I'm still able to drive, remember," Grandpa interrupted. "I'll take my own car to Otto and Joan's where you can contact me if you need. It would be nice to have someone get my luggage."

"I'll get Christopher on it."

There were hugs and a few tears as Grandpa got into his car. All the families were scattering to safe havens, never out of touch but not in the same close proximity as they had been living. Their immediate destinations were all stopgaps, temporary sites to get them clear of threat while more permanent plans could be made. There was hope that eventually some of them would end up close together again, and a sliver of a possibility that this would all blow over and they'd be able to return safely to Rivendell. But there seemed to be something final about Grandpa himself getting into his car and driving away. Suddenly the whole site seemed less like a home and more like an operations center that was being evacuated.

*   *   *

Luke wearily pulled his ATV into the shed and killed the engine. Much as he'd love to just go collapse, he needed to check in. But first he checked his oil and refueled his vehicle, just in case. Then he grabbed his bags and headed for his apartment.

The plan had been that as the ranches were evacuated and their residents transported to safety, Luke would remain disengaged from the mechanics of the moving in order to be free to respond to any medical crises that might arise. But there had been no medical crises, and as the plan execution had fallen further behind schedule, he'd increasingly been pressed into helping with the basics of packing and loading and getting people on the road. He didn't mind the work, but it was tiring, and with every truck or van that he saw drive away, Luke wondered what would happen to him once they were all gone. Whether the plan addressed that, he hadn't heard. It didn't help that much of the packing and driving off had been done after nightfall or in the early morning hours, under cover of darkness. As a result, Luke's sleep schedule had been hopelessly fouled up, and he was stumbling with exhaustion.

Clumsily Luke banged his way through the door to his rooms, burdened by his heavy duffels. Slinging his medical gear onto his desk, he dropped his personal things on the floor at the foot of his bed and looked around. The air was cold and stale and every surface dusty. Such had been the pace of the last couple of months that he'd hardly stayed here at all, only bunking occasionally if he was passing through the area, stopping only long enough to restock his supplies, wash his laundry, and pick up more gas cards. The stash of snacks he kept in the small refrigerator had certainly gone bad, which meant that he'd have to go to the Big House to find something to eat. He fired up the room heater and reluctantly headed over to see what edibles might be available.

"Hello?" Luke called as he came in the back door. There was nobody in sight, so Luke started poking about the kitchen. Before long Gil breezed in, staring at his tablet and muttering.

"Oh, hello, Luke," Gil said. "Did you get everything squared away up in Brown City?"

"Yes – and in Marlette, and Snover," Luke replied curtly.

"Great, great," Gil said absently, ticking some things on his tablet while Luke assembled his sandwich. "That puts us closer to being back on schedule."

"Wonderful," Luke replied blandly.

"It is. We got the wing emptied out today, at long last," Gil rattled on. "Took some doing, with as many guests as we had, but it's finally finished."

"I bet that's a load off your mind."

"It is, but there's still a lot to tackle," Gil bemoaned. "That's one reason I'm glad you're back. We've got a couple of sites that have asked for some help." He pulled a slip of paper out of his tablet case and laid it on the counter beside Luke. "Anvard, and then the Farriers over by Croswell."

"Anvard? That's up near Peck, isn't it?"

"Right. It would really help us get back on track if you could go give them a kick start. All our goals of having this completed by last Friday are in tatters, of course – we'll be doing well if we get this done by this Friday."

"Sure, Gil," Luke replied, then added hesitantly. "Is...is Grandpa around?"

"Dad? No, he left about an hour ago. You could call him, though. Is there anything I could help you with?"

"No," Luke answered. "No, I don't think so."

"I need to chat with you about a couple of other things –" Gil began, but just then his phone rang. Glancing at the caller, he said, "Ah, at last. I'll be with you in a minute, Luke."

While Gil went into the next room to take the call, Luke put his dishes away and wandered outside, feeling more abandoned and alone than ever. Listlessly he walked over to the first house he'd visited here at Rivendell, which had been occupied by the Schaeffers at the time. When they had been forced to flee, the Hagerstroms had moved in for a while, but now they had departed as well. Luke went up the front steps and across the wide porch. He wistfully recalled the friendly conversations he'd had with Kent and Linda while seated on the swing that hung there. He tried the front door, found it unlocked, and entered the empty house. The rooms seemed heavy with silence and his footsteps echoed as he walked through them, remembering when they had been filled with life and love and laughter. Once this had been a home, one that had welcomed him and given him hope and purpose in life. Now it was just an empty house containing nothing but bare walls and fading memories. Unable to bear the weight of the silence, he went out the back door.

Luke made his way along the covered walkways to the stable. This was, if possible, even more depressing. Not long before it had been full of the sounds and smells of livestock, but now it was cold and silent, with only a faint musty odor lingering. He walked among the horse stalls, remembering when Martha and Christopher had introduced him to horses and riding – the day he'd worn the unsuitable footwear. Luke felt an odd sensation that those events had happened only yesterday, yet at the same time that they'd taken place long ago during some other age. Martha was a wife and mother now, and Christopher had moved away, and there were no more horses at Rivendell. The saddles hung forlornly on their bars, looking like nothing more than tavern decorations.

Luke wandered out of the stable and along the side of the workshop, heading for his apartment door. Glancing up, he saw the white stone monument standing in the yard, surrounded by flowers. The monument had become backdrop by now, part of the scenery that he passed by routinely without thinking or stopping. He stopped now, remembering the brilliant, headstrong, quirky Sam Chapman, whom Luke had only known for a few weeks. Daring Sam, unpredictable Sam, ultimately sacrificial Sam, who'd given his life to protect those he loved.

Luke remembered well the day they'd dedicated the monument, the friends and family standing around on a chill November morning. Luke had been fraught with grief, yet also buoyed with hope and promise. Despite the trauma and loss it had seemed that a new day was dawning for him. He'd found a family to which he belonged, a home, and meaning to his life. He was doing valuable work helping with something greater than himself, something noble and heroic. It had seemed like his life had turned a corner, that he'd traded in bleak solitude for fellowship and love.

Now all that was being hastily dismantled. Of course, it had started last summer, when those terrible things had happened to the Schaeffers and they'd been driven from their home. Now, it seemed, everyone was being driven from their homes. Luke had no idea what would happen to this property, but he felt like Sam was being left behind, unremembered while the whirl of life passed on to other arenas.

Luke could sympathize.

Sighing, he turned away and made for his apartment. Good thing he hadn't unpacked – hopefully he'd be able to do his laundry at Anvard. The sun was still high enough in the sky, and it would only be about an hour's ride under these conditions. He lugged his gear back out to the ATV and eased off along the trails toward Peck.

*   *   *

The knock came gently at the office door. "Come in," called Sister Joseph Marie. The door opened and Teresa stepped through. "Ah, Teresa. Please come in." The sister beckoned to a seat.

"You wanted to see me, Sister?" Teresa asked.

"Yes, and thank you for making time," Sister Joseph said, folding her hands on her desk and looking at her young volunteer carefully. Teresa did look weary, with bags under her eyes and a sagging posture that bespoke exhaustion. But there was something more, something Sister Joseph had never seen before – a lingering sadness that haunted her eyes, a sadness that seemed to rise from deep in her soul.

"I'll get straight to the point, Teresa – are you all right?" Sister Joseph asked kindly but frankly.

"Am I all right?" Teresa echoed. "Why? Have I done something wrong?"

"Not at all. You've been your usual competent and diligent self. But many of the sisters have been concerned about you, especially since Margaret and Kateri had to awaken you from whatever was distressing you in the kitchen. A couple of them have approached me today, specifically stating that you seemed sad and downcast. Is anything wrong?"

Teresa wrung her hands and looked at her shoes, and seemed to be struggling to say something.

"Have you been having more visions or dreams?" Sister Joseph prodded gently.

"Yes," Teresa admitted in a choked voice. "My...my sleep has been terrible. I'll wake up and have the most horrible imaginings, and then I'll go and pray. I had one Saturday night – or early Sunday morning, I guess."

"Are they frightening?" Sister Joseph asked, trying to discern whether she was dealing with exhaustion-induced nightmares or something more sinister.

"Parts of them. I can't always tell what they mean. There's a man, though, a man in all of them. His name is Jason."

"How do you know that?"

"I just…know," Teresa shrugged. "I saw him, though, and spoke to him."

"Saw him?" Sister Joseph was confused. "In your dream?"

"Well, I saw him in my dream, but I saw him in real life, too. On a bench in Sandusky, last Wednesday when we went for supplies."

"Really?" Sister Joseph sat up and looked at Teresa more sharply. "This man in Sandusky, you saw in your dreams?"

"No, the other way around – I saw him in my dreams, and then in real life. Oh, and I've seen him once more in a dream, or vision, since then."

Sister Joseph didn't know how to handle this. Had it been any of the other sisters, she would have discounted the story as fancy, perhaps arising from confusion due to stress. But Teresa was as non-fanciful as they came. Furthermore, these seeings were very unusual for her. Teresa probably dreamed as much as anyone, but had never spoken of her dreams until recently. Also, if she was seeing men in her dreams whom she later encountered on the street, it raised some very sobering questions. Sobering questions, indeed.

"Is the presence of this man all that is distressing you, Teresa?"

"No," Teresa shook her head, her eyes still downcast. "I saw other things, things that gave me the impression that…that things are about to get very bad, maybe even dangerous."

"I see," Sister Joseph said. She was not surprised. This squared not only with the word she'd received that the ranches were being evacuated and St. Anne's was advised to do likewise, but with hints she'd received in her prayer and consultation. It seemed beyond question that something was hanging over the little community; the only issue was when the blow would fall, and what form it would take. "And this is distressing you? This foreboding?"

"Somewhat," Teresa admitted. "But that's not the biggest thing."

"It's not?" Sister Joseph was taken aback. "There's something worse?"

"Not…worse," Teresa choked. "It's hard to describe. It's like…" she trailed off, struggling for words. Then she lifted her head and looked at Sister Joseph with eyes brimming with joy and anguish at the same time. "Sister, have you ever known beauty? Beauty so fierce that it will tear you apart, yet so lovely that you'd embrace it even while you're being torn? Beauty so heavy that you cannot bear it, passing quickly so you won't be destroyed by its intensity, yet crushing you by its departure? Beauty so deep that once you know it, nothing on earth will ever frighten or satisfy you ever again? Have you ever known beauty like that?"

Sister Joseph gazed at Teresa for a long while before shaking her head slightly. "No, not personally. But I've heard of it."

"That's what's upsetting me most," Teresa admitted. "For the briefest of instants, I held that beauty – or it held me. But it passed, and I…I…" She trailed off again and hung her head. "I'm left with nothing."

Sister Joseph didn't respond immediately, letting the words hang in the air. After a minute she rose from her seat and came around her desk to kneel beside Teresa and gently place her hand on the sobbing woman's arm. "Nothing? Perhaps for a little while, but not forever."

*   *   *

Luke made it to Anvard well before sunset, and the Drake family who lived there welcomed him warmly. He got a good dinner and helped them with their packing, and was even able to get his own laundry done. This household was scattering to different destinations – their guest Dave Grandy was heading for a home in Southfarthing, the rural region in northwest Ohio, while the Drakes were headed for Westfarthing in Indiana. They were taking it all casually, especially the kids, acting as if it was a vacation and assuming they'd be back soon. Luke wasn't sure about any of that, but he kept his opinions to himself.

The packing lasted late into the night, and was followed by an early morning, hours before dawn, when the car showed up to take Dave away. Shortly thereafter the Drakes piled into their truck and headed off. Luke tried to catch a bit more sleep, but all the activity had so completely wakened him that the effort was futile. He brewed some coffee and breakfasted on the last of the bread and peanut butter while awaiting dawn. He'd be closing up the house, but since Anvard had been an administrative site for the network of ranches, some of the equipment would be left running. Mostly this meant leaving powered the communications equipment that facilitated the private phone network. At some later point someone would come by to shut it down – or not. As the sun rose, Luke locked up the house and headed for Croswell.

The trip didn't take long, and the Farrier family gave him their usual warm greeting when he arrived. They had their packing well in hand, which was good, because he had to spend most of his time stabilizing their guest, Mrs. Landon. He did what he could, which wasn't much because his medical supplies were getting low. While he was there, he got a terse message from Gil asking if he could run up to Beaversdam, another administrative site just west of Minden City. This would take less time than a usual transit, since Luke could travel up there by means of an abandoned railroad track that ran up the eastern Thumb. He was at Beaversdam by midafternoon to help a slightly less organized Tim and Allison Kettleman with their packing and preparations. Fortunately, their guest Mrs. Reichert was in reasonable health and full mental acuity, so she was able to assist. Even so, it was after nightfall when the van arrived to take them all away to their destination in Northfarthing, leaving Luke alone in the empty house.

Luke hadn't heard anything from anyone since the message from Gil, so he wasn't sure what was expected of him now.

Lacking instructions or other ranches to visit, he was at loose ends. Then he realized he was less than twenty miles from Gagetown where the Schaeffers lived, just over an hour away by trail. He called Linda and ascertained that they had not yet evacuated, and made plans to come in the morning.

Settling down in the empty house proved difficult for Luke. He was accustomed to sleeping by himself, but the Kettleman's home had always been full of laughter and lively chatter, so the silent emptiness was disquieting. He dozed fitfully, finally waking well before dawn. He made a meager breakfast of snack bars and black coffee and took one last walk through the unoccupied house to ensure everything was secure for a long vacancy. His footsteps echoed in the empty rooms as he checked faucets and windows. When he was certain that the only thing still running was the communications console, he turned off the furnace, secured the kitchen light, and went out into the chill morning air. Locking the door and tucking the key in the stowage spot, he fired up the ATV and turned west.

Since some of the trails were still boggy and hindered by winter-fallen limbs and trees, Luke had to take more circuitous paths, so it was closer to two hours before he was pulling up at the red brick house where the Schaeffers lived. The youngsters piled all over him, eager to share the latest excitements in their lives. Luke listened to them all, holding little Miriam while Matthew earnestly related how he'd found frogs *and* turtles in the nearby brook. Tabitha and Elizabeth displayed their array of Easter crafts while Jude updated him on how his studies were going. As a mature lad of nearly thirteen, Jude's interest in medicine had been piqued by the times he'd accompanied Luke on rounds, so now he was seriously pursuing high-school level advanced biology and physiology. He confided that he hoped to be into college-level material by the time he turned fifteen, and Luke could well believe it. Luke had a jolly morning, feeling for a while that he was back in his old home, and that things had never changed.

But when Luke got a chance to sit down with Kent and Linda over lunch, it became clear that matters were not as settled as he might be led to believe when just dealing with the children. Kent seemed to have recovered some of his equilibrium after the traumas of the prior year, but there was a brittle superficiality about his demeanor, particularly when the conversation turned to Martha and her newborn son Leo. Kent bravely tried to play the part of the proud grandpa, and to reassure Luke of what a fine husband young Evan Stover was, but Luke could see the pain Kent bore. Every mention of Martha as wife or mother was a small reminder of the events that put her in that situation at such a young age. Some healing took time.

Unfortunately, the conversation got even more difficult when it turned to Phillip's whereabouts.

"Have you heard from him at all?" Luke asked.

"Not recently," Linda said as lightly as she could manage. "We hear from Ruth that he's still bunking with Cletus and Sixtus, though apparently that's not going too well."

"In what sense?"

"I've no idea," Linda shrugged. "That's all we've heard."

"I tried to warn them that what they were trying wouldn't be as easy as they were imagining," Luke said. "But they weren't listening to me."

"They weren't listening to anyone," Kent growled. "So now they're finding out the hard way. Ah, to be nineteen again, when you know everything!"

"Now, Kent," Linda soothed him.

"Does he know you're moving? Has he a way to reach you once you do?" Luke asked.

"We've left messages on his phone, and he's got the current contact information for the folks at Fangorn as well," Linda explained. "He should be able to get in touch with us."

"If he does so before we have to leave," Kent said moodily, then stood up. "Excuse me." Without explanation he walked away. Linda looked after him with a sad expression.

"I'm sorry if I brought up a painful subject," Luke apologized.

"It's all right," Linda waved. "This will be our second move within a year, both under less than ideal circumstances, with a lot of other trauma thrown in as well. It seems like he just gets back on his feet when he's hammered with another blow. Truthfully, I'm proud of him for keeping things together as well as he has."

"Where will you be moving?"

"Somewhere up in Northfarthing," Linda sighed. "They haven't told us exactly where yet. Steve and the Fangorn crew are coordinating for the ranches in Huron, as well as northern Tuscola and Saginaw counties. I get the impression things are not coming together as smoothly as they'd hoped. Of course, they've got Annette's condition to deal with, which is undoubtedly distracting Steve, and I'm sure the evacuation is proving a lot more complicated than anyone anticipated."

"I think that's what they were finding at Rivendell," Luke said. "You don't actually have to move, do you?"

"Strictly speaking, no, because we're not a ranch. But it's Gil's opinion, and we agree, that any threat which imperils the ranches doubly imperils us," Linda replied. "But what about you? Where will you be heading?"

"Well..." Luke began, but just then Elizabeth ran in toting Miriam, who needed some kind of attention, and Linda had to bustle off.

In the midafternoon Evan and Martha and Leo arrived, and though the house got a little cramped, there was much merriment as the aunts took turns holding the baby and getting updated on all the milestones. Luke was struck by how mature Martha looked. He still thought of her as the vivacious young teen who'd taught him how to ride horses. Yet here she was, comporting herself as a wife and mother, confident and competent and working well with her husband. Evan was clearly smitten with her and with little Leo. The dinner table was crowded and the laughter plentiful that evening. Kent seemed to be putting the best face on things that he could, but even the addition of Evan at the board could not make up for the absence of Phillip, and no amount of levity could obscure the fact that this was, in a sense, a farewell dinner. Wherever the Schaeffers were being evacuated to, the little Stover family was staying behind. Given that nobody knew what the final outcome of all these changes would be, the evening's ambiance was bittersweet.

It wasn't until after the Stovers had taken their leave and evening prayers said and the girls settled down that Luke and Linda had time to resume their conversation. Kent and Jude were off attending to some details that needed resolving in preparation for the move, and Miriam was nursing herself to sleep on Linda's lap.

"So, Luke, we got interrupted earlier," Linda began. "What are your plans? Where will you end up when all the dust settles?"

"Well, I'm not really sure," Luke admitted, cringing a little internally. This wasn't a topic he wanted to discuss.

"Not sure?" Linda asked sharply. "You mean you haven't talked this over with Gil or Fitz or anyone?"

"Well, they've got a lot on their plates right now. I didn't want to be any trouble – I'm sure I'll figure out something."

"Trouble?" Linda persisted. "Who told you that you were trouble?"

"Well, nobody said that," Luke admitted. "It's just that there's so much going on, and so many unexpected problems – I didn't want to be a bother. I can take care of myself."

"'A bother'?" Linda flared briefly, unsettling little Miriam enough that she had to take a minute to calm her before continuing. "Derek Stevens, who has been feeding you this crap? A bother, indeed! You're as loved and valued a member of this community as anyone else! And beyond that, you've been so helpful, so sacrificing over the past two years – you've been a lifesaver, quite literally, many times over! Nobody thinks you a bother. I'm going to call Gil right now – I'm sure this is a communications mix-up. I know they'll have made some provision for you."

"No, no, please, Linda," Luke pleaded, feeling grateful and embarrassed at the same time. "It's really late, and he's had a crazy day."

"Well, it is late," Linda admitted. "But first thing in the morning, either you call him or I will. I won't be going anywhere until I know exactly how you're being taken care of."

"Linda, please, it's no big deal. I'm on top of it."

"The hell," Linda snapped back. "Derek, we love you like a son, or a younger brother. We've lost so much in the past year, we're not losing you."

"Okay, okay," Luke said. "And speaking of morning, it's not that far away, and I've had a couple of rough nights. I think I'll turn in."

"All right," Linda conceded, eyeing Luke warily. "But first thing tomorrow, we resolve this, right?"

"Right."

Confrontation

Pete was the first to arrive at their next meeting, though he was soon followed by Gerald, who handed out the next set of translated pages without comment. Though Pete didn't know Gerald well, it seemed to him that the First Nations scholar was unusually pensive. This made Pete disinclined to pursue small talk, so he quietly inserted the new pages into his binder and started paging through them as Gerald did the same.

Unfortunately, Dr. Harris missed this subtle atmosphere when he breezed in late, greeting them both with a cheery "Howdy!" Slinging his jacket over the back of the chair, he picked up the new pages.

"Well, are we ready for another round of ghost stories?" he asked lightly.

Pete grinned at this, but Gerald looked at Dr. Harris darkly before erupting. "Ghost stories?" he rumbled, then slammed his fist on the table as he rose to his feet. "Ghost stories? This is how you modern Europeans deal with anything that does not fit into your tidy categories!" he cried furiously, throwing his hands into the air. "You mock and scorn and dismiss, for what cannot be explained by your rationalism and empiricism must be mere legends and ghost stories! How well that works can be seen from what your culture has become. At least we had families, and lands, and an identity – what do you have any more? Shows on the internet and fast food and children who do not know their own fathers! When was the last time you ate something you raised on your own land, or caught with your own hands? Do you even know your great-grandparents' names? You buy what you are told to buy and think what you are told to think and scoff at whatever challenges your neatly canned world view. Thus you are caught helpless when faced with what is real and dangerous, but which you refuse to believe exists. Reality is much deeper and darker than your materialism acknowledges, Doctor! What will you do when what you say cannot exist rises to stalk you?"

Dr. Harris was sprawled back in his chair, blinking and gaping at this unexpected outburst. "I…I'm sorry," he stammered. "I never meant –"

Gerald collapsed back into his chair and buried his face in his hands. The other two men looked at one another, wondering what to say or do. Gerald saved them the trouble by speaking in a low, exhausted voice.

"My apologies, Doctor. I didn't mean to jump down your throat. It's just been…a trying couple of days."

"That's all right," Dr. Harris said. "I quite understand –"

"No, you don't," Gerald interrupted. "Not enough, not yet. I've been reading ahead a little, looking over what we'd be covering tonight. The material has resurrected some…disturbing memories." He fell silent and rubbed his face with his hands before continuing in a subdued voice. "For all the honor of my tribe, and all the pride I take in my heritage, there is no people on earth that does not have shameful tales, and chapters of their history in which they take no pleasure. For we Anishinaabe, there has always been a shadow lurking about the edge of our history, a shadow that has overcome some of us from time to time, such as the darkness which drove us from *Mooningwanekaaning*, of which the lore masters do not speak.

"I am about to tell you some things that I have never told anyone else. I ask you not to speak to any others about them, for the matter is rather…personal."

The other two muttered assurances while Gerald continued.

"I wouldn't mention this at all if it wasn't germane to what we have to cover tonight. Many years ago, when I was still learning what it meant to be First Nation, I explored many paths in my search for knowledge. I had not yet learned enough of the wisdom of my fathers to be wary. I had been schooled in the assumptions of the modern rationalists that knowledge was simply neutral, that there was never any harm in knowing; the potential danger lay only in how that knowledge was used.

"I learned better.

"It was when I'd just returned from finishing my studies in England. I was proud of my accomplishments and smug in my education. I returned to my reserve to the acclaim of my people, who had great hopes for my future.

"I spent that summer and autumn getting reacquainted with the land. In my pride I decided to defy the wisdom of my elders. Years before, I had heard whispered, furtive mention of a rogue member of the tribe who had scorned our heritage and sought out the darkness, the forbidden knowledge. Though he was eager to claim the name and heritage of the Anishinaabe, he was shameless and defiant toward tribal authorities. In the end he was driven out, and lived by himself up the coast in the woods near Michipicoten. He pretended he was living in the noble spirit of our ancestors, simple and close to the land. The tribe knew he was living in disgrace and squalor, and shunned him. All peoples have such rogue members, do they not?"

"They do," Pete affirmed.

"In my folly and youthful arrogance, I sought out this man. I went up the coast and found the overgrown two-track that led back to his cabin. Even as I drove it, I was revolted by the foulness of the meagre property, littered with scraps and trash. My instincts began to tell me to flee, but I was too sophisticated, and was afraid of appearing cowardly. The man greeted me warily, but when I told him my purpose, he welcomed me into what he called his wigwam – a shabby, ill-tended hut. Inside it was dark, and stank, but he stoked the fire and began to hold forth at length about the mysteries he'd learned, and the hidden history of our people, and a great deal of other nonsense. He flattered me for my foresight in seeking him out, and assured me that he could put into my hands great powers, lost powers that were our rightful heritage. I listened in a superior manner, convinced that I could hear his talk yet remain aloof from it, a detached and critical observer, able to withdraw at any time.

"The man said it had been long since he'd had a proper apprentice. Decades before, one had come, a short, skinny man eager to learn. He had taught this apprentice much, but they'd had a falling out, and knives had been drawn, and the apprentice had gone away. Since then it had only been petty visitors seeking Indian magic, until the man had grown tired of them.

"But in me, this man assured me, he saw potential for greatness, if I would come under his instruction. At that point he threw some sticks on the fire that began to fill the room with a sweet, heavy aroma. He also brewed a tea of some nature which filled my nostrils with a sharp scent when he put the cup beside me. Becoming suspicious, I only pretended to sip, but he drank eagerly while speaking of the things he could teach me, and the power I could have, especially over the Europeans.

"He spoke of an ancient power, one that long predated even our people, a clinging darkness that could fill the land and entrap people. He told of dark rituals and obscene rites by which this darkness could be summoned, and that the Europeans would be powerless before it. He told me that if I became his apprentice, he could teach me all this and more, and that I could be the vehicle by which our people could return to greatness.

"Even as I scoffed inside, thinking just what you said, Dr. Harris – that these were but ghost stories to frighten children – part of me was allured, and my feigned interest became less feigned as his flashing eyes and enticing words began to draw me in. Wild fantasies started to roil in my imagination about how I could be the one who would unite our scattered and diminished people and reclaim our heritage from the Europeans. And there, in the reeking dimness of that dark shaman's hut, I began to feel stirring within me a gnawing emptiness, an insatiable hunger for that glory and exultation. I was barely aware of it at first, but as it grew I found myself increasingly eager to take in, to gobble up, this man's words and find through them the greatness that I hungered for.

"The firelight was low, but the cloying smell was thick in the room. My mouth was dry, and the tea which sat at my elbow called to me, urging me to drink. But suddenly, sharply, a great dread rose within me, and I knew that I was in grave peril. Whether that dread came from *Giche Manidou* or the Holy Spirit of the Christians – if there is a difference – I know not, but whoever it was I thank Him for that warning. Casting aside my immaturity, I pushed myself to my feet and crashed from the hut, swaying like a drunkard while the man laughed at me and mocked my flight. For flight it was – I stumbled to my car and raced off, heedless of what any man said, thinking only of putting as much distance between myself and that accursed place as I could.

"I returned to my people and spoke to nobody of where I had gone or whom I had visited. In fact, I have spoken to nobody else of my folly until today. I know that I avoided great danger by fleeing when I did, but I also know that in my pride I injured myself by even going to that place and listening to that man.

"Not all knowledge is neutral. There are some thoughts no man should ever entertain, some words that should never be spoken, some things that should never be summoned for any reason. On that day I sustained a wound to my soul, a wound that remains unhealed to this day. I wish I knew how it might be healed. Perhaps someday it will. But I hope you can see, Dr. Harris, why I do not automatically scoff at ghost stories. I have come near one, and it was almost the end of me."

Dr. Harris said nothing, but nodded somberly.

"I mention my experience because it may have some bearing on what these next pages of the journal recount. As you can see, Fr. Thomas's next entry is two days after the lengthy and detailed entry we examined last time. As of its writing, the village is still in a great deal of agitation, and Fr. Thomas can only guess as to why. Something was learned from the Cree before they died, but his Ojibwe is not good enough to discern what. He suspects that it has some connection to the violent fits that overtook the Cree. He wonders if it was some sort of plague, but he cannot reconcile that with what Mygizi said of the darkness and hunger.

"Nikikouet is nearly frantic with worry about Jean's whereabouts, so Fr. Thomas doesn't wish to disturb her with questions. Meanwhile the other villagers treat him with a curious combination of fear and respect. He guesses that they are still in awe of how his god protected him from the mad Cree.

"The following entry is three days after that. Jean has safely returned, much to Nikikouet's relief. The village is still in turmoil, with the men speaking at length around the fires, and Fr. Thomas hopes that Jean can find out what is going on and apprise him. Jean mingles with the village men all day and then returns to report.

"Jean is very grave. It seems the hunger and hollow darkness to which the men had alluded referred to an ancient condition which afflicted regions of the forest. They did not name it, but since Jean had not heard that bit of tribal lore, they filled him in as best they could."

"I presume this isn't a natural condition, but something considered supernatural?" Dr. Harris asked.

"Those categorizations mean more to Europeans than they would have to my people, but in the sense you ask, yes, that's true," Gerald affirmed.

"So we're talking about…a curse, or something?" Pete added.

"That's how Jean explains it to Fr. Thomas, but he goes out of his way to mention that the village men use distinctive phrases to describe it. It is like a mist, a clinging darkness, that they call the earth's blood. They also speak of it shrouding, and one of the great fears about this clinging darkness is getting lost in it and falling prey."

"Falling prey to what?" Pete asked.

Gerald tapped the page and pondered a moment before replying. "It seems that's where the ravenous hunger comes in. Along with this shrouding, or in the midst of it, is some thing or things that devour. It's unclear whether the darkness creates the hunger, or the hunger creates the darkness, or some mixture thereof, but they go together. Remember that we're getting Fr. Thomas's summary of Jean's sketchy account of his conversation with men who didn't want to talk about it."

"Did the Cree create this darkness? Or bring it?" said Pete.

"Jean inquired after that, and got a firm no. Whatever the source of the darkness, no First Nation bore any responsibility for bringing it. Apparently it was older, a terror from before any people came to the land. However, it was more common in the north, so the Cree would have seen more of it," Gerald explained. The men were talking in subdued voices, as if reticent to expose this taboo topic.

"You can see, perhaps, some congruity between this and the legends of the wendigo hunting grounds," Dr. Harris offered. "You didn't want to stumble into those, either."

"I'd noticed that," Gerald nodded. "Perhaps the tales of the wendigo and its grounds were partly this legend filtered through European preconceptions? Who can tell? But you're right, there are distinct parallels."

"So – if the Cree didn't start this, what was going on with them?" Pete asked.

"Apparently that very question was what had the village men so concerned," Gerald replied, scanning the page. "Seems the two Cree had been part of a band which stumbled into this area of shrouded forest. The two got separated from the others and were able to flee, but not before they 'passed beneath the shadow', as Jean relates to Fr. Thomas. Apparently that was enough to somehow taint them, for the men said their violent outbursts were a sign that they were being 'devoured by the hunger'."

"So this – ravenous hunger, whatever it was, got into them somehow? Like an infection?" Pete asked.

"So it would seem – a spiritual infection, if you will, though they had no understanding of such a concept. They were concerned enough to start talking about moving the village."

"Moving the village?" Dr. Harris asked.

"Not so radical as it sounds," Gerald explained. "They moved seasonally anyway. With winter approaching they'd customarily shift from fishing at the Sault to hunting north of Lake Superior. The difficulty is that the section of shadowed forest through which the Cree had stumbled lay right along their usual migration route – along the lake, in the vicinity of Michipicoten." Gerald stopped, and silence lay heavy in the air.

"Couldn't they go around it?" Pete asked.

"They had no idea where the boundaries of the shadowed area lay. Whatever happened, had happened recently. Jean reported passing through that region just a few months before with no difficulty. Now, for whatever reason, a shadow of indeterminate size lay across their path – a shadow they considered fatal to enter. And it gets worse."

"How so?" asked Dr. Harris.

"Apparently, this mysterious darkness spreads, occupying more and more of the woods over time. Only water – enough water to separate the trees – hinders it. The way the men speak of it, it sends out tendril-like threads that not only find prey, but serve to expand the edges of the darkness. According to Jean, the men say that the trails become confused. The men are afraid that even if they find their way around it on the way to the winter hunting grounds, it'll spread so far behind them that they won't be able to make it back to the fishing grounds in the spring."

"So, they'd be trapped up there," Pete observed.

"Exactly. Even staying at the Sault would be risky, if the Shadow spread far enough south. Apparently, there was some discussion of removing to beyond the St. Mary's River, into hunting grounds in what we would today consider the Upper Peninsula of Michigan. There'd be more risk of encountering other tribes there, but that wasn't their greatest worry. But look here – it seems that Fr. Thomas is getting bold. Read at the top of the next page:

> *Hearing of the tribe's distress, I asked Jean to accompany me to where the men were gathered and to translate for me. He brought me, knowing that the men do not think much of me. I asked him to tell them that the God of the Cross had conquered death and darkness, and had driven evil spirits before him like defeated warriors. This same God who had routed death could defeat this dangerous shadow as well. The men received this news soberly, for they recalled how I had been protected from the demonic fury of the possessed Cree. They asked how I could do battle with darkness and mist, or wrestle with a hunger. I answered that I did not*

yet know, but that I would think on the matter and consult my God. Recalling the Gadarene demoniac, I was confident that the Holy Ghost would guide me to the proper way to exorcise this evil.

"Gadarene demoniac?" asked Pete.

"Looking it up," Dr. Harris tapped on his tablet. "Ah, here. A story from the Bible where Jesus heals a man who was supposedly possessed by a demon – a demon that made him violently attack people."

"So, Fr. Thomas thought this a case of demon possession?"

"Not necessarily," Gerald replied. "He only references this as an example of Jesus's power over evil. He seems mystified by the exact nature of the threat, and even what exactly to do about it, but he's confident that the Christian God is strong enough to do the job.

"Reading a little further, we see that the men tell Fr. Thomas to talk to his god, that they will delay their plans to uproot the village for three days. He goes to his wigwam to – oh, my, he embarks on a three-day fast to pray and ask for divine guidance. That must have taken effort."

"Why so? I mean, other than not eating for three days," Dr. Harris said.

"The diet he'd been on was none too abundant at the best of times, and far less than he'd been accustomed to in France. He was probably eating barely enough to survive as it was. Fasting for three days on top of that would push him close to the edge of starvation. Let's see, here...he says Mass...he prays. Ah, toward the bottom of the next page:

Having beseeched the Holy Ghost on the matter, I am convinced that the answer lies with the Blessed Sacrament. Whatever this curse might be, it will be broken by the Holy Eucharist.

"'The Eucharist'? Isn't that the body-of-the-god issue we were talking about earlier?" Dr. Harris asked.

"Yes," Gerald confirmed.

"How, exactly, would this Eucharist help break the curse?" said Pete.

"It's a quandary that Fr. Thomas is struggling with himself, as you can see on the next page," Gerald answered. "He tells of how he prays for guidance, and only toward the end of the third day does he mention anything certain."

"But, what does this mean here?" Dr. Harris asked. "*I have no monstrance, and even if I had, I would fear desecration. Perhaps it is I who must be the monstrance.*"

"It is cryptic," Gerald admitted. "So much so that I contacted Fr. Allan West, who is the Jesuit scholar reviewing this translation even as we are. I asked him if he could explain Fr. Thomas's words. Here is a portion of his response." Gerald pulled a slip of paper from his binder.

A monstrance is a receptacle solely for the public display of the Blessed Sacrament in the species of a consecrated host. The host used for display is usually of a slightly larger size than common Communion hosts, in order to be more easily viewed. The monstrance is typically round, between twelve and eighteen inches across, and made of a precious metal like silver or gold. It often takes the form of arms or blades extending from a center, to give the effect of rays radiating from a source. There is a small window in the center through which the host can be viewed, and is mounted on a pedestal made of similar metal.

Though a monstrance can be used in something like an outdoor Eucharistic procession, normally it resides in a sanctuary or chapel where it can be protected from harm. For though the monstrance elements have some innate value, infinitely more precious is the One it contains.

Fr. Thomas's quandary springs from his conviction that the Eucharist must, somehow, be brought into the area stricken by this mysterious shadow. He cannot simply tuck it into a pack and carry it, for that would dishonor the host. But even if he had had a suitable vessel such as a monstrance, the problem of protection remained. Unlike a sacramental agent such as holy water, or a symbol like a crucifix, the consecrated host is God Himself, who cannot be used as a tool to any man's end. A consecrated host must either be consumed or handled with the highest honor and propriety. As a Christian and especially as a priest, Fr. Thomas was bound to protect the Blessed Sacrament from desecration, even at the risk of his own life. Hence his dilemma: though he perceives that the presence of Christ in the Eucharist is the key to defeating the darkness, he cannot simply carry a host into it, even if he had a suitable vessel. The risk of losing the host, or exposing it to abuse and desecration, is too high.

But a Christian who receives the Eucharist worthily, that is, in a state of grace, becomes in effect a living monstrance, bearing God's divine life within him. This, I believe, is what Fr. Thomas means when he speaks of himself being the monstrance.

"So...Fr. Thomas is thinking of taking this Eucharist and then going into these woods himself?" Pete asked.

"It would seem so," Gerald answered quietly. A stillness fell on the room for a minute before Dr. Harris stirred in his seat and cleared his throat uncomfortably.

"Look here, now," he said in an artificially lighthearted voice. "We don't really believe all this, do we?"

Gerald turned his head and looked at him dispassionately. "To what are you referring, Doctor?"

"Well, I mean…all this," Dr. Harris blustered, waving at the binder. "This whole haunted woods and magic bread and ancient curses stuff. I mean, it's a nice legend, but I'm a historian, and…well, you know…" He trailed off to a mutter, still fixed by Gerald's steady gaze. Silence fell again, this time heavy and uncomfortable.

"The issue is not what a postmodern materialist might think," Gerald responded. "The issue is what my ancestors, and Fr. Thomas, thought. My ancestors were strong and cunning, facing lethal danger on a routine basis. Fr. Thomas so strongly believed in his message that he gave up the world he had been raised in to share the life of my ancestors and teach them. One view they shared was that of a multilayered reality filled with things not only visible and invisible, but good and wicked, benevolent and malevolent. Based on their experience and understanding, they discerned a mysterious but very real threat. To comprehend their motivations and actions, we have to examine them from this shared view, not from the viewpoint of materialistic rationalists – and certainly not from our view of their view."

"Well, but of course…" Dr. Harris muttered, fading into incoherence and retuning his attention to the binder.

"So," Pete said after a minute's difficult silence. "What does Fr. Thomas decide to do?"

"That's where we have to guess," Gerald replied, turning a page. "His journal entries grow scant from here on out. The next one is two days later, where he records a conversation with Jean and Nikikouet. The only hint he gives is, *I have told them of my decision.* From his description of their response, they did not take it well, which lends support to Fr. West's speculation that he had decided to go himself. Jean seems saddened but resigned, possibly because he knows the gravity of the threat. Nikikouet is more adamant, insisting that Fr. Thomas is much too valuable to be lost. When Jean points out that the dark hunger must be stopped, Nikikouet offers to go herself, since she is now a Christian. At this point Jean asks Fr. Thomas to step outside the wigwam, which he does. The subsequent discussion between Jean and Nikikouet can be heard even there. When they ask him back inside, he records:

> *Nikikouet sat to one side, holding her daughter and sunk into that deep silence that serves the Ojibwa woman as tears do a French woman. Jean stood by the fire and informed me that he will become a Christian and do the deed instead of me, for he knows the woods about that area better than any of the tribe. This was his firm decision, from which he would not be dissuaded.*

"I wonder how hard Fr. Thomas tried to dissuade him," Dr. Harris mused.

"Probably not too hard," Gerald said. "Though not out of concern for his own skin. Think about it: Jean would represent another convert, a 100% increase in his adult conversion rate with the tribe. These frontline missionaries had to take what they could get." He turned to the last page. "Here we see his final entry for this set of pages. It's a few days later, and Fr. Thomas is lamenting the scant instruction he's able to give Jean: just a few basics on the Sacraments he'll be receiving, the Creed, and the Paternoster."

"Paternoster?" asked Pete.

"The Our Father – the basic prayer of the Christian faith," Gerald explained. "Hmm – seems that one concession Fr. Thomas was able to wring out of Jean was marrying Nikikouet in the Christian rite, which would legitimize their children in the eyes of the Church. Apparently, this influenced where the baptism would take place – I'm not sure why. Toward the bottom of the page we see the Latin inscription with the date and place of baptism, followed by the record of Christian marriage between Jean and Nikikouet, with the names of their children. After the Latin is one brief entry: *Light, cold rain all day. Nikikouet made me a bitter potion to help with the cough that has been troubling me. Plan to depart in the morning.*

"'Depart'? Depart where?" said Pete.

"Not sure," Gerald said with a shrug. "Certainly somewhere to do with the empty darkness. It's certain there was a lot of discussion going on within the tribe that Fr. Thomas didn't record in his journal, either because he didn't have time or space, or because his focus was elsewhere. But we've reached the end of the translated pages for now. We'll have to wait for the next set to learn their destination, and where and when they depart."

Assault

Monday morning Jason received a message from Ethan that the Selfridge people wanted to meet soonest; apparently they had some major developments to report. Jason had him set up a meeting in Port Huron for 11:00 a.m. Ethan suggested inviting a couple of the officers in charge of the Domestic Terror Division forces, since they'd be the ones coordinating the field activities. Jason okayed that and headed down to Port Huron.

Major Collins and his staffer were set up and ready when Jason arrived. Ethan was seated with a man and a woman, both in fatigues, who were introduced as Captain Katy Touma and First Lieutenant Craig Nealson of the DTD. Jason waved the meeting to order, and Sergeant Danvers gave an overview of how they'd been using the two addresses to clarify the existing overflight analysis. This had produced a set of points of interest, but with relatively low confidence probabilities.

"However," Danvers explained as she projected a map of the region onto the wall. "Later last week we did some educated guessing about a few more potential addresses. We fed these into the NSA model, which required some reevaluation of our existing calculations.

"The results surpassed our wildest hopes. The network analysis including the newer addresses – the educated guesses – produced a good number of points of interest with confidence levels over 90%, several over 95%." Abigail pointed to two glowing red spots on the projected map. "These were the initial addresses provided, one near Mayville and another south of Ruth. Better than nothing, but limited utility. When we added in our additional addresses, located here in western St. Clair County, things really opened up." A bright cluster of red dots appeared on the map toward the bottom center, followed by a busy network of dots and lines of varying brightness blossoming all across the map. Several dozen bright red dots stood out, connected to other dots by bright red lines. The glowing indicators nearly covered the region, from the farthest northern tip down to I-69, and from Lake Huron in the east over to I-75.

"Keep in mind," Abigail warned. "That these are all potential points of interest, including those with probabilities down under 50%, which are probably useless. But even if we thin those out," she clicked a controller and the dimmer dots and lines vanished, leaving only the brighter dots, "that still leaves us with a good number of viable sites to work with."

"Do we have a list of these sites?" Lieutenant Nealson asked.

"All the data are in the presentation files on your devices, both in list format and geospatially mapped," Abigail confirmed.

Touma and Nealson looked excited, and were talking rapidly with Ethan in low tones.

"So, just to be clear," Jason interjected. "Based on the addresses we have, or are estimating, this is the computer model's best guess as to where the other nodes in the terrorist network are?"

Collins and Danvers gave each other cautious looks before Abigail responded carefully, "It's best to say that based on analysis of traffic patterns involving these addresses, we've identified probable points of interest to the network participants. Some might be where these hidden people are located. Some might be coordination centers or supply depots. Some might be everybody's favorite coffee shop. Some might be total mistakes. But based on the best data we have, which is the addresses and observed traffic, these should be good starting points."

"Hell, that's good enough for us!" Nealson said with a fierce grin, then turned to Ethan. "So, this is what we can use as the basis for our assault plan?"

Ethan looked embarrassed and turned to Jason, who spread his hands.

"I'm not sure about assault, but these spots look like good places to start with the investigation," Jason said. "Go ahead and draw up a plan and timetable. Is there anything else you aerial folk have for us?"

"Well," Collins replied, "We should probably be included in the tactical planning, to coordinate surveillance and support for the ground forces, but we can probably do that offline."

"Good idea, Major," Touma said. "They've given us temporary offices down the hall. You could join us there, if you have the time."

"Sure, unless you have anything further?" Collins turned to Jason, who shook his head. "Good, then. Danvers can stay to address any intelligence questions."

"Good job, Major!" Jason said.

"Happy to help, sir," Collins replied smugly. Jason noticed that Sergeant Danvers threw a sharp look in the major's direction as he headed for the door.

"Hot damn!" Nealson muttered to Touma as they rose to go. "Time to kick a few and take a few!"

A little alarmed by this, Jason called out, "I want to approve those plans before anyone executes anything!" This garnered nods and waves from the officers as they bundled out of the room. Ethan accompanied them, which mystified Jason, but since he couldn't think of anything he wanted Ethan for, he didn't object.

This exodus left Jason alone in the room with Sergeant Danvers, but this didn't last long. As Jason was preparing to ask some minor question, another door opened and agents Sanderson and Harris came in.

"Sorry we're late," Sanderson said. "Did we miss anything?"

"Just some stuff that doesn't concern you," Jason explained. "Any developments?"

"Only this," Sanderson handed Jason a piece of paper with some details scrawled on it. "The owner of that purse was Frieda Pelton, seventy-four, married for five years in her thirties, divorced, never remarried, no children. Lived in Flint most of her life, on and off public assistance, employed sporadically. Moved to the Vassar area, north of Flint, about fifteen years ago. Started to draw Social Security at sixty seven, kept working at low-wage jobs, primarily at a cleaning service out of Caro.

"About three years ago she vanished. A trust was set up in her name to receive Social Security payments, but she disappeared. Any correspondence went through the executor of her trust, a lawyer in Lapeer. She didn't even file taxes because her income was too low.

"Just about three weeks ago she called an assisted living facility outside Caro to book a contract. The following weekend she moved in, helped by 'some friends', as the facility owners put it – no names or details. She promptly made an appointment with her old cardiologist. No credit cards, checking and savings accounts in the name of her trust, no driver's license, expired state ID with the address of record being her lawyer's office."

"So," Jason mused. "A typical OPEL, who'd been hiding for several years."

"A what?" Sanderson asked.

"Never mind. No hint as to why she reappeared just now?"

"Nothing documentary. Given the speed with which she made the cardiologist appointment, I suspect that she was looking for medical care. But that's just a guess."

Yeah, thought Jason, that didn't work out too well. But he said, "Thanks, guys. Anything more on that woman who was killed in the blast?"

"Just the basics: parents divorced, father lives alone and works as a staff accountant at a firm in Columbus, Ohio; mother remarried and living near Atlanta, no siblings, no friends, never married, no assets except an older car. Moved around with her parents in her younger years, attended high school and college in Port Huron, stuck around when her parents divorced and moved away, got a job at the hospital. About as vanilla as it gets. Want us to keep looking?"

"No, thanks."

"Anything else?" Sanderson asked.

"Not right now," Jason said. He wrapped up and headed for his car, wondering whether he should hunt down Ethan and the officers. But he didn't know what he'd ask them, and participating in detailed technical planning of that sort didn't interest him. Well, he'd told them they had to come to him for approval before taking any action, so he'd see any end results at least. He turned north toward Sandusky to attend to the day's tasks.

The next couple of days passed quietly for Jason, which was fine by him. He caught up on his write-ups and messages and status reports. He didn't hear much from the HHS people, since his contribution to their effort had pretty much concluded, but they did drop him a line from time to time to thank him and inform him that the initiative was proceeding well. There had been no further green-tagged parties since the first two, though Jason was assured he was still on the notify list.

As far as his own sphere of responsibilities was concerned, Jason was hearing very little directly. He was being copied on numerous messages, most of which were in either intricate legalese or highly technical paramilitary Field Op jargon, and none of which required any decisions from him – or, at least he hoped not. Some of the messages left him confused, seeming to allude to discussions which he couldn't remember having or decisions that couldn't have yet been made. His e-mails to Ethan regarding these either went unanswered or got quick responses assuring him that he'd misunderstood, and that things were proceeding apace. Jason began to wonder just how long this planning would take, and how much of it could be conducted remotely, and whether he'd need to convene another meeting in Port Huron or Selfridge just to get everyone in the same room at once. He decided to give it another couple of days. Hopefully they were getting close to the final presentation that he could either sign off on or send back for further work.

On Monday evening Jason rang up Cassie for a video chat, which went surprisingly well. Her stepbrother Zach was over visiting, which kept Cassie on reasonably mature behavior. When another call pulled Cassie away for a while, Jason and Zach held a lengthy conversation on a wide variety of topics. Jason got his contact information and resolved to get in touch with him once he returned – Zach seemed like a friendly and levelheaded guy.

Despite sensing that he was a bit out of one or more planning loops, Jason appreciated the days to work by himself, partly because he could take breaks whenever he wished. These usually found him strolling down to the courthouse lawn to drink coffee and look around. He tried to tell himself that he wasn't looking for a red-haired woman or a white van, neither of which he saw. He tried to assure himself that he was just enjoying the warm spring air and fresh green all around. But part of his mind kept gnawing on the fact that if a woman they "knew" was dead was actually alive, that cast everything into question. It unsettled him – not enough to cause him to put the brakes on the aggressive planning, but enough to wonder if he should, at least until they learned more. But how could he explain such a move? So he let the planning continue, reassuring himself that he'd have to give final approval to any plans before execution, which gave him time to stall and think.

Or so he thought.

Until Wednesday.

*   *   *

Well before dawn on Wednesday a small fleet of unmanned aircraft launched from the Selfridge airfield and headed north. These were observation drones, and they were the limiting factor in the evolution. It had been decided that every strike team would have close observation support, and since there were only fourteen drones available, that restricted the number of teams. Three of the newest models, with the best optics and longest duration, were sent to loiter over the locations with the highest levels of confidence – the three sites for which they had addresses. These would eventually be hit as well, but the plan was to take them last. As the strikes progressed, word was sure to get around. If the known sites were control or coordination facilities, the assault coordinators wanted to observe responsive activity before moving in.

About an hour after the observation drones launched, a smaller fleet of drones lifted from the runways. There were only six of these, and they were larger and heavier than the observation models. They looked sleek and deadly as their wings knifed through the morning air. They had optical capabilities, but their main features today were much more lethal. These were deployed as secondary support, distributed across the six areas into which the region had been divided. They would fly at higher altitudes, ready to be called upon if needed. Their heavier payload restricted their in-theater time to four active hours, but that should be plenty.

The plan called for this operation to be wrapped up well before then.

*   *   *

Isaac Bailey felt downright grown-up as he led his younger brother Andrew out to the goat barn for the morning milking. After all, it had been Dad who'd taken Isaac out when he was just six, to learn the basics of managing the goat herd. Now Andrew was six, and Dad had entrusted Isaac with teaching him how to do the feeding and milking.

"Come on, now, stay close," Isaac encouraged Andrew, who was lagging a little behind. They were taking the side path, under the row of pines, partly to avoid drenching their trousers in the thick dew on the grass that lined the meadow path and partly because Isaac was more consciously trying to mimic the habit his parents observed of keeping under cover whenever possible.

"When will we get there?" Andrew whined. Isaac said nothing, remembering Dad's admonition to have patience with his brother. Isaac tried to recall what it had been like when Dad had first taken him out, and how he'd had to face his fears of the familiar yet alarming animals. At age six, Isaac had still been skittish of how pushy and jumpy goats could be, and of their eerie square pupils. Now all that was familiar to him, and he could push his way through them and shoulder them aside when they came crowding about, and even shove and drag them to where he wanted them. Dad had shown him all that, and had been patient with his fears. Now it was Isaac's turn to be patient with Andrew.

"Here we are," Isaac announced as they got to the barn gate. The goats were already crowded on the other side, jostling and butting one another. They knew what morning visitors meant, and were anxious for breakfast. As Isaac unhooked the gate, Andrew hung back, his eyes wary. "Just push into them, see?" Isaac demonstrated. "They get out of the way. Come on in, don't be scared. Always remember to latch the gate behind you. Like this, see? Okay, now you try it." Isaac shoved a nosy goat aside with exaggerated firmness, mostly to reassure Andrew that they could take a little rough handling. Andrew latched the gate and followed Isaac with more confidence.

In the kitchen, Maureen Bailey was just setting the waffles on the table. Jack was upstairs helping Mrs. Gauss to the bathroom while Catherine was bouncing in her high chair. Maureen gave Catherine the edge of a waffle to pacify her. Liz was sitting beside little Rose in the living room, which was a service but not so necessary now that the baby was asleep again. Of course, Liz took every opportunity to hang out near baby Rose.

"Liz, breakfast is almost on – you can leave her for now," Maureen called. Then she cocked her head at what sounded like heavy tires crunching on the gravel drive outside.

"Jack?" Maureen called up the stairs as she stepped toward the window. "Were the evacuation vehicles supposed to come today? Because we're not anywhere near ready."

"Not until day after tomorrow," her husband's voice came back.

"Then why – oh!" Maureen was reaching to part the curtain when a black-clad figure dashed past the window. The implications of this clutched her heart in an icy grip. "Jack! Trouble! Liz! Get in here and get Catherine!" She almost collided with her daughter as she dashed to the crib in the living room.

"Mom, what –" Liz began, but Maureen cut her off.

"Just do it!"

Out in the barn, Isaac chanced to look up while he was pouring food into a trough. He had a clear view of the house, and his brow furrowed at the sight of the two large, black trucks in the drive. He saw dark figures darting from the trucks toward the house.

Dark figures carrying rifles.

Isaac dropped the bucket and ducked behind a stack of bales, hooking Andrew's arm and pulling him close.

"Isaac, what –"

"Hush!" Isaac said sharply. His mouth was dry and his hands were shaking. He knew what those trucks meant. Dad had talked to him about why Mrs. Gauss lived with them, about why so many of their supplies were delivered, about why they lived such quiet and secluded lives. Dad had explained how what they were doing was difficult and possibly dangerous, but they had to do it to protect people like Mrs. Gauss. Dad had warned him that the day might come when he would need to be brave, because things might happen.

It looked like things were happening.

Isaac peered around the bale, his heart hammering. He didn't feel at all brave – he felt weak and sick, but he had to take care of Andrew. He could see three men in dark clothing up against the outside of the house in different places – one at the back, one by the kitchen door, and one by the living room window. All were crouched low, as if trying to hide. Suddenly the man by the living room window made a quick movement with his arm, and one of the side windows smashed. A light wisp of smoke hung near him, then all the windows shattered as a bright flash and loud boom split the morning air. Shrieks and screams followed, and the man by the kitchen door kicked it open and pointed the gun at the opening.

"Oh no, oh no," Isaac cried, tears streaming down his cheeks.

"What is it, Zak? What's going on?" Andrew tried to push around him, but Isaac shoved him back.

"We need to stay out of sight, Andrew," Isaac insisted. "Hush!"

"But I want to look!"

"You can't look! It's dangerous!"

"But you're looking!"

"Hush!" Isaac crouched low, pushing Andrew further back and down lower. Instinctively Isaac understood that lower was better, and from lower down he could see through the bars of the goat gate. Now many men were moving around the house, six or seven of them, all carrying rifles and wearing black clothes and some kind of helmets. The kitchen door was standing open but all Isaac could see through it was white smoke. Was the house on fire? But no – two more men dashed through the door into the smoke.

"No, no, no, no," Isaac moaned as figures started to come through the smoke and out the kitchen door, jerkily and clumsily as if being pushed. There came Liz, clutching a howling Catherine. Isaac thought he saw blood streaks on their faces. Them Mom stumbled out the door, bent low over a limp form in her arms. Oh, no! Not little Rose!

"Mama!" Andrew cried, and Isaac realized he'd crawled around so he could see around Isaac.

"Hush!" Isaac said, roughly shoving him back. "They'll hear us!"

"But...but *Mama*!" Andrew sobbed, struggling against Isaac's hold.

"Shh, Andrew," Isaac hugged his brother, trying to console him. "We can't let them hear us!" His curiosity overcame his shock and grief, and he turned to watch the horrible scene. It looked like little Rose had been strapped to a board of some type, and someone was looking her over while Mom stood near, with one of the black-clad men standing at Mom's shoulder. Another man stood over Liz and Catherine where they clung to one another sobbing. Then there was some noise and fuss at the back door, and suddenly Dad stumbled through the smoke, his hands cuffed behind him. Right behind him came one of the black-clad men, who pushed Dad roughly with his rifle. Dad stumbled and fell facedown on the drive, and Mom shrieked and tried to run to him, but was grabbed by the man standing beside her. Then two more men emerged from the kitchen door, dragging between them a slightly struggling Mrs. Gauss. She looked small and weak beside them, her wispy white hair all messed up. But the two men shoved and yanked her recklessly, causing her to stumble and nearly fall. Dad yelled something from where he knelt in the gravel, and the man standing over him clubbed him savagely with his rifle butt, sending him sprawling. Again Mom cried out and tried to run to him, and was again pulled back, this time to be slammed up against the side of the truck.

"Mama! Daddy!" Andrew cried at Isaac's elbow, and lurched forward as if to run to them. Isaac pulled him back and sat down behind the bales, hugging him tight. Andrew sobbed and struggled, but Isaac held him firmly.

"We can't go out there. We can't, Andrew," Isaac choked against his own tears. He sympathized fiercely with his brother. Had it been an option, he would have charged out there himself, knowing it would mean his capture as well, just to be with his family. But he knew that Mom and Dad would want him to stay hidden, to keep himself and Andrew safe. That was his responsibility right now.

"But – Mama!" Andrew howled, struggling harder.

"Shh, Andrew, or they'll hear us!"

Now there was renewed screaming coming from the direction of the house, high pitched and panicked, so Isaac bent around to see what was happening. Mom and Dad were being forced into one truck, while men pulled Liz and Catherine and Mrs. Gauss toward a different truck. One man was carrying the board onto which baby Rose was strapped, but she didn't appear to be moving.

"Oh no, oh no, oh no," Isaac sobbed some more. The harsh sound of slamming doors cut off the cries.

"Where are they going? Where are they taking them?" Andrew asked, near hysteria.

"I don't know, buddy, I don't know," Isaac moaned. He felt like there was an empty place where his heart should be. He wanted nothing more than to run to some trusted adult, to find shelter and reassurance, to find someone who could fix this terrible mess. But there was nobody – and he was responsible for keeping Andrew safe.

The trucks started their engines and pulled out of the drive, but not all the men left with the trucks. Some stood outside the house, holding their rifles, while others went back inside. Hot panic seized Isaac, burning through his grief. They were still looking! Maybe they knew there should be more of them, and were hunting for the missing ones! Maybe it was only a matter of time before they came to search the barn with their rifles and handcuffs! Isaac looked down to where Andrew lay curled against the bales, sobbing "Mama, Mama, Mama." No matter how scared or sad Isaac felt, he had to protect Andrew. That's what Mom and Dad would want, he knew it.

"Buddy, listen," Isaac shook his brother gently. "We need to get out of here. They may come back here, so we have to go."

"Go where, Zak? Where can we go? We don't know where they're going!"

"No, we don't, buddy, but we have to get to safety ourselves, so they don't catch us. C'mon, let's crawl to the back door." Isaac still felt like he had a huge, aching hollow spot inside, but having a plan of action distracted him. The boys crawled across the dirty, straw-strewn floor toward the rear of the barn. Isaac was already thinking of a path which would take them out the back of their property while keeping them mostly under cover. They could keep low and make their way to the drain, and then follow that to the windbreak, and take that over to Mrs. Parker's house. Surely Mrs. Parker would help them. The goats would have to wait.

Now that activity was keeping his grief and panic at bay, Isaac's mind could engage the questions that plagued him: What had just happened? And why?

*   *   *

At the home of Terry and Julie Mills, just outside of North Branch, the strike was swift and clean. Terry had just finished morning prayers, and was pouring himself another cup of coffee before heading upstairs to rouse Casey for the day's studies. Julie and Mrs. Fowler could sleep a little longer. He didn't hear the tires in the driveway or the agents creeping into position around the house. The first clue he got was the flash-bang grenade smashing through the kitchen window. He turned to see the smoking, hissing thing bouncing on the floor, and didn't even have time to react before it detonated in a blinding, thunderous flare. Terry was blinded and deafened, and the coffee pot smashed in his hand, splashing scalding liquid down his front. Crying in shock and pain, he stumbled backward and tripped over one of the dining room chairs. His head came down hard on the edge of the table and he fell to the floor unconscious.

The Domestic Terror agents found cleaning up that site to be easier than expected.

*　　　*　　　*

Just outside Melvin, Al Becker was finishing his morning rounds of the property. He'd checked the garage and outbuildings for varmints, and walked around the garden just to keep in practice. Of course there wasn't anything in the ground just yet, but once there was, the damned deer would come around to chew it off as soon as it sprouted. Gary and Olivia had repeatedly assured him that his morning and evening property patrols weren't necessary, but dammit, a man felt like he needed to be contributing even a little, that he wasn't just dead weight.

Al was just about to head inside for a little breakfast when the trucks pulled up the drive. What the hell? Who were these people, so early in the morning? Had to be some kind of contractors, maybe called by the township about that ditch issue they'd been going round and round with Gary about. Who the hell did they think they were, pulling right in like that without so much as a knock on the door? Completely blocking the drive, too! Grumbling and cursing, Al reached inside the door and took down the .410 that hung there, which he kept loaded with bird shot to drive the raccoons away from the garbage cans. He'd show them. He'd take out a windshield if he had to.

"Hey!" Al blustered, waving the shotgun and walking toward the trucks. "Hey, there! You get outta that drive, y'hear?"

Sergeant Tonge had just been about to exit the vehicle when he saw Al coming. "Carlisle," he asked, pointing at the old man. "Does that look like a weapon to you?"

"Sure as hell does, Sarge," Private Carlisle confirmed.

Tonge wasted no time, but touched the button on his headset. "This is Team Seven, Team Seven. Encountering armed resistance. Request aerial intervention."

"Roger, Team Seven, confirming that you are encountering armed resistance and request aerial intervention. Are any friendlies exposed?"

"Negative, all under shelter."

Down in the command center at Selfridge, Sergeant Danvers was monitoring the video stream from the drone overhead of Team Seven's position. She turned to where Major Collins sat surveying his staff.

"Sir, Team Seven reports armed resistance and requests aerial intervention in accord with Threat Level Three conditions. We have video confirmation of armed resistance. Request authorization for weapons loose and active response."

Yes! Collins had been waiting years for this. "Authorize weapons loose. Respond at your discretion."

Danvers turned back to the console and keyed some commands. The armed backup drone was nearby – it would take less than a minute to vector it into range. She issued the preparatory commands while the drone moved into position. There – coordinates all locked in. Just coming into range…now. She tapped her keyboard to send the command.

Al was still standing in the driveway, holding the .410 and staring down the black trucks. He had to be scaring them – they weren't even coming out of their cabs. Good. Maybe they'd just go away.

The side door of the house opened, and Gary's voice called out. "Whatcha doing out there, Al?"

Al was just going to explain about the trucks when he heard a noise that sounded like a cross between a whistle and a shriek. He never heard the blast that took out the house, killing him along with Gary, Olivia, Jeffrey, Madeline, and little Tony.

Abandonment

Teresa had been working hard from before dawn to well after nightfall. She wasn't consciously avoiding sleep, but there was a part of her that shied away from turning in. It wasn't that she feared the ominous and threatening visions – those, she could deal with. But the prospect of experiencing that ecstasy only to lose it again was more than she could bear. She was still mourning the first time.

But sleep would come for her nonetheless, sometimes right where she was sitting. Thankfully it brought with it no dreams of any sort, enabling her to rise somewhat rested and return to her work. The sisters were gracious and respectful, working with her cordially but giving her time and space to grieve.

This night, however, a vision came. It was not threefold as most of the others had been. Teresa found herself standing in the bright open space, surrounded by the milky opalescence she'd seen before. The pedestal stood a short distance before her. This time, to her delight and amazement, she was wearing a beautiful dress. She didn't remember how she'd been clad in her other dreams, but this dress was impossible to miss. It was a long, graceful white gown with simple lines but embellished with insets of satin and delicate lace. It was light and comfortable and fitted like it had been tailored. Teresa turned this way and that, delighting in the quiet swishing of the fabric as she moved. Slowly the truth dawned on her.

This was a bridal gown.

Awed and a little frightened at what this might mean, she approached the pedestal, pleased by how gracefully she moved in the dress. As she drew near the now-familiar tableau, she was again smitten by the simple, elegant beauty of the bouquet and veil. Looking more closely at the veil, she noticed that the lace pattern was the same as the trim on her gown. Her eyes widening, she gently lifted the veil to examine it more closely. There was no mistaking it – the pattern matched down to the smallest detail. This was the veil that went with this gown.

"Teresa," came the voice, not loud, but soft and heavy like thick velvet draping.

"Sir?" Teresa replied, turning toward where the voice had seemed to come from.

"They are yours. Take them and come. Today is the day."

A thousand protests swarmed in Teresa's mind. Hers? Take them? But the weight of the voice lay upon her, and it had not been permission, but command. With trembling fingers she lifted the veil to her head. The cap fit like it had been measured for her, and the veiling fell into place over her face and across her shoulders. Picking up the bouquet, she lifted her chin and began walking toward the voice.

Teresa's eyes opened, but there was no break, no disruption of continuity. The Teresa in that gown and veil, obeying the voice that had summoned her, was the same Teresa who lay here in her bunk. It was not like she had come out of that reality and back into this one; she was living that reality and this at the same time. In fact, the Teresa in the gown, answering and obedient, dwelt in a truer, firmer reality than the Teresa lying in the chill dark listening to Sister Elizabeth breathing quietly in the upper bunk.

It was time to be up and on her way. Teresa checked her phone – 5:00 a.m. She slipped from her bed and into the bathroom – a quick shower would suffice. Afterward she began to give a little extra attention to her hair, then stayed her hand. It wasn't these appearances that mattered. She eased quietly into her room and selected her usual simple white blouse and skirt. Clean and plain was the order of the day. Easing on her light jacket and slipping her phone into her pocket, she glanced at where Sister Elizabeth lay peacefully. Teresa gently stroked the mattress by her head, praying for peace and tranquil sleep for her. Teresa would miss her; she would miss them all. But she would never lose them.

Sister Joseph Marie was just straightening her veil when the quiet knock came at her door. Opening it, she saw Teresa dressed for outdoors.

"Yes?"

"Sister Joseph," Teresa announced. "I'm leaving."

"Leaving?"

"Yes. I have been summoned, and I have to go."

At this unexpected answer, Sister Joseph looked more closely at the young woman. Superficially there seemed to be nothing unusual about her – the same workaday outfit, simply arranged hair, no makeup. But this morning she seemed to be walking in a lightness, an effervescence that Sister Joseph had never before seen. Her eyes seemed to shine and her smile, which was seen too seldom, came readily to her lips.

"Summoned?"

"Yes. My Bridegroom has called me, and I must go to Him." Teresa's smile was brilliant now, and she seemed to be struggling to keep her feet still.

Sister Joseph extended both her hands, and Teresa took them. "I've suspected this day would come. I knew you were never ours, that we were only your home for a time."

"And a wonderful home you have been," Teresa said. "I thank you for all your kindness and assistance, and am sorry for any ways I may have taxed you or the other sisters."

"You have been more than a blessing, and a tremendous help," Sister Joseph assured her.

"Please tell all my sisters how much I love them and how much they mean to me. I will miss them, and I would say that I will be sad without them, except that I don't think I will. How could I be, when I am going to meet my Groom?"

"None of us would have it any other way. When the Groom calls, you must answer."

Teresa leaned forward and gave Sister Joseph a tender kiss on her cheek. "That is from Him. He will give you everything you need when it is asked of you. Your call will come soon."

"I'm sure it will. Now go, with our blessing and best wishes," Sister Joseph gave her a quick embrace, and then Teresa passed out of the doors of St. Anne's and into the dark predawn, where the sun was just lightening the eastern horizon. The stars were a blaze of glory across the heavens, and though the breeze was chill, it held the promise of warmth once the sun's rays came to touch the fields.

*   *   *

Luke awakened abruptly, still tired but knowing that he wouldn't be able to sleep any more. It was dark and the house was quiet. His phone told him it was 5:00 a.m., which got him thinking – he had time to execute a plan he'd fallen asleep pondering.

As much as he loved his family, part of him dreaded what dawn would bring. Linda would pester him about contacting Gil, while Kent would bluster indignantly on his behalf. If he didn't contact Gil, Linda would do it, and would browbeat Gil into making provisions for him. Gil would give in, and set aside other pressing concerns to make plans for Luke, mostly to get Linda off his back. Everybody would be gracious and accommodating, but the truth is that he'd be just one more hassle, one more problem to burden Gil and everyone else.

But not if he moved now.

If Luke slipped away before anyone was awake, he wouldn't be around for the embarrassment of having people make a fuss over him, and he wouldn't be a trouble to anyone. He could take care of himself. He didn't need people going to bat for him. His mind made up, he slipped out of bed, grabbed his travel kit, and headed quietly for the bathroom. He'd been sleeping in the same room as Jude, who was insensate in the sleep of the young. In ten minutes, Luke had washed and dressed and was quietly making his way downstairs. He gathered his gear and slipped out into the cool morning. He packed the ATV and turned down the trail. Looking over his shoulder, he was grateful to see no lights on in the house. He breathed a quiet farewell to the family he loved so much as he slipped away.

Luke's main problem was that he didn't know exactly where he was going. He'd done everything he'd been assigned yesterday, and didn't have any rounds to do because the ranches were all being evacuated. He could head back toward Rivendell, but the trip would take him most of the day, so by the time he got there it would be vacant. On a whim he turned northwest, toward Bay Port, where some trails he knew would take him near the beach. He often found it calming to linger near the water.

Luke hadn't been on the trail for half an hour when his phone rang. It was Gil. Luke sighed – certainly some other assignment. He thumbed the button to route the call to voice mail. Maybe he'd check it later. Right now, he had too much to think about. Sure enough, within five minutes the phone chimed again, this time with a message from Gil: "Please call ASAP." Luke dismissed that as well. He felt weary and overtaxed, unable to cope with more demands. Not ten more minutes had passed before his phone rang again. This time it was Linda, and Luke knew what had happened: the Schaeffer family had awakened, his absence had been noted, and now Linda was calling to try to talk him into returning or calling Gil or something. Luke sighed in exasperation – why was everyone trying to push him around and meddle in his life? He had some critical decisions to make! Impulsively he turned his phone off and tucked it away. Let them talk to the voice mail until he was ready to pick up the messages.

The sun was just rising as he came to the water's edge. The trail took him to a secluded spot where a break in the trees let him down to the beach along Saginaw Bay. The shore was wild and desolate, as well as a bit chilly – the air was warming, but winter's touch still lingered on the water. Luke strolled along, listening to the birds among the reeds cry to each other and thinking about his life.

It had seemed like such a great idea two and a half years ago. Take the inconveniently "dead" people and conceal them in a secret world among the other hidden ones. They could live undetected and undisturbed by hostile parties, and could even be useful in their exile. Such a tidy and elegant solution! Luke had embraced it enthusiastically, happy to leave behind his lonely life and immerse himself in this new, accepting community.

But nobody had considered what would happen if the hidden ones had to flee and the secret world had to be dismantled. What would happen to the "dead" people then? Where could they hide when all the hiding places were gone? What could he do now? It wasn't like he could just drop into an employment office and start submitting applications. He was officially dead, with a death certificate and everything! That was the reason for all the skulking and secrecy of the past couple of years – if he were to be discovered, it could endanger the entire operation!

But what, Luke mused, if there was no longer an operation to endanger? With everything shut down and everyone fled, would it matter so much if he were to turn up again? Sure, there would be difficult questions, but he could think up some story. Maybe he could feign amnesia. After all, it wasn't like getting killed was a crime. What could anyone do to him, really?

So Luke pondered as he walked alone by the edge of the water, watching the flocks of fowl rising from the water to circle in the morning sky and then settle back among the reeds.

*   *   *

The dire reports were flooding in to Gil so quickly that he was struggling to keep track of everything. He was missing the communications and coordination setup they'd had at Rivendell, with the giant map of the region on the wall and the ample communications and computing resources. Here at the evacuation site just outside of Yale they had three phones and a couple of tablets. Fitz would soon be arriving with more resources, and Shelly and Steve were handling what they could within their areas, but it was still a nightmare.

Gil was numb with shock. At right about dawn, their phones had gone off with emergency alerts from a couple of the ranches. They'd called back for further details, but nobody had answered. They'd tried remotely activating the phones to use as monitors, but with limited success. One hadn't responded at all, and the other had shown no video but the audio had been a terrifying mix of

422

screams, thumps, and distant shouting. This had been enough for them to send out a general alarm, requesting all ranches to check in. The results of this had been confusing, since the ranches were still in a state of flux, with many recently abandoned or in the process of evacuating. Once the dust had settled, there were between six and ten sites about which there was some question. They'd scrambled to find people to drive past the suspect sites. Some of the sites had indeed been evacuated, but from others had come ominous reports of black vehicles, armed troops, and raided houses. This had caused them to trigger a full SCRAM of all the ranches, and now it was a race against the timetable of an unknown number of unknown enemies, rushing to evacuate what ranches they could before more people were taken or killed.

It was Gil himself who ended up calling the Schaeffers to warn them to evacuate immediately. Fortunately, he got Linda – Kent still had a tendency to be high-strung about emergency situations. Gil briefed Linda on what they knew and advised them to pack up and get out, but to stay in touch for further instructions. As he was getting ready to ring off, Linda asked, "Have you heard from Luke?"

"Luke?" Gil replied. "No, I haven't. I've called him three times and messaged him twice, with no response. I haven't heard from him since he shut down Beaversdam yesterday morning."

"He spent much of yesterday and last night here with us," Linda said. "But he'd left by the time we got up this morning. I've no idea where he went. I've called him twice, but have only gotten his voice mail."

"Oh, goodness," Gil groaned. "I hope he's all right."

"I doubt he's been arrested, if that's your fear. But last night he was indicating that he was feeling forgotten, and that nobody was considering the effect all these changes would have on his life."

"What?" Gil blustered. "That's ridiculous! Forget Luke? How could we forget Luke?"

"I said he was *feeling* forgotten," Linda emphasized. "He had no idea what he was going to do once all the ranches were evacuated."

"But...I have a plan for him right here! I have it all worked out!"

"Did you ever take the time to discuss this plan with him?" Linda asked sharply.

"Well," Gil paused. "I...I guess not. I meant to on Monday, but things were getting right out of hand, and he headed off before I had a chance. It was one of the things I was going to talk to him about this morning, except I haven't been able to reach him, and then everything hit the fan."

"So, you mean –" Linda began hotly, then paused before resuming in a slightly calmer voice. "All right. What's done, or not, is done. We can hope he's in no trouble, and can keep trying to reach him. But if I know Luke, when he's convinced he's on his own, he tends to make decisions based on his own perceptions and priorities without consulting anyone." She sighed. "We can only pray he's safe, and doesn't do anything rash before someone gets in touch with him."

"Will you keep trying?" Gil pleaded.

"I will," Linda assured him.

"Gil," Janine said sharply at his elbow, a phone at her ear and a panicked look on her face, "nobody's answering at St. Anne's."

*   *   *

"Are you sure? You've only been here a couple of days."

"I'm sure, Otto," Michael Peterson replied. They were standing on the Fletcher's front porch in the morning sunshine. It looked like the start of a beautiful May day. Michael was holding his small suitcase and shaking Otto's hand. "I appreciate your hospitality, but I've other places I need to be. Convey my thanks and love to Joan, if you will."

"Certainly, Mike," Otto said. "Best of luck and Godspeed."

With that Mike got in the car, giving all the appearance of settling in for a long drive. Though the drive itself would be short, Mike suspected the journey could be longer.

Teresa was in bliss. She was wandering the country roads, delighting in the scents of the growing plants and the caress of the sun upon her skin. By midmorning it had warmed up enough that she no longer needed her jacket, so she'd taken it off. After carrying it for a few miles, she'd realized that she had no reason to do so, and had left it hanging on a fencepost. Now she traveled with just the clothes on her back and her phone in her pocket, though she kept that turned off. She needed no phone right now. Her only desire was to be right where she was, experiencing what she was experiencing.

Of course, she was "here" in a manner she'd never been before, for she was also "there", wherever it was that Teresa the Bride was proceeding toward her Groom, obeying the summons. She was at the same time both there and here, yet somehow being there made her more completely here.

So Teresa danced along the dusty dirt roads, reveling in the breeze and sunshine, heading nowhere in particular and not concerned about it. She'd stop for random periods to watch the flow of water through a drain tug at the reeds, or turn off the road to stroll along the edge of a freshly plowed field just to relish the scent. She knew she had a destination, but did not fret about arriving. She would be brought there in good time. Every once in a while, she had a dim sense of events happening in the distance all around her, events impacting people she loved. She had the impression of carefully laid plans in motion, and parties being maneuvered into place like pieces on a chessboard. At times she was tempted to grow anxious about these events, to wonder if she should be elsewhere or doing something. But then she would calm herself, putting her thoughts back with Teresa the Bride, sure of her steps and her path. Then she could rest in being Simple Teresa, strolling along in the springtime sun, biding her time, living in the moment.

Teresa was not dependent solely upon her feet. A friendly farmer's wife gave her a ride for one long stretch, and the two chatted merrily until they arrived at the town the woman was heading for. There Teresa began walking again, but got no farther than the outskirts of town before a helpful plumber in a rusty pickup with a water heater in the back offered her a lift. He was a kindly old gent, who shared his sandwich and chips with her for lunch. She'd not even considered meals until she began to eat the half sandwich and realized how hungry she was. She devoured the sandwich and chips, finding them the most delicious meal she'd ever had, satisfying her completely. She had the plumber drop her off at an intersection where he was turning east, for she knew, somehow, that her path lay northward and a little west. She ambled along, whiling away the hours, not knowing exactly where she was going or when she would get there, but trusting that everything would come together in due time.

*   *   *

Luke was also frittering away hours, which weighed much more heavily upon him. Leaving the Saginaw Bay shore, he drifted south and east in a random pattern. He paid no attention to his direction of travel; he was gnawing on the question of what he was going to do next.

Evaluated frankly, he seemed in dire, if not desperate, straits. The only resources he had were what he had with him, and that was barely anything – a few gas cards with trivial balances, a bag half-full of contraband medical supplies, his clothes, and an old, trail-worn ATV for which he didn't have the paperwork. He had barely enough to fuel himself and his vehicle for the day. He had nowhere to go when night fell.

Of course, Luke still had his phone, his sole link to the world to which he'd belonged, a world which had now folded up and vanished. He took the phone out every so often, turning it over in his hands. A couple of times he was tempted to cast it away, to pitch it into a river he was passing or drop it into a flooded ditch. He never quite did that, but neither did he turn it on. He didn't want to deal with the inevitable messages and voice mails, requesting him to call, asking him to do things, appealing to him to return. He didn't doubt that once the ranches were completely dismantled and everyone else had been taken care of, they'd cobble together some kind of accommodation for him – probably under pressure from Linda. It would be the same old pattern: Luke the afterthought, Luke the inconvenient detail, Luke the overlooked problem that needed a quick fix. Well, not this time. He wouldn't be any trouble to anyone ever again. He could take care of himself.

The difficulty was, Luke had no idea where to begin. Surely an unexpected reappearance from beyond the grave would evoke some kind of official response, possibly even getting him arrested and charged with some offense. He was sure he could handle that – whatever they'd charge him with couldn't be very serious. But he had no idea how to trigger that response. Walk into his old place of employment, the St. Clair County offices? Show up at a bank or post office? He considered going to his mother's house, but dismissed that idea. He hardly had the resources to get all the way to Upstate New York, and he guessed that his mother wouldn't be happy to have him reenter her life after he'd been written off as dead.

So Luke drifted along as the day wore on, evaluating options and imagining scenarios, resolved to do something but unclear on what it would be, or how to go about doing it.

*   *   *

The atmosphere was still tense around the makeshift communications center where Gil, Janine, Fitz, and a few others were scrambling to collect information, coordinate activity, and resolve last-minute problems. The still-occupied ranches and other sites of interest had been given their instructions and were complying as rapidly as they could, which was a welcome change from the procrastination and foot-dragging they'd encountered before. Nothing like a few casualties to light a fire under people, Gil reflected grimly.

Over the course of the morning a picture of the catastrophe had emerged from direct reports, scraps of online conversations, and eyewitness accounts. At just about dawn, eleven sites had been struck by paramilitary troops in SWAT fashion. No local law enforcement units or any other first responders had been informed, much less involved. When police or others attempted to engage the paramilitary units, they were told it was a Department of Homeland Security Domestic Terror Division operation, and to stand clear. The troops had gone in against the homes heavily armed with aerial support which had, indeed, resulted in one deadly missile strike.

The only silver lining to this calamitous cloud was that of the eleven sites struck, five of them had been vacated, some as recently as the day before. But that still meant five families and their guests had been arrested and taken off to unknown destinations, though Steve had received word that some children from one of the families had eluded capture and were in safe hands. But worst of all had been that the eleventh site had been St. Anne's. Sister Joseph Marie had been warned as part of the general evacuation, and had even managed to send off some of her guests over the past few days, but most of her patients had been too weak or frail to move easily. The gallant sisters had made clear that none of them would bolt for safety until all of their guests were taken care of. Now they were all in custody somewhere.

The pressing question was how these mysterious forces had known where the ranches were. That they had known was beyond question – this had not been a geographic sweep or door-to-door action, but a targeted move against specific addresses synchronized across an entire region. Fitz strongly suspected that the enhanced surveillance they'd been warned of had played a major role, but the presence of an unknown party with a broad mandate and virtually unlimited resources raised the question of what other factors were in play.

The frantic period immediately following the attacks had been under the shadow of threat: where, and when, would the mysterious troops strike next? Surely they weren't engaging all these resources to take out a mere eleven sites, half of them vacant. So, the team of Gil, Fitz, Steve, and their helpers hustled to get the word out and SCRAM the remaining ranches, working in constant dread of when the other shoe would drop. And indeed, it seemed like the next wave was about to unfold when observers reported two more sites being hit about an hour and a half after the initial attacks. Fortunately, both sites had been vacated, though it didn't take long for Fitz to realize that the addresses were of the families where the two vanished guests, Frieda and Willard, had lived. But after those secondary strikes, there had been nothing – no further attacks, no public announcements, no official notifications to local authorities, nothing. The team was certainly grateful for whatever respite they could get, and spent the time resolving minor problems and reestablishing communications with scattered parties. They were slightly encouraged when word began trickling in from the other Farthings of the safe arrival of some of the earlier evacuees. But far too many people were still in the open, and the threat still hung in the air: when would the next wave of strikes come, and where would it hit?

It was just after noon when Gil's phone rang. It was Shelly with a panicked question. "Gil, do you know where Dad is?"

"Dad? Isn't he at–"

"Joan and Otto's, yes, he's supposed to be. But he isn't answering his phone, and Otto says he left there about seven thirty this morning," Shelly replied in a frantic voice. "Nobody's seen or heard from him."

"Did he tell Otto where he was going?" Gil asked.

"No – just that he had other places to be."

Cold fear gripped Gil. Dad vanished? On such a catastrophic morning?

"What's up?" Fitz asked quietly at Gil's elbow.

"Dad's missing," Gil explained quickly. "Headed off about seven thirty, left no details, isn't answering his phone."

"Hmm," Fitz mused for a moment, then asked, "Do you have anyone watching Rivendell?"

Gil turned slowly with wide eyes. "No," he whispered. "I hadn't even thought of it."

"Might want to check it out," Fitz advised. "But be careful. If it's been hit, it may be being watched even if it isn't actively guarded."

"Shelly, do you have anyone you can send over to eyeball Rivendell?" Gil asked. "Very carefully?"

"I'll scare up someone," his sister promised.

The next hour was the most tense Gil had ever known. He sent another message to Luke, and followed up on a hundred details. They had scouts all over the Thumb watching for any troop activity, but none was reported. More accounts of safe arrivals were rolling in, and the last of the ranches that had been struggling was finally evacuated and on their way. Through it all, Gil kept pacing and awaiting word.

Finally Shelly called back. "One of my friends did a drive-by. There were no guards, but she didn't want to risk stopping and getting out. There were no signs of anything that she could see from that distance: no cars, no open doors, no property damage, nothing. She wondered if some of the bushes in the front yard looked a little bent, but couldn't be sure."

"Damn," Gil muttered. Even a minor sign of trouble would have told them something, but instead they were left in suspense.

"My friend is hanging about in the area, if you'd like me to have her go back for a closer look," Shelly offered.

"No, no," Gil said. "Maybe after nightfall, but right now it's still too dangerous. We may yet have more strikes. Give her my thanks – I'll be in touch." He rang off and slammed his fist against the table. "Damn!" First Luke and now Dad, vanishing. Of all the losses on this terrible day, those stung the worst.

*   *   *

Teresa's spirits were still buoyant, but her body was getting a little weary. She'd walked much of the afternoon, enjoying the warmth and sunshine. Basic bodily needs still called for attention, but a little party store had served once, and another time she'd knocked on a farmhouse door and asked for a drink and the use of their facilities. The friendly couple had given her lemonade and some cookies, and they had parted friends. Teresa felt like a songbird, riding the breezes from tree branch to fencepost, finding whatever she needed along the way.

As the afternoon wore on, Teresa's muscles began informing her that she hadn't walked so much in a very long time. She was wondering what to do about this when she spotted a tree just off the road, at the edge of a field, with a broad, soft patch of grass beneath it. How lovely! She wandered over and stretched out beneath the spreading branches, looking up at the leaves just out of their buds. Their light, delicate green in the sunlight was soothing and restful. Busy little birds whirled among the branches, filling the air with their piercing cries. She lay back and closed her eyes.

She awoke rested, though a little thirsty, and stiff from sleeping on the ground. The sun was below the horizon, though the western sky still glowed orange and gold. Overhead the sky was deep blue, fading to black as it stretched east, where brighter stars were visible. The moon, just past full, was rising in the eastern sky.

Teresa's heart was still light with joy, but now she also felt a determination. She had idled through the day, meandering along while others were moved into place and events beyond her influence unfolded. She had been hidden, kept out of sight while other actors in the drama played their roles and paced their appointed steps. Now, as this fateful day drew to a close, it was time for her to come out of hiding and begin moving more decisively to her designated spot.

And, she realized, to begin moving others.

Teresa pulled her phone from her pocket and turned it on. When it came up, she saw that there had been no calls, and only one message, from Sister Joseph Marie. Its wording was as terse as it was ominous: "Do not return." Teresa bowed her head and prayed for her sisters in their hour of trial. They would remain true, she was assured, and earn their own veils.

And now, for her hour of trial. Who to call?

Todd.

Todd? She barely knew Todd.

But she did have his number in her phone, and he was one of the actors that needed moving. But what to say to him? She bowed her head and listened, joining with Teresa the Bride in her obedience. And then, she knew. She called Todd.

"Hello?" came the answer.

"Hi, Todd. It's Teresa, from St. Anne's. Do you remember me?"

"Oh...ah, yeah, sure I remember you. It's been a while. Are you all right? I mean, are you safe? It's been a crazy day!"

"Indeed it has, and it's not over yet. Listen, I need three things from you. Ready?"

"Fire away."

"First, I need you to dump out that beer you're holding, and not to drink any more. You need to be sober."

Todd gulped. "Ah...sure, no problem."

"Second, I need you to get in touch with the Huron County sheriff."

"Sheriff Keller? Sure. Why am I doing that?"

Teresa told him what to pass along to the sheriff. When she was finished, he repeated it back to her for confirmation, then cautioned her.

"He may need more than keys. I think some of that has been welded."

"Then have him bring a cutting torch," Teresa instructed. "Third, I need you to come pick me up."

"Pick you up? Um...sure. Where are you?"

"I've no idea," Teresa laughed.

"Well, then, can you send me your position?" Todd asked, so Teresa keyed the sequence that transmitted the phone's location to Todd. "Okay, that's not far," he assured her. "I can be there in forty minutes."

"Great," Teresa replied. "I'll wait here for you. And, Todd? Dump the beer."

She rang off and pondered her next call. Even from here she could sense the turmoil and confusion. She smiled. Her oldest friend and dearest brother. His confusion was about to end. She keyed his number.

*   *   *

The day had ground on for Luke, drab and oppressive. Now night had come, and he had to do something. He'd dithered and vacillated until he'd finally reached a decision, but now he had to muster the determination to act on it.

Luke had concluded that the most sensible thing for him to do would be to turn himself in to the Lapeer County sheriff. That was the office in whose jurisdiction the blast had happened, and they were the ones who had announced his "death". Even though the Feds had quickly taken over the blast site, it had been the sheriff who had opened the initial investigation, thus it made sense that he should go there and end all this where it had begun. The past couple of years had been a challenging and rewarding chapter in his life, but now that chapter was ending. He would give up being Luke and return to being simply Derek, and accept the consequences of that.

But turning himself in to the sheriff meant going clear down to Lapeer, to the west of town where the jail was. He knew trails that would get him close, but he'd have to park his ATV and walk the last couple of miles. Unless, he thought with grim humor, he wanted to ride the ATV all the way in, and risk getting stopped for riding on a public road. That would also get him to the sheriff's office.

As he'd pondered this course of action through the day, Luke had meandered southward. The truth was, the closer he came to the point of final decision, the more he hesitated. It wasn't that he wanted to hang back – he had nothing to hang back for – but because the move would be irrevocable. Whatever followed, there would be no going back, no saying "just kidding" and vanishing again. This action would be final, and even though he had no choice, the very irreversibility spooked him. He wished he could do nothing at all, but that wasn't an option, so he had continued rambling southward.

As he was approaching the spot where he'd have to turn west toward Lapeer, his phone rang. His phone? Startled, he pulled it from his pocket and saw that the caller was neither Gil nor Linda but Teresa.

Teresa? What on earth? "Hello?" he answered hesitantly.

"Hello, my dear brother. How are you?" came a familiar voice. It was certainly Teresa, but she sounded – how could he put it? – richer? Fuller? More like her?

"I…I'm fine, I guess. It's just that…" Luke trailed off.

"It's just that what?" she asked mischievously.

"Just that I could have sworn I had turned this thing off."

Teresa laughed heartily, sounding more alive than he'd ever heard her. "It is a night of wonder and mystery!" she announced. "But tell me, where are you?"

"Where am I?" Luke was taken aback – he hadn't expected that question. "I'm…I'm a little south of Brown City, west of M-53. Why?"

"Can you make it to Woody End?"

"Woody End?" It was one of several unmanned storage sites and supply depots scattered across the Thumb, located just a few miles northwest of Rivendell. How did Teresa even know about Woody End? "Sure, I could make it to Woody End. It's not the direction I was going, but it's not far. Why?"

"Wonderful. Could you go there and wait? Somebody will be by to pick you up. God bless you, brother. I'll see you shortly."

"Pick me up? Wait, Teresa – what's all –" Luke began, but she had rung off, leaving him staring at the dark screen of his turned-off phone.

What on earth?

Just to be certain, Luke switched the phone on. Sure enough, it went through the start-up cycle – it hadn't been sleeping. When it came up, the screen was flooded with the messages that had been piling up all day. Luke sighed. This was precisely what he'd intended not to do. In fact, he'd planned to ditch his phone before going into the sheriff's office, for obvious reasons. But now that he had it on, he might as well see what was there. He thumbed down through the list of text lines. They were only a few words, parts of the first lines of messages or transcriptions of voice messages. Most of them were from Gil or Linda, with a couple from Fitz, and read like, "Luke, please call when you..." or "When you get this, please..." There had been a steady stream of them rolling in through the day, and he flicked past them all until he came to the last one. It was from Linda, and the transcription read, "Derek, Derek, please come..." His resolved weakened, and he tapped the text line to play the message.

"Derek, Derek, please come back," came Linda's distraught voice, clearly through tears. "Please, please come back. We may have lost Phillip, and it would tear our hearts out to lose you as well. Please come back to us." The message ended, leaving a stunned Luke staring at the screen. His vision started blurring, and he bowed his head to his handlebars and sobbed.

*   *   *

Beneath her tree, Teresa smiled and prepared to make a couple more calls.

Uproot

Jason was just sitting down to breakfast when his tablet chimed. The red band across the top of the screen told him it was an immediate priority, high security message, which puzzled him. At this time of day? He thumbed the biometric pad and saw the face of Chad Collins appear.

"Major Collins?" Jason said, still mystified.

"Hello, Mr. Pelletier," Collins replied in a grave voice, though his expression looked rather satisfied. "Sorry to bother you so early, but I thought you'd want to know immediately. One of the teams encountered armed resistance this morning, and was forced to respond with a missile strike. All of our personnel were under cover and are safe, but the threat was completely destroyed. No survivors."

Jason stared at the screen. What the hell was this? Missile strike? No survivors? "Collins, what are you talking about?"

Collins looked confused. "As part of Operation Uproot. This morning. Most of the site cleanups are proceeding without incident, but at one site the team met with armed resistance and requested aerial intervention. According to standard engagement protocols for Threat Level Three, we responded in force."

"Wait – Operation Uproot? Aerial intervention? What in the hell is all this, Collins?"

Now the major looked thoroughly bewildered. "Operation Uproot kicked off at 0500. You know, what we've been planning since Monday. The troops were in theater and primed for action. You've been in on all of it – I have the messages right here."

Jason's head was spinning. Messages? He'd seen lots of long-winded stuff over the past couple of days, but he didn't remember any – "Wait," he said. "You said 'most of the site cleanups'. How many sites are there?"

"Well, the first wave was fourteen in total, though we're holding off on the final three until the optimal moment. The dawn action hit eleven."

"Eleven sites? Where?"

"All over the Thumb. This was a regional evolution, remember?" Collins answered. Seeing the expression on Jason's face, he continued somewhat defensively. "This was all in the messages. You can't say you didn't see them – hell, you sent many of them!"

"Right now, I can't say what I have or haven't seen," Jason snapped back. "But I had no idea anything was coming down this morning. The last instructions I gave were for you all to draw up a plan for us to go over together before I gave final approval. There's clearly been a major screw-up. Missile strike? What do you mean 'no survivors'? Were there casualties?" He was still struggling to grasp what he was hearing.

"Well, yes, of course there were," Collins seemed shocked that he'd asked. "The team encountered armed resistance, requested support, and we responded."

"How many casualties?"

"None of ours. Of the enemy, six – three adults and three juveniles."

Jason reeled – *juveniles*? "Wait – you fired a missile at a residence with kids in it?"

"It's part of the protocol!" Collins pleaded. "Threat Level Three – immediate threat. Engage proactively if deadly threat perceived. The team met armed resistance."

Jason dimly remembered discussing that threat level business with someone – Ethan, that was who had spoken of that. He needed to get hold of Ethan pronto. "Let me get to the bottom of this," he said to Collins. "In the meantime, I forbid you to fire any more missiles at anything or anyone!"

"You're changing the Threat Level?" Collins protested. "But the deployment plan presumes –"

"I don't care what the damn deployment plan presumes! No more firing! Ground those drones right now or I'll have your ass!"

"Yes, sir," Collins acknowledged, and rang off.

*   *   *

Down at the command center, Sergeant Danvers had overheard most of the high-intensity conversation. Tactfully she turned to her boss.

"Weapons tight, sir?"

"Weapons tight, Sergeant," Collins confirmed glumly. "Recall the birds. Notify OpCom."

"Yes, sir."

*　　　　　*　　　　　*

Back in Sandusky, Jason's pulse was racing as he punched up Ethan. Operation Uproot? Juvenile casualties? When Ethan picked up, he seemed to be in a moderately noisy room with an unusual amount of background activity.

"There you are, chief. I was about to contact you to report–"

"Can that – what the hell is going on? What's this about missile strikes?"

Ethan grimaced. "Yeah, well – bad business, that. But the steps are prescribed in the response protocol, so –"

"Shut up!" Jason barked. "What the hell's all this about a regional evolution? I said I wanted any plans to be explicitly cleared by me before anyone did anything!"

Now it was Ethan's turn to look befuddled, a response that was starting to alarm Jason. "But…you did clear it. I have the message right here."

"You do? When was it sent?"

"Yesterday, just after noon. They had the plan all worked up, and wanted to bring it up to present to you, but you messaged back saying you trusted them and authorized the execution."

Jason's brain raced – yesterday about noon? What had he been doing? Had that been one of those interminable document messages? But no – whatever he'd read, he'd never said or written the words "I authorize". He would have remembered that. "Look – forward me that message, and all others in that thread. In the meantime, I'm countermanding anything anyone thinks I've said.

I'm pulling authorization for this operation and ordering everyone to stand down."

Ethan looked crestfallen. "Pulling the plug on the whole evolution in mid-execution – I don't know if I can do that, chief."

"You'll do it – I'm ordering it!"

"I meant, I don't know if they'll take it from me. You'll probably have to tell them yourself."

"Fine, I'll tell them myself. Patch me through."

Shaking his head, Ethan punched some buttons. The screen blurred and then refocused, showing a young man in some sort of helmet and sunglasses who seemed to be outdoors.

"Area Three TacCom, Lieutenant Simmons," the man said briskly.

Simmons? Jason asked himself, but forged ahead. "Listen, this is Jason Pelletier. There's been a terrible misunderstanding. Cease operations and stand down immediately."

The lieutenant, who had been distracted by some off-screen matters while Jason was talking, suddenly gave him full attention. "Cease operations? Who the hell is this?"

"I'm Jason Pelletier, and I'm in charge of the whole area!" Jason exploded. "Cease operations immediately!"

"Look, buster," Lieutenant Simmons replied bluntly. "I don't know who you are or how you got on this TacNet, but this is an official circuit and we've got stuff going down. Clear this line immediately!" The line went dead, leaving Jason fuming. He started to dial Ethan back, then changed his mind and keyed a different number.

"Major Collins."

"Yeah, Collins, do you know where I can find Nealson or Touma?" Jason asked.

"Sure, they're at OpCom. Let me patch you –"

"No, don't patch me through. Give me the number and I'll key it directly."

"All right, sir," Collins replied, and provided the number. Jason keyed it, fretting at the delay. At last, it was answered by a young woman whom Jason didn't recognize.

"UPROOT OpCom, Corporal Oliver speaking."

"Corporal Oliver, this is Jason Pelletier. Please let me speak to Captain Touma immediately."

"I'm sorry, sir, but Captain Touma is heavily occupied at the moment. I could take a message and have her get back to you at her earliest convenience."

Jason erupted. "Here's your damn message! Get her on this line right now or I'm driving down to fire every one of you!"

The shocked corporal muttered something and stepped away to leave Jason to ponder the emptiness of his threat, since he had no idea where this OpCom was. Shortly Captain Touma came on the line.

"Captain, do you recognize me?"

"Yes, sir, you're Jason Pelletier of DHS DTD."

"Very good. Do you acknowledge that I have plenary authority over all activities related to this investigation, including over you and all your personnel?"

"Why, of course, sir," Touma responded in a surprised tone.

"Then listen clearly: I am ordering you to cease and desist all operations immediately. Halt execution and stand down."

Again the look of bewilderment. "But, sir, we're deep into the plan you authorized –"

"I know what you're in the middle of," Jason cut in. "But there's been a serious miscommunication that I've yet to unravel. In the meantime, a missile strike has killed a family, including three children."

Captain Touma looked saddened, but her tone was defensive. "That was too bad, sir, but our personnel were threatened, and the protocol stipulates –"

"I don't care what the damn protocol stipulates!" Jason barked. "I want no more chances for such misunderstandings until we get this sorted out! Stand down immediately!"

Looking like a child who'd just had her Christmas toys taken away, Touma replied sullenly, "Yes, sir. Be advised that some of our personnel are in exposed positions, and simply walking away may increase their risk. May I suggest an expedited but orderly stand-down that would maximize personnel safety?"

"Very well," Jason acquiesced. "But do it as quickly as possible. And what is the address of the home that was struck by the missile?"

Captain Touma provided it, and Jason rang off. He forced himself to sit back and breathe calmly. He was reacting; he needed to calm down and take the initiative. This was clearly a full-on cluster, but it wouldn't help anything for him just to react impulsively. He needed to get a handle on things, not charge around blindly. He checked his message box and saw several messages that Ethan had forwarded. He flicked through them until he found the damning one – a response, from his address, to a message outlining the operation and requesting a meeting for full explanation and approval. There, at the bottom, was the response purportedly from him: "Seems acceptable. No meeting necessary. Execution authorized." It closed with his initials, which was his usual manner of ending messages.

Now Jason was beginning to question his own sanity. The message addresses were all in order, and the timestamps were correct, but he couldn't for the life of him remember seeing a message like that, much less answering it. Had he unthinkingly tossed off that response? He checked his sent message bin, and there the message was, right where it should have been. Everything indicated that he had, indeed, received that message, and sent a response that authorized this paramilitary action.

Still questioning his mental stability, Jason dashed off a couple of messages to D.C., including the questionable messages as attachments. Then he headed for the address of the destroyed home. The morning sun was rising, and if the area citizens were yet oblivious to what had been unleashed in their midst, he doubted that state of ignorance would last for long.

Thankfully, the site of the missile strike was not far – near the crossroads named Melvin, which was just south of Sandusky. His nav system told him it was thirty minutes away; Jason made it in seventeen, thanks to the early morning emptiness of the rural roads. Even without the nav screen to tell him, he could spot the place at a distance from the wisps of black smoke curling into the morning air.

As Jason turned onto the road, he saw a cluster of emergency vehicles parked along the edge – a sheriff car, a fire truck, and an EMT vehicle. But the responders were all standing around their vehicles talking, and as Jason pulled up he saw why. At the edge of the property, along the road, walked two men in what looked like full battle gear – helmets, flak jackets, rifles, gear belts, the works. They could have been soldiers on any overseas deployment, except that they were here.

Beyond this picket, a dark truck was parked in the drive, and a couple of figures were walking around the charred and scattered wreckage of a house. They were talking with each other, jotting notes on their tablets, and snapping pictures of the destruction. To Jason's horror, six long bags, three full-sized and three smaller, lay side by side at the edge of the driveway, zipped up and tagged, like sacks of waste awaiting pickup. The local responders were eyeing all this darkly as they talked among themselves, and gave Jason similar looks as he pulled up, clearly associating him with the forces that were preventing them from tending to their dead.

Well, thought Jason as he walked toward the drive, time to see about that. Seeing the guards eyeing him keenly, he fished his department ID from his pocket as he approached them.

"By Federal order, access to this site is restricted –" one of the guards began barking as Jason approached. Jason didn't even break stride, flashing his badge at the man as he walked past.

"Jason Pelletier, DHS DTD. I'm authorized –"

"SIR!" the guard barked in a commanding voice. "Halt immediately or I will open fire!" Jason stopped in exasperation and turned to see himself staring down the barrel of a rifle.

The first thing Jason felt was cold fear, but hot fury rose swiftly to dispel it. He strode right up to the guard and shoved the barrel aside.

"You point a gun at me again, buster, and it'll be the last thing you do as a federal employee," Jason growled. "What's your name?"

"Corporal Ellis, and I've been ordered –"

"Well, Corporal Ellis, you scan this ID badge and send it to your headquarters," Jason handed the man his badge. "I'm Jason Pelletier, and I have plenary authority over all DTD operations in this region. That means, Corporal, that I give your bosses orders. Half an hour ago I gave them an order to stand down all troops in the Thumb. You obviously haven't gotten the word yet, so I'm giving it to you now: you and your buddy stand down right now and let these responders do their jobs."

Corporal Ellis looked a little less cocksure, but he could still bluster. "I have received no orders to that effect, sir," he said, though he held Jason's ID up to his eyepiece to scan it. "Until I receive orders through my chain of command, I must maintain my station."

Jason allowed how that could be reasonable. "Well, you just wait a minute, and you'll get confirmation. In the meantime, you don't point that thing at anyone – not them, not me, not anyone – or I'll have your ass, understand, Corporal?"

Corporal Ellis said nothing in response, but kept his rifle elevated. After standing for a long minute, Jason asked, "Well?"

"Sir?"

"Well, what have you heard? It can't take that long to confirm my credentials."

"I have forwarded your information to TacCom, sir. I have not yet heard back. Until such time, I am required -"

"Yeah, yeah," Jason interrupted. "Check again."

The corporal spoke briefly into his mouthpiece. "TacCom reports receiving your data and is processing it. They will respond when they have completed their verification."

"Did they say how long they expect that to take?"

"No, sir."

Jason fumed. He recognized a stonewall when he encountered one, and didn't have time to burn. He stalked back to his car where he pulled out his phone and redialed the headquarters.

"UPROOT OpCom, Corporal Oliver."

"Corporal, this is Jason Pelletier again. Please put me through to Captain Touma."

"I'm sorry, sir, but the captain has stepped out of the center briefly. Can I have her contact you when she returns?"

"Lieutenant Nealson, then."

The corporal looked around quickly. "No, sir, he's not around either. Could I have him –"

"Yes. The minute either one becomes available, have them contact me. Highest priority."

"Yes, sir. Highest priority," Corporal Oliver echoed in a nonchalant tone that conveyed little urgency.

Jason rang off, his fury being displaced by a deep, cold dread. He looked at the two sentries still walking along the roadside, rifles at the ready. Missile strikes. Grim-faced soldiers preventing responders from discharging their duties. Juvenile casualties. If that was what was happening here, God knew what was unfolding across the region. His dread deepened. He was supposedly in charge of this travesty, but that was clearly a fiction.

But if he wasn't in charge, who was?

Jason started as the car radio spat static again. Stupid thing! He'd intended to exchange this car because of that malfunction, but had never gotten around to it. He punched the radio off and thought furiously. What could he do to get this disaster back under control? Contact D.C., to be sure, but what could he do *right now* to prevent any further carnage? He looked at the sentries and was certain his stand-down order was not being heeded by anyone. Any enforcement of his will was going to have to be done in person.

But where? He didn't even know where the OpCom was, and was certain that nobody was going to help him find it. He could drive down to Port Huron and hunt, but that might waste all day. The problem was these maniacs out here, right now!

Then Jason remembered – Collins had said they were "holding off on the final three". That had to be the three highest confidence sites, the addresses they'd known for certain. Maybe those hadn't been hit yet! But where were they? Wait a minute – Jason pulled out his tablet and flicked back to the presentation files that Danvers had provided on Monday. Network analysis…addresses… there they were! The known or highly suspect addresses. One over by Mayville, one not far from Ruth, then the three properties in close cluster northwest of Emmett. That last one wasn't far – he could be there in fifteen minutes. He threw the car into gear and pulled away.

As Jason turned onto the dirt road along which the three addresses were located, he saw nothing out of the ordinary – no sentries, no trucks, no people at all. The house on the corner was a trim two-story, then next house was a large, low brick ranch, and the one beyond was a friendly-looking brown-sided farm house with a porch stretching across its entire front. The houses all looked peaceful and quiet in the morning sunshine, with no vehicles in evidence and no sign of activity.

Jason pulled up in front of the furthest house, the brown farmhouse with the porch, unsure of what to do. He guessed that he wanted to warn any residents that they were at risk, and perhaps stay with them to ensure they weren't mistreated. But if these addresses were suspected of being involved in the terror network, wouldn't he be in danger coming here? Would he be aiding them by giving them warning? Then he thought back to the destroyed house, and the body bags, and knew that nothing these people had done deserved being dealt with like that. Let anybody try to charge him with hindering an operation – he'd have plenty to say in response to that.

Jason went up on the front porch and knocked on the door. After a minute of no response, he knocked again. He could hear no sounds from within the house, and on a chance tried the knob. Expectably, it was locked. He considered going to the next house, but decided to look around back of this one, just in case someone was in the yard. Walking around the side, he saw a neat and orderly back yard, but no sign of residents. A covered walkway ran from the back door of the house to a barn.

"Hello?" Jason called tentatively, and his voice seemed to echo among the trees that shaded the lawn. The property was empty, but it didn't have the derelict air of a place that had been forsaken. It seemed vacated, as if it should be alive with people, but they had left, and the premises missed them. Jason walked through the trees into an open, lawn-like space beside a long building made of cinder blocks that stood next to the barn. Jason was scanning the open space when his eyes fell on something that made him freeze in his tracks.

There in the lawn, beside the cinder block building, stood a white monument that looked something like a gravestone but was of the wrong proportions. A bed of flowers encircled the stone, and there was an inscription on the front:

SAMSON JOHN CHAPMAN
APRIL 17 2001AD - OCTOBER 4, 2033AD
'THE LORD IS MY STRENGTH'.

Jason's dream, which he'd almost forgotten in the day's turmoil, began to come back to him, and his pulse started pounding. This morning had brought its share of emotions, but he now felt a fear of a totally different type. On top of that, something was nagging him, like there was something he should remember but couldn't. Something about the stone, or the inscription, was tugging at him but eluded his recall.

Whatever it was, it could wait. Remembering more details, he turned his back on the stone and started walking. There it was, just as it had been in his dream: the lawn, the trees, the benches, the gazebo, the little pond. His sense of awe and foreboding deepened – what if she was there, walking along the edge of the pond? But there was nobody, just the morning sun filtering through the leaves. Only the singing of birds broke the peaceful stillness.

Looking about, Jason saw that the pond and trees were in the back yard of the ranch house. There was still nobody around, but there was a large deck on the back of the house, and a set of glass double doors that opened onto the deck. Jason crossed the yard and knocked on the doors.

That got a response. From somewhere inside came an answer that Jason couldn't understand. He tried the handle of the door and found it unlocked. He slid the door open far enough to stick his head in. "Hello?" he called.

"In here!" a man's voice called. Jason stepped into a kitchen so large that it had an industrial stove and refrigerator. "I'm up in front, in the living room," the voice continued, giving Jason something to follow. He went down a short hallway and came into a tidy front room with a large bay window overlooking the front yard and road. In a rocking chair sat an older man with white hair, a full white moustache, and smiling eyes.

"Welcome," the man said, beckoning to the couch. "Please sit down, make yourself comfortable."

"You...were expecting me?" Jason asked, no longer able to be surprised.

"I was expecting somebody," the man replied with a smile. "I admit to anticipating a somewhat more martial intrusion, but I always appreciate pleasant surprises. I'm Mike Peterson, by the way."

"Jason Pelletier," Jason shook the extended hand. "I...I'm from the government. DHS Domestic Terror Division."

"Ah, yes – that, I was expecting," Mike replied. "Tell me, do I appear as ominous as you'd expected?"

"I...beg your pardon?" Jason asked.

"Me," Mike replied, spreading his hands. "Do I look like a dangerous domestic terror mastermind who's been leading you in circles for years?"

Jason was dumbfounded. "You, sir? I hardly think –"

"Ah, but appearances can be deceiving, can they not? I am indeed the man you're looking for. It was all my idea from the start – the ranches, the guests, the supply and communications network, the snatches – all of it. Of course, I must credit my sons and daughters and their spouses, as well as numerous other friends, but the original idea was mine."

"You're...admitting all this? I must warn you, sir –" Jason began, but Mike simply smiled at him.

"I understand all about my rights, but do you honestly think any of this is going to end up in a court of law? Besides, I'll freely admit this to anyone, anywhere. I'm not ashamed of what we did – in fact, I'm rather proud of it. It was a good run."

"Why did you do it?" Jason asked, though he was sure he knew the answer.

"That should be obvious," Mike replied. "To save lives. Your secret government program was quietly executing people for no reason other than that they were inconvenient and expensive. We spirited them to safety."

"And provided them with medical care, even though it was illegal to do so?"

"As you should be aware, the original purpose of governmental control over health care was to contain costs – hence the laws restricting care provision. I suspect that your execution program was implemented for similar reasons. When we removed the potential victims from the medical care system, their expenses went with them. Hence, we were honoring the spirit, if not the letter, of the law. Not that it will make a difference, but it never really was about the money, was it?"

"But... somebody had to be paying for their care," Jason protested.

"Indeed," Mike agreed. "We did. Out of our own resources. There was some pooling of assets, of course – properties, pensions, savings, and the like. We were forced to get very creative with our supply channels. But it was worth the cost."

"Where did they get this medical care?"

"In their homes. We had more intensive facilities for those in serious condition, but that was usually end-of-life care."

"In their homes?" Jason was astonished. "What quality of care did they expect to receive there?"

"A quality that was typical a few generations ago," Mike replied. "And I'm sure you'll understand that our guests were willing to accept a lower quality of care to avoid the risk of a lethal injection in the night."

Jason had no answer to this.

"Besides," Mike continued. "The ranches were more successful than we anticipated in many ways. Lonely people devoid of purpose found belonging and acceptance. They loved and were loved. We hosted many of them here over the years, and gained far more from them than they cost."

Jason looked around the empty room, listening to the unseemly silence that filled the house. "Where did they go?"

"Dispersed," Mike smiled. "We knew this day would come, and made some provision for it. Whether that will be enough..." He spread his hands and shrugged.

"There has been some activity this morning," Jason admitted hesitantly. "Including some...casualties. It happened without my knowledge, and I'm doing my best to control it."

"That's the thing about these kinds of forces," Mike replied. "They're always easier to unleash than contain. That's part of why I'm here. When I received...notification of the attacks, I returned with the intent of providing you with a high-value target in hopes that you would call off your assaults elsewhere."

"Returned here?"

"Yes – we evacuated this site several days ago, after we deemed it was unsafe to occupy any further. But I see our time for conversation draws short," Mike said, pointing out the front window.

Jason turned and saw dark vehicles pulling up in front, and armed figures dashing into position around the house.

"Dammit," Jason growled, standing and pulling out his ID. "I ordered them to stand down!"

"Do you really think they're taking orders from you?" Mike asked. Even as he spoke, the front door burst open and several men bearing rifles charged through. Toward the rear of the house Jason heard glass shattering as the sliding doors were smashed in.

"They could have just knocked," Mike said with a sigh as he pushed himself up out of his rocker. Jason started to say something, but one of the armed men shoved him to the ground, and for the second time that morning Jason found himself staring down the barrel of a rifle.

"Stay down –" the man began, but Jason's anger boiled over.

"Jason Pelletier, DTD!" he cried, holding up his ID. "I'm in charge of this operation, and you were ordered to stand down over an hour ago!"

The man eyed the badge then, keeping his weapon trained on Jason, tapped his earpiece. "Sarge, got a guy here who claims to be DTD. Yeah, all right." He gestured for Jason to stand. "You keep your hands where I can see 'em. Sarge'll be along in a minute."

"Hey!" Jason cried as two other soldiers slammed Mike face-first up against the wall, twisting his arms back to handcuff them. "That's an old man! He's no danger to you!"

"Shut up, you!" the man guarding Jason said, gesturing sharply with his rifle. Jason watched helplessly as Mike was shoved and dragged from the room. The old man was enduring the ordeal stoically, but could not avoid the occasional wince or groan of pain as his joints were twisted or yanked. From the far reaches of the house Jason could hear crashes and thumps, as if the rooms were being searched and ransacked. Finally, a burly looking man wearing sergeant's stripes came through the front door. The man guarding Jason handed the sergeant Jason's ID. He eyed the card and then Jason.

"Look, mister, I don't know what you're doing on this site, but you'd better clear out, pronto, if you know what's good for you," the sergeant growled, thrusting the ID back at Jason.

"I'm the DHS coordinator with plenary authority over all DTD activity in this region!" Jason exclaimed.

"Sure, you are," the sergeant replied. "Look, we take our orders from the TacCom, who gets them from the OpCom, who reports to regional authority under Colonel James down in Fort Wayne. I've never heard of you, civilian. Now clear out before we haul you in for being on a target site." He nodded to the soldier, who started nudging Jason toward the front door with his rifle.

Jason's temper flared again, but he damped it quickly. The bruises to his pride would have to wait. He couldn't affect anything here, under these circumstances where brute force was speaking loudest. Also, a heavy blanket of fear was settling on him, fear that had nothing to do with the rifle muzzle inches from his face. This was out of control. The whole thing, completely out of control. Martial law had been unleashed on this rural population, at least pockets of it, and he had no idea who was giving the troops orders.

Jason needed to get this thing in hand quickly.

If that was even possible.

Jason turned and walked out the front door. There were several vehicles about, but no sign of Mike or those who had taken him. Several sentries stood along the road watching him as he walked to the neighboring house and got into his car. He drove away just to be clear of their scrutiny, but didn't go far before he pulled over.

Jason laid his head on the steering wheel, his mind numb with shock, his heart sick with horror. Body bags lying beside driveways. Kindly old men bullied and beaten for no reason. Faceless enforcers strutting around waving rifles and muttering into headsets.

What the hell was going on?

A thousand urgencies stormed Jason's mind, each clamoring for attention. Where had they taken Mike, and why? How could he clarify the chain of command, to get this catastrophe under control? What was happening at the other addresses, wherever they were? How was he going to explain this to D.C.? What would the public reaction be? He forced himself to quiet the emotional din. His grief and shock and outrage would have to wait; right now he needed to focus his efforts for maximum effectiveness. He came back to the starting point which had served him so well to this point: what did he actually *know*?

The problem was, that whole category was in question. Ever since a supposedly dead woman had walked up to him in front of the Sanilac County Courthouse, what Jason thought he knew had been upended. What Mike had told him had made it even worse.

What if those running the clandestine network hadn't been doing it just to sabotage a government project? What if those who had sought hidden shelter hadn't done it to frustrate bureaucrats, but to stay alive? What if the hidden ones hadn't been exploited, but protected? He thought back to the display viewer he'd found in the purse of the green-tag woman who'd shown up at the Fairgrove RCC. Those hadn't been pictures of someone oppressed or exploited, but of someone who'd loved, who had found a family. What was the reality here? What did he actually *know*?

But – the Imlay City blast. That had surely happened. Of course, even what he thought he knew about that was in question, since Janice Boyd clearly hadn't died, but the blast itself was undeniable. Over twenty people had died at that remote site on–

Then it struck him. Jason had known something was familiar about the date on that monument! October 4th – that was the date of the blast! Then who was Samson Chapman, and did he have anything to do with it? Jason now regretted that he hadn't had time to discuss that event with Mike. He was certain the old man would have truthfully relayed all he knew. Where had they taken him? They were certain to interrogate him – would they ask him about that? No, the fact that the blast had been other than an industrial accident was a closely guarded secret. They wouldn't know to ask, and he certainly wouldn't volunteer any information.

Jason forced his skittering thoughts to focus. It was possible that this Samson Chapman was irrelevant to the blast, and the date only a coincidence, but he doubted it. Was that a grave? Who'd put a grave in their back yard? And it didn't look like a grave, but a monument. Why would anyone erect a monument in a yard instead of a headstone in a cemetery?

Maybe because they didn't have a body to bury.

Jason thought of the mysterious body the forensics people had discovered on the site of the blast, the charred and mangled corpse that had raised more questions than it had answered, the man who had been shot from below. The man, maybe, who had been involved in placing the explosives in the plant.

If that man was Samson Chapman, implicated in an act of domestic terror, then who would erect a monument to him? Monuments were placed as a sign of love and honor – who would honor a terrorist implicated in a massacre?

Maybe people who loved and honored massacres.

The same people who rescued helpless old people from being executed for being helpless and old?

Maybe nothing in this whole situation was as everyone had thought.

Again Jason disciplined himself to focus. This all bore further investigation, but nothing effective was going to happen until he got control of the players in this ugly drama. That was going to call for clear communications – clear, *direct* communications – and no small amount of damage control.

That would best be accomplished from his office in Sandusky. Tempting as it was to race all over five counties locating command centers and halting raids, Jason needed to get a grip on this at a high level. He pulled back onto the road and headed north.

*   *   *

To the west, a grim interrogator faced the white-haired old man whose arms were strapped to the chair.

"And that's all you have to tell me?" the interrogator asked, tapping his tablet.

"That's all I know, and it's all true," the old man replied. With a sigh he flexed his arms against the straps. "These really aren't necessary, you know. I won't go anywhere."

"Yeah," the interrogator said absently, focused on the tablet. The old man sat in silence while the interrogator tapped away, and said nothing when he stood and left. Alone in the room, the old man tried to remain calm. He knew what was coming; he had invited it for a reason.

At length the door opened again, and a nurse wearing a surgical mask and holding a tourniquet came in. She wore no name tag, only a small badge with a number and bar code printed on it.

"Good morning," the old man said, but he got no response. The nurse tied the tourniquet tightly around his arm, then pulled a syringe from her pocket. The old man leaned his head back, closed his eyes, and began to murmur quietly.

"*Nunc dimittis servum tuum, Domine Secundum verbum tuum...*"

Damage Control

As Jason drew near Sandusky, his tablet chimed with an incoming message. Once the message had been read to him, he nodded and sent a reply saying he'd respond within the hour.

Back in his office, Jason swiftly sent the messages he'd been composing in his head. One to Cynthia in D.C. full of the expected bluster about being cut out of the loop, communications foul-ups, breakdowns in command lines – everything that would be expected of him under the circumstances. Then he sent messages to Touma and Nealson requesting immediate updates on the raids, and a couple of messages to Chad Collins at Selfridge. Then he called a number in D.C. that was becoming distressingly familiar.

"George Spader, Public Opinion Management."

"George, this is Jason Pelletier with DHS up here in Michigan."

"Jason! How good to hear from you."

"I hope you'll think that after I'm done," Jason grumbled. "George, your people have done stellar work, and the campaigns you've worked up have been great. But I'm in need of some serious damage control here."

"Oh, my," George said sympathetically.

"You mentioned that you sometimes have to redeem a situation after it's already smashed all over the floor, and this is one of those," Jason replied, and proceeded to tell George everything he could about the raids and casualties.

"That does sound serious," George commiserated when he'd finished. "We've had to work with worse, though."

"I hate to ask such a big job of you, particularly since you're not even in my department, but I don't know where to turn, and minutes matter here."

"Pah," George said dismissively. "I've been told that after all you've done for our department, I'm to give you any help you need. You're right, this is a tall order, which we may need help from DHS POM to fully resolve. It may need press releases and

457

talking heads, but you let me worry about it. I know some people over at DHS. I'll get started on this and get back to you."

No sooner had Jason rung off that call than his phone rang with a call from Sheriff Keller up in Bad Axe. He'd been dreading this, but picked up quickly.

"Sheriff Keller."

"Mr. Pelletier, do you mind telling me what the hell is going on?" Chip's grim expression matched his ominous growl. "I've got two boys up by Pigeon reporting that their family was kidnapped by men in black trucks. Al Corrigan in Sanilac is dealing with a house explosion that's rumored to be anything from a propane tank to a missile strike, but his people can't get to the site because of some kind of sentries. We've got reports trickling in from St. Clair to Tuscola of unmarked vehicles carrying strike teams. Do you have anything to do with all this?"

Jason was tempted to bark a sharp negative, but he knew he couldn't do that to the sheriff. "Sheriff Keller, I knew that something would be happening, but I wasn't aware...that is, there have been some communications problems, and...I've been working to get things back under control."

"'Back under control'?" Chip broke in. "Do you mean they're not under control?"

"Not as much as I'd like, Sheriff," Jason admitted

"Well, that's just great!" Chip exploded. "I've got armed Federal agents driving all over my county, and the man who's supposed to have authority over them tells me they're not under control. What the hell am I supposed to tell my deputies? What the hell am I supposed to tell my colleagues?"

"I know, Sheriff – I saw some deputies at that blast site, and–" Jason's mind started clicking. The sheriffs. The deputies. "Listen, Sheriff, I have plenary authority over all DHS DTD activity in the region. I have ordered a general cessation of activity and a full stand-down, but that word isn't getting out consistently – that's part of the communications foul-up."

"What? You guys are supposed to be able to coordinate multiple activities from across the continent! How can you not control people right in the same county?"

"I don't know, Sheriff, but I suspect several factors. But this is what you can tell your deputies: if they encounter any DTD troops, they're to tell them that I'm the legitimate authority under DHS DTD Director Miller, and I have ordered this general stand-down. Give the DTD people my name and direct number, and encourage them to call me."

"Really?" Chip looked skeptical. "You're encouraging my deputies to say that? Can you give me a signed document to hand them?"

Jason thought fast. "A document would require input from our legal department, which would delay things. Here's what I can do: let me record a message that you can pass on to your men for them to take with them. Give me a few minutes to pull it together – I'll call you right back."

Jason took care in drawing up an official-sounding script, which he recorded and then called Chip back to play it for him.

"Well," Chip admitted. "That certainly sounds ominous, especially that last part about how if they ignore your order, the Department may disavow responsibility for their activities, and they could face arrest and prosecution as private citizens. Could that happen?"

"I'm not sure of how legally secure that is, but it's possible," Jason explained. "The main point is to rattle them, to sow doubt. That's why I put my contact information in – I want them calling me, if they have the courage."

"So, I can distribute this video to my deputies, so they can show it to these soldiers?"

"Distribute it as far as you can – other sheriffs, fire departments, EMTs, whomever. When it's shown, try to make sure at least two of your people are there, and if possible, take a video of the troops watching the recording, so there's a record of when it was seen."

"Do you want my men to confront these troops?" Chip asked skeptically.

"No, not at all. Not even a hint of confrontation, just a friendly discussion. Behind the bluster, these troops are just like your deputies – guys trying to make it through a workday. They're caught in this, too. Your deputies can sympathize, show them the video, assure them that nothing will happen if they obey orders. If they don't listen, your men should walk away."

"All right, then," Chip replied. "I hope this helps."

"I'm pursuing other avenues as well, Sheriff, quite aggressively. Something's badly wrong. This is out of control. The abruptness, the…brutality goes beyond anything I've ever seen. Something's been unleashed and it needs to be reined in."

"I'll say. Anything else?"

"Yes. Those boys up by Pigeon who escaped? Hide them until this blows over."

"You bet," Chip said.

There, thought Jason as Sheriff Keller rung off, I've thrown a ticking bomb out there, well clear of approved channels. Let's see what response it generates. Then he took his tablet, the new one he'd acquired here in Michigan, the one that he'd been careful never to take into any DHS facility, and went to the local coffee shop where they had online access. There he picked up several messages he'd been expecting. He wrote and sent a few more, then took out his phone. Ensuring it was using the coffee shop's network, he made a call to a number that not even the recipient knew he had – except that he made a point of knowing such things about the people he worked with.

"Hello?" came the mystified response.

"Hello, Sergeant Danvers. This is Jason Pelletier. Do you recognize me?"

"Of course, sir – I just wasn't expecting you to call my personal phone. Is there something I can do for you? Should I get Major Collins?"

"No, you're the person I want. I'm going to need some assistance – a small recon drone for a special task. Can you manage that?"

"Sure, sir. We've got recon drones in the air all over the region. I can vector one wherever you wish."

"Great. I'll be contacting you shortly with coordinates and instructions. You can inform Major Collins that I've requested your help, but I don't want to trouble him with details. It'll just be a minor flight."

"Umm…sure, sir," Abigail replied, still puzzled.

"I suspect we'll need to start somewhere near Port Huron, but I can't be sure."

"I'll make sure I've got one nearby, sir."

"Thanks, Sergeant."

Jason headed back to his house, where there were several messages waiting on his workstation, mostly from George Spader at HHS. Jason was just copied on most of them – it was clear that the POM people were running with the problem. They'd engaged their colleagues at DHS, and were swapping plans and timelines at a speed that amazed Jason – he hadn't known that bureaucrats could move that quickly. Many of the exchanges were in jargon and acronyms that were opaque to Jason, but he gathered that the departments were moving quickly to manage public opinion about the events.

Jason realized that he felt woozy, and a glance at the clock told him why: the day was well along, and he'd had nothing to eat yet. The coffee that he'd mindlessly gulped at the shop was sitting harshly in his stomach. He needed to get some lunch, or he'd be useless.

At the local diner, Jason noticed that most of the patrons were focused on the two television screens mounted on the walls. They seemed to be tuned to a standard news site, with a split screen interview that Jason couldn't quite hear. Amazed to see the locals so absorbed in a news broadcast, Jason brought up the site on his tablet while his lunch was being prepared. Slipping in his ear buds, he was astonished to see that the news site was out of Detroit, the host was interviewing a DHS spokeswoman, and the topic was the events of the morning.

"...with us this morning is Karen Farnsworth of the Department of Homeland Security. We're discussing the reports of DHS activity across Michigan's Thumb region, just north of metro Detroit," the host intoned. "Ms. Farnsworth, could you fill us in?"

"Well," Farnsworth said with a deprecating chuckle. "I'd hardly characterize our activity as 'across the Thumb' – that makes it sound like we've got trucks sweeping from Saginaw Bay to the Huron shore. Nothing so dramatic. At about dawn today, protectors from the Domestic Terror Division executed a targeted action of limited scope against about a dozen sites in the five counties of the Thumb region. It's true that the sites were scattered throughout the area, but I wouldn't characterize the DTD's activities as 'across the region'."

"Domestic terror troops?" The host asked in astonishment.

"Yes," Farnsworth affirmed. "Though the protectors from DTD are usually focused on major urban areas, activity in less populated regions does not escape their notice. This action was the culmination of a low-key but lengthy DHS investigation into a clandestine terror network that has been lurking in the area for some years."

"Clandestine terror network? In the farmland of the Thumb?" Now the host sounded skeptical.

"Subversive activity knows no boundaries," Farnsworth cautioned gravely. "Sometimes the isolation of a remote area well suits criminals. It was less than a year ago that a crime ring operating in the Thumb area was uncovered. They'd been engaged in human trafficking, slavery, smuggling, government corruption – things as bad as anything you'd find in Detroit or here in Washington. Small-town police and sheriff's deputies can hardly be expected to cope with that level of sophistication."

"So there's evidence that this crime ring was connected to domestic terror activity?"

"We have no proof at this time, but the investigation is ongoing."

"Then what prompted these – 'targeted actions', as you call them? Why now?"

Farnsworth's expression became somber. "I've been authorized to reveal something that hasn't been public knowledge until now. Do you remember an explosion a couple of years ago at a rural site in Lapeer County? An industrial accident that claimed the lives of two workers?"

"Dimly," the host admitted.

"Well, that was a cover story. In actuality, it was an act of domestic terror that claimed the lives of twenty government officials," Farnsworth said grimly.

The host looked stunned. So was Jason, but for a different reason. Just a few weeks ago this had been DHS top secret. Why was it now being discussed in a broadcast interview? The restaurant crowd was also surprised, and were talking among themselves with great animation.

"I can't go into much detail for security reasons," Farnsworth continued. "But I can say that these officials were pivotal in a pilot project intended to bring better health care service to the region. Their loss set the project back years, and it's only now getting back on track."

"So that's what caused this activity? Response to this terrorist act?" The host asked.

"Not exactly," Farnsworth cautioned. "The terrorist act drew the long-term attention of our investigators, but the immediate cause was a breakthrough we had recently, one that enabled our investigators to better track the suspect activity and identify where the terrorists might be hiding."

"Ah. We're running short on time, but one more question," the host replied. "What of reports of homes raided and drone strikes destroying buildings? Is there any truth to these rumors?"

"Well, you'll never lack for speculation online," Farnsworth replied with an indulgent smile. "How much substance there is to these stories remains to be seen. As far as explosions destroying buildings, keep in mind that the domestic terrorists we've been seeking are experienced with demolitions and aren't afraid to use them. People should be wary of believing everything they hear."

"That's straight-up horsecrap!" cried one viewer from across the room. "My sister lives near Yale, and there was a clear missile track leading right down to that house near Melvin. A track visible for twenty miles around!" This generated a storm of response that drowned out the show.

Jason closed his tablet and pondered. This interview and other spots had to be part of the POM quick response to the raids, but he hadn't expected anything so blunt. Were they going to lay bare the whole project? He hoped his name wouldn't be mentioned. He was just about to pick up his phone to call George with a few questions when it rang. Seeing who the caller was, he smiled. He'd been expecting this one, but considering circumstances, he'd better answer it outside.

"Mr. Pelletier," came Captain Touma's sharp voice. "I'd like to know why you're putting recorded messages in the hands of locals that undermine my command authority!"

"Ah, Captain Touma," Jason replied. "I was just attempting to resolve a lingering problem with *my* command authority, which you are under, and the conveying of my instructions to your forces."

"Mr. Pelletier, martial command structure exists for a reason, and if circumvented –"

"Captain, I ordered you to stand down your troops and cease operations early this morning. Over an hour after I gave that order, one of your squads kicked in the door of a private home and violently dragged away an unresisting old man. I was right there, and your troops refused to obey my orders, or even acknowledge my authority. Clearly, there are serious communications breakdowns in your command, and I had to address that somehow."

"Sir, I'm not denying that there will be foul-ups in any large-scale operation, but still –" a slightly chastened Captain Touma continued.

"Leaving aside the point that DTD is *supposed* to be able to coordinate much larger operations than this with real-time oversight and instantaneous communications, I agree that we need to rectify the communications failures. I intend to come down there and talk to you directly, so we can ensure that consistent word gets out through proper channels. Agreed, Captain?"

"Agreed, sir," Touma replied with a surly expression. "We look forward to your arrival. Touma out."

The captain hung up so abruptly that Jason had no chance to respond, which he was sure was intentional. Fortunately, he had anticipated that, and consulted the utility program he'd left running on his phone during the conversation. Calling the captain back would be futile, and she'd had the geolocation feature of her phone turned off. But, as expected, she'd been using the site's network for her call, which happily spilled its location to Jason's utility. Ah, the Border Security site in Marysville, just south of Port Huron. How clever – near to other DHS offices, but just enough out of the way to be hidden. He called Sergeant Danvers.

"Yes, sir?"

"Hi, Sergeant. Do you know who Captain Touma and Lieutenant Nealson are? Would you recognize them?"

"Yes, sir, I could spot them."

"Good. At least Captain Touma, and I'm guessing Lieutenant Nealson, are in a facility at the coordinates I'm sending you now. I suspect that within ten minutes they'll be leaving, and I'd like you to track them and keep me updated on where they go."

"All right, sir."

"And Sergeant? You don't have to fill Major Collins in on this task. This can stay between us."

"Yes, sir," Danvers replied, her expression betraying a little impish excitement at being able to spy on her superiors.

Jason got in his car and headed west out of town. He didn't know exactly where the DTD officers were heading, but he had guesses, and wanted to be in optimal position. He was barely out of town before his phone rang with a message from Sergeant Danvers.

"They were at that site, sir, and both got into a vehicle and left. They're now heading north on I-94 toward Port Huron."

"Very good. I'm guessing they'll turn west on I-69. If they do, could you call me back with a list of DTD tactical sites north and west of Imlay City?"

"Sure thing, sir."

Jason had reached the truck stop at M-53 before Danvers called again. "They did turn west, sir, and are cruising out I-69. I looked up the TacCom sites, and there are two – one on the east side of Marlette and the other near a spot called Millington, in the western part of the Thumb. The other two are in Port Sanilac and Bad Axe.

"Thanks, Sergeant. When they get to the Imlay City exit, please let me know if they turn north or continue west on I-69."

"Will do, sir. I may have to vector in another bird, this one's getting low on gas."

"I leave that in your capable hands, Sergeant."

Jason lingered at the truck stop, checking his messages and planning. He didn't know for certain whether the two fleeing officers were headed for one of the tactical command centers, but his instincts told him that they'd seek out a familiar environment from which to continue their game of cat and mouse. That probably meant an official setting with lots of communications capabilities and underlings to order about. But there were two probable options, and he didn't know which one to head for until he knew how they'd turn.

Jason's phone buzzed with a message from Sergeant Danvers: "*Headed north at Imlay.*" Jason nodded and smiled – it was as he'd hoped. They thought he was coming from Sandusky down to Port Huron, so they were going in roughly the opposite direction. Figuring Danvers must have had a reason to message instead of calling, he messaged back. "*Great. Please text vehicle type & color, & address of TacCom in Marlette.*" Then he headed south on M-53 toward Marlette, which was just a few miles, and made his way to where he could watch the parking lot of the building where the TacCom was located. It looked like a typical small office building, a little shabby, with the marquee advertising an insurance agency and a brokerage. Jason watched and waited. Eventually a message came in from Danvers: "*Entering Marlette & turning east.*"

"*Well done. I'll take it from here. Tx.*" Jason messaged back. He watched as the unmarked black sport utility vehicle turned into the parking lot and the two officers got out and entered the far door of the building. Jason pulled into the lot and walked along the face of the building. When he got to the door, he readied his ID and took a deep breath – this could either go very well or very badly. He yanked the door open and strode confidently through.

The corporal behind the table that had been set up as a reception desk stood in alarm. "Sir, this area is –"

"Stand easy, Corporal," Jason interrupted, holding up his ID. "I'm just here to see your bosses."

"Oh, well...I could –" the corporal began, reaching for the phone.

"Don't bother, I'll talk to them in person," Jason said, pushing through the doors into the operational area.

The room was open and unfinished, with desks and lights and wiring all about. There were projections on the walls and people at workstations. Just in front of him stood Captain Touma and Lieutenant Nealson, discussing something with a sergeant holding a tablet. They looked up at him and the captain's expression filled with surprise and rage.

"Ah, Captain, what a happy coincidence," Jason said blithely. "I was hoping I'd find you here."

"Who let him in?" the captain blurted out in fury.

"That would be the duty corporal, but he was just following orders, which I understand the DTD excels at," Jason replied. "And on that topic, while I'm here we can clear up this little misunderstanding."

"Mr. Pelletier," the captain said in a firmly controlled voice. "You are untrained in field operations, and you have no idea –"

"I might not have training, but I do have full authority over you and all your troops, as confirmed by Director Miller's office this morning," Jason interrupted. "Your concern might have more weight if I was ordering your troops to do things, but I am not. I am ordering them to cease doing things and return to their staging areas. I have given this order repeatedly and it has yet to be obeyed. Now will you give that order to your troops here and now, or will I have to relieve you and give your command to someone who will?"

Captain Touma glared at him with unbridled wrath, and for a moment Jason wavered. He was keenly conscious of the fact that the room was full of troops, some of them with sidearms, all of whom knew her and none of whom knew him. The memory of his treatment by the last team he'd encountered was painfully fresh. But then he remembered how they'd shoved and punched a white-haired old man, and the body bags in a row on the driveway, and he knew he had to stand his ground. Somebody had to stop this. He held the captain's gaze until she turned away.

"Very well, *sir*," she spat fiercely. To the room at large she announced, "General notice to all field units: abort operations and return to TacComs. Repeat, from OpCom to all units, abort operations."

There was a moment of silence, and then the room became a flurry of activity as troops started talking into headsets and keying things into workstations. Jason breathed an internal sigh of relief.

"Will that be all, *sir*?" the captain forced out, looking like she'd swallowed a hornet.

"One more thing, Captain. I want a detailed briefing on every site that was hit this morning – damages, injuries, fatalities, detainments, everything."

"Very well, *sir*," Captain Touma granted. "Sergeant!" A young, frightened-looking sergeant stepped forward. "Provide *Mr. Pelletier* with all information he wishes regarding any of the day's strikes, including live feeds and raw footage." With that, she turned on her heel and stormed off, leaving the sergeant to guide Jason to a workstation and provide him the basic details on the raids.

Jason soon saw why Captain Touma and her forces were so anxious to continue operations: nearly half the sites hit in the first wave of assaults had been empty. Five of the eleven addresses had yielded no captives, and according to the raiding troops, there was evidence that the houses had been recently evacuated. This had stoked the officers' fury, and they'd been readying plans for a second wave of raids when Jason had finally caught up to them. The sergeant explained that the captives taken in the raids had been transported to different locations, segregated by type. Those with documentation were held at detainment centers, while the undocumented people were taken "elsewhere", though the sergeant wasn't sure where.

Jason flipped through the photos and videos of the raids – Melvin, which had been the missile strike site that he'd seen firsthand, Pigeon, North Branch, Deford, Fargo. All the sites had been simple homes, most had children, and all showed elderly people being shoved into waiting vans. The sergeant explained these videos dispassionately, in terms of personnel deployed, ordnance used, and total action time. Jason thought of gentle, white-haired Mike being yanked from his home, and wondered how things could have gotten so badly out of hand. But then, Jason reflected, hadn't he been part of the planning? What had he expected? Behind all the abstract discussion of probabilities and network analysis and points of interest, what had he expected there to be at those addresses, other than people living their lives?

It was the videos from the final raid that caused Jason to sit up sharply. The house was a big ranch on a rolling hill, with wheelchair ramps and a large garage. The grounds were well manicured, with tables and chairs scattered about them and a small pond in front of the house. What caught Jason's attention was the footage of the troops leading some of the detainees out of the front door. They were women wearing long white robe-like dresses and draping headdresses. The images piqued his memory – he'd seen women dressed like that recently, somewhere, but only briefly. Jason was wracking his brain to recall where, when the video panned toward the driveway and he saw the outline that brought it all back sharply.

The van! There it sat in the driveway of the house, a white utility van with a distinctive silhouette. That had been the van into which Janice Boyd had gotten after approaching him on the Sandusky Courthouse lawn. And there had been two women by the van, dressed in those long white dresses! He hadn't taken careful note at the time because he'd been so startled, but it came back to him now.

"Sergeant, these last videos here – where was this site?"

"That one? Over by Deckerville, sir. It was probably the most successful action of the day. We think it might have been some sort of care facility. The women in white uniforms seemed to be caretakers, and there were a number of parties in the facility, many of them bedridden. No resistance from either group."

Deckerville. Just a few miles from where he was staying in Sandusky. He watched the video to the end, first the troops rudely herding the white-clad women into a bus-like vehicle, and then about a dozen older people being led out and loaded into a couple of gray vans. The older people looked confused, and some were wearing nightclothes over which long coats had been hastily thrown. Some were asking questions of the troops, but were getting no answers – just curt gestures and ungentle pushes and lifts. Finally, everyone was loaded and the vans drove off, leaving a couple of sentries pacing in front of the house while other troops went in and out of the house, lugging workstations and boxes of things to waiting trucks. Jason scrolled the video back a couple of times to review the footage of the caretakers being brought out. He scrutinized every face but didn't see her, though he couldn't see anyone's hair, because it was all covered by those draping veils.

"Sergeant!" Jason called.

"Yes, sir?"

"These women – the ones you call the caretakers. Where were they taken?"

The sergeant tapped his tablet. "I'd guess to the detainment facility just west of Port Sanilac, sir – it would be the closest."

"You'd guess? Why don't you call and find out?" Jason suggested. The sergeant returned shortly.

"Verified, sir. The detainees are being held at the Port Sanilac Center for now."

"Very well. Inform the Center to hold them for my arrival. I want to talk to them. Wait – who are you talking to over there?"

"Corporal Bauer, sir."

"Tell Corporal Bauer that when I arrive, I will ask for him personally, and I will hold him responsible for ensuring that all the women are present and available for me to interview. If I encounter delays, or if any of the women are unavailable for any reason, he and his immediate superior will answer to me for their failure. Understand?"

"Yes, sir," the sergeant said with wide eyes.

"Good. Convey that and ensure that Corporal Bauer understands."

"Yes, sir," the sergeant replied, then stepped aside to speak urgently into the phone. "He says he understands, sir."

"Good. Tell him I'll be there within half an hour," Jason said, making for the door. He glanced at the corner where Captain Touma stood muttering into her phone and looking daggers at him. He ignored her – he had much larger issues before him.

Jason made it to Port Sanilac in something less than half an hour, again grateful for the nearly empty country roads. The detainment center had been set up in an old, decaying building that looked like a giant pole barn. Waiting at the door was not only Corporal Bauer, but also Sergeant Reid, senior noncom at the site. Both eagerly assured him that his instructions had been followed, and the detainees were waiting for him. They led him into the cavernous main area of the building, wherein sat a chamber that looked like it had been assembled from panels brought in from elsewhere. The chamber looked like a bloated shipping container sitting in the center of the vast, empty space. Corporal Bauer unlocked a door in the side of the chamber and led him inside.

The interior of the makeshift prison was bleaker than the exterior. The walls were a uniform dull gray, and the only light was from temporary LED fixtures fastened about the walls. These were grossly inadequate to illuminate the space, so the corners and center of the chamber were in shadow. The air was stale, chilly, and clammy. Clustered to one side, sitting on what appeared to be crates, were about a dozen women. They were dressed in wrinkled, ill-fitting orange jumpsuits and their heads were bare, showing hair that was close-cropped, in some cases close enough to look like it was just regrowing after having been cut completely off. They looked at Jason with apprehensive eyes. One of them, who looked older and wore an air of authority despite the circumstances, stood and looked at the men.

"Yes?" the woman asked quietly.

"This is Mr. Pelletier from the Domestic Terror Division!" Sergeant Reid barked in a harsh voice. "He's here to ask you some questions, and he expects full cooperation!"

Jason winced, but the woman just looked at them placidly. "Sergeant, that will be all," Jason said. "I'd like to speak to the ladies alone."

The soldiers looked shocked. "Sir," Corporal Bauer cautioned. "Protocols require at least one guard in attendance while visiting–"

"Please, Corporal, I appreciate the protocols, but I'm in no danger from these women," Jason interrupted. "I note your advice and take full responsibility for my actions. Please leave them with me – I'll call when I need to be let out."

Looking skeptical nearly to the point of rebellion, the men turned to leave. "Calling won't work, sir," Corporal Bauer advised. "The chamber walls ground the signal. Just knock, I'll be outside the door." They exited, the sound of the lock snapping shut echoing in the shadowed chamber.

"There, I'm at your mercy. If you harm me, Corporal Bauer will never let me hear the end of it," Jason joked lamely, but nobody laughed. The women just watched him with steady gazes, the older one standing with an air of quiet dignity that was enhanced rather than diminished by the humiliating circumstances.

"How may we help you, Mr. Pelletier?" the older woman asked quietly.

"Oh, well...I...that is," Jason stammered, realizing that he didn't know where to begin. "Won't you sit down, ah, Ms. –"

"Sister Joseph Marie," the woman replied. "And I'll remain standing, if you don't mind. As you can see, our accommodations leave something to be desired."

"Yes, well, ah...sorry about all this," Jason gestured at the dreary surroundings. "This wasn't...that is, I'm going to see what I can do about it."

"Never mind us," Sister Joseph said. "Our patients are our greatest concern. Please focus all your efforts on protecting them."

"Oh, well, I'm not exactly sure where they are," Jason offered. This was technically true, but given that they were only a few miles from the Forester RCC, he had a guess. From the way that Sister Joseph looked at him, he suspected she had a guess, too.

"I'm certain someone in your position would have sufficient authority to discover their whereabouts and condition," Sister Joseph pressed.

"I'll do what I can," Jason assured her. He glanced about at the other women, most of whom were watching him, though a few had their heads bowed. None of the faces looked familiar, though some of them were in shadow.

"Please forgive the condition of our hair," Sister Joseph said after seeing where Jason was looking so intently. "We normally wear veils, and given the nature of our work, short hair is much more convenient."

"Oh, ah...it wasn't that...that is, I wasn't looking at your hair," Jason fumbled. "To be honest, I was looking for someone I thought might be with you. She was just shorter than me, close-cropped reddish hair, brown eyes, bright smile. She was wearing white, but not one of your long dress outfits. I'm sure I saw her with a couple of you, getting into your van, over in Sandusky not long ago. Do you know who I'm talking about? Have you seen her?"

Jason looked imploringly at Sister Joseph and at the others, but all he got in return were steady gazes and closed mouths. It took him a minute to figure out why he'd gotten such a stony response.

"Look, I don't want to hurt her, and I won't turn her over to anyone. I just…well, she came up to me a couple of weeks ago and said something mysterious, and I wanted to ask her about it."

"Came up to you?" Sister Joseph asked sharply, now looking at him with keen interest.

"Yes. I was sitting on a bench on the courthouse lawn, right by the gazebo, drinking coffee. She walked up and said something about there being a way out, but not by the paths I was looking down, or something like that. I've got it noted down here somewhere."

This statement seemed to mean something to Sister Joseph, because her guarded expression was now touched with surprise. One of the other women in the group stood up. "He's right, Sister Joseph – I remember that. I was with her, as was Sister Margaret here. It was on the last supply run, when we got the coffees."

"See?" Jason said sharply. "They remember. And then I had a dream where she spoke to me again –"

"Wait," Sister Joseph had been turning to speak to the woman who'd stood up, but abruptly turned back to Jason. "You had a dream of her? Can you recall what she said in this dream?"

"Yes. She was walking beside a pond, dressed in black, not white. She looked sad. She told me…that I could stop all this. But I didn't. I did find the pond, though, behind a house not far from Emmett, but she wasn't there," Jason explained.

"When did you have this dream, Mr. Pelletier?" Sister Joseph asked.

"A few days ago – just this past weekend, I think," Jason said, then stepped closer to Sister Joseph so he could speak in a lower voice. "I know who she is. She's Janice Boyd, the woman who was supposed to have been killed in the Imlay City blast."

Sister Joseph's steady dispassion could not mask the flicker of alarm in her eyes at this revelation, so Jason continued, "Don't worry, I'm the only one who knows, and her secret is safe with me. I just need – want – to talk to her, if that's possible."

Sister Joseph studied him for a moment before responding. "If you don't mind my asking, Mr. Pelletier, what is your given name?"

It took Jason a minute to understand what she was asking. "Oh. Jason. My first name is Jason," he responded, wondering why she'd asked that. There was another flicker behind her eyes before she spoke again.

"Stay here for a minute, if you will, Mr. Pelletier." Then she went over to speak in low voices with the two sisters who had been with the van. After some while she returned.

"I have spoken with sisters Margaret and Elizabeth, who confirm the incident in Sandusky. The fact that your stories align, and your dream, and discussions I'd had with the person you're seeking, and the fact that you know so much already, and the witness of my spirit, all convince me that something mysterious is going on."

"Well, that's certainly true," Jason commented.

"I do not know you, Mr. Pelletier, and would have little reason to trust you even if I did. But I am going to trust my Lord and tell you what I can, hoping that you will be true to your word and not willingly bring harm to Teresa. You and your men can scarce do more harm to us," Sister Joseph said.

"Teresa?" Jason asked.

"Teresa, as she is known since she began her new life in Christ, is not with us, and has not been since early this morning. Before dawn, about an hour before your troops struck, she came to my door. She told me that she was leaving because she had been summoned."

"You mean she could just...leave like that?" Jason asked.

"Teresa served with us faithfully and willingly, but never took any vows to become part of our community. We all agreed that her calling was ultimately different from ours, and that her sojourn among us was temporary. I suspect that her true calling was what summoned her early this morning, and she responded."

"Ah," Jason said, puzzled. "You don't...have any idea where she went? Or who summoned her?"

"What she said was that her Bridegroom had called her. I have no idea where, geographically, He called her to."

"Bridegroom?" Jason was even more mystified.

"For those who commit their lives to Christ, He is among other things their Bridegroom," Sister Joseph explained. "This is especially true for vowed sisters such as ourselves, but mystically true for all Christians. I suspect that the Bridegroom was calling Teresa very specifically this morning."

"Do you think she went...off?" Jason asked.

"Teresa was not insane," Sister Joseph assured him. "But the circumstances out of which she came, and the... extraordinary...situations that the Lord put her in over time gave her a mystical bent. She tended to see life differently, to respond to urgings in unpredictable ways. Approaching a stranger in public was just the kind of thing she would do, far more than any of the other sisters. That, plus her appearance in your dream –"

"But in the dream, she wasn't wearing white, she was wearing black," Jason interrupted.

"Teresa recently suffered the loss of a dearly loved one. She wore a black dress for mourning, and would have been wearing it near the pond you described. The precise details you provided lent credence to your account."

Jason felt a cold shiver at this. "So, you think she went away because...Jesus called her?"

"Jesus is always calling all of us, Mr. Pelletier," Sister Joseph responded. "The only questions are to what, and how will we respond. I have no doubt that Teresa responded to what she understood as a personal summons. I do not know precisely what she was being called to, but that is between her and her Lord."

Jason again felt like he was caught up in a vortex, with circumstances and events whirling about him with increasing speed and violence. He'd thought that finding this mysterious woman would help settle him, and possibly provide him some answers. But he had only discovered her to learn that he'd just missed her.

"So you have no idea where she might be?" he asked weakly.

"None," Sister Joseph replied. "What we know of her whereabouts, you now know."

"Well, I...thank you for that," Jason said. "Is there – that is, can I do anything to help you?"

"You mean, aside from getting us released?" Sister Joseph asked with a cocked eyebrow. "Though I doubt you have the authority to do that."

With shock Jason realized that Sister Joseph was probably right. For all his supposed plenary authority, he doubted that any effort on his part could effect the release of these or any of the prisoners taken that day. He felt more keenly the sense of having unleashed something uncontrollable.

"I doubt it, too, though I plan to investigate. But if I can't do that, is there anything else I can do?"

"Access to water and sanitary facilities would be pleasant," Sister Joseph said. "And though we are accustomed to deprivation, some food eventually would be welcome."

"Wait – they haven't let you go to the bathroom?" Jason asked in astonishment.

"Perhaps it has slipped their minds. I get the impression it has been a busy day all around."

"What – dammit, this at least is going to change!" Jason swore as he headed for the door.

"Oh, Mr. Pelletier? I realize getting our habits may be asking too much, but could we have a rosary back? Or a Bible?"

"Right," Jason said as he started hammering on the door. "Ah...what's a rosary?"

"A long cord in the form of a loop, having beads set along it at intervals. We each had one when we got here, but they were taken from us with our habits."

"I'll see what I can do," Jason assured her as the catch rattled and the door opened.

Once Corporal Bauer had let Jason out, he turned to the hapless young man and said in a tone of barely controlled fury, "Summon Sergeant Reid, and every other person on this site, *immediately*."

As Jason drove away, he felt a little remorseful for unloading the frustrations of the day on the detainment center personnel, but only a little. While it was true that they weren't responsible for all that had happened to him, they were certainly responsible for the humane care of those in their custody. Jason recognized the problem – they were so obsessed with the protocols and checklists and performance metrics that they'd completely lost sight of their primary function. Hopefully he'd reordered their priorities – he'd made sure the women had a chance to wash, and that this would happen on a regular schedule. Rations were being brought even as he was departing. But he'd encountered a stiff wall when he'd tried to get their uniforms – apparently 'habits' was the term – returned to them, and their rosaries as well. Regulations regarding prisoner garb, and possession of cords of any type, were apparently inflexible. Jason had been able to insist on finding them some Bibles, though that had sent one of the low-ranking staff away on a hunt to find one. He'd departed with strict orders for Sergeant Reid to learn the DTD protocols for handling detainees and be in full compliance with them by the end of the day tomorrow, at which time Jason would be checking back. He wanted to investigate just what these women were being charged with, and see what he could do about getting them moved to better quarters.

As he turned his car south toward Port Huron, Jason bowed his head with weariness. His body was exhausted and his heart was sick – and he still had one more issue to resolve before the sun set. He hadn't found Janice, or Teresa as she was known, but she was out there somewhere. As he drove, the last words she'd spoken to him echoed accusingly in his mind, and he knew she'd been right.

He could have stopped this.

The sun was dropping toward the horizon as Jason pulled into the main DHS office in Port Huron. There were many more lighted windows and cars in the lot than was usual for a government office this long after quitting time, but that was expected with all the activity in the area. Jason was greeted at the front desk by a supervisor and the director of security, who had been expecting him. Once the arrangements had been made, the supervisor told him that Ethan could be found out back in the break area. Jason took a deep breath and headed there.

The break area was nothing more than a couple of picnic tables and a trash can, well away from the building doors and windows. Smokers congregated here, but there was only one now, sitting on one of the tables, his back to the building and its bustle. Jason tapped out a smoke and lit it as he walked to the other table and took a seat facing the same direction. The man glanced over at Jason, grunted, and turned away to take another puff. There was a moment of silence as both men smoked in silence.

"I gotta hand it to you," Jason finally said. "That was an excellent job. Those messages were byte-for-byte identical to real ones. My tech said they were the best forgeries he'd ever seen. He was very impressed. I think you've earned a place in his gallery of samples."

"Thanks," Ethan muttered. "Nice to know my effort paid off."

"Almost," Jason corrected him. "I was particularly impressed by how you handled the response sequences. All of the genuine messages reached me, but never any of the forged ones. If you don't mind my asking, how did you manage that?"

Ethan looked at him and shrugged. "Server-side intercept. Small code pocket that I was able to slip into the distribution policies. It could detect which messages were written by you and which were written by me, and route them accordingly."

"This script has since been deleted, I presume?"

"Of course."

"Clever," Jason acknowledged. "And that was only part of it. The timing was perfect, and you even mimicked my idioms and style – impressive job." They fell silent again for a while.

"If you don't mind my asking, how did you figure it out?" Ethan finally asked.

"You had to know that it would be found out eventually – or were you figuring I'd be ruined and run out before then?" Jason replied. Ethan gave no answer, so he continued. "I have a friend in

D.C. who has a stepbrother named Zach, who works for a private security firm in their deep-tech area. Zach knows how to read portions of messages that most people don't know about, the parts that are hard to reach. It's in those parts that the hardware addresses of the originating devices are stored. I had someone forward some of the forgeries to me using private servers, so your clever little script was avoided. Once I got those to Zach, he was able to distinguish the real messages from the forgeries by the device addresses.

"Ah," Ethan replied. "I guess you can't anticipate everything." There was another long pause, during which bird songs could be heard piercing the evening air. Finally, Jason spoke again.

"So, what did Whitman offer you?"

"A clean record. A promotion. A transfer out of this shithole."

"And he never mentioned the consequences? Interfering with official communications. Forging classified messages. Hindering execution of critical departmental operations. I'm sure they'll think of more. That's high-level felony stuff, way beyond simple administrative action."

Ethan looked at Jason with a sneer. "You'll never pin any of that on me, even with all your proof. I've been around this block before. My union will negotiate, and I might get an extension of my probation. That's all."

"You were willing to unleash that on all these people just to help Whitman sink me?

Ethan glanced at him again, his expression ugly. "You think I give a flying about these people? Dirty, ignorant peasants with their rusty pickups and pissant little towns and empty fields and gloomy woods. T'hell with 'em all. I don't care about them any more than I care about you or Whitman. You're just a couple of jacked up 'crats from D.C., breezing into town just long enough to get what you want then flying off, leaving your messes for the rest of us to clean up. T'hell with you and Whitman both."

Jason pulled out his phone and tapped it a few times. "Well, you'll get part of your wish. Even as we speak, agents are closing in to arrest Whitman – just as agents are on their way out to arrest you. Your workstation and tablet have already been seized, but I'll need your phone."

Without even looking at Jason, Ethan pulled his phone from his pocket and tossed it dismissively on the table. Jason picked up the phone then turned and walked back toward the building, handing it as he passed to the security staff who were on their way for Ethan.

Back in his car, Jason sat for a minute, leaning back against the headrest. God, what a mess. This was going to take weeks to sort out. He'd only seen a couple of the forged messages, and part of him sympathized with the frustrated and confused Captain Touma. How could she have known which Jason Pelletier she was trying to satisfy? The sharp, decisive Jason who had given the go-ahead to her most forceful and aggressive plans? Or the wary, cautious Jason who seemed to only want to rein her in and hinder her operations? There was a folder full of forgeries awaiting him at his workstation back in Sandusky, and he'd best get to them. Throwing the car into gear, he turned back northward and headed for his temporary office.

What a day! What a hellish day! He'd gone to bed the night before without a hint that any of this would hit him, yet here he was, right in the thick of it. It was taxing and frustrating, but there was more to it, more than just the administrative confusion and betrayal and miscommunication. Jason couldn't quite put his finger on it, but it seemed to him that something poisonous lay at the root of everything. There was an extremity of violence, a seething brutality that underlay all that had happened, triggering responses madly out of proportion to what the circumstances warranted. Paramilitary teams executing maneuvers against private homes? Flash-bang grenades and drone strikes against families with children? When a couple of agents with sidearms knocking on the door would have sufficed? He'd gotten a personal taste of it when Mike had been arrested and he'd been curtly ejected from the house. There had been a sense that things were right at the edge, and could explode into uncontrolled savagery at any moment. It was infuriating and mystifying and frightening.

Jason had worked closely with violence before, major operations in urban areas renowned for being dangerous and lawless, but he'd never felt the kind of lust for destruction that seemed to mark operations in this remote rural area. What the hell was going on? And what could be done about it?

Suddenly a great weariness swept over Jason, a fatigue that rose out of physical exhaustion and emotional distress and heart sickness. He nearly nodded right there at the wheel, and began to swerve in his lane. He shook himself awake – fortunately, he was nearly home. He forced himself to focus on the road, shoving aside the other concerns that churned in his mind. His inbox would have to wait – he'd have to take a quick nap before tackling that. He pulled into his driveway and barely made it to his sofa before collapsing into a deep sleep.

Fulfillment

Luke stood in the shadow of the storage shed in which he'd parked the ATV. He had no idea who he was waiting for, or how long he'd have to wait. He would have liked to call Teresa back for more details, but he'd gotten the impression that her hands were full, and he didn't want to disturb her. For that matter, he didn't want to talk to anyone, as confused and upset as he was. He still didn't understand – how had his phone rung? – but it had been Linda's message that had shattered him. She had left it three hours earlier, and even now he didn't trust himself to speak to her – it would be too overwhelming. He'd sent her a message to the effect that he was returning, just to relieve her anguish, but as of yet had gotten no response from anyone.

From where he stood, Luke could see up and down the dirt road to where it intersected with roads to the north and south. Woody End was on a quiet road in a seldom-traveled area, so there wasn't much traffic in sight. But when a car approaching on the southern cross road doused its lights before turning onto the dirt road, Luke knew that was his ride. Killing headlights was a simple counter-surveillance trick for night driving. Luke watched the car come up the road toward him, its lights still extinguished. Whoever was driving had experience, and was being very cautious. He wondered who it was. Maybe Kent or Linda? One of Shelly's people? He stepped out to greet the car as it turned into the pull-off by the shed, catching a glimpse of the driver.

It was Felicity.

She gave him a quick smile and unlocked the doors so he could climb in. Once he was settled, she grabbed his hand fiercely.

"Thank God, thank God, Derek. We've been worried sick about you! Dad's been about frantic – we thought you might have been picked up."

"Picked up? By whom?"

Felicity stared at him, dumbfounded. "By the troops, of course!"

"Troops?" Luke asked in alarm.

"Have you no idea what's happened today?"

"What's happened?"

Aghast, Felicity gave him a quick summary of the day's events. As she spoke, Luke was smitten with remorse for the anxiety his impulsive actions had caused his friends.

"...and when you didn't answer, and didn't message, and nobody had heard from you, we feared the worst. Didn't you get all the messages?"

"Well," Luke answered sheepishly. "I had my phone turned off."

"Turned off?" Felicity said with surprise. "Why would you turn off your phone, especially with so much going on?"

"Well, I didn't know what was happening," Luke replied. "I guess I just wanted some time to think. There's been so much pressure lately, so much piling up."

"What kind of things?" Felicity asked.

Reluctant as he was to discuss it, Luke felt like such a mess of loneliness and regret and tension and heartache that before he knew it, it all came tumbling out – how he'd felt alienated and taken for granted, his early departure that morning and aimless wanderings through the day, his tenuous status as one who was officially dead, his decision to turn himself in to the Lapeer County Sheriff, and how close he'd come to actually doing that. Even as he recounted everything, his decisions and the impulses that had driven them sounded increasingly petty and immature, and by the time he was finishing he was almost ashamed. As he lamely wound down his explanation, he half expected Felicity to laugh at his silliness or admonish him for putting everyone to such trouble.

Felicity did neither. Instead she pulled to the side of the road, unbuckled her seat belt, and turned to enfold Luke in a fierce hug, pressing her damp cheek against his.

"Oh, Derek, Derek, I'm so sorry, we're so sorry," she whispered into his ear.

"Well, I'm the one who's sorry, for putting you all –" Luke began, but Felicity cut him off.

"No, you're right. We were taking you for granted. Dad sure thinks so. He was about spitting nails all afternoon – I've never seen him so mad at himself. He had an evacuation plan all worked out that he meant to go over with you."

"He did?"

"Of course he did! But a hundred little brushfires kept interfering, and he kept sending you off to attend to some of them." Felicity pulled back and looked at him, holding his face in her hands, tears glistening on her lashes. "That's what you get for being so blasted reliable, Luke Peterson. You were my dad's most dependable field worker, and he kept using you unthinkingly, without even stopping to thank you, much less let you know what provisions he'd made for you. Then you dropped off the face of the earth, and he was so remorseful, especially after Aunt Linda called back and ripped into him for treating you so badly. I felt sorry for him, but I could see her point. I've never been so relieved as when Teresa called to tell me to pick you up! And to think you came within an ace of turning yourself in to the sheriff! It gives me chills just thinking about it!"

"But...you mean..." Luke stammered, overwhelmed by these revelations. "I thought –"

Felicity startled him by leaning over and stopping his mouth with a firm kiss. She pulled back, keeping her eyes inches from his, and spoke in a slightly scolding tone.

"Luke Peterson, don't you ever think that you're not loved, or appreciated, or wanted. You are family. Don't you understand what that means?"

"I...I guess not," Luke said. Felicity sighed, then dropped her eyes and nodded.

"You wouldn't, would you? A couple of years can't offset a lifetime. Well, one thing it means is that you're never forgotten. You may be overworked, and occasionally unthanked for a time – both of which are wrong – but you're never forgotten. You matter, you matter to all of us." Her firm tone faltered. "You especially matter to me."

"I do?" Luke whispered.

Felicity looked up, straight into his eyes. "Most of all," she replied quietly, then gave a wry smile and leaned back a little. "Though Aunt Linda might contest me for that." Then she settled back in her seat and pulled back onto the road, leaving Luke stunned and reeling, not least from the unexpected kiss.

"What a mercy Teresa reached you in time," Felicity continued, then paused. "Wait – if your phone was turned off, how did her call get through?"

"I've no idea," Luke admitted, pulling out the device. "It was off when the call came in, and was off after she hung up. I turned it on just to be certain, which was when I found the messages that had been piling up – especially the last one from Linda."

Felicity shook her head. "She was nearly beside herself, but I gather the rest of the family wasn't much better. They almost refused to leave until you were found. It was all Dad could do to talk them down."

"They did leave, didn't they?" Luke asked, again smitten that he had not only caused his family such anguish but had nearly put them in grave danger.

"Yes, they're on their way to the refuge site, and may have even arrived by now. You could try Linda or Kent – they'd probably be able to pick up. You should also call Dad, to let him know you're safe."

"Well, I can't use my phone, because the battery is nearly dead," Luke said, checking his gage.

"So drop it on the charger and use mine. It's in my purse."

Luke spent some embarrassing and tearful minutes talking to the Schaeffers, who were beside themselves with joy to hear from him, and with Gil, who was abjectly apologetic and reassured Luke repeatedly that he'd be taken care of. By the end of it, Luke was feeling chills of his own at how close he'd come to shutting himself out of this world forever. After those calls, he felt he needed to take a rest and give himself some time for the emotional turmoil to settle. Through it all Felicity kept to herself, steering decisively along the dark and empty country roads. When he finally set the phone down, she gave him a smile.

"See? You're loved and appreciated, even if we're not always good at communicating it." She sighed sadly. "You were one of our missing people for the day. If only we could find the other."

"Who is that?"

"Grandpa," Felicity said grimly. "He left his haven early in the morning without telling anyone where he was going, and hasn't been heard from since."

"Grandpa?" Luke's breath felt labored. The beloved patriarch was another whom he hadn't considered in his self-absorbed maundering. "Grandpa's missing?"

"Yes. He'd been sent safely away, first to a local friend's house, with the intention of moving him to a refuge in Westfarthing. But he left the friend's house on his own. We suspect he returned to Rivendell, which may have been struck by the enemy. Nobody knows – once it was evacuated, we didn't think to keep a watch on it."

"So, Grandpa might have been taken? Does anyone know by whom?"

"No. Some of our sources report that the troops are identifying themselves as Domestic Terror Division, but there are no insignia, and no identification presented. Apparently Department of Homeland Security is warning local law enforcement to stay clear."

"Do we know where they've hit, and where they're taking people?"

"We've no idea where people are being taken," Felicity said grimly. "They hit thirteen sites that we know of, possibly fourteen if they got Rivendell also. The good news is that over half the sites had been evacuated. The worst news is that one of the ones that hadn't been was St. Anne's."

Luke leaned his head back and clenched his jaw. St. Anne's! The weakest guests, and the beloved sisters. He gasped. "Teresa! Was she – but no, then she wouldn't be able to call us. Wasn't she there? How did she escape?"

"I don't know," Felicity admitted. "We only spoke briefly, and didn't discuss St. Anne's. I intend to ask her when we meet."

"Is that where we're going? To where Teresa is?" Luke asked.

"Well, I think we're converging on the same place, but she asked me to make one more stop first – we're picking up Grace. We're nearly there now, but before we arrive, I've one more thing I want to clear up with you."

"What's that?"

Felicity sighed and proceeded hesitantly. "A couple of weeks ago, when we were...when we were out in the gazebo...I behaved very inappropriately. I'm sorry for that, and for any pain and confusion it might have caused you."

"That's all right," Luke replied, embarrassed. "I must admit I was a bit confused. It was so unlike you."

"It was very unlike me," Felicity said with a blush. "To this day I'm not sure why I did it. I don't want to hide behind the tired old 'I don't know what came over me' excuse, but in this case there's a germ of truth in it. I've been very confused and...disjointed recently, especially since returning from school. It's like I've been under a cloud of some sort, and you haven't been the one who's gotten the worst of it. My relationship with Grace had almost been destroyed before Teresa stepped in and helped us."

"I understand," Luke said. "I think that I – and others – have been having similar experiences." He remembered the dejection and discouragement that had overwhelmed him the moment he'd awakened this morning, and how uncharacteristic it was of him. How could he have so easily forgotten all those people who loved him? How could he have ever thought his family would overlook him? The more he considered it, the less sense it made.

"Since that day," Felicity continued. "I've been avoiding you, mostly out of embarrassment. I had no idea what to say to you, how to begin to apologize."

"You've done just fine," Luke assured her.

"I was afraid that what I'd done had helped drive you away." She took his hand and squeezed it. "I'm so glad you're back."

"Let's not talk about it anymore, okay?"

"Okay!" Felicity replied with a smile. "Well, here we are at Grace's." She pulled into the drive, and Grace came out of the house and got into the back seat.

"Where to now?" Luke asked.

"Remember the last time we were all together? Up in Huron County, before we went back to school?" Felicity asked.

"Who could forget that night?" Grace replied.

"Well, that's where we're headed now. Apparently we're going to meet up with some others there."

"What for?" Luke asked.

"Teresa didn't tell me," Felicity responded.

*   *   *

Fr. Gabriel was eastbound on Sanilac Road, heading for Deford, where one of the attacked households was located. He'd just spent a futile hour at the Detainment Center outside of Port Sanilac trying to get in to see the sisters held captive there. The official in charge had called several parties to determine if he could let Fr. Gabriel in, or to even let him know the status of the captives. There had been so many half-replies and unanswered phones that in the end the official had informed Fr. Gabriel that he didn't think he had the authority, and to try back tomorrow. Trying to salvage the evening, Fr. Gabriel headed for Deford, all the while talking to Fr. Vincent up by Pigeon, who was trying to make arrangements for the stranded Bailey children.

Never in his years of ministry had Fr. Gabriel known such a tense and frustrating day. Paramilitary raids and air strikes in his own parish! What was the world coming to? Saginaw wanted answers and Detroit wanted answers and Fr. Gabriel wanted answers, too. He'd gotten help from many, like Pastor Gene over in Marlette, but he still felt stretched and battered. The support teams he normally drew on for resources had their hands full evacuating the ranches, about which he was supposed to know nothing, which meant he had to stretch further.

He'd just passed through Sandusky and was approaching the crossroad named Elmer on the map – actually no more than a few houses scattered along the road – when the dark tension inside his car began to lighten. Despite the burden of his concerns, he began smiling and tapping the wheel as a favorite tune from his high school days began playing in his mind. Soon he was humming, and before he knew it, the space was filled with the frothing jollity which had overwhelmed him several days before. Part of him bristled indignantly at the impropriety of it all. On a day filled with such violence and tragedy! But his resistance was swept away, and shaking his head he succumbed to chuckling, which turned into guffaws, and before he knew it he was belly laughing.

"Enough! Enough!" he cried when he could catch a breath. "You clearly have no sense of decorum. What do You want of me?"

To turn north.

"What, on Ubly Road?"

Yes.

"But – Deford is further along."

Deford can wait. Turn north.

"Toward Bad Axe?"

You need not pass through Bad Axe. Go north. Tonight you shall have the last laugh.

Fr. Gabriel thought for a moment. Ubly Road would take him to Ubly and beyond, to where it hit Sand Beach Road just east of Bad Axe. That was where most people turned left to go into town, but you didn't have to. You could keep going straight, on what became Plumber Road, which continued north through the fields.

Until it hit Nathan Road.

Fr. Gabriel's eyes narrowed, his levity replaced by fierce determination. Turning right at Elmer, he headed north at a most unpriestly speed.

*   *   *

As the three friends drove north through the night, Felicity told the others all the details she knew of the strikes on the ranches earlier that day: which of them had been empty, which had been occupied, and how many people had been lost.

"I can't believe they fired a missile at a residence," Grace gasped. "How many died?"

"If everyone was there, it would have been six – three adults and three children," Felicity said. "There were two waves of strikes, the biggest at dawn and a second one about an hour and a half after that. We don't know exactly what damage the second wave did. Two addresses we know they hit had been vacated, but it's possible they hit Rivendell as well. That had been evacuated, but it's possible that…someone had gone back. We don't know."

"Any other activity besides that?" Luke asked.

"Not that we know of," Felicity replied. "Of course, we were scramming everyone we could even with the risk of overhead exposure, so it's possible some sites were hit without our knowledge. Those would have been vacated ones, though, since we got positive contact with all the occupied ones before midmorning. But since the second wave of strikes, we've heard nothing.

"Doesn't that seem odd?" Grace asked. "All those resources, all that coordination – I would have expected more action."

"That's what we thought, too," Felicity assured her. "That's why we took the risk of scramming everyone in broad daylight. We don't know why the assaults ceased so suddenly, or what to expect next – and we don't want to wait around to find out."

"So, everybody has been evacuated?" Luke asked.

"Just about. Some are staying, though with a lower profile – Steve, Lawrence and Annette, a few others. Your family is, Grace, though they've always been on the periphery. Mom and Dad and all of us are going to slip away sometime in the next couple of days. Aunt Ruth and Uncle Travis are leaving tomorrow."

"Any word from Cletus and Sixtus?" Luke asked. Felicity only bit her lip and shook her head, a little teary. Luke thought of

Linda's anguished message, and wondered what "We may have lost Phillip" might mean.

Meanwhile Felicity kept driving northward, and from the back seat Grace cleared her throat. "Ah, Feliss," she said in an edgy voice. "I've…ah…heard some rumors about this place we're headed toward."

"I've heard a few myself," Felicity replied. "But it's where Teresa told me to come. We'll just have to trust her, like we did last summer. Ah, here we are." Felicity stopped at an intersection, and Luke noticed the sign said "Nathan Road". She turned left. They traveled the last few miles in tension-tinged silence, Felicity focused intently on the road, her lips moving silently. Luke struggled against a deepening sense of threat, a threat that seemed to lie ahead of them. He also noticed that the plowed fields and tended ditches were giving way to fallow stretches and choked, unkempt roadsides. They were entering an area where people rarely came.

Finally they saw taillights ahead. A car was parked by the side of the road, and Felicity pulled up behind it. She left the headlights on as they all got out and approached the two figures standing there, who turned out to be Teresa and Todd. Felicity and Grace rushed to Teresa, so Luke approached Todd, who was looking disheveled and smelled vaguely of beer.

"Hey, man," Luke gripped Todd's hand. "What brings you here?"

"She does," Todd jerked his thumb over his shoulder in Teresa's direction. "She seems to be running everything this evening."

"Well, good to see you. It's been a while," Luke said, thinking that it had been far too long. Todd was wearing scruffy jeans and a dark, stained work jacket over a tired looking t-shirt. He seemed dispirited and looked at the ground more than he looked at Luke. "How have things been?"

"Well…ah," Todd stammered, but he was saved from having to respond by the approach of Teresa, who came up to enfold Luke in a great hug, then stepped back, taking his hands and looking at him with sparkling eyes.

Luke was taken aback. He had never seen Teresa look as joyous, as effervescent, as radiant as she did now. Her smile, always her loveliest feature, seemed to illuminate not only her face but her entire being. Adding to the luminous effect, she was clad in her usual plain white blouse and simple white work skirt which she wore like a princess would wear a gown.

"Luke, thank you so much for coming. I'm so glad you could make it. Isn't it a glorious night?" Teresa asked, releasing one of his hands and sweeping her arm toward the heavens.

Looking up, Luke saw that she was right – it was a glorious night. The sky was mostly clear and carpeted with stars. A nearly full moon hung overhead, bathing the land in pale light that was bright enough to cast faint shadows. A warm, gentle breeze idled from the southwest, wafting scents of flowering meadows and budding trees, aromas which were familiar and welcome to Luke. It appeared to be just as Teresa had claimed, a glorious spring night.

But over Teresa's shoulder loomed the blight on the idyllic scene – a dark, ominous mass of trees thrusting into the sky to the west, occluding a large patch of stars. The gentle moonlight was unable to penetrate the shadows shrouding the woods. Luke was unsettled to see that despite the mildness of the breeze, the tops of the trees were waving and tossing as if buffeted by a gale. The low moaning and rushing from this waving was the only sound in this otherwise quiet evening.

Luke recognized where they were. He had not been back here since that night last summer, though he had heard enough rumors to stay clear of the area. Beyond Teresa, about a quarter of a mile away, he could see the glint of the tall security fence that he'd heard had been thrown up around the woods.

As Luke gazed at the waving mass of dark branches, the apprehension which he'd been feeling seemed to deepen, and he found his body tensing. He wanted to be anywhere but here. He wanted to get back in the car and drive somewhere that the breeze blew unhindered and nothing blocked the view of the sky and the moonlight fell onto the fields and woods without shadow.

"Luke?" Teresa's voice broke his reverie.

"Oh, ah, yes," Luke replied clumsily, his eyes still lingering on the woods. "Lovely...lovely night."

Teresa followed his gaze, then turned back with a silvery laugh. Even as she did so, the trees seemed to buck and bow as if struck by a blast of wind, and a noise that was something between a moan and a shriek rose from the depths of the shadow. Luke supposed the sound might be made by two tree trunks blown against each other, but he still gave a little start.

"Don't worry," Teresa said casually, waving a hand. "It's just upset because it knows its time is short."

Luke didn't know what to make of this, so he asked, "Is this as close as we're getting to...that?"

"Oh, no. We'll need to get right up to the gate. We're just awaiting another party, and that may be him." Teresa pointed over Luke's shoulder at some headlights that were coming from the same direction Felicity had come. Squarely illuminated by the headlights, Teresa grinned and waved at the car, which stopped just in front of her. To Luke's surprise, Fr. Gabriel got out and smiled at Teresa.

"Well, am I in time for the festivities?" he asked.

"They wouldn't be able to proceed without you!" Teresa said cheerily. "Thank you all for coming."

"The summons was...compelling," Fr. Gabriel assured her. He clapped his hands together and rubbed them in anticipation. "So, what's next? Are we ready to proceed? What are we doing, anyway?"

"We are nearly ready," Teresa replied. "We're expecting a couple more arrivals to trickle in, but most of the main participants are here. We should be getting into place, so let's move closer. Father, if you could lead, we'll follow. Please park sideways across the road in front of the gate – we'll want to illuminate your hood with our headlights."

"Illuminate?"

"Yes," Teresa responded. "Altars should be illuminated, should they not?"

"Altars? Yes, yes, they should," Fr. Gabriel replied, getting back into his car. Teresa called Felicity over and explained what she wished done. Then everyone piled into vehicles to follow Fr. Gabriel down the road toward the dark woods. Luke watched nervously as they came to the chain-link fence, and the peripheral light from the headlamps showed some kind of solid metal fence beyond the chain-link, right up against the woods. He didn't remember that being there. Above the top of the solid fence twisted branches swayed, casting strange shadows as the light passed by.

Fr. Gabriel parked so his headlights pointed directly at the tall gate in the security fence, and the gate in the fence beyond, the gate through which the three women present had passed last summer. Weeds had grown up around the gate and the foliage was thick on the other side. The video camera that had monitored the gate, which had been destroyed on that fateful night, still sat on its platform, a shattered mess. Nobody had taken the trouble to remove it.

The other two cars pulled up in the middle of the road, training their headlights so they bathed the hood of Fr. Gabriel's car. He was rummaging in his trunk, eventually coming forward with a medium-sized board in one hand and what looked like a small suitcase in the other.

"I carry this with me because I never know where I might have to say Mass," Fr. Gabriel said, holding up the board. "However, I've never had to use the hood of a car before, so perhaps I could borrow some jackets to stabilize it?" Luke and Todd stepped forward, shedding their jackets and folding them up to place beneath the board on the hood while Fr. Gabriel fished around in the suitcase. When he stood up, he had a stole draped around his neck.

"Teresa tells me that we're still awaiting one more important party, and doesn't want to begin until he arrives. Until then, I'm open for confession," he announced.

"I'll go first!" Teresa said, almost bouncing where she stood.

"Very well, then – if you'll step into my confessional," Fr. Gabriel said, gesturing to his car. Then he turned to Luke and Todd. "Gentlemen, if you'd be so kind as to place the items in the bottom of this case out onto the makeshift altar, it would save time." He got into the car while Luke and Todd set out the Mass items and altar cloth. They tried not to look at the woods behind them, where the trees were now writhing and pitching furiously. Felicity and Grace stood nearby, holding hands and talking quietly, their backs to the woods. Luke focused on his task, trying to ignore the unease hanging around him, the sense of looming threat. This was probably the last place in the entire world he wanted to be, yet he was here at Teresa's summons. He glanced at Todd, who seemed to be having even more difficulty. Todd was sweating and muttering to himself, and his hands were trembling slightly as he set out the vessels. Luke sighed – clearly, he wasn't the only one who'd been having struggles of late.

Presently the passenger door of Fr. Gabriel's car opened and Teresa hopped out, leaving it open as she went to the far side of the road to stand quietly with her back to them, her head bowed. The other four looked around at each other before Todd spoke.

"I…I'll go next," he said, and got into the car. Luke continued as best he could, though he had no experience setting up altars. When he'd finally placed everything in the case somewhere on the board, he sensed someone standing at his elbow. Still a little jittery, he jumped a little and turned to see Teresa.

"Oh, it's you," he breathed in relief.

"Of course it's me, right here with you," Teresa said with a smile, then threw her arms around his neck and hugged him tight. "Oh, precious friend, dearest brother, what joy it brings me to have you here on this wonderful night!" She pulled away and stood at arm's length, still holding both his hands and beaming at him.

What exception Luke might have taken regarding the wonder of the night died on his lips. Teresa was, if possible, more radiant than she'd been just a few minutes earlier, seeming to glow with passion and excitement. Though she was still the same Janice he'd always known, tonight he felt like he'd never seen a more beautiful woman – in fact, it was like he'd never seen a woman at all.

"You...you're looking uncommonly good," Luke stammered clumsily.

"How could I not? My Groom comes for me tonight." She hugged him again. "Beloved friend, you who have seen me at my worst, how suitable that you should be here. You loved me when I was scattered in a thousand pieces, and it was often your hands that were used to gather me back together. Now, I am nearly complete. I am yet two, but soon, very soon, I will be one, no longer disintegrated but a harmonious whole."

"Oh...ah, that's great," Luke fumbled, not knowing how to respond. "That's just great."

"It's glorious!" Teresa exclaimed, throwing her arms wide and lifting her face to the heavens. Then she looked at him with grave sympathy and caressed his cheek. "Dear brother, how deeply you are loved. I know you cannot receive that yet, at least not all of it. You are still in too many pieces. I understand. All things in proper time. You shall be gathered back together and unified. Even tonight a large part of it shall be begun. Have patience, and trust."

"Um...okay," Luke replied, only understanding about half of that, but appreciating the part about being loved. "It's great to see you so happy."

"I am happy, and soon will be even happier. Remember that, for my path may seem difficult, but it is the path I have been summoned to, and the path I have chosen."

"Sure," Luke replied. Just then Todd got out of the car and went to the side of the road, where he crouched down with his back to everyone. Teresa looked at Todd lovingly, but Luke glanced at the door, and then at Felicity and Grace, who were still talking.

"I guess it's my turn, then," Luke said, getting into the car for his confession.

Grace was standing closer to Felicity than she'd normally stand to anyone, and they both had their backs turned to the towering, shadowed menace of the trees. It was hard to recall the giddy triumph of that summer night, when they'd passed illuminated through the choking mist and led all those poor youngsters to freedom. Grace could remember the facts of the event, but could not taste the experience, the exhilaration, the sense of victory. It seemed she could not tap any positive memory or feeling, not here, so near the eaves of these haunted woods.

Here came Teresa, smiling and holding out her hands to them both. Her spirits didn't appear to be dampened at all by the looming threat. "My dear sisters, how wonderful and suitable it is for you to be here tonight," Teresa proclaimed joyously. "I know it is short notice, but will you be my bridesmaids? There's nobody in the world I'd rather have."

"Sure, Teresa, we'd be happy to," Felicity replied with a quick glance at Grace. It was the kind of glance that might convey uncertainty about someone's stability or grasp on reality, but neither of the women could shake the impression that, of the three of them, Teresa was the most stable and perceptive right now.

"Wonderful," Teresa smiled with just the hint of a wink, as if she sensed her friends' uncertainty. "We shall have the nuptial Mass shortly. Fr. Gabriel is hearing confessions now, if you wish to avail yourselves. Currently the men are, so we have some time."

"Luke seems to be just finishing," Felicity pointed out. "I'll go now." She walked over to the car, leaving Grace with a beaming Teresa swinging her shoulders with excitement.

"I know!" Teresa said. "I'll want a bouquet. It won't compare to my real one, but it'll be something to hold."

"A bouquet would be nice," Grace admitted, looking around for any flowers that might serve.

"What about these? They're delicate and lovely," Teresa said, walking over to the masses of Queen Anne's Lace growing by the side of the road. Grace followed hesitantly with a puzzled expression, her suspicions about Teresa's stability beginning to resurface.

"Oh, come on, Teresa," Grace prodded gently where Teresa was selecting the stalks with the largest flowers. "Surely we can find something more suitable than a ditch weed to make into your bridal bouquet."

"Why would that be unsuitable, when my Groom has chosen a ditch weed to make into His Bride?" Teresa paused to fix Grace with an innocent gaze. Grace had no answer to that, so proceeded to help harvest flowers. They found a few sprays of small daisies to fit in here and there, and by the time Felicity returned the bouquet was large and surprisingly beautiful.

"How lovely!" Felicity exclaimed.

"It's amazing how pretty even ditch weed flowers can look," Grace admitted. "But what shall we do for a veil?"

"I need no veil, not here," Teresa said quietly, touching her hair while her eyes got a faraway look in them. "There is none on earth as fair as the one my Groom has provided."

Giving Felicity another skeptical glance, Grace asked, "Teresa, are you sure you know exactly what you're doing here?"

"I'm not doing anything," Teresa answered with serene confidence. "I'm simply following my Groom's call. He is moving pieces into place, some by my hand, and some more directly. All is nearly ready – only a few moves remain. But, my sisters," a vulnerable note crept into her tone, and for a minute she looked less like a confident princess and more like their familiar Teresa, "the last step will be the greatest, but will require the most courage. My Beloved has called me to make it for His sake and for many others. Pray that I would have the strength to be faithful, and not to falter at the last."

Felicity and Grace assured her that they would, then Grace went for her turn at confession while Teresa and Felicity strolled back toward the makeshift altar. The men were off by themselves, presumably doing their penances. Felicity couldn't help but notice that the dark trees to their right were waving and thrashing more violently than ever, though the evening breeze remained mild, and more moans and thumps could be heard coming from the dark eaves. She also saw that Teresa took no notice of these phenomena, but chatted as easily as if they were strolling through a park on a peaceful afternoon.

"Ah," Teresa said, pointing down the road. "Here comes another of our expected pieces. Would you be so kind as to take my bouquet?" A pickup was approaching, and Teresa walked over to it confidently while Felicity stayed back holding the flowers. The pickup stopped just short of the gate in the fence, and the man who got out of it wore a brown sheriff's uniform. Felicity recognized him from that night last summer, though he hadn't been wearing a uniform then. It was the Huron County sheriff – Keller, that was his name. The men had been working with him. Felicity had no idea what he was doing here, but Teresa seemed to, for she was talking to him briskly and he was nodding. She finished whatever she was saying and started back toward Felicity while the sheriff began fetching something out of the bed of his pickup.

Confession had been hard for Luke. He remembered having all sorts of good intentions when he'd begun his spiritual journey – daily prayer, diligent Mass attendance, confession at least once a month like Grandpa had recommended. Over time those intentions had fallen by the wayside, starting with confession and eventually extending to Mass attendance, particularly lately. He finished the prayers he'd been assigned with the resolve to return to all those practices, whatever direction his life took him from here.

Luke turned back toward the altar to see that Fr. Gabriel was out of the car and vesting for Mass. He was also surprised to see that Sheriff Keller had arrived. What was Chip doing here? He would have walked over to chat with him, but Teresa was standing with the women, and was beckoning both him and Todd over to join them.

"My dear friends, you who have been closest to me, the time is short," Teresa said to them all, her eyes shining. "My time of union is mere minutes away. On this, my wedding night, my Groom has granted me gifts to bestow." She handed her bouquet to Grace and took Luke's hand. To his stunned amazement she walked him over to where Felicity stood. Taking her hand, she laid it in his and folded his hand around hers. "Beloved, I give you each other. All that is past, is past. Your lives begin anew tonight. If you accept the burden, you shall embark together, and help one another through the trials to come."

Luke could hardly believe his ears. That which he'd never dared dream, coming true here on this country road! He looked down at Felicity and saw not the unattainable goddess of his fantasies, but a real woman – beautiful, to be sure, but simple and human and even a bit bedraggled. As his fears and hopes and embarrassments and idealizations faded away, he felt like he was truly seeing her for the first time.

"I accept the burden, if she will have me," Luke found himself saying.

Felicity blushed a little and dropped her eyes, then raised them again and spoke clearly. "I will have you, and will accept the burden as well." Luke expected his heart to soar at these words, but circumstances were too grave. There would be time for excitement later; just now they felt the weight too keenly.

"Then you are betrothed," Teresa pronounced with authority. She then kissed them both tenderly on their cheeks, then took her bouquet from Grace and handed it to Felicity, and turned to Todd and Grace. Laying her hand in his, she said again, "Beloved, I give you each other. Begin anew. Help one another in charity, and bear one another's burdens."

Luke noticed that Grace was looking frankly at Todd, but Todd was looking at the ground. "I…I'm willing, for my part," Todd forced out. "But I don't know if you'd want me, damaged goods that I am."

Grace smiled and reached out to lift his chin. "I'm rather damaged myself, Todd. If you'll have me, I'll have you, and with the Lord's help we'll repair each other's damage."

Todd looked up, and Luke could see the tears standing in his eyes. Then he and Grace were embracing and sobbing on each other. Felicity stepped next to Luke, who put his arm around her as she leaned her head on his shoulder.

"Then you are betrothed," Teresa announced. "Now, beloved, the time draws near. I see that Fr. Gabriel is vested and ready. Let us go up to the mountain of the Lord, to celebrate the Wedding

Feast of the Lamb." Taking her bouquet back, she led them all toward where Fr. Gabriel stood in the headlights, the vessels ready on the makeshift altar, the candles burning, and his Missal in his hand.

Sacrifice

At their next meeting, Gerald seemed more than normally subdued as he passed Pete and Dr. Harris the newest set of translated pages. As the men snapped the pages into their binders, they noticed that there were fewer of them.

"As you can see," Gerald explained. "This set of pages is the final translation – the task is complete. Dr. Picotte is very excited."

"Do we find out what happens to Jean? And Fr. Thomas?" Pete asked as he flipped through the pages.

"Yes, though it's not a happy ending, at least for them," Gerald replied. "Only two entries remain in the journal, one rather lengthy one and the other quite brief. The lengthy one is a deliberate history written for a specific purpose, which Fr. Thomas records at the outset. Take a look at the top of the page:

> *It is now four days since we returned from our journey, and my health has only gotten worse. I can wait no longer, nor presume that I shall survive to make my report in person. I must write the account of our journey north, and of the noble sacrifice of Jean LaPenseé, Christian, lest I die and all record be lost.*

"That doesn't sound encouraging," Dr. Harris noted.

"No, it doesn't, and it means that Fr. Thomas's record is much more focused, so we don't have to wade through extraneous personal details. Let's look at what he said:

> *We rose well before dawn the next morning, for we had much paddling ahead of us. The rain had ceased and the wind was coming up the river, which the men said boded well for our journey. Jean bid Nikikouet and his children farewell, and spoke of returning in a week.*

We took two of the lightest canoes, for speed was the purpose. Two men and Jean were in one, while I was in the other with two men paddling. We passed swiftly up the river and were on the great lake which they call Gitgee Goomi by dawn.

I sat huddled in the center of the canoe, coughing and wrapped in furs. Jean was able to assist in paddling his canoe, but I was not, so I tried to stay as warm and dry as I could, and offered the discomforts of the journey to our Lord for the salvation of these people and the success of our journey.

The day passed long and dreary, and as the sun set we put into a small bay with sandy beaches. Fires were lit and Jean sat by me, smoking and chatting as if he had not rowed all day. He said that we were well more than halfway to our destination, and if the wind and weather held we would be in the Michipicoten area the next morn. He seemed little concerned about what would happen when we arrived.

We rose long before dawn the following day to get out on the water. So great was my exhaustion and illness, and so unsettling the motion of the canoe, that I did not give my morning devotions the attention they deserved, especially in light of our goal. I asked Our Lady and St. Joseph to pray for me.

As we proceeded, the wind swung so that it blew off the shore, making rowing a bit more difficult, but the men made light of it. After several hours one of the men in the other boat pointed and shouted. Our boat drew close to theirs and the men spoke rapidly to each other while Jean explained to me that we had come to the area of the forests around Michipicoten. One of the men spoke to Jean as he pointed to a beach not a league away. Jean agreed, so we paddled the canoes in.

The beach was a narrow sandy strip that quickly merged into one of the vast flat marshes so common in this land. From the marsh a stream flowed across the beach and down to the lake, just south of where we landed. To the east the fen stretched to the edge of a distant forest, but to the southeast stood a line of tall pines. The sun was rising beyond the distant trees, which were casting the usual morning shadows. At the north edge of the beach stood an outcropping or rock perhaps one and a half to two perches high [Trans: about 10-14 meters] The face of the outcropping was steep but climbable, with many boulders, shelves, and crags. The top was clearly flat, for woods ran right up to the edge of the outcropping, looming over the beach.

As we drew near the beach, the trees on the outcropping above us increasingly drew our attention. They were deep in shadow, but as the sun rose and scattered his rays through the misted woods to the southeast, those same rays did not seem to penetrate the woods atop the outcropping. No light pierced the darkness that wrapped about the boles of those great pines. As we drew closer, I thought my eyes must deceive me, for it seemed like a thick mist churned and roiled amidst the trees, a mist unlike the light morning mists of this coast, or even the heavier fogs that roll in at times. This mist was dark and murky, and no light could penetrate it, much less dispel it.

As the men beheld this, they began pointing and speaking rapidly among themselves. Though I could not comprehend their words, there was no mistaking the edge of fear in their voices. These were men who held steadfastness and courage as the greatest virtues, yet their terror was manifest.

They rowed to the beach, their eyes ever straying to the woods above them. Jean leapt ashore bearing his pack and musket, while I was put out of the canoe and my pack thrust roughly into my hands. The canoes pulled quickly away from the beach, to stand off in the lake at some distance, where the men spoke rapidly among themselves and continued pointing at the mist. I asked Jean to translate their words, and he told me that they were saying that the land bleeds. The thick mist among the trees was the gore of the land rising to darken the woods and shroud what lurked therein. He said their gesticulations and gestures were warding signs, intended to keep the evil at bay.

I asked him if he still intended to follow his plan, and he assured me he did. I planted in the sand my Cross, the sign by which Hell is defeated and darkness scattered, and at the foot of it I heard Jean's brief confession. Then I set out the elements upon a rock and said the sacrifice of the Mass as the sun rose higher in the eastern sky, shedding his light on the world. I gave Jean Communion, knowing well it might be his Viaticum, and also gave him to drink of the Chalice, given his chosen mission. Then he knelt in the sand for the final blessing. I embraced him like the brother he was, and he slung his musket. Telling me to look for him within the week, but to wait no longer, he turned his face to the outcropping and began climbing it. I watched his intrepid progress as he ascended, never looking back, until he attained the top and plunged into the wood.

I gathered up the Mass vessels and packed them away even as one of the canoes put in to shore to fetch me. I boarded clumsily but was sure to hold the Cross high. As we pulled away from the shore, I did my best to stand in the boat and hold the cross erect and facing the shadowed wood. When my canoe rejoined the other, the men quickly turned the bows southward. They wished to quit the area as quickly as they could, no matter how I tried to make clear that I wished to wait. Their wills prevailed, so I watched the rocks for any sign as they began to row swiftly for home. We had not gone half a league before we heard, muffled across the water, a musket shot. This made the men row yet harder.

The return trip to the Sault was soon beset by steady rain that chilled me to the marrow as I crouched in the canoe. My cough worsened and I could not eat, even ashore. When we landed, the men went to the tribal leaders while I sought Nikikouet and told her all.

That was now four days ago. Spurred by the report of the men who rowed to Michipicoten, the tribal leaders made the decision to move the tribe south, across the river, and the village was packed with the speed the Salteaux can exhibit when they desire. Now only a few remain – some stragglers, as well as Nikikouet and her children, awaiting the return of Jean. My cough has not departed, and I awaken weaker every morning. I write this in case I will never present my report in person, most especially that the sacrifice and heroism of Jean LaPenseé should not be forgotten. I pray that he survived and may yet return, but my heart forebodes otherwise. Nikikouet also is certain that he is lost. If that be so, I am convinced that this rude trapper has been received by all the saints and angels. He gave his life to protect his people and heal the wounded land. Greater love hath no man –

"What does that mean?" Dr. Harris asked, pointing at the page.

"What does what mean?" Gerald replied.

"That last sentence – it looks like a fragment."

"It's a quote from the Bible. Jesus said it, 'Greater love has no man than to lay down his life for his friends.'"

Dr. Harris looked puzzled. "What does he mean by that? Why would he partially quote Jesus?"

Gerald looked at Dr. Harris in silence for some while before responding. "He's suggesting that Jean's actions be interpreted in that light. He's saying that Jean walked into those shadowed woods and lost his life out of love for his family and tribe, and that he should be recognized as a martyr."

Dr. Harris muttered something and looked back at the binder.

"There's only one more entry, very brief," Gerald continued.

Now eleven days, no sign of Jean. My health worsens despite Nikikouet's ministrations. I entrust this journal to her, that if I perish, she may return it to a Jesuit, or to any who can return it to my superior in Quebec. My mission has failed. May God have mercy on my soul.

"And that's the end of the journal," Gerald pronounced. "The last line is in Latin. Clearly the journal was never returned, and it's very nearly a miracle that it survived at all. It had to have been handed down by Nikikouet to her children, but how it ended up in your aunt's attic, Pete, is anyone's guess. I don't think there's any question as to its authenticity."

"Was it as big a find as everyone was expecting?" Pete asked.

"A discovery such as this, especially an original document, is always a big find," Gerald explained. "There weren't any startling revelations, but that doesn't lessen the value. I think scholars will consider this more evolutionary than revolutionary. We knew that missionaries were working in the upper Great Lakes about that period; this gives us more detail. We knew that by the 1650s the Salteaux Ojibwa had moved south and west from the Sault area. We'd thought the impetus was Iroquois pressure; this sheds more light on why they migrated, and possibly on why they ultimately felt free to return. They retained a presence in the Sault area, and were resident when Marquette and Allouez arrived some decades later."

"Perhaps the journal became an artifact in the hands of the tribe?" Pete suggested.

"Probably not, for which we can be thankful," Gerald said. "If it had been a tribal artifact, it would have moved west during the successive centuries when the Salteaux were pressured to resettle into Manitoba, Saskatchewan, and Alberta. It would almost certainly have been lost. I suspect it stayed in family hands, which probably means that some of your ancestors were descended from Jean and Nikikouet, or had close contact with those who were. Is there any word of First Nation or *métis* blood in your family?"

"Not that I've heard," Pete replied.

"But," Dr. Harris struggled to articulate. "But...do you *believe* all this?"

"'Believe' what, Dr. Harris?" Gerald asked.

"This...this whole thing about a haunted woods and this trapper breaking a spell, and...all of it, I guess."

"The record is what the record is, Dr. Harris," Gerald replied coolly. "Regardless of what we postmoderns think of the outlook and motivations of the Salteaux and Fr. Thomas, his account of the activities is clear and relatively dispassionate. You can form your own opinions of what you think was happening there four centuries ago. But as I've said before, we have to judge their actions based on how they understood reality, not how we do. Unless you wish to contend that the Salteaux Ojibwa and Fr. Thomas were childish, ignorant savages, *something* influenced their behavior. We have only this account to relate what that was."

Dr. Harris nodded, again preoccupied with his binder.

"So...what's next?" Pete asked. "Now that the translation is complete, what happens?"

"That's somewhat up to you, Pete," Gerald replied. "The ultimate disposition of the journal is your decision. I know Drs. Newell and Picotte are hoping to have an announcement event at the University of Western Ontario. They especially wish to thank you, Pete, and Dr. Harris and Lake Superior State. If there's enough interest and input, it may turn into a weekend seminar. I know that Anishinaabek representatives from across Canada and the U.S. are very intrigued. The Jesuits, of course, wish to attend."

"Wow," Pete said with a grin. "That sounds like a lot of trouble for a simple journal."

"You'll be welcome at all of it, of course – both of you, as guests of honor," Gerald continued. "I'll be in touch as plans firm up. It may be months away, given all the coordination that must happen."

With that the men shook hands, promising to stay in touch. Tucking his binder into his briefcase and his passport into his pocket, Gerald stepped into the warm evening air and strode toward his car, pondering as he went whether that which healed a wounded land could also heal a wounded soul.

Revelations

Jason was in another dream that was indistinguishable from waking. He was standing at an intersection he remembered well, the corner of M-53 and Nathan Road. There were the tumbledown buildings and the street sign, dimly visible in the lone streetlight that hung over the road. The streetlight swayed in the night breeze, but other than that there was no movement. M-53 was empty as far as he could see, and toward the east Nathan Road stretched into the distance, a pale dusty line between the dark fields, edged by tall weeds being blown by the wind. In the distance, shadowy outlines of woods lurked on the horizon. Jason turned away – he knew what lay in that direction, and didn't want to think about it.

Jason saw a white-clad figure coming toward him from the north, walking along the side of the road. From her bearing and silhouette he guessed who it was even before she was close enough to recognize. It was Janice, or Teresa, coming down the shadowed road as if it was broad daylight. As she drew near, he could see that she was dressed in a long, flowing white dress and veil, and holding a beautiful bouquet. Her eyes were slightly downcast and her lips were moving in silent speech.

"Janice! Janice, it's me!" Jason called out, but she didn't notice him. She was engaged in what seemed to Jason not so much an attitude of diffusion as one of intent focus, fixation to the exclusion of all else. Jason was standing on the southeast corner of the intersection, watching her approach. He would have run across to meet her, but he feared to set foot on that cursed road, lest he be led astray.

She was approaching the intersection now, and Jason was desperate to have her acknowledge him. "Teresa!" he called. Finally she looked up and gazed at him, her eyes full of tenderness and love.

"I'm…I'm sorry!" Jason called. "You warned me, but I didn't listen! I could have stopped it –"

Teresa said nothing, but gave him a brilliant smile which somehow reassured him that he was forgiven. Having reached the intersection, she turned and began walking down the center of Nathan Road toward the shadowed east.

"No, Teresa!" Jason cried in alarm. "Not that way! It's too dangerous! You'll get lost!" But if she heard him, she gave no indication, but kept walking straight, her white dress receding into the night.

Jason came fully awake, his heart pounding. He knew that woman and he knew that road. He grabbed his phone and looked at the time – just past eleven. He'd slept for a little over two hours, but he knew what he had to do. Dream or no, he had to find her. He ran to his car.

The roads were empty on the drive toward Bad Axe, and the stoplight in the center of town had gone flashing yellow. The signs for the stores and restaurants along M-53 north of town quickly faded in his rear view, leaving dark open country before him. Jason slowed as he approached the Nathan Road intersection, looking for a white-clad figure walking along the roadside, but he saw nobody. Steeling himself, he turned on Nathan Road and drove straight east.

"Please don't let me get lost. Please keep me going straight," Jason muttered as he drove. Last time the moon had guided him eastward, but tonight it was too high in the sky to be of any use. Doubts nagged him – was he just chasing a fantasy? He dreaded what might happen to him if he got lost on these roads, but he yearned even more to find this mysterious woman who was the key, the missing component that would bring order to all this confusion.

Jason drove slowly, trying to keep his wheel straight and focus on the road just in front of the car. He didn't know how far he'd come when he spotted some cars ahead. They were parked oddly, their headlights illuminating another car that stood in the middle of the road with people gathered around it.

With a mixture of dread and amazement Jason stopped and got out of his car to better observe the curious scene. Towering overhead on his left stood the great, dark woods, looking more menacing than ever. The trees were bucking and waving as if buffeted by a windstorm, and Jason could hear the moaning and scraping of the branches. The chain-link fence shone in the headlights, and near the gate in the fence was parked a pickup, beside which stood a man in the shadows whom Jason could not clearly identify. But what drew his eyes were the people in the pool of light around the car in the road. Jason had no idea what was going on – there seemed to be something flat on the hood of the car, like a desk or table, that held a few items, including a couple of lit candles, of all things. A man in a white robe stood beside this, but everyone else was kneeling in the road. It was hard to count the people, because some were behind the car, but there seemed to be five of them.

One of them was clad all in white.

Everyone had turned to look at Jason as he pulled up, but then returned their attention to what the man in the robe was doing. Whoever he was, he was speaking and moving in a formalized manner. Jason seemed to have arrived in the middle of some sort of ritual, something that not even his presence could interrupt. He walked forward, but halted just at the edge of the pool of light formed by the headlights.

Now the man in the white robe seemed to be bending over the table-like thing on the car hood and saying something inaudible. Then he did something Jason didn't expect at all – he lifted up something small and white and held it high in the air. Jason peered at the thing, looking for something unusual, but all he could see was a thin, round disk a couple inches in diameter. This baffled him – what was that thing, and why was it being held up like that? The man seemed to be elevating it for a very long time, and everyone else was looking at it, as was Jason. There seemed to be something about it that drew his attention, and as the seconds passed Jason found himself thinking more and more that it looked like an eye in the air, one that was as much looking at him as he was looking at it.

Then the man lay the round thing down on what looked like a gold plate, knelt briefly, and took up a small gold cup that looked like a wine glass. Again he bowed over it and seemed to be saying something, then held the cup up in the air. As he did so, it seemed the trees of the woods overhead twisted and writhed worse than ever, but he held the cup steady like a glittering beacon in the shadowed night. Eventually he set the cup down, knelt briefly, turned the page in a book that was lying on the table, and continued reciting.

Jason had no idea what he was witnessing. It was clearly a ritual of some sort, but it seemed strange to be holding it in the middle of the night on a country road. But that was hardly the strangest thing of this night. He could see that one of the kneeling people was Janice, all in white, though wearing a simple blouse and skirt rather than a long gown. She was watching the standing man and his movements with rapt fascination, her eyes glowing. She was holding a bouquet of white flowers, and was flanked by two other kneeling women. On either side of them knelt two young men, their heads bowed. Jason looked to his left at the man standing by the pickup, and recognized Sheriff Keller, who simply returned his glance then continued watching the ritual.

Jason held his place, no matter how badly he wanted to rush in and start talking with Teresa. He felt like whatever was going on was too important for him to interrupt. The man in white was now holding up both the white thing and the gold cup and chanting something. Then he put both things down and everyone stood, which made Jason wonder if the ritual was finished, but apparently it wasn't, because presently everyone began reciting something in rough unison. This was followed by a brief pause where everyone gave each other hugs. Jason almost started forward at that point, but was glad he didn't because things weren't quite over yet. Again the three women and two men knelt in the road, and again the man lifted the white thing and the gold cup in the air and sang, to which everyone responded in unison.

Just when Jason was wondering if the ritual was finally finished, something very unexpected happened – the standing man in the white robe bent low over the table and seemed to eat part of the white thing, and then to sip from the gold cup. As Jason was wondering if he'd seen correctly, the man stepped toward the others and fed each of them little pieces of the white thing, which apparently had been broken into pieces. They opened their mouths where they knelt, allowing the man to put the pieces directly on their tongues. Then he took the golden cup and gave it to Teresa to drink from. Jason, who'd never been into religion or ritual, could make no sense of what was happening, though it seemed to mean something to the participants. He'd never heard of a religion that practiced ritualized eating.

Now things seemed to be drawing to a close, as the man in the white robe was busying himself about the table while the five participants remained kneeling in the road, their heads bowed. The man was quickly finished and then said a few more things, after which everyone stood up. He traced some sort of figure in the air, and the others responded with some gestures. That seemed to finally end things, for the three women stood and seemed to fall into each other's arms, sobbing and clinging, while the two men stood by looking uncomfortable. Jason noticed that it was the other two women who seemed to be doing most of the crying, and though Teresa was as well, she seemed more to be consoling or reassuring the others.

Jason hesitantly stepped forward, uncertain of how to approach the party. He was swiftly intercepted by Sheriff Keller, who glared at him and said gruffly, "Mr. Pelletier, I don't know what you're doing here, but this is a private meeting, and –"

"I'm not here in any official capacity, Sheriff," Jason tried to explain. "I'm here on a...personal basis." That didn't sound quite right, but how could he say it? Mission? Quest?

"Oh?" Sheriff Keller replied skeptically. "What 'personal basis' would that be?"

"I'm here to see her," Jason said, pointing to Teresa, who was now hugging one of the young men, and seemed to be saying something into his ear.

"Oh? For what reason?" the sheriff persisted. There he had Jason, for Jason didn't know precisely himself. How could he explain his compulsion to seek out this woman who had haunted his waking and sleeping hours? He could hardly tell the sheriff that it was none of his business, since the sheriff's business was protecting people, and he had very good reason to protect everyone he knew from Jason.

Fortunately, Jason's quandary was solved by Teresa herself, who came up as they were speaking. "It's all right, Sheriff Keller. I've been expecting him."

"Really?" Sheriff Keller replied, surprised. "You know Mr. Pelletier?"

"We've met," Teresa replied, looking at Jason with a glowing smile. Jason felt crushed and strengthened at the same time.

"I...I'm sorry," Jason stammered. "You were right, I could have stopped it. I just...I don't know."

"It's all right," Theresa said gently, laying her hand on his arm. "Your path will be more difficult now, but if strengthened you can still walk it. And now, for my path. Sheriff, if you please – the gate?"

"You're sure about this?" Sheriff Keller asked.

"Yes," Teresa replied, then turned to Jason. "Go in peace, Mr. Pelletier. Find your way home. There will always be a path, difficult though it may be." She stepped close to kiss him on the cheek, then turned and walked back to the man in the white robe. She knelt in front of him, and he made that gesture in the air again while muttering some words over her.

While this was going on, Jason saw with alarm that Sheriff Keller was unlocking the two locks that fastened the gate in the security fence. Swinging that gate wide, he picked up the kit that lay against the fence and went through to the inner gate. The trees bucked and heaved more violently then ever as he put on some goggles and pulled something clear of the pack. Only then did Jason discern what the kit was – a portable cutting torch. The sheriff sparked a flame at the nozzle and began attending to the latch that held the inner gate.

Meanwhile, Teresa had stood again, and had given the white-robed man a hug, then the other young men kisses, and then both of the women lengthy hugs. Lastly she smiled at Jason, then squared her shoulders, held her bouquet tightly, and passed through the gate in the security fence. Coming to the inner gate, which now stood open with Sheriff Keller beside it, she nodded to him and walked through it into the shadowed woods beyond.

Jason didn't know how to respond. He wanted to run after her, to warn her, to pull her clear of the peril. But the others, who seemed to have a much keener sense of the danger, did nothing but stand and look after her, sobbing. Even Sheriff Keller, who had erected these protections in the first place, had only cautioned her, then had stood by and let her walk through them. How could Jason interfere?

Then, it seemed, things were finally finished. The sheriff looped a short chain around the inner gate and padlocked it, then came out and relocked the gate in the security fence. The man who'd been wearing the white robe was removing it and folding it up, while one of the young men was busy packing away the items on the table. The other young man came over and greeted Jason.

"I'm Luke Peterson."

"I'm Jason Pelletier," Jason replied. Then he suddenly remembered why the man looked vaguely familiar. "Are you the other person who is supposed to be dead, but isn't?"

Luke looked at him warily. "Look, she told me to trust you, and to answer your questions, but this is going to take some time, and we need to get out of here." He gestured toward the trees overhead, which were now rocking and swaying so badly that the rush of the rubbing trunks was approaching a roar.

"Get out of here? But...aren't you going to wait for her to come out? You're not just going to leave her in...in there, are you?"

At first Luke gave no response, instead turning to look at the woods for a long time. His features worked as if he was trying to collect himself. He finally spoke in a husky tone. "She...she told us to go. If she comes out again, and needs help, one of us will be notified."

Beyond Luke, Jason could see that everyone seemed to be departing. One of the women was getting into one of the cars, while the young man and the other young woman were getting into the other. The man who'd been in white but was now wearing a black shirt and trousers was packing gear away into the car on which the table had been resting. Sheriff Keller had gotten into his pickup and was pulling away. Soon Luke and Jason would be the only ones left on the dark, lonely road.

"I came with her," Luke pointed at the woman who was driving the car by herself. "Unless you're willing to give me a ride, I need to either go with her or with Fr. Gabriel."

"Sure, I'll give you a ride wherever you need. Hop in," Jason said. Luke waved to the woman, who pulled away, then climbed into Jason's car. "Where are we headed?"

"The best spot would be my old home, though we'd have to be gone again by dawn, because they're watching it," Luke said. "It's in a workshop behind a house down toward Emmett."

"Is that the three houses with the barn in back, and the pond and gazebo in the back yard?" Jason asked. Luke looked at him sharply.

"You know the place?"

"If that's the spot, then yes, I know it. The one with the monument to Samson Chapman in the back yard. I was there earlier today – or yesterday, now."

"What were you doing there?"

"Trying to head off a DTD raid. I was unsuccessful – they hit the place anyway, and weren't taking orders from me."

"Good thing we evacuated in time," Luke said with relief.

"Almost," Jason replied. "There was one guy there."

"Really?" Luke asked in alarm. "Who?"

"An older guy named Mike. We were able to talk for a while before they arrived."

"Oh, no," Luke breathed, his voice hollow. "Oh, no. We...we'd wondered what happened to him. We'd gotten him away, but then he disappeared. We feared he'd gone back. What… did they…"

"They took him, I'm afraid," Jason admitted. "I tried to stop them, but they weren't listening to me. They came within an ace of taking me, too – I don't know what was wrong with them." The car fell silent as Luke buried his face in his hands. He said nothing, but Jason thought he could see his shoulders shake from time to time. "Look, man, I'm really sorry," Jason finally added, unable to bear the painful silence.

"It's…I just need –" Luke began thickly, then sat up and took a couple of deep breaths. "Sorry, you're dealing with a guy who's lost his father and his sister in the same day. Not that they didn't prepare us for it, but it's still…it's a blow when it happens."

"Your father and your sister? Really?" Jason was mystified, for Mike had looked too old to have a son Luke's age, and he seemed to remember that Janice Boyd had had no siblings.

"Adoptive, in both cases," Luke explained. "But more precious to me than blood relatives. Did Grandpa say anything?"

"He was really nice to me, even though he knew who I was," Jason replied. "He explained why you all had been hiding those people, and that you'd anticipated the raids and mostly dispersed. That was about as far as we got."

"So he turned himself in? That would be like him," Luke said. "He was a great man. That's something you hear all the time, but in his case it was true. He was very quiet about it, and when I first came I thought it was the others who were running things. But the more I learned, the more I saw that he was the backbone of everything. He was a true patriarch, in the best sense, just as Grandma was a matriarch. She died just a few weeks back, did he tell you that?"

"No," Jason replied.

"That hit him hard, but he was still strong through it, comforting everyone, especially Teresa. Grandma was more like a mother to her than Grandpa was a father to me. Saved her life. But now she's gone, they're all gone – Grandma, Grandpa, Teresa. I'm left, and I have to start over – again."

Luke fell silent, and Jason left him to himself. They'd come through Bad Axe and Jason had turned east in order to catch M-19 south toward Emmett. The roads were expectably empty at that time of night, and Jason drove along in silence while Luke just sat beside him, head bowed, mostly silent but occasionally muttering something under his breath. Jason felt a little uncomfortable, as if he was intruding on this stranger's grief. He could appreciate Luke needing a little time to recover – yesterday hadn't been kind to either of them, and Jason was still trying to figure out what to do once dawn came.

Finally Luke sat up straight, took a deep breath, and rubbed his face. "Well, I guess I'm supposed to answer questions. I can't guarantee I'll answer all of them, but you can ask."

"How about we begin with, 'Why aren't you dead?' You or Janice – Teresa – for that matter. Everything I'd heard about the blast, right up to the briefing I got before leaving D.C., counted you both among the casualties. I was shocked enough when she walked up to me on the courthouse lawn, and speechless when I figured out who she was."

"She walked up to you on a courthouse lawn? When was this?" Luke asked.

"Just about two weeks ago," Jason replied, and told how Teresa had found him on the bench, and the message she'd relayed.

"Hmm... 'A way out, but not by the paths you think'," Luke mused. "Yeah, that sounds like the sort of mystical thing she'd say. Cryptic and personal, that was what she'd get. Apparently she'd sometimes get messages for the guests at St. Anne's, who were usually close to death."

"St. Anne's?"

"The house where she worked with the sisters. The one your troops hit yesterday morning," Luke said frostily. "But to your original question: Teresa and I were rescued by a couple of other workers. They came along the trails through the woods and slipped up to the office door. We were being held in the office for...interrogation...but fortunately when the rescuers arrived, everyone but a sympathetic guard was in the other room, preoccupied with Sam."

"So was that the trigger for the detonation? Your rescue?"

"No – we barely got away in time. Nobody had any idea that Sam had rigged that building with explosives. Believe me, many things would have been done very differently if anyone had understood just how dangerous the situation was. For that matter, we think Sam would have done things differently had he known that Teresa and I were in the building. Piecing things together afterward, we can only conclude that he didn't know."

"This is adding even more confusion to an already confusing situation," Jason pointed out.

"You're right. Let me back up. Sam Chapman –" Luke began, then fell silent, pondering. "No, let's take it all the way back to a man named John Holmes, who ended up having tremendous impact on many lives, including mine, though I didn't know about him until after he'd been killed."

"Killed?"

"Yeah – by one of your eradication teams. John was a kind old man who'd never had any children with his wife Angie. So over the years the couple took neighborhood children under their wing, nurturing and mentoring them when nobody else would. They helped a lot of lost children find their way in life – I've met a few of them.

"One of these children was Sam Chapman, a moderately cerebral-palsied child who barely made it past birth. Through an unusual set of circumstances, Sam and his teenaged mother came into John and Angie's care. John pretty much raised Sam, teaching him to overcome his disability and giving him many practical skills. This was no small service, for Sam was a genius who only needed to be equipped and turned loose to do a lot of good for a lot of people. John was even more of a father to Sam than Grandpa was to me.

"But eventually John and Angie grew old. She finally died from complications of diabetes, and Parkinson's was taking him. But apparently somebody's algorithm decided he wasn't going quickly enough, because a few months after Angie's death, a snuff team showed up at John's house and killed him with an overdose of amitriptyline, staging it to look like a suicide. That was when I first 'met' John – I worked at the county coroner's office and was called to the scene. I did the medical exam on him, and was ready to write it off as the suicide it appeared to be, until I met John's executor. That man's steadfast determination that it wasn't in John's moral character to commit suicide was what convinced me to take a closer look at the irregularities in the situation. And though it didn't change the official finding, I found enough evidence to became convinced that he hadn't killed himself.

"My involvement in the inquest into John's death brought me into contact with some of the families who'd loved him, and who'd been part of the network who'd been –"

"Hiding people," Jason filled in. "Mike explained that much to me."

"Ah, so I won't have to go into the reasons for that," Luke replied. "Though you probably know more than I about the circumstances that made that necessary."

"Actually it was an HHS initiative, but I was briefed on it before being sent up here."

"Yes. Well, by the time I came along this secretive network had been running for a couple of years, and I didn't find out about it right away. I did get to know Sam, though, who was a crazy and wonderful guy, and phenomenally competent in a surprising number of disciplines. He lived at Rivendell –"

"Wait," Jason interrupted. "'Rivendell'?"

"A code name for the campus of households that we're heading for. We had code names for all the major communications centers, as well as our own communications and supply network. Grandma and Grandpa lived at Rivendell, as did Sam, as did other families. It was one of the other families who sort of adopted me, so when I first got involved I was out there a lot. I began helping with things like supply runs, though I wasn't aware of what I was doing until later. But that put me in close contact with Sam.

"But unknown to any of us, Sam had spied out a factory right at the edge of our circle of concern, a factory that had stood empty for years but which had begun to be used as a meeting spot for the people running your extermination operation. Sam didn't know this at first. But being inquisitive and independent, he decided on his own to bug the place, and capture video and audio of what was going on inside."

"Ah, so he was the one," Jason interjected. "The forensics people found some of the monitoring equipment, but couldn't figure out who'd placed it, or why."

"Yeah, that was him. And because Sam never did anything by halves, he rigged up the equipment to transmit the video footage back to his workshop ten miles away. It didn't take him long to figure out not only that he was listening in on the people running the extermination operation, but that they were responsible for killing John Holmes.

"We think that's what triggered him to mine the building. In fact, we suspect we know the exact conversation that put him over the edge, though that's after-the-fact conjecture."

"Wait," Jason interrupted. "Nobody else was in on the planning of this? This Sam guy did it solo?"

"Yup. Sam could play things pretty close to the chest when he wanted, especially if he suspected the others might take a dim view of his activities. The leaders might have put up with him bugging the factory, but they never would have allowed him to rig it with explosives."

"So...what did he hope to accomplish? What was his goal?"

Luke sighed. "We're not sure he knew. We suspect that when he found out who he was eavesdropping on, he just gut-level reacted: he had to do something. According to those who knew him longer than I, Sam could be like the proverbial dog chasing cars who wouldn't know what to do if he caught one. He was always thinking up these projects – sometimes very intricate ones, which he'd execute perfectly – and only after they were finished would he step back and consider how they'd fit into the grand scheme. We suspect he may have intended to destroy the complex, and only after he'd placed the charges did he stop to think that destroying the facility was the *last* thing he'd want to do, given that his bugs and the occupant's ignorance of them were providing him a gold mine of information.

"Nobody thought that his intentions might have included killing about twenty innocent people?" Jason couldn't resist asking.

"Given what they were coordinating and executing, the people in that building hardly qualified as 'innocent'," Luke shot back. "However, even then, Sam offered them a choice and spelled out the consequences. Had they listened to him, or even followed their own engagement protocols instead of shooting him, they'd all be alive."

"Hah," snorted Jason. "How could you possibly know that? You weren't there, and nobody who was survived."

"From the video," Luke said simply. Jason looked at him in wonder.

"Wait – there's a video?"

"Yes. That's what I'm taking you to see. The same video-monitoring setup that Sam used to spy on the building also recorded and transmitted the final minutes before the explosion, including Sam's arrival and confrontation. We have it all on chips."

Jason rocked back. The solution to this vexing mystery had all been captured on video, and he was going to see it? This could resolve a lot of things very quickly. "But, why was it being recorded, when Sam was at the building?"

"Wait – let me lay this out chronologically or we'll be skipping all over. Where was I?"

"Umm," Jason thought. "Where Sam learns who was responsible for John Holmes' death and decides to rig the building."

"Right. At about the same time, an incident happened at the hospital in Port Huron where I worked that alerted the people running the exterminations that something unusual was going on. One of the snatch teams – the folk who'd secretly remove from the hospitals people who were in danger of extermination – nearly got caught. Until that point, the entire operation had been able to fly under the radar. But once the extermination people were tipped, they could go back and look for instances where victims had been snatched from under their noses. With enough diligent digging they found evidence, which goaded them to look more aggressively for this group that was hindering their plans. Ultimately, they connected some dots and discovered my involvement, and figured once they arrested and interrogated me, that I'd betray my friends and they could uncover the entire network of ranches. In anticipation of this, they initiated a large movement of strike troops into the area, poised in Sandusky to fan out and hit whatever sites were revealed."

"I know about that," Jason confirmed.

"Meanwhile, the head honcho of the operation flies in and calls his chief exterminators to meet him at the factory. They were expecting things to move quickly once I was arrested, but I gave them a scare by slipping away after having been warned. But they caught me again using Teresa as bait, and took us both out to the factory.

"What nobody knew was that Sam was monitoring all this, and by the time the honcho got to the factory, we think Sam was watching in real time. We've had to do some guessing and back-figuring from the evidence we were left, but the best we can figure, Sam was actively monitoring the meeting at the factory, and when he heard of the plan to attack the ranches across the Thumb, he immediately set out to stop them using the only weapon he had: the charges he'd planted on the site. Fortunately for a lot of us, he left the video monitoring on and recording when he left his workshop.

"Shortly after Sam headed for the factory, a couple of friends came looking for him. They didn't see the footage about the area-wide assaults that had motivated Sam, and knew nothing about the explosives, but what they did see was real-time images of Teresa and me being brought into the factory for questioning. Guessing, but not knowing, where Sam had gone, they set out for the factory themselves, in hopes of catching up to him and helping us."

"What did they imagine they could do?" Jason asked. "There were armed guards at that site. Did they bring weapons?"

"No weapons. They had no idea what they were going to do, they only wanted to help," Luke explained. "They came on ATVs along hidden trails that we used to get around. Sam took the same route.

"Reconstructing the timing from the videos, Sam arrived at the factory first. He went in the main door, using an opener he'd configured to send the proper code. He went right up to the rafters and began shouting condemnations on everyone from above their heads."

"Wait," Jason interrupted. "The rafters? What on earth?"

"Sam's palsy made him slow and clumsy on the ground – he needed canes to walk. But he had incredible upper body strength, and could pull himself around with ease. Also, he was amazingly adept with his whip, which he used in many different ways. His initial intention seemed to be to disrupt the meeting, and boy, did he. As you'll see in the video, he began by smashing overhead lights. That got everyone's attention in a hurry, and caused most of the people to go from the office to the factory floor, which turned out to be good for Teresa and me."

"The rafters!" Jason exclaimed. "Who would have thought? Well, that clears up one major mystery."

"What's that?"

"The bullet trajectory. The investigating team found Sam's body, which was puzzling enough, but the fact that he was shot from below really stumped them," Jason explained.

"Yeah, you'll see that on the video," Luke said glumly. "The bastards just started shooting at him. No talk, no questions, no attempt to reason, just shooting. He warned them, told them not to kill him or they'd regret it, but they kept shooting until they got him."

"Is that when he detonated the explosives? When they started shooting?"

"No. He had the detonators tuned to a dead-man's switch he was clutching in his hand. Only when they hit him did he drop it, as he was falling from the rafters. His warning to them was completely honest and accurate. In the end, they died by their own hands, after having been warned repeatedly."

"Yeah, but..." Jason began, then fell silent. It was hard to contest that point.

"You'll see it. Anyway, while Sam was doing his rafter performance, Teresa and I were in the next room, being watched by a security guard who was sympathetic to our plight – or at least unwilling to tolerate what the honcho was proposing, to get me to cooperate. We had no idea what the fuss was about, and would never have guessed it was Sam. For his part, Sam certainly had no idea we were on the premises. Fortunately, it was right then that our friends arrived to rescue us. They were as shocked as we to find us alone in an office, guarded only by a man as eager to see us gone as they were to take us. We were less than five minutes away when the factory blew," Luke concluded.

"Wow," Jason said. "That was...unbelievable timing."

"One might be tempted to say divine," Luke answered. "I know it's a lot to believe, but I can show you the video, on synchronized split-screens, so you can see it unfolding. Even now it gives me the shivers if I consider how close we were to death. The poor, noble security guy who let us go was blown to bits."

The car fell silent while Jason stirred this vat of information. It certainly upended a lot of assumptions he'd had about the situation, and he was finding it hard to let go of some of them. Finally, he spoke again.

"What about this connection to the human trafficking network that was exposed about a year ago? Isn't that –"

"Pah!" Luke scoffed, glaring at Jason with naked scorn. "I caught one of those inferences in the spots you've been putting out. You should know better than to believe your own lying propaganda, Mr. Pelletier. There was a family-run crime operation out of Huron County, as you well know, but not only were we not part of it, we actively fought it – and were substantially harmed by it. The direct damage that Ray Hubbart and his family did to the area was severe, and the indirect damage was incalculable."

"What…what do you mean by that?" Jason asked, mystified.

"The whole affair has nothing to do with our past or current operations, except in the damnable lies of your propagandists," Luke replied fiercely. "Thus, I'm not obligated to explain it to you. Suffice it to say that thanks to Ray Hubbart's dark hobbies and demonic friends, the worst part of it didn't end when his empire was uncovered, but only began. Hopefully…hopefully you saw the end of it, just tonight, on that dirt road, which hopefully also means you saw how much that cost." Luke fell abruptly silent and bowed his head, and this time Jason could see the tears dropping onto his clenched hands.

Jason left him to his grief for some miles before speaking again. "I'm really sorry. I only spoke what I'd been told."

"Yeah," Luke nodded, sniffing. "As Grandpa used to point out, webs of sin and deceit entrap everyone, and then we end up clawing and stabbing at each other when we should be cutting the web. We're getting close, and I have an idea. Just because night is safer from surveillance doesn't mean we should tempt fate. Rivendell is certainly being watched. We should come and go by hidden trails."

"Ah…those are being watched, too," Jason explained reluctantly.

"I know, but cover is cover, and using them will be less obvious than pulling into the driveway. Shortly we'll be at an intersection where you can drop me off. My ATV is parked at a shelter nearby. You can then go to a spot on a road that I'll explain to you, and I'll come pick you up. From there we can approach Rivendell using covered trails."

Thus it was that about forty five minutes later Jason found himself approaching the homestead he'd visited less than twenty-four hours before, only this time stealthily, riding behind a man who would be in custody if he wasn't considered dead. The nighttime ride through the woods helped refresh Jason – his stressful and exhausting day was beginning to catch up with him.

Luke steered the ATV into a sheltered area behind the long cinder block building, which he called the workshop. He guided their way with a small flashlight that cast a soft red glow. With unconscious ease, Luke moved so as to stay hidden from overhead surveillance, leading Jason from the shelter to a side door in the workshop.

"This used to be my apartment until just recently," Luke explained as they entered some empty rooms. "It was Sam's before that. Let me get the chips." He removed a shelf from an empty bookshelf set into the wall and felt in the dark slot at the back of the bookshelf into which the shelf had fit. Finding something, he straightened a paper clip and inserted it into the slot. Out popped a small wooden card to which were affixed five storage chips.

"The videos are on these chips?" Jason asked. "Why not store them online?"

"There may be copies online, but I don't know where they are," Luke answered. "These videos are pretty hot, and online storage leaves trails no matter how diligently you cover your tracks. We decided that physical storage would be safest."

"But – on a site that might be raided and ransacked?"

"Sam built that hiding spot," Luke grinned. "Would you have found these?" Jason smiled and shook his head. "We also sent chips to other locations. And they all have safety interlocks on the media – too many failed access attempts will destroy the files."

Luke pulled a tablet from the duffel he'd been carrying and set it up to project onto the wall. He went through a few security steps, and a shadowed, grainy image of a large room appeared. There seemed to be a lot of vehicles crowded about.

"This is a video of the main factory floor," Luke explained. "I'm showing you the annotated version. The audio pickup was never good in that cavernous space, and Sam's speech was slurred on top of that. We've added text at the bottom of the frames that spells out what he's saying."

As the video rolled, Jason watched the main door open and close again, a shadowed form ascend with astonishing agility to the rafters, people cry out in alarm as they spotted the intruder, and Sam destroy the first bank of overhead lights with a startling crash.

"The video quality starts to degrade here, as Sam takes out the light sources," Luke cautioned. "The camera does some compensating, but not enough." Jason nodded, watching the captions. Sam was certainly calling attention to himself, and it didn't take long for people to respond. A crowd was gathering on the shop floor, occluding the lens at times, clustering together to point at and murmur about the intruder.

"There – notice how he mentions John Holmes?" Luke pointed out. "He's talking to someone specific, who we think was the head honcho. There's some byplay off to the side that I didn't quite catch."

"I did," Jason said. One of the guards was being ordered to shoot, but refusing. "My, this Sam is certainly laying it on, with the wrath of God talk."

"Yes, that's how he thought. But notice that he was warning them – 'You'd better not shoot me! If you shoot me, it'll be the last thing you do!' At that point he was already holding the dead man's switch. In just a couple of minutes the shooting starts."

Both men watched as the drama unfolded, with Sam's slurred shouts punctuated by the sound of smashing glass, and the image darkening and then coming back as the camera adjusted to the lower lighting level. Then at the bottom of the image people could be seen moving about to find better aiming points, and the hollow popping began.

Jason recognized that sound. It always heightened his heart rate and senses. Looking over, he saw that Luke was staring at the projection with glistening eyes.

"At this time, you were in the adjacent office?" Jason asked.

"Yeah, I...we can look at that shortly," Luke replied. "The honcho took the first guard with him when he went out, but then the first guard came back and sent the other guard out. Then our friends showed up, and we were surprised that the first guard let us go. Earlier the honcho, or his people, had tried to sweet-talk me into collaborating, and when that failed the honcho ordered everyone but the guards from the room and threatened to have the guards rape Teresa right in front of me if I didn't talk. The first guard didn't like that at all. But here – this is where they get Sam." Luke pointed at the video, where Sam's shouting and the popping were both ongoing. Suddenly the small dark figure in the rafters jerked awkwardly, seemed to stagger, and toppled from his place. Before he hit the ground the image went white with static.

"And that's it," Luke said. "You've now seen how the blast unfolded."

Jason shook his head. "This has puzzled a lot of people for years, and to think it was on video this whole time."

Luke then showed the video clip of the office, from the point he and Teresa were brought in until the blast obliterated the cameras. Then he showed the images synchronized split-screen so Jason could see how the events fit together. Luke answered all of Jason's questions, and when that was finished he went through a few security steps with the tablet, scanning Jason's face and getting his thumbprint.

"So," Jason ventured warily. "Any possibility I could get copies of one or two of these videos?"

"They're yours," Luke announced, holding them out and dropping them in Jason's palm. "That's what the security steps were for – they've been unlocked for you."

"Don't you need them?"

"For what? We have copies elsewhere if we ever need to reexamine them."

"Aren't these top secret, at least for your operation?"

"Our 'operation', as you put it, is no more. We've shut down. We were in the process of evacuating the ranches already, and were a little more than half done when your troops struck. The events of yesterday have accelerated things – all through this night, families and guests have been being removed from their homes. By dawn, there won't be any operation to protect."

"Where will they go? What will they do?"

Luke gave him a steady look before answering. "Do you really need to know those details?"

"I guess not," Jason replied.

"Hopefully, to safer quarters," Luke continued. "It's not them we're most concerned about. It's those we leave behind, those we could have sheltered but now must leave to the tender mercies of your staff at the RCCs."

Jason had no answer to this. Luke glanced at the time. "It'll be getting light soon, by which time we should both be far away from here. It's been a long night after a taxing day, and the day dawning promises to be no gentler. I can return you to your car, unless you have any further questions."

"Only one, which I don't know if you can answer," Jason replied. "What happened there at the woods tonight?"

Luke bowed his head and was silent for a minute, and when he spoke it was in a thick, choked voice. "God alone knows exactly. All we have is guesses. Suffice it to say that almost a year ago, two very foolish and wicked men for their own selfish reasons unleashed something they did not understand and could not control. It was barely contained at the time, but the damage was done, and it strengthened as it festered. Only a heroic act of obedience could defeat it, and we hope that has been accomplished."

Jason nodded, and the men headed out. The darkness of the woods was just beginning to lighten as they pulled up to Jason's car.

"So, what's next for you?" Jason asked conversationally as he dismounted. Again, Luke fixed him with a steady gaze.

"Do you really need to know those details?"

"I guess not," Jason admitted. "If it makes any difference, I never intended the assaults to be that brutal. I helped plan them, but – well, things got out of hand. Had I had been in control, there wouldn't have been that level of violence, certainly not against families."

"That's a lesson, then, isn't it?" Luke replied. "Sometimes when we turn things loose, they can end up doing a lot more damage than we intend."

"Yeah," Jason acknowledged. "I...I'm sorry we had to meet under these circumstances. I feel odd saying this, but I think that had we met under other circumstances, we could have been friends."

"Maybe," Luke replied with a skeptical shrug. Then he gave Jason a half-smile. "Or at least friendly, perhaps." He offered his hand. "Mr. Pelletier, may God bless your paths and lead you closer to Him."

"Call me Jason," he replied, gripping Luke's hand. "The best of luck to you, wherever your future takes you."

"Thanks," Luke replied, starting the ATV. He waved as he drove off into the woods, leaving Jason standing in the gray dawn, feeling crushed and battered. Wearily he climbed into his car and turned toward Sandusky, and what would surely be a day of demands and decisions.

Turning and Returning

The alarm on Jason's tablet chimed, and he forced himself up through layers of unconsciousness that felt like sodden wool blankets to stagger across the room and silence it. It had been only two hours since he'd stumbled through the door of his house just before sunrise and toppled onto his couch. Two hours was all he could allow himself, he reckoned, before the day came crashing down on him.

Nor was he wrong. He'd just finished washing up when his phone chimed. He brought it up to see an impeccably uniformed sergeant wearing DTD insignia.

"Mr. Jason Pelletier?"

"Yes," Jason replied.

"Good morning, sir. Are you able to take a call from Colonel Pelowski and Major Serrano? It would require activation of your security chip."

"Oh, fine, but we'd best shift to my workstation. It has a bigger screen, and my device batteries are nearly dead."

"Very well, sir."

Jason scrambled for a minute to transfer the call to the workstation and activate the security features. He was wracking his brain trying to remember why the colonel's name should sound familiar. When the images came up side by side on his screen, he was reminded, for there were names and offices displayed below the images. The slightly graying man on the left was identified as Colonel Gerald Pelowski, Commander, DTD Fast Response Center Fort Wayne, while the swarthy man on the right was Major Miguel Serrano, District Adjutant. Jason wondered what a District Adjutant was, and why these serious-looking men were calling him at eight in the morning. He was sure it would have something to do with his forceful actions yesterday, and hoped he wouldn't have to get too firm with these guys as well.

"Mr. Pelletier? I'm Colonel Pelowski of the Fort Wayne Fast Response Center, and this is Major Serrano, newly appointed adjutant of the Eastern Michigan Special Protectionary District," the colonel said gravely.

"Good morning," Jason replied, his mind churning. Special Protectionary District? What the hell? "Sorry if it's taking me a bit to spin up this morning – hectic day followed by a crazy night."

"We understand, sir," the colonel assured him. "And before we get any further, I'd like to apologize for the crossed lines and hasty plans that might have brought about any confusion yesterday. This evolution was laid on rather quickly, and we apologize for any inconvenience it may have caused."

Apologize to the dead kids, Jason thought, but simply nodded in response.

"Captain Touma and Lieutenant Nealson have been recalled to Fort Wayne, and Major Serrano will be assuming authority there in the Thumb area. We intend to ensure that there will be no repeats of yesterday's missteps."

This appeared to be proceeding in a much less contentious direction than Jason had feared it would. "Colonel, Major, you should both be aware that no small amount of yesterday's confusion was due to some forged messages that were part of a concerted effort by…certain parties to undermine me and my work in the region."

"We've been apprised of that, sir," the colonel assured him. "D.C. tells us that internal security is investigating aggressively. In the meantime, we've assigned a liaison officer to you, so there's unimpeded communications to and from your office as long as you occupy it."

As long as he occupied it? Odd phrasing, that, but he simply asked, "Liaison officer?"

"Yes," Major Serrano chimed in. "First Lieutenant Bonnie Hammond. She's being briefed right now, but we could conference her in if you wished."

"No, no," Jason waved them off. "Before we get any further, are you guys and your troops performing any – activities this morning?"

"No, sir, your stand-down order remains in effect until you rescind it," Major Serrano said. "We'd want to consult with you before making any changes, because we want to take the results of yesterday's operations and feed them back into the predictive algorithms to hone our future planning. It's a prudent move anyway in a time of command flux. All troops are mustered at the TacComs awaiting orders."

"Good, good." This alleviated Jason's concern about more dawn raids and missile strikes. "If you don't mind my asking, what the hell is a Special Protectionary District? This is the first I've heard of it."

"That's because we first envisioned it last night, sir," Major Serrano replied eagerly. "We've been conferencing with some of the D.C. operatives, pulling an all-nighter, frankly, about the challenges of maintaining order across such a broad and sparsely populated region. We've decided to implement an array of protocols to bring about –"

Jason realized he'd made the mistake of asking an enthusiast to hold forth on his favorite topic, but this morning he had no patience for gushing.

"Please, Major," Jason waved a hand. "I presume that this District is a new administrative entity that's been created for the region?"

"Well, yes," the major said in a disappointed tone.

"And I'll be briefed in full at some later point?"

"Certainly, sir," the major assured him.

"Great. Then let's hold the full explanation until I'm better able to grasp it. Question, though – who's in charge of this Special Protectionary District? You?"

"Why, no, sir," the major looked shocked. "You are."

"I am?"

"Well, for the time being," the colonel added. "As Major Serrano mentioned, matters are in a state of flux at the moment. We anticipate more clarity within a couple of days. But that brings up the reason for our call: we want to rectify any errors with all expedience. We will be moving administrative and other assets into the district over the upcoming week, but we want to get resources at your disposal as soon as possible. Lieutenant Hammond is ready to proceed to your location immediately, if necessary. She can be there in four hours."

"No, no," Jason waved them off. "Later today, or even tomorrow, would suffice. I need to do some regrouping and assimilating myself. As long as nobody's doing anything rash, we've got time to proceed carefully."

"Very well, sir," the colonel nodded. "I have one more matter – an interrogative by Major Chad Collins of Border Patrol Aerial, requesting permission to resume low-level reconnaissance overflights."

"No," Jason said, and then had an idea. "In fact, I want all overflights halted for now, and all assets grounded. The RA asset should be vectored out of the area and returned to NSA control."

The officers looked puzzled at this sweeping order. "Very well, sir, but –" the major began, but Jason cut him off.

"Major, we had unnecessary fatalities yesterday – *juvenile* fatalities – due to confusion between ground and aerial operations. I want every asset grounded – high level, low level, everything – until things are sorted out to my satisfaction. Understand?"

"Yes, sir," the major snapped.

There, Jason thought, that should give the evacuees a little breathing space. "Listen," he continued, "we've all had a long night, and you're still pulling things together. I need to arrange some local details and consult with D.C. myself. Perhaps we could communicate later in the day about progress, and make further plans then?"

"That sounds great, sir," Colonel Pelowski replied, and the two officers rang off.

Jason staggered into the kitchen to brew and down a mug of coffee, then took a long hot shower in an attempt to clear his fogged mind. He needed to fire off an update to D.C. as well as get their take on what was going on. Clearly there'd been a lot of planning and decision making done without his input, and he needed to get back in the loop.

Jason sat down at his workstation and laid on the table the five storage chips which Luke had given him. Those little devices contained explosive stuff, intelligence that upended many assumptions and filled massive gaps in understanding. He now faced the task of explaining it all to D.C. As he was pondering how to approach this, he came to a realization.

He'd succeeded.

He'd come up here intending not only to solve the mystery of the blast, but to get the Chengdu Project back on track for HHS. Against all odds, he'd accomplished both goals.

But victory didn't feel at all like he'd expected it would.

Jason tried to feel excited about his success. He imagined returning triumphantly to Tysons Corners to detail his success to Cynthia. He even tried to generate some dark satisfaction at the mental picture of Whitman being escorted from his office in ignominy by a pair of security guards. But none of it seemed to matter. The images that kept forcing their way back into his mind were of a woman in white walking with chin high into a shadowed wood, or of a genial old man sitting in a rocker, chatting casually while awaiting the troops that would haul him away to his death, or of a sentimental old woman sobbing over a chintzy red purse, or of a dark-haired young man bowing his head in grief. Jason was also haunted by images he'd seen only on video: of families being herded into waiting vehicles, parents into one and children into another, or aged patients being loaded into vans for a one-way trip to the nearest RCC. Then there was the image he knew he would carry to his grave – that of six body bags lying in the driveway of a gutted and burned home, three large and three small.

No, victory didn't feel at all like he'd expected it would.

Jason realized he was feeling dizzy, and that hunger as well as fatigue was contributing – he hadn't eaten since lunchtime yesterday. He fired off a short message to Cynthia about major developments and details to follow, then headed out for breakfast.

The diner was full of what Jason recognized as regulars. His waitress, Becky, brought him his coffee and juice without being told, and asked if he wanted his usual. As he awaited his breakfast, he looked around and realized he was, in a way, seeing his fellow diners for the first time. The two elderly women chatting over their toast and coffee with great animation. The heavy-set guy in a John Deere cap seated at the counter, working away at his hash browns while watching a video on his tablet. Two middle-aged men conversing earnestly in low voices, their breakfasts half-finished and shoved aside. Jason wondered how many of these people knew that scores, maybe hundreds, of their neighbors had slipped away from their homes yesterday lest they be assaulted and taken captive. Some knew, Jason guessed. Maybe they weren't in the room right now, but certainly some of them had passed through this diner over the years. He also wondered how many guessed that even as they ate their breakfasts and planned their days, people living hundreds of miles away were making decisions that would impact their lives in ways that nobody could foresee. This was where it came down, Jason realized. People who walked the proverbial halls of power – which he had walked, and had planned to walk again – made life-and-death decisions that impacted people like these in their homes, their towns, their workplaces.

Becky brought Jason's eggs over medium, sausage, and crisp hash browns, placing them before him with a cheery smile. He watched her as she walked away. He'd never noticed how kind she was toward everyone, and how she stopped to chat with the patrons, like the two men who'd finished their breakfasts. That wasn't even her table, yet she took away their plates and had some friendly words for them both. How unlike the D.C. coffee shops he usually frequented, where everything was about brisk efficiency and trying to upsell you to the featured product of the month.

Jason's phone rang, and he saw it was Major Collins from Selfridge. He was probably trying to appeal the order to ground all the drones. Jason let it roll to voice mail – let Collins deal with the Fort Wayne people on that. Jason ate his breakfast slowly, savoring every bite and sip, while he pondered the tumultuous events of the day and night before. His phone didn't ring again, and when he finished his breakfast and returned to his house, the only message awaiting him was from Cynthia acknowledging his message and advising him to stand by for further instructions.

Jason realized that he had nothing to do but paperwork. No troops to stop, no drones to ground, no assets to coordinate, not even any mysteries to unravel. He needed to write up a detailed report about yesterday's events, of course, but there were still a lot of unresolved issues and partially executed activities. He could scrape up all kinds of make-work to fill his time, but instead he decided to do what he truly wanted – to revisit the houses down near Emmett, the site Luke had called Rivendell. So he drove down to the properties he'd been to twice in the past twenty-four hours, wondering as he approached whether he'd have to face down some sentries, or park so as to remain hidden from overhead surveillance. Then he checked himself – neither were active threats, because of his orders.

Parking in the circular driveway in front of the brick ranch, Jason went to the front door and tentatively tried the latch. To his surprise he found it still unlocked, allowing him to enter the quiet house unhindered. He came into the living room where he'd conversed with Mike. A few scuffs and smudges on the walls were the only evidence of the harsh arrest and removal. Jason gently touched the arm of the rocker where Mike had been sitting, trying to recall the old man's soothing voice and courteous manner. Their brief conversation had left Jason longing for something he hadn't even known he lacked.

Jason's bowed head snapped up – what had that been? The thick silence had been broken by what sounded like voices from farther back in the house. No, there was only silence – but there it was again! It sounded like the busy chatter of several voices, but right on the threshold of hearing, as if from a distance. It seemed to be coming from the direction of the kitchen – but then it was gone again. A little spooked, but even more curious, Jason slowly walked toward the kitchen, only to find it as empty as it had been yesterday. But even as he was slowly turning, listening attentively, he caught a whisper of some low conversation that seemed to be coming from a sitting room just off the dining room. He couldn't discern specific words, but there was definitely the low murmur of people speaking. But when he went over and looked through the door, the room was dark and empty.

Now more than a little apprehensive, but sharply intrigued, Jason walked back to the kitchen, only to hear the sound of laughter and chatter coming from the rear of the house. It was the briefest of flickers, gone even as he caught it passing. The glass doors leading to the outside had been roughly boarded up where they had been broken the day before, but they still worked. Sliding them open, Jason stepped out into the gentle spring morning and walked back toward the pond which he'd seen in his dream. Just after passing one of the benches which were scattered about the grounds, he distinctly heard behind him two female voices, an older one speaking in querulous tones and a younger one soothing and reassuring. He whipped around and, of course, saw nothing.

The sharp thrill which shot through Jason had nothing to with dread. It wasn't ghosts he feared, but being ghostly. Ever since that day at the blast site, but especially after encountering Teresa, and speaking with Mike, and learning all he had last night, Jason felt increasingly like he'd come into glancing contact with a world much larger and more solid and more real than anything he'd known. He'd thought he'd come from the important world, the environment where real power was wielded and significant decisions were made and substantial consequences realized. When he'd been sent here, he'd thought that he'd been exiled from that world to an insignificant backwater where petty people fussed about trivial matters as they faded into obscurity. At first it had seemed that way, but the more he'd learned and the deeper he'd delved, the more he'd found a world of truth and courage and sacrifice and love. It was a real world, a solid world, for all that it was hidden. No wonder it had left impressions on the places where it had been. That was to be expected, in the same way one would expect that a real man walking along a beach would leave footprints in the sand. Nobody would expect a ghost to leave footprints, and that was what Jason felt like: a ghost. He'd lived his life among ghosts, playing at doing serious things. Here he'd met real people living real lives and doing truly important deeds. Whom had he ever rescued from death? What had he ever sacrificed to protect someone else from harm? Where would he have found the strength to walk into that darkness?

Jason stopped in his tracks. He had to know. He had to see for himself, to know for certain. Swiftly he returned to his car and turned it northward toward Bad Axe. He tried to be patient, to slow down properly as he passed through all the little towns like Yale and Peck and Sandusky, but he was anxious to know. Finally he passed through Bad Axe and approached the Nathan Road intersection. Breathing deeply, he turned east and watched the road as he drove. He tried not to concentrate on keeping the wheel straight, but simply drove naturally, though on edge for even the slightest sound from his radio.

After a few minutes of seeing nothing but fields and ditches, it came into view: a wooded patch surrounded by a tall security fence. He'd reached it straightaway, without any confusion or wrong turns. There stood the fence and the wood, just as they had last night – and yet, somehow, different. Jason walked to the fence and peered through at the trees. The morning sun was streaming down through the spring leaves, dappling the trunks and underbrush with patterns that shifted and flowed with the warm breeze. Jason could see all the way to the leaf-covered ground. There were no murky shadows lurking amidst the bushes. The woods looked just like – woods. They held no darkness or terror.

Jason stepped back and looked at the gate in the security fence, with its two locks, and the chained gate beyond. He thought of calling Sheriff Keller, of asking him to come and unlock the gates so Jason could go in and search the woods. But he knew he would not find her, and the prospect of searching in vain filled him with sadness. She had been right – she had her path, and he had his. He returned to his car and headed for Sandusky.

Back at his workstation, there were nothing but routine messages awaiting him, though he'd been copied on many of the messages flying back and forth between Fort Wayne, D.C., and Port Huron. He recognized the mood of these exchanges: of people dealing with a small project that had somehow escalated into a Major Initiative, so now everyone wanted to ensure they were included in the Big Decisions. Not that long ago Jason would have felt the urge to jump in himself, to ensure that his opinions were considered and his influence exercised. Now he viewed the message threads with detachment – he couldn't muster any interest. He wondered how these people would react when it came out that much of the case was solved. That wasn't his worry. His short night was starting to catch up to him, and the sofa looked very inviting, but he dashed off a quick request to Agent Sanderson before collapsing for a long overdue nap.

Jason was awakened in late afternoon by a call from Lieutenant Hammond, who cheerfully informed him that she'd been completely briefed and was ready to serve as his liaison, and wondered whether he wanted her to drive up that night or wait until morning. He assured her that the next day would suffice. Then his conscience smote him, and he called the Port Sanilac Detainment Center to follow up on his orders from the prior day regarding the treatment of the women. Sergeant Reid assured him solemnly that routines had been established and protocols implemented that ensured proper and humane treatment of all detainees. There was just enough desperation in his voice that Jason was tempted to drive over to examine these routines and protocols personally. But that would mean he'd feel obligated to speak with Sister Joseph Marie, and that would remind him of his great loss, and he found that prospect unbearable. He settled for assuring the sergeant that he would be following up, and then shut down his workstation and headed over for dinner. It would be an early bedtime for sure tonight.

The next morning his inbox was unusually quiet, though he did get a message from Lieutenant Hammond informing him that she was on her way and should be there by 10:00 a.m. This gave Jason time to wander over to a diner for a leisurely breakfast, to organize his thoughts for the presentation about the blast, and to type up the document he'd been pondering. That he tucked away in a hidden pocket in his briefcase, still uncertain as to what he would do with it.

Lieutenant Hammond arrived right on time, eager and excited about her duties. She saluted him when he met her at the door, which made him feel downright odd, but he asked her in.

"Forgive the casual working space," Jason apologized. "These are also my temporary living quarters, and it was more convenient to use the living room as an office than to intrude on the Port Huron offices."

"Perfectly all right, sir," Hammond assured him. "I'm sure the District will be setting up more permanent administrative facilities before long."

"Yes, well...you'll have to forgive me, but I'm still a little unaccustomed to this whole Special Protectionary District thing, much less the idea of being director of it, or whatever I am," Jason explained.

"Understandable, sir. It is my honor to convey the first official communication to you as director: you're being summoned to Washington."

"Me?" Jason replied. "I haven't heard anything like that."

"I was assigned to bring you the message, sir. A plane is waiting for you at Selfridge. Director Miller is hoping to receive your briefing by the end of the day. I understand," Lieutenant Hammond's voice took on a tone of insider confidence. "That the director is extremely pleased with your achievements."

Well, Jason thought, that would be a first. But he had enough experience to know that "Director Miller" in this context probably meant Cynthia, which was no more than he'd expected. And whereas there would have been a time when the knowledge that a plane was awaiting his arrival would have filled him with excitement and urgency, now his response was more measured.

"That's great," Jason replied. "But I have a few questions before I go. Could I get a few more details about this Special Protectionary District? I've worked in DHS for years and never heard of such a thing."

"That's because it's a new innovation, a dynamic reimagining of governmental responsiveness to intractable situations," Lieutenant Hammond gushed. "It's an interdisciplinary, interdepartmental solution for addressing the toughest problems faced by government. There have been theories and proposals floating around for the longest time, but now they have coalesced into an agile, responsive reality. If I may say so, sir, it has been your activities over the past few weeks which have paved the way for this new vision."

"Mine?"

"Why, of course, sir!" Hammond replied with surprise. "Your creative approach to attacking stubborn situations, your willingness to think and act beyond departmental boundaries, your take-no-prisoners attitude toward obstacles – why, you were a proof of concept in action, sir! HHS could never have imagined using those FEMA assets any more than DHS could have so adeptly deployed the POM resources you leveraged. All within a tight timeframe with almost no budget! If I may be so bold, sir, I think your execution here will be used as a case study in management seminars for years to come."

"That's all very well, Lieutenant, but it still doesn't explain what a Special Protectionary District *is*. What is the purpose?"

"Ah. Well. The SPD is still something of a work in progress, but the guiding principle is swift and effective response to intrinsic threats. The citizens have a right to be protected from disruptive and seditious elements in their midst, and we shouldn't hesitate to employ the most innovative and forward-thinking synergies to provide this protection. Dangerous situations call for proactive solutions and bold initiatives. Again, sir, you've blazed the trail for us, with your brilliant use of NSA resources to bring resolution to seemingly irresolvable situations. That's what we hope will be the hallmark of the SPDs – aggressive, goal-oriented action."

"'SPDs'?" Jason asked. "There is more than one?"

"I believe the vision is that this district will be a pilot, with the protocols and definitions ironed out here to be deployed wherever necessary," Hammond explained.

"And I'm in charge of this District?"

"For the time being, sir. As I mentioned, it's a work in progress, a dynamic initiative adapting as it grows. But don't worry, sir, your place in it is secure no matter what that ends up being. In my opinion," once again her voice took on that tone of husky confidentiality, "I think the only question is whether you'll be in charge of just this District, or the entire SPD initiative."

Seeing that he was fighting a losing battle, Jason didn't attempt to explain that job security had been the least of his worries. "Well, if D.C. is expecting me, I'd best be on my way. But a couple last questions before I go. First, what about the captives? What happened to them?"

"Captives, sir?" Hammond asked in bewilderment.

"Yes! The captives who were taken in the raids yesterday – no, Wednesday morning," Jason replied forcefully. "They were herded into vans – where were they taken?"

"I'm sorry, sir, but I'm not completely current on that status," Hammond tapped her tablet rapidly. Jason waited in silence, making no attempt to mitigate her embarrassment, while she scrambled to find the information.

"Ah, here it is, sir. Seems the NDs were remanded to HHS for evaluation and treatment, while the active suspects are being held in DTD detainment centers pending arraignment."

"'NDs'? What's an ND?"

"Non-documented, sir. Not exactly sure of the definition – it's an HHS phrase – but it indicates a party without proper or complete personal documentation. Mostly these seem to be minors and elderly," Hammond said dismissively.

"I see," Jason replied, guessing he knew the nature of the "treatment" that some of the elderly would receive. "Well, I know about the detention centers, since I've visited one. Here's my first assignment for you: I want you to visit every one of the Regional Detainment Centers to personally ensure that they're in compliance with all DTD protocols regarding humane treatment of detainees. I want you to inspect everything: accommodations, sanitation, environment, diet, everything. The centers are to be in conformance with all protocols or you're to shut them down on the spot and file charges against the staff. I gave a direct order to this effect on Wednesday afternoon and had intended to follow up on it yesterday, but things got away from me. They've had plenty of time to come into compliance, and if the staff hasn't used that wisely, I want them booked. Understand?"

"Yes, sir," Hammond replied tersely, scribbling madly on her tablet.

"Humane treatment of those detainees is of primary importance to me, so I want your personal report on every Detainment Center, including photographs and videos, by the end of the day. Fail this, and you may as well drive back to Fort Wayne."

"Of course, sir."

"All right, Lieutenant. One more issue, and it's a personnel matter. As director or whatever I am of this SPD, does that give me authority over DHS employees within its borders?"

"Again, sir, the SPD is a work in progress, with boundaries of authority a bit in flux at the moment. However, the working model currently being implemented allows considerable latitude in that regard."

"Good. There is an employee I want out of the District. He's expressed dissatisfaction with his assignment here, and I want to accommodate his desire to depart as soon as possible," Jason explained.

"Of course, sir. What is his name?"

"Ethan Patterson. He's currently under disciplinary action, so I can't send him across the country, but I'd like to get him out of the immediate area."

"Do you have a specific location in mind, sir? The Detroit area?"

"Too close, Lieutenant," Jason said, glancing at a map of DHS sites on his tablet. "We want far, but not too far. Somewhere like, say, Sault Ste. Marie. Can you arrange that?"

"Certainly, sir."

"Excellent. Then I'm on my way to D.C. It's been a pleasure meeting you, Lieutenant."

"The pleasure is all mine, sir."

As Jason drove down toward Selfridge, his phone rang. It was Agent Sanderson.

"About those questions you sent, sir: there was a Samson John Chapman born on April 17, 2001, as recorded by the St. Clair County Clerk. I've forwarded you full details, but the record notes one oddity: it was a walk-in registration."

"Walk-in?"

"Yes, sir. Most births are recorded from hospital documentation, but people can just walk in and swear that their baby was born on a date. It's usually done for something like a home birth."

"I see. Anything else?"

"Just routine stuff, and it's all in the message I sent. Normal records for immunizations, but no school records other than a GED certificate. That indicates he was probably homeschooled."

"Very well. I'll check your message for details. Thank you, Agent Sanderson. It's been good working with you."

"Thank you, sir."

"So, Jason, in your estimation this evidence proves conclusively that the blast was a one-off event, an act of vengeance by an individual, rather than part of a greater plot?" Cynthia asked after Jason had shown the video of Sam's last actions and death.

"I wouldn't say it proves it conclusively, but I think it provides enough evidence that we can rest easy," Jason answered. "From the outset, we've never had any actual evidence that the blast was part of a concerted effort. There was no advance notice, no claim of responsibility, no follow-up activity, no other attacks on agents or property, nothing that would indicate broader domestic terror activity. We were concerned that it was part of a conspiracy, but concern has been all we've ever had. I think this footage is sufficient to allay our fears, and let us write this off as the work of a solo operator."

"He was using some fairly explicit religious language," Cynthia cautioned.

"Sometimes religious fanatics operate by themselves," Jason pointed out.

"True," Cynthia acknowledged. "And…you can't be more specific about where you obtained these videos?"

"We know from the ATF Forensics examination that the site was being monitored and the footage being transmitted elsewhere. It's a reasonable guess that this Sam Chapman was the active agent – planting the bugs, monitoring the videos, and ultimately reacting as you saw. Obviously, this footage was some of what was captured. I met my contact indirectly – a friend of a friend sort of thing – and he was very coy. I'm sure he gave me a pseudonym, and he didn't specify how he'd obtained this footage. I suspect he'd known this Sam fellow, and heard I was investigating."

"Any chance the footage might be falsified?"

"Always possible," Jason shrugged. "But it squares with what else we know. It also explains some formerly inexplicable details, such as the bullet trajectories entering Chapman's body from below. How could a forger have known about that? But your video forensics people can examine it to be certain." Jason had only provided Cynthia the video of the shop floor activity. The videos of the office, showing Tasker's brutal interrogation and the rescue itself, were gracing the bottom of the Belle River back in Michigan.

"Very well, Jason," Cynthia snapped her tablet shut and stood. "Please remain seated for a bit – I'll be right back."

Jason sat alone in the conference room, wanting a smoke. It was all so enticing, so alluring – but he'd seen the brutal end result. He was tempted to call or message Cassie, just for a human contact, but he didn't know when Cynthia would return. So he sat there, his briefcase on the seat beside him, trying to strengthen his resolve.

Finally, the door opened again, and in came not only Cynthia but Director Miller himself, trailing some aides. Jason stood, but the director waved him down, collapsing into a seat himself with the sort of hurried breathlessness that accompanied him everywhere. Cynthia sat on his right while the aides hovered in the background.

"I haven't much time, ah, Jason, but I wanted to stop in to congratulate you personally on a job well done. Cynthia tells me you worked miracles up there, absolute miracles. Solved a problem that's been nagging us for years, jump-started this stalled HHS initiative, made good use of a wide variety of resources – initiative by the truckload, seemingly."

"Thank you, sir –" Jason began, but the Deputy Director kept going.

"That's what we appreciate around here: initiative. Why, Jessica Boldrey from HHS – we golf together, you know – she just couldn't get over what you'd managed. Damned logjam that had them stymied for years, and one of our guys goes up there and blasts it loose in a matter of weeks. Weeks! Jessica couldn't get over it. Said to say thank you from her personally, and I told her I would. Damn straight I would!

"Initiative! That's what we need more of around here. I said to Cynthia, we need to turn this guy loose, that's what we need to do. Wherever we've got problems, that's where we need initiative. Tell him, Cynthia."

"The Director is pleased to offer you a choice of assignments," Cynthia said with a smile. "After Mr. Whitman's removal, we're going to be restructuring the departments. Something could open up here in a few weeks, or we have immediate needs up in Oregon, Arizona, or Boston. In recognition of your successful effort, you'll be supervising a large staff and have a substantial budget."

"I'm sorry," Jason said in mystification. "I thought I was being considered for director of this new district."

"Aw, hell," the Directory waved his hand. "We wouldn't dream of sending a go-getter like yourself back to a dead-end like that. That's a small-time assignment we can hand off to some petty functionary - we've got much bigger fish for you to fry."

"I see," Jason said. He took a deep breath and stood. Seeing his hesitation, the Deputy Director plunged in again.

"No need to make a decision now," he assured Jason. "Cynthia's got all the details. Plenty of time to look things over, plenty of time. No rush."

"Thank you, sir, for your gratitude and generous offer," Jason said, withdrawing a paper from his briefcase. "But I have considered things carefully, and have made my decision. I'm resigning." He slid the letter across the table.

"Resigning?" the Deputy Director asked in surprise.

"Yes, sir. I think it best," Jason replied, placing his ID card and official phone on the table as well. "Thank you for all the opportunities." He nodded at the Deputy Director, then at Cynthia, and then at the stunned aides. Cynthia said nothing, but glared at him with eyes of cold fire as Jason strode to the elevators.

The Friday afternoon traffic was its usual horrendous mess, so Jason had plenty of time to ponder his actions. One corner of his mind was already berating him for the folly of taking a huge torch and hurling it right in the center of a bridge he'd spent over a decade building. But another part of him answered that if he didn't cast it all away with one throw, if he'd tried to live with part of it, he would have slowly given in over time, accommodated, and looked the other way. He forced himself to recall the image of the body bags lying in the driveway, or of the sisters huddled on crates in a barren cell, stripped of the most basic human dignity for the crime of caring for the dying. He thought of the nameless NDs, and the "treatment" they had certainly received at the hands of HHS functionaries. He couldn't be part of that.

Jason's nav console beeped with a traffic alert – the route ahead was jammed, and would take at least an hour to pass through. Jason felt depleted. He had nothing left, not even to sit through traffic or follow the intricate alternative route the console was suggesting. He pulled off onto a side street and into a narrow parking lot – he'd wait this one out. He had nothing left. As he leaned his head back to rest, he caught a marquee out of the corner of his eye. It said *St. Rita's*, and had some times on it, but in the space for the message of the week, the block letters read "My strength is made perfect in weakness."

What the hell? That made no sense. Strength was the opposite of weakness.

As he was puzzling over this contradictory statement, Jason spotted something that caused him to sit up sharply and get quickly out of his car. A woman had walked up to a door in the side of the stone building and gone inside, a woman wearing one of those long dresses like he'd seen on the women from Deckerville as they were being arrested. Their dresses had been all white while this woman's was gray, but it was the white draping headgear, the veil, that caught his attention. Jason strode to the door through which the woman had passed – maybe he could catch up and talk to her.

Passing through the door, Jason found another door which opened into a large, dim interior with stone walls, high ceilings, and rows of long wooden benches. This had to be a church – Jason hadn't been in many churches. He couldn't see the gray-clad woman, but there were a handful of people scattered about among the benches. A faint fragrant smell lingered in the air.

Off to Jason's left was the most brightly lit thing in the place, which was a big table of some sort, covered in a bright white tablecloth with lace edges. In the middle of this table stood the oddest thing Jason had ever seen. It had a broad base with a thick, ornate stem holding up a round thing that looked something like a sunflower, except the proportions were all wrong. Instead of a broad face and short leaves about the edges, this thing had a much smaller center, just a few inches across, and long leaves fanning out to a diameter of about eighteen inches. It was all gold and shone in the small spotlights that were trained on it, and was flanked by two candlesticks each holding seven lit candles. The center of the golden flower-thing was clear glass, like a little round window. In this window Jason could see something round and white, displayed in the center of all that gold and light.

Round and white. Why did that seem familiar?

Jason gasped as it all came flooding back. The middle of the night on Nathan Road, with car headlights trained like spotlights, lit candles and golden vessels and people kneeling on the ground while the man in the robe lifted a small round white thing into the air. What had that been? Why was there another round white thing here? Were they the same? But no, they'd eaten that other one, consumed it completely. Yet here was another round white thing, in the middle of all the gold, looking just like the one he'd seen on Nathan Road. What did all this mean?

Wanting a closer look, Jason unconsciously started moving toward the gold thing, but between him and the big table a short wall or fence, just taller than knee height, ran across the front of the room. There was some sort of gate in the middle of this wall, but the gate was closed. It seemed like the golden thing with the white disc in the center should not be casually approached. He considered stepping over the wall, but noticed a man sitting in one of the benches toward the front who was watching Jason intently, maybe a little warily. Glancing about, Jason saw that nobody was close to the golden thing, though they were all oriented toward it. Jason nodded at the man and smiled, then went to sit in one of the benches. The man smiled back and returned to whatever he'd been doing.

Jason sat looking and wondering. What was that round white disc in its golden holder? Why was it there, and why were these people here in its presence? Some were gazing at the golden thing while others had their head bowed, or were looking at books. A few were holding cords with some kind of beads on them, like he'd seen Teresa doing in his dream. That caused him to remember the woman whom he'd followed in here, and he looked around but couldn't see her. There were relatively few people in this space that was obviously made to hold many more, and they all seemed to be here for that golden stand, or what it contained.

Jason's eyes were drawn back to the golden stand and the white thing in its center. As he gazed on it, he felt again the curious feeling of inversion, as if the white thing was watching him more keenly than he was watching it. This feeling intensified as the minutes passed in the still silence, until Jason felt that whatever this white thing was, it had always been watching him – here, on Nathan Road, everywhere – and only now was he getting a chance to watch back.

As he sat in the dim quiet, Jason's mind grappled with the tumultuous events of the past three days. True though it was that he'd been betrayed and undermined, that didn't change the fact that he'd been the architect of the entire project. Those people had been arrested, and those families torn apart, those innocents killed because of his plans and under his authority. He'd been the driving agent. It wouldn't have happened without him. His thoughts reached further back, over the prior weeks, and he saw clearly what a fool he'd been. He'd used the resources to identify the sites across the region, and had commissioned the plan to raid those sites. What had he expected those troops to do when they hit those addresses? Issue tickets? Of course they'd make arrests – and he hadn't put a bit of thought into what would happen to those arrested. He'd been so efficient about setting up the RCCs that he hadn't considered what would happen within those clinic walls. And the missile strike? Collins had been itching to fire his toys ever since they'd first met – how foolish had Jason been not to expect him to do it at the slightest provocation? It had been Jason's oversight, Jason's dedicated attention, that had set up the entire debacle.

Following this line of thought, Jason realized with horror that that made him responsible for Mike's death.

That really hit home. Jason had coordinated the overflights and analysis that had identified that house. Jason had brought in the troops who would kick in Mike's door and drag him away. Jason had set up the facilities where the clinician had certainly given him the pill or injection or gas that had killed him. Mike, and many others, had died by Jason's hand, however indirectly.

Still under the relentless gaze of that unblinking white eye, Jason's thoughts turned to the mystery of the woods, and what he'd seen along Nathan Road. There had been one of these little round things, and Teresa and the others had been kneeling in front of it. Glancing furtively about Jason noticed that many of the people here seemed to be kneeling as well. Was this some sort of magic talisman or token of power? But then the white-robed man and Teresa and the others had *eaten* the white thing. What was with that? And that had been almost the last thing that had happened before Teresa walked through the gates into the shadow-wrapped woods. Jason knew full well that he'd never have had the courage to do that. Whatever had been in those woods had been something Jason never wanted to get close to, yet Teresa had walked right in. Somehow, she'd gotten the strength to do what he never could – and it had worked. The shadow, whatever it was, had been driven away.

Suddenly Teresa's parting words sounded in his ears, not as a memory, but as clearly and plainly as if she'd been right beside him.

Your path will be more difficult now, but if strengthened you can still walk it.

Startled, Jason whipped his head around, but there was nobody near. There was only the white eye in its golden stand, gazing at him, the candles burning steadily in their silent vigil, and the occasional rustle as somebody arrived or departed the warm dimness. He felt torn, like he could bear that unblinking scrutiny no longer, yet could not leave this quiet haven for the harsh, cold world outside.

Yet, somehow, Jason knew that he was finished for now. His remorse and pain had not lessened, nor were his questions answered, but his inner turmoil had somewhat calmed. It was time for him to go. He rose quietly and headed for the exit, getting a nod from the watchful man as he departed.

The traffic had cleared, and Jason made his way home with no more than the usual delays. As he was driving, a thought came back to him, a memory from his brief but illuminating discussion with Mike.

It never really was about the money, was it?

Jason was tempted to dispute that. Of course, it was about the money! The money had been the primary impetus, the driving force from the beginning! But another part of Jason recalled Mike's calm wisdom, even as the destruction he'd invited swooped down upon him. Mike had seemed to know much more than his simple demeanor indicated. What had he known that Jason hadn't? If it wasn't about the money, what was it about?

Jason finally pulled into his parking lot and made for his apartment door, but even as he was unlocking it, a voice came from behind him.

"Mr. Jason Pelletier?"

Jason turned to see two stern-looking men in suits standing behind him, blocking the sidewalk.

"Well," Jason said. "That didn't take long."

"You need to come with us, sir."

"Of course," Jason nodded, and turned away from his door.

Resolution

Luke was nearly toppling with exhaustion as he wove his way along the trails. He'd now been awake for twenty-four of the most taxing hours of his life, and that on the heels of a short and unsettled night. He'd known plenty of exhausting circumstances over the past couple of years, but he'd never before had to worry about falling asleep while driving his ATV.

The site he was heading for was codenamed Bamfurlong. It was a farm southwest of Yale, not far from Rivendell, and was one of the sites that had never been used for anything. Hopefully this meant that it would not have been located by whatever method the government had used to identify the ranches. It was a bolt hole, a last-ditch refuge for extreme emergencies, intended for transient use. That's where Gil and Fitz were right now, coordinating the final stages of the evacuation before they departed themselves.

Luke hoped that he'd find Felicity there. He couldn't ask, because sometime during the long night he realized he'd left his phone charging in the car Felicity had driven. That meant he was heading to Bamfurlong blind, unable to warn anyone he was coming. He just had to trust that they'd be ready for him.

When Luke finally pulled out of the woods into the shaded area behind the house, he saw that he needn't have worried. The car was parked in a shelter near the pole barn, and Gil came out of the house wearing a relieved expression.

"Luke, thank God, we were so worried! Felicity told us how you'd driven off with that government man, and when she realized you hadn't taken your phone, she nearly panicked. She'll be glad to hear you're safe."

"Where is she?" Luke asked.

"Sleeping. She got here late, and told me everything that had happened." Gil clapped him on the shoulder. "You look like death warmed over – let's get you some food and rest."

"Sounds good," Luke agreed. "But first: I got definite word on Grandpa. He was taken from Rivendell by government troops."

Gil bowed his head and nodded slightly. "So, he did go back. Did this government guy hear about it?"

"His name is Jason, and he was there when it happened. He claims he tried to stop them, but was ineffective. Take that for what it's worth."

"I don't doubt it. Somehow, I knew – many of us knew – that once Ma went, Dad wouldn't be far behind. We just weren't sure of the manner."

"I'm sorry, Gil," Luke offered.

"I'm sorry for you, too, brother," Gil replied. "He was your adoptive father. Just one more grief in these trying days. But c'mon, let's get you some chow and rest."

Luke awoke in the late afternoon, still weary but rested enough, and feeling the call of other bodily needs. After a shower he made his way downstairs in search of food and coffee.

The house indeed had the appearance of transient quarters. It was sparsely supplied with the plainest furniture, and provisions were packed in boxes. Fitz sat in the living room, a phone to his ear and a tablet on the table in front of him. On a counter in the kitchen sat a pot of coffee and a tray of sandwich fixings. As Luke was wolfing down his hastily assembled ham and swiss, Gil came in.

"Ah, there you are," Gil greeted him. "I was going to come wake you shortly. We've washed and repacked your clothes, and stowed them and your other gear in the car. We want you to be ready to depart as soon as it's fully dark."

Just then Felicity came through the back door. Spotting Luke, she unselfconsciously walked over to him, wrapped her arms around his waist, gave him a light kiss, and leaned into him, resting her head on his shoulder. Luke was a little taken aback, but slipped an arm around her and rested his head on hers. Gil just smiled slightly and quietly left the room.

"Did you sleep well?" Felicity asked.

"Well enough for now," Luke answered. "I feel like I could use about a week of sleep before feeling properly rested again, but I doubt that's in the offing."

"Not any time soon, I'm guessing," Felicity replied. "I've been packing – only a few things left." She stepped back, gave him another quick kiss, and swept out of the room.

Gil, who seemed to have been lingering in the next room awaiting Felicity's departure, stepped back into the kitchen and handed Luke a tablet. "Stare at the green dot now," he instructed, which Luke did, slowly turning his head from side to side to facilitate the recognition encoding. When the tablet beeped, Gil took it back, tapped a few things, then returned it to Luke.

"There, all set. Your instructions and destination are encoded in there. You and Felicity both have access. I've already stashed the travel pack in the car – cash, some gas cards, a few other items."

"Thanks," said Luke. "Have you...ah...got a minute? There are some things I need to discuss with you."

"Sure," Gil replied with a fatherly smile. "Let's step outside."

The two men sat on the front porch while Luke gave Gil his perspective on the prior night's events. He also explained what he'd shown Jason, and how he'd given him the video chips of the blast. That was the easy part. Broaching the final topic was a bit less comfortable.

"There's, ah, one more issue to discuss," Luke said. "You mentioned that Felicity has told you about the events at the wood?"

"She did, but she hinted that there was more that I should take up with you," Gil affirmed.

Luke nodded, and explained about Teresa's final gift before her departure.

"And so," Luke concluded. "Though this is a conversation I never dreamed I'd be having – I mean, I dreamed about having it, because I dreamed about marrying Felicity, though I hope you don't take that the wrong way –" Luke felt like he was fumbling every word, but Gil just grinned.

"That just makes you red-blooded. Marrying young women is what young men should be dreaming about. I was one myself not too long ago, if you can believe it."

"That's true," Luke acknowledged. "But I've always thought Felicity rather…special. Even so, nobody was more shocked than I when Teresa put her hand in mine last night. But to do things in proper order, I'm asking your permission to marry Felicity."

Gil sat quiet for a minute before responding. "In truth, such a significant action by such a special person just before such a towering sacrifice – the permission seems to be already granted by a much higher authority than I. Nonetheless, for myself and on Jan's behalf, I thank you for your courtesy, and grant you permission."

"Thank you, sir," Luke replied.

"Truthfully, I'd already guessed something like that from Felicity's hints," Gil said, tapping his chin thoughtfully. "It's a welcome development, but it does complicate things a bit."

"How so?"

"We're all headed to various sites in Northfarthing, and we'd planned to have Felicity stay with us while placing you closer to the Schaeffers. The problem is that there's some distance between the two sites, and travel is going to be more difficult there for a variety of reasons. No matter – we'll figure out something, even if it does discommode the Schaeffers a bit. They're so giddy right now that they'll not notice any minor inconveniences we suggest."

"Why is that?"

"Phillip," Gil said with a broad smile. "He showed up today while you were sleeping, and he went off with Jan, who'll be dropping him at the Schaeffer's site."

Luke breathed a sigh of relief. One shadow looming over the hasty departures was getting in touch with the "lost" members who had cut themselves off sharply from their families. It was unsafe to try to contact them too aggressively, and unthinkable that the families could leave behind even the most oblique information regarding where they'd gone. Given the turbulent conditions and the fact that the families might have to flee again if the pursuit proved too hot, it was possible that family members might lose track of each other for years, if not permanently. Luke was unspeakably relieved that Phillip had turned up in time, but that raised another question.

"Any word on Cletus and Sixtus?"

"None," Gil shook his head grimly. "Phillip said they were 'thinking things over', but hadn't arrived at a decision. Ruth and Travis headed for Westfarthing on Monday. There are only two sites still active – this is one of them, and we're evacuating by midnight. I'm not sure if they know where the other one is, and it's vacating tomorrow."

Luke shook his head sadly, but there was nothing he could do. "We can hope they make it to that one, or something. At least Phillip came home."

The hours until nightfall were spent packing the three vehicles – Gil and Fitz were going to different destinations after eradicating any trace of their presence. They had a simple supper, and just before sunset some visitors showed up to say farewell: Todd and Grace. They, too, had spent the day resting and making plans. They intended to stay in the Thumb, though Todd would have to find more work in order to support a family. Luke was impressed with how much better Todd looked already – much more like the alert, attentive Todd he was accustomed to. Grace looked radiant, and she and Felicity spent most of the time chatting and laughing like schoolgirls. There were tears when Todd and Grace departed, and promises to stay in touch as best they could.

Once enough of the sunset had faded, Fitz headed off to his destination in Southfarthing. Half an hour after that, Luke and Felicity got into their car and headed along their arranged route. Gil was staying a couple more hours to make some final calls and then shut the house up before departing himself. Given that the last two cars were headed for the same destination, they were separating their departure by time, and taking different routes.

As Felicity navigated the dark roads, Luke felt too exhausted and shattered by the events of the past several days to reflect much on the fact that his life was being uprooted and radically altered for the second time in less than three years. In one sense he dreaded the prospect of starting all over from nothing in a completely new environment, but in another sense it wouldn't be completely new. There would be some familiar pieces. Besides, he thought as he glanced over at his betrothed, he had something now that he hadn't had before.

*   *   *

The tall man in the dark suit swept into the conference room with an authoritative air, and Lieutenant Bonnie Hammond stood to greet him.

"Mr. Buchanan?"

"Yes. And you must be Lieutenant Hammond?" The man shook her hand and turned to the other officer in the room.

"This is Major Chad Collins, DHS Border Patrol Aerial Division," Bonnie said. "Chad, this is Mr. Pierce Buchanan, who just arrived from D.C." The men shook hands before Mr. Buchanan was seated and picked up the tablet which Bonnie handed him.

"So," Buchanan began. "As the new head of the Special Protectionary District, I need to get up to speed in a hurry."

Chad and Bonnie exchanged a quick glance. This was an unwritten cue: if the new director mentioned the old one, even with stock phrases like "seeking career opportunities", that indicated it was safe to refer to him. But if no mention was made of the prior official, then the subject was taboo. Nobody had heard from or about Jason Pelletier since he'd flown off to D.C. the previous Friday. Bonnie had only received word of the new director's existence, and imminent arrival, at eight o'clock that morning. Whatever had happened to Jason was clearly not open for discussion.

"Hmm," Buchanan murmured as he skimmed the pages on the tablet. "Good start, but a lot of work ahead of us. So, are we it? Are you two my command team?"

"Well, no, sir," Bonnie squirmed a little. "Fort Wayne recalled the original command team after some miscommunications, and is still assembling a replacement team. Major Serrano, at least, will be part of it, but others are being named. They hope to dispatch them to the district by the end of the day."

"Yes, I heard about the miscommunications. How about you, Major?"

"I'm technically not in your chain of command, Mr. Buchanan," Collins admitted. "However, my unit was providing close support for the field units of the DTD, and were integral in providing vital intelligence to the effort. It is my hope that we can continue to provide those essential services, regardless of how the administrative details sort out. My unit stands ready to resume surveillance overflights at your command."

"'Resume', Major?" Buchanan asked. "Aren't the flights ongoing?"

"No, sir," Collins replied. "The last order we received from the office of the director was to ground all flights."

"Really? That's...unexpected," Buchanan mused, looking at the tablet. "There are nearly a hundred sites here categorized as extremely suspect, and over four hundred highly suspect. Are you saying we haven't been watching any of them since—"

"Since last Thursday, no, sir," Collins interrupted.

"Well," grumbled Buchanan. "That makes no sense. Regardless of what we do or don't do on the ground, we need good intel. Get those flights up in the air, with concentration on watching these sites." He tapped the tablet screen. "You have this list, correct?"

"Yes, sir," Collins replied enthusiastically, getting to his feet. "Will that be all, sir?"

"Yes, Major. Oh, one last thing."

"Sir?"

"No armament. Until we straighten out the communications and clarify some protocols, I want surveillance flights only."

Only the briefest flicker of disappointment crossed the major's face before he nodded and saluted. "Understood, sir."

"Now, Lieutenant," Buchanan said after Collins had departed. "Let's see about establishing a little order in this new Protectionary District, shall we?"

*   *   *

The twins cut the chatter as they approached the end of the trail. The instinct of secrecy was too ingrained, even though they knew that nothing remained at their destination to endanger. They'd parked a mile away and walked this last stretch of the trail under cover of the finally leafed-out trees, waving off mosquitoes all the way, simply to be able to approach the property unobserved. It was a route they were accustomed to, though they'd traveled it more often on motorcycles or ATVs. They paused behind the thicket of bushes at the end of the trail. Even though they doubted there was any immediate danger, they were still cautious.

"You ready?" Sixtus asked in a quiet voice.

"Damn, Six, you don't have to whisper. Anything that could hear us out here already has," Cletus replied, though even while saying it he pitched his voice more softly than usual.

"All right, then," Sixtus replied, and the two stepped from the trail into the carefully covered area around the stables. The stillness of the property was unnerving – they'd lived here most of their lives, but had never heard it so quiet. They could hear the breeze barely rustling the leaves as it passed overhead.

"C'mon, let's look inside the stable," Sixtus urged, so they walked around to the side door and slid it open. They were greeted by the dank, still air of the empty building. Where there had once been the lowing and thumping of livestock, the least sound now echoed hollowly. The twins quickly backed out and closed the door.

"The houses?" Cletus suggested weakly, and Sixtus shrugged. In truth, neither of them knew why they were here, except that they'd both felt a keen longing to return to their old home, a longing that neither had wanted to admit openly to the other. So the venture had been casually suggested, and nearly dismissed, and nonchalantly revisited, and tossed about indifferently, and finally agreed to without any clear discussion of what they were going *for*.

But now that they were here, it seemed reasonable to have a look around. Staying under cover, they went around the walkway to the back of what they still thought of as the Schaeffer's house. They tried the back door, which was locked, and peered through the window at the empty utility room. A glance through the window next to the door told the same story: the kitchen, once so full of life and noise and love, was stark and empty. Some of the cupboards stood open, adding to the air of desolation.

Cletus took a slow, deep breath while Sixtus discreetly rubbed his eye. They stepped to the edge of the porch and looked across the yard at the Big House, which had been their home as long as they could remember. It looked unnervingly dark and still, shadowed under the trees as the daylight faded.

"Want to...ah...take a closer look?" Sixtus suggested in a thin voice. Cletus didn't respond, but swallowed hard and shook his head slightly. Seeing the stable and the Schaeffer's house empty had been hard enough. They might not be able to bear seeing their childhood home abandoned. A sense of the gravity of their situation and the severity of their isolation settled more heavily upon them.

They had to admit they'd been warned. Phone calls, messages, hints to both them and Phillip, even a visit from Mom and Dad, all with the same theme: things were happening, nothing was certain, change might come suddenly. No more could be said, because of operational security, and the twins had scornfully dismissed the warnings, not least because they were so closely linked to the operation and its precious security. That lay at the heart of their grudge – how the operation had consumed everything for the past several years, looming over all the families and influencing every decision. Escaping the ever-present demands of the operation had been the biggest motive behind their strike for independence, and they still bridled at doing anything because the operation required it.

But independence had fallen short of their expectations. What jobs they could find paid little, and rent and utilities were expensive. They couldn't afford to go out much, even if they had the energy after a day of work, so most of their eagerly anticipated free time had been spent at home eating bad food and watching inane shows. Of course, they'd been less than an hour's drive from home, and could have driven up on evenings or days off to visit, but to their minds that would have been admitting defeat, "running home", proof that they couldn't make it in the world. They'd even speculated that the oblique warnings were no more than attempts to get them home, and had laughed them off.

But a few days ago, something had changed. Their scorn and disdain had softened, and suddenly going home hadn't seemed like a sign of weakness any more. They found themselves scoffing less and yearning more. On Friday evening, unbeknownst to the other, each had tried to call home, only to make the terrible discovery that nobody could be reached. They'd tried all the numbers – home, Uncle Gil, the Hagerstroms, even Uncle Kent up in Gagetown. All their attempts encountered the same message: dead line. At first, they thought it might be more OpSec, so they'd kept trying through the weekend, hoping that something would change, or that it was just a temporary glitch. It wasn't until Monday that they'd entertained the possibility of driving up to look around, and now on Tuesday they were here.

As the twins looked out over the abandoned campus the implications were sinking in. They both knew the protocols for a full SCRAM – no outgoing contact, no messages, no traces, nothing. The foe was presumed to be so cunning and resourceful that all tracks had to be eradicated, all lines cut, and all data erased, because even the most oblique clue could be followed. Those who were inside the operation were given the new locations and contact numbers, those outside were given nothing. Cletus and Sixtus had placed themselves outside, and had ignored the warnings to return until it was too late.

"Well," Cletus offered in a too-brave voice, "nothing much here, from the looks of things."

"Unless you want to check out the Peterson house," Sixtus suggested, but Cletus shrugged it off. It would serve no purpose other than to remind them further of their isolation.

"Head back, then?" Cletus continued, and Sixtus nodded. They had no idea what they were going to do. All they had left to cling to was the façade of their independence. They turned and headed back for the trail that had brought them here.

Halfway to their destination, Sixtus stopped in his tracks. "Do you want to check behind the Board?" he asked.

"Oh!" Cletus said. "Sure, why not?"

The Board was a loose plank in the back wall of the horse stable. It didn't feel loose to casual inspection, and the crack that enabled you to remove it was inconspicuous. You had to know exactly where it was, and precisely how to lift it, to expose the hollow spot in the wall behind it. Once the section of plank was seated back in the wall it was indistinguishable from the boards on either side.

The Board, or more specifically the space behind it, had been their hiding place during their growing up years. Goodies and pops snuck from the kitchens ended up there, as well as more potent contraband as they got older. It had been a useful stash for small items that could be smuggled onto the property and stowed until they could be more safely relocated elsewhere. They were fairly sure that they were the only ones who knew of this hideaway, though they occasionally found items in it that they had not placed there, or missed items that they'd been certain they'd safely stowed. Thus, there was a shadow of a question of just how secret their secret stash was, though as twins there was also a shadow of a question about just how truthful they were being with each other about mysteriously appearing or disappearing items. They hadn't used the Board in years, and Cletus was surprised Sixtus had thought of it. It was unlikely, a fool's chance, but it was worth a try.

The twins slipped back into the dark stable. Not daring to turn on a light, they located the spot by flashlight on Cletus's phone. Sixtus applied the proper lift and pressure to slide the Board clear and expose the space behind it. Eagerly they peered in, not knowing what to expect.

The space was empty.

"Oh, well," Sixtus said with exaggerated nonchalance. "Slim chance, anyway." He made to replace the board when Cletus stopped him.

"Hold it. Let me see the back of the board."

"The back?"

"The side facing in," Cletus said in exasperation. "Here, hold it so I can look at it." Sixtus held the Board so that Cletus could scan up and down it with his flashlight. Suddenly he stopped and held the flashlight still. "There – look at that."

Sixtus looked more closely and saw written there a long number. It was barely legible, light pencil on gray board, but the numbers were clearly written.

"Was this here before?" Cletus asked.

"I'm not sure, I never looked," Sixtus replied. The number could be years old – or it might have just been written there a few days ago.

"Why don't I take a picture, and then you read it to me so I can jot it down, in case the picture doesn't come out?" Cletus suggested.

"Why don't you take a picture, and then you read it to me, so I can jot it down on my phone, in case something happens to yours?" Sixtus countered. So they did, and then replaced the board.

"Shall we try the number?" Sixtus asked.

"Not here," Cletus replied, his security instincts kicking back in. "No signals from the site. Let's get back to the car."

The walk back along the darkening trail went more quickly than the walk in, so eager were they to get to the car. Once there, they decided to let Sixtus dial, though they put the phone on speaker. Tersely they listened to the rings until the destination number picked up and they heard a familiar voice.

"Hello?"

"Mom?" Sixtus asked hesitantly.

"Sixtus?" came the excited response.

*   *   *

The meeting room was bustling with activity. Mr. Buchanan had had a full week to get into the swing of directing the Special Protectionary District, and the vision was beginning to take shape. Major Serrano and his aides were present, Lieutenant Hammond was deftly moving everyone through the agenda, and minor functionaries were slipping in and out of the room attending to various tasks. Earlier they'd heard Major Serrano's plan for redistributing his troops in light of the latest decisions, and they'd just wrapped up a videoconference with D.C. about finessing the POM aspect of the new District. Everything was sounding positive, things were clicking nicely, and the meeting looked to be on track for an swift wrap-up, freeing everyone to head home early on this fine Friday afternoon.

"So, Bonnie, what's left for us?" beamed Director Buchanan.

"Report from Major Collins regarding surveillance overflight results," Lieutenant Hammond ticked off on her tablet.

"Ah, Major, thank you for coming. Please," Buchanan gestured to the presentation lectern.

Major Collins had been the only party in the room not joining in the festive mood. Throughout the meeting he'd sat in his chair, pulled a little back from the table, looking sullen. Now that it was his turn to present, he heaved himself to his feet and walked to the front of the room. As he stepped behind the lectern, a now-familiar map of the Special Protectionary District flicked onto the screen behind him. An array of spots of various colors were scattered across the map in no particular pattern.

"Here we have the District, with all suspect addresses with an 85% or higher probability illuminated," Collins began in a dull voice, waving at the map. "The legend on the left explains the color coding: sites we hit productively, sites we hit unproductively, and suspect sites to be hit at later times. Since Monday we've been running surveillance overflights of all the sites, particularly the ones we've not yet hit." The major sighed before continuing.

"Unfortunately, with two exceptions, all these sites have been evacuated. They're empty."

"Evacuated? All but two?" Buchanan asked in amazement.

"Yes – and we're now suspecting that even those two were false positives, and never had anything to do with the clandestine network," Collins confirmed.

"How certain are we of the data?" Major Serrano asked.

"As certain as we can be using only aerial assets," Collins explained a bit testily. "We have footage of human activity at these sites as recently as two weeks ago. Since resuming overflights, we're seeing only vacant properties. We've even sent low-level assets – helidrones and such – in for closer inspection. Every indication is that the addresses have been vacated."

"Do we know how quickly this happened?" Buchanan asked.

"That's not the kind of thing aerial assets can determine after the fact. A ground investigation may yield some clues. Had I been able to get some assets in the air, I might have been able not only to get that kind of data, but alert everyone that it was happening. Unfortunately, my assets were grounded for a five-day window. I suspect it was during that window that most of these evacuations happened."

The atmosphere of elation in the room dampened markedly as the principals looked at each other, dumbfounded. "Well," Buchanan finally said, "that was unexpected."

Unexpected? Major Collins smiled thinly but said nothing. He didn't know what he could say to people who launched limited attacks on a well-ordered network run by disciplined parties and then naively expected their targets to linger around waiting for the next round. Of course, the network was going to evacuate! Given how organized they'd proven to be, they'd probably had several levels of response plans ready to hand, and had only to execute them when the hammer fell. The only hope that DTD had had was to hit them in as many places as possible as quickly as possible. Not only had they not done that, they'd grounded their surveillance assets during the most critical period. Collins sighed as the ground-pounders discussed among themselves the implications of this intelligence. What good was a sophisticated urban assault force with no targets to assault?

Realizing that the major was still standing while they discussed options, Buchanan addressed him. "This is clearly going to require us to rethink a few things. Unless you have any further information, thank you for your input, Major Collins."

"Nothing further. Good day, sir," Collins saluted and walked from the room, shaking his head slightly.

*　　　*　　　*

Agent Brian Sanderson slammed the door to his apartment, threw the handful of mail on the table, and set the bag containing the burger and fries beside it. Damn, he had to stop doing this. He couldn't let his eating habits slide like he had so often in the past. But he had few options – he was ravenous, it was pushing eight o'clock, and he was too weary to fix a proper dinner. He grabbed a beer from the fridge, ripped the bag open, dumped the fries on the torn remnants, and began unwrapping the burger.

Sanderson's whole life seemed to be going down the tubes recently. It had been a week since everything had hit the fan, on what everyone was coming to refer to as Hell Day. The PR fallout from that was still falling, some new operational district had been created across the region, and issues like whether the Border Patrol units were part of this new administrative monstrosity were still being sorted out. That meant long, stressful days for everyone. Jason Pelletier had been recalled to D.C., where he'd vanished, which disturbed Sanderson. He hadn't liked the guy much, but he didn't deserve whatever he was certainly getting now. Some honcho had been appointed in his place as director of this newly formed district, and there was the expectable friction between him and the existing DHS managers. And, of course, there were Stan's problems, which were becoming increasingly harder to ignore.

What nobody was talking about was exactly what had happened on Hell Day. It was common knowledge that some "sites" had been "hit", but it had been special agents – troops, some said – brought up from Fort Wayne who'd done the hitting. The local agents had had no part in any of it, and had been told nothing in the aftermath. That there had been a missile strike was clear, and Sanderson suspected the trigger-happy Major Collins had had something to do with that, but everything else was under wraps. Why the sites had been targeted, what had happened to those detained, what could be expected next – nobody was providing those details.

Sanderson had his own suspicions, and had driven by Counselor Fitzgerald's office the other day. His sign was still up but there was a For Lease sign in the window. Sanderson hoped that meant what he expected it meant. He also hoped that the warning he'd discreetly provided to Counselor Fitzgerald had been enough to do some good.

Damn, Sanderson thought as he worked away at his meal. As if there weren't enough real crooks around, that the higher-ups had to go targeting ordinary people! He was starting to truly hate his job, and to wonder what he'd do in a year if it continued along the trajectory it seemed to be following. On top of that, he'd had to move out of his house into this chilly, smelly apartment where the neighbors yelled at all hours of the night.

In a mindless way Sanderson began flicking through the mail. He didn't know why he picked it up any more – it was all junk anyway. He got his bills electronically, but the department – and probate court – wanted to be able to mail him things, so he had a mailbox, which meant he got junk mail. He'd worked most of the way through the pile when his fingers felt an item of different texture than the flyers he'd been glancing at before pitching. It was a bright yellow envelope, hand-addressed to him, with no return address. He tore it open and found an invitation to Jasmine's upcoming birthday party. Inside was a sticky note with "We need to talk" scrawled in Kayla's hand, along with her new phone number.

Kayla saying they needed to talk. An invitation to Jasmine's birthday party. Sanderson stared at the paper until his vision blurred and tears began to drip down his cheeks.

For the first time in months he began to feel a glimmer of hope.

*   *   *

The church basement was dimly lit with aging fluorescent bulbs which were doing no favors for the yellowing linoleum. The folding chairs were standard brown institutional issue, stenciled with the church's name and dented with long use. The obligatory coffee service had two pots hot and one brewing, and the people milling about it smelled of the cigarettes they'd just been smoking outside. Only people with very low standards, who had seen much worse, would find the surroundings tolerable, much less appealing.

Which was probably true for almost everyone here, thought the visitor, including himself.

The leader called starting time and chivvied attendees to their seats. The leader then introduced himself and led the group in a prayer. Then another person stood and read from a book for a while. The visitor tried to pay attention, to truly listen, not to let his mind wander and look at the other attendees and start to think that he didn't belong here. After all, he was wearing much nicer clothes, and had a steady job, which was probably more than most of these could say.

No! He thrust those thoughts away and forced himself to listen. He did belong here, yes, here, with all these scruffy, down-and-out people. Difficult as it was for him to swallow, he was in the same boat they were. He saw that now. About a week ago he'd finally faced that fact, and knew he had to take this step. Brian had been hinting and nudging for half a year, and he'd dug in his heels and resisted. No more. Tonight, he was facing it, right here among these people.

The man had finished his reading, and the speaker stood and asked if there were any visitors or new members who'd like to speak. Nobody looked at the visitor, though he guessed that he was the only new face. Taking a deep breath, he stood and spoke.

"Hello. I'm a visitor, but I'd like to become a member. My name is Stan, and I'm an alcoholic."

*　　　　　*　　　　　*

Angel Stockwell glanced at her tablet, then out across the waiting room teeming with cases awaiting their turn. Sighing, she began tapping her way through the list. It was shaping up to be another long Monday.

Angel and her coworkers understood the necessity of the RCCs, even though it hadn't been explicitly spelled out for them. She approved of the concept, though she couldn't understand why the clinics needed to be so far out in the sticks. She supposed part of the reason was restricting access, which was fine – anything to help them work better. There needed to be a lot more of these clinics, and fast. Angel was getting toward the age where she was beginning to think about retirement, except there wouldn't be any retirement for her if the government kept flushing scarce funds to provide medical care to people with no future. Something had to be done, and if it took RCCs, so be it.

Take the first patient Angel had dealt with this morning: fussy, whining Agnes Milburn, who'd been driven here by her carping daughter Margaret. Agnes was very old and Margaret was close enough. Angel shook her head as she watched them snipe at and bicker with each other out in the waiting room. Both of them should have been yellow-tagged.

Oh, yes, it hadn't taken long for Angel and her coworkers to figure out what that yellow tag on the patient's record meant. They'd even done a fair job of figuring out the profile components that lay behind the telltale yellow square. It had become almost a game among them to guess which of the day's patients would be yellow tags, since the tags wouldn't actually appear until after the patient checked in. After only a few weeks, Angel's predictive accuracy was above 70%. She could almost smell a yellow tag patient coming through the door.

Those same instincts caused her to look askance at Agnes and Margaret. They were textbook candidates for yellow-tagging, but they wouldn't be, for the simple reason that Agnes had Margaret and Margaret had Agnes. A close living relative was an automatic disqualifier. What they were doing here, Angel didn't know – they'd probably been roped in as decoy patients, just for appearances. But damn! They were such ideal candidates! If only…

Angel sat down at a workstation for some quick research. Sure enough, both of them fit the profile almost exactly. Angel drummed her fingers on the desk and thought. When it came down to it, the yellow tag itself wasn't the important thing – it just told the clinic staff what protocol to use for the patient. The protocol was what mattered.

And as primary clinician, Angel made the decisions regarding protocols.

It only took a few minutes to make the requisite adjustments to the records. Now Margaret was a patient as well. Next, the appropriate codes were entered into both sets of records to designate the protocols Angel wished them to receive. A few more taps and everything was set up. All that remained was a *pro forma* office visit for each of them, signing off on the recommended treatment, and sending them on their way with their pre-loaded dispensers. Who needed a complex computer algorithm when a little human ingenuity would suffice?

"Agnes Milburn?" Angel called out. The elderly woman hobbled to the door, assisted by her fretting daughter.

"I'm Agnes Milburn."

"If you'll come this way, please. Oh, and are you Margaret?"

"Me?" the daughter replied in surprise. "Why yes, yes I am."

"How fortunate! Your records indicate that some of your prescriptions are about to expire, and you're due for a reevaluation anyway. If you'd like, we could take care of that while you're here."

"Now? Today?" Margaret fussed. "But my doctor…I have an appointment."

"Well, you can keep going to your doctor if you wish," Angel said sympathetically. "But we do have an opening today, which is likely to fill soon. We could examine both your mother and you, make any adjustments to your medications, and send you both home with a two-week's supply at no charge. Your call."

"No charge?" Margaret asked anxiously. "And you can fit me in today?"

"This very morning," Angel assured her.

"That sounds wonderful," Margaret replied. "What do I have to do to –"

"Nothing at all," Angel said. "You just wait out here while we take care of your mother, then we'll call you in to take care of you. Then you can both leave with your new medications, and you won't need to come back. Our care model is very efficient."

"Really, now? Why, that's wonderful, wonderful," Margaret mumbled as she wandered back to her seat.

"Come along now, Agnes," Angel took the elderly woman's elbow to guide her down the hallway to the exam room. "We'll have you taken care of in no time."

There, thought Angel. Piece of cake. Have to look for more opportunities to do this.

*　　　　*　　　　*

Fr. Gabriel checked his watch. Fifteen more minutes of confession time before he had to go vest for Mass. The "traffic" had been sporadic, enabling the confessional door to stand open a good portion of the time, relieving some of the stuffiness of the little chamber. *This* was the summer, he vowed, to have something done about the ventilation in here. It was quite warm already in late spring, and could get stifling in high summer. Of course, proper attention would have to be paid to soundproofing.

The door clicked shut and a penitent knelt on the other side of the screen. Fr. Gabriel reflexively made the sign of the cross and waited for the person to continue.

"Bless me, Father, for I have sinned. It's been several months since my last confession," the voice began.

It's been nearly a year, Jake Kyle – I remember the date precisely, Fr. Gabriel thought. He wondered how many of his parishioners would be horrified to know how well he could recognize their voices. Not that it mattered.

"I...I'm afraid I have some grave sins to confess," the voice went on, and Fr. Gabriel settled in to listen. He'd heard it all before, and rather than being scandalized, he was happy to help people get rid of the burden of their sins. It was one of the best parts of being a priest.